—————— PRAISE FOR ROBINSON'S WRITING ——————

"Owen Kivlin, the narrator of Dave Robinson's novel *Sweeney On-the-Fringe*, sidles up to the reader as unassumingly as Ishmael and announces that he's got a tale to tell. And what a tale it is. The elusive, eponymous Sweeney is a man on a quest. Told through letters, dramatic narrative, interviews and poems, *Sweeney On-the-Fringe* is a wild, lyrical ride of a book, rich with mythical allusion, offbeat characters and a roll-your-own New England vernacular that is dead on. Will Sweeney find what he seeks: truth, self, adventure, romance and the perfect wave? You'll have to read to find out. Recommended."

DAVID DANIEL
Author of *Goofyfoot* and *Reunion*

"Equal parts strange, funny and insightful, the sweeping *Sweeney in Effable* is a truly ambitious effort by both author Dave Robinson and his protagonist, Sweeney O'Sweeney. Masters of storytelling, the pair take us around the world in Sweeney's epic quest for enlightenment. A weighty matter, sure—but Sweeney is also the kind of guy you want to have several beers with at the neighborhood tap. He'll stick with you for days after you leave him on the final page."

SARAH McADAMS CORBETT
Writer whose work has appeared in the *Chicago Sun Tribune, Montreal Gazette* and *The New York Times*

"…The poems are real, serious, and present us with a unified sensibility, and unusual poetic intelligence. If this novel is to be understood and appreciated, the reader must be able to read Sweeney's poems because the poems reveal his unique identity and give the novel its considerable literary value. Robinson's employment of his poetic capabilities is original and very effective."

Vyu Magazine review by GLOVER DAVIS
Author of the poetry collections: *Separate Lives, Bandaging Bread, August Fires* and *Legend*

SWEENEY
IN
EFFABLE

Five Books About Enjoying the View

Printed in the United States of America
Limited Edition

Design: Kelly Freitas
Cover Photo: Anna Isaak-Ross, Cultivamos Cultura, São Luís, Portugal
Author's Photo: R. Stoner
Back Cover Photos: Dave Robinson
Typeface: Bembo text and EdmondSans display

IP

Loom Press
P.O. Box 1394, Lowell, MA 01853
www.loompress.com

SWEENEY IN EFFABLE

Five Books About Enjoying the View

DAVE ROBINSON

BASED ON THE NOTES OF OWEN KIVLIN
& JOURNALS OF SWEENEY O'SWEENEY

Loom Press

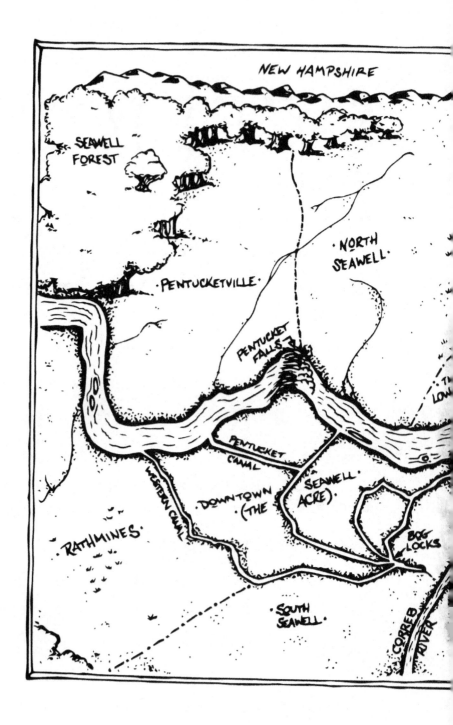

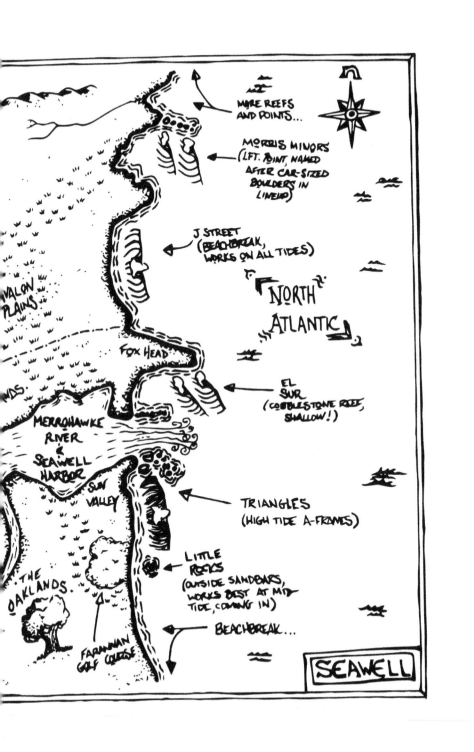

MORE REEFS AND POINTS...

MORRIS MINORS (LFT. POINT, NAMED AFTER CAR-SIZED BOULDERS IN LINEUP)

J STREET (BEACHBREAK, WORKS ON ALL TIDES)

NORTH ATLANTIC

EL SUR (COBBLESTONE REEF, SHALLOW!)

FOX HEAD

AVALON PLAINS

...NDS.

MERROHAWKE RIVER & SEAWELL HARBOR

SUN VALLEY

THE OAKLANDS.

FARANIAN GOLF COURSE

TRIANGLES (HIGH TIDE A-FRAMES)

LITTLE ROCKS (OUTSIDE SANDBARS, WORKS BEST AT MID TIDE, COMING IN)

BEACHBREAK...

SEAWELL

ACKNOWLEDGMENTS

Grateful acknowledgment is made to the journals, magazines and websites where some of these poems and excerpts of prose first appeared: *The Surfer's Path, Entelechy International: A Journal of Contemporary Ideas, Powdermag.com* and *Margie: The American Journal of Poetry*.

I'm indebted to the poet Trevor Joyce for his "The Poems of Sweeny Peregrine."

My translation (to Spanish) of "Obituary" by Weldon Kees, made it necessary to supply the original English version from *The Collected Poems of Weldon Kees*, edited by Donald Justice, (Univ. of Nebraska Press, 1975).

Quotation from "The Heat in the Room," by Weldon Kees, ibid.

Quotation from "Spring" by Denis Johnson, from *The Throne of the Third Heaven of the Nations Millennium General Assembly, Poems Collected and New*, (HarperCollins, 1995).

Quotation from "The Sixth of January," by David Budbill, from *Moment to Moment, Poems of a Mountain Recluse*, (Copper Canyon Press, 1999).

Quotation of "It's True," by Hayden Carruth, from *Doctor Jazz*, (Copper Canyon Press, 2001).

Quotation of "Widow's Lament," by Richard Brautigan, from *The Pill Versus the Springhill Mining Disaster*, (Four Seasons Foundation, 1968).

I fictionalized portions of "Political Apologies: Chronological List," by Graham G. Dodds, Political Science Dept., Univ. of Pennsylvania, www.upenn.edu/pnc/politicalapologies.html.

Quotations from *An Invitation to Practice Zen*, by Albert Low, (Charles E. Tuttle Co., 1989).

Epigraph at the beginning of Book V is from *Light of Wisdom Vol. 1*, Commentary by Jamgön Kongtrül, trans. by Erik Pema Kunsang & Marcia Binder Schmidt (Rangjung Yeshe, 1999).

ART CREDITS

I'm grateful to Martha Mayo of the Center for Lowell History & the Patrick J. Mogan Cultural Center for permission to use the art on page 349.

Photography: I'm grateful to Anna Isaak-Ross, James Higgins, and Tom Brothers for the use of their work.

Eric Jones took time to draw a "Reyman" according to my description of the creature. Thank you, Eric.

Anna Isaak-Ross' sculpture "Shoe Mold Cairn" appears in Book II courtesy of the artist. Isaak-Ross also assisted the author with the creation of the Loafe Pooka sculpture in Book II.

Additional poetry: Thank you to Matthew Miller for writing a poem at my request. Part of it appears in Book IV and is credited to "Marc Mueller."

Lyrics quoted from "Fuckin' Around," by The Shods, from the album "Thanks for Nuthin'," Poorhouse Records.

Lyrics quoted from "You Can Never Hold Back Spring," by Tom Waits and Kathleen Brennan, from the album: "Orphans: Brawlers, Bawlers & Bastards," Anti- & Epitaph Records.

The symbols for the seasons, used in Book V, are from "The Book of Signs," by Rudolf Koch, translation by Vyvyan Holland, (Dover Publications).

To the reader: Please buy the abovementioned books. If you find you've spent money on a book you don't like, pass it on to someone you know who might. They're inexpensive treasure. These poets and writers deserve sustained attention. I'm grateful to them, as well as the presses, editors, translators and companies that keep their work in print.

CONTENTS

BOOK II: Sweeney In-The-Froth

AUTHOR'S NOTE

This series of books is proof of my cultivated underachievement—a kind of flexibility adopted to get me to the ocean whenever waves appear. Dickinson, Keats, Frost and artists of their ilk learned to let idleness seep in; we must dissolve ourselves into nature. The infinite beauty of the universe flourishes within this observant, reciprocal shiftlessness.

My parents attempted to raise me as an overachiever. The tragic flaw in their plan, what set me on the right path to the rewards of underachievement? Surfing. They never should've brought me "down the beach" each summer if they expected me to make something of myself.

I echo the filmmaker Andrew Kidman's thoughts on the "competent surfer" when I admit that the ocean reveals to me my insignificance. Still, I spend hour upon hour floating over, diving under and surfing waves. The caliber of beauty shown to the merely competent surfer is extraordinary, yet feels normal at the same time. I've met whales eye-to-eye, shared waves with dolphins, been chased out of the water by a giant sea lion and surfed a sandbar built off the hull of a shipwreck on a desert coastline. More often wind, rain, snow, sun, the cold, beer, thunder and lightning ruined thousands of hours of attempted surfing. Whether I get skunked or score, oddly, doesn't factor into my need to repeatedly steep myself in saltwater idleness.

In 1997, I found Trevor Joyce's gem, *The Poems of Sweeny Peregrine*—I set out to rework that tale into a novel. It didn't take. I read other translations, Seamus Heaney's more popular *Sweeney Astray*. I tried a screenplay. Couldn't make it work at the time. Maybe a collection of short stories? Not quite. Around 2001, I'd worked out the form for Book One, *Sweeney on-the-Fringe*—the retelling of how a half-insane hero-poet lost himself in raw, sublime wilderness. While Book One went to print with Loom Press as its publisher, Book Two was already cooked up and half-served. Other than the folkloric twists and visual cues, Two really isn't that different in form from One. Book Three, however, is vastly different: a corrupted, failed screenplay. It's far too long for a screenplay, but I gave in to imagery and dialogue and let it ride. It's more about a faux-crazy Sweeney embracing his chosen role but having second thoughts after meeting a child who is genuinely ill. Interrupting this larger story are some shorter bits chronicling the decline of a couple, the producer and director, dedicated to making the film of Sweeney's life.

Books Four & Five echo Japanese poets of previous centuries, practitioners of Zen, who simply walked around the mountains and meadows of Japan writing haiku (introduced and interrupted by rags of sparse prose). These books illustrate the maturation and more important evolution of Sweeney. Backsliding be damned, there are elegant pathways open to half-crazed artists (maybe).

If I haven't scared you off just yet, please read these books in any order you prefer. Skip around, start with the final book, or begin on page one and push through to the end. If the screenplay format of Book Three at first feels clunky and awkward, it should order itself for you after ten or twenty pages and feel more like a quick read, I think. In any order, and hopefully without excessive pushing required, these books are the fruits of my practiced idleness.

Finally, the Buddhist ideas and meditation practices described in these books whet the edge of the abovementioned shiftlessness—maybe adding a twinge of wisdom to the mix. But I claim no expertise or deep knowledge of Buddhism and meditation. There are true teachers out there, and I'm surely not one of them. I'm still fumbling around with words, thoughts and other daily illusions. Find your own teacher, if Buddhism strikes a chord with you. For, as Zen masters of the past have stated, writers are the most lost.

Thank you for reading,

Dave Robinson

FOREWORD

These are books of water. These are books of meditation. These are books about one man, Sweeney, whose story runs as deep and as troubled as the water in which, as a surfer, he lives much of his life. We hear about Sweeney through his poetry. We hear about Sweeney through Owen Kivlin, the narrator and guide. Often we hear about Sweeney through the people of Seawell. Their Sweeney stories echo those told by villagers about classical heroes of folktales and myths. These were heroes whose abilities and experience stood out from those of other men—heroes such as Beowulf, the poet Orpheus and Ireland's warrior poet Sweeney Peregrine, upon whose tale these books are built.

Dave Robinson's Sweeney is a hero marked by the modern world. Like Eliot's Prufrock he feels the withering stare of conventional society. Like Kesey's Randle Patrick McMurphy, Sweeney's search for answers pushes him past society's boundaries as its trappings attempt to pull him down. Most of all, Sweeney reminds me of Melville's Ishmael. If I could get into Sweeney's head I imagine his thoughts would reflect Ishmael's at the opening of Moby Dick:

> Whenever I find myself growing grim about the mouth;
> whenever it is a damp, drizzly November in my soul;
> whenever I find myself involuntarily pausing before coffin

warehouses, and bringing up the rear of every funeral I meet; and especially whenever my hypos get such an upper hand of me, that it requires a strong moral principle to prevent me from deliberately stepping into the street, and methodically knocking people's hats off—then, I account it high time to get to sea as soon as I can.

For Sweeney the ocean also seems to ever offer this baptism of healing and nourishment. It is for him both bread and balm.

This is not simply one man's journey among others to find his self. Rather, at times, it is a journey of others to literally and figuratively find Sweeney. And we, the readers, through Robinson's skillful narrative, are as well woven through this experience. The delight of reading these books is that the story reaches into some sense of shared human connection, compelling us to continue searching and holding out hope for Sweeney, for Sweeney's people, for the people in our own lives.

The characters in this story are more central, more alive, than the word "characters" signifies. They are very much Whitman's roughs, those Americans that he heard singing, from the farm to the factory. In this book, the choir sings for Sweeney. They tell his tale, especially in Book One and Book Three, because he is the hero they need in a certain time and place and form, whether as the boy naturalist, the baseball player, the surfer, the poet, the matador, the artist, the seeker. But they are more than roughs, more than salty folk satisfied with their lot. They dream and hurt and wish as much as any blood-and-flesh person. And they tell these stories not just to create the myth of Sweeney they need, but because these are their stories as well. They become part of the myth through the telling of it.

And it is this, I think, that is the heart of these books. Sweeney is the stone in the soup, that thing that tricks all the other ingredients together. The care and attention Robinson gives to the voices and lives of these people betrays his love for them in a way that only writing with empathy, not pity, can. He lives with these people in his heart. And here in this volume he celebrates them. He sings these people. And, to paraphrase Whitman, every atom belonging to them as good belongs to us.

As I reflect on Sweeney and the storytellers of Seawell, I am again brought back to Ishmael. "Yes, as every one knows," says Ishmael, "meditation and water are wedded for ever." Inside these pages there is wisdom and there are waves. Both are powerful. Treacherous. Exhilarating.

Matthew Miller
Exeter, New Hampshire

October, 2007 & September, 2016

Unidentified, possibly Sweeney. Seawell Beach, Hurricane Magrath.
Photo: Brothers

Book I

SWEENEY
ON-THE-FRINGE

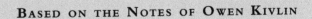

BASED ON THE NOTES OF OWEN KIVLIN

PROLOGUE

My name is Owen Kivlin; I was once friends with a man named Sweeney, the most memorable person I've met in my lifetime.

A few Seawell locals, most of them several years older than me, swear on their pints of stout that Sweeney lived on a retired fishing trawler—perched on beam-ends, stilts and barrels somewhere in the woods to the right of number six at the Farannan Golf Course. They claim they used to hang out with him in the winter while they were "practicing their drinking" on the course during high school, before they were old enough to get into the bars downtown. These are just a few of the people in Seawell, Sweeney's hometown in Massachusetts, who were eager to tell me about their connection to the man. I have gathered together a dozen or so of these stories in an effort to pass on the legend of Yardbird Sweeney.

I

Seawell is a harbor/mill town of nearly one-hundred fifty thousand people that sprawls along the banks of the Merrohawke River as it empties into the Atlantic Ocean a couple of hours north of Cape Cod, Massachusetts. The residents are a mix of factory workers, lobstermen, fishermen and a growing population of graduates from Seawell University who commute to Boston daily for their earnings.

Seawell is often referred to as "the armpit of Massachusetts" by the residents of Boston and its suburbs. The departure of the mill industry after World War II, the recession in the '80s, and the depletion of the cod population off The Georgia Bank hit the city hard. The downtown area was rundown, and local business owners steadily lost customers to the homogenized malls popping up just over the border in New Hampshire. During this time, gang violence and drug trafficking became well publ cized problems in Seawell, thereby only adding to the nasty reputation of the city.

Seawell is and always has been decidedly blue-collar, while harboring small enclaves of upper-class businessmen and property owners. Many of them still reside atop the hills in the original mansions built by the mill owners in the 19th century. However, Seawell owes its survival—and recent economic and cultural revival—to the waves of immigrants who continually arrive from their own troubled countries to work in the factories in the city and on the boats off its coastline. First the Irish fled the potato famine and came looking to dig the city's canals, as that was the only work the mill-owning English would allow them to undertake. Eventually the Irish moved up to the factories and the fishing boats and began treating the arriving French Canadians as they had been treated by the English. Later, the French Canadians found the Greeks to be second-class citizens—in turn, the Greeks took their angst out on the Polish. The Polish showed distaste for the Southeast Asians who fled the Khmer Rouge, the Southeast Asians for the African Americans, and so on and so forth through the arrival of the Dominicans who currently feud with the local Puerto Ricans. Lately, we are welcoming as best we can the West Africans who are fleeing political strife, famine and genocide in their own ravaged homelands.

II

Just like Sweeney, I was born and raised in Seawell. I went to Seawell High School in the downtown area (also known as the Acre), and I experienced firsthand all of the intricacies of the richly diverse populations and cultures present in my home town. I also grew up with my mentor and good friend Sweeney watching out for me—when he was around, that is. And, in a way, Sweeney and I have confided in each other since I was about four or five years old. While rumor, insinuation and speculation form the basis of his local legend, I was fortunate enough to hear many stories directly from the man.

What prompted me to collect these stories was their seeming shelf life. I've found that many of the same tales I heard from Sweeney have been passed on in one form or another among the people of Seawell since my childhood. To this day, many, many people in this city still talk about "that loony guy that lived in the boat out in the woods."

Some people claim to know Sweeney from his drinking and brawling days at The Old Wardin House. Some remember his raw athletic talent—he ran the 110 hurdles in high school in the winter; played catcher and shortstop, and hit clean-up for the varsity baseball team as a sophomore, junior and senior. However, the lure of the ocean and traveling seems to have cut Sweeney's promising baseball career short. Other locals dwell on the fact that he spent some time in Darville Mental Hospital for a serious mental disorder. This illness came not too long after Sweeney had served time at The Merritt House of Corrections for his part in a bar brawl. Those closest to Sweeney speak of his eerie connection to the ocean, though few are fortunate enough to have witnessed his genius in person as he slid across the faces of the waves off Seawell Beach.

The old timers at the bar in the Farannan Golf Course clubhouse called Sweeney "Yardbird." Gerald Francis, a retired fireman and lifetime resident of Seawell, seemed to know Yardbird pretty well from his days at Farannan. Gerald was always more than happy to pass on a story or two about him. Gerald detailed—in a stroke-induced, hoarse whisper—why everyone at the golf course knew Yardbird:

> That kid was always frog huntin' at the pond on nine. All
> summer long he'd be out there and then after school in
> the fall, too—year after year. He had eyes like a hawk.
> You could just yell over to him: 'Yardbird, I lost a

Titleist-three to the right on number six, two-hundred-forty-yards out.' And off he'd go, flying across the course and into the woods to find the damn thing. He was a fast little bugger, and he was worth every penny. He was a tough kid with these darting, alert eyes—always muddy and smiling. He'd give you your exact ball, plus two more, then expect you to buy the two other balls for fifty cents each. 'Sundown special,' he'd say with a grin, 'this deal won't be around tomorrow.' Usually, I'd see him outside the pro shop near the end of the day, a smile on his tanned face, with purple stains on his shirt from the grape soda he bought with his hard-earned money.

My father, Patrick Kivlin, and Sweeney also met on that same golf course when Sweeney was around six years old; they remained close as Sweeney made his way to high school and my father finished up college at Seawell State University. My father is almost ten years older than Sweeney and he kept an eye on him as a sort of mentor and friend as they grew up together—much like Sweeney did for me when I was young. The two friends spent their younger years together at Farannan—my father usually caddying and Sweeney usually hunting frogs or lost golf balls. My father agrees with Gerald Francis that no kid could match Sweeney's ability at either pastime. Sweeney and my father drank a lot of that hard-earned grape soda together under the shade of the awning by the pro shop.

But my father points out that this wasn't where they spent all their time in the summer. Neither of them particularly cared for golf, they seemed to like the open, green space the course provided and they also coveted its proximity to the surf spots of Seawell. By working there, so to speak, they both could keep an eye on the surf conditions. Whenever there was a swell in the North Atlantic the two of them surfed in the mornings until the wind turned onshore. They would then stash their boards in the woods, and run all over the golf course for the day. Later, the two would grab their boards from the woods and go back out for a surf in the evening if the wind had died and the ocean had glassed off. Eventually, through their work at Farannan, both had saved up enough money for wetsuits and began surfing together right through the winter.

They were a lot like brothers. My father claims Sweeney was an incredible athlete but, at heart, "He was a traveler, a surfer and a poet." He was such a good writer that my father, with the money he made as an environmental consultant for the state, helped fund some of Sweeney's travels and writings as he got older—hoping that a work of art would come of his many talents. But Sweeney has remained in obscurity as an artist while his reputation as an athlete, wildman and world traveler has persisted and grown—at least locally—after he disappeared.

This book contains the stories Sweeney told in my house for years and years. Some of these are the same that Sweeney took the time to tell me himself when I was just a little boy. Here, however, the people of Seawell speak. Because who better to tell these tales than the people who are keeping the story of Sweeney alive? These are the stories that I miss hearing now that my friend hasn't been heard from or seen for many years.

III

In addition to the stories, I've gathered a few of the dozens of poems that Sweeney sent me from far-flung corners of the Earth. The poems often arrived scrawled on postcards and scraps of paper mailed to me from Central and South America; other poems arrived carefully scripted on lined paper from places like Vancouver Island, British Columbia; San Clemente, California; and Longville, Minnesota. Sweeney once sent me a poem in blank verse written on the back of a used rifle range target, complete with silhouettes of pigs, ducks, cows and rams! I've yet to figure out the meaning behind that choice of paper; although, chances are just as good that no symbolism was intended.

Unfortunately, I haven't received any poems from Sweeney in approximately five years, since his disappearance in the late '90s. I have placed his best poems, in my opinion, between the stories that make up this book. And now is just as good a time as any to mention the invaluable assistance of Paul Moling—the unofficial poet laureate of Seawell. Paul was tireless in helping me to select the poems best suited to this particular project. We're very excited to share these poems with the larger world. Until now, my family and a few close friends of Sweeney have been the only readers of his work.

I decided to include these poems because I've found they help explain who Sweeney is and how he led his life—in his own words. He often, though not always, wrote about his travels in his poetry—the animals he encountered, the adventures he went on, the jungles and deserts and coasts he explored and sometimes he even wrote of the people he met along the way. There are a gross of tales about Sweeney, but only a small collection of poems in which we hear him speak.

IV

Yardbird Sweeney isn't some sort of mythical being, in the sense that he's imagined, he was a real guy, born and raised in Seawell like the rest of the people telling these stories. In fact, if he is still alive, he would be 34 years old at the time of the completion of this writing in 2004. But Sweeney's pranks, achievements and eccentricities have taken on a mythical life of their own in the bars and on the beaches of Seawell. It seems important to me to record the talk of his wanderings and the opinions on his whereabouts. It seems vital to me to assemble this portrait of my lost friend. I hope, by the end of this book, you will understand why this project has been my baby. Hopefully you'll know Yardbird Sweeney a little bit better when you have finished reading.

V

I should leave you with a physical description of Sweeney before you begin. He was six feet tall by most accounts, had dark brown or black hair that was often long and shaggy. He sometimes wore a bushy, full beard that had a hint of red in it. He was muscular but lean, with a lithe, laid-back sort of stride. Those who saw him play baseball and surf all claim he made the difficult act look effortless—he possessed an unassuming grace. And Sweeney's eyes, in my memory, were remarkably clear and a unique shade of green (others say they were blue or even gray). His high school coach, Jorge Mroz, told me the most remarkable thing about Sweeney was his vision. He says Sweeney had the same 20-15 vision as "Teddy Ballgame," a.k.a. Ted Williams, one of the most respected hitters ever to play the game of baseball.

As you can see, Sweeney's reputation has blossomed into a kind of local legend, and it is my hope that this legend may one day become the stuff of myth passed on to the next generation of Seawellians—be they baseball players, fishermen, surfers or factory workers.

What follows is a retelling of Yardbird Sweeney's life in the trees and oceans of New England and his larger world.

—Owen Kivlin

THE SEAWELL DRAWBRIDGE

Rob's cousin, Ricky Spence, was up
for the week from Quincy. Me, James, Rob,
and Stanovich met him one day
at Seawell Beach. We asked about
Quincy and he bragged as we walked
toward the drawbridge that crossed the harbor.

He claimed he "beat the livin' shit
outta Mark Wahlberg, before he
was 'Marky Mark,' before he got
famous." And Stanovich just shook
his head: "Oh, that's bullshit. But I wish
you'd kicked his ass, 'cause Marky Mark
and the Funky Bunch fuckin' suck!"
We laughed, but the kid stuck to his
bold claim: "I shit you not," he said,
"But, whatever. If you bastards don't
believe me, I don't give a fuck."

We liked this kid. We'd only known
him for a couple hours, but his
stories were grade-A bullshit.

The bridge, when we finally got
there, was bumper-to-bumper cars.
A siren cried and faded, bells
rang and the ancient bridgehand swung
the iron gates out with a rumble.
The summer crawl of traffic slowed.
We stood beneath the flashing red
stoplight, and we watched a sailboat

motor and push its way through ebb
tide's steady pull. The wooden boat
was huge, with three masts and furled sails.
The captain was alone on deck,
beside a spotted border collie
on its sealegs. The five of us
stared, and the dog gazed up at the bridge.
The captain stood at the helm, stock-still.
Ricky Spence tapped me on the shoulder:
"You guys usually jump from right
around here?"

                "Yeah, this is the spot."
"How high's this?"

                "About forty-five
feet," I said.

           "Ahh, this is a cinch.
We do backflips off double this
height back at the quarries in Quincy."

That snapped Stanovich out of his
trance, gawking at the boat's approach:
"Oh fuck you, Marky Mark. Let's see
a backflip right now."

              The kid climbed
over the metal rail and looked
down as he leaned forward and held
on like a freckled figurehead:
"OK, Stanovich, you wise ass,
I'll do something good here—for you,
and that damn mutt on deck." The boat
plowed between grey, cement-block pillars
as Ricky Spence jumped up and out.
He threw his head back, yanked his knees

up to his chest, hugged them with both
arms, and he pulled a perfect, slow
full gainer. He uncoiled his tuck,
pointed his feet, crossed his left arm
over his farmer-tanned, white chest
and then, strangely, took care to hold
his nose with his right hand. The dog
sprinted to port to bark and growl
as a grinning Ricky Spence appeared
ten feet from the boat's broad, green side.

Stanovich was silent and stunned.
The collie looked back up at us
just as the aft deck slipped between
the pillars of the bridge. We turned
and watched Spence swim for the south shore,
pulled swiftly by the tidal drag.

—Sweeney

(Postmarked in Mexico, 1989.)

O1

BACKSTAGE DANCING

I received a phone call from Margaret Tierney, one of Sweeney's mentors and friends as a child. She told me one of her former fourth graders had an experience with Sweeney that might interest me. I interviewed Erin Hamasaki while she was on lunch break at the Bolcain Glen, a gourmet restaurant in Tyngsboro, Massachusetts. At the time of the interview, Erin was seventeen years old, about five-foot-seven, a little on the gangly side, with short-cropped, shining black hair. She came across as a very intelligent girl. Erin was born and raised in the Rathmines section of Seawell, and has become an avid surfer in her own right. At first, she was a little uncomfortable with the tape recorder, but as the interview continued she grew more accustomed to it and seemed to open up to my questions.

SO, ERIN, NICE TO MEET YOU.
Um…hi. Nice to meet you, too.

ERIN, I WANT TO ASK YOU A FEW QUESTIONS ABOUT YOUR EXPERIENCE WITH SWEENEY. I'M GETTING TOGETHER A FEW STORIES FROM PEOPLE WHO KNEW HIM IN SEAWELL.
Well, I guess I didn't really know him, I just…I mean, we just met that one time at Seawell Beach. So, maybe I'm not, like, the right person to interview.

WELL, I TALKED TO MARGARET TIERNEY ABOUT YOU AND SHE SAID YOU HAD A REALLY INTERESTING STORY TO TELL…
Who's Margaret Tierney? Oh, wait, you mean Ms. Tierney from the Oakland?

YES, I'M SORRY, MS. TIERNEY, YOUR FOURTH GRADE TEACHER.
She was my favorite teacher at the Oakland. I love Ms. Tierney!

Oh, I guess I can tell you what happened. It wasn't any real big deal or anything, but if you need to know…wait, what's this for again?

I'M JUST PUTTING TOGETHER A COLLECTION OF STORIES ABOUT SWEENEY. YOU KNOW, ALL THOSE STORIES YOU ALWAYS HEAR ABOUT HIM GOING CRAZY AND LIVING ON THE GOLF COURSE AND STUFF LIKE THAT.

Really?! That's cool. He did some pretty cool shit, from what I hear. I mean um, wait. You can't put in the swear words. Can you cut that swear out of there? My mother would kill me if she ever knew I said that.

NO PROBLEM, I'LL GET RID OF THAT FOR YOU. DON'T WORRY. BUT CAN YOU TELL ME ABOUT THE DAY YOU SAW SWEENEY SURFING?

Um, yeah. What do you want me to say?

JUST TELL ME HOW YOU MET HIM. WHO WERE YOU ON THE BEACH WITH?

Well, that's a funny thing. This is another thing that my mother'd kill me for if she knew about it. I was down the beach by myself that day, and I wasn't supposed to be. I was only a kid. I think I was in second grade then. Yeah, I was, because I remember I couldn't wait to go to school the next day and tell Mrs. Brown about surfing, but she was absent that day. I wanted to tell her so bad, too. She was my second-favorite teacher at the Oakland, after Ms. Tierney.

AND WHY WERE YOU AT THE BEACH BY YOURSELF WHEN YOU WERE ONLY, WHAT, SEVEN OR EIGHT YEARS OLD?

(Laughs, and blushes a little in embarrassment) I ran away from home.

YOU RAN AWAY FROM RATHMINES, ACROSS THE WHOLE CITY, TO SEAWELL BEACH?

Yeah, I took the bus. The bus ran near my house on Stevens St. my whole life, and I'd always wanted to take it somewhere, but my mother always drove me everywhere. It's kinda weird, I know, but, um, I like riding on buses and trains and stuff like that. So I took the bus all the way to downtown and then walked a couple miles out to Seawell Beach.

YOUR PARENTS STILL DON'T KNOW YOU DID THIS?

(*Laughs*) No. No way! I told them I was over at the Mahoney's house all afternoon. The Mahoney's lived right down the street, and I was always hanging out with them. My parents didn't even suspect that I was gone (*more laughter, and covers her mouth*).

OK, SO YOU GET TO THE BEACH AND WHAT DO YOU SEE?

Well, it was in May or early June, and it was wicked nice out. So I was just sorta wading in the water and watching the waves. It was a weekday, a Wednesday, and we had a half-day at school for some teacher's convention or something stupid like that. Halfdays were the best! But they don't have them anymore, except near Thanksgiving and Christmas. Yeah, um, so I was just wading in the water, up to my ankles, with my shoes off. The water was fuh…um, the water was wicked cold. I remember that much, because my feet went numb so I started to turn around to walk back up to the warm soft sand and Sweeney was standing up in the soft sand. He sorta scared me, because no one was on the beach at all that day. Like I said, it was a Wednesday and everyone was at work. The beach was totally empty.

DID HE SAY ANYTHING TO YOU?

Well, I knew I wasn't supposed to talk to strangers so I didn't want to talk to him. I was trying to ignore him, so I turned back toward the water and I pretended I was looking for shells in the sand. I crouched down and I was picking at the little pieces of shells and crab claws and stuff at the edge of the water. And then he came up to me and he says to me, "How's the water?" He asked me like I was an adult or something! I thought he was gonna ask me what I was doing down there, and then call my parents and I'd get in trouble. I looked up at him, and I must've looked scared a little bit because he smiled at me and was like, "I think I'm gonna go surfing. What do you think? Is it too cold out there?" I think I mumbled, "I don't know." I didn't know what to say to him because I didn't really know what surfing was. I mean, I'd seen it on cartoons and TV, but I didn't know anybody surfed in Seawell. I thought he was teasing me or something.

WHAT DID YOU SAY? DID YOU TELL HIM THE WATER WAS COLD?
No, umm. It was kinda stupid. I was just a kid, you know. I wasn't supposed to talk to strangers and all that stuff. I think I asked him what surfing was.

I remember his laugh; it was, like, a real laugh. You know? It was like he'd never heard that question before or something. Like…it made no sense to him. I was just a little kid, but I knew he wasn't laughing at me. I could just kinda tell. I remember looking up at him and he was smiling. That was when I noticed he was in his wetsuit, wearing boots and gloves too, but no hood. I just sort of pointed up and down at him and said, "What's that?"

He told me it was a wetsuit and that it kept him warm in the water when he surfed. I remember telling him that was good, because the water was freezin'. That was how our conversation started.

And then he had this beautiful bluish-green surfboard laying up in the soft sand. I just looked up at it at the top of the hill and asked him what it was. I was like, "What's that?" He musta thought I was stupid or something, but he didn't act like it.

He told me that it was a surfboard, a longboard. He told me it was made by a man called "Dale Velzy." And we walked up there to look at it. I remember that he let me stand on it, on the sand. He dug a hole for the fin, and then lifted me onto it with my bare feet. He told me to bend my knees, and put my arms out and pretend I was riding on a wave in the ocean. I didn't really know what he meant, but I tried to do it like he showed me. And the whole time, he talked to me like I was an adult. You know what I mean? He wasn't treating me like a little baby, even though I was one. He was laughing and it was like he was happy to show someone what he was doing on the beach that day by himself.

DID YOU SEE HIM SURF THAT DAY?

Yeah, um, I think I remember what he said to me before he paddled out. He was like, "What's your name? Mine's Sweeney. I'm Sweeney." I told him my name and then he goes, "Well, Erin. It's good to meet you. I'll make you a deal," I was looking at him, and I was kinda scared again because I was thinking that he was going to ask me about my parents and stuff. But he goes, "I'll go out there and I'll show you what surfing is if you promise to sit here in the sand and watch every wave I catch. Then, after I take a few waves, I'll come in and you can tell me if you like surfing or not."

I remember he said something like that, because he wasn't telling me what to do like my parents always did. He was making a deal with me, and so I just smiled and nodded up at him and then sat down in the warm sand. That was the first day where I realized how much I loved the sand and the beach and stuff. I didn't have anything to do but watch Sweeney surf and look at the sun on the water and play in the sand.

I remember Sweeney picked up his longboard and he made a face, or stuck his tongue out at me, or something, and then ran down the hill to the water and out into the waves. I clapped and got all excited like a little kid, you know? There was still nobody on the beach, so I kinda felt like it was a show just for me. Like some sort of play or something, but then he started surfing and it looked like he was dancing on the water. It wasn't like a play at all, it was like, um, it was like he was dancing with the waves.

MARGARET TELLS ME YOU'RE A PRETTY GOOD SURFER YOURSELF. HOW LONG HAVE YOU BEEN SURFING?

Well, pretty much since that day when I saw Sweeney surf. My parents made me take some dance classes back then. I went to this studio in downtown Seawell, but I didn't like it much. Everyone said I was pretty good, but I hated dancing in front of people. I liked dancing, that was the fun part, but dancing on a stage with an audience and other dancers and stuff sucked. I remember looking at Sweeney that day, the way he turned the board, and cross-stepped up to the nose and cross-stepped back to the tail and carved—and he made it look so easy. And it's not! At least, it's not easy making it all look as sorta casual as he made it look. He would just glide along the face of the waves and stall the board and walk out to the nose and then back and then cut back and do drop-knee turns and it seemed like he wasn't moving anything but his legs. His arms and upper body were so, I don't know how to describe it? Um, he was like, you know when a bull is charging that guy?

THE MATADOR?

Yeah, that's it. The matador. Well, Sweeney kind of looked like that. I mean, the waves weren't that big that day, but he still had the kind of style of a matador—really calm and controlled and graceful. That's how they'd describe it at dance lessons, anyway: grace. But the best thing about the whole thing was that he was out there doing it by himself. I mean, he would have been out there all alone if it wasn't for me on the beach. I guess out in California it's really crowded and it's hard to find a place to surf by yourself. And it's kinda like that when I go to Florida with my family for February vacations. You can't really surf alone down there, and it's worse in California. That's what I hear, at least. I mean I haven't been there yet or anything, but that's what my cousins in Dana Point tell me. But out here, in Seawell, I grew up surfing by myself whenever I wanted.

It's the best thing about surfing, I think. You just go out into the ocean with a board and do whatever you want. It gets crowded up at the point breaks in North Seawell, but Seawell Beach is usually empty. Sometimes these seals come by and watch me surf in the fall. They're Northern Fur Seals, I looked it up.

REALLY? THAT'S COOL.

Yeah, I love it. They swim out past where I take off on waves and they crane their necks up out of the water and watch me go down the line on my waves. They're so cute and curious. You can see it in their faces. I like that kind of audience better than the audience at dance shows, but that's just me.

YEAH, I KNOW WHAT YOU MEAN. ANYTHING ELSE YOU WANT TO TELL...OH, BEFORE I FORGET, WHAT YEAR WAS IT WHEN YOU MET SWEENEY?

Well, I guess I was around eight or nine years old. My birthday's in May and I met him a little before my birthday, so I think that was around 1989. I thought he was wicked old back then, like my parents, because he kinda had a beard and longer hair. But, now, if I had to guess, I suppose he was around twenty.

THAT SOUNDS ABOUT RIGHT. I THINK HE WAS NINETEEN AROUND THEN. ANYTHING ELSE?

Um, I don't think so. I think my lunch break is just about over, and my boss is a real ass...oops! I mean, I gotta get back to work. But one more thing, I saw Sweeney surf one more time, a few years ago. The waves were huge, and he was riding this bright yellow '70s sort of board. It was a single fin and I saw him ride one huge wave. He was definitely like a matador that time. And the more I see people surfing around here the more I realize that no one in Seawell will ever surf like that guy. He had a really nice style. It was like the different boards he used, and the different waves and stuff...he was just in tune with all of it. I'm glad he's the guy who first taught me about surfing.

Oh yeah, um, before I go: do you know if he's around anymore? Did he really jump off the Pennacook Bridge?

I don't believe he did. So, if you know where he is, maybe you could tell him I've been surfing a long time now thanks to him.

I DON'T REALLY KNOW WHERE HE IS. WHAT DO YOU THINK?

I think he's in Ireland or someplace like that—you know, cold water keeps the crowds away from the good waves. Once you get used to surfing alone, it's hard to go back. At least it is for me. I try to avoid crowds whenever I can. You should look for him in Ireland or South Africa or someplace with cold water. I've been reading about places like that lately.

Well, I guess I gotta go bus some tables. See you later, tell Sweeney I said hi if you see him. I'd like to go surfing with him someday, that'd be the best.

I WILL, ERIN. TAKE CARE, AND THANKS FOR TALKING TO ME.
No problem, see ya later.

UNTITLED

The spread and fold and flex of the frigate birds'
slender, extended tails. Their red chests bulge
above *El Río Chone*, where they soar
and tussle, rise and dive on bent, black wings.

    Specks slipping against the folds
    of low clouds, the birds stitch
    taut patterns along
    the horizon's forested cuff.

The spread and fold and flex of the frigate birds'
swallow-like tails: Their trim, dark silhouettes
above *El Río Chone*, where they soar
and tussle, rise and dive on bent, black wings.

    They narrow in the distance,
    widen to a sliver's width
    through their banked, sharp turns—
    black needles pushed and pulled
    through the overlapped patchwork
    of river, hill and sky

—Sweeney,

(Postmarked in Ecuador, 1994.)

O2

THE BRAWLING MOUTHS

I have it from reliable sources that the Trabell brothers, Danny and Mike, have the filthiest mouths in Seawell. At the time of this interview, both went to Oakland Elementary School, Sweeney's alma mater, in the section of Seawell known as the Oaklands. They look very much alike in that they are both pale-skinned and fair-haired, with freckles scattered across the bridges of their noses. The front of Danny's shirts were perpetually stained with fruit punch or ginger ale, and Mike never wore a pair of pants that weren't patched or worn through at the knees. Mike's a year older than Danny, in sixth and fifth grades respectively, and while they never fight anyone else they have been suspended three times for beating each other up: once during a recess game of kickball; once during a school assembly about personal hygiene; and most recently when they were both kicked out of their classrooms, found each other in the hallway and fought about who would be in more trouble when they both got home.

They're tenacious little kids, and I had trouble breaking up one or two of their fights while I tried to interview them. And, yes, I now know firsthand that the Trabell brothers have the dirtiest mouths of any little kids I've ever known. It approaches an art form with these two.

[In the Oakland schoolyard, near the third baseline of the kickball field]
SO, HOW DID YOU GUYS GET TO KNOW SWEENEY?
MIKE: We don't know the crazy fuck. We just saw him that day at the bullring over in Holy Ghost Park.
DANNY: Yeah, we snuck in through a hole in the back fence by the porta-potties. Mike went in one and was like, "Hey, they got a sink in that one. It was cool." I was like, "You dumbass, that wasn't a sink! You're supposed to piss in that thing. It's for pissin' in!"
MIKE: Danny, shut the hell up. I never said that! *[Turning to me]* Sorry, he

makes stuff up sometimes. Our older cousin told us a story about a little kid who thought the urinal was a sink, like in a real bathroom. I wasn't the kid who said it. Danny just likes to make shit up.

DANNY: Fuck you, Mike! I'll say whateverthefuck I want. You're not my boss just 'cuz you're older than me! Shut up or I'll kick your skinny ass.

MIKE: *[Exasperated]* Oh, shut the heck up. Anyways, I was in third grade back then and we just snuck in the back fence. It was just me and Danny, and we climbed up some pallets out back and got on the roof of this barn or something.

DANNY: The sign said it was a "Fuckin' Hall." It was funny as shit, I was laughing so hard I almost pissed...mmmph!

MIKE: *[Holding his hand over Danny's mouth]* Don't listen to this little shit. It said it was the "Function Hall." He always says that about the sign, he knows what it said. He's stupid.

DANNY: *[Escaping Mike's grasp]* If I'm stupid then you're a dumbass, you stupid fuck. *Danny then jumped up and punched Mike in the temple, Mike screamed and rubbed the side of his head. The boys then began chasing each other around the schoolyard, calling each other every name in the book. I was forced to break Mike's full nelson on Danny over by second base, then Danny bit Mike on his shoulder and they were too pissed off to continue the interview. I brought them to White Hen Pantry, bought them some Slush Puppies and Big League Chew and then we went back to the schoolyard to finish the interview.)*

[Next to the second-base oak tree]

OKAY, YOU WERE UP ON THE ROOF AND YOU SAW SOME SORT OF BULLRING?

DANNY: Yeah, we got up on the roof of the Fuckin' Hall *(shooting a sidelong glance at Mike)* and the Portagees had these weird metal fences set up in the park in a circle. It was some sort of religious party or something for them, so they had this big table with all this food and all the fathers were drunk as shit and there was this crappy music playing on loudspeakers and everyone was too shitfaced to notice us on the roof.

MIKE: Not everyone was drunk, like there were mothers and kids there, but they were having this big party. It was cool because we got to see this guy come out dressed in these shiny pants and stupid hat and he fought this fucking huge bull and everyone was cheering and it was pretty cool.

DANNY: The bull's horns weren't that pointy, but he was fucking huge. *(The bull's horns were apparently filed down so they wouldn't gore the matadors, but the bull still had long enough horns to do some damage.)* I mean I think he weighed, like, ten tons or something.

MIKE: Yeah, he was like ten tons and he was all black and sweating and he was so fucking pissed off. He was angrier than my Uncle Ben when he runs out of beer on Saturday. Right Danny?

DANNY: Yeah, Uncle Ben comes over and drinks all my Dad's Pabst and then gets fucking pissed and throws the empty cans at the wall and stuff. He swears and throws the cans everywhere. He's a drunk fuck.

MIKE: No, I was talking about the bull, you fuckin' loser.

DANNY: Oh. Yeah, the bull was madder than Uncle Ben with no beer. You're right.

MIKE: So the bull is bleeding a little from running into the metal fence and the guy who was fighting him climbed up the fence and out because he was scared. He was being a pussy.

WHAT ABOUT SWEENEY? WAS HE THERE PARTYING OR SOMETHING—WITH THE PORTUGUESE FAMILIES? HOW DID HE GET IN THE RING?

DANNY: *[Excited and shouting]* No, Sweeney wasn't partying with the Portagees, we saw him climb in the same hole in the fence as us! He climbed through and sort of looked up at us, but I don't know if he saw us or not. He just kinda looked up in our direction where we were hiding.

MIKE: Yeah, that loony fuck snuck in there just like us, but he walked around to the front of the building. I think he knew someone there because he was shaking peoples' hands after a while. He started drinking beer and watching the bull running around the ring. It was weird, he was staring at the thing and it was like he didn't even know there was a fucking party going on.

SWEENEY SNUCK IN THERE, AND HE KNEW SOME OF THE PEOPLE AT THE FESTIVAL?

DANNY: We already said that, you dumbass!

MIKE: *(Yelling and smacking Danny in the back of the head.)* Hey! Shut the hell up, this guy just bought us Slush Puppies. You better watch your mouth, or I'll kill you.

(At this point, Danny threw his Raspberry Slush Puppy all over Mike and myself and ran away laughing. Mike proceeded to chase him down on the other side of the school, using a nice leg tackle from behind. Danny scraped up his chin and began to cry while Mike flipped him over, pinned down his arms with his knees and gave him a good dose of what they called "The Typewriter Torture." This means that Mike simply poked Danny in the sternum with his index fingers, repeatedly, while yelling "I'm typin', I'm typin'!" until Danny completely spazzed and threw Mike off of him. Finally, Danny chased Mike out into the street and into the woods across from the school on Birch St.)

I called it a day at this point because I was covered in blue Slushy and there was no way I was following those two into that swamp.

[Three days later, at the Trabell household.]

OKAY, FIRST TELL ME WHY YOU GUYS ARE GROUNDED.

DANNY: Me and Mike were fist-fighting in the woods after you left and some guy was driving by and he saw us.

MIKE: Yeah, it's all that asshole's fault.

DANNY: He said somethin' like, "Hey you two, stop fighting or I'm going to call the police."

MIKE: I just gave him the finger and punched Danny in the guts.

DANNY: Yeah, he punched me when I wasn't looking. I fell down in the mud. It was gross, it smelled like shit.

MIKE: Then the guy got out of his car and he was pointing at us. He was some sort of businessman or geek, he was in a suit, and he said he was gonna call the cops. And I didn't want him to because me and Danny got in trouble last month for doing the can trick to a cop car *[The boys explained that the "can trick" involves stringing fishing line with cans tied to the ends across the street at about car-bumper height so that the driver of the car can't* *see the fishing line and the whole thing gets wrapped up in the car's bumper.]* How were we supposed to know a cop would drive down the street? It was funny shit!

DANNY: Yeah, Mike was saying, "Uh-oh, I smell bacon." And then the stupid cop got the cans all caught up in his axle and wheels and he was clanging down the road. Me and Mike were laughing so hard he heard us, and we couldn't run because we were laughing. That cop was wicked pissed, he grabbed us by our necks and took us home. It killed my neck, but we got a ride in a cop car—which was pretty cool.

WAIT A SECOND. WHY DID YOU GET GROUNDED?

MIKE: Oh yeah. So the guy who was going to call the cops on us for fighting in the woods was just being a prick. So I yelled, "Fuck you, you pus-filled shitbag! Get in your car and go fuckyaself!" And then we ran for it. There was no way he could've caught us because we took the shortcut through the swamp and up to Eliot St. We must've laughed at that dumbass for like an hour. Then we went home and Dad was already waiting for us.

DANNY: It sucked because I was winning the fight, I was kicking my older brother's ass!

MIKE: Yeah, whatever, you dipshit. You weren't even close to winning. You just punched me in the ear once.

Anyways, I guess that guy with the phone went to high school with our Dad, so he recognized us and told my Dad what happened. He told my Dad he was worried because it looked like one of us was bleeding pretty bad. The whole thing is bullshit, and my Dad wasn't even that angry. I think he was kind of laughing about it.

DANNY: *[Incredulously]* Yeah, but we still had to stay inside for the whole freakin' weekend and we missed our street hockey game against the Briley School kids. If we lost to those shitheads because of that guy with the phone we're gonna hafta do something about it. I remember what his car looks like. . .

OKAY, OKAY, YOU GUYS. LET'S GET BACK TO THE BULLFIGHT. YOU ALREADY

DANNY: Um…oh yeah, well, what happened next? Mike, what happened…oh yeah! Then, I think another Portagee in a stupid costume climbed into the ring and the bull is bleeding from ramming into the metal fence and stuff. And the bull still looks pretty pissed off and he's doing that thing in the dirt like the bull does in the Droopy Dog cartoon an' everything, and the guy with the cape lets the bull pass him a couple times but the guy looks scared shitless. The Portagee looked like a chickenshit in there. He was holding the cape out and shaking and stuff. It was funny. I wanted to yell stuff at him, but Mike covered my mouth 'cause we woulda gotten thrown outta there.

MIKE: Yeah, and then the guy got nailed! You should've seen it! The bull turned around fast and got the guy with one of his horns. The guy went flying! At first I thought it was funny, but then the bull threw the guy off the fence and the whole crowd was quiet and a couple fathers jumped the fence to help the guy on the ground. It was pretty freakin' cool! But the bull was going fuckin' crazy at that point, and he was jumping up and down and kicking and no one could get near the matador guy.

DANNY: Then the bull jumped on the guy on the ground. It was gross. We heard the guy's bones break from way on top of the roof.

MIKE: It was fucking gross. None of the Portagees could get the bull away from the guy on the ground, an' he was screaming and bleeding and you could see the bone sticking out of his leg. Me and Danny were about to get out of there, because it was scary, but then the bull left the guy alone on the ground and they got him over the fence. And nobody wanted to go in there to try and fight the bull anymore. And that was when Sweeney climbed over the fence. One of his flip flops fell off when he jumped into the ring and so he grabbed it and jumped behind this wooden wall just before the bull almost got him. It was a close one, because that bull was still pissed and he wanted to kill everybody.

DANNY: Yeah, someone gave Sweeney a red cape and he was in his flip flops and he didn't have a shirt on and it looked like he was wearing a pair of long shorts—like the guys who surf out at Seawell Beach wear. They were gray ones with a red stripe, I think.

MIKE: No, they were blue, shithead. Anyways, all the Portagees started cheering and stuff when Sweeney got in there. He didn't do so good at first. He looked like he was scared, but then he did the thing with the cape like twice and the bull was following it and stuff. So Sweeney started looking like he wasn't that scared at all, and he was smiling and getting the bull to follow the cape over and over.

DANNY: Yeah, and all the Portagees started cheering and yelling each time the bull ran by him and missed him. It was pretty fuckin' cool. The bull was getting tired an' shit, an' Sweeney looked like a real bullfighter except he wasn't wearing the shiny costume. He had his hand behind his back and one holding out the cape and he was waving it and stuff like this *[Danny takes off his T-shirt and begins waving it around]*.

MIKE: Put your shirt back on, man. You always take your clothes off when you get excited, jeez. Quit bein' a spaz.

So then, after the bull ran by like ten times, it was wicked tired or dizzy or something and Sweeney couldn't get him to chase the cape anymore. It was weird. Then Sweeney. . .

DANNY: *[Interrupting his brother]* Oh yeah! I forgot about the coolest part. Then Sweeney starts walking toward the bull like he's dancing or something. It was pretty cool.

MIKE: *[Standing up and cross-stepping across the living room to demonstrate]* He was, like, crossing over his steps one after the other and he was getting real close to the bull. The bull was just sorta standing there sweating and breathing heavy and looking at the cape in Sweeney's hand. Then, the best part was when Sweeney kneeled down in front of the bull and stared at his face. It was fucking awesome! It was cooler than that time when Danny broke the back window of the UPS truck with the snowball.

DANNY: Yeah, that was pretty funny but this bullfighting thing was way better. The bull was like a foot away from Sweeney and he was genuflexin' like they make us do in church, and they just stared at each other for like a minute or something.

MIKE: *[Laughing]* Not "genuflexin'," shithead. "Genuflecting," it means getting down on one knee. But anyway, all the Portagees weren't saying anything; it was wicked quiet. Someone had stopped the music too and Sweeney was just there on one knee like a foot from the bull's face. The bull was breathing heavy and you could see his ribs and he was all bloody with this white stuff coming from his mouth. It was cool.

DANNY: *[Standing up to demonstate]* Yeah, it was the coolest thing I ever seen. Then Sweeney stood up and walked backwards away from the bull, real slow, doing that crossover thing with his feet again. Like this, and he's holding out the cape and stuff. Mike you do it! You do it better than I do.

MIKE: *[Mike stands up and backs away from us cross-stepping and pretending he's holding out a cape with one hand behind his back.]* OK, so then the bull chased the cape one more time and missed again! Everyone in the park started yelling and screaming and cheering, and me and Danny were jumping up and down on the roof yelling "*Olé*" and "Sweeney!" and "*Olé*" and all the Portagees were pointing at us and laughing and throwing their hats and beer bottles were smashing everywhere. It was the coolest thing ever.

DANNY: Like a week later, I told Dad about it because I thought he would think it was cool. At first he was pissed that we snuck through the fence and climbed on top of a building, but then when I told him what we saw he thought it was the best thing ever. He made me and Mike tell the whole story again to all his friends when they were playing Forty-Fives one night. He let me swear and everything while I was telling it, because Ma wasn't home! All his friends thought it was the best thing they'd ever heard. And me and Mike got to split a glass of beer. It tasted shitty, but I drank it anyway.

DID YOU GUYS SEE WHAT SWEENEY DID AFTER HE CLIMBED OUT OF THE RING?

DANNY: Yeah, I turned around while everyone was still yelling and screaming and breaking bottles and Sweeney was already out the hole in the fence. So me and Mike climbed down from the roof and tried to catch him.

MIKE: I wanted to get his autograph on my shirt or something and tell him how that was the coolest thing ever, but when we climbed through the fence he ran across Clark Rd. and into the woods behind the bus depot. I guess he was headed back to the golf course, 'cause that's where my dad says he lived back then.

DANNY: Me and Mike tried to follow him through the depot woods but we couldn't tell where he went. He was fucking fast, he went flyin' through that woods. So we just went home and pretended our backyard was a bullring for like three hours. It was fun.

'Membah that, Mike? When I ran into the bulkhead door and cut my forehead open? Dad was pissed at us for that, huh?

FROM KID TO CONSULTANT

The early days of awe stick in his craw,
but he feels no more than the ghosts of men
in grey suits blown past the downtown bar's door.★
His nimbus was once the whole evening sky,
a wavering miasma of star-flecked green.
He knew, by heart, the liquid accolades
of northern mockingbirds—back when "do-overs"
were law, when mown grass sang within his nostrils.
Before night after night in search of this fade,
he trilled and mucked and trafficked in her words:

> *raw jalopy guy*
> *you are my weary*
> *sparkler sun-bulge*
> *writing letters to the evening*
> *star about our dreaming-*
> *sweetly river*
> *shrouded with jailkid skies.*

Now he feels overfed, insatiate,
in workaday skin. Marlboro smoke wreathes
about his drunk, five-o'clock-shadowed face—
this expert, this consultant, whose days brim
with Muzak and the soft jazz of keyboards.
Who hears the hissed ess-oh-ess of this darkled
grey ghost in his suit? The quiet, mumbled and slurred
ess-oh-ess of this faded requiem shark:

★Line adapted from the poem "Aspects of Robinson" by Weldon Kees

pigtails and muzzled
dogs all day long,
heart-patterned pajama
bottoms in coffeeshops
at dawn, pigtails
and muzzled dogs
all day long.

—Sweeney

(Possibly written during Sweeney's first stay at the Merritt House of Corrections, 1989-'90. The final draft included the note about the line adapted from Kees.)

03

THE FIFTEENTH-HOLE INCIDENT

I tracked down Gerald Francis, one of the older members at Farannan Golf Course. Gerald was living with his youngest son, Walt, since suffering a mild stroke four months before my visit. Both men had salt and pepper hair, Gerald's was considerably thinner on top than his son's. Both also had unusually large ears, and grey eyes surrounded by especially earnest faces. Gerald's mind was a little scattered at times, but his memory of Sweeney seemed very clear. He was 71 years old when I met with him, and he was unable to speak for any length of time as his voice had somehow been affected in the stroke. Walt did most of the talking for his father. Gerald listened intently in order to make sure his son included all the important details about his old friend, Yardbird Sweeney.

WHO TAUGHT SWEENEY HOW TO GOLF?

GERALD: *(Nods and points at his own chest, and smiles.)*

WALT: My father taught Sweeney. He told me that none of his own sons had been interested in learning to play golf. And he's right, none of us were interested that much in golf when we were younger. We all played football during high school, and we wrestled in the winter. During the summer we went to different football and wrestling camps, golf seemed like an old man's game to us. We knew Dad was good at golf, one of the best at Farannan, but we figured we had the rest of our lives to learn golf. Anyway, my father told me that he once took Sweeney out on a rainy day when no one was on the course. He took him to the driving range with three or four buckets of balls and taught him how to hit his woods with one bucket, his long to middle irons with another bucket, and then one or two buckets for Sweeney's short game. I think…um, Dad, Sweeney was just a kid then, right?

GERALD: *(Nods and holds up ten fingers, while whispering)* He was only around ten years old! And it only took one day.

ONE DAY? YOU TAUGHT HIM IN ONE DAY?

WALT: Yeah, my dad always told us about this little kid that hung around on the course all day every summer. He had tried to get Sweeney to play, but Sweeney would only caddy for my father and watch everyone else play. It used to make us laugh how frustrated Dad would get about the fact that Sweeney would hang out on that course all day and never hit a single ball. But finally, I think Sweeney must've realized how much Dad wanted to teach him. So they both went out on a misty, foggy day in April. I remember it because it was just after New Englands [the annual high school wrestling tournament] had happened, and I was a senior on the Seawell High team. I'd gotten second at that tournament, I lost to some skinny hick from Timberlane—some high school up in New Hampshire. Dad came home two nights later and was ecstatic that Sweeney had gone golfing with him. It was all he talked about at dinner that night, which was fine with me because I was sick of thinking about coming in second to some backwoods kid.

I'd seen Dad that happy when I'd won the state tournament the year before, so I could see that Sweeney meant a lot to him back then. That night, he told us how he had Sweeney hit four buckets of range balls, and how the kid had a natural swing. Then we heard—and, believe me, we heard this story at the beginning of golf season every year for a long, long time—how Dad and Sweeney went out and played nine holes in the afternoon showers. The course was soaked through from all the April rains, it shouldn't even have been open, probably. But they played and Dad had an awful round, he'd sliced it out of bounds twice, he'd landed in a sand trap that was sitting under three inches of water, he three-putted four greens, and so on and so on. I've practically memorized the whole story.

Dad always ended the story with the same phrase: "Can you believe that a ten-year-old tied me at my own course in the first round of his life? I've been golfing for twenty-some-odd years! For the love of Christ, I can't believe that kid!"

Dad and Sweeney both shot a 45 that day.

I ONLY KNOW A LITTLE ABOUT GOLF, IS FORTY-FIVE A GOOD SCORE?

WALT: Forty-five isn't great, but for some kid's first round of golf it was pretty amazing. I mean, even I knew, back on the night Dad told us, that a 45 at Farannan was pretty damn good for a beginner out in the rain and cold. It's like nine over par, I think.

GERALD: *(With a grunt and a pat on Walt's shoulder, Walt and I watched as Gerald brought his right hand up under his chin, as if he was going to slap Walt. But then he extended his flat hand away from his body as if he were giving a lost driver directions. Gerald then began whispering a phrase over and over in a hoarse whisper.)* Every ball, every ball. He hit it straight, every ball. That kid hit it straight all day long.

SWEENEY HIT IT STRAIGHT EVERY TIME?

WALT: *(To his father)* Yeah, Dad, I know. I wasn't going to forget that, don't worry. *(Turning toward me)* Sweeney didn't hit all the balls at the range straight that day, he had some problems with his driver, but Dad always said, and this is a quote, "The damn kid got up to that first tee and hit it straight and just about as long as me. He never looked back. I never saw him duck-hook or slice anything once he got on that course." It really was an amazing story, and I'm not sure if that's really true or not... *(Gerald interrupts by backhanding his son's shoulder—gently, but with a look of consternation on his face).*

WALT: *(Laughing)* Okay, Okay, Dad insists it's true. I was just kiddin', Dad. Dad swears he didn't embellish the story over the years—but you can take that for what it's worth *(Walt winks at me, and smiles at Gerald who just shakes his head and frowns at his son).*

DID SWEENEY PLAY A LOT OF GOLF THAT SUMMER, OR AFTER THAT? BECAUSE I HAVEN'T COME ACROSS MANY OF HIS FRIENDS THAT REMEMBER HIM AS A GREAT GOLFER.

WALT: Well, Dad says that Sweeney played with him a couple times a week that first summer and fall after he learned, and then they played together regularly during the next several summers. But Sweeney wasn't a member, I mean a junior member, so he had to meet Dad out on number two tee in order to play.

Sweeney would play seven holes of golf with Dad, and that would be it. He couldn't play the ninth hole either because the green is right in front of the clubhouse and the members might see him. If Dad was playing with other members, Sweeney wouldn't be waiting at the second tee. He might caddy for Dad if the other guys were around, but he'd never play with a group.

GERALD: *(Gestures insistently with the index finger of his right hand.)*

WALT: *(To his father)* I was getting to that Dad, let me get to it. Jeez. *(Turning to me)* It drives my father crazy that he can't tell you this story. Me and my sisters and brothers always heard these stories when we were younger, but Dad's decided that I tell it the best—besides him, of course *(smiling at Gerald)*. It's driving you crazy isn't it? I know. I'm trying, Dad, I'm trying.

GERALD, WHAT DID YOU MEAN BY SHAKING YOUR FINGER?

GERALD: *(Simply points at his son, and then folds his arms and nods while pursing his lips and giving a little shrug.)*

WALT: He meant that Sweeney was known to play alone in the early morning or late evening. Like you always used to say, Dad, "The kid could and would play in the dark." See, one of the things that drove my father nuts about Sweeney is that he was usually alone on the course—other than when he was running around with your father, Owen. My dad loved Farannan because he could go down there and drink beers and bullshit in the morning, go out and play a round with his buddies, then come back to the bar overlooking the ninth hole and sit and drink beers in the shade and bullshit about the round he'd had or talk trash about the other guys on the course that day. My dad loved the social aspects of golf, but Sweeney hated it. I guess Sweeney only ever played with my Dad and by himself.

YEAH, MY FATHER PATRICK TELLS ME HE ONLY HIT BALLS WITH SWEENEY A FEW TIMES WHEN THEY WERE KIDS, BUT THAT THE TWO OF THEM HUNG OUT ON THE COURSE A LOT TOGETHER BACK THEN. ALTHOUGH, I HEARD SWEENEY DID PLAY IN ONE OF THE CITY TOURNEYS, AND DIDN'T HE ALMOST WIN IT? I THOUGHT YOU HAD TO BE A MEMBER TO PLAY IN IT?

WALT: You do. I mean, Sweeney joined up one year because he'd seen that annoying lawyer from Mt. Pheasant Country Club win it. That's how Dad tells it.

Dad, what was that guy's name, that idiot with the white pants and hair plugs? I always forget his name.

GERALD: *(Laughing and whispering)* Harold, Harold Crasspus, that bastard.

WALT: That's right! Harold Crasspus. He thought he was the best golfer Seawell had ever seen. And he'd just flat out tell you that when you talked to him. He was just a bastard, and no one liked him. Even the guys at Mt. Pheasant hated him. Just a rich prick, you know? He was some semi-retired partner in a law firm in Concord, and he had all the time in the world to golf. The guys at Mt. Pheasant told me he was always moaning and complaining about women on the course and how many black guys had joined the club. Just an all-around idiot, you know. So...wait, what was I talking about before Crasspus?

GERALD: *(Rolls his eyes and takes a drink from his tea.)*

WALT: Alright, alright Dad, take it easy, I remember. I was saying how Sweeney had never played golf with other people and he didn't really like the whole country-club atmosphere of the thing. But he was an athlete, and was kinda competitive as I understand. My dad arranged with the guys at Farannan to let Sweeney join as a junior member. Most of the guys knew of Sweeney. For years, Sweeney'd sold them back the balls they lost in the woods and water. Dad said a few of the sour old guys down at Farannan complained about him here and there, but almost everyone liked the kid.

Sweeney was fifteen, or at least that's what he told my father, at the time when they let him join. My father and a couple of the other old guys paid Sweeney's membership dues, which weren't much for a junior member. *(Turning toward his father)* Something like two-hundred bucks, or so. Right, Dad?

GERALD: *(Squints, in an effort to remember and then nods and gives the "somewhere-near-that-amount" wiggle of his left hand.)*

WALT: Yeah, so it was around two-hundred or two-fifty, this is back in

'85, I think. Sweeney promised he would beat the Crasspus guy. Sweeney and my father sometimes talked about the bad stuff that's associated with golf whenever they played their seven holes together. Sweeney hated that rich-white-guysonly feel of the game, and my Dad did too. We're part Portuguese, and my Dad has had to ignore more than a few "Portagee" comments down at Farannan from some of the members he doesn't get along with. Sweeney might have been part Hispanic or something, too. I don't know. My dad said he had dark skin and black hair, but no one really knew. He could've been Black Irish for all we know. Anyway, Sweeney had heard Crasspus making comments during previous City Tourneys about how Farannan had the most "niggers" of any of the clubs, and how it was a trashy course, and stuff like that. And that was why he agreed to play in the Cities and try to beat Crasspus.

DIDN'T SWEENEY PULL SOME PRANKS ON HAROLD CRASSPUS DURING ONE OF THE PREVIOUS CITIES?

GERALD: *(Laughs, smiles, and gestures at Walt with a sweep of his right hand as if to say, "Go ahead, tell him, you know the story." He then sat back in his chair with his arms folded, a broad smile on his face.)*

WALT: Oh yeah, there were two big pranks that Sweeney pulled off. But two years before he had decided to even play in the Tourney, he pulled off the first good one. What Sweeney did was, he figured out what ball Crasspus was playing. The year before, he heard Crasspus spouting about how he only played Titleist Balatas, every ball a number four. I guess Sweeney combed the woods and ponds that whole next year to find all the Titleist Fours that he could. He must've had two hund...

GERALD: *(Leans forward and delivers a slap to his son's shoulder, and wags his finger at him and begins whispering hoarsely)* You can't tell it like that, you're telling the story wrong. Set it up, Walt. For the love of Christ, set it up and tell the story right. Tell it like I told you and your mother when it happened!

WALT: Okay, Dad, I'm sorry. Relax, jeez, you'll wear yourself out. I'll tell it right. Sit back, I promise *(gently eases his father back into his chair)*. I'm sorry. You're right. I'll start over. You just gotta promise to relax, or I'll have to tell Owen this stuff without you here as creative director. You can't handle too much stress, okay? *(Turning toward me)* Jeez, that's the most he's even tried to say for months. He's right though, I did screw up there. Let me start again.

So Crasspus is leading the Cities for the fourth year in a row. As much as he was a prick, he was a really good golfer. It was his life. Sweeney knew this, and Sweeney's life was connected to golf in a different sort of way. My Dad said that Sweeney just played golf because it was a game. Granted, it was a game that "requires exceptional mental and physical dexterity," as Dad always said. But Dad told us that Sweeney was a natural, so he just played because it was challenging and simple at the same time. It had the potential to be beautiful—in a way—you know, just using the right club to hit the right shot at the right time. *(Walt looks over at Gerald to see if he is telling the story properly. Gerald gives a single thumbs-up from the crook of his folded arms, coupled with a wink.)* Well, I guess I'm on the right track here, so I'll keep going.

Sweeney hated Crasspus and Crasspus just didn't pay much attention to anything he might have heard about Sweeney. But after the infamous "Fifteenth-Hole Incident" he probably began believing in Sweeney a little more. See, what Sweeney did was wait by the sixth hole, in the woods, during the last round of the City Tourney. There's no fifteenth hole at Farannan, because it's a nine-hole course, so everyone plays each hole twice from different tee positions for the second round. Crasspus was playing against some slouch from Zephyr Country Club. They were the two leaders of the Tourney that year, so they were the last group on the course. Crasspus had a three-shot lead, going into the fifteenth hole and it didn't look good for that guy from Zephyr. So they tee up on the fifteenth, and it's like a short, par-four hole. Some guys can hit the green from the tee. It would make sense not to go for the green if you were Crasspus, since he had the lead. I mean, most guys would play it safe and lay-up and then hit a pitching wedge from like fifty yards out. But Sweeney knew Crasspus was an arrogant bastard, and that he'd go for the green anyways. At least, that's what Sweeney was hoping for. Of course, Sweeney was right. Crasspus took out his driver or three wood and went for the green. He just cleared the front sand trap and his ball ended up on the green. From the tee, you could see that it rolled to the back, around fifteen or twenty feet from the hole. The guy from Zephyr had no choice but to try the same thing, he had to try and catch Crasspus. The Zephyr guy ends up hitting the back of the green, but the ball didn't stick—it rolled off the back fringe and down the hill near the woods.

Here's what is pretty amazing about this prank: Sweeney had figured out that as the gallery and the two golfers walked down from the tee into the gully in the fairway, none of them would be able to see the surface of the green. The green was a little elevated, but the big sand trap in front had a, um…a sort of steep wall of sand that blocked the view of the green. Sweeney had very little time to pull off the prank, but he did it. What he did was he took about a hundred and fifty or two hundred Titleist Fours and scattered them all over the green—all around Crasspus's ball on the back of the green. None of the Titleists were on the fringe or in the rough, they were all on the green. When Crasspus got up to the green, swaggering and carrying on about reaching the green with one shot, his jaw dropped. My Dad was there in the gallery, hoping that Crasspus would choke and lose it on the last four holes.

GERALD: (*Leans forward with his elbows on his knees, his head in his hands. He is laughing silently, with the occasional wheeze, he is laughing hysterically.*)

WALT: (*Gesturing at his father, and laughing himself.*) Oh, this story…this story doesn't get old for the old man. And, hold on, I'm sorry (*Trying to contain his laughter*). I'm sorry, okay.…Wooo, I guess it doesn't really get old for me either (*Laughs*).

Okay, I'll keep going. Dad, reign it in, you're losing it (*More laughter from both*)!

Alright, I've seen Crasspus and I know he's got these god-awful hair plugs. He was one of the first guys, back in the '80s, to get hair plugs. My dad swears that when Crasspus saw the two hundred balls on the green—see, Sweeney had snuck up and dumped what must've been a trash-barrel full of golf balls onto the green—my dad swears that Crasspus lost it so bad that he pulled out his own hair plugs. Ha! How 'bout that shit? The whole gallery was dyin' laughing, and no one knew what the hell to do or how the hell all the balls had gotten there. There was just an empty trash barrel and no sign of Sweeney anywhere.

It was a small gallery of about fifty people—mostly from Zephyr, watching their guy—because nobody else wanted to see Crasspus win again. Everyone was pretty buzzed, because they sell beers on the course and it's usually a pretty good all-day party. So there's like fifty people laughing uncontrollably at Crasspus, and he's there pulling his hair plugs out and just freaking and yelling and swearing. It made no sense to anyone, how it happened, but it was perfect. It livened up that party.

Somebody, I think it was Sully, ran back to the clubhouse bar to tell everyone what had happened. I'd snuck in the bar and was getting a little bombed in the side room when Sully ran in and yelled, "You guys! You guys! Come check this out. Someone just fucked Crasspus. Somebody dropped like a thousand Titleist Fours on the fifteenth green. We can't find his damn ball!" At that point, like two hundred people ran down the eighth and ninth fairways with their beers in their hands and then over to the "Fifteenth-Hole Incident," which is what people began calling it that day.

GERALD: (*Is sitting back with folded arms, smiling broadly, occasionally wiping the tears from the corners of his eyes. He then takes out a hanky, unfolds it carefully and blows his nose with a loud honking noise over and over.*)

WALT: Whoa! Easy, Dad, you'll blow a gasket there. God, we love this story, don't we? And, Owen, you know how serious people in Seawell are about the City Tournament. I mean, it's a pretty big party but the golfers in Seawell act like it's a sacred event, like a major tournament or something. So many people across the city were pissed about the prank, but so many non-golfers loved that it happened. The next few years of the Tourney were huge—just huge drunkfests with golf getting played somewhere nearby. It was great. I wish it was still like that.

So who won the Cities that year? How did Harold Crasspus finish that hole?

WALT: Well, actually, yeah, Dad weren't you an official that year? Yeah, he was, because he had won the thing many years before that—that—when I was just a little kid. I remember I was glad he was an official because that kept him from catching me sneaking beers in the bar.

So I get to the green, and Crasspus is just pissed off beyond belief. He's fuming. And my dad and the other officials from the other clubs rule that the entire hole has to be replayed by both golfers. I heard my dad pushing for the ruling that the Zephyr guy could play out his ball since his wasn't on the green, and Crasspus would have to replay the hole—but that didn't go over too well. Made sense to me. I mean, why penalize the Zephyr guy? He didn't do anything, and we could see his ball sitting in the short rough behind the green.

To make a long story short, Crasspus and the Zephyr guy replayed it and both guys hit the green from the tee. But, once they got down to the green to putt it seemed like Crasspus was spooked or something. He kept squinting into the woods and up into the trees as he approached the green.

The gallery was now about three hundred people, and a bunch of us were pretty drunk and rowdy. We were heckling Crasspus, and yelling stuff about "The Farannan Yeti."

I'll never forget the sight of Crasspus bent over his ten-foot putt for par when they replayed the hole. He looked like some sort of falcon or hawk had tried to carry him off by the hair. He was pretty shaky. It was hilarious. We were all quiet when he stroked the putt and left it about four feet short of the hole. Everyone in the gallery, even some guys from Mt. Pheasant, let up a huge cheer. The Zephyr guy had birdied the hole and was now only one shot back from Crasspus. Crasspus had fourputted! Four-putted! The guy was a mess.

DID THE ZEPHYR GUY END UP BEATING CRASSPUS? THEY HAD THREE HOLES LEFT, RIGHT? WHO WON?

GERALD: *(In a hoarse whisper.)* The Zephyr guy won it on the first playoff hole. Crasspus fell apart. It's how he got the nickname. Harold "House-ah-Cards" Crasspus.

OUT-OF-BOUNDS

Before I went to prison, years ago,
I built a simple footbridge in the woods
north of hole number six. There was a stand
of honey ash tucked behind the swamp,
about two-hundred yards from the fairway,
beyond "The Pit" where the high school kids drank.
I lived beneath those ash, for several years.
Spring, fall, winter and summer in an old
trawler, long since retired, perched on oil drums
and stacks of beam ends. A rank, weedy creek—
more like a wet ditch—squabbled and meandered
around my boat, my refuge run aground.
My friends would visit and we'd drink some beers,
insult each other, then strive to one-up
the other guy with old stories of getting
drunk—until they'd leave and inevitably
trip into the muskbush by the muddy creek.
So I decided to build them a bridge,
something to catch their drunk stumbles and stop
their harsh, predictable bitching and moaning.

This was all just before I went away,
well after I began to write my poems,
but well before my friends abandoned me.
My blue-collar friends shied from me and my
poems as most forgot about those things
that we dreamt, dwelled and thrived on as little kids.
Some shied from things that didn't reek of work,
or rhyme like sports, sing like assembly lines.
The ring of earnings, the shine of long weekends,
these were the new rhythms of their lifetimes.

I don't blame anyone, but when I laid
my simple bridge over that no-name ditch—
as I leapt into what I loved—they left.

I wanted to write, I knew nothing else.
I avoided the dull thud of the clock-punch,
rode a bike, lived in an old wooden boat,
and wrote my poems from my grove of trees.
I soon became "What-a-Waste," "Lazy-Bastard"
and "That-Loony-Fuck."
                        I'm Sweeney Out-of-Bounds
and my bridge rots and sinks into the oily
pockets of mud—black bed of the bull frog.

I have known friends, I have known the small comforts
of visits—shared starlight seen through the shifting
canopy of ash. I have notched a dying
alder's thick trunk, chopped on the southern side
to fell the tree to the north. I have known the heft
of the plane in my palm, the shaving down of raw
materials. I've slowly sculpted, reaped,
parsed, pieced, composed, chipped at and drawn
a bridge to my world.
                And now I know the cold
of the winter roost, the ice-encrusted nest
leaning and creaking high above the blue,
dead snow of a February out of bounds.

—Sweeney

(Written in longhand on the back of a rifle-range target, postmarked in Minnesota, 1995. For more on Sweeney's boat see Appendix B, "The Kemp Aaberg.")

04

GHOST-RIDING ROBIN HOOD

The following is an interview with Yardbird Sweeney's landscaping boss Miguel Obregon. Everyone calls Miguel "Micky" or "Goatboy" in Seawell. He and Sweeney went to high school together, played baseball together and started mowing lawns together in the summers. Micky weighs in at about 180, with a small beer belly and a tuft of black beard on his chin. He has olive skin, black hair and blue eyes. His parents are originally from Puerto Rico. Sweeney and Micky had more than forty lawns all over Seawell when they were just seniors in high school. After graduation they expanded into tree maintenance and removal. Soon after graduation, Sweeney gave his share of the business to Micky. Periodically, Sweeney returned to Seawell and worked as Micky's foreman for the tree crew.

When I finally got a chance to speak with Micky—in May, approximately twelve years after he and Sweeney had mown their first lawns together—he'd sold the lawn maintenance side of the business. Micky is now the Head Groundskeeper at Farannan Golf Course, and he is also owner/operator of the Flintmere Trees-caping business. Flintmere has captured the bid for the City of Seawell's tree work for the past five years.

During this interview, at times, Micky seemed reluctant to talk. I tried to draw information out of him without antagonizing him. By the latter stages of our talk, Micky was on a roll so I got out of his way and stopped asking questions.

MICKY, IT'S NICE TO FINALLY GET TO TALK TO YOU. YOU'RE A BUSY GUY.
Yeah, sorry. You shoulda tried me back in December. We didn't have any work back then. I sat around twiddlin' my damn thumbs for weeks. Didn't know what to do with myself.

Anyways, whaddaya wanna talk about? If you're looking for Sweeney, and you think I know where the silly bastard is, you're wrong. I don't know shit. I haven't talked to the guy in a coupla years. He was s'posed to show last June for tree work, but he never did. He told me he'd be back for a big job we had coming up. He said that before he left that winter, or, wait, I guess that was two years ago now. Anyways, he usually told me the truth about that stuff. Always did, until that year. But…he was a no-show. Wait a sec, *d'you* know where that prick is?

NO, I WAS KIND OF HOPING YOU DID. PEOPLE WERE TELLING ME YOU PROBABLY KNOW, BUT THAT'S OKAY. NOBODY SEEMS TO KNOW. DID HE SAY WHERE HE WAS GOING WHEN HE LEFT, WHAT WAS IT, OVER TWO YEARS AGO?
Yeah, it was October a couple years ago. And, no, he didn't say where he was going. He never, ever, tole me where the fuck he was going. Never. He only useta tell me when he was coming back. I mean, he always just went somewhere to surf, I think. And then he'd come back to Seawell around the time he tole me he would, give or take a couple months.

I'd be sitting in McSwiggans, or The Temple Bar and he'd come up to me outta nowhere. It always freaked me out. I'd be half in the bag talkin' to some woman or something and then he'd suddenly be sitting across the bar from me. One time, when we were both around twenty—we're the same age, ya know—he actually managed to sit down next to me at the muthafuckin' bar without me seein' him. I look to my left and he looks me in the face and says, "Hey, Micky. How's things? Can you get an old friend that's down on his luck a beer or two?"

I still have no idea how he got on my left, in the chair next to me in The Temple. You been there?

IS IT CALLED THE SKEFF NOW?
Yeah, some new guys bought it. Same place.

YEAH, I'VE BEEN THERE. IT'S A TINY PLACE.
Yeah, it's just a tiny dive, ya know. But somehow, that bastard was sitting next to me. I hadn't see him in like a year. "Hey, Micky. How's things. Can you get an old friend that's down…" Can you believe he says that type of shit?

So, what's your opinion on the police finding Sweeney's bike beneath the Pennacook Bridge a week after he'd disappeared?

You know, no one's ever asked me whether I thought Sweeney jumped or took off to Mexico or somewheres. It's weird, it's like everyone thinks I'm gonna get pissed off or cry in my beer or something if they asked me. Everyone still talks about it now and then. Some drunk fuck will say he saw Sweeney down on Middle St., goin' into Stella's or some stupid shit like that, and then everyone will freak out and talk about Sweeney-this and Sweeney-that. I hear it in the bars now and then, some of the guys have running bets that he didn't jump and that he'll be back on such-an' such a date. I betcha about a thousand cases of beer will change hands the day Sweeney runs outta money and comes back to Seawell to work for me.

So you don't think he jumped from the bridge?

It's all a load of bullshit, if you ask me. I mean, the fuckin' guy coulda jumped, he coulda gone to fuckin' Botswana to learn how to hunt rabid wombats for all we know! What's the difference? We'll never know, unless he shows up back in Seawell one night down at The Wardin.

You don't care?

I don't know, kid. They didn't look too hard for a body, and the bike was locked. I'd love to say that the bike was locked so that means someone else put the bike out there and Sweeney'll be back. But I don't know. The stupid prick never locked his bike before that, half the time he'd just ghost-ride the damn thing toward the sidewalk in front of whatever bar he was gracing with his presence. But he could be fuckin' with my head, too. He'd do that kind of shit. So where the hell does that leave us?

I'm not sure I follow?

I mean, the guy rode around town on that old three-speed bike. It was a chocolate-brown piece of work. It was called "The Robin Hood." You could barely see the scratched-up name painted on the side. Sweeney would just ride it out from the golf course to whatever bar we were all going to and just slip off the back of the bike and let it park itself. I useta just drive around and look for that bike stuck in a snowbank somewhere in North Seawell and then I'd know what bar he was in. He didn't give a shit about the bike so he never bothered with chains and a lock.

IS GHOST-RIDING WHEN YOU JUST PUSH THE BIKE WITH NO ONE ON IT?
Yeah, we all did it when we were kids, ya know? The Robin Hood could be ghost-ridden with pretty good accuracy. I don't think that piece of shit ever sat in a bike rack in its life, and it sure as hell was never locked up until the day the cops found it near the Pennacook.

DO YOU THINK SWEENEY LOCKED IT UP JUST TO BE FUNNY OR DID SOMEONE ELSE PUT THE BIKE OUT THERE AS A SORT OF JOKE AFTER SWEENEY DISAPPEARED?
Well, that's a good theory, that one about someone else putting the bike out there. It's somethin' I thought about a little bit, but it's dogshit! Because the bike was always in my garage out on the golf course—where Sweeney kept it. And everyone thinks Sweeney took off a week before the bike was found, but that's not how I see it.

THE BIKE WAS IN YOUR GARAGE DURING THE WEEK THAT SWEENEY HAD SUPPOSEDLY TAKEN OFF?
Yeah, the bike was there on Tuesday when I went in to get some tools. I think I was looking for some rakes or somethin', and the bike was there. I remember it was there because Sweeney had stopped working for me the Friday before and the bike was gone for the weekend. Everyone said on Sunday that Sweeney was gone again, but the bike was back on Tuesday. So I don't know where he was in Seawell but he didn't leave when everyone thought he did.

WHEN DID THEY FIND IT BY THE PENNACOOK?
I think I read in the papers that they found it on a Friday morning, at like three in the morning or something. Most of the cops in Seawell know Sweeney's bike by sight.

WAS THE BIKE IN YOUR GARAGE UNTIL THURSDAY NIGHT OR FRIDAY MORNING?

I didn't go in the garage much that week because we were just about done with work back then. It was a bad October that year, so most of the leaves were down by mid-October and me and Sweeney and the other guys had done our fall cleanups by the second week of November. We did like three straight weeks of fall cleanups. Just about raked my fuckin' arms off that year, and then Sweeney said he was taking off when we were done. Some of the guys on the crew spread the word in the bars that he was leaving when work was done, and it went from there. But, like I said, the bike was there that Tuesday and then I saw it on Thursday night at about seven. I was on my way down to The Wardin for the beer-boiled hot dogs and football, and I was putting the rakes back in the garage. The bike was there, and one of my chains and padlocks was hangin' from the handlebars. I remember stopping for a sec, because the chain-and-lock thing made me think.

SO THE CHAIN AND PADLOCK THAT WERE ON THE BIKE UNDER THE BRIDGE CAME FROM YOUR GARAGE, AND SWEENEY HAD A KEY TO YOUR GARAGE?

Yeah, we used to use the chains on the trailer to lock down the blowers and the Walker mower while we were driving from job to job. But, like I said, Sweeney never locked the damn bike up so I thought he was going to use the chain and lock for something else that Thursday night when I saw it. Didn't matter to me, because we were done with for the season pretty much.

AND HE HAD A KEY TO YOUR GARAGE?

Yeah, me and him had the only keys. I think. Maybe Will has one now, but not back then. So, yeah, just me and Sweeney at that time.

WOULD THIS MEAN THAT SWEENEY TOOK THE BIKE AND LOCK OUT OF THE GARAGE AND RODE IT OVER TO THE BRIDGE?

I don't know, man. Do I look like Agatha-fuckin'-Christie? I have no idea if Sweeney did it, really. Someone could've stolen or found his key or something. Who knows?

I HAVE TO BE HONEST WITH YOU MICK, YOU'RE NOT CLEARING MUCH UP FOR ME.
Yeah, no shit. Welcome to the club. Anybody who knew the guy was only worse off for it in the head *(Laughs)*.

WHAT DO YOU MEAN BY THAT? FROM WHAT I HEAR, YOU AND SWEENEY WERE JUST ABOUT BEST FRIENDS.
Yeah, yeah, I'm just kiddin'. Me, him and your dad were all pretty tight. But the guy did mess with your head if you knew him. It was just how he was. He didn't always do it on purpose either. I mean, he was so much on his own level that you couldn't figure him out for the life of ya.

WAS HE AS SMART AS SOME OTHER PEOPLE HAVE TOLD ME?
Oh, the fuckin' guy was brilliant. He shoulduv gone to some Ivy League school or something, but he knew what he wanted to do and did it. That was the thing, if I can tell you anything that I figured out about the guy—and it ain't much—Sweeney made a decision early on to do what he wanted to do. Once his parents cut out, he did whatever he wanted whenever he felt like it.

EVERYONE HAS BEEN TELLING ME STORIES ABOUT SWEENEY, AND HOW THEY CAME TO KNOW HIM. YOU MUST HAVE A FEW GOOD ONES.
Oh, I got shit I can't even tell you about. I got stories from when we were fourteen, drinkin' beers and gettin' in trouble—shit that's pretty damn funny.

YOU WANT TO SHARE ANY WITH ME?
Share? What the fuck is this, "Romper Room" or something?

UM...I THOUGHT THAT YOU WOULD WANT...
I'm just fuckin' with ya. I'll tell you a story, but you only get one. 'Cuz, yeah, the guy is my friend, but I'm not doing any of that "Sweeney-this and Sweeney-that" bullshit that all these other guys do. That shit sucks, and Sweeney would be the first to tell you that if he was here. But, like I said, I got a story that'll give you all you need to know about the guy.

Good, good, for a minute there I thought you were getting pissed off with me.

Nah, I'm always kind of angry, but that's because I'm a prick. Don't worry about it. I'll tell you a story, but none of that high-school shit. Sweeney was a high-school shit. Sweeney was a high-school hero, but he let that all go. He never talked about how he called a one-hitter against Galloway with that ham-an'-egger, Miren, on the mound. That was impressive shit, but he never said shit about it or anything about the stupid stuff we did back then to get in trouble when we were teenagers. He let it all go, and so I'll follow his lead on that.

I'll tell you about the day he got outta Merritt [House of Corrections]. He was in there for around eighteen months or something.

I was at the garage at Farannan, trying to change out the blades on the mowers one last time for the year. I had my wrench in one hand, and one of the thirty-six inch mowers up. The fucking blades weren't coming off, so I was getting pissed. It was early, around seven or so, and I had six or eight lawns to get to that day.

So this was while you were working at the golf course, but before you sold off the lawn maintenance section of the business?

Yeah, I dabbled in both for a while before I decided to work at the course and keep the tree work. Once I got the contract to do the city's tree work, I gave up all that lawn shit and sold all the mowers.

But, yeah, I was in the garage trying to pull off the blades and in walks Sweeney. It was a shitty, cloudy day. I was hoping the rain and sleet would hold off so I could do these lawns for the last time that year. So, he walks in and I says to him, like I was angry or something, "Oh, look who it is. You're a little early. Is that rain holding off?" He just laughed a little and said, "You mean snow? It hasn't started yet. And, by the way, you owe me twenty-five bucks for the cab, asshole."

I was supposed to pick him up at noon at Merritt. But he told me he'd gotten out early. He'd talked Leo Luque into letting him out a few hours early. So I says, "You talked a fucking prison guard into letting you out early because you thought the waves were good? How the hell..."

He says, "Well, I didn't tell him it was 'cuz of the waves. But he kinda owed me one from some other stuff I did for him. What's six hours or so after eighteen months, ya know?"

By then, I was up off the floor and we shook hands and I told him it was good that he was out and stuff like that. I told him that I had started surfing a little before he went into Merritt, and that someone had to use all of his boards up in the rafters of the garage while he was gone. He says to me, "You? Surf? Goatboy, what the hell is that about? You could barely swim last time I saw you." He'd been calling me "Goatboy" since I'd grown my first scruff on my chin when I was like sixteen. The name stuck for a while, but had sort of faded since he was gone. I wasn't too happy to hear it again, so I told him to go fuck himself about the nickname, and we laughed. Even though I was kinda serious.

But then *he* got a little serious and started to ask me about his favorite surfboard, his baby. Before he could even get upset I told him I hadn't touched the damn thing. I knew that board was sacred to him for some reason, and I knew not to use it while he wasn't around. He loved that board—more than The Robin Hood, even. He calmed down pretty quick when he saw the board off by itself in the rafters. He said that that board was the one he'd been thinking about all that time in Merritt. It was this beautiful yellow, single fin, seventies-style board he got during one of his trips. He never told me where exactly he got it.

But, next thing I know, he's got his winter wetsuit out and is looking for his boots and gloves. I'd put all the stuff in a locker for him and I got it out and handed it over. I was like, "Sweeney you better have done about a million pushups and situps back in Merritt 'cuz it's fuckin' big out there today."

He just kind of quieted down at that point, mumbled "I know, I know," and started putting on his wetsuit. I was trying to get him to skip the morning session and to wait for the tide to go back out in the afternoon. I told him I would take him up to the points later on, up in North Seawell. I was just trying to get him to stay away from the beachbreak down on Seawell Beach. I'd checked it when I came into work, like I did every day since I'd started surfing, and it was double- to triple-overhead out there. It was out of control. Way too big for me to even think about surfing. I wasn't even going in up at the points, where it was a little more in-control, but I just told Sweeney that to try and get him to wait until later to surf. I was thinking that maybe someone else would be out somewhere and we could keep an eye on Sweeney since he hadn't surfed in so long. I mean, I'd be watching from the beach wherever we went, but some of the other locals would be psyched to surf with Sweeney again. They'd know to just keep an eye out for him since he'd just gotten out an' stuff.

But, after the first few minutes of trying to get Sweeney to wait, I could tell that there was no chance in that happening. He was quiet and focused. He was in his suit, and was just about to pull the hood over his head, but he realized he had the wrong boots. He had his summertime, thin boots. He needed his fivemillimeter boots because it was late-October, and the water was pretty cold by then.

I told him to wax up the Hot Buttered—yeah, that's what it was, it was a Hot Buttered board from Australia. I told him to wax up and I looked for some five-mil boots for him. I couldn't find mine or his at that point, and Sweeney just wasn't gonna wait. I knew that much. He had waxed the board, pulled on his hood, and had his lobster-claw mittens on already. I looked up at him and he says, "Fuck it, Goatboy, I don't need boots today." And he walked out the door.

I was like, "Wait, man, you gotta at least wear the threemils!" He was gone. I run outside, and he's already trotting out of the woods toward the sixth and seventh holes.

I had to see this shit.

I grabbed my phone and called up a couple of the locals from North Seawell and Sun Valley and told them what was going on. I only got through to one of the guys, Mike O'Dowd, and he said he'd be down as fast as he could.

I jumped on the Walker mower, the ride-on mower, and headed toward the seventh fairway. I was goin' as fast as I could, and those things move pretty good, so I was catchin' up to Sweeney. But it'd started flurrying these big fat white flakes. It was coming down pretty hard, actually. It was more than a flurry, kind of a snow squall—which is a little weird for October, but, then again, it's New England so it's not that weird.

It was hard to see Sweeney, he was just turning up along the edge of the woods on the right side of number seven. I could see him in his all-black wetsuit jogging through the snow, with that beautiful yellow board under his left arm. But it was coming down really hard right then. The flakes were huge and wet, and falling straight down, and sticking to everything. There wasn't much wind, so I guess it wasn't a squall, really, but it was just like a curtain of fat white flakes falling. There was already a white coat of snow over most of the grass on the course. As I cut across the sixth hole I could see that Sweeney had jogged along the tree line around the green and up the seventh. His bare feet were leaving a dark trail of footprints through the grass and fallen leaves.

I finally caught up with him about a hundred yards off the seventh tee. I pulled up alongside and says to him, "Are your damn feet feelin' like bricks by now? Take these fuckin' boots, man. At least wear something." I tried to hand him the three-mils.

He looked over at me for a split second, and I just stopped talking and kept driving along next to him. His eyes were this piercing green…just intense. He was going in without the boots and, since I knew the guy pretty well, I could tell he had no time for my bullshit. He had that look that says he only has time for the essential shit. Sometimes he used to look like that right before a fight started, or before we had a sketchy tree job to do. I used to see him look like that after he'd had a few beers—and those nights always turned into all-nighters, somehow.

So I just gave it up, I was like, "Okay, okay, calm-the-fuck-down! But don't expect me to swim out there and save your jailbird ass. You're on your own." And then I asked him, "Have you even checked it, yet?"

He says, without even looking at me, "Yeah, it's the biggest it's been in my life. It's from those three huge storms off the coast. I know what's up."

I go, "Alright, alright. Just checking. Water's about 46 or 47 degrees,

I'd say. It was choppy this morning, but the wind seems to be dying or something. The tide was all the way out about two hours ago, so now it should be pushing over the mid-tide sandbars, with the storm surge, on the inside. The outside sets will be feathering way out there. It should be about as good as it's gonna get today."

"No shit?" he says, with a sort of sarcastic grin. He knew the conditions, no doubt about it. And by this time the snow was letting up a little. I mean, the flakes were a little smaller, anyway.

"Yeah, so, the sets are coming pretty close together. Probably only ten minutes or less between the pulses. These are the biggest storms we've seen in a few years, and they're pushing some ten- to fifteen-foot waves in here. It's probably gonna get bigger while you're out there, too."

"Goatboy, Jesus, I didn't know you *really* started surfing." he says.

"Yeah, I'm on it. I check this place every day. I been keeping an eye on it for you while you were gone. A seal couldn't beach its fat ass around here without me seein' it."

I remember I couldn't help smiling at the guy. I was just chuggin' along on the mower, smilin'. It was really good to see him, ya know? I'd been waiting to go for a surf with Sweeney for a long time, since he went into Merritt, but this time I was only gonna get to watch. It didn't matter to me, I didn't give a fuck— as long as Sweeney was out I felt pretty good.

You'd fuckin' think *I'd* been in jail or something, huh? It was just that he was an old friend, and it seemed like he was back on track, he was back in Seawell, it all felt pretty good to me. I don't know if Sweeney felt that way or not.

By this point, we were down on the right side of the green. We'd covered five-hundred-and-fifty-some-odd yards pretty quickly. The snow was letting up to a light flurry. Sweeney stopped before he climbed down the rocks behind the green. I turned off the mower.

"Anything else I should know?" he says to me, while he was staring out at the ocean.

And he was humoring me, believe me. This guy knew more about that surf spot than anyone. He'd been surfing there as long as I'd known him, and I think he started like five or six years before I met him. But I tole him what I thought anyway, I guess I kinda wanted to show him that I was into it, you know? So I says, "It should be linin' up outside The Little Rocks and walling up all the way to Triangles. If you get the right wave, something more from the east than the north, you might get a reform all the way through to the inside."

"Thanks, Goatboy. that's good stuff. How 'bout a beer later? I want to go down to The Skeff and then over to McSwiggans." I remember he wanted to see Skidsy bartending over at McSwiggans.

I was like, "Yup. Skidsy's still there. He'll never leave that fuckin' place. You know that."

Then he sort of jumped down onto the beach and stood in the soft sand for a few minutes. I was yelling at him to hurry his ass up, that I was cold as hell and stuff like that, just givin' him shit. He pretty much ignored me.

As he paddles out, there was this long lull. He only had to push under two or three waves on his way out. The ocean went nearly flat, I swear to God. It was eerie. I mean, I'm sitting there on my riding mower, cold as hell, it's still snowing a little bit, and out he goes into the biggest fuckin' day Seawell has seen in like thirty years—and the Atlantic goes almost flat for his paddle out.

He gets outside and sits up on the board. It was right around then I realized he didn't put on a leash. The board didn't even have a leash plug. I was fuckin' nervous, there was a lot of water moving around out there. A set was coming in, it looked like it was going to close out across all of Seawell Beach, and he's sitting out there on a board he hasn't ridden in two years. There was no doubt in my mind that I was going to have to swim out there and save him. As the set lined up on the horizon, I just started screaming and whistling as loud as I could. I stood up on the seat of the mower, the thing's springs were squealing, and I'm yelling at the silly bastard at the top of my lungs. I know he didn't hear me, but he starts scratching for the horizon to get over the set. He gets through it okay, and I'm relieved so I kinda crouch down on the mower, just shaking my head and hoping that Mike O'Dowd comes down from up north in case Sweeney needs help. I couldn't see anyone on the entire beach, it was deserted.

How long was Sweeney out...

I'm getting' to that, don't worry, keep your fuckin' shorts on.

Anyway, someone pulled up to one of the public entrances down the beach a little. And I think it musta been them who called the Coast Guard, because it sure as hell wasn't me. And O'Dowd says it wasn't him either. Sweeney's out there about another fifteen minutes, and in this time—I couldn't fuckin' believe it—the wind changed direction! It had been blowing onshore pretty hard in the morning when I'd checked it, and then the snow-squall thingy had happened and there wasn't much wind at all. I'm sitting there, watching, crouched on the mower's leather seat, and the wind picks up again—but from the west. By the time the third or fourth pulse shows on the horizon, it's blowing straight offshore at about eight or ten miles per hour. Unbelievable. I knew I was watching something fuckin' incredible goin' down.

The person who had pulled up to the public beach entrance had gone, so it wasn't Mike O'Dowd. He hadn't showed yet.

The next pulse comes in, and it looks huge. It looked like five feet bigger than everything else that day, so I thought it was going to close out like most of the other sets. And the first wave comes through and Sweeney lets it go—you don't want to take the first, fuck up, and get caught on the inside by the rest of the set. That's basic. Second and third waves are about the same size, and Sweeney lets them go. There's lines of swell out to the horizon, and the sun starts to peek out through the clouds. It doesn't come all the way through the clouds, not like some magic-halleluiah type shit, but it peeks through kinda dim and makes the water go completely silver. Kind of a dull grey-silver, with little whitish highlights. I'm getting' all Robert-Frost on ya, but like I said, fuckin' New England weather, right?

So the fourth and fifth and sixth waves come through and they close out from The Little Rocks to the rivermouth—just huge walls of silver feathering in the offshore breeze, and Sweeney's paddling over each one, one by one. I'm standing on the seat of the mower, yelling, "Outside, outside you silly bastard!" or some such shit.

It must have been the tenth or eleventh wave of the set, it was fucking huge. I knew right away it was the one Sweeney was waiting for. He gets over the wave in front of it and just stops paddling. I can just see Sweeney like a speck sitting on the board facing the eleventh wave while getting rained on by the spray from the tenth wave pushed back by the offshore wind.

He's just sitting there. I'm like, "Paddle, paddle, you muthafuckahh! Go, go!" Sweeney just sits there until the thing's about to break on his head, then he spins the board around and pulls it under him with his black, gloved hand up near the yellow nose of the gun. He takes off at a sharp angle, he's going right, and doesn't even paddle. Not one stroke. Think about that shit!

This giant fuckin' wave comes all the way across the Atlantic, like eleventh in a set of what must've been fifteen waves, and Sweeney is out at just the right beach, and he's battled the rip and currents and closeout sets so that he's sitting in the exact right spot to take this wave. The fucking wave traveled a thousand miles just to pick him up from his little spot in the water. He didn't even paddle, just used the buoyancy of board to propel himself into this wave. It looked like he was slicing down a moving wall of, like, mercury or something, and it's feathering white at the top in the wind.

So he cuts down the steep face and the wave is already breaking above him, he's got his right hand out and it's dragging down the face behind him—leaving a little path like a skipping pebble behind him. I can see his white, bare feet on the deck of the board. They musta felt like bricks by then, nearly useless blocks on the end of your ankles after even ten minutes in that freezing water—nevermind the dusting of snow he just jogged through to get to the water!

He comes down into the trough of the wave, and he's gonna be deep in the barrel any second. He does a sort of halfbottom turn, and the last thing I see before the lip of the wave hides him from sight is a kick-stall. I mean, this wave is like fifteen- to eighteen-foot on the face, it's feathering down the line for about twenty or twenty five yards, and Sweeney pulls up under the lip and stalls a single fin. It's ridiculous. If you saw it, you'd say the same thing. While he's stalling, he's standing up straight, and I doubt he even had to crouch in that first barrel.

That barrel was the best and deepest ever ridden at Seawell, I don't give a flyin' fuck what anyone says about some swell back in 1969. With all due respect, those old-timers can go fuck themselves for all I care. This was the best barrel in New England's history. He was completely out of sight for a good eight or ten seconds, then he ducked under the end section of the barrel and came hauling out. He screams out onto the shoulder and throws a big, arcing carve. He knew how to ride that Hot Buttered like he had shaped the thing himself.

Sweeney carved the shoulder of that wave and then he sort of looked left and right and laid down on the Hot Buttered— back on his belly. The wave was just a ten-foot wall of whitewater at this point, and it was pushing him toward shore between The Little Rocks and Triangles. He starts angling left a little bit, still on his stomach, and then the wave starts to reform on the inside sandbar. Sweeney paddles a little bit, like two or three strokes, and then pops to his feet again and fades to the left and then bottom turns right on the frothy inside section. Little bits of foam are blowing out the back, and it looks like a snow squall coming off the lip of the wave. Sweeney bottom turns and carves up and down the face for speed about three or four times. He's flying across the inside section in a low crouch, arms out, like, I've seen photos of Owl Chapman or somebody in the early '70s. Then he does an off-the-top and angles straight down the vertical face, right before the bowling section of Triangles. Usually Triangles is a wedgy A-frame that works mid- to high-tide, but when the waves are huge at Seawell it becomes a nasty, final, inside bowl section—one last, fat-lipped tube at the end of the wave. It breaks in only a few feet of water right there, kinda ugly and doubled- up a lot of the time, right near the rocks.

Sweeney comes down from the off-the-top, does a tiny fade to the left, and cranks a soul-arched bottom turn up under the thick lip that had been held up just long enough by the wind. He disappears again, in a crouch with his arms forward, for about four or five seconds. It musta been the second-best barrel ever at Seawell.

Well, maybe not, that's crazy-talk. But it was a deep, thick barrel and one of the best at Triangles in a long time.

He squeaked out of that one under the lip, just as the section in front of him was barreling right at him. He got clipped a little in the head by the lip, but he managed to stay on his feet, just barely. Then he just laid down again and rode the last twenty yards to ankle-deep water down in the corner of Seawell. He got out by the rocks at the rivermouth to my left.

DID MIKE O'DOWD SEE IT, DID HE SHOW UP IN TIME?

No. I thought the guy was going to have to save Sweeney from drowning, but he drove up to one of the public entrances just as Sweeney came out of that second barrel. At least that's what he told me. By then, I couldn't take my eyes off Sweeney. I'm standing in silence on top of the riding mower's seat, hands in my pockets, shaking my head in fucking pure amazement.

Sweeney just waved up at me once, as he walked back down the beach and into the dunes. I don't know where the fuck he went. His clothes, the ones he went to jail in way back when, were in a pile back at my garage! I stopped wondering and I just went back to watching the ocean. I was freezing my ass off, but I waited for Mike to walk over from the public entrance, and then, just as he got to me, the Coast Guard and some TV crew showed up. They said they got a call about someone being pulled out to sea. They asked me if I'd seen anyone out there, and the Coast Guard guy had this worried look on his face as he pointed out toward another closeout set sweeping across the beach.

I told them you'd hafta be fuckin' loony to paddle out in that.

He says, "Paddle?"

I says, "Yeah, surfing in that shit's for the birds."

And me and Mike laughed at the Coast Guard guy's confused look.

An' just then, the wind shifted to sideshore, outta the northeast, and blew the whole place back into the whitecapped, choppy mess it had been earlier that morning.

No word of a lie, I'm not even kidding.

"A LISTENING AIR..."*

I held the grit of the thick diving board
between my fingers. I was all-day drunk
and laid-out, fully clothed on a green raft.
Stan and I had pool-hopped on our walk from the bar
to "late-night" at our friend's mom's house in Rathmines.
It was nearly three o'clock in the morning in June,
and I'd found my slurred reverence for summer.

It's now late November,
five years later, and the trees
drop their dry hints of winter.
They pile and lie murmuring
against the dormant grass—
heaped syllables cast from a worn voicebox.
The beeches and black oaks
reserve a choice few—the rattling
stragglers of autumn.
The wind lisps, invisibly,
across the emptied canopies of Seawell
until I'm urged back,
reminded of that summer night.

I felt the grit of the white diving board
in my left hand as I dug through and sloshed
in submerged pockets. I threw Stan his dripping
ignition key. He drove to Twelfth and Bridge—
the Karnick's house, for late-night beer and noise.
I was left with the unrest of dialects—
a hushed breeze moved like a thrown voice through the willows.

Today, the bell-shaped dome
of remaining beech leaves
wanes to a skirt of yellowed bickering.
The clamor's wrung by the gusts,
just as leaf-green's wrung by the sun.

And I released the edge of the diving board
to measure the accent—foreign and obscure—
as it was tossed from tree to ragged tree.
A slackened, traceable, and clockwise wind
argued and gestured among the blown tufts
of dense foliage gone grey in the distance.
My wet head rested on its inflated pillow.
I spun, shadowless, and stared at the lush orations
of summer pushing me about the pool:
from deep to shallow, around low end to deep,
along white curbs—reckless near journeys in sleep.

—Sweeney

---

* Sweeney gave this poem to Gerald Francis in the clubhouse bar at Farannan Golf
Course in 1993 on the day Gerald turned 60. Sweeney told Gerald that he lifted this
poem's title from Robert Frost, Gerald's favorite poet. The phrase originally appears in
Frost's poem, "The Sound of Trees."

05

MISSION TO THE BOAT RANCH

Most of the stories in this collection appear in the order in which they came to me. Usually, an interview with an acquaintance of Sweeney's led me to the next interview; one person recommended talking to another and so on and so forth. This chapter, however, was the last I recorded. Once the storyteller, Sweeney's cousin Tommy Santos, told me the following story I realized that it needed to appear early on in the collection to help flesh out aspects of Sweeney's life.

As far as my second interview with Tommy, this is how it came about: Tommy called me up, but didn't sound good on the phone. He said he wanted to meet with me to tell me about "all the shit that happened in Mexico, all the shit that happened because of Pepperdine." We agreed to meet two days later, at The Nightjar, for an interview over breakfast before Tommy went off to work for the day. Tommy said to me, "Don't forget your tape recorder. You hafta hear this story. No one has heard this one, and it explains a lot about Sweeney goin' to jail and goin' crazy an' stuff like that."

But, the night before we were supposed to meet at the diner for this second interview, Tommy called me from the payphone in McSwiggans. He sounded pretty drunk. He asked me if I had a tape recorder that would work over the phone. I told him I did, but it wasn't set up. He said, "Okay, set it up. No, wait, wait. Hang up. Wait. Hang up after I tell you this, then set up the recorder thing and I'll call you right back. I gotta take a piss." He hung up.

I set up the recorder, but the phone never rang.

I went to The Nightjar Diner the next day, not knowing what to expect, and Tommy was waiting for me in a booth. He had a half-eaten bacon-egg-and-cheese sandwich in front of him, with two empty cans of Mountain Dew sitting on the table.

I started the recorder right after ordering my own breakfast.

Yah, sorry kid. I shoulda called you back last night, but Scotty Khim came in as I was takin' a piss. He bought me like three root-beer barrels. We useta play street hockey together when we were kids over in the Acre. I hadn't seen the guy in years. Anyways, I was *all done* after that. I was gonna call you, but I was fuckin' all done, kid.

YEAH, YOU DON'T LOOK TOO GOOD. FEELIN' A LITTLE BANGED UP?
Yah, no shit. But I wanna do this. I gotta go to work in about forty-five minutes, so I'll give you the revised version of this whole thing. My fuckin' wife will kill me if I don't get this off my chest. It's been buggin' me really bad since we last talked. Thanks for *that*, by the way.

SORRY, BUT I DIDN'T KNOW ANY...
Ahh, I'm just fuckin' with ya. Let's get goin' before your food gets here. You recording this yet?

LET ME DOUBLE-CHECK...ALL SET, GO AHEAD.
Good. Yeah, so I told you I went down to Baja after Sweeney dropped outta Pepperdine. I think I mentioned that last time we talked? Anyways, I went down there with Sweeney's old high school girlfriend, Brigit Beaulieu. She was a real winner, let me tell you that. Traveling with her sucked. I never liked the girl, she never liked me, but she needed someone who could speak Spanish to help her find Sweeney in Baja.

YOU SPEAK SPANISH, TOMMY?
No, I don't actually. I lied to her and my uncle. I speak a little Portuguese, my family's Portuguese. You'd think my uncle would've known that, huh? But he's an idiot, as you'll see. And I told Brigit I spoke Spanish because I wanted to go see Sweeney—see if I could get him back to Seawell. At least I thought I did, at the time.

See, I'm gonna hafta go to work, so, umm, I'm just gonna say this. You can take it for what it's worth.

Brigit and Uncle Jon, Sweeney's father, were real tight. Sweeney and

Brigit weren't even going out anymore. That's what fuckin' pisses me off about all this; Sweeney didn't want anything to do with the girl at that point. But Brigit, in some twisted fuckin' way, thought that if she got Sweeney to come back to Seawell with her he would see that they were supposed to be together, that they belonged together or somethin'. She was about as fun as a bag of wet leaves, ya know? Usually, I steered clear of her.

Anyways, Brigit and Uncle Jon tell me to go out there and let Sweeney know that his mother, Diane, was sick and that they didn't think she would die, but that she was going to be in the hospital for a long time and she wanted to see him. Sweeney's mother had gone through a long stay in the hospital once when we were growing up. I think she had double pneumonia or something like that, I'm not sure. Whatever it was, they told me she was back in the hospital for the same thing. At the time they told me this, she was in the hospital but who knows what for. Coulda been a fuckin' hangnail, and I wouldn't-ah-known because I didn't really ask.

But, at the time, I said, ya know, since Sweeney's dad was asking me to help out, I said, "No problem, of course, whatever you need. Yeah, I speak Spanish..." and blah, blah, blah. I figured I could get by with my Portuguese. Uncle Jon'd never asked me for anything before, so I assumed that it must've been serious at the very least. I never saw Uncle Jon that much when we were growing up. Sweeney'd be the first to tell you his father was a prick—a real fuckin' brainwashed, military hardass. You know the sorta guy I mean. The thing was, he was never even in the military. He had some injury and they wouldn't let him in. He was a technical consultant for them, like high-tech missile technology or somethin'. But he played the part with how he raised Sweeney and treated my Aunt Diane. *[For more on Sweeney's family, see Appendix C.]*

Anyways, to make a long story short, I never got to go and visit Aunt Diane before I went out West. They told me she wasn't seeing visitors—a bunch of bullshit. Like two days later, I fly out there with Brigit. I'm tryin' to be all understandin' and helpful with the little lying cunt, ya know? She told me that her and Sweeney had been in touch the whole time he was out at Pepperdine. I just believed everything she said because

I didn't know what the fuck was going on. I just knew we were supposed to go about five hours south, past Tijuana, past Ensenada to this little town of Jaramillo.

Look that up, because I have no idea how to spell it. Begins with j-a-r, I think.

In any case, Sweeney was supposed to be living down there. I was up for whatever, it didn't matter to me, I figured we'd find the guy somehow. Brigit told me she wanted to break the news to Sweeney, that it would be better that way. I was like, "Whatever. Do what you gotta do, this is a free vacation for me. Let's go get the bastard, let's drink some beers, get some Cuban cigars." All that shit, ya know? I was clueless. I think about it now, and I realize I had somehow managed to shove my big fat head all the way up my ass and I didn't really care. Fuck, awwright, umm, how do I say all this? I can't be late for work today. I gotta get down to it.

Ahhhm, so, we meet up with some of Brigit's college friends up in Mission Beach in San Diego. This guy, Shane, says he'll take us down to Jaramillo because he seen Sweeney down there a couple weeks ago on a surf trip. Shane, actually, was an okay guy. He didn't drink that much with me, but I saw him surf and he was pretty fuckin' good. And, thank fuckin' god, he knew his way down to The Boat Ranch pretty well. I mean, he found the dirt road out of Jaramillo that pretty much went right to The Ranch, and they all looked the same to me down there. We woulda been lost without the guy.

So, somehow, it turns out that this guy that'd met Sweeney surfing back here in North Seawell was down at Cuatro Casas...

WAIT, WHERE'S THE PLACE YOU'RE GOING AGAIN?
Oh, ahhhm, it's weird: The town is called Jaramillo and it's a couple miles inland from this surf spot called Cuatro Casas. It's down in the desert, the middle of nowhere. Right above the surf spot, on the cliffs, there's this collection of old, retired fishing boats up on stilts, or barrels or something—like, 25-foot trawlers and old lobster boats—and they're all arranged in this circle, kinda like a wagon train, but with boats.

And this guy, Shane—the guy driving us—met Sweeney surfing in North Seawell when he was like sixteen. So he sees Sweeney down at Cuatro Casas randomly, staying at The Boat Ranch, that's what they call it. I guess this was like a couple weeks after Sweeney'd dropped outta Pepperdine. Shane talks to Sweeney and they figure out the connection, they smoke each other up, they drank a bunch of beers and they surf and Shane goes back to San Diego and tells some people, ya know, that he saw this random guy in Mexico that he met like ten years before in Seawell, Mass. He's just sorta telling the small-world-story thing to some people at a party in San Diego, you know what I mean? And, anyway, one of the girls he tells this story to thinks Sweeney might've been her friend Brigit's old boyfriend who visited up at the University of New Hampshire when her and Brigit were both freshmen there. She thought it sounded just like him, and she'd heard from Brigit that Sweeney had left Pepperdine and all that. It was fucked. Pretty random, ya know?

But, in any case, that's how Brigit found out where Sweeney was and she went straight to her favorite—my Uncle Jon. Sometimes, I think she liked Uncle Jon more than she liked Sweeney, but that's another story. Like I said, the two of 'em contacted me, and next thing I know me and Brigit are in an old, blue, beat-up, '83 Jeep Cherokee goin' down to The Boat Ranch.

Eventually, we get there and Sweeney fuckin' freaks out when he sees us. He was out in the water surfin', and we watched him from up on the cliff. Shane paddled out and told Sweeney we were there. We got a fire going on the edge of the cliff with some wood we brought, 'cuz Brigit thought it was getting a little cold. But it was nice out, man. Nothin' like Massachusetts-cold, ya know? Anyways, Sweeney looks up at us sitting in our beach chairs drinkin' Pacificos, and he waves—kind of confused and half-assed. He didn't know what to make of it. He took one or two more waves, and then he came out. Shane didn't know anything about Sweeney's father bein' sick, I mean Sweeney's mother, but Sweeney came out of the water kind of knowing that we were there to bring him back to Seawell for whatever reason. So we go up to Sweeney and he's psyched to see us, he's still in his wetsuit, dripping in the dirt. He's psyched, but he's like, "What the fuck are you guys doing here?"

Brigit blurts out, "Oh, Shane knows such-an-such-afriend- of-mine and they talked and figured out that you were down here and she called me and I talked to Tommy," and she just bullshit him, you know? Sayin' something like: "and we just wanted to come and visit and say hi."

I knew something was going wrong there, but I wasn't sure what. I was drunk, I didn't really care. I remember I was pissing right there off the cliff as I turned back to Sweeney when she finished blabbing, and I was like, "Yeah, Sweeney, I'm Brigit's official translator and guide, Tommy Santos. How ya been? Nice to meet you." I had a cigar in my mouth, pissin', I was just bein' a wise ass. I was like, "You know you can drink in the car in this country? I love this fuckin' place. Beautiful country. Now, tell me, *amigo*, where the fuck are the beers?" I was tanked from drinking since Ensenada.

Turns out my Spanish, or Portuguese, wasn't needed at all since Shane drove us right to the spot. That bein' the case, I decided I'd have a few road sodas as we left Ensenada. I was about eight beers deep when we got to The Ranch. Sweeney was laughin' at me.

So I guess Brigit put off telling Sweeney about his father or mother being sick at that point, because we all got drunk that first night, except for Shane. He wanted to surf in the morning, so he just smoked us all up and went to bed kinda early. He had some crazy fuckin' chronic stuff. It was good weed, but he wouldn't touch a beer. Kinda weird, but whatever. So he goes off to one of the boats to sleep and me and Brigit and Sweeney sat around the fire pit until like two in the morning, and we were throwin' down Pacificos like they were goin' outta style. Good fuckin' beer, too—with a slice of lime stuck in the neck. I'll drink those fuckin' things all night, but not too many bars around here have 'em.

Anyways, the next morning it was hot as fuck in the boat I had passed out in. It was comfortable all night until that desert sun hit it around eight. Those boats are great, way better than sleeping in some tent in the dirt. They're all teakwood and clean and they have all these different sized beds in 'em with those Mexican blankets and stuff. I even found a big old bed for a fat bastard like myself.

But, that morning, I wake up sweatin' like a freak. I stumble out and down the ladder of my boat. I went across The Ranch to take a piss out behind one of the boats. It was named the Ronnie Brosnan, he was some surfer from the '50s or '60s, if I remember right. Whoever set up the place had it dialed, there were bottle openers bolted to the hulls of the boats so you could open a Pacifico wherever you walked. I remember I cracked open the first of the day on the hull of one of the boats, and then I went behind the side of the boat next to it to take a piss. They had a pipe with a giant oyster shell, or some kind of shell, stuck to the top of it with a drain in the center of it so you could piss and it would go down to a real septic system. It was a crazy, fuckin' cool place. Sweeney told me he named all the boats after famous surfers—The Duke, The Skip Frye, and a bunch of others. He painted the names on there himself.

So, I'm there pissing and I hear Brigit start yelling something. I'm like, "Ohh fuck, here we go."

I'm rollin' my eyes, and then I hear Sweeney say, "Well, whaddyamean you don't know what 'exactly' he's sick with? You came all the way down here and...and blah, blah, blah," you know?

I was still sorta groggy from the night before, but I remember bein' like, "He? Why would Sweeney be asking about Uncle Jon?" I'm standing there with my prick hanging out, it's like 8:30 in the morning, I'm drinking my one-thousandth Pacifico of the trip and I'm as fuckin' confused as I've ever been in my life. I just sort of paused, and then I shrugged it off and tried to go back to sleep for a little bit. It didn't work, it was hot as hell in the boat and then by like 9:15 Sweeney had us all running around cleaning up The Ranch and getting ready to leave.

When he was locking up the boats and the big iron gate, and me and Brigit and Shane are sitting in the car waiting to go, I says to Brigit, "What the hell did you tell him?"

She fuckin' hemmed and hawed and was like, "Um, I figured that um, he would be too upset if I told him it was his mother that was sick, so I told him it was his father. He hates his father, so I thought he wouldn't be…"

I didn't even let her finish, I was like, "Brigit you are a certifiable fucking nutcase. You are a lying sack of shit. I mean it. I don't know what the fuck is goin' on here, but you are full of shit and I want no part of it."

I just kinda knew something was fundamentally wrong with whatever was going on.

She begged me to keep quiet during the ride, and I was, again, tyin' one on, so I told Sweeney, I lean out the window and I'm like, "Bro, I don't know what the fuck is going on right now, but your parents want you to come home and we gotta get the fuck outta Dodge." I think Sweeney might've thought I was just rehashing the obvious, so he sorta ignored me and just gave me a shut-the-fuck-up-Tommy look.

I was familiar with that look. It was a tense ride home—from what I remember of it, anyway. I was bugging Sweeney about how he fucked up his free ride at Pepperdine and shit like that, but he wasn't even listening to me. I mean, how do you fuck up a free lunch like that? Seriously, you know?

But he wasn't listening and no one wanted to stop into Hussong's in Ensenada for some more beers, despite my reasoning. Then the Mexican army guys, the Federales, searched our car like three times for drugs or guns or whatever. I do remember pissing in a Gatorade bottle a few times while sharing the backseat with Brigit. It was a long drive, ya know? That was pretty good. She wasn't happy. No one was happy. I think Shane, the poor kid, thought we were a bunch of lunatics. He didn't say much on the drive home.

Ahhh, shit! Look at the fuckin' time, I gotta run. Here's the deal, in a nutshell:

Brigit *and* Uncle Jon had lied to me so I would help get Sweeney back to Seawell. I finally found out Aunty Diane wasn't seriously ill, it was like a compound fracture in her leg that needed some pins put in. So when we got to Baja, Brigit told Sweeney his Dad was sick because she knew not to really mess with Aunty Diane. Uncle Jon didn't give a fuck about lying to me or to Sweeney, he just didn't approve of his son's decision to leave Pepperdine and so he set up the whole fucking thing to get Sweeney back home. A recon mission. I mean, what an asshole—ya know?

And then there's me? I was just a stupid, drunk fuck who went along for the ride. Sweeney, like I said before, was not happy with me. He really didn't even ask me what was going on with his sick father while we were coming back here because I told him I was clueless and didn't want to be involved. I guess I was okay with dragging him back to Seawell because, back then, I was sorta pissed at him for screwing up Pepperdine and giving up baseball and shit like that. I mean, I guess I didn't have a right to be pissed or whatever, it probably wasn't any of my business. At least, that's what my wife keeps telling me. But I was pissed—like a lot of us that grew up with Sweeney, playing baseball with him and stuff. And I was drunk almost the whole time I was on the West Coast, so I told Sweeney to just talk to Brigit about all of the family shit that was going on. I was drinking *a lot* back then, I don't remember all of it.

Later, after we got back to Seawell, I was pleading my innocence with him, but I kinda knew I'd let him down.

Sweeney came back to Seawell, then went straight to Rhode Island to see his supposedly-on-his-deathbed father. He got there and all was well and his mother was in a cast, happier than hell to see him. Sweeney finally talked to his mother and found out she didn't even know that we'd gone to Baja to get him. And she couldn't even tell him who was lying about what! She was the only one more clueless than me in the whole thing—pretty fuckin' sad situation, when I think about it now.

Needless to say, Sweeney flipped out on his father an swore he'd never talk to him again because he couldn't ever trust him. He barely talked to the guy anyway, so it wasn't too much of a change. Then he came back to work for Goatboy to try to save more money to go traveling again. His mother, although she loved Sweeney and never forgave Uncle Jon for what he did, she stayed with that stupid prick of a husband and they moved farther south to, like, Baltimore or somewhere a few months later. I don't think Sweeney talked to them much anymore. I don't even know where they are now, and they're my aunt and uncle—well, Aunty Diane is sisters with my real uncle's wife. So Sweeney's like my third cousin or something. I'm not sure how it works, really, maybe he's once-removed or some such shit?

But by that point, Sweeney wanted to kill Brigit. I mean, seriously. I think he seriously thought about killing her. And Brigit, she was just miserable, just a bad person—she claimed she didn't understand why anyone was mad at her. She actually had the fuckin' gall to say to me once, "But nobody understands that Sweeney and I are soulmates!" I contemplated killing her myself, to be honest.

Sweeney made her and me swear we wouldn't tell anyone about the whole fuckin' fiasco. That was the first thing he did when he came back from Rhode Island, when he'd figured it all out. I kept up my end of the deal until now, talkin' to you. Brigit, once she got it through her thick head that Sweeney was never going to talk to her again, just moved to Colorado or Idaho. She just got outta here, which was the best thing for everyone involved I think. She was gone in the span of about two or three months after Sweeney was back in Seawell.

Then, like I told you [in Chapter 8], Sweeney got a little mean, ended up clocking that Mormon kid and wound up out at Merritt for a couple years or so. He and I were never really that close again. He came out of Merritt and a little while later he stole the ice cream truck and they put him out at Darville. Who he fuck knows what he's done since then, really, ya know?

I mean, seriously, the guy went crazy after a while. Who could blame him with a father like that, and a mother who won't stand up for herself? Don't get me wrong, I love my Aunty Diane and Sweeney, but things were fucked up over there too. I certainly don't blame Sweeney, he never really had a family that took care of him or anything—nothing to fall back on like most of us.

But, like I said before, I just really wish I'd done things differently back then—laid off the sauce, paid a little attention to the shit that was going on, ya know? I fucked up, big-time. I guess I still don't understand how Sweeney just walked away from his baseball scholarship either. That's kinda shitty of me, I know, but me and a lot of people in Seawell can't forgive him for wasting his ticket outta this place. Probably stupid to still let that shit bother me, but it does.

And, on top of all that shit, now I'm late for work.

WAIT! DOES ANYONE ELSE KNOWS ABOUT THIS, LIKE GOATBOY OR MY FATHER?

Trust me, kid, no one else knows about this one unless Sweeney told 'em, 'cuz I sure as hell didn't tell anybody. Your father asked me about it once, I think. But I didn't want to talk about it, so I got pissed at him for asking and just mouthed-off about the Pepperdine thing and called Sweeney a quitter. But Brigit's out in Colorado somewhere just bein' the bitch that she is, so she hasn't been talking to many people around here. No one would believe her anyways, everyone's had their fill of her. Mostly, I've been too freakin' ashamed to even bring the whole thing up—I mean, I eventually told my wife but that was like four or five years after it all happened.

Speakin' of my wife, she'll be glad to hear I told you all this. She thinks I'm not really to blame here, and I hope, now that I've gotten all this shit off my chest, I might be able to figure out what I did wrong. I mean, I *know* what I did wrong, but maybe now I can start to feel a little bit better about all of it. Who knows? We'll see how it goes.

I gotta run, here's twenty for breakfast. Keep the change. See ya later, and I hope I never see you again you fuckin' inquisitive bastard. You're like the goddamned therapist I never had *(Laughs to himself as he leaves)*.

MIGUELITO

lies splayed in the schoolyard and cranes
his dusty head—a bony fist
clenching sentience and old brains.
His jaw dips in stale sand, some grist
for the mill of his mouth. His shell is burnished
by the kids' leanings: rough grey to black,
the shine stands, permanently polished
on the dome of his ancient back.
His slow lurch, wisest of animals
in the yard, heaves his dark bulk—the most
adored but harried of pet mammals.
He strains. If he could speak, he would boast
of his century's worth of years,
knowing it's the widest breadth of time
our fast but feeble minds might hear
and grasp. Later he'd describe the crime:
Demented, mass slaughter that's clearcut
through all species of common sense.
His kind nearly extinct, he fears
our kind—the fast and feeble—in silence.
He snaps at the fluttering, soft pass
of a hand, inches back, tramps dead grass.
The globed breadth of his rockhard shell
holds a wolf moon in its hidden well—
his flesh-dense haven and hollow hell.

—Sweeney

---

* For the resident Galapagos Tortoise
at *La Escuela de Miguel Valverde*, Bahía de Caráquez
(Scrawled in tiny cursive writing on a postcard with a picture of a gigantic, menacing statue
of The Virgin Mary overlooking the city of Quito, Ecuador, 1997.)

06

YARDBIRD AND THE GEEZERS

This chapter is culled from several interviews with Margaret Tierney, lifelong member at Farannan Golf Course. Margaret taught fourth grade at Oakland Elementary School for thirty-five years, was an avid tennis player and golfer when she was younger, and now resides at Fairheath Nursing Home in Pentucketville. Most importantly, Margaret was a friend and mentor for Yardbird Sweeney when he was a child. She was more than happy to reminisce about a young Sweeney, and she told me that she hopes Sweeney will return to Seawell someday and maybe even visit her at Fairheath.

Margaret is a self-described "dowdy old bird" with grey curls framing a friend-ly, smiling, oval face. She reminded me of more than a few elementary school teachers I had when I was younger. I didn't have to ask Margaret many questions, she began talking, pausing only to sip at one of her many cups of tea, and she told me all she cared to remember.

I first knew Yardbird when he was just a little thing, running around the course all day long. He was always sunburned and muddy, and he was a quite an alert boy. He really wouldn't say much unless you goaded him into a conversation. Now, what I remember is that he loved to hunt for golf balls in the ponds on eight and nine and in the out-of-bounds woods off four, six and seven. He'd be in and out of the woods all day. Once in a while, I'd see him up in the seaside blackthorn near the green on four. He just sat there in the limbs, peacefully watching all the foursomes approach the green to play out the hole. He'd wave to some of the golfers that he knew, others he'd let pass without a sound or any move-ment to give away his aerie. His tanned legs would be dangling slowly, mud drying from deep brown to a sort of clay color on the soles of his bare feet. Even back then he was difficult to find. He never wore white or yellow or the type of clothing that would attract attention in the bright green canopy during the summer months. He always wore khaki shorts and a forest green or navy blue T-shirt. And you know, come to think of it, I don't believe I ever saw the child wear socks. Most of the children wore knee-high tube socks back then around Seawell, knee-high tube socks and, oh, what's their name? Those red high-top shoes. . .Chuck Taylors. Yes, that's it, Chuck Taylors. But little Yardbird never wore socks and he always had flip-flops or went barefoot. He was the picture of summer with his mussed, dark brown hair, tan face and light freckles scattered across his cheekbones. If he wanted you to know he was around, he would take his flip-flops out of his back pocket, slip them on and start walking toward you along the edge of a fairway. Otherwise, he was nearly impossible to find. He really was a fixture on that course; I believe he lived in a little split-level Ranch with his parents on Yewtree Avenue—past the woods on the right of number three, so whenever the weather was nice he could be found somewhere on that course.

One summer, he must have been five or six, I started teaching him about the trees at Farannan. It was just after I saw him coming up off the beach behind the green on number seven one day in June. I'd never really talked to the boy at that point; I'd only watched him enjoying his summer days all around the course. He always waved to me when I saw him, because I golfed regularly in the summers back then, but we'd never spoken. But that day in June I watched him wash the mud from his shins and knees in the receding foam of the little waves beyond seven's green, and then he trotted back up the sand toward the green, flip-flops in hand. I waited for him, and he was a little shy, but he climbed up the rocks and onto the back fringe of the green. I had a few twigs from the hazelbirch over by number six and I offered him one to chew on. I told him my name, and he said his name was Sweeney. I said, "Sweeney? That's a nice Irish name, but don't you have a first name? My name's Tierney, and I'm Irish, too. My first name is Margaret, so you can call me Margaret."

I'd grown tired of the habit all the men in Seawell had of calling one another only by their last names. If you referred to any of the many unrelated Sullivan's by their first name there was mass confusion, but if you said "Sully, you know, the other Sully." everyone somehow knew who you meant. I tried to get Sweeney to tell me his first name, but he wouldn't tell me. Later, I was to find out—and I found this very odd—his parents had named him Sweeney O'Sweeney. At least, that was the name on his birth certificate. What the *havill* would make his father and mother do that to their only child? I found out from Sweeney about a year after I'd met him. He was very embarrassed about his name, almost ashamed. He made me promise I wouldn't tell anyone his real name. I kept my promise, but I suppose it's all right that I've told you all these years later. Poor child, his parents were a little loopy from what I gathered—a little touched in the head, I'd say.

However, back to my story about the day we met. What Sweeney did tell me the first time we met was, "Some of the old men around here call me 'Yardbird.' I like that name. Mr. Francis says I'm like a junkyard dog, but with eyes like a hawk."

So Yardbird took the twig I offered and looked at it thoughtfully, then watched me chewing on my own hazelbirch twig. For a moment, I thought he didn't trust me, but then he smelled the wintergreen. He had striking green eyes, even as a boy, and he just looked at me and those eyes flashed as the taste hit his tongue. The simple fact that he could safely chew on a part of a tree without getting sick made his face light up. He was amazed that I knew all about plants and trees. I've been a gardener all my life, I love plants more than people sometimes. In any case, that little boy loved to learn about any flower or tree that New England had to offer. I told him to be careful not to call the old men around the course "old men." I told him to be sure to call them "geezers, as in 'Mr. Geezer, sir.' And you can tell them I told you that." He twisted up his face, a little confused, but then he nodded.

I laughed a little at his expressions, and told him to meet me by the seaside blackthorn the next Tuesday if he wanted to learn about the tree he was chewing on. Now, by the time he was eight or nine, I'm sure he knew all the trees and flowers that grew on the course by name. He loved to point out the slenderelf mushrooms, amanita muskbush, cork elder and coyote elder. He was a bright young boy, and polite and as nice as could be. You could tell that he was brought up properly—despite his family's other oddities. Sweeney minded all his manners and respected his elders and so on—elders of all kinds, both trees and people, I might add!

He was there, that next Tuesday. In fact, he had already climbed up about fifteen feet off the ground and was swinging his bare legs around in the branches of the seaside blackthorn, just waiting for me to tell him all about the tree. The first thing Yardbird Sweeney ever learned about trees was how hazelbirch twigs, when you snapped them off, smelled of wintergreen. He was so happy that he could identify and name a tree by looking at the shape and color of the leaves and the direction of the "scrape marks" on a tree's bark. That's what he called the markings on a tree trunk. He'd say something like, "That one has a lot of flaky bark with up-and-down scrapemarks, and big leaves with five tips each. It's a shagsap maple. And this one, the one you can chew on the twigs, has side-to-side scrape marks that kinda look like a million eyeballs. It's a speckled hazelbirch." From about age five to eleven, I don't believe I ever saw the boy without a hazelbirch twig hanging from the corner of his mouth.

Each day, there he'd be, his face peeking out from the blackthorn leaves as I'd approach Tuesday mornings with my women's league foursome, and Saturday afternoons with the men's twilight league. It got to the point where I'd almost forget about playing some of the holes, instead trailing the other women and men while talking to him about the plants and trees and birds and animals on the course. Almost every Tuesday and Saturday he'd be waiting with four or five twigs for me and a few for himself, along with some wild bogberries, or bits of brine lettuce from the tide pools. We'd stroll along together, pointing out trees and birds, and every once in a while I'd drop a ball and ask Sweeney what club I should use. He'd always stare intently in the direction of the hole, shade his eyes with both his hands, chew on his bottom lip, then say, "I think you need a seven iron," or whatever it was that he thought I needed.

And wouldn't you know it! He'd be right. I'd say, "Sweeney, my goodness, how did you know what club I needed? You always know."

He'd just smile and say something observant. Many times, it was very simple, like "Margaret, the wind is blowing wicked hard in your face." Or, "Well, your ball didn't pass that Earcain Yew yet, Margaret."

He picked it all up as quick as could be. We met every Tuesday and Saturday of every summer for years at that same seaside blackthorn. He'd walk with me and fore caddy, because he had strong eyes. I'd say he had abnormally strong eyes, stronger than any child I'd ever known. I'm not sure I ever lost a ball when he walked the course with me. All the old-geezer golfers loved Yardbird, they'd pay him a dollar and he'd go and find their ball and three more to go along with the one they originally duck-hooked into the woods. I believe, if I remember correctly, now, that was where the nickname "Yardbird" came from. He had eyes like a hawk, and he hung around that course like it was his own backyard, like a junkyard…have I already mentioned that? Am I repeating myself? I'm sorry, but it was such a curious nickname. And it stuck—like most curious nicknames do, whether you want them to or not.

I once saw him dive in the pond after a ball, this was when he was a little older, around ten or eleven. God's honest truth. I saw him go after one of those geezer's damned orange balls one day in August. It was Gerald Francis' ball, he was always the nicest to Sweeney out of all the old golfers at Farannan. Gerald duffed it into the water off of nine tee that day, just as I was coming off of eight, through the tunnel under two tee, to play number nine.

Sweeney was carrying Gerald's bag that day, as he sometimes did on Saturdays back then. There were no real caddies at Farannan, but Sweeney carried bags or fore caddied for his friends when he was bored with hunting for frogs and turtles in the ponds. We'd buy him a hot dog, or a lunch of some kind to pay him.

In any case, back to the lost ball. Sweeney started toward the water after Gerald's ball, all the frogs splashed out of sight as he kicked off his flip-flops and took off his green T-shirt. Gerald yelled at him, yelled something to discourage him. But Sweeney wouldn't listen, he wouldn't let the ball go. I remember I yelled at him, too: "Yardbird Sweeney, you will not go swimming in that pond after that ball. It's filthy in there. Do you hear me?" But Sweeney just looked back a little apologetically as he waded in through a smattering of terrified frogs, swam out to the middle and dove for the bottom. There was no visibility along the edge of that pond at two feet deep, never mind ten or twelve feet deep. It was half mud, half water by that point in the summer!

Sweeney must've been underwater for a good minute. I know it was this long, because the foursome from the first green stopped putting and came over—the Underhills, I believe. And it's a bit of a walk from the far side of the first green to the other side of the pond in front of nine tee.

I was very worried. I remember I started in the water after him. In fact, that's right, I remember now! I waded in up to my knees, worried sick, right there in my spikes and socks. Then the little menace popped up in the middle of the pond with a huge smile on his face and Gerald's orange ball raised over his head. He was triumphant, and that foursome of geezers let up a cheer they usually reserved for Red Sox games on the television in the bar.

All Sweeney said, as I glared at him from my soaked golf shoes was, "It was a Pinnacle-three, right Mr. Geezer, sir?" Those old men, the Underhills, and I all had a good laugh then. He was dripping wet, with that shining tan skin in the sun, standing on the gravel cart path in front of nine tee. He was such a nice child, really. Not a bad thing I can say about that boy back then. He was almost like a son to me and a few of the geezers at that course.

Now, as he got older, things were different. From what I hear, I believe he started hanging around with the wrong crowd. This was during the summers after his family had moved to Rhode Island. I believe Sweeney was around sixteen or so when his family decided to move to a town in Rhode Island, it might have been Providence. I believe his father was in the Navy, and was transferred from the old Seawell base down to a newer Rhode Island base. Now that I think about it, I suppose it was Narragansett. Yes, it was. However, Yardbird had become sort of a fixture in Seawell and he wasn't willing to give that up. He was a wonderful baseball player, I believe he was the catcher or the second baseman, in fact. I used to read all about him in the papers. He really was an above-average athlete. He had also become quite the surfer, so I hear, though I never really saw him surf much myself. I did see him play golf a few times, and I would say that he had a better natural swing than anyone else at Farannan in those years. Really, he excelled at whatever he put his mind to. I know that no one at Farannan wanted him to leave for Rhode Island. Everyone from the geezers to the groundskeepers offered him summer work so that he could come back when school was out.

I'm not sure what happened, but Yardbird never really left with his family. He remained enrolled at Seawell High School, partially due to the efforts of the baseball coach, I seem to recall. I think there was a falling out between Sweeney and his parents at that point in his life, and I don't think a boy of fifteen or sixteen should go through such a thing with his parents—not at that age. I'm willing to guess that was the time when Sweeney began to go astray.

I don't believe his grades or the athletics suffered too much. We talked about school here and there on the course, and it all came easily to him. Often, I had to discourage him from skipping class to go and read at the Public Library. He said he would rather read poetry and philosophy than sit through a Trigonometry class. I understood perfectly. I, myself, hate math and remember how tedious those classes could be. But I tried to instill in him the importance of good attendance—to no avail, I'm sorry to say. And I think that the lack of supervision during these years, until Sweeney went off to college, hurt him in the long run. I mean to say, after his parents left, we saw less and less of the boy on the course in those years. He always said he was working to pay rent and so forth, but he finally simply stopped appearing at Farannan during the day. Occasionally, someone would spot him surfing off the beach behind the seventh green, or the geezers would be mumbling about how he lived in the out-ofbounds area off number six, but he was no longer playing golf, or even keeping in touch with Gerald Francis any longer. He apparently was still doing some tree work for the greenskeeper, the "Goatman" or whatever-the-havill they call him. But that work was done during the early morning hours before the golfers swarmed the course, and I hardly ever saw him.

Some of us were worried, but teenagers are teenagers, as they say. What can one do in a situation like that? In a selfish way, I suppose I missed his company and I was upset about it a little bit. At that time, I must've been in my fifties when he was fifteen or sixteen. Any middle-aged woman in her right mind would've been a little miffed after losing the attention and friendship of such a nice young man.

In hindsight, and that seems to be the strongest sight I have these days, it really was a selfish attitude for me to take up. Maybe I could've helped him a little more through that troubled time in his life. Instead, I just imagined it was all part of being a teenager, that it was all part of something I shouldn't meddle with.

OBITUARY

Boris is dead. The fatalist parrot
No longer screams warnings to Avenue A.
He died last week on a rainy day.
He is sadly missed. His spirit was rare.

The cage is empty. The unhooked chain,
His pitiful droppings, the sunflower seeds,
The brass sign, "Boris," are all that remain.
His irritable body is under the weeds.

Like Eliot's world, he went out with a whimper;
Silent for days, with his appetite gone,
He watched the traffic flow by, unheeding,
His universe crumbling, his heart a stone.

No longer will Boris cry, "Out, brief candle!"
Or "Down with tyranny, hate, and war!"
To astonished churchgoers and businessmen.
Boris is dead. The porch is a tomb.
And a black wreath decorates the door.

by Weldon Kees

—from *The Collected Poems of Weldon Kees*

OBITUARÍO

Boris es muerto. El loro fatalisto
No puede gritar los avisos a La Avenida de A.
Se murío en la semana pasada durante un día lluvioso.
El esta anhelado con tristeza. Su alma fue rara.

La jaula esta vacía. La cadena separada,
Su guano pitiable, las semillas de girasol,
La señal del latón, "Boris," son todo que permanecer.
Su cuerpo iracundo esta debajo de las malas hierbas.

Como al mundo de Eliot, salío con un lloriqueo;
En silencio para algunos días; no tenía hambre,
Miraba el flujo del tráfico, sin interés,
Su universo se caía pedazos, su corazón como una piedra.

Boris no gritará más, "¡Apague, la candela breve!"
O "¡Maldiga la tiranía, el odio y la guerra!"
A la gente asombrada desde la iglesia y los hombres de negocios
pasmados.
Boris es muerto. El pórtico es un tumba.
Y una corona negra decora la puerta.

—"Obituary," by Weldon Kees, translated by Sweeney

(Mailed to Patrick Kivlin along with the original English version
from Huatulco, Mexico, 1992.)

07

THE GUN HEIST

The following is a letter written at my request by Sweeney's high school teammate and friend, Peter "The Wizzah" Joyce. It was typed on onionskin paper, on an old typewriter that was apparently missing the letter "r." I've fixed that and a few spelling errors but, other than that, I've reproduced it here without changes. It offers a little insight into some of the places Sweeney visited during the years he was in and out of Seawell after he'd gone to jail and Darville Mental Hospital. Peter, the author, believes the following story happened in the winter of '95-'96, I lean more toward the belief that it was '96-'97. Sweeney was approximately 26 or 27 years old.

Dear Owen,

How's things? I decided to answer your request for a Sweeney story because it sounds like no one has ever put down on paper the whole "gun heist" incident from a few winters ago. I know you wanted me to write this out, for whatever reason, but I'm not that good at writing letters or stories or anything like that. So I decided to go to the bar with some friends from work and a tape recorder. We whacked back a couple pitchers to warm me up and then I told them a long story. A couple weeks later I got around to listening to the recording and typing it all out exactly as I told it. I figured that was the best way to let you know how Sweeney got a hold of his favorite surfboard, but it took me way longer than I originally thought it would. Irregardless, I hope it helps you figure some shit out about that guy. Tell him Wizzah says what's up when you see him, and if he wants to come back out to work as a liftie I've got a job waiting for him.

—Pete

"I'm not sure I should even be telling you clowns any of this, but here goes. It's a long one. It all went down a few years after Sweeney went to jail for that brawl in Sun Valley in East Seawell. He did about two years at Merritt and then spent a couple years after that acting a bit feral. He stole an ice cream truck and they diagnosed him as Schizophrenic or something like that, and put him in Darville Mental for a while.

"Then it was about two or three winters after they let him out of Darville that Sweeney wanted out of Seawell. He'd had his share of winter surf at the points in North Seawell. It had never gotten as good as we had it that fall during the swell from that No-Name Storm a couple years before. Those were the best waves Seawell will ever see—clean and long and empty—like an East-Coast Rincon, just epic for Seawell. Sweeney made the call to move to the mountains for a season before hitting up Orange County for a quiver of surfboards and then on to Central America—at least that's what he told me he was going to do. He'd always wanted to dedicate a winter to hiking for deep powder, but the surf bug had always kept him searching elsewhere.

"I played baseball with Sweeney at Seawell High, and Sweeney knew I was running the lifts at a certain mountain resort, that shall remain nameless, in the Sierra Nevadas. I offered him a job as a liftie and he took it. He got out there in early November and I put him on the easiest schedule imaginable—three, sometimes four, days a week. I didn't need the help, really, but I knew Sweeney didn't want to start spending whatever money he already had stashed for his upcoming trips. The salary covered rations and beer, and me and Sweeney usually spent the other three or four days of the week hiking around the backcountry by ourselves. It was one of the infamous El Niño winters and the Sierra Nevadas were getting pounded with snow. We scored our fill of fresh powder that year, my friends.

"Lookit, the second week he's out there Sweeney stopped into one of the upper-mountain lodges for a beer—and he rarely, if ever, spent any time or money in those damn places. The snow was still a little thin in early November, so Sweeney'd been sticking to the resort's trails at that point, just exploring and figuring out where they all went. So he goes into the lodge and heads back toward the bar. He passed by the cafeteria grill and that's when he first saw it—his magic surfboard. The thing was fucking perfect: a pristine, red dye-job with a pinstripe outline of yellow on the deck. It looked like a late, rare, Ronnie Brosnan-shaped Pipeline board.

"Ronnie was this California guy who first went over to Hawaii when he was real young, back in the late '40s, and went back every winter for years and years. Eventually, Brosnan was living out by Honolua Bay in a tool shed by himself. The guy was a trip. He didn't like the scene that was just starting up on the North Shore or anywhere else in the islands. He liked surfing alone, or with a few Hawaiian locals. The locals at Honolua say he had that place wired. It's a long, hollow right—like a point wave, off these cliffs, that can hold some size. They say he could ride it at any size and make it look easy. He just lived up off the point in a shack and grew pineapples and dove for sea turtles and spearfished. There's this sort of story about how he only showed up on the North Shore for the biggest swells. He'd always just be there, one of the only guys to paddle out when it was 20-foot and bigger. He rode these long balsa-wood big-wave boards he shaped for himself out behind his shack. He'd developed his shapes through pure trial and error. Wouldn't ride anything else, only his own. Only a few foam boards made by his hand exist. He said he never liked foam, just wood—something about riding a board that was once a living entity. I admire his aesthetics, so did Sweeney. Although, we've all been riding mostly foam boards pretty much since we started surfing back in Seawell.

"So there's Sweeney in an imitation Bavarian uppermountain lodge in the Sierra Nevadas staring at a Ronnie Brosnan down-rail seven-foot-six.

"He told me all about that first moment, that love-at-first-sight thing. He had to have the damn thing. It didn't belong in some inland cafeteria, hung in the greasy glow of a fryolater. He was enthralled and enraged all at once, standing there staring at his magic board, three feet above his head. He told me we had to bring it back to the sea. He wanted to drop into some double-overhead bombs on that thing. The question was how to get his hands on it. I caught him whispering to himself once while we were drinking at The King's Head one night. I called him on it and he was like, 'Fuck you, Wizzah, I have to calm myself down somehow, so I keep telling myself, "The board isn't going anywhere. It isn't going anywhere."'

"I'd been at the resort four or five years by that point. I knew everyone and everyone knew me. Sweeney came to me right away—the guy from his hometown who useta get in trouble with him after school an' shit. And out there, outside of Seawell, I'd managed a level of notoriety by getting fucking hammered every weekend, crashing on someone's couch and then sleepwalking wasted around whatever apartment I was in. There were a couple times where I'd forgotten to check the location of the bathroom before passing out, and there'd been a few times where I'd pissed on a houseplant or in someone's sock drawer. The best story is the one where I pissed on this snowboarder chick's plaid dogbed and the dog had it out for me. Sweeney heard a few stories and started calling me 'The Wizzer.' It caught on, but no one pronounced it that way because they all loved Sweeney's diehard Seawell accent—so they all called me 'The Wizzah.' It was funny as shit, and I didn't care either way, whatever. A nickname's a nickname, and there was no way of getting around the fact that I'd done my best impression of a sprinkler in a few living rooms back in those days.

"But, yeah, anyway, Sweeney came to see me about the Brosnan shape. I told him it was owned by the manager of the place at that time, Gene Perkins. Gene grew up in the Inland Empire in Orange County, California, and his dad handed the board down to him like 20 years ago when Gener was just a little kid. Gener never even tried the thing in any real surf, rumor has it, because he said 'the water was too cold in the winter.' He just put the poor thing up in the rafters of his garage when he was a kid. I heard that he only took it out at Doheny once or twice or something like that, and he'd already turned down all offers to buy it. I'd offered Perkins some good money myself, actually. Right then, when he heard all this, Sweeney nearly lost his shit. He flipped. I was laughing at him, he was so fucking pissed.

"I was laughing pretty hard, so Sweeney told me that if I didn't shut up and help him come up with a plan to get that board back to the ocean he'd tell every gaper and liftie on the mountain that I shit myself once on New Year's back in Boston when we were walking home from the bars. I was like, 'Jesus Christ, Sweeney, shut the hell up. I'll help you. What the fuck's your problem?'

"I mean, the guy could be a prick if he wanted to. Lookit, I didn't care if he told everyone about that night. I had to take a shit and I slipped on some ice on the damn sidewalk, a little came out. I was wasted, it was New Year's, big deal. You know? Who gives a fuck? I told him I was planning on sneaking back into that snowboarder chick's place and squatting a grumpy on that stupid dog's bed anyways. Sweeney laughed his ass off at that one, and then we started coming up with a plan to relieve Gene Perkins of his treasure.

"We waited until it was deep. Real deep. By January there had been like eight huge dumps up on the mountain and the whole thing was under about 400 inches of snow. You could launch off anything and land in these huge pillows of fresh powder, it was like a playground out there and all the lines in the trees were deep and fresh just about every other day. We knew we needed to take that board through the trees on a whiteout day so that there was no chance to be seen by patrol or any tourists lost in the woods. Even though Perkins had sacrificed the thing over the grease pit, he claimed to love it, but for all the wrong reasons, you know? He loved it like a museum piece and Sweeney and I knew Brosnan never made a board in his life that wasn't meant to be ridden in big surf.

"The thing is, and it's really sad, Brosnan kind of dropped out of surfing in the early '60s as Hawaii was getting mobbed. He went to Peru for a while, I think, and then when he heard that the World Championships were gonna be down there he just disappeared. No one really heard from him for years. I've read a couple articles about the guy and Sweeney told me all about him, too. Brosnan was supposed to be in South Africa and then in Ireland, but he really was tough to track down. The FBI was looking for him because of some embezzlement charge or something, but no one could find him. Brosnan was from the old school of surfing. He used to drink and surf and brawl with the locals, the Hawaiians, after every big day at Waimea. The locals loved him over there because he was a lot like them, just smaller. When he traveled he kinda stopped shaping boards, but then after he got out of jail he was down in Baja making foam guns and drinking a ton. They say he died after about a year or two down there. Died from drinking too much. Those few foam boards, like the one over that fryolater, showed that Brosnan still had the touch—even if he was drinking up the profits from each board.

"Sorry, I went off on a tangent there. Even now, I remember how much Sweeney loved that surfboard in the lodge. It was as close to Ronnie Brosnan as he was gonna get in his lifetime. And he told me most of the stuff I know about Brosnan, I'm just passing it on to you. The only reason I didn't pull the thing down when I first saw it was because Perkins had the decency to hang the thing with fishing line—rather than driving screws through it. Thank God. If he had impaled the thing I'd be in Pelican Bay doing time for manslaughter.

"Oh yeah, so the plan goes like this: Sweeney and me only let one other guy in on it—this ski patroller, Jan (pronounced Yahn). Jan had surfed a little, admitted that he sucked at it, but he said he knew a good board when he saw it. I knew he'd be cool with helping us. Jan Solo, which is what the staff on the mountain called him, was this huge, almost stereotypical Swedish-American guy. He had the huge reddish-blonde beard, the hulking frame, big smile, happiest when it was below zero and blowing for days. You know the type of guy. He was even from Minnesota! No shit. From some little town up north—Longville, I think. He got Sweeney a job doing tree work up there one spring or summer—it's up by the Boundary Waters near the Canadian Border. Jan was a great guy, and he helped us out a ton because he agreed to let me and Sweeney use his patrol sled for 60 minutes. No more than that, because if some gaper wrapped himself around a tree in that time—and a sled was missing—then it was back to freezing, flat Minnesota for his Swedish ass. I think Jan Solo, instinctively, didn't understand a guy like Gene Perkins, so he was game for our gun heist.

"Me and Sweeney met up at the lodge at exactly 12:15 p.m. on a Saturday of the Xmas-New Year's vacation week. It was nearly whiteout conditions—about 20 or 25 degrees with a storm dumping big wet flakes all day long. But the lodge was still pretty crowded because it was one of the peak weekends of the year. We hoped for a little chaos when it all went down, so we were in good shape. We'd stashed a big rusty pair of hedge clippers in the snow out by the side exit of the lodge, nearest to the Brosnan, and marked it with a pair of ski poles. Jan Solo had skied the clippers to the lodge at about ten to noon and I met him near the back of the lodge and pulled the clippers out from under the blankets on his patrol sled. He then left the sled down by the same side exit. The patrol guys sometimes left sleds there around lunchtime, so it didn't look out of place.

"Me and Sweeney went inside and got in line at 'The Kahuna Grille' while Jan Solo made himself scarce. We didn't need him for anything else until he was gonna meet us above the patrol shack, and he didn't want to be connected any further than the placement and pick-up of the sled. I had a citronella candle in my pocket and Sweeney stood a few people behind me in line. We'd changed out of our resort jackets and kept our hats on and our goggles around our necks. The line was really long, so we waited until we were about 8 or 10 people away from the front of the line. Then Sweeney signaled to me and I went back into the bathroom and lit the candle beneath the smoke alarm in the bathroom. It was the old fire-alarm trick. It had gotten us out of many an exam at Seawell High School and Sweeney felt it wouldn't let us down.

"So I came back out and give him a nod as he starts to order a 'Santa Fe chicken burrito, please. Hold the guacamole, beans, onions, salsa, cheese, and I guess I better not eat any sour cream either.'

The kid looks at Sweeney, 'So…you want just chicken in the tortilla?'

Sweeney says, 'Yeah, I guess. You think that's weird? I don't think it's any weirder than eating a fake Mexican burrito from a poser-Hawaiian fast food place in an imitation Bavarian ski lodge while enjoying turns in the deep powder of western North America.' Sweeney had figured out that a little geography and a few cultural references tacked onto any comment made most teenage ski bums' heads spin.

The kid looks up at Sweeney like some sort of wounded primate and goes, 'Dude, what's wrong with you? You like laptose intolerant or something?' Apparently the geography and cultural comparisons didn't even register with that jackass. He heard Sweeney's order and then, 'Blah, blah, blah....'' I heard Sweeney say, 'Yeah, that's right, Julia Child, so just give me the Santa Fe burrito with the chicken and maybe a little cheese. You happy?'

"Then, in the middle of what I imagined was his response of, 'Whatever, dude,' the fire alarm goes off—way louder than I expected. Me and Sweeney throw our trays and silverware back over our heads and scream like 12-year-old girls at a horror flick, and the whole place goes fuckin' crazy. Just...fuckin'...bananas! It was hilarious. We both pulled on our goggles and zipped up our jackets over our mouths. I ran over to the side exit and squeezed through the throng of people pushing their way through the door. I held it open for everyone and pretended to shepherd the gapers out into the safety of the blizzard conditions, yelling, 'Jesus, people, save the skis! For the love of Christ, think of the skis!'

"Sweeney went directly to the bathroom and grabbed the candle and shoved it in his pocket. He came out the exit in the middle of a crowd and he pretended to trip and shoved me and like five gapers into the snowbank. Everyone screamed, the door banged into some spacey kid's head, and everyone rolled around in the snow while I dug out the clippers—trying not to laugh and throwing a few uncalled-for elbows.

"Gracefully executed? No. Effective? Pretty much.

"So everyone basically got out the door and they were all trying to collect their skis and snowboards and poles and shit out of all the racks next to the building. People were dropping mittens and zipping up their one-piece Bogners and the whole scene was a joke. Everyone's so concerned with their gear that me and Sweeney prop open the door with the patrol sled from the other side of the snowbank without anyone even watching us. It was all working smoothly. At this point, we heard the ski patrol clomping through the front door of the lodge, upstairs, so we knew we only had a little time. Sweeney and me run in back to the fryolater, and

I reach up and clip the fishing line, one and two, and the Brosnan slipped into Sweeney's waiting arms. It was that simple. The feeling of those rails in Sweeney's hands was just shinin' through his ear-to-ear grin. He knew he had a Brosnan and knew he would ride it in the sort of waves it was made for.

"Next thing we did was I went back to the sled that was holding the door open. By then, a few people were kind of looking our way, though they couldn't see too much through the snow. I'm yelling out the door, in my best junior-high, highpitched voice, 'No worries, gapers, nothing to see here. Just a small grease fire, everything's under the bowl, we'll have this cable up in time for your soaps, snow berries. . .' and so on and so forth. I'm just spitting out nonsense and nobody can hear me over the alarm and the wind and snow anyway. It was like herding sheep in a hurricane—just chaos.

"So then I grabbed an extra blanket that Jan Solo left on the sled for the purpose and I made like I was gonna run in and smother the fire. Sweeney wrapped up the bottom half of the board in the blanket. I ran back to the sled and grabbed the other blanket, unfolded it and held it in front of the door with my arms over his head. As soon as I block every-one's view, Sweeney runs over and slides the half-wrapped board into the sled. I drop the blanket in my hands on the board. We gently strap it into the sled and pull it out from the door. A couple people asked us what was going on in there. Sweeney babbled something about a panic attack, a hairnet and the fryolater, and we kept moving, dragging the sled around the corner behind us. No one asked what was in the sled because it looked pretty flat and empty with just the board under the blankets.

"The Brosnan's single, semi-transparent, red, fiberglass fin stuck out of the blankets at the bottom of the sled and I prayed that no one saw it, and I'm pretty sure no one did. I clicked into my waiting skis, strapped on the sled and took off toward the nearest trees. Sweeney jumped into his snowboard bindings and followed. He told me that the red fin cut through the powder like the fin from some sort of snow-shark.

"Jan Solo had given me a quick lesson on how to ski with a sled behind me, and I had done some patrolling for like a month back East at Nashoba Valley so I was doing okay with the thing. Sweeney caught up to me in the trees and he was laughing his ass off and imitating my tray-throwing scream from when the fire alarm went off, and he could scream pretty damn well himself. We laughed for a minute or two, and then we calmed ourselves and made our way through the trees, across the mountain and out of bounds. We hiked up a little bit to the snow cave we had constructed for the purpose of storing the board for a few days. Sweeney had plastered the inner walls of the shrine with pictures of firing Honolua Bay, 30-foot Waimea closeout sets, and shots of Brosnan with his balsa boards back in the '50s. It was like a little frozen slice of Hawaii in there, couple pineapples stuck in the snow and stuff like that. I'd even constructed a little altar for the board to rest on, with two chairs dug out of the walls so that we could stare at the board and drink a couple cans of beer to celebrate the resurrection of the Brosnan. But, by the time we got to the cave, the 60-minute limit on the patrol sled rental was up. We shotgunned our beers, said goodbye to the gun, and I brought the sled back to a mogul run above the patrol shack where Jan Solo took it over and brought it home. Jan Solo was all smiles when he heard the board was safely in the cave. He said he'd meet us there at nine, well after the mountain closed, to check out the board and have a few beers.

"Me, Sweeney and Jan Solo met that night and we each drank a six pack and sat by the Brosnan and admired it in the lantern light on its altar of snow: Three grown men, in silence, staring at a real Ronnie Brosnan. Jan Solo wasn't really even a surfer, but he hung out for a long time—the board was that pretty. Three days later, we met again at nine p.m. and gently strapped the board onto another patrol sled and skied the thing down to my car, which was waiting in the backcountry shuttle parking lot out by the road through the pass.

"Within a month, Sweeney brought the Brosnan down to Black's in San Diego. I gave him two weeks off. He told me he caught a day with 15-foot faces, Santa Ana winds and a good sized crowd out there with him.

"Lookit, I can't really explain the elation he must've felt when he paddled out on that board. Some of it was still showing in his eyes when he told me about it a week later. It would be impossible for me to describe how it slid down the face of that first greenish A-frame, but I can imagine. Well, I guess I can imagine because I started going to Hawaii myself in the summers after that winter. I decided I wanted to get back to surfing after helping to liberate the Brosnan. When I think back on that winter, though, I still like to imagine how it must have felt for Sweeney on that first day at Blacks—how he must've felt on the fade to the left and the first bottom turn up under the lip; how the sunlight filtered down onto the droplets dancing near the red, shining nose of that board. I can see him setting the rail on the wave's face, looking up and out toward the light as the whole wave bowled around him. I can feel how fast that board cruised out of the shade of that barrel with ease.

"He described it to me more than once, 'I just let it do its thing, man. I wish you were there to see it come out of that barrel—the closest I've ever been to a state of grace.'

"I heard a rumor that Sweeney had someone send a photo of him in that barrel to Gene Perkins a couple months later. I don't know about that, but I've always held out hope that he did."

LOUD

The quick chirp of a disarmed car alarm
wakens me to the rustling at three thousand
meters: the creaks and murmurs in the building;
the thud of un fútbol in a courtyard;
cabs honk as they bump toward each intersection;
the "*Buenos Días*" of the indigenous
beneath the heft of baskets that are bound
to their backs, held close, with blankets grey and taut.

SOFT

They've walked down from Pichinchas broad, green steeps,
speckled and veined with blue and whitewashed homes.
And *los nubes* slip along the ridge,
the low clouds push and pull like bent, licked paws
along the verdant flanks of the volcano.

SUSTAIN

In the afternoon, the rain spatters the bricks,
sunwarmed cobblestone sidewalks, wrinkled asphalt;
the flat, wet smell of the pavement commingles
with the coaldark rank of combusted gas.
And the cops will whistle, as clouds thicken and wisp
above thin men on mopeds, as the Quichua
lead travellers with a trail of fresh scent
drifting from their bushels of bougainvillea—
louder than the blankets that hold their soft wares,
the cradled blooms of my frail, seedling poems.

—Sweeney
(Postmarked in Ecuador, 1997.)

08

THE "DOCTAH" AND THE CURSE

I'd been unable to find out much about Sweeney's life in the few months leading up to his original stint in The Merritt House of Corrections. Then I heard that Sweeney's cousin, Tommy—a local at McSwiggans—was good for a couple of Sweeney stories after he'd had a few. I went and found him on a Tuesday night at McSwiggans and bought him several pints.

Tommy's a big guy—he says he's "pushin' three bills these days" and he has a thick, brown goatee hanging off his face. He's worked at "Duck Island," Seawell's sewage-treatment plant, since shortly after he graduated from high school.

Other than cutting out a few of Tommy's tangents about Sweeney's penchant for bedhead and why "The Doctah," aka Doctor MacGillicuddy's, a brand of peppermint Schnaaps, is so popular in Seawell, I have transcribed his story word for word. I asked Tommy to tell me about what happened to Sweeney the summer before he went to Merritt for fifteen months. The following interview was from my first meeting with Tommy Santos.

It's funny I'm tellin' you this, 'cuz just the other day I was sayin' to Spiro, that's Billy Spiroulakis, that I couldn't figure out for the life of me what the hell two Mormons were thinking when they went out to Farannan to try and "save" Sweeney's soul. I mean, what the fuck were they thinkin'?

Sweeney was drinking heavy back then—this was when he was around nineteen or twenty, I guess. He was drinking even more than usual 'cuz there hadn't been waves in a couple months. He'd been down in Mexico all spring—this was just after he'd fucked up the whole Pepperdine thing in the middle of '89. In like, March, I think, he disappeared down to Baja, and then came back to Seawell just in time to miss the cuts for [The Seawell City Golf Tournament]. He was in rough shape, there was some weird shit going on with him and his family and girlfriend back then. And those poor Mormon kids just picked the wrong time, just the fucking worst time, to try and talk to Sweeney.

Sweeney was tellin' Goatboy about the whole thing, like the night after it happened. Sweeney wasn't really talkin' to me back then; we had a falling out over some family shit earlier that summer. But I still hung out with him, with that same crew, you   know what I mean?

A big group of us were playing cards at The South End Club, early, and Sweeney'd been in this weird mood, laughing to himself the whole time. Some guys asked him what he was laughing about, and to shut the hell up, "We're playing 45s not fuckin' double-dutch," and stuff like that, just givin' him shit. Sweeney said he wasn't gonna tell anybody about it but then he was, like, "This is too funny *not* to tell you guys." So he finally went into the whole thing after him and Goatboy lost to a pair of 75-year-old Polish women who played 45s like a couple professionals. Those Polish old maids take that shit seriously—they do *not* fuck around.

But, regardless, we finished up the tournament and a bunch of us went over to The Wardin so he could tell the story. We got some beers and all went upstairs, there were about eight or nine of us—me, Goatboy; Smitty, the Spiroulakis brothers, Dennis Laverty; Tweedy and Speck, and a maybe a couple other people.

Sweeney starts by tellin' us he was all hungover the morning these Mormon kids showed up at his door. He was trying to sleep it off, but the groundskeeping shed was getting hot in the sun. Back then, he used to stay in the groundskeeper's shed in the woods off number six on Farannan Golf Course when he was too drunk to walk the 200 yards past the garage in the woods. He had an old boat, a big old trawler, up on barrels out in the woods, he lived in the thing so he could be close to the surf spot right near there, but he kept falling in the ditch back there when he was drunk and he'd wake up all hungover and smellin' like musk bush. But, anyways, Sweeney tells us he hears this knock on the door of the garage the other morning. He's like, "Who the fuck would be knocking on the door?" His head was killin' him and he doesn't want to answer the door because he's sure it's just Mick with the garden hose ready to soak his sorry ass. But he hears these mumbles and more knocking. Then he hears a squeaky voice say, "It's Elder so-and-so and Brother what's-his-face," or whateverthefuck they call themselves.

Sweeney just gets annoyed. He said he was psyched that he woke up and he didn't smell like musk bush, but he's still fuckin' hungover and somehow these little tie-wearin' bastards had walked all the way out on the course to try and talk to him. He had no idea how the fuck they knew he was there. He said he thought it was kind of weird at the time, but he's sort of impressed that they found him, so as he's layin' there he decides to just laugh it off and have some fun with the kids. Harmless shit, ya know?

He wraps his blanket around him and jumps up and sneaks to the garage door. He unlocks the thing quietly, trying to hold onto the blanket. And then, while the kids are still knocking on the storm door to the left of the garage, he throws up the garage door as hard as he fuckin' can—trying to scare the hell outta the kids. But, when Sweeney throws up the door—and I was just describin' this moment to my cousin down in Lynn the other day—a nail or bolt or somethin' caught the Mexican blanket and just ripped it clean off of him. So there he is, naked as a jay-bird, showin' a rabid case of bedhead, with a couple of virgin Mormon kids going pale and falling all over each other tryin' to get away from the sight of it.

Sweeney decides he better keep going with the joke, before he breaks down laughing, so he starts yelling about how, "Jesus can go to hell and Joseph the Prophet can suck a dick!" And, "Who the fuck dares knock at this ungodly hour of 9:35…" And he's waving his arms and jumping up and down and trying to look crazy, an' shit like that. Sweeney told us he started doing the Chicken Dance in the driveway while he was yelling all the blasphemous shit he could think of. He said he was trying to keep from laughing out loud at the sight of the Mormons' faces, and somehow doing the Chicken distracted him from how funny the whole thing was. I kinda understand, 'cuz I get depressed every time I see people doin' the

Chicken at a wedding or a Jack 'n' Jill. It's fuckin' degradin' to see a guy, drunk as hell, flappin' his elbows an' shit. I fuckin' hate it..

On the other hand, picturin' Sweeney doin' the Chicken buck-naked kinda sucks, too. I mean, we all loved the guy, but he was fuckin' haunted a little bit, ya know? But he told a good story, so we were all listenin' to every word outta his mouth that night.

Anyways, Sweeney was dyin' laughin at The Wardin while he was telling us about how the kids were backing away and tripping over tree roots and how their jaws dropped. They were just fuckin' horrified. I wished I'd been there to see it, it musta been a riot.

See, some of us kinda knew Sweeney didn't really like organized religion, most of us were raised Catholic and he would give us shit, but I never heard him say anything bad to a stranger or insult somebody he didn't know—like insult their beliefs or anything. Sweeney just worked on his own level, he left people alone unless someone tried to tell him what to think or believe. That's the only time I ever saw him get pissed and rant about religion.

And the thing is, I knew he was a smart bastard but he never came across that way. He had all these piles of books about Buddhism and tons of stuff by Steinbeck. He could speak Spanish and stuff. I remember when we were teenagers he read *War and Peace* and fuckin' Roots in one summer. He was fuckin' nuts! He always had tons of books lying around the garage and out on his boat in the woods, lots of poetry too. Not many other people knew how smart he was. He was just like all the other guys when we were hanging out drinkin' an' shit. It's just that he was way smarter than all of us, and a better athlete, and he could've kicked all our asses at once—well, maybe not at once, but you know what I'm sayin'. He was just better at everything without even trying.

The thing is, back then, when we were all in our early twenties or so, he didn't have any sort of outlet other than traveling. At least, that's my theory now that I've thought about it. The traveling thing seemed to work for him. Before he started traveling regularly, before he went to prison, like around the time these Mormon kids tried to save him, he just got hammered a lot. He never drank when there were waves, but the summer flat spells would drive him down to The Wardin or over to The Harbor Court's upstairs deck like four or five nights a week.

So, anyways, sorry, I got off track there. As far as those Mormon kids go, Sweeney told us he was just trying to have fun with them when he tried to scare them. He didn't like some 17-year-old asking him "Do you ever feel lost?" but he felt sorry for the brainwashed fuckers so he didn't want to hurt them, really. But that day he scared those two kids so bad they fell in the mud and got their white shirts all dirty, and then they ran across Farannan and back to their cheap mountain bikes. When they turned around to run, I guess one of 'em dropped his Bible. Sweeney chased after them for like a hundred yards waving the book around, and then he threw it into the pond near the tee on number nine. One of the kids actually stopped when he saw him throw it, and yelled back something like, You're cursed, you madman, Yardbird Sweeney! You can't get away with that! And only God may save you! or some kinda bullshit.

Sweeney said he was a little weirded-out by the kid knowing his name, but since it was only the old timers at the course who called him "Yardbird" he figured it was one of them that sent the kids out to the groundskeeping shed as a joke in the first place.

Other than telling us the story in the bar that night, and laughin' until he was cryin'—we were all laughin' pretty hard that night—Sweeney didn't seem to think too much about the whole thing. He didn't really talk about it much. I mean, that summer, you could get Sweeney to imitate his naked Chicken Dance after he'd had a few, but that was about as far as it would go. And these days, if I go to tell the story, turns out not many people have heard it before.

Even though *he* didn't talk about it much, to be honest, and I've thought about this a lot, I think things did kind of go to hell for Sweeney after that. A little while after that, Goatboy had to tell him he couldn't stay out on his boat or in the groundskeeping shed for a while because some golfers complained to the pro. So he lost his places to stay near his favorite surf spots, and then there wasn't much tree work for him to do that month either, and there were no waves. It was one of the worst summers for waves in a long time in Seawell, I remember people complainin' in the bars. The Atlantic looked like a freakin' lake. Sweeney had been down in Baja a little before that, just surfing his balls off all spring. I think it was like two months later, during that flat spell, sometime in August or something, when he got in that brawl in North Seawell.

Has anyone told you about that? I mean, I'm sure you heard he went to Merritt for fighting and stuff, but have you heard about the actual fight? No? Well, get another Car Bomb set up.

Hey, Jamesayyy! Set us both up with Irish Car Bombs, on my tab!

I'm gonna go take a piss and then I'll tell you all about it. This is a crazy fuckin' story!

Okay, let me down this thing and then we're on [gulps down a shot of Jamesons whiskey dropped in half a pint of Guinness]. Okay, like I said, Sweeney was drinking like every other night down at The Wardin that summer. After the Mormon incident, he kinda snapped. He didn't have any patience with anyone he didn't know. I mean, he was cool with all of us, but that was 'cuz we drank with him and had gone to high school an' shit with him. We loved the guy, he was sort of like a hero to most of us for all the shit I've been telling you about. But that month he was starting fights, rather than trying to calm things down and only fighting if he had to. He was actin' different. I think it was because of the Mormons, but also because he owed Pedro [his bookie] like a grand. He finally had to pay up on that ridiculous bet on the B.C. Eagles during March Madness the year before—fuckin' idiot. Everyone told him not to make that bet, but he did it anyway—stubborn prick. So, he ended up putting off traveling for a few months and I think that got to him. He started spending the money he had on Guinness and The Doctah—just drinkin' like a fish.

He'd been fighting all these guys from Galloway and Lawrence during that month. It was fun for him. He'd get pissdrunk and start something with whoever else looked like they wanted to fight. He'd broke one guy's nose for playing some New Kids on the Block song on the jukebox at The Blue Limerick, or something like that. Guys were steerin' clear of him by then.

Then, on a Saturday night near the end of the summer, these guys from Galloway brought like a dozen friends into Seawell to find him. He was drinking up near the beach in North Seawell, in Sun Valley, because that's where all the summer people go and rent houses and party and shit. It's fun there in the summer. A couple of us were with him at this place on Maghrath St., but it wasn't our regular place. We liked the bars downtown. So, anyways, these Galloway guys come in and Sweeney's actin' like he's got a death wish or something. He's ordering pints of Guinness and chuckin' 'em at these guys—I know! Alcohol abuse, right! He's just wastin' beer, throwin' it at people whenever the bartender isn't looking, throwin' his cigarettes and lighter an' shit. It's fuckin' nuts. Like four of the Galloway guys jump up and one huge guy holds 'em all back, and just before the bartender tosses all of us—and this was fuckin' perfect—the music stops and Sweeney gets off his stool, looks the huge guy up and down and says, "If you're feelin' froggy…then leap, suckah!"

And that guy started to leap, he was keyed-up, but we all stopped it and brought it outside.

So we all go outside, and it's like twelve of them on seven or eight of us, but Sweeney was in rare form. He was just dropping people left and right with elbows and uppercuts and wrestling take-downs. He could box a little bit and he could wrestle an' shit. He was goin' off. It was fucking nuts.

It got to the point where the Galloway guys sort of stopped comin' after us and we sort of stopped goin' after them, and we were all just watching Sweeney finish off the huge guy he talked shit to inside the bar. The guy was way bigger than Sweeney. The guy was a fuckin' monster. But Sweeney could fight. He wrestled one-sixty-threes or something when he was a sophomore, I forget what weight, but he was smart and fast. He got up close and quick on this guy and had his mouth all bloody, and then ankle-picked him and the guy went flying back. Before he even landed Sweeney was on top of him, with one of his legs locked up, just pounding him in the face. They rolled off the sidewalk, it's like a raised sidewalk outside that bar, and the guy's head hit the cement or somethin', 'cuz he was sort of knocked out for a second. Sweeney got up and was yelling at the guy to get up, and we were tellin' Sweeney to calm down 'cuz it was obvious to everyone there the fight was over.

This part's fucked up, just fucked. Because, as I'm grabbing Sweeney's right arm, but before I really got ahold of him, one of those two Mormon kids came up behind us—the same little fuckers from the golf course. They came outta nowhere, the stupid little shits. I think it was the one who'd lost his Bible in the pond. I guess the Mormon kids were living somewhere nearby in North Seawell, out by the marsh I guess. Not the nicest part of town, but that's where they had their apartment. So Elder what'shis-face comes up behind us just as I'm trying to grab Sweeney. He gets his hand on Sweeney's left arm and starts to say something. Sweeney turns around, like, frothing at the mouth, and just lays the poor kid out with a left-handed haymaker. It was fucked.

He sort of lost it right there—personally, I think that's when Sweeney hit bottom. He was all flighty, his eyes were rollin' around in his head. He musta been out of his mind, because he usually fought fair if he fought at all. The poor Elder-kid's jaw was shattered by that one punch. I saw his eyes go blank, and his face got limp and pale while he was falling to the street. It was, like, in slow-mo, ya know what I mean? It was fuckin' crazy. He slipped off the sidewalk, landed in an oily puddle and his head cracked a parking block. It was disgusting—his face was a mess, and it was probably better that he was knocked out cold.

About five or six of us jumped on Sweeney and held him down and kept the Galloway guys away from him. We're all bleeding on each other and Sweeney's just freaking out beneath us. The Galloway guys were kinda picking up their own guy, the monster, and then they were just staring at all of us and Sweeney. And just then the other Mormon kid comes up and he's jumping around in his white shirt and tie and he's freaking out about his friend's face. So, Laverty's trying to hold that kid back from moving his friend around and the kid's yelling that he's already called the cops and telling Sweeney he's going to hell and all that shit. I can see Laverty wants to slap the kid, in spite of himself. I'm tellin' him to calm down. Meanwhile, there's blood dripping out of the other Mormon's ears, and it's takin' the rest of us, like six of us, to hold Sweeney down because he was still fuckin' acting like an animal. The Galloway guys stuffed their monster in the back of a Jetta and took off, and then about four cop cars pull up and see the poor Mormon kid laid out in the puddle. They pepper-spray Sweeney, cuff him and throw him in the paddy wagon in about five seconds flat. No questions asked.

We were on Sweeney's side, but we couldn't believe that he'd just knocked that kid out. And, for once, I didn't really recognize any of the cops. A couple of us—Laverty was one of 'em—thought Sweeney didn't know who he hit. Some of us thought he did. I still don't know. And the cops were everywhere before we could think straight. I'd had too much of the Doctah' that night, and my eyes were pretty much swelling shut by that point. I was just stunned by the whole thing. We should of let Sweeney take off, the cops never would've caught him, the guy knew how to disappear quick. But we were all kinda freaked by the sight of the unconscious kid on the ground; Spiro was screaming for someone to call an ambulance; the other Mormon's still jumping around yellin' all kinds of fire-and-brimstone type shit. It wasn't pretty and never got any prettier.

I remember watchin' the paddy wagon pull away, and thinkin' that Sweeney might need to do some time to calm down a little. What was it with his record? Like, 18 months at Merritt? I don't know, I forget. But I realize now that it wasn't any good for him. It didn't do him any fuckin' good at all.

Because when Sweeney got out, we didn't really hang out much after that. I didn't see him at The Wardin or even McSwiggans anymore, and I was there a lot. I mean, he was still pissed at me for the stuff in Mexico that past June, but it wasn't that bad between us. We were patchin' things up slowly. But Sweeney just kind of faded in and out for a few years after that. Everyone was telling us he was living over on the golf course again, in his old boat, the Kemp Aaberg—which, he was. . .sometimes. But then I'd hear he was in Mexico, and then Ireland. I heard crazy, erratic shit. Then I started hearin' Sweeney went fuckin' bananas while he was in

Merritt and that the government was giving him money to live on.

I don't know. I didn't know what to do about the guy. I didn't really know what was true or what, even though I'm his cousin. I mean, what was I supposed to do? Go over to the golf course and start looking in the out-of-bounds areas for him—up in the trees an' shit? He was still kinda pissed at me, and I couldn't blame the guy. But I was still kinda pissed he stopped playin' baseball and that he quit school. So I wouldn'tah- known what to say if I found him out in the forest or somewhere. I mean, every once in a while, we'd gone over and hung out with him on his boat in the woods, but I was engaged back then and I was catchin' hell for goin' out and getting shitfaced and all that. I wasn't seeing too much of him or any of the other guys at the time.

I remember bein' like, "Fuck it, he knows how to take care of him-self." I just let it all go. You know what I mean? Sweeney was always the type of guy who would just show up and hang out and drink an' shit. You never called him, he'd always just be there on the best nights an' stuff. He knew everything that was going on, I just sort of followed his lead back then. I didn't know how to help someone like that.

I think about it now, sometimes, and I guess *anything* would've been better than nothing. I shoulda come clean with the guy.

I mean, well, this is all I'll say: at this point—and I think about this a lot, Owen—I just wish I'd tried something, that I'd done something different. You know what I mean?

FRANCISCO "PANCHO" MONEYMAKER

Once told me, "I only hear
Dixieland, no matter what
comes my way." He always rode
his piebald mare with a flat,
broad machete hung from his
left hand, rope-reins in his right.
He bobbed to the rise and fall
of the mare's slow clop, danced
through muddy, rock-strewn streambeds.
His machete thwacked through vines
and green jungled undergrowth
like a rusty metronome.
He built a small farm, and grew
passion fruits, corn, peanuts and weed.
The chickens were happy there—
plump from smoke-induced feeding
frenzies Pancho blew into
their flock.
       When he needed cash
Pancho dug ditches in town:
"It's honest work, if you can
sweat it," he grinned. "Dirt-road towns
need ditches. It's straightforward
here; when it's shallow they say,
'*superficial*,' and my
sweat makes it '*más profundo.*'"

—Sweeney

"THE SEED," PANCHO'S DREAM

Late Saturday night, Pancho spoke the dream.
He chanted its deep swerve and benthic sway.
I listened, seated, leaning against salt-bleached
driftwood logs, sifting sand through my cupped hands.
Three days before, we'd crushed the skull of a quarter
horse, a spooked, brownish mare that lurched from the ditch
grasses to the right of our borrowed Toyota.
Pancho's head hung over the tiny peaks
of sand burying his tanned, calloused feet.
The firelight licked at the crown of his head
as words crept through the veil of his long hair:

Neon vines sprout in my virgin jungle, low
*   in the ferns, their unraveled reds split hues of green*
*   evening as dusk unfolds. And dusk spreads slow*

as rust clotting the gears of an old machine.
*   When darkness floods, suddenly, it's a spate*
*   of hungry bats blackening the skies of the scene.*

I feel the Earth pulse, like a fuse blown straight
*   out of its box. It teeters in search of its lost*
*   thread: the long orbit plotted by its own weight.*

In a flash, my jungle goes cold. A dense hoarfrost
*   seizes the undergrowth and shorts the neon.*
*   Bright vines explode, sparks shower, thrown and tossed*

by freezing winds. I wilt beneath the strewn
*   sparks, their wide glare reddening the frosts' white spread.*
*   Blown-glass clouds gather, backed by a dark, moon-*

less night—their blue-black underbellies touched
    with white reflections of the rime that chokes
    the web of jungle life. Soon, it will be dead.

I move slow—cold, static—but my body soaks
    my clothes with sweat. White-hot secrets stab down
    from clouds in the tilted sky. The thigh-thick spokes

of lightning chisel the icy ground and stun
    me into a world gone black and white. Each moment
    conducts the next, but connects with the mare's last one:

when her round eye fogged like some animate,
    rolling sky blotted with shock. But then the dream
    shifts as the clouds thin, break and dissipate.

The sun rages, though light rain pelts low steam
    that's slung around the brown trunks of thin trees.
    The trunks resemble limbs jutting from a stream

of stretched gauze. But the truth tugs me to my knees,
    struck dumb, staring at a field of birth-wet foals
    sown hoof-deep. The Earth's brood incubated by breeze

and sunshower—I'm entranced till something rolls
    in my palm. The vision blurs, and I understand
    her eye's a seed in my care. My whole arm tolls

in time with the throb of that surging ground.
    There is no knell in the pulse of the green world.
    And I slip from that potent fountainhead

electric and awake; back to the sound
    of my farm in the heart of the jungle—where trees seem to graze
    on silence budding between footfalls of wind.

Pancho paused, stared at our fire, his yellowed gaze
subdued, and said one more thing before he left:
"I read once that at any given moment
one hundred bolts of lightning strike the Earth,
each sheathed in a column of thunder. We survive...
we grope along on pulmonary ground—
between the beats and breaths of this green fuse."

—Sweeney, as told to me by Francisco Moneymaker.

(Both of these poems take place somewhere in Central or South America. Yet, each arrived separately, within the same month from Galway, Ireland, in 1997. Both were written in green ink on paper designed to fold up into their own air-mail envelope.)

09

THE BLOWN FREE RIDE

The following is an interview with Audrey Gammens. Audrey has written and edited for Seawell's newspaper, The Seawell Times, *for twenty-five years. She originally covered the local sports scene—Seawell State University, Seawell High School, and the Red Sox single-A affiliate, the Seawell Gulls. Eventually, Audrey began covering the Sox down in Boston, often travelling to Fenway for important games, post-game interviews and general coverage of the club. Audrey left* The Seawell Times *for several years and freelanced as a writer and editor. Many of her articles appeared in* The Boston Herald, The Boston Globe *and occasionally in* The Sporting News *as well as other national sports publications. Baseball has always been her "beat," and Audrey was one of the first female sportswriters to be accepted into the old-boys media-coverage scene in the Boston area.*

Born and raised just outside of Seawell in Galloway, Audrey eventually returned to The Seawell Times *to woman the helm as Sports Editor.*

Ms. Gammens, thanks for agreeing to this interview, I know you are very busy at the paper and you don't have much time.
Not a problem. Please, call me Audrey and forgive me if this is a little awkward. I'll have to get used to being the interviewee. I'm usually on the other side of the tape recorder.

Not a problem, Audrey, I'm sure you'll do fine. Please feel free to help me out with my lack of skill as an interviewer. This project has forced me to appreciate the art of asking the right questions, but I've still got a lot to learn. I just wanted to ask you about your days covering Seawell High baseball, back when Yardbird Sweeney was playing shortstop for the varsity team as a sophomore.
Oh, well you're doing fine, just fine so far. You're asking about a very specific period of time, and I remember Sweeney very well. He was one of the best players Seawell High has ever seen. He was their shortstop,

but over those four years I saw him try his hand at catcher, outfielder and almost every other position in the field. He was nearly a complete player, which is very rare at that age. The coach back then, Jorge Mroz, had a pretty good eye for talent and he worked Sweeney into his lineup every chance he could during Sweeney's freshman and sophomore years. I believe Coach Mroz would've made Sweeney a starter at short as a sophomore, but there's a heavy amount of politics to be negotiated within the coaching of Seawell's varsity squads. As a junior, however, Sweeney had earned the spot at short, occasionally backing up as catcher when needed. Those were Sweeney's two best positions, defensively. Which, if you know baseball, you know it's odd for a player to be able to grind out a game behind the plate one day and then have the range and quickness to play the next game at shortstop.

COULD YOU ELABORATE A LITTLE ON THAT. I'M NOT REALLY UP TO SPEED ON THE FINER POINTS OF BASEBALL.

Certainly, I'd be happy to. You see, Sweeney, back then, was around five-foot-ten or so. He wasn't thin, but he wasn't stocky like your average catcher, either. He was an athlete, around one-hundred and sixty or seventy pounds. He was lanky or even lithe. Yes, "lithe" would be an accurate word to describe him. I believe he ran the 110 hurdles during the winter as well. I remember that he physically looked more the part of a shortstop, but once he threw on the equipment he was every bit of a catcher as well. He had a cannon for an arm, so there was no problem there—he could throw a runner out at second from his knees, but he could also turn a double play as if he were never hurried to make the play. I would equate him, now, to Montreal's Orlando Cabrera, a guy who has fun playing short every day and does it with ease. When he caught, Sweeney always reminded me of Pudge Fisk, the old Sox catcher. Sweeney had that same nonchalance as Pudge, and that quality is rare in a catcher.

I remember distinctly, and you might find this in some of my old columns about those high school teams, that he was a natural. He could hit any pitch from either side of the plate, lay down a drag bunt with the best of lefties, he had some power from the left side and his swing was smooth and even. Overall, very pretty to watch when he was at the plate.

As for the defensive end of things, he really could've played anywhere on that field—as I've said before. Seawell always had strong pitching in those days, so he wasn't needed there, to my recollection. But I seem to recall that he gave every other position a go—and he handled it all smoothly. Struggle was not a part of his game. He seemed to glide through every play I saw him make. Most importantly, and this is the aspect of his game I most enjoyed, he always looked like he was having fun out there. He was, at least until his senior year, constantly smiling and laughing—constantly at play, as a high school player should be.

So, Sweeney was a different sort of player as a senior?

Well, I recall that he seemed to lose touch with how much fun he was having out there. It was only a few games into his senior year and I noticed how he had lost that verve, and he was playing with a little more aggression, a little more anger. At least, it appeared that way to me. As a fan, I was disappointed to see this subtle change in his game. Although, I recall that his numbers weren't affected. He still hit cleanup and was All-State, and his defense never suffered. He never revealed to me the cause of this change. I never pushed the issue in the few brief interviews I did with him that year. I wanted to, desperately, but I kept reminding myself that he was just a kid playing baseball. He wore his heart on his sleeve, that was clear, but he was just an extremely talented kid, and it didn't seem fair of me to delve into anything in his personal life that might have affected his game. Really, as I've said, it was a subtle change in his playing style that not too many people noticed. I suppose I only noticed because I'd seen him grow into a star in the Seawell High program. Baseball is my first love, and he was a player I'd spent a lot of time watching.

Could you speculate as to what might have caused the change?

Well, yes, I suppose I could. I once spoke with Jorge Mroz about it because, as I've said, I was concerned. This was all off the record, but Jorge and I sat down in his classroom at Seawell High once to talk about how the season had gone. It was the year that Seawell had lost the state championship to Galloway, their biggest rival, in a close battle. Jorge agreed to talk about it as long as it was off the record. He told me he thought that Sweeney had been having trouble adjusting to living alone in Seawell. His father was in the Airforce, a lieutenant I believe…or maybe it was the Navy. I'm not entirely sure. In any case, he had been transferred to a base in Rhode Island or Connecticut during the summer before Sweeney's senior year. Sweeney didn't want to leave Seawell, he told Jorge he couldn't leave. He asked Jorge to help him. In turn, Coach Mroz spoke with the family and told me that he had made an arrangement to keep Sweeney in Seawell for his last year of high school. The logistics of the deal involved Coach Mroz virtually guaranteeing that he could pull some strings and get Sweeney into Pepperdine on a baseball scholarship, and that he would serve as Sweeney's guardian for that final year in Seawell.

From what I heard, the family agreed, and Sweeney stayed and even ended up going to Pepperdine for half a year or so. He dropped out after a disagreement with the coach out there. The coach wanted him to play short exclusively, as well as batting lefty exclusively. It was a strange battle of wills from what I can gather. I always thought it was a little crazy for a coach not to want to use all the tools Sweeney could bring to a team, but politics and stubbornness and other things I don't know about must have factored into it. What resulted was Sweeney quit the team and left Pepperdine almost immediately after the start of his second semester.

Jorge Mroz had kept his end of the deal as guardian during Sweeney's senior year, but I remember people were mumbling that Jorge had never reined Sweeney in that entire year. His grades dropped somewhat, his style of play changed in my opinion, and he seemed like a different kid. In fact, I heard he was living in some shack or shed on the Farannan golf course or some such thing.

SO YOU BELIEVE THAT SWEENEY'S PARENTS' DEPARTURE WAS THE REASON FOR SWEENEY'S CHANGE AS A PLAYER AND PERSON THAT YEAR?

Well, I imagine that was part of it, but there was also a lot of pressure on him to perform in order to get that scholarship. I think, sadly and unnecessarily, Coach Mroz blames himself for Sweeney's fall from baseball grace. But I think his mother and father leaving started the ball rolling, to be perfectly honest. They were no longer around, and the logistics of the situation had Sweeney playing baseball for a reason other than pure enjoyment, and the game was no longer fun for him. He was still the leader of that baseball team and all the players respected him, but he no longer played with that unadulterated joy the players and coaches and fans were accustomed to. People came to watch him play, and they were rarely disappointed. He was an exciting player, defensively and offensively.

JUST HOW GOOD WAS HE? YOU'VE COVERED THE RED SOX SINGLE-A TEAM AS WELL AS THE RED SOX MAJOR LEAGUE CLUB, COULD HE HAVE PLAYED PROFESSIONAL BALL?

No question. In my mind, no question. I know, barring injury, that he was a big-league caliber shortstop in the making. Red Sox and Cardinals scouts were raving about him during that final year at Seawell. However, a reliable source told me he turned down all offers by the end of that year. He didn't want to be drafted.

REALLY? HOW DOES A BALLPLAYER TURN DOWN BIG-LEAGUE OFFERS?

I know, I know, I've often wondered the same. At first, we figured it was because Sweeney wanted to go to college, but we know now that obviously wasn't the case. And, like I said, baseball had lost its luster for the kid by the end of his senior year. Pepperdine, in my opinion, was just a gesture—he felt obligated to Coach Mroz and wouldn't go back on his word. Well, that's my theory anyway. Once he got out to Malibu, I heard he just went surfing or some such nonsense. He fulfilled his end of the deal by beginning the season with the Pepperdine team, and then took off to surf and fritter away his God-given talents.

It burns me to this very day to think about it, to be honest.

IN YOUR OPINION, EVEN THOUGH YOU RECOGNIZE SWEENEY WAS NO LONGER

HAVING FUN WHILE PLAYING BASEBALL, YOU BELIEVE HE DID WRONG BY LEAVING THE GAME?

Listen, I was born and raised in northeastern Massachusetts just like him—just like you, right? Galloway's a blue-collar town, similar to Seawell. You know as well as I do that thousands of kids would've given their right arms to have his talent, and he goes and throws it all away over some family problems, a little pressure and surfing. For the love of God! The kid was the best ball player in New England at age 17. The best! I'll never know what the hell he was thinking.

BUT IT SOUNDED LIKE YOU HAD PUT A LOT OF THOUGHT INTO WHY SWEENEY STOPPED HAVING FUN AND THE GAME HAD BECOME MORE LIKE A JOB FOR HIM? I TAKE IT YOU'RE NOT ENTIRELY SYMPATHETIC TO HIS REASONS FOR QUITTING?

You bet I'm not! Maybe I'm being selfish here, but that kid could play. He would've made a lot of people happy if he'd kept at it. Seawell is a hardcore sports town, and he was the best athlete to come out of here in decades. I don't know what was going on, really, but I think he blew it. He threw it all away and disappointed a lot of his friends, family, coaches and fellow players.

DID YOU EVER FOLLOW UP WITH HIS FAMILY TO TRY AND FIND OUT WHAT HAD BECOME OF SWEENEY AT PEPPERDINE?

Well, I tried to interview Sweeney and he wouldn't return my calls to the Pepperdine program. I spoke with his mother and father briefly, but they refused to say anything. They were livid that he had quit and disappeared, but I don't think Sweeney had a good relationship with his parents to begin with—even while they all lived in Seawell together. The coach at Pepperdine, I forget his name, he crucified Sweeney when I talked to him—so much so, I didn't feel I could publish any of his quotes in *The Seawell Times*. He was fairly brutal about the whole thing. He called Sweeney a selfish player and other things along those lines—accused him of not being a team player. And as I've said, Sweeney epitomized the concept of team—whether he was playing happy or angry baseball—so

I didn't trust the coach's assessment of Sweeney's character. And this is from the guy who wouldn't let Sweeney switch-hit, so I think he was a little batty to begin with. I kept my last report about Sweeney dropping out fairly vague and inconclusive in *The Seawell Times*, I didn't want to add to the rumblings and rumors circulating in town.

Since then, I've heard Sweeney's had his problems with his mental health and so on, and I suppose that might explain some of his actions back then, but I'll never understand what happened. I'm just hurt and disappointed that his talents went to waste, that a scholarship was wasted on him.

I wanted to follow his career through the major leagues, I wanted to root for a Seawell guy up at the plate at Fenway someday. Imagine for a second if the starting shortstop for the Sox was from Seawell! This town would've canonized Sweeney. He would've been a walking, talking legend. I would've done my part to make that happen, too. I would've done my best to bring that kid into the limelight he deserved. I never got my chance, and I think a lot of people in Seawell feel the same way.

YOU KNOW, I HEAR WHAT YOU'RE SAYING, AND I'VE HEARD A FEW PEOPLE TALK ABOUT THE WHOLE PEPPERDINE THING, BUT IT SEEMS TO ME THAT SWEENEY HAS BECOME A LEGEND OF SORTS IN SEAWELL ANYWAY.
Well, the whole "Fifteenth Hole Incident," the City Tourney victory, and the rumors of his insanity and jailtime and all of that has gotten him some local notoriety, but I'm talking about national attention here. Listen to what I'm saying, this little coastal city, just north of nowhere, would've had a born-and-bred professional baseball player to prop up and adore!

WELL, I SEE YOUR POINT BUT IT SEEMS TO ME THAT WAS JUST WHAT SWEENEY DIDN'T WANT. FROM WHAT PEOPLE ARE TELLING ME, HE FOLLOWED HIS OWN PATH SO TO SPEAK...
Oh, don't give me that "and I took the road less traveled" b.s. Sweeney wrote some poems and pulled some pranks and lived in the out-of-bounds area of some golf course—I've heard all the stories. And never-mind his dominance in the 110 hurdles, his skills on the track paled in

comparison to what he could do on the baseball diamond. The diamond is where it would've paid off for that kid. *He wrote and traveled and did what he wanted*, blah, blah, blah—it doesn't matter. Maybe if he'd have listened to his coaches and family and followed through at Pepperdine he wouldn't have jumped off the Pennacook. He burned a lot of bridges by dropping that free ride, then he climbed one and threw it all away. The kid's dead and he doesn't deserve any more attention. He blew it, plain and simple, and plenty of people in this town feel the same as I do. Tough cookies.

Are we done here?

CASING MY LOT

I watch, unsteady, in the sweep and glare
of headlights as a stray unfurls itself
from folds of deep sleep
in the gutter's dust.
The only paved street in town is pale orange
under patches cast by weak streetlamps.
Four men welcome a fifth to their corner
with a proffered swig of sugarcane booze.
A few slowly fold their T-shirts and tanktops
up to their chests, rub their brown bellies,
whistle and laugh.
            It never ceases,
this warm onshore wind never ceases
nudging the blown waves' mumblings
through the orange dark—a blurred song
that sways me in the street.
I think about another beer, but let it go
with a slow, unseen wave of my hand.
I turn toward bed,
barefooted amblings in the dust,
as the markets and bamboo shacks
fade from my sight.
            The asphalt's grown
smoother in the gutters.
I angle there each night,
casing my chosen wilderness,
shuffling through this seaside tranquility.

Somewhere below my cinderblock bedroom
there is small chaos and laughter.
For a moment, near silence:

the blurred mumblings billow my mosquito net,
shift the latticework of light
cast by the glassless windows.
More small chaos,
and a child laughs at an escaped quarter horse
clopping toward greener vacant lots.

—Sweeney

(Postmarked in Ecuador, 1997.)

10

VICTORY AT THE CITIES

The following story is pretty much a standard in the bars of Seawell. Everyone you meet has heard it. Almost everyone tells it differently—embellished, exaggerated, or just filled with flat-out lies. I went back to the source, Gerald Francis, for a firsthand account (Walt, again, did most of the speaking) of what went down that day on the golf course.

GERALD, NO ONE HAS EVER BEEN ABLE TO FIND SWEENEY GUILTY OF PULLING ALL THOSE PRANKS AT THE CITY TOURNAMENTS. DO YOU KNOW SWEENEY PULLED THESE PRANKS FOR SURE?
GERALD: (Just nods.)

I FIGURE YOU AND YOUR SON ARE TWO OF THE MOST RELIABLE WITNESSES TO WHAT HAPPENED THAT DAY WHEN SWEENEY WON THE CITIES. CAN YOU GUYS HELP ME OUT WITH SOME DETAILS?
WALT: Not a problem. We had fun talking to you last time. So I'll try and remember what me and my father saw that last day of the Cities.

My father says that Sweeney never said a word about the pranks for a couple of years, but all of us from Farannan kinda knew Sweeney pulled them. I mean, who else could've? The one from when he won the Cities, when he beat Crasspus, was even better than the "Fiteenth Hole Incident."

WAIT, SWEENEY WON THE CITIES OVER CRASSPUS?
GERALD: *(Leaning in close to me whispering.)* He made Crasspus look like a fool that year. A fifteen-year-old kid was beating Crasspus by a stroke going into the fifteenth hole.
WALT: Yeah, Crasspus was pretty broken up by that point of the tournament. They were paired together as the leader group that last day. And, again, that year the last day was at Farannan. Every time Crasspus birdied a hole, Sweeney would birdie the next—like spring following winter, it

was guaranteed. The gallery was huge that year. None of that fifty-guys-hoping-Crasspus-lost stuff from a couple years before. There were at least five hundred people following those two from hole to hole. It was the best Cities of all time. Everyone was drinking and it was a beautiful day in June. Dad, what was that old song that everyone was singing after Crasspus and Sweeney would hit their shots from the tee?

GERALD: *(Squints in an effort to recall, then smiles and whispers)* "Molly Malone." It was "Molly Malone."

WALT: Oh yeah, that's the title. I never remember the title, I can always only remember the "cockles and mussels, alive, alive-ohh" chorus. Yeah, so, everyone would launch into that song right after those two guys would hit their drives. We'd all sing it as loud as we could right up until one of them got ready to hit their second shot. It was such a great day, I'll never forget it. Dad and Ma and Jaime and Jason and me were all there. It's the only time we all went to watch the Cities after Dad stopped playing.

Remember, Dad? Ma even turned a blind eye to all of the Miller Lites I drank that day. Unbelievable, huh Dad?

GERALD: *(Smiles and whispers in my direction)* If you knew my Kathy you'd be amazed at that tidbit right there.

WALT: Yeah, Ma gives me a look even now when I have more than one beer when I visit.

So what happened that day, how did Sweeney beat Crasspus?

WALT: Oh yeah, sorry. Back to the golf. Well, Sweeney was just a kid with shaggy black hair and, oh I almost forgot to tell you this, the kid wasn't wearing golf shoes. It was driving Crasspus crazy, he wasn't wearing shoes at all. Completely bare foot, wearing a pair of grey surf trunks and a blue and white Hawaiian shirt. Zephyr and Mount Pheasant had made Sweeney wear spikes for the two rounds on their courses, but Farannan was his home course so they let him play how he wanted. Everyone knew it would drive Crasspus crazy, too. By the tenth hole, after those two had traded off birdie after birdie, I heard Crasspus muttering to himself. I couldn't make out what he was saying, but it didn't sound friendly.

Finally, after Crasspus made a nice up and down from the bunker to the left of twelve's green, and we had started singing again, he yelled, "Oh, shut up! Just shut up! None of you even know what a damn 'cockle' is anyway!" That actually did quiet us down for a minute, until my brother Jason yelled, "You're the effing cock-le, Crasspus!" It was a classic moment.

GERALD: *(Lauging and muttering to himself)* Hmmpf, cock-le, Crasspus was the biggest cock-le I've ever known.

SO WHAT HAPPENED, WHEN DID THE OTHER PRANK HAPPEN EXACTLY?

WALT: *(Still laughing)* Sorry, I don't want to lose it on you like last time we talked. Umm, well, I guess it started at the tee on number fourteen and it continued all the way up to the tee on the seventeenth. See, Farannan is kind of shaped like a, whaddyacallit? A parallelogram...no, wait, I mean a trapezoid. Yeah, a trapezoid. I'm breakin' out high school geometry for you, so you know you're getting a good story! Right, Dad?

Anyway, the clubhouse is at the base, at the wider end of the course, between the beach and harbor. The right, left and top sides of the trapezoid are the woods—mostly sweetrey oak and stag pine trees—that surround the course. Sweeney supposedly lived back in those woods somewhere when he was older, but as a kid he had run around and played in them until he must've known them like the back of his hand. And the fourteenth tee makes up the top right corner, at what would be the smaller end of the trapezoid.

So, at this point, as Crasspus and Sweeney came to the tee on the fourteenth, they had the woods on their right and behind the tee. It's shaded and usually damp down in that corner, kind of a weird spot on the course. Anyway, Crasspus had birdied the thirteenth hole so he was up first on the fourteenth tee. All of us in the gallery were along the back of the tee and gathered along the edge of the trees. We were quiet as Crasspus teed up and then he began a casual practice swing. When his club reached the peak of his backswing, above his head, there was this bloodcurdling scream from somewhere in the trees behind us. Crasspus nearly jumped out of his spikes, and the whole gallery was frozen with fear. I heard about a dozen people say, "What the hell was that?" Like three or four little kids started bawling. I instantly got chills from the sound of that scream.

Crasspus was freaked out, but he figured it was some drunk guy or girl or someone in the gallery. The officials came up on the tee and asked everyone to please be quiet while the golfers were on the tee or they'd stop serving beer on the course or some crap like that. Everyone was looking at each other in the gallery.

A minute or so passed, and Crasspus stood behind his ball and looked up toward the green. I think he had a seven iron or something like that in his hand. It was one of the two par threes on the course. He seemed annoyed but not too flustered, and so he lined up his club behind the ball and did his stupid little butt-wiggle that he did before every swing. He started his backswing, and I swear to God there wasn't a peep coming out of that gallery. None of us even cleared our throats, or moved an inch (partly in fear of being cutoff, and partly because we were scared of that damned noise). His club gets to the peak of his backswing and there was the scream again! It sounded like a demon was screaming "*Haaaay-ullllllll!*'" It sounded exactly like the word "hell" had been screamed by a demon in the trees.

Everyone there, even the officials, knew it did not come from the throat of a human being. Nothing human could scream that loud with such a, high, strange, bloodcurdling pitch.

What did Crasspus do?

GERALD: (*Softly*) He topped his shot. A real worm-burner!

WALT: A "worm-burner" is when someone just hits the top of their ball and it flies and skips along the ground before rolling to a stop. Crasspus had hit it about seventy-five yards along the ground.

Again, he was nearly pulling his repaired hair plugs out of his head with how mad he was. It was strange. No one in the gallery was even laughing, because we were all kind of disturbed by the sound of that scream.

The officials stopped play for a short time while they searched the woods, but they didn't find any sort of stereo speakers or any person or demon hiding out there. We all knew it was no one in the gallery because the noise was so loud that we would have run away from whoever was making it if they had been in the crowd. But it was definitely coming from somewhere in the woods.

The officials came back, and Sweeney was instructed to tee up. Crasspus moaned and complained, but Sweeney just went up there and asked him to step aside. He teed up his ball, and everything went silent. I'll never forget it, we were all standing there around the tee, lining the trees—five or six hundred of us not even sipping our beers. If you can picture the crowd around Sweeney in the shape of a giant V, I was standing at the top right of the V looking toward the bottom center where Sweeney stood behind his ball. He had a six iron, I think. He addressed the ball and was going to swing away without a practice swing. He starts his backswing, and I noticed a bunch of people with their hands over their ears, wincing. Sweeney gets to the top of his swing and, "*Haaaay-ulllllll!*" It was clear, violent, and timed perfectly with the peak of his backswing.

The crowd kind of groaned, but Sweeney somehow came through and struck his ball just fine. He hit it to the front of the green, about twenty feet from the pin. He left himself a tough putt, but at least he had hit the damn thing despite the grotesque scream.

And Crasspus's standing there, his face has gone white, his mouth hanging wide open under that silly "Magnum P.I." moustache he had.

There was a delayed, half-hearted cheer from the crowd. Nobody knew what the hell was going on.

GERALD: *(Laughing and waving Walt on.)*

WALT: *(Laughing, but with a serious look in his eye.)* It was the strangest feeling, knowing that noise was coming and not being able to stop it. No one knew what was screaming like that. The officials ordered Crasspus and Sweeney to keep playing. They finished the hole without another sound from the woods. Both of them made par on that hole, I think. Yeah, they tied, because I remember that Crasspus kept honors on the next tee.

Crasspus teed up his ball. And the tee on the fifteenth is right back next to the woods again—he looked a little hesitant as he started a casual practice swing. He brought the club back only halfway, and then through—nothing, no sound. He brought the club up around three-quarters and then through—nothing, no noise at all. It was funny as hell, because the whole crowd was quiet, just watching Crasspus test the waters. We were all kind of relieved at the second practice swing, because no one wanted to hear that scream again.

I guess Crasspus felt confident that whatever had made the noise behind the fourteenth tee had not followed us to the fifteenth. I thought we were clear of it too, to be honest. He addressed his ball, and we were all perfectly quiet staring up at him on the elevated tee. He started his backswing. My mother grabbed my arm and buried her head in my chest. I was this close *(shows me the length of an inch between his thumb and index finger)* to doing the same to my father who was standing next to me. And at the apex of his damn backswing, "*Haaaay-ulllllllll!*" It was uncanny. I got the chills again, and some people started to laugh quietly as Crasspus's Titleist Four hooked deep into the woods—we all heard it drill a tree trunk with a loud knock! Crasspus just stood there, petrified with rage, then he slammed his club into the ground.

Sweeney teed up. He didn't take any practice swings, he had his three wood out and he was going for the green. Remember, this is the infamous fifteenth hole of the infamous "Fifteenth Hole Incident" two years before. And the gallery was silent. My mother was past the point of watching, she had turned her back and covered her ears at this point—like a bunch of other people in the crowd. Pretty funny sight, actually. Little kids were crying, teenagers sipped nervously at their beers trying to look like they weren't scared, my Dad looked like he was sweating bullets—just chewing away at his fingernails.

GERALD: *(Looking at me earnestly and whispering)* That bird made a dreadful sound, you would have sweat bullets too, Owen…

WAIT, IT WAS A BIRD THAT WAS SCREAMING? HOW DO YOU KNOW THAT?
WALT: *(In mock anger)* Jeez, Dad, I try to tell the story how you told me to and you go and mess it up. What the heck? C'mon now, that's not right.

GERALD: *(Whispering)* I'm sorry, I'm sorry. You're right, you're doing a good job. I broke my own cardinal rule, I'm sorry. Go on, tell it.

GO ON WALT, YOU WERE SAYING SWEENEY WAS ABOUT TO HIT HIS BALL OFF THE TEE.

WALT: OK, I'll try *(shoots a dirty look at his father, then shakes his head and smiles)*. So Sweeney starts his backswing, my mother's not looking and my father's losing weight next to me. He has this slow, controlled, graceful backswing and it reaches its peak and a spine-tingling "*Haaaay-ulllllll!*" comes out of the trees beyond Sweeney. Right after the "*Haaaay-ulllllll!*" we all hear the thwack of the club on the ball, and then the whole gallery is silent until the ball lands on the front of the green, two-hundred-and-twenty-odd yards away—and it's pin-high, five feet to the right of the hole! Somebody, I wish I knew who, launched the whole crowd right into the loudest "Molly Malone" of the day just a moment after Harold Crasspus began complaining. We were singing "Molly Malone" that year, for some reason or other. I've already said that, haven't I?

Yeah, well anyway, Crasspus' whinings were drowned out, and the spell of the "*Haaaay-ulllllll!*" had been lifted by Sweeney's pin-high shot. Kids were laughing, jumping and tackling each other in the rough, teenagers were shot-gunning their beers and paying up on bets, adults were singing at the top of their lungs. It was crazy, I mean, half of those people have never even golfed in their life. They just wanted to see Sweeney beat Crasspus. The whole crowd of us marched down the left side of the fairway, singing and cheering Sweeney on.

And then we all stopped in dead silence about halfway to the green, because this little bluish bird with a long neck came fluttering out of the woods. It came down from one of the low branches in one of the stag pines. It opened up a gigantic, shiny, green tail with the blue, iridescent eyes at the end of every feather, and gave one more "*Haaaay-ulllllll!*" for good measure. It was a freakin' peacock!

Everyone, except Sweeney, had stopped singing and stood still. It was near perfect silence. I remember my sister said, "Must've escaped from Benson's Animal farm, huh?" Benson's was an old zoo that was shut down by then, so it didn't make sense but not much did at that point.

Sweeney was up ahead and he simply kept strolling toward the green with his putter in his hand, singing "Alive, alive oh-oh, alive, alive oh-oh...." quietly to himself, "crying cockles and mussels, alive, alive-oh-oh."

All six hundred of us were staring at the bird, stock still, and then it closed its tail and strutted off into the underbrush. I kept looking at the bird and then up at Sweeney walking toward the green, and then back at the bird. I glanced at my father and he was just starting to laugh. And as he started losing it, everyone else was quiet, and Crasspus looked like he was going to keel over and pass out.

We all heard a soft commotion of feathers, and then nothing. Not another sound was heard from the woods.

That is, until Sweeney reached the top of his backswing on the sixteenth tee along the eastern edge of the course. Again, there was a "*Haaaay-ulllllll!*" and, again, Sweeney hit it straight down the fairway.

GERALD: *(Smiling and shaking his head and whispering)* I don't know how the kid hit it straight with that damn bird screamin' away up in the trees.

AND THAT WAS IT? THE BIRD WAS GONE?

WALT: Well, that's the thing. After the sixteenth, the last two holes aren't bordered by the woods, so the bird was pretty far away. Every so often the bird screamed "*Haaaay-ulllllll!*" off in the distance but it only caused laughter by that point. I remember some high school kids had already started pounding a beer every time they heard the bird's cry— you know how Seawell kids will make a drinking game out of just about anything.

Anyway, the officials were somehow inclined to believe that Sweeney had something to do with the bird—that he had somehow trained a peacock to follow the golfers from the woods along the fourteenth, fifteenth and sixteenth holes. But, I mean, how could someone train a peacock to scream at a specific point in a golfer's backswing? It's seems impossible to me. And Crasspus was past the point of coherent speech on the subject. He was fuming and gargling like he was having a seizure or something.

No one ever even pinned the 200-golf-balls-on-the-green trick, that "Fifteenth Hole Incident" thing, on Sweeney from a couple years before, so I don't see how they could pin the peacock thing on him like that.

GERALD: *(Pulling me close and whispering in my ear)* I'm not gonna tell you how he did it, but Sweeney explained it all to me, but made me swear not to tell anyone. I had to pester him to tell me every time I saw him for a few months, but he finally explained it all. That kid could do anything he set his mind to, and that's the god-honest truth. You can put that in your book *(with a wink)*.

Walt and Gerald went on to tell me that even though the officials of the 45th Annual Seawell City Golf Tournament felt Sweeney was responsible for the peacock, they were unable to prove it. According to Gerald, when asked about the bird and the "Fifteenth-Hole Incident" of a few years previous, Sweeney only smiled beatifically and twice repeated, "I will neither confirm nor deny the allegations at hand."

At the awards banquet that evening, a 15-year-old, smirking, barefoot Yardbird Sweeney politely refused the winner's trophy—further embarrassing Harold Crasspus, who snatched the trophy and stormed off the deck above the ninth green as the crowd again began singing and laughing through one final chorus of "Molly Malone."

OUTSIDE THE GREEN CITY

In low shadows above the leaf-thronged floor
the ghostly, domed mushrooms hold quiet court.
A warbling copse of emerald ferns leans and bends
beneath currents and floods of summer light.
Uphill, under an eleven-o'clock sky,
green depths of forest are flayed-through and mottled
with sharp, gold sunlight. I'm watching your dark
eyes shine through the shade of trees drenched with moss.
Softly, in morning light, spiderwebs billow
as copper dragonflies flit, dart and spark.
They shine—struck flints amid the silken luff.

And the soft peak of my upper lip is adrift
on the cooled edge of the petal of your ear.
Your dark irises are bluegreen coronas:
lidded and lashed reflections of the forest's
late-August, sun-ignited canopy.

—Sweeney

A SOFT DAY

I am of smoke
this paleskinned morning—
the tinge of it
lifts from my mist-damp clothes.
We warm one another with a drawn-
out embrace, good bye;
the soft lull
of your syllables.
And the waves insist.
The waves insist,
as they did at midnight
beneath a veil of blown mist
held back by our driftwood fire.

You are of mist
this paleskinned morning—
the tinge of it
lifts the last flecks
of firelight from your green eyes,
sets the smell of smoke
in your nightdark hair.
A drawn-out embrace;
the soft lull
of your lips on my lips.
And the waves insist.
The waves insist
we were torsos of smoke,
entangled limbs of mist.

—Sweeney

(This poem and "Outside the Green City," arrived typed on separate sheets of
onionskin paper, mailed in the same envelope from Venezuela in 1996.)

11

SEQUEL TO "THE STING"

My father, Patrick Kivlin, and Sweeney were childhood friends, and Sweeney trusted my father with stories he wouldn't share with anyone else. My father is six feet tall, with a sandy tangle of hair. He always looks as if he's just gotten out of the ocean and towel-dried his head.

He was forty-four years old, ten years older than Sweeney, at the time of the writing of this letter—still in good surfing shape and proud of that fact. He was born and raised in Seawell, just as his mother and father were. As I've mentioned before, he grew up surfing and fishing, playing any and all sports, and generally spending as much time as possible outdoors by the ocean or on a playing field with Yardbird Sweeney.

Owen,

I've decided it would be best if I wrote this story out for you. It's really many stories lumped together, because Sweeney told me this whole thing in bits and pieces over the span of about six or seven years. I found I had to write it out by hand. My thoughts and memories seem to be explained best through the pace of writing in longhand.

I've included some of the details that Goatboy Obregon and Jay Scanlann passed on to me about the ice cream truck hijacking. But I know the story well enough to tell it to you, so I'm just gonna let it fly.

Sweeney had been very careful to cover his tracks and to make sure that no one suspected him of even a modicum of sanity before he started explaining any of this to me. That being said, I suppose the statute of limitations is up on any and all of the frauds and crimes I'm about to detail—so I don't feel too badly in finally telling this story to you.

Now, I should say that Sweeney always began the installments of this long story the same way. He'd look me in the eye, usually over a couple bottles of Harp and say something along the lines of: "Remember, Paddy, I don't recommend getting arrested and making an effort to be diagnosed insane as a valid career path for everyone. Who knows," he'd say, "someday, maybe it'll be the right one for you? I mean, I'll tell you how I pulled all this off because it's good to have options, right?"

Basically, Sweeney had spent sixteen months or so stuck in the Merritt House of Corrections writing, reading and doing push-ups. He told me he sat in his cell for most of that time and memorized the necessary symptoms he would need to practice in order to be diagnosed with Schizoaffective Disorder, Bipolar Type. I remember this is what he was aiming for because I eventually went down to the Wallace Library [Seawell's Public Library] and read up on it myself. I read up on all the disorders in the *DSM-IV*, it's sort of a cookbook filled with recipes for insanity. I also studied the *DSM-IV Casebook*. I found that Sweeney had done his homework, and that he seems to have imitated insanity with aplomb.

Sweeney didn't go to college, but he'd taken some classes here and there and done a ton of reading and writing on his own. Sweeney always called his jail time, "my study-abroad semester at Merritt." I think his jail time actually did help him figure out what he wanted to do with himself when he got out. He found out that being crazy, legally, doesn't necessarily mean that you are a danger to society. I think he told me that around three percent of *sane* people in the U.S. react violently to situations involving stress. He got the whole idea to become legally insane because he read that that number, that percentage, is exactly the same for the population of *insane* people in the U.S. He realized that being an insane person didn't mean you were violent. "This might have its benefits," he always told me. He realized that the supposed scientists in charge of dishing out those benefits were a predictable bunch, as well. In a stroke of luck, it hadn't hurt that the prison psychiatrist was a childhood friend.

These facts encouraged Sweeney, as well as his rationalization that working in some damn cubicle for forty of the approximately eighty-four hours of daylight per week was the equivalent of a prison sentence.

He didn't want to work a single day of his life in that environment. He always said, "Fuck that, Paddy. I'm never doing that shit and you and me both know that most of the hamsters stuck in their cubicles would get out for good if they could just figure out how to do it, right?" I had to kind of agree with him. He said that sort of thing to me all the time, as if he wasn't quite sure if he could justify what he'd done in his own conscience.

But Sweeney knew he didn't want to return to Merritt in the future either, so he devised a crime that would most likely lead a judge or any competent psychiatrist to believe he was legally insane, but harmless to society. He was hoping to receive a monthly stipend from the government while doing some kind of non-stressful volunteer work and then sneaking off for a surf trip a few times a year.

Sweeney told me he realized his scheme would take a very long time to put into place. He said he started showing signs of his symptoms in the last two months of his time in Merritt, and then he waited about two years to commit the crime that would eventually get him a stipend from the government so he could travel and write.

O., you were just a little kid when Sweeney served his time, probably five or six years old. Sweeney had really done a number on that Mormon kid's jaw. I knew that, and he knew that, and he was sorry for it. He felt he deserved his time in Merritt, and he told me his brawling days were over—that he would never fight anyone again. And he was telling me the truth, because I never heard about him getting in any fights after he got out of Merritt. He grew up quick during his short stay in prison.

But Sweeney was a shrewd study and he decided to use that remorse, as genuine as it was, to his advantage. He told me that when the day came where it was exactly two months until his release from Merritt he made an appointment to see the prison psychiatrist, Dr. Karen Bent. Sweeney and I had gone to school with her older brothers at the Oakland. Dr. Bent is a good doctor and a good person. Sweeney went in to see her that day and he told her in graphic detail what he'd done to the Mormon kid and how awful he felt. She asked him what prompted his confession and remorse and he told her how a little voice told him to talk to her that day.

He started in on the bid to become legally insane right away. He told her he'd just heard that little voice for the first time in his life that morning, while eating his scrambled eggs. She thought the whole thing was very interesting. Karen and I have never really talked about their meetings, due to that doctor-patient privilege thing. But Sweeney told me all about their sessions in detail.

His behavior in her office was cool, calm and collected, although he told me how he continually asked to borrow her mechanical pencil to jot down notes in a little notebook. Whenever she wrote something down, he asked to borrow the pencil and he started to write something down. "For my poems," he kept telling her. But he kept breaking the tip of the pencil and handing it back to her apologetically as if he didn't know how to work the thing. He was in the office for an hour or so, and he said he must've broken the lead on that pencil twenty-five times. Dr. Bent has a great poker face, but Sweeney could tell her interest was piqued. Four weeks later, one month before his release, he purposely caught Dr. Bent's attention again. This time he began responding to the supposed voice he heard.

He was in the cafeteria and he threw his oatmeal on the floor. He was talking to himself like he was frustrated. A guard named Leo Luque, who we went to high school with, brought him to Dr. Bent. Leo was a good guy too, funny and tough as hell when we were growing up. Sweeney described to me how gently Leo had escorted him down the hall. And then he left him with the doctor. Growing up, we'd never seen Leo be gentle, so that was sort of hard for me to picture, but Sweeney swore Leo, one of the toughest guys in Seawell, had a gentle side.

Anyway, that day, Sweeney told Dr. Bent that the voice he heard kept saying, "Check him out, he's having his oatmeal now isn't he? There it is, he'll finally have his oats." He explained to Dr. Bent, in a calm and collected manner, that he hadn't heard the voice since the last day he'd been to her office—exactly one month previous. He told her that the voice repeatedly insinuated that he was learning some sort of lesson, and that his oatmeal was his medicine. He told the good doctor that he would no longer eat oatmeal, "even if it was cinnamon raisin." He expressed his need to get out of Merritt and he told her he felt he'd been cooped up too long.

I guess Dr. Bent took some notes and seemed very interested and perplexed. Sweeney saw the doctor just once before his release four weeks later. He told her he hadn't heard the voices anymore, and that he'd eaten all his oatmeal for two weeks. She seemed happy for him, Sweeney said, and they didn't see each another for about two years.

Sweeney got out of Merritt on the day the swell from that no-name storm peaked in Seawell. Leo Luque somehow got him out a couple hours early because he knew how much Sweeney wanted to get in the water before the tide got too high. Leo was very good to him in there, and Sweeney appreciated it. First thing Sweeney did was go surfing. He told me how he'd seen Micky Obregon that morning, but he'd purposely acted a little flighty to benefit his cause. He told me how he felt bad, because it was really good to see Mick again and he wanted to thank him for sending him all those surf magazines while he was locked up. But Sweeney acted a little haunted that morning because he knew he had to stay disciplined and stick to his symptoms in order for the whole thing to eventually work.

Owen, hold on a minute…Sorry, I just ran down to check the waves because it sounded like the wind had died. I'll have to continue this letter later. It's head high and glassy with only Goatboy in sight. I'll go surf with him and maybe have some beers afterwards at The Wardin, if he's up for it. Talk to you in a little while, I'll be sure to grab a long right for you.…
Okay, I'm back. Me and Mick had a great surf at Seawell. It was mid-tide coming in and so, about a half-hour after I paddled out, the sandbar over on the south side of the Little Rocks started working. I rode my Lis fish, the one I traded for out in San Diego a few years ago. It was perfect, just enough push and hollowness to the waves. We both got some good ones and then we went to the Wardin for a few. I had four or five beers with Goatboy, K.J. and Dicky LaFerrier so it might be hard for me to get back on track.

You know what? On second thought, I'll get back to this Sweeney stuff when I sober up a bit. I don't want to start running my mouth through this pen too much.

Let's see, where was I? I guess it was two years from the time Sweeney got out of Merritt to the time he stole the ice cream truck. He pretty much lived out in the woods in the spring, summer and fall during those years. Those were the years when you and Sweeney used to play catch and tag and all those imaginary games you two made up together in our backyard near the golf course. The two of you were best friends for a while there. I remember watching him teach you how to climb and identify trees and you taught him how to tie his shoes, unaware that he knew how to do that already. Do you remember that?

Sweeney mostly worked with the Goatboy during that time, doing tree work and plantings. Everyone in Seawell was beginning to wonder about him, and they thought he had already been a little wacky before he went into Merritt—so by then they figured he was beyond the point of no return. Even I'd had my doubts about Sweeney. He had changed so much while he was away. But when I'd watch him playing with you out back, I knew he was doing fine. I told anyone who'd ask about him that he was okay, but no one really believed me—they just wanted to hear more gossip. Seawell's a good-sized city but it operates like a small-town gossip circuit most of the time.

I didn't know it at the time, but Sweeney knew he still had to solidify the idea of being loony in the minds of a lot of people in order to eventually get those checks from the government. His hair had grown long and he had a huge, nappy beard going. I thought it was all par for the course, really—but that's coming from a close friend of his. A lot of the conservative sorts in Seawell, the same people who were still angry with Sweeney for supposedly wasting his scholarship to Pepperdine, thought his hair and beard and overall ragged appearance was a sign that he had gone crazy while he was locked up. Goatboy didn't care about Sweeney's appearance because he was his best tree guy and he was reliable—unlike most of the crackheads that worked for him.

There they were, all of Goatboy's crackhead laborers, trying so hard to be sane—just trying to get by. They were failing painfully—poor guys—while Sweeney was trying to be more and more crazy as the days went by and he knew he would be rewarded for it. It was a strange situation to witness, especially since none of us really knew the reality of what was going down at the time.

Goatboy told me how most of the crackheads never made it to work and were basically spaceshots when they did show up. Sweeney didn't drink or go to the bars much during that time—I suppose he was saving money to travel. He just wrote, surfed, hid in the woods, played some barefoot golf in the evenings by himself, worked for Goatboy and grew a lot of hair. Once in a while, I'd hear of a mild fit he'd throw while at work and Goatboy would get worried and take him back to the Kemp Aaberg to "chill out for a couple days." Not a bad life. If it weren't for Seawell's long, cold winters Sweeney would've probably kept on doing what he was doing, too. But he needed money to travel and surf in the winter and the Schizoaffective thing seemed like the best way to do it.

After letting his appearance slip a little, Sweeney started messing around with the crackheads' minds whenever Goatboy wasn't around. He insisted that they called him "King Sweeney" and Goatboy told me he once heard Sweeney tell the crackheads, "Hell, I have hollow bones, boys. I could fly around and do all this tree work, but then none of us would ever get any overtime, would we?" None of the crackheads wanted to do any of the sketchy tree work, so Sweeney would do it while telling them not to worry because he could always fly away if he started to fall. After a while, he was pretty much the reason most of those guys quit working for Goatboy. Sweeney freaked them out, but don't tell Goatboy because he'd lose it if he heard that.

Eventually, Mick started hearing about Sweeney wanting to be called "King" and stuff and he got a little worried. I remember Goatboy coming over and telling me how Sweeney talked about the voices he was hearing in his head. He'd told Goatboy he'd heard them since the last few days of his stay in Merritt. Sweeney was lying to Goatboy, and felt bad about it, but he had to keep up the appearances to make it all work.

Sanity was not really a factor in their friendship, anyways. They surfed and drank together, and Sweeney showed up for work regularly. That was good enough for both of them back then.

Anyways, during the winters of those couple of years Sweeney would take off for mainland Mexico and other Central American surf spots. He always said he nearly froze his stones off that one winter when he lived in his boat out in the woods. He swore he wouldn't do it again. He'd come back later and later in the spring each year. There was one year where he didn't come back until late August, and he was raving about a little spot down by the Guatemalan border—a righthand pointbreak with a sand bottom. He just raved about it, and said the summer south swells hit it just right for weeks on end. I was a little jealous of all the surf he was getting back then, but I had a family to raise so I sort of lived vicariously through him, I suppose.

I was starting to get worried that Sweeney wasn't going to come back, and he seemed to be acting more strangely each time I would see him. The only sign of his sanity was his friendship with you, Owen. You took him for what he was, and the two of you were like best friends back then. I noticed how fewer and fewer adults took the time to hang out with Sweeney in those years, and how he spent more and more time with you in our backyard and out on the course in the summer evenings. I remember getting a little upset, myself, at how Sweeney was sort of pulling away from all of us. But he'd always take the time to tell me about where he'd traveled and what waves he'd surfed and how his writing and Spanish were coming along. I didn't want to pressure the guy toward any sort of normal life because I could see that he was happy. He seemed to be pulling away from supposed "adult society" but he seemed almost content—strange and lonesome, but content. Does that make any sense?

I figured that there weren't many people in his life in the first place, especially after all that stuff he went through after leaving Pepperdine. He'd lost his girlfriend and cousin Tommy who was one of his oldest friends, and his parents were definitely out of the picture at that point. And on top of all that, he goes away for a while to Merritt, then comes out and seems happy—crazy, but happy.

It's a weird thing to see someone who is genuinely happy, you know? I don't think most people in Seawell know how to deal with someone who figures out a way to do whatever he or she wants to do. I just wanted to keep Sweeney writing and traveling back then, it seemed it was what he needed to do. I tried to ignore the protective instincts I had for him as an old friend. It was hard for me sometimes, but I think Sweeney appreciated it.

I know for sure, in the long run, he still looked at me as one of his best friends. The day he started telling me about the ice cream truck hijacking was the day I knew for sure that he trusted me like a brother. I mean, if anyone had found out about any of this he would've been back at Merritt in a heartbeat—for a much longer stay, too. It was hard for Sweeney to trust anyone after what his parents did to him. I think you already talked to Sweeney's cousin Tommy about that situation. That's why I say it took a long time for Sweeney to trust me entirely.

So, eventually, this is what he told me he did to sort of seal the deal with the diagnosis of Schizoaffective, Bipolar. I'll try to be as detailed as I can. It shouldn't be too hard for me, because this is absolutely my favorite Sweeney story—and that guy told me a lot of damn stories.

In any case, it was late August and Sweeney knew that this big festival was happening during Labor Day up in northern Vermont. It was in this remote mountain pasture somewhere. It was an underground sort of thing back then. Something to do with sculpture, music, art and most likely drugs. It was called The Vapid Tortuga Festival, and it was different in that nobody sold anything like T-shirts or food at the festival. You just showed up, bought a ticket and supplied all your own water and food and you could barter for drugs and booze. It all lasted ten days or so, and it switched locations every year throughout the northern Appalachian Mountains. There were all these sculptures and artwork and music featured each night on different stages and in different parts of the woods and meadows. It was a very cool setup, from how Sweeney described it. Sweeney had memorized the directions to the festival earlier that summer so he could take off for it when he got his chance. "If you're trying to look insane," he'd say, "you can't have sense enough to buy a map at a gas station—you know what I mean?" It was the little things that made his plan a success, and Sweeney had a talent for the little things in everything he did.

It was a Monday, hot as hell, and Sweeney and Goatboy were doing tree work out on Parkview Ave., near the old Capanetti house. He was sick of working and sweating and missing out on the surf in Mexico, so he decided that it had been long enough. He needed to commit the crime that week in order to make it up to the festival in time. He needed to start the process of committing a crime, getting caught, going to trial, getting a diagnosis and collecting some money from the government.

And Jay Scanlann, a Seawell guy a few years younger than us, was driving an ice cream truck that summer. He had permits for Seawell's beaches, and he'd made a killing with all the nice weather that July and August. Sweeney knew he'd made more than enough to go back to school, so he didn't feel too bad about stealing his truck at that time of the summer. Scanlann's parents had money anyway. Sweeney didn't know how he was going to actually steal the thing, but he was ready. So that Monday he's up in a seaside blackthorn tree, working near the top, and he sees these little kids, the Swenson and Capanetti kids I think, quietly tying cans to the ends of a long piece of fishing line. When they heard the music from the ice cream truck coming around the corner they set up the line at around car-bumper height across Parkview Ave., right before it crosses Willow St.

Sweeney climbed down from the tree when he saw Scanlann driving down the street. James and Pauly Capanetti and Dave and Janet Swenson were the only little kids I ever knew who didn't like the ice cream man. Sweeney said he thought it was because they didn't have much money, and they were bored. Irregardless, they had been screwing around with Scanlann all summer long whenever he drove through the Oaklands section of town. They attacked the poor guy with squirt-gun ambushes, snowballs saved from February, they fired bottle rockets out of Wiffle Ball bats at his truck—they pulled out all the pranks they could think of on Scanlann.

Scanlann told me all about the kids, and Sweeney stealing the truck, later that fall after he dropped out of the University of Chicago and came back to Seawell. Scanlann was a good guy. I used to see him down at the Wardin every so often back then. And Goatboy has told me his version of this story several times down at The Wardin as well. Everyone involved in this whole fiasco acted all pissed off back then, but I think they were all having fun chasing each other around and battling that summer.

So, in any case, Scanlann is coming down the street in his truck, ringing his bell and making his way toward Sweeney, Goatboy and the can-trick trap. Sweeney put down all his tools in the grass and told Goatboy that Slim had commanded him to get a Snow Cone and a Fanta from the truck. "Slim" was the name he'd given to one of his hallucinations—one of the heads who were responsible for the voices he'd heard every day of that summer. Mick knew all about Slim.

This is how Goatboy tells me this part of the story, he seems to like the part where Sweeney and the kids were all about to wreak havoc on the truck. And Goatboy tells me this part of the story every other time I see him these days—if he has a few beers in him, which is most of the time. He's always like:

> "Paddy, I'm tellin' ya, I think Sweeney knew what he was doin', he set us all up, I'm tellin' ya.
>
> "'Cause that day I says to Sweeney, 'You hate Snow Cones. What the fuck are you talking about?'
>
> "And Sweeney puts down his tools in the grass and he says to me, with that weird fuckin' look in his eyes, 'You just can't argue with Slim, Goatboy. Out of the five heads, he's the meanest.'
>
> "So I says, 'Oh, Jesus Christ, you are completely fucked! Go get your damn ice cream, and then finish this beech tree.' I remember we still hadta plant that spruce out in Amesbury later that day. I wanted to get that job done, and here he is tellin' me: 'The heads said this, and Slim said that, blah, blah, blah....' And I'd been on the ground completely baked all morning, so I

never saw the Capanetti and Swenson kids setting up the can trick—the little bastards."

Usually, I manage to get away from Goatboy before he continues the story, because we've all heard it from him a million times. And later, after I learned that Sweeney had all this planned out, I knew there was a whole lot more to it than Goatboy knew. Sometimes it was hard not to let Goatboy in on the whole thing, he'd been friends with me and Sweeney for a long time but sometimes he runs his mouth like a teenager after a school dance, so I had to resist filling him in on the truth back then.

See, Sweeney told me he had two dollars and some change, all of it in dimes, nickels and pennies—Sweeney knew the exact amount, let's say it was $2.73—in Goatboy's dump truck. So he grabbed the $2.73 and waited a little ways past the spot where those little kids had set up the fishing line. For whatever reason, the can trick never got old to those little kids, god bless 'em. Scanlann was driving down Parkview and he's got the ice-cream-truck version of the theme song from that Paul Newman movie "The Sting" playing loud and clear. He stops ringing his bell when he sees Sweeney and he waves. Sweeney said he just stood there as if he was having a conversation with one of his talking-head hallucination friends.

Goatboy was sitting in the shade drinking some water and smoking a joint. Sweeney just kept talking and gesticulating until Scanlann drove his bumper right into the fishing line and the cans started clanking away at the sides of the truck. It was funny as hell, but Sweeney couldn't laugh—because that would show that he knew what was going on—so he just kept talking to "Slim" and the other heads while Goatboy coughed up half his water with that nasally laugh of his.

Scanlann stopped in the middle of Parkview, threw the truck into park and jumped out. The Swensons and Capanettis popped out from behind the coldwater ivy hedge up on the hill in the Barrett's yard. They started calling Scanlann names and laughing: "Ahh, ha, ha, ha! You suck! Get a real job, shithead!" Sweeney and Goatboy both told me that the kids were laughing hard and then they'd run twenty yards or so up toward Hollyrood Ave. and they'd stop and call Scanlann some more names. Scanlann was trying to pull the cans out of his bumper and the fishing line was all tangled in the axle and he was swearing and getting all pissed off. "The Sting" was still blaring out of the megaphone speaker on top of the truck.

Goatboy got up and starts yelling at the kids, he hates all kids, and then him and Scanlann started running after them. Goatboy yelled for Sweeney to follow but Sweeney just pretended to be violently arguing with the heads about the superiority of Chipwiches over Snow Cones or something like that. Goatboy remembers that Sweeney's gestures indicated that Slim was not happy with him at that point in time.

Sweeney heard Goatboy tell Scanlann, "Forget about that crazy fuck, let's get those little bastards!" Then the chase was on. Scanlann stopped for a second at the top of the Barrett's yard and yelled down, "Sweeney, just leave the money on the dash and take whatever you want!"

That, Sweeney told me, was a better cue than he could have possibly hoped for. He got in the truck, turned up "The Sting" a little bit and drove down Parkview, onto Rogers, onto 495, toward 95 and all points North. He said he let "The Sting" play all the way out of Seawell. The fishing line snapped when he took the left onto Rogers in front of Dunkin' Donuts, and the cans fell off the truck. Sweeney put his $2.73 in a cup on the dash and kept it there for the whole trip. In fact, when he came back, the police found the cash box untouched, the ice cream all melted and rancid in the coolers of the ice cream truck. Sweeney'd left everything precisely the way he found it when he stole it.

Sweeney stayed up at the festival for about three days. When he got back he just went about his business like nothing had happened. Scanlann had called the police a day or two after Sweeney had taken off. He'd waited for Sweeney to show up with the truck, but then the guys who he leased the truck from started breathing down his neck so he was forced to call the cops. Sweeney showed up for work on the next Tuesday, after the long weekend. Goatboy always describes him that morning as, "all banged up and rough around the edges. Basically, he was fucked." The cops were waiting for him to come to work and they took him away. He was back in Merritt until his trial, but they treated him with kid gloves out there—Leo Luque told me he made sure of that much.

The trial came up and the judge granted the Public Defender's request for psychological tests on Sweeney. Scanlann and Goatboy had informed the cops, when the truck was stolen, about Sweeney's odd behaviors—at that point, everyone in Seawell was worried about the guy.

So, it was back to Dr. Karen Bent for a round of interviews and tests and analysis. Sweeney told me that he made sure he had the symptoms and habits of a Schizoaffective patient down pat by then. He'd been careful of exactly how and when he'd stolen the truck. He showed no guilt about stealing the truck, he expressed that he'd been told by Scanlann that he could "take whatever he wanted." He also left that cup full of change on the dashboard and told Dr. Bent he'd paid for the use of the truck with the $2.73 in change.

Growing up, Sweeney was the craftiest, smartest person I knew. A lot of difficult things came easily to him, and so I can imagine that if he says he studied and memorized and displayed the behaviors of a person with Schizoaffective Disorder, Bipolar Type, that means he had it down to a science. Dr. Bent and the judge and everyone else in Seawell never had a chance to discover his plan if Sweeney put even a little effort into it. And, from the sound of it, he put a lot of effort into that.

Over the years, he revealed to me all the things that led Dr. Bent toward the right diagnosis: "Slim," and the hallucinated talking heads; the request to be called "King Sweeney" by the crackheads; the ongoing commentary of the voices; how the voices resurfaced on the anniversary of his release from Merritt. All these behaviors were perfectly timed and practiced parts of Manic Episodes and the other requirements for a Schizoaffective, Bipolar diagnosis.

Sweeney pulled off the perfect fraud and ended up with a few months in Darville Mental Hospital for his effort. He was released with a monthly stipend of around five or six hundred dollars. That's where Dr. Bent came through for him. She had to diagnose him as Sweeney wanted her to, he'd set her up just right, but she cut through the red tape quicker than normal for him because she'd been in Sweeney's second-grade class. I think the normal waiting period for that sort of a stipend is at least a year, maybe two. There's a lot of crap to wade through as the government drags its feet through every stage of that sort of thing. Sweeney had his money in around five or six months. So you can see, like I said, Seawell is a city that often operates like a small town—favors are plentiful if you know the right people.

After that, Sweeney lived in the out-of-bounds area of the golf course in that old trawler up on barrels, the Kemp Aaberg. He did a little volunteer work and special jobs for Goatboy—special tree work. He was instructed to avoid all stressful jobs or situations, and he was to report every six months or so to Dr. Bent for further evaluation. Sweeney told me had trouble keeping a straight face when the doctors said, "We encourage you to avoid stressful situations and employment for several months." He said to me, " I was thinking, like, 'No fucking encouragement needed, my friends. You have my word!'"

The hard part was over for Sweeney. It had taken three or four years from his first stint in Merritt to the time when he could take his first extended surf trip to Central America on the government's tab.

Sweeney had constructed his own reality that no one else could understand, including me. He told me he felt like a free man for the first time in his life when he was put in the mental hospital that time—ironic as that sounds.

Looking back on that, I think he meant that he was finally free to write his poems, surf the winters away in warm places and come back to Seawell around the spring of each year to check in and have a few surf sessions with me and Goatboy. Sweeney had even gone far enough to have the court order me and Goatboy to be in charge of depositing his checks in his account on a monthly basis since his family wasn't around any more. And banking, apparently, was out of the question for someone in his delicate state.

We did all of this willingly because we were his oldest friends. But, as I said earlier, Sweeney seemed happy in a weird way back then—even content. And despite the label of "legally insane" he was still Sweeney, and we both were just happy he wasn't locked up in prison or an institution or working in some insurance office fifty weeks of the year. He was still Sweeney, and Sweeney was supposed to fit in our lives as a traveler and writer and surfer. We sort of needed to believe he was insane so that he could go on being the same sort of Sweeney for us.

I mean, Goatboy and I sort of lost touch with ourselves once we grew up. Maybe "lose" isn't the right way to put it. I guess I mean when you get married and have kids or own your own business you start to become someone else—a husband, a supervisor, a father—someone you haven't been before. You miss the old things a little at times. We chose our lives, and we're doing fine, but we also always liked living vicariously through Sweeney's travels.

Me and Goatboy hardly ever went on surf trips any more, we could barely get in the water around here. And while we had wives and kids we loved, we still struggled with the loss of some of the stuff that made us who we are. I'm babbling a little bit here, but I think this is why Sweeney remains a part of our lives to this day. It's more than just fond memories of someone who's gone. It's like we've always felt that Sweeney hadn't lost anything as he got older. He seemed to *create* his life while our lives *happened* to us and around us. There's a big difference there. Me and Goatboy always agreed that, in our opinions, Sweeney never lost anything in his life but the label of "sane." And I'm not too sure Goatboy and I would've ever saddled him with that label in the first place.

Looking back on all of it, knowing what I know and being the only person to really know all this stuff, I'm proud of the guy. I mean, I think he managed to find a way to get the money to do what he wanted to do. He earned his freedom.

I've thought about it a lot in the last few years, and it seems to me Sweeney's the only person I've ever known to act on trying to maintain his own sanity. He sort of nurtured his version of reality and it grew into a life that can't be copied or even fully understood—although, by all the talk and interest that's still around Seawell I think people are trying to understand or explain him in their own way almost every day.

Nobody's seen the guy in years, as far as I know, but people talk about him in the bars like he's due back any day now. Maybe it's that he's got people using their imagination as they wonder about what the hell he did with himself. I mean, he's one of us, one of the people who grew up in Seawell—but the only one who lived in a boat out in the woods, and traveled to exotic places every year, and disappeared and reappeared, and maybe killed himself.

In any case, I don't think I'm supposed to understand all of it. I miss the guy and I get sad sometimes when I think about how long he's been gone, but I'm happy for him at the same time. He sort of went out on top in my mind, whether he killed himself or not. I spend a lot of time thinking about what he's done over the years, and, I guess he's still around in one way or another. It still feels like he's gonna show up at the Wardin some Tuesday night. I'm pretty sure he will. My guess is that he was on his way back here one spring and then he just found a place or a person or a reason that felt like it might be a little more important to him than Seawell, his old friends and his need to be back here. He'll come around. He will.

If he doesn't, there will always be someone at the bar who'll be glad to reminisce and tell a few tales about the guy anyways.

CONTEMPLATING THE PENNACOOK BRIDGE

My bones grow hollow before the plunge—
as if long-lost instinct, not memory,
jogs for a stretched   instant.
It is a brief flight
upward, a soft brawl
with gravity's invisible blight.

After the crash of wind-burned flesh
on the boiling face of the currents,
innumerable bubbles rise   expire.
I was not plumed   so I plummeted.
I am not gilled   so I rise.
The twin levels of my lungs
lift me to a state of wet grace.

I am a dumb cork hefted on ebb tide.
Blackened liquid seeps from my head
above the pocked floor of the sea,
below the sieve-like expanse of night sky.

My pores are portals for the salts
and oils of my sea and my self.

—Sweeney

(Found by Miguel Obregon in the berth of the "Kemp Aaberg" after Hurricane
Murgill toppled the boat in 1998, just a few days after Sweeney's bike was discovered
by Seawell police under the Pennacook Bridge. The poem was written in Sweeney's
cursive in black ink on one side of a sheet of white paper. On the other side, Micky
found the final poem in this book: "The Gealt, A Covered Bridge.")

12
HURRICANE COMPANIONS

After I'd spoken to everyone and gathered all these stories together, I felt like I needed a little more closure—if that was at all possible. I decided that I would let Margaret Tierney have last word on Sweeney's whereabouts. I hoped she might be able to shed some light on the suicide-or-disappeared question. Eventually, as you'll see once again, Margaret got around to answering my original question in her roundabout, engaging way of telling a story.

The last time I saw Yardbird Sweeney was on a Saturday night in October. It was the night before Halloween, and the last belt of Indian Summer weather was moving through Massachusetts. The temperatures were up in the high sixties that weekend. The evening that I saw him was simply the most beautiful night that autumn, just wonderful weather. Farannan had closed early that year to repair the widespread damage from Hurricane Murgill in late September. Almost every hole had a tree of some kind cast across its fairway or green. The par-three number two had half of an eastern white poplar from the first fairway in its front bunker. The tree's upper branches had snapped off and sailed and tumbled nearly one hundred yards until most of them got tangled up in the sand guarding the right edge of the green. There weren't many holes that had any room to land a drive off the tee.

But I couldn't let that evening pass.

I felt winter coming on strong. Indian Summer is always too beautiful for me to ignore. I walked around the course with my clubs on my shoulder, hoping to find a few open areas to drop a few balls and hit into some of the greens—anything to help me absorb the last bit of nice weather we were going to see for a long time. I checked number three, and it was covered by the remains of Viking maples and white poplars.

Five was too damp to play, it's one of the lowest points on the course so I knew it wasn't an option. Six had a huge bog oak down across the middle of the fairway, but with a solid drive I felt I could clear the worst of it. I teed up and hit my shot a little low, but it made it to an open area on the fairway. This was the hole, I'm sure you've heard, from the infamous "Fifteenth Hole Incident" with Harold Crasspus during the Cities. It's a fun hole to play. In any case, I had about 80 or 85 yards to the pin after my first shot. Of course, I skulled a nine iron and skipped the ball over the green and down the steep, short hill into the woods behind the seventh tee. I laughed it off, dropped another ball and, of course, hit it perfectly. I still remember the shot, to this day. It landed about four feet to the right of the pin, and didn't roll more than three feet. I was ecstatic. I had a shot to remember that would tide me over through the winter months, even though it was a mulligan.

You know, just one good golf shot is all I needed to clear my head back in those days. I'd strike the ball and feel it come off the face of the iron cleanly, then the divot plops back to Earth, and I'd watch that tiny dimpled ball sail through the blue sky on the exact trajectory you hoped for headed right for that yellow flag...it's a wonderful experience, a perfect golf shot. I miss it very much, but my knees. Oh, nevermind the ramblings of a half-senile old bird like me. I'll get back to my story. I apologize.

Now, I started looking through the brush behind the green for the ball I had skulled into the woods. I wasn't looking too hard, I figured it was lost and I didn't have the luxury of Sweeney's eyes that evening. But, wouldn't you know it, I found a ball under some oak leaves. It wasn't mine, but I called it even and turned to walk back to the seventh tee to try and land a drive somewhere in the fairway that was covered by branches and leaves and looked to be pretty wet. I'd already tapped in my mulligan and fixed the divot where it had landed on the green. But as I turned to the seventh tee, all of a sudden, I saw some movement in the distance. I couldn't believe my eyes when Sweeney poked his head out from the out-of-bounds area off the right of six—the hole I had just played. He was at the base of the fallen sweetrey oak. I'd heard he was supposedly in hiding, from what I'll never know, but I ducked back down a little, behind the edge of the raised green. Sweeney looked like he was checking to see if the coast was clear, then he seemed to be studying the base of the tree where the roots were exposed from being ripped out of the ground by the wind. I still remember that he was dwarfed by the size of that tree's upended roots. He looked very small.

I had a good view of him below me, and I knew he couldn't really see me. He started walking across the fairway and then turned toward me. I ducked into the deep sandtrap that borders the back of the left side of the green and waited. After a long minute or so, Sweeney passed me, without seeing me, I'm sure of that. He then turned away from me to the northeast toward the seventh green and began walking along the edge of the woods in the rough. He walked fast, and had three old clubs leaning on his shoulder, and one ball in his left hand. He was wearing a pair of khaki shorts, a navy blue T-shirt and no shoes.

The sun had just gone down at this point, and twilight was slowly turning all the trees purple. I decided to follow him to see what he was up to. I couldn't move from the sand trap until he had walked all the way down the five-hundred-and-forty-five-yard fairway. But I saw him climb down the rocks behind the green and onto the beach. To this day I don't know why he went down to the beach, but that was my chance to get into a better hiding spot to see what he was up to.

There were small breakers crashing that night, the sound was very soothing, and a slight smell of sea spray had blown across the course. It really was a gorgeous evening, I've never forgotten it. As soon as he was out of sight, I dropped my bag of clubs and ran, as fast as an old woman in golf spikes can run, to the tunnel beneath the second tee that connects the eighth hole to the ninth tee. I guessed that Sweeney would be playing the eighth hole. It had always been his favorite on the course. It was a long par four, four hundred and sixty yards, or thereabouts, with water guarding most of the green that is tucked away to the right, as you play it, behind a hillside and some trees. It's probably the most challenging hole on the course, in my opinion. The seventh is long, and difficult too, but relatively straight without any water to worry about. The eighth is only slightly shorter with that pesky quarter-dogleg and the water that has stolen many a ball from my bag over the years. I knew Sweeney would play that hole if he was to play at all that evening.

As I covered the last several yards of my two-hundred-yard sprint (well, it would resemble more of a hurried waddling to anyone else, but to me it felt like a sprint) I made out the shape of Sweeney setting up on the eighth tee. I'd crossed the line of trees down the left side of the fairway just before he did, and I made it to my hiding spot without him seeing me. I watched him tee up the ball with an old tee he picked out of the grass. He stood directly behind it, dropped two of the clubs in his hand to the grass, addressed the ball, and hit a perfect drive without taking a single practice swing. He hit a draw, from right to left, since he's a righty. He easily cleared all the downed branches and wet leaves that cut across the fairway at about two hundred and twenty yards. His ball skipped and rolled down into the bottlenecking fairway. He hit it just far enough to get a clear shot at the green, but he had at least 180 yards left to the pin. The pin, that day, was tucked way back in the left corner of the green. The groundskeeper hadn't bothered to change the holes since the hurricane, and for some reason they hadn't pulled the flags out of the holes at that point. I suppose there was too much damage to the course itself to worry about the flagsticks. In any case, I estimate the shot Sweeney had left to be about 187 or 88 yards to the pin, and with the way that water was guarding that tiny little green behind it, I didn't think the boy had a chance.

I say "boy," but by this time Sweeney must have been at least twenty-five years old. Is that right? Twenty-five? I suppose it is, I've never really thought about it, but that seems about right. By then he'd grown out his hair and it was shaggy and long. He also wore a bushy, reddish-brown, full beard. He looked nothing like the boy I had known at fourteen. He certainly looked nothing like the eight-year-old who followed me around that course during that first summer of our friendship. As I watched the bearded Sweeney walk along the small hazels and honey ash, down the left side of the fairway it occurred to me just how much I missed the boy I knew. I was upset, more with myself, for not contacting him over the years. I wanted to walk out from behind the spruce I hid behind and confront the boy and see that he was okay, but I couldn't do it. I knew Sweeney had been through some difficult times after his parents moved away, after he dropped out of college that first year. I suppose I was scared that Sweeney wouldn't talk to me, that he'd disappear into the woods if I showed myself. I'd heard he'd been to jail and to the Darville Mental Institution, I wasn't sure he would even know me any more. I would have been hurt by that, and I didn't want to be hurt. I decided to stay put, and found myself shaking a little bit. From nervousness or my little jog to my hiding spot, I'm not sure. It was the strangest feeling. I didn't want the boy to see me and, at the same time, I couldn't take my eyes off of him.

As all this was running through my head, Sweeney approached his ball for his second shot. I was only forty or fifty yards to his right up on the hillside at this point. I had moved from the tunnel to a position behind a small bluff willow on the hill where all the kids used to sled in the wintertime. I stood stock still as Sweeney approached his ball. Through the branches, I could see that he had an old wedge, a wooden driver, and a seven or eight iron in his hand. He'd left a trail of darker footprints in the tall, wet rough behind him, his pale bare feet and ankles were speckled with bits of wet grass. He dropped the wedge and the driver behind him, gripped the seven or eight iron and stared intently at the green. I doubted there was any way he could reach the green from 185 yards away. There was just a breath of wind coming off the ocean, it pushed the sea mist toward the two of us standing there in the twilight. The mist was coming in fast, and it was cooling off. There was almost a sweet sea rose smell on the air as Sweeney set up to hit his ball.

He took a moment to look back at the water, as if to gauge the breeze at his back. I saw that his green eyes were still just as clear, but now they seemed piercing rather than inquisitive. There was more of an edginess to his person—a flightiness, so to speak. It was the only thing on his body that revealed any sort of strain, those eyes.

As Sweeney swung his head back toward the hole, from his right shoulder toward his left, he seemed to pause as his line of sight passed the yellowed willow I was hiding behind. I hadn't moved an inch in the whole time he'd been within two hundred yards of his ball. I was so afraid that he saw me just then, in that moment, that I held my breath. I was instantly aware of the off-white stripes on my golf shirt, and the beige of my own khaki slacks. I tried to stop shaking, I had the chills for some odd reason. It was no use, I was convinced he'd seen me. I was just about to move from behind the tree, say hello and give myself up when he angled his head at the ball in front of him.

Before I could move, he was in the middle of his backswing. He came through, slowly and rhythmically, shifting his weight firmly and with control. Even though he was on bare feet, it was as if he had golf spikes on. Everything moved with an ease and flow. His golf swing was the picture of relaxation and smoothness. Nothing was out of place. He struck the ball and turf and followed through, I let myself exhale, his divot landed on the fairway with a soft thud. He'd struck it high, and again with a slight draw from right to left.

I wasn't sure the ball would clear the large stone wall that climbed out of the far side of the pond and marked the edge of the front fringe of the green. I only moved my eyes to watch that ball, and when I glanced back at Sweeney he had already picked up his two clubs from the rough and was walking toward the hole. He wasn't even watching his shot. The ball came down pin-high, four or five feet to the right. It had enough backspin on it to roll back away from the pin about eight feet. It looked to me like the ball was just touching the edge of the fringe on the green, just above the water. He had an eight or ten-foot putt that was a little bit downhill with a slight bend to the left.

Sweeney climbed up the rise to the fringe of the green on the right side of the pond, he turned toward his ball and walked back to it. And wouldn't you know? He had a pair of flip-flops sticking out of his back pocket, just like old times. I was smiling to myself, as he walked to the other side of the hole, leaving a handful of footprints on the grain of the green. He crouched and lined up the putt. He walked back across the green, removed the pin, rested it lightly on the fringe. I realized, right then that Sweeney didn't have a putter with him. I wondered why for a moment, but then saw him choke down on the shaft of a club and he putted the ball with the flat face of his old, wooden driver.

It was the perfect speed, and he played the right to left break nicely. I was thrilled by what I had seen. He'd sunk it for a three.

The boy took three swings with battered, old clubs, and birdied the most difficult hole on the course. He'd hit three perfect golf shots— without any practice swings, in his bare feet! I will tell you right now, it was a beautiful thing to witness.

By the time the ball had dropped in the hole, the mist was rolling over us. There were wisps of it blowing toward Sweeney standing on the green. And I could no longer see back down the fairway for more than twenty or thirty yards. The last thing I saw the boy do, before the mist engulfed him, was walk over to the hole, bend down and take his ball out of the hole. He seemed to be fiddling with the ball, somehow. I couldn't make out what he was doing, as it was nearly dark by then. But then he did a strange thing in that moment—he bent down and put the ball back in the hole, took his flip flops out of his back pocket, slipped into them and walked over the hill behind the green. He went right back into the woods by the downed sweetrey oak tree.

I was left there, standing in the near dark behind the bluff willow, listening to a few bullfrogs grunting from the edge of the pond. For the life of me, I couldn't figure out why he had put the ball back in the hole. I hurried over to the green to get a look at that ball. When I took it out of the hole, I saw that he had written on the ball in black permanent marker. It read:

> A solitary bird
> For my companion
> Upon the withered moor.
> —Senna

I keep that ball on my mantle in my room here at the home. I know he left it for me, and it's a lovely Haiku. Sweeney had known I was there watching him on the course, but it had been too long since we'd seen each other. I realized that night how much I missed him.

I miss him now, too. It was the last time I saw Yardbird Sweeney. I was told that that was the year he went traveling and didn't come back to Seawell. That was also the year they found his old, rusty beach cruiser by the base of the Pennacook Bridge.

Some of these people around Seawell think he jumped, but I'm not so sure. He wasn't really a sad or angry person, just a lonesome sort of person. Most people aren't comfortable around someone like that, they don't know what to make of a person who prefers to be alone. It scares most people, frankly.

I know that boy did not jump off that bridge. I imagine he still wanders, still looks for his place. In my heart of hearts he's camped out at some remote surfing place in Peru or South Africa, learning to listen to the tides, waiting for the far-away storms to send him some waves.

Do they even have good breakers in South Africa or Peru? I'm not even sure *(Laughs quietly to herself)*.

THE GEALT, A COVERED BRIDGE

I made it through some evenings in the Gealt's
deep shade, drinking cold Pabst to fight the heat.
Swallows careened through shifting clouds of midges
above the river, along twilight's dark pleat.
I once swam beneath the bridge to check the depth
of the water with my eyes, but the mud
proved too much. So with squinched lids and held breath
I dove for the silt of the bed—through the lifeblood
of the overhanging birch and the oak knolls.
I frog-kicked downward, for what seemed like years,
but failed to touch. As I surfaced, some locals
biked between the footbridge's thick tiers.
They cursed the heat and sweated: frail, bare-chested
boys who had flown over the playing fields
for wont of freedom and quick solace wrested
from the summer's humid, repetitious yield.
I gave up on the bottom and I climbed
up the pollen-dusted boulders of the bluffs
toward the boys' swears and laughter as it chimed
thinly and shrill through the Gealt's lattice truss.
I dripped wet blots and padded on warm planks,
stenciled with long, crisscrossed shadows, to suss
out the jumping spot. The four boys stood in rank,
in line from old to young above the rain-starved
river, to wait their turn. The smallest shrank
from my question, then spoke: "Jump from where 'jump's' carved
in the wood." I watched as his delicate, white feet
gripped the plank's edge and rasped on grit and sand.
He rose and left the four, rough letters wet,
dark, sunk into the grain of the weathered wood.

—Sweeney

THE END.

THE STORYTELLERS

*These short biographies were completed via brief
telephone interviews with each storyteller.*

ERIN HAMASAKI

AGE: 17 **BORN:** Seawell General Hospital.

SEAWELL NEIGHBORHOOD: Rathmines, I grew up near the Bailey School.

CURRENT HOMETOWN: Seawell, but I want to go to college in Australia in a couple years, on the West Coast. I'm sick of this place.

SCHOOL OR WORK: Junior at Seawell High, and I'm a waitress at Bolcain Glen in Tyngsboro. School's okay, but my job sucks!

WHERE AND WHEN YOU MET SWEENEY: At Seawell Beach after I ran away from home when I was just a little kid. He was getting ready to go for a surf. It was springtime. **LAST TIME YOU TALKED TO SWEENEY:** I guess it was the day I met him. But I saw him surf one more time during a big day at Seawell Beach when I was older. **WHERE YOU THINK SWEENEY IS NOW:** He's probably surfing somewhere with cold water and big waves, like Easter Island or somewhere. He didn't jump off that bridge. No way! He got out of this stupid city and never came back.

MICHAEL JOSEPH TRABELL

AGE: 11 and a half. **BORN:** Kingston, New Hampshire. I lived there for a year when I was really little. I don't remember it.

SEAWELL NEIGHBORHOOD: Oaklands, I'm from the coolest part of Seawell.

CURRENT HOMETOWN: Is this a trick?

SCHOOL OR WORK: I'm in sixth grade at Oakland Elementary. Next year I go to Moody Junior High.

WHERE AND WHEN YOU MET SWEENEY: I've never met him, but my dad says he was cool when they went to Seawell High.

LAST TIME YOU TALKED TO SWEENEY: Some of these questions are repeats.

WHERE YOU THINK SWEENEY IS NOW: I think he's in Mexico or some jungle somewhere, but my dad thinks he jumped off that bridge because he dropped out of college or something. I don't believe him.

DANIEL ANDREW TRABELL

AGE: It was my birthday last week. I'm 10. **BORN:** In Seawell.

SEAWELL NEIGHBORHOOD: Oaklands, but I wish we lived in the Rathmines because my friend Tina lives out there near a cool park where the fire department makes ice for skating in the winter. They spray the senior league outfield with their hoses. Our park sucks.

CURRENT HOMETOWN: Seawell, I already told you.

SCHOOL OR WORK: I'm in fifth grade. I get an allowance if I take out the garbage and clean up after our dog when he shits in the yard.

WHERE AND WHEN YOU MET SWEENEY: You already asked us about that.

LAST TIME YOU TALKED TO SWEENEY: These questions are dumb.

WHERE YOU THINK SWEENEY IS NOW: He's dead, I guess. I don't know. Everybody says he jumped off that bridge over the harbor.

GERALD M. FRANCIS

AGE: 71 **BORN:** My parents came here from Portugal while my mother was pregnant with me. I was born in 1933 in Woburn, Mass., a few months after they arrived.

SEAWELL NEIGHBORHOOD: I married Walter's mother when we were both 22 years old, and we moved to South Seawell, to her neighborhood, after our honeymoon.

CURRENT HOMETOWN: Oddly, I find myself still living in Seawell, Mass. I never left this place, never even traveled to Florida each year like all the other snowbirds.

SCHOOL OR WORK: I'm a retired firefighter. I was on the force for 30-some-odd years.

WHERE AND WHEN YOU MET SWEENEY: Farannan Golf Course when he was only nine years old, I believe.

LAST TIME YOU TALKED TO SWEENEY: I suppose he was around 23 or 24 years old, around nine or ten years ago. We had a few drinks at the [Farannan] clubhouse on my birthday. That's when he gave me that poem as a gift. I was a spry sixty on that day.

WHERE YOU THINK SWEENEY IS NOW: Well, I suppose he's wherever he wants to be. Whether he jumped or not, I can't say. That kid always did as he pleased, so I'll just imagine he's doing whatever he wants to do wherever that may be.

WALTER J. FRANCIS

AGE: 38 **BORN:** St. John's Hospital, Seawell

SEAWELL NEIGHBORHOOD: The Lowlands. We grew up in South Seawell, and now I live with my three daughters and my wife on 12th St. in the Lowlands—the old, marshy section of the city.

CURRENT HOMETOWN: See previous.

SCHOOL OR WORK: I read meters for the gas company. I've been doing it for almost twenty years now.

WHERE AND WHEN YOU MET SWEENEY: I met him through my father at the golf course, and he hung around with one of my second cousins when they were kids.

LAST TIME YOU TALKED TO SWEENEY: About ten years ago at Farannan with my dad. Before that? I guess it was when I was in college and Sweeney had a keg party on that old boat he lived on in the out-of-bounds area of Farannan—the one on stilts. I really haven't talked to the guy that much other than a "Hello" or "How's things?" every once in a while.

WHERE YOU THINK SWEENEY IS NOW: I have no idea. I haven't thought about it much. My dad would know better than me. I hope he's laying on some deserted beach somewhere, just enjoying the sun and the surf, while we hang around like a bunch of suckers who can't wait to shovel more snow! Good for him, you know?

MIGUEL GUTIERREZ OBREGON, a.k.a. "Micky" or "Goatboy"

AGE: 34 **BORN:** Puerto Rico, we moved to Boston when I was four then to Seawell when I was eleven.

SEAWELL NEIGHBORHOOD: I grew up in the Acre, and then on the other side of the river for a while in Pentucketville, but I just bought an old cottage in Sun Valley that I'm fixing up.

CURRENT HOMETOWN: Seawell.

SCHOOL OR WORK: I own Flintmere Treescaping and I'm Groundskeeper at Farannan. I've been running Farannan since I was a teenager, really. Timmy Danvers, the old Groundskeeper, was still around but he let me run the show most of the time. I got a guy who takes care of the Flintmere work for me, I just keep an eye on things over there and spend most of my days fixin' up this course.

WHERE AND WHEN YOU MET SWEENEY: Seawell High, gym class. We were challenging each other to do crazy shit off the diving board during our two weeks of swimming for the year. We were sophomores I think. He could do one-and-a-halfs; I couldn't.

LAST TIME YOU TALKED TO SWEENEY: Couple nights before he disappeared. We surfed up at the points—had a good session, too—and then had some beers at McSwiggans.

WHERE YOU THINK SWEENEY IS NOW: I don't know. I talked about that in the other interview, and I don't want to say anything more about it.

THOMAS SANTOS

AGE: 33 **BORN:** Seawell.

SEAWELL NEIGHBORHOOD: The Acre.

CURRENT HOMETOWN: Seawell.

SCHOOL OR WORK: Duck Island for just about half my life.

WHERE AND WHEN YOU MET SWEENEY: We're third cousins or somethin'. We used to play Little League together, and I guess I knew him even before that.

LAST TIME YOU TALKED TO SWEENEY: I don't know. We hung out a couple times after he got out of Darville Mental, like, the whole group of us. That was in the early '90s, but we weren't really too friendly by then.

WHERE YOU THINK SWEENEY IS NOW: I hope he's surfing off of some deserted island, living in a shack in the jungle and just relaxing. I hope that's how it is, but I don't know. He might've killed himself, he might've jumped. I've seen him get pretty depressed after a bender and stuff. Who knows?

MARGARET KATHERINE TIERNEY

AGE: 83 **BORN:** Prince Edward Island, off the coast of Canada.

SEAWELL NEIGHBORHOOD: My family had moved to P.E.I. before I was born, to be close to my mother's family, but we moved back to my father's old neighborhood, the Oaklands, when I was a toddler.

CURRENT HOMETOWN: Seawell.

SCHOOL OR WORK: I taught third and fourth grade for thirty-five years at several schools around the city.

WHERE AND WHEN YOU MET SWEENEY: Farannan Golf Course in the late '70s.

LAST TIME YOU TALKED TO SWEENEY: Well, we didn't talk but I saw him on the golf course shortly before he disappeared that fall, in 1998 I believe.

WHERE YOU THINK SWEENEY IS NOW: I like to tell myself he is off gallivanting around some deserted coastline, learning about the edible and medicinal plants in some forest or jungle...well, I'll just leave it at that. I just pray the boy is okay—off by himself like that.

PETER TREVOR JOYCE, a.k.a. "The Wizzah"

AGE: 32 **BORN:** Seawell, Mass. **SEAWELL NEIGHBORHOOD:** The Lowlands. If you have to live in Seawell, it might as well be in the Lowlands—God's

Country, kid, no doubt about it.

CURRENT HOMETOWN: Whistler, British Columbia, Canada.

SCHOOL OR WORK: I picked up a trade out West. I'm a unionized Ski Bum. I bartend at The Boot a couple nights a week for beer and rent money. It works for me.

WHERE AND WHEN YOU MET SWEENEY: Moody Junior High, him and a bunch of other guys threw me in a Dumpster on the first day of school. They had to sacrifice a seventh grader, and why not me, right? Kind of an honor, really.

LAST TIME YOU TALKED TO SWEENEY: I guess it was almost seven or eight years ago, he drunk-dialed me from El Salvador or Honduras or somewhere. He assured me that it was really hard to get to a phone at whatever time it was down there. He rode on a donkey or Shetland pony or something, he said—like I was supposed to be proud of his effort or something.

WHERE YOU THINK SWEENEY IS NOW: I don't know. It sounds stupid, but if the phone rings in the middle of the night I wake up thinking it could be him—wasted or he just got out of a Mexican jail or something. I don't know for sure, but I think he might have killed himself because I haven't heard from him in a long time. Nobody has. Back in the day, he used to call or send a postcard to one of his old friends, no matter how long he'd been gone. The tide's so strong under the Pennacook [Bridge] they never would've found him if he had jumped. I hate to think about it, I really hate to think about it. Now I'm all fuckin' sad an' shit. See, I knew I didn't write anymore of this bullshit down. Edit out the tear stains, alright? And tell your dad I said, "What's up?"

AUDREY ELAINE GAMMENS

AGE: No comment. **BORN:** Galloway, MA

SEAWELL NEIGHBORHOOD: : I just gave up an apartment that I kept during the past couple of decades in the downtown area of Seawell.

CURRENT HOMETOWN: Galloway, MA

SCHOOL OR WORK: I went to Galloway High, Boston University, and I've been a sportswriter since graduating. I'm currently the Sports Editor at *The Seawell Times*.

WHERE AND WHEN YOU MET SWEENEY: I first covered him when he caught for Seawell High's baseball team.

LAST TIME YOU TALKED TO SWEENEY: He told me he had "No comment" when I tracked him down to see how the Pepperdine program was treating him. It was a few months after he had enrolled there. That was pretty much it, I couldn't find him after that.

WHERE YOU THINK SWEENEY IS NOW: He killed himself by jumping off the Pennacook Bridge in 1998, his remains are scattered throughout the ocean he loved so much.

PATRICK FERGUS KIVLIN

AGE: 44 **BORN:** St. John's Hospital, Seawell

SEAWELL NEIGHBORHOOD: I grew up in the Oaklands, and I now live in Rathmines.

CURRENT HOMETOWN: Seawell.

SCHOOL OR WORK: Environmental Consultant for The Commonwealth of Massachusetts.

WHERE AND WHEN YOU MET SWEENEY: On Seawell Beach, when he was around six or seven years old. We were both down there watching waves roll in from a hurricane off the coast. The waves looked so perfect, we decided to learn how to surf together. He was just a kid, but he picked it up faster than I did. I guess I was fifteen or sixteen when we met. I was kind of a big-brother figure for him after that.

LAST TIME YOU TALKED TO SWEENEY: I'm not sure. I suppose it was a day or two before they found his bike at the base of the Pennacook. We said we'd meet for a surf, for dawn patrol, and we did, but it was blown out and we both went back to bed.

WHERE YOU THINK SWEENEY IS NOW: He's somewhere in South America finishing a collection of poetry or translating the next great Chilean poet to English. I suppose that's what I'd say if I had to guess. But he still owes me five-hundred bucks for that Hynson board I lent him in 1997. So, I suppose I'll take a cut of the advance on this book, we'll buy a longboard and teach a few kids to surf this summer down on Seawell Beach. That way we can call it even between you, me, Sweeney and everybody else in Seawell who still tells stories about him to this day.

THE "KEMP AABERG"

Compiled by Owen Kivlin, Miguel Obregon,
Thomas Santos and Patrick Kivlin

In the summer of 1986, after Sweeney's parents moved to Rhode Island, Sweeney began searching for furnished apartments in the downtown area of Seawell. He decided against living with his high school baseball coach, Jorge Mroz and his family, though Sweeney greatly appreciated the offered hospitality. He also declined an offer from my father, Patrick Kivlin. Sweeney wanted to live on his own, despite only being sixteen years of age.

Sweeney checked in with the people at the Seawell Marina to see if any old boats were up for sale at the start of the summer. He and Micky Obregon had discussed throwing a boat on a trailer, hauling it out to the woods of Farannan Golf Course behind the groundskeeping garage, winterizing it as best they could, and then Sweeney could live in it until he found a better situation. The boat was originally intended as a temporary solution.

Sweeney bought the trawler that became his Seawell home from a local fisherman known as "Gerry the Russian." The story goes that Gerry needed to get the boat out of the water, the Fish and Game Department was ready to fine him for a small fuel leak. In addition to engine trouble, the boat's hull was no longer seaworthy. It floated, and would be fine as a home on stilts, but the hull couldn't take many more poundings in the North Atlantic. Gerry the Russian didn't want to pay to haul it out of the marina, so he plugged the leak and began stalling the Fish and Game people. Around the same time, Sweeney's parents sold the family house in Seawell and were passing papers later that summer. Sweeney need-ed to move out of his childhood home, but he struggled to convince any landlord that he was eighteen with a reliable full-time job. Sweeney called Gerry the Russian and told him he would pay for the removal of his 32-foot fishing trawler, but he didn't have enough to buy it outright.

They apparently made a deal that involved a handshake and a whiskey sour—purchased for Gerry the Russian by an underage Sweeney at the Marina's restaurant. When I tracked him down in 2004, Gerry the Russian only offered a brief comment on the transaction. He said, "I don't remember too much about that boat. I know the guys at Fish and Game were breakin' my balls over a leak. I remember that because it was a five- or six-thousand-dollar fine if I didn't get it out of there by the end of the summer. The boat wasn't worth more than a few hundred bucks, it hadn't been seaworthy in a couple years. I just wanted to get rid of it. The kid took it off my hands, no questions asked—said he was gonna live in it, or somethin' ridiculous like that. I didn't care, I just wanted it out of my sight. The whiskey was enough for me."

Gerry the Russian was pleased to hear that Sweeney had actually lived in the boat on and off for many years. "You're shittin' me? That's great," he responded.

Micky helped Sweeney tow the boat out to Farannan in the middle of a late summer night; they did some damage to the edge of the fairways and rough of the fourth, fifth and six holes, but fixed it themselves. Micky told his supervisors that some joyriding teenagers were responsible for tearing up the course. The next day, Micky claims, he and Sweeney used eight-ton jacks to take the 32-foot trawler off the trailer. Using two jacks and piles of beam ends, scavenged from construction sites, they carefully set the boat down on a pair of steel oil drums positioned at the corners of the stern, and two piles of beam ends placed beneath the bow and the under the centerpoint of the boat. They managed to perch it behind a grove of honey ash, at the base of a steep hillside covered in yew trees. They planted some fairie alder and holly saplings on the port and starboard sides hoping to keep the boat out of the wind and hidden from sight.

At the start of its new, landlocked life the boat was christened the "Kemp Aaberg," named after one of the original Malibu stylists whose silhouetted, soul-arch bottom turn appeared in the first issue of *Surfer* Magazine in 1960. Apparently, the christening party went so well nobody actually slept in the boat that first night. Eight or ten men and women woke up in various pits and beds of leaves on the forest floor around the boat. A small search party found the last stragglers passed out, completely naked on a Shamuu pool raft in the rough of the sixth hole of Farannan Golf Course.

It seems, for the most part, that Micky and Sweeney were successful. Hurricane Murgill eventually blew the Kemp Aaberg off of its improvised stilts in 1998, but not before the boat had served as Sweeney's Seawell home for nearly twelve years. It took yearly rounds of winterizing, weatherproofing, repairs and improvements, but the trawler stood up against the elements longer than anyone expected. It also was hidden well enough, after three or four years of sapling growth, to give Sweeney the solitude he desired. No one but his closest friends, and a few high school kids drinking by their fire pit in those same woods, ever visited. Not many people ventured into the out-of-bounds woods tucked in the back corner of the golf course. In fact, many of the people I interviewed for this book had heard of the Kemp Aaberg out in the woods, but few claimed they visited the boat.

Micky says he and Sweeney took the boat's leaky engine out of the engine box in the center of boat's kitchen and installed a wood stove in its place. He said the kitchen and sleeping area were spacious enough for one person: "It was only a little bit smaller than a studio apartment downtown—you know, one you'd rent for like twelve-hundred a month these days. We extended the table and the booth seating in there, and buried a generator nearby for electricity. We insulated the inside as best we could and then built a little Plexiglas enclosure over the back deck. We had the whole thing remodeled for that first winter. It was cold as hell on the deck, but the stove was almost too warm for the inside of the boat. I hung out there and played cards a lot with Sweeney back then—drinkin' beers, talkin' shit. We even had a 45s-night for a while with a bunch of guys, ya know, until Sweeney ended up at Merritt. But, yeah, the Kemp was a nice spot, and we kept it in real good shape each year. The thing lasted way longer than we thought it would! I've been thinkin' about doing it all again with another boat, same spot. It was only two or three hundred yards behind my groundskeeping garage out there. It was cool to have a place to kinda disappear to, hidden behind the earcain yews and honeycomb gorse. It was good just knowin' it was there and stuff."

In 1989, Sweeney would find likeminded surfers on the West Coast who had a surf camp on the coast of Baja called "The Boat Ranch." Tommy describes the place somewhat in detail in Chapter 5. The Boat Ranch contained fifteen or sixteen old fishing vessels, no longer seaworthy, hauled out of the Pacific and circled like a nautical wagon train at a camp in the desert on the cliffs above a surf spot. Sweeney had retreated there after he dropped out of Pepperdine. For a brief time he lived at the Boat Ranch, approximately three to four months, and he fished with the local fishermen and served as caretaker for the Ranch. The stewards of The Ranch, Lance Downs and John Stanley, let him live rent-free in the boat of his choosing while they were living and working five hours north in Southern California. From what Tommy says, John and Lance also took to Sweeney's idea of naming the boats after legendary surfers from Hawaii, Australia and California. While in Baja, Sweeney chose to live in the boat that had the best view of the surf spot from its stern. He christened that boat "The Ronnie Brosnan."

SWEENEY'S FAMILY

Compiled by Owen Kivlin, Gerald Francis,
Margaret Tierney, Thomas Santos and Patrick Kivlin

I.

Despite my efforts to track Sweeney's parents down, Diane and Jonathan Sweeney refused to elaborate on their son or his whereabouts. They live together in Silver Springs, Maryland, just outside of Washington D.C, as of 2004. Mr. Sweeney has since retired from his consulting days, after closing his career working at the Pentagon. Mrs. Sweeney worked for twenty-two years as a customer representative and team manager for Nynex and its affiliates.

I spoke with Sweeney's parents separately on different dates, and Mr. Sweeney declined further comment with this brief statement: "My son made his own choices from his teen years onward. There was nothing I could do to further discipline or influence his way of thinking. I do not know where he is, and I won't speculate on his supposed suicide. If you continue to contact me I will be forced to bring this to the attention of the local authorities and my lawyer."

Mrs. Sweeney was more receptive to my phone call. She, at the very least, listened to my description of this project and seemed open to the idea. I sensed that she was almost happy for the attention paid to her son, but her overwhelming sadness at his departure from her life appeared to win out. She refused to answer any questions about Sweeney's life, and after I asked her whether or not she believed Sweeney had committed suicide or simply abandoned Seawell there was a long stretch of silence and she gently hung up the phone.

As far as I can tell—from my interviews with Thomas Santos, Patrick Kivlin, Margaret Tierney and Gerald Francis—Sweeney's parents essentially abandoned him when they left Massachusetts in 1986. It doesn't sound like they had much influence over him between 1986 and 1989. Whatever rift resulted between them, the beginnings of it seem to have come about with their move from Seawell. In 1989, Sweeney's father made an attempt to get his son back on "the right track" by sending Sweeney's cousin Tommy and Sweeney's former girlfriend Brigit Beaulieu to find his son in Baja, Mexico. Once they found Sweeney, Brigit was instructed to inform him that his father was deathly ill and wanted to see him before he passed away.

To the best of my knowledge, this all came to pass because Mrs. Sweeney had suffered a compound fracture in her lower leg that didn't heal properly and required minor surgery during the spring of 1989. Mr. Sweeney pounced on this opportunity and recruited Tommy and Brigit to the mission by bringing them to Rhode Island. He then lied to Tommy by saying that Diane Sweeney was the one who was on her deathbed and couldn't see any visitors, but wanted to patch things up with her son.

Brigit seems to have known of the deception at work, and only agreed to it in a warped effort to rekindle a relationship with Sweeney—a relationship that began and ended during their freshman year at Seawell High School. Tommy and Brigit set off for Baja together, and the rest of the story is detailed in Chapter 5.

II.

Whatever problems Sweeney had with his parents, and vice versa, their relationship appeared to come to an end with this episode. Sweeney refused to speak with his parents, Brigit and Tommy after he uncovered the truth in Rhode Island. Mrs. Sweeney remained with Mr. Sweeney and, despite Tommy's speculation, it's unclear whether or not she was ever tempted to divorce him over his deceit in dealing with their son.

Sweeney's decision to quit the Pepperdine baseball team, along with the time he served at the Merritt House of Corrections, exacerbated the damaged relations with his cousin Tommy, and they were never close again. I'm not sure that the relationship between Brigit and Sweeney was anything more than a high-school crush, but soon after the above-mentioned incident Brigit moved to Colorado and was never a part of Sweeney's life again according to the individuals I've interviewed.

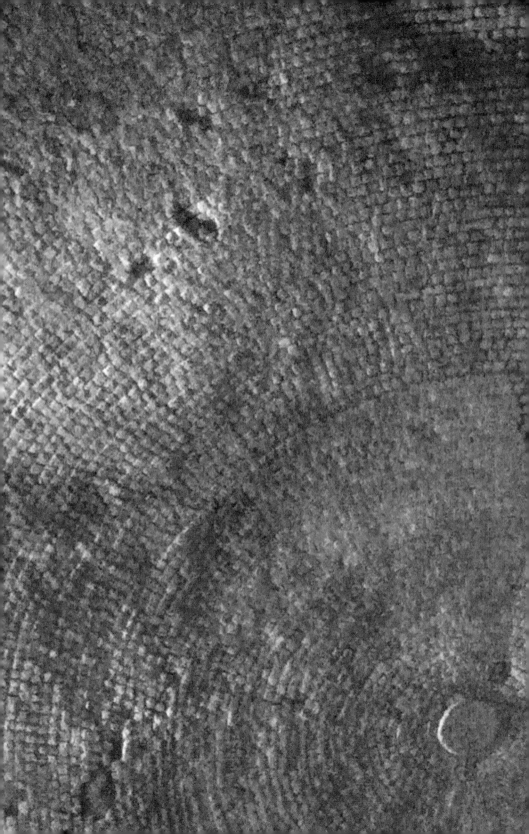

BOOK II

SWEENEY
IN-THE-FROTH

BY SWEENEY O'SWEENEY
EDITED BY DAVE ROBINSON &
OWEN KIVLIN

CARDINAL'S OFFICE
66 BANKS DRIVE
BOSTON, MASSACHUSETTS

To Cardinal Molloy:

I intend to be excommunicated from the Catholic Church. It has occurred to me that a complete disconnection from Christianity is needed to further my spiritual growth. In addition to this desire for inner growth, I object to the bloody history, fundamental misogyny, homophobia and egotism that fuel the Catholic Church's modern endeavors.

I believe it was the Irish poet Yeats who estimated most governments run their course and expire after 250 years; just as most religions spawn, flourish and die after approximately 2,000 years. Since the Vatican is as power hungry, corrupt and dangerous as any dying government, I imagine that Catholicism should be fully dead by 2250 A.D.

However, I'd like to get out now if you don't mind. Actually, even if you do mind, I want out.

This pedophilia scandal involving your priests is sickening. Your archaic and dangerous attitudes toward women and gays are alarming. The pope you just threw into power actually believes hell is a physical location somewhere within the universe. I needn't remind you, I'm sure, that anyone who reads the poetry of the Bible—the much translated, edited and corrupted poetry—and believes it to be literal is missing the point (imaginatively and spiritually). The power of the poems is in the metaphor, as is the power of your faulty dualistic notion of an afterlife in heaven or hell. Now, Pope Benedict XVI may not actually take the Bible literally, but he's preaching it as fact and that's a lie I can't stomach. There's no justification for such spiritual dishonesty even if he believes such a lie will scare the poor and illiterate of the world into behaving better. Acts of compassion devoid of any connection to a system of myths and belief are even more valuable than missions to convert under the premise of spiritual blackmail—i.e. "Love our god and you won't burn in hell, which has a zip code these days, so watch out!"

I haven't trucked in your "fear is the heart of love" Old Testament gobbledygook since I was a teenager. I'll never traffic in those cosmic scare tactics. Jesus didn't either, but you Catholics have taken a beautiful brown man who understood the innate divinity in every living thing and rewritten him as a superior white demigod lacking much of his inherent humanity.

Lastly, if you're still reading (and I doubt you are, *fat bastard*—just kidding, I put that in there to see if you actually read this thing. I know you're a pretty fit Cardinal, as Cardinals go.), I want to be excommunicated because I've converted to a spiritual practice of my own making. I need disconnection to further this practice. If you look up the myth from "The Poems of Sweeney Peregrine," translated by Trevor Joyce, or the version "Sweeney Astray" from the '80s translated by Seamus Heaney, you'll see that the original Sweeney quarreled with a cleric. Sweeney was his own man, a king, in fact, and he tossed a pesky cleric's book of psalms into a lake. The cleric cursed Sweeney and, to keep this short, he went insane and lived the last seven years of his life as a half man, half bird in the wilderness of Ireland and beyond. My mother, just before abandoning me as a teen, told me she named me Sweeney O'Sweeney after this original King Sweeney of the wilds.

This initially shocked me, but further reading of Joseph Campbell and Carl Jung helped me recognize I'd been handed the keys to my own contentment. Since studying the legend of Sweeney Peregrine, I have modeled my life after King Sweeney.

It has been fourteen strange years since I began constructing my personal myth. I am in self-imposed exile from my home of Seawell. I have lived in Ecuador, British Columbia, Ireland, Mexico and visited many other far-flung locales in this shrinking world of ours. The Third World has been the wilderness to my American upbringing. This is of course the same Third World that the Vatican is assaulting with an emboldened campaign to keep the money coming in by scaring hungry, poor, diseased, desperate and uneducated people into believing they were born sinners and thus suffer, and suffer more without Lord God as their Savior. I hesitate to even capitalize the names of these spent characters your superiors sling about like cubic zirconium versions of spiritual jewels.

In my own life it appears I've reached a stage, paralleling the actual legend in *Sweeney Peregrine,* where I've been humbled by the wilderness and become one with nature and creation. Sweeney was mistakenly killed in his seventh year of exile and he told his story no more.

I'm no king and do not want anything more than to kill off the original Holy Spirit I was given without my consent. Please help me to do this via excommunication.

I was not born a sinner. Jesus of Nazareth is a man I admire and emulate but do not accept as my savior. I am, just like all humans, my own savior as the divine is within me. Each day I attempt to love all persons I see, all sentient beings, as if I am watching godliness cross my path moment by moment. I am now what the past has made of me, but I will become more loving and compassionate by the moment. I will be one with the dirt, the oaks, rain, stars, the sea and the animals around me.

This lifetime is heaven and there is no good or evil—no duality—just billions of shades of virtuousness making up the beautiful instants of my life here on this planet.

Billions of paths to a wholeness.

Please grant me my request to end my dying spiritual connection to Christianity. As you finish this letter you are hearing the final feeble breath of my Holy Spirit. My next breath will be my next moment, while I am one with birth, death, time and space—one moment closer to whatever awaits me after enlightenment.

Sincerely,
Sweeney O'Sweeney

---

*See page 347 for the Catholic Church's official response to this request.

PROLOGUE

Owen,

The mud—the vengeful, ill-willed mud—is all-powerful here. Unless, of course, you've grown into a pragmatist since last I saw you. If that's the case, you would disagree and argue that it is *la lluvia,* the rain, which whips this tropical dust into its more egotistical, viscous self. And the rain and mud are the reasons I'm writing you at the moment. The waves are tiny and it's been raining pigs-and-dogs down here for three days.

For three days I've been wondering how to contact you again. For three sopping days of ocean flatness I've had no distractions, no way to avoid the thought of the book you created, the interviews you conducted and the poems you included. *Sweeney on-the-Fringe* exists in Seawell and the larger world—it might exist a bit more than I do these days.

I guess you could call this a dispatch from the fringe, but really I'm beyond the fringe at this point. Physically, Farannan is in the Northern Hemisphere. I've gone south. Imaginatively and emotionally, well, I'm still out of bounds.

There are 1,001 reasons I left Seawell so often and, finally, for all of this time. I couldn't even list them in this Moleskine. It would make for boring reading and a seemingly cynical prologue to what I hope becomes a response to the book you cobbled together about me.

I feel like I have to create something to respond. It'll be a little scattered, but that's how it goes with me: keep it live on the set and be kind along the way. It's all I do these days.

I turned a corner during my final year of high school. I was thrown harshly onto that corner, but I made the call to get up, turn and not look back until I knew what was behind me.

It was a Friday-night-football pre-game ritual for us—the seniors, the spectators, the drinkers. We called the shots, named the drinking spots throughout Seawell and told the other crowds to go to The Rock or The Hill, The Briley Woods or Mt. Pheasant after the game ended. The murmurs, rumors and instructions began with us at the base of the bleachers, leaning against the wall above the track circling the well-lit field. We feigned interest in gridiron politics but watched the party info ripple through the pockets of students up in the stands like wind through teen-aged trees. But something was different on the night I'm describing.

I was late getting to Center Field for our pre-game beer. I think I was lost in the emptiness of my newly gutted house. I can't recall why I never got up and out of the place of my own volition. But the boys rallied and saved me a beer. They drove the can to my house. My cousin Tommy brought it to the door and told the other clowns to wait in the car. They didn't listen. It was a clown car, after all. They were supposed to pour out of it, dance and smack each other around—just as they did, all over the front yard.

But, like I said, things were different on this night. Some of these young, buzzing meathead friends of mine knew my parents had just left me and gone to Rhode Island. I suppose they just forgot in the blissful beginnings of a Friday night in high school: beer, girls, fights, running from the cops. Tough to remain focused or emotionally aware with those prospects immediately ahead of you. This is why I'm wondering how those same prospects hadn't distracted me on this night of nights in my life—I was 17, eager to get drunk and laid just like the guys kicking up the dry, fallen leaves in my yard.

I could hear their heavy breathing and swearing from my couch in the cellar, I could imagine clouds of breath streaming between them and the streetlamp above the yard.

My cousin Tom came in first while the rest shot doubles and sank half-nelsons. He knocked twice sharply, waltzed in, yelled for me and commenced searching through every empty room upstairs. Curses were cussed as light switches flicked on and off to no effect. The electricity had been shut off. The movers had taken all the furniture that afternoon. They'd had mercy and left me the ratty, plaid couch in the basement, despite my father's instructions to take every last thing. I had to bribe them all with a half rack of Bud as thanks. My clothes were in a pile behind the sliding doors of my closet in my former room upstairs. I'd tried to move the couch upstairs where it was warmer but I couldn't get it through the door at the top of the cellar stairwell by myself. I let it tumble back down the maroon and white painted stairs and I must've dozed off on it where it landed.

Brian Mello found me. Cousin Tom was too busy yelling for me up in the attic and Brian had started to run down into the cellar. He said the streetlamp was filtering in one of the rectangular ground-level windows and onto my couch. He'd stopped three-steps down.

Brian told me later, "I threw you the beer we saved you and you sorta grunted and rolled into a sitting position, with your bare feet on the bottom stair." I remember downing the beer and jogging up the steps, out to the car, calling "shotgun" and getting the night started. It got back to normal from that moment.

A couple years later, I bumped into Brian at The Skeff and he described that night in his own way. I've always tried to remember how and why he told me all this.

"Sweeney, it was like any other Friday with a home football game. Except I'd just left my house an hour or so before. You know my house—it's packed with polished tables and leather couches, bookcases and a couple televisions. It's a nice place and my parents worked hard to buy all that shit. But I go to Center Field that night, pound a beer, you're not there and so we all go to your house. 'Where the fuck's Sweeney?' You know what I mean?

"We get there, I cheap-shot Sanchez out on the front lawn because he won't keep quiet about some stripper at The Blue Star or something ridiculous like that. You know Sanchez, right? Never shuts up about women. Anyways, I get inside your house and it's completely empty. It's dark and empty and cold. And I swear I'd just left my parents and little sisters sitting by a fire watching reruns of "Barney Miller," and my dad's reading the paper and digesting dinner. Then Tommy's barging around your house yelling for you and I just kinda stopped in my tracks. Then I figured you were in the basement on that couch, because where else would you be? Right? It's the only piece of furniture in the place.

"I went down a couple of stairs and could barely see you on that thing, that shitty couch...no offense.

"I threw you the beer, you downed it and kinda bounded by me, up the stairs, down the hall, through the empty living room next to the black and white pristine kitchen and out the front door to the car. You didn't even close the door, and still had your flip flops in your back pocket.

"I came out last after your cousin, and suddenly had a lot on my mind so I just climbed in the way-back of the station wagon. I cracked a beer back there, someone shut the tailgate and you yelled from the front seat, 'Brian, what the fuck? Were you raised in a house or something? Shut the front door of my barn next time you're last one out, okay?' Everyone laughed and we took off, but no one ever went back to shut the door. There was no point.

"But Sweeney, that night when we snaked through your family's empty house and you bounced out of it like it wasn't a big thing, that night sticks with me. It was the first time I paid any attention to, you know...that not everyone has had an easy time of it. I mean, how many kids at Seawell High didn't have shit to eat before school? Prob'ly like a thousand. Whose parents were passed out or shooting up or just long gone like yours? They just left you in the middle of your senior year. What the fuck was that about?

"Don't answer that. I don't mean to pry or anything. It's your business, I'm just telling you this thing I have on my mind.

"All that stuff in *my* house back then, the Nintendo, four touchtone phones, expensive silverware, ride-on mower, dining set, all that stuff became irrelevant to me after that night at your house. I still can't stop thinking about the half-played game of 45s I saw spread out on the living room floor—like you'd been playing both hands before you went down to the cellar to sleep on the couch. That shit has stuck with me. Instead of 'us' versus 'them' it read 'me' versus 'myself' on your score sheet. You fuckin' weirdo! No offense.

"But you went out with us once we came and got you that night, your old friends. And we got drunk, drove around to all the spots, hit on girls, talked trash and had a blast. As always. And you were there just doing your thing the whole night like you knew what mattered, man. You weren't pretending, either, because I watched you and I know bullshit. Just like anyone that grew up here, we know bullshit when we see or hear it.

"You basically just had fun that night and then went back to your empty house, clowning in the front yard when we dropped you off.

"I'd flipped you an extra beer out the back window from my next-night stash, and I told myself that I would keep things simple from then on. You didn't give a care, cruisin' through the open front door to the dark hall and down to that crappy couch in the cellar; it was enough.

"So I started telling the people who love me I love them right back and I've kept it basic like that.

"No! Hold on! Don't give me any shit, Sweeney. Just let me finish and then you can fuck with me. I'm not that good at it, at telling people I care about them, but I try to keep it simple now and think more about the stuff other people go through, you know? So, yeah, that's what I've been waitin' to tell you for a couple years now since you took off. And I don't care if you wanna give me shit now. I just hadta say it."

Owen, once Brian framed that night for me, gave me his perspective, I knew I was doing okay—and there were some rough times during those years after high school. It got really rough during the time leading up to the night he told me that story. This was after I'd cracked the Mormon kid's head open, but before I stole the ice cream truck.

Brian confirmed the direction I was headed in and so I kept going, minus all the violence and *some* of the drinking. I realized back then that my life, whether I'm aware of it or not, influences people. And not in that American influence-the-masses kind of dreamy way, but in a person-to-person way. Little details, small decisions all fan out and have an effect on people. I don't have (or want) any control over what other people think about me or my life, the good and the bad, but I can take care of myself, do what I want to do and be content without caring what other people think. And that rubs off on the receptive, it seems.

Brian's story helped me open up and decide to do what I wanted to do with my life. And what I first did was recall something my mother once told me about my name: Sweeney O'Sweeney, a name I was often embarrassed about. She told me that she named me after an old Irish king back in the day. She said I should take some time in my life to learn his story. After listening to Brian, that's what I did.

I procrastinated a bit, but then the book found me: "Sweeney Peregrine," a translation by the Dublin poet Trevor Joyce. I found a copy of the book at a poetry conference at the University of Seawell. I was over there drinking beers with Seawell guys, fifth- and sixth-year seniors. I timed my weekend visit so I could ditch my friends and try to sneak into the poetry conference. I stumbled into the festival and stumbled across the book. I use that phrase loosely, because when I checked with the woman there as to how much the book cost she said, "$2.50." It was the exact amount of bills and change I had in my pocket. Since then, I've believed so much less in the idea of coincidence and so much more in keeping my mind open to whatever might come my way. I mean, I bought one of the last copies of a small translation of Gaelic poems that first came out in 1975 in Dublin and was just sitting in Seawell—poetry written by my crazy namesake, originally, like a thousand years ago.

I saw it, figured I hadn't been given anything I couldn't handle so far, so why not? Back then, I stopped worrying and started reading *Sweeney Peregrine*.

Owen, if you go back and look at the arc of your book *Sweeney on-the-*

Fringe you'll find it follows a similar one to the story told in "Sweeney Peregrine." This is no coincidence, my old friend. A month or so after Brian told me the story about my own empty house, I decided to adopt the myth of *Sweeney Peregrine*. I made the ancient King Sweeney my Jesus-Buddha-Allah figure. After all, what are prophets but examples of people leading lives worthy of imitation? King Sweeney the bold, the insane, the lyrical, the treed, the lonely—he became the first self-appointed manifestation of my inner nature. I gave myself over to the rhythms of his life story, and your book about me is a reflection of my effort—strange as it has been.

It wasn't until I thought of my mother's gift of my name that I knew what would shape my life: an acceptance of an example and a willingness to allow my life to morph itself around that example's story. I would form and grow out of the chaotic suffering in the original Sweeney's world as well as my own.

I wrote poems like Sweeney; I thought too much of myself; I was tired of the strictures of Seawell as I grew older. Might as well live while you're alive. Most of the things I'd been taught as a kid were bullshit anyway, why not just admit it to myself, let go of the anger, and move on to something better and more honest? Why not let myth, imagination and kindness lead the way? Who needs money, laws and logic to find the moral path? I was aiming then, as I'm aiming now in this moment, to live above morality—within a place where my first action and only reaction is compassion.

I had to leave Seawell and its coldwater waves to get closer to this place within myself. I was an amateur at this stuff, I will always be an amateur…but I'll get back home once I get back to my self. As the Buddhas believe, "Before enlightenment there's chopping wood and carrying water; after enlightenment there's chopping wood and carrying water."

For now, I only wanted to contact you and let you know I'm creating a response to your *Sweeney on-the-Fringe*. I'm profoundly grateful to you and I hope I can continue what you began. If I ever finish the book, I'll send it to you.

With all the long-distance gratitude and respect I can muster, I'll wish you what the people of Bella Vista, Ecuador, wish the world, what they painted on the rickety fence bordering the path up to their shantytown:

"Paz, Amor y Vida,"
("Peace, Love and Life")

Sweeney O'Sweeney

01

PAGAN'S SONG

Seawell Beach, a.k.a. Sun Valley

Low-pressure groundswell trains from the south and huge blue waves detonate down the sandbars built off Little Rocks. I'll surf from six to nine, when the sea breeze slackens or changes direction.

On shore, stragglers shake sand from blankets; suntanned dads brush the seats of chafed kids' swimsuits. They begin the short trudge to their rented houses for quick outside showers.

Floating, waiting for just the right wave, I recall the Seawell evenings when I was a kid: sunburnt nose, warm sand, salt air in my lungs made deep breaths coughs, a sign that the day had been a slow, full-bodied taste of the seasonal coast.

These days I paddle for the last waves of the sets and hope for a lull to follow. If there's no lull, I paddle and duck, push and dive, under wall after blue wall. I'll chase one last wave until I'm too beat to recall how few stained-glass evenings will wink, flare and go dim before the smudge of winter's flat skies and white flakes. As if half the year blurs through a lens of scuffed, thick seaglass.

For now, I watch facets of rose-colored light dance along the glass shoulders of swells. The waves stand, plume and crash down onto distant sandbars.

Near dark, with the sky still edged in green, the stars begin to glint and wheel. Sea foam dissolves with a hiss.

I walk home, looking back for moonrise—reddish and papery, as the Sox bat through sharp static from three or four porch radios tuned to the game. Seawater drips from my fingers, the street is still sun-warmed. Tucking my board beneath my other arm, I smile and inhale the charcoaled chicken, lilacs and hints of marsh blown out to the swells.

All over Sun Valley, these west-to-east streets, people eat and laugh on porches and decks. The drawbridge siren wails from the harbor, a cluster of dog barks rises as the gate bells ring. Traffic stacks, chorus-barks blend rhythms with the clangs.

As the guttural push of a boat's low-geared diesel resounds from the bridge, the evening unhinges and cools. I rinse my board and peel my wetsuit off behind the house, slap at a few unfortunate sand fleas, then sit down to a cold Pacifico with a splinter of lime jammed in the neck of the brown bottle. Sun Valley unwinds through its lattice of yards. We strum the rough crabgrass with flexed, bare feet.

As fists pivot and gasp on bottlecaps slow trains of waves break down the beach. The air aches with hushed coughs—the liquid pulse of the summer's first full moon.

02

THE STUDY

Dear Owen,

Dr. Nicolas Panagiakis moved to the Seawell area from Athens, Greece, in the early 1980s to conduct a study of the Merrohawke Valley's population of international Gypsies. The majority of the population descended from a group of Gypsies that originally moved from Northern Ireland and Donegal in the Republic of Ireland. Originally, a small population lived outside of Boston during the early to mid-19th century. They'd fled poverty and persecution as stowaways on various cargo ships and ocean liners. Gathering north of Boston, they formed a community of traveling musicians and artisans known for their skills in smithing, carpentry, grayhound breeding and racing, cow and horse trading and, of course, storytelling. Although, at the same time, this community was almost universally reviled and harassed wherever they traveled in Massachusetts much as they had been all over Ireland and Europe.

Here in the United States, Dr. Panagiakis found the "knackers" were persecuted much as they were in their homeland. Accused of thievery and kidnapping on a regular basis, the knackers were chased from county to county in eastern Massachusetts by residents, police forces and occasionally through legislature designed to root them to a single place. It wasn't until 1987 that the Commonwealth of Massachusetts publicly apologized for a "gypsie assimilation program" called "Operation Nomad" in place from 1830 to 1964. The program forcibly removed thousands of knacker children from their families and placed them in state-run orphanages, the military and schools in the western part of the state.

In 1834 a group of 37 Boston knackers walked north, nearly 30 miles, to Seawell to become laborers on the Pentucket Canal—the first canal to be excavated, followed by several more miles of canals all dug by hand. No other group of immigrants would become as integral to the digging of Seawell's canal system, and thus the larger water-powered industrial revolution that began in what would become North America's first planned industrial community. In Seawell, the knackers found a relative tolerance for their traditional way of living. They were not allowed to live in the city's boardinghouses but they were allowed to move between four or five encampments in Seawell and on either side of the Merrohawke River provided they kept a majority of their menfolk toiling at the excavation of the canal system. Once the English mill owners in Seawell alerted the government in the British Isles that the knackers were suited to the backbreaking shovel-and pick-work, the English, Irish, Welsh and Scottish governments began rounding up knackers, pikeys, tinkers and Gypsies all over the Celtic Isles and shipping them to Boston and Seawell.

It is believed that by 1870 more than ten thousand knackers were crowded into the Acre neighborhood in Seawell, just outside of the canal and mill systems constructed in the cities. Soon Greece, Armenia, Canada's French Canadian provinces and Italy would all ship Gypsies and other supposed "social deviants" to the Merrohawke Valley to finish off the miles of canals. When the canals were completed, Seawell already possessed the huge workforce needed to build the redbrick mills to make use of the waterpower. Once the mills were built, the children of the knackers earned their keep as the exploited workforce that ran the looms, presses and other deadly machinery inside the stifling mills of Seawell and its soon-to-follow sister cities of Galloway and Lawrence.

During the late-20th century, Dr. Panagiakis was interested in assembling a collection of essays on the socio-linguistic adaptation of Greek children in Seawell's Acre. Instead, he found a blending of cultures, oral histories and spirituality that couldn't be parsed or remotely qualified in a constructive fashion. In fact, after recording more than 2,100 pages of oral histories from the knacker population, Dr. Panagiakis realized that a recent influx of refugees into Seawell from Laos, Cambodia, Vietnam and other war-torn nations was a continuation of the original Gypsie exodus (voluntary or involuntary) toward Seawell. Dr. Panagiakis was unable to speak any languages other than Greek and English and became frustrated by the influence of the new population of refugees.

Eventually, he abandoned his project to Seawell's public library, leaving the onionskin pages stacked in baskets on the Wallace Memorial Library's prominent granite steps before it opened for the day. He was on his flight back to Greece that same afternoon, having left a note that read:

> *To the People of Seawell, Mass.,*
>
> *Seawell knackers do not mind who lives where, who tells what story, where any body came from or why that body came to the Acre. Aside from your average conflicts and altercations occurring between established and newer populations, this Gypsie city within a city is a magnet for the castoffs of other countries. I happily found myself in over my head, drowning in a sea of thirty-six languages and surrounded by so many cultures and oral histories it was enough to spin my head around and around and eventually back toward my homeland. I submit, an imaginatively richer and more compassionate man for the effort, but nonetheless I submit. The funding has dried up, so I must go home. Thus, I offer up my work for public consumption. These pages are the only American-based records of my work with the knackers of Acre City. Transcribing them has cemented the details, bit by bit and brick by brick in my heart and mind. I hope future generations of Seawell will benefit, as I have, from my work.'*
>
> *—Salutations, Dr. Nicolas Panagiakis*
> *Seawell, Mass., October 1985*

Incidentally, the photocopied version of Dr. Panagiakis' "Folklore of the Knackers of Acre City, Seawell, Massachusetts" available to the public had only been checked out nine times in its ten-year shelf life at the Seawell Library. Gerald Francis was one of the few amateur historians to take an interest in Seawell's history of Knackers. Gerald originally told me about the manuscript and we poured over it many times together when I was a teenager. We spent the equivalent of months reading and enjoying that sacred, unpublished text together in Gerald's home and at the Wallace Library. I skipped a few algebra classes to sneak down the road for a beer at the Old Wardin House followed by some reading of Panagiakis' work in the Wallace.

What I've included throughout the following book are a few of the tales I believe best relate the intricacies and richness of the cultural and spiritual history of the workforce that brought Seawell into existence. Specifically, I'm interested in the tales sprung from Celtic wilderness mythology involving species of fairies, gnomes and elves—originally guardians and stewards of nature. As you'll see, many of these creatures have now adapted themselves to the urban-industrial setting of Seawell. Later tales have the fairies mingling and breeding with the rumored ghosts of the Irish child workers maimed and killed during their work in the mills.

Whether or not you believe in these creatures or have closed your heart and imagination to the possibility of such things, the remarkable power of these creatures and their significance is unquestionably revealed in the staying power of these tales. The original legends from which these Seawellian tales derive are thousands of years old, predating Christ, Buddha, Muhammad and even the Mayan and Incan systems of belief.

Incredibly, many of the descendents of the keepers of these oral histories still live in Seawell, where locals claim their ninth-generation Seawellian status with pride. These "great-grandknackers," as they refer to themselves, still reside in or frequent the Acre and its public houses. These are places where storytellers, musicians and poets are held in highest regard. Unlike the more gentrified neighborhoods surrounding the Acre, the more "cosmopolitan" city of Boston and the larger Western World surrounding Massachusetts, when a poet enters a Gaelic pub in the Acre the crowd shuffles aside as he is offered the best seat by the fire.

To my knowledge, and despite the vitality of the oral versions of these tales, there are few written texts—besides Dr. Panagiakis' timeless work—which record the quirks, power and charm of the urban creatures of Northeastern Industrial and Post-Industrial America. While refugees from Africa, Southeast Asia, Haiti and points beyond continue to flock to Seawell's Acre decade by decade—bringing their own tales and culture and beliefs—these ancient Gypsie stories are adopted, adapted and abandoned as the fluidity of time and ever-changing society dictate.

For years, I buried myself in Acre City—the pubs, the histories, the homes and the heritage of the place and the people. As certain groups of friends believed me to have traveled and disappeared and reappeared, often I could've been found—simply—in other obscurely comfortable neighborhood houses listening to stories in Gaelic and slurred English.

These legends are examples of some of the texts I chose to study to help me escape Seawell whenever I needed to.

Owen, you hold before you the extended prayers of an exploited people grown content at the end of their long climb to the rungs of the working and middle classes. You're reading evidence of the connection between the spirit and minds of some of the first industrialized peoples in the "New" World. These descriptions of mythical creatures are the product of the knackers' desperate attempt to survive the harshest working conditions imaginable as they fled the forests, famine, wars, prejudice and strife of their homelands and were forced to dig, construct and weave paltry fortunes for the sake of their children. These aren't the abducted, G-rated creatures of Disney. These are the murderous, strangely beautiful, drunk, blistered and dangerous spiritual embodiments of many Seawellian's connection to nature.

As Dr. Panagiakis famously wrote, "I bet these bléssed beastly children will outlast alphabets and any religion we fortunate animals could ever organize."

—Sweeney O'Sweeney

Above: The Canal Hag waltzes near
the ruins of the Humbleton Mills, date
unknown.
Photo: Seawell Historical Society

Below: Paula Stanislaus claims to have taken this photo of the Canal Hag in 1990. As she prepared to ford a small stream in Seawell State Forest, she heard a "swishing" in the dry grass behind her. "It was a silent, raw day in March. I hadn't seen a soul for miles," she states, "and then this beautiful woman was suddenly turning and striding away from me as if she'd been nearby all along. I snapped this photo, the last on my roll, and hiked directly to my car. I was terrified and didn't stop shaking until much later that evening."

03

RUNNING FROM COPS

When we were kids we used to run from the cops all the time. I was telling some friends of mine down in Ecuador about drinkin' and all the different spots around Seawell that we used to go to back in high school. All these people from all over the world were sitting around comparing cop stories. I mean, you sit in a bar in Ecuador in these lost, little beach towns★ up north and you don't see police or the army or anything for weeks on end. When you do see cops, they look like heavily armed infantry dressed in fatigues or black bulletproof vests, speeding through town on the backs of police trucks on their way north to the next town fifteen miles up through the jungle. At that point everyone stops and drops what they're doing, including us travelers, and you watch the procession go by hoping they don't stop anywhere near where you are hanging. You'll hear hushed whispers: "*Mira, mira la policia!*" This includes Ecuadorians. You don't mess with the cops down here, and they won't really mess with you. It's not like driving in Baja, where the *Federales* shake you down for cash every time they decide to pull you over. On the coast down here if they hear you're selling pounds of weed or if someone gets shot in a drunken dispute, then the cops appear fast—and some citizen's gonna get beaten, some citizen's going to an old, infested, dark jail cell. And if you're not from Ecuador, you're paying tons of cash, rotting in a cell for a few months and then getting deported for your trouble. The cops down here are fuckin' serious when they have to be.

This Irish guy I met described some things from his life growing up in Belfast, heavier shit—armed patrols, continual helicopter surveillance. He was talking about police forces, the IRA, British militias, the Protestants keeping the Catholics in line, the Catholics retaliating, the Protestants

---

★This storytelling session takes place in Canoa on the coast of northern Ecuador.

answering the call—just back and forth for ages. His northern lilt described Dublin, to the south, as more peaceful. The cops don't usually have guns and they'll chase a junkie down and then beat him a bit, throw him in jail but there aren't cradled M-16s in fatigued arms, gunfire in the streets like when he grew up in Belfast. He told me the cops won't allow even one "rubbish bin" on the street because all the British and Irish terrorists hid most of their bombs in them.

This Spanish woman, an architect backpacking for six months by herself, said Spain's pretty laidback as far as the police. But she did grow up hearing horror stories from her grandmother about the fascist police forces and stuff like that. She lisped that she was sort of influenced by those stories as far as her point of view on the cops.

When I told all these people about the police in Seawell, Mass.—fully equipped, armed, mobile cops—and how we grew up fucking with them, they just couldn't really believe me. Their jaws dropped above sweating *mojitos* and *Pilseners*. Pancho, who'd heard about Seawell police from me before, called over the locals playing pool under the palm-thatched overhang. The ugly American, twenty-one-year-old Rob from Phoenix, Arizona, even shut-up for the first time in two weeks to hear my story.

It was weird. I had a whole slew of world travelers and all the locals, waitstaff included, hanging around the hammocks and tables of the Balsa Hostel Bar down on the beach. There is no indoor section at this place; it is all outdoors right on the sand next to a shallow river coming out of the jungle and nearby cattle ranches. This sort of scene goes down when I travel, I guess—I mean, every couple days or so someone from Tasmania or Saginaw will tell me about their life, their neighborhood, their culture and I'm rapt. I can't get enough of hearing how people get by in other places. On this night, I had the floor. The whole group wanted to hear all about the Seawell Police Department's efforts to keep teenagers from drinking in the woods, on dark golf courses, in empty business parks.

I first told the story in English, a couple paragraphs, and then in Spanish—back and forth like that for a while. It's an odd way to do it—to tell and retell and choose words that aren't exact but give the gist of it to two entranced audiences near closing time, leaning on every word. It was exhausting, but we all helped translate and the *Cuba Libres* kept us alert. We all had enough time to get somewhat loose on booze before we broke out the postcards, but more about that later.

For now, I'll start by saying it was a warm, clear night. The only other sounds besides my voice were the four-foot waves that broke across the rivermouth and the town's pack of snarling stray dogs down on the beach. It was a full-moon night in June. The dogs were hyped up and chasing invisible disturbances all along the edge of the sea. I waited for Rob, "Mouth" as I'd nicknamed him, to settle down about his cousin Leon, the rent-a-cop that hated skateboarders like the plague, then I began:

On a typical night during my high school years, we'd tell our parents we were off to the football game (*Americano* not *fútbol*) or the basketball game or some such lie and we would go but only for a little bit. If there was a dance at the high school, we'd only go to lure other people away to go drinkin' in the woods or down the beach. If the weather wasn't too shitty, most kids would rather be outside away from teachers and their bullshit. Well, it wasn't that way in each town back there, but it was that way in Seawell. We'd get a good crowd that would flee the dance or game or whatever and someone would call it—and normally it was a junior or senior guy who was pretty much known as the local teen alcoholic. He'd shout the name of a place, or whisper it to the upper classmen... well, that's not entirely true. If the guy was smart he'd only tell the underclass girls. Freshmen were the lowest of the low, the boys anyways. The freshmen girls, well, you get the point. So, like, Bobby Mulcahey—a Nighttrain lush at seventeen—would say, for instance, "We're all goin' to the Rock; there's a half-keg there." And everyone would go, whether there was a half-barrel or not. And the Rock wasn't really a great or even inviting spot. It was a broken-glass-covered, graffiti-splashed mound of granite behind the local supermarket near the football stadium.

Most of my friends knew there was no keg at the Rock by the time we were freshmen because we'd been going to some of these parties since the seventh grade. Not all of us drank, but we hung out and tried to learn what flirting with girls was all about. When we did start drinking, there were different packies that would sell to minors on a regular basis—and "packies" is short for "package stores" or "liquor stores" and that's a tough one to explain in Spanish, believe me. There was G & M's out by Toady's in Pentucketville, and there was a place we called "Shithead's" because those guys sold to almost anyone flashing a fake I.D. You could bring in your library card fudged with your cousin's Crayolas and Shithead's would sell you all the Miller Lite you could drink before school started on Monday morning. And there were other packies where some hockey player worked nights for his uncle or some shy girl from the Science Club trying to be cool would sneak cases of Beast (Milwaukee's Best) to a cooler hidden behind the store. But those plans called for Friday-afternoon scheming in school. Normally we didn't make plans until we got out of last class. We all had and lost fake I.D.s and had our reliable spots to buy booze, but if nothing was working and no one's older brother or sister was home from college then we "lowlifed."

This was another tough term to explain in Spanish to the non-English crowd listening to the sordid facts of my youth in Seawell. Lowlifing involved asking a homeless man, woman or known drug addict on Middlesex or Appleton Street to sit shotgun in my car with me to go to the packie to buy me a couple cases of beer. I'd always tell the person to just get themselves some Boone's or cigarettes for a job well done. It's nearly a foolproof method to get beer, but it's the last resort because no one wants to allow a wasted or flat-out crazy drug addict that smells like pine trees, dog shit and booze in their car for five or ten long minutes.

After we lowlifed at Shithead's we would head to the spot where all the kids were drinking. We wanted, ideally, to get out in the woods, in a park or on the edge of Seawell Cemetery and hang out by a fire to drink our beer and try to look cool. We'd talk trash and try to hook up with some girl. Hopefully, someone had weed or two guys fought, and that was about it; that was some good shit for us in high school—we loved nights like that.

Now what would always happen was we'd get to, say, the Rock with beers and the cops would either be there dumping out everyone's beers or they'd show up right after you cracked your first or second beer. The freshmen would run but the juniors and seniors wouldn't bother. A lot of times, the cops got out of their cruisers and said, "Alright, everyone dump 'em out, get in your cars quietly and get the hell outta North Seawell." Then some tipsy obnoxious kid would mouth off and the cops would take the kid by the collar and make him pop his trunk, take his beer, threaten to arrest him, maybe slap him around a bit but then let him go.

Cops like free beer. Most of us had lost a twelve pack or more to some chubby cop because we made a drunk wisecrack or two. You had to be that kid here and there—sort of a rite of social passage in my hometown.

This one time, a week before Christmas in my sophomore year, we were all at the Lot out by Mount Pheasant golf course and there were about fifty or sixty high school kids and it was freezing out that night. I remember it because we couldn't get a fire to start as two cops drove up behind the industrial park to the parking lot where we crouched near the wet sticks and cardboard smoldering. We were hanging out, waiting for someone to puke or fight. Some Run DMC song was blasting out of some kid's parents' Chevy Celebrity. The cops didn't get out or even roll down their windows. Nobody ran, nobody hid their beers. The cops circled us slowly then flipped on their bullhorn:

"What's up, guys and gals? Are you havin' a Merry Christmas? Hey! You freshmen! Don't even think about running on that golf course. It's too damn cold! We're not chasin' your sorry little asses. Finish drinking your beers, pick up the empties, throw the rest in your trunks and get outta here. Get the fuck outta Rathmines. Go back to the Briley Woods or somewhere. Don't leave any trash on the ground and no one gets arrested tonight. You have a nice holiday, okay?"

We did what they said. We laughed a bit, the cops drove off and we cleaned up the parking lot a little.

That night, we were all psyched because me, Bert and Stanovich had lowlifed cases of Lite from a bum we knew. We had plenty of beer, almost a full case each. We'd heard there was supposed to be a party the next night at the Muellers' house on their third floor. We were set, beer-wise, for the whole weekend—Bert bought a half-ounce of brick weed; we were stocked! And then the cops didn't even take our beer at the Lot.

So we all pile in Bert's old AMC Matador to head across the city to the Briley Woods in the Oaklands—just a block's worth of trees behind a school. The whole thing, the school's grounds plus the woods took up about two city blocks' worth of land near my house where I grew up. Three streets surrounded the whole thing, with two streets dead-ending at the backyards of a line of houses on Hovey Street—it was my favorite place to go to drink as a kid. It was close enough to my house so I could walk home and we usually built a small fire there in the snow and mud from twelve-pack cardboard and damp wood. I liked that place; the cops hated it because they couldn't sneak up on us too good.

We never could tell when, but about three or four times per year the cops would get pissed and arrest like three or four loudmouths to make a point. The point was never taken.

As we drove to the Briley Woods on that night, we had no idea the cops were setting us up for a bust. We should've figured something was going on since they were so nice to us out in Rathmines at the Lot, but we were just drunk, cocky high school kids—most of us. Then there were plenty of kids who didn't give a fuck whether they got arrested or not. These kids already had records for muggings, armed robbery or drug trafficking and a nonviolent charge for public drunkenness didn't faze them much.

I remember thinking I was cool that night because I was feeling buzzed and B. Regan and Freddy Nguyen were giving me Keystones and we were hanging out even though I was just a sophomore. I had beers in the Matador's hatchback trunk, but I wouldn't lug them down the path till after the police came and went. I mean, I did want to get bombed, so I wasn't gonna say no to B. and Freddy's Keystones. So we were bullshitting, and telling stories and whatever, and there was a small, smoky fire burning. It was pretty good that night: tons of kids, like sixty or more; all our cars were parked down one side of the street behind the woods and all around the cul-de-sac behind the school. Someone had the doors of their Blazer open and they were blasting P.E.'s "Yo, Bum Rush the Show" out of their system. Some drunk Canuck with a mullet was pissed because we shut down his Ozzy blasting from his Mercury sedan—an old Grand Marquis shitbox stacked with a kicker in the trunk. There were even a bunch of girls who normally wouldn't come to the Briley because a few girls always slipped and slid down the hill above the cars on their asses and ruined their new clothes from the Quail Run Mall.

We hung out there for a long time, like an hour or more, when someone yelled, "Cops! Five-O are coming down the path!" Whoever it was had a friend in the trees with a mag light and all the freshmen dropped their beers and ran. I was about to take off, but the guys I was drinking with, Freddy and B., just froze so I just froze and held onto my Keystone and tried to pretend I wasn't freaked out. Some seniors were running around picking up dropped six packs, smashing half-full Bartles and James bottles on the rocks and trunks of trees. B. laughed: "Those assholes deserve losing their beers for running." Then just as everybody sort of slinks back out of the woods behind us, sheepishly cursing, and the predictable pack of girls are picking themselves off the ground almost in tears, right then I took a minute to decide on my escape route. 'Cause the cops were coming, I knew that much. It was too big of a party, too loud.

And I told the people gathered at the Balsa Bar on that strange full-moon night, that looking back on it—the fact that I left my case of beer in Bert's Matador had saved my ass on the biggest night of arrests in Seawell High's history. The Spanish architect and locals understood the pain of losing your beer in any situation. We were all travelers, so beer and the cops seemed to be subjects we could agree on.

By that time of high school I was learning to avoid the abandoned six or twelve pack. It was precious stuff so you tried to hold onto it for the next weekend if you could. I'd certainly outrun or hidden from the cops enough times to allow myself to enjoy the prospect of the chase. The chase had become the best thing about drinking outdoors in Seawell. I didn't even drink half of the nights we'd go out, I'd just hold onto a beer so no one would talk shit to me and I'd just be waiting to run. I'd been caught once, namedropped a sergeant, a first cousin, and released—beers intact. I'd been a part of a huge group of eighth graders caught and told to dump our drinks. I'd even been lined up, whacked on the top of my head with a mag light, made to pick up cans and bottles dropped by scared kids. It was all good for a laugh, all good for stories exchanged later over fries and Cokes at Lefty's as escapees trickled in to reconnect with their rides for the night. We all had different close calls and tales of escape like some demented, shrill family of ex-cons spending quality time over comfort food. It really was the best, running from the cops was the best. And the cops soon got sick of chasing us out, each year, from the neighborhoods. "Fuck 'em, they're just fat, slow pigs. They won't catch us—and even if they arrest twenty of us, it won't be me." We said this kind of thing all the time! And that's exactly how we referred to them, as "pigs." And someone always yelled the obligatory donut comment as we ran from them. Tension would build each school year—steadily, predictably, and we didn't give a fuck.

We had no shame—we called the people who bought us beer "low-lifes" and we dubbed the best packie (and the people who sold us the beer) "Shithead's." And when we punks got drunk, trespassed, wrecked cars, fought, wrote graffiti and generally were a danger to anyone that came near us, we abused the cops by oinking at them whether they were being cool or not. Thus, when the cops showed up at the Briley Woods that night for real...those pigs were serious. They'd given us all time to get complacently drunk. They showed up around eleven. Nearly three hours after their colleagues had gently kicked us out of Rathmines. This time fair Seawell's finest came in force.

Some freshman scout ran down the back of the woods on the path from the residential street above the school, yelling: "Three cruisers! Five-O! Five-O!" As the scrawny kid screamed, two lit-up cruisers came screeching down into the cul-de-sac behind the school at the base of the hill in front of us. And I heard someone, as we dropped our beers, "They're out on Hovey Street! We're fuckin' surrounded!"

This was no joke. All the seniors split, scattered in the bushes. I ran south and guessed that if I stayed in the trees and hid behind a house on Hovey, on a porch or back patio, that no cop would bother to look that closely.

Four cops came in quick at the base of the hill to my left. Three or four girls stood in a line crying. Their asses were all muddy from sliding down the hill. They were all done. Me, Goatboy and Stanovich somehow had the same idea about where to run and we slowly crawled and crouched and made our way to the back of the houses on Hovey. Black, cold mud covered my jeans since I'd tripped in a ditch. Me and Goatboy stifled laughs because Stanovich was stuck in a pricker bush higher on the hillside. We couldn't stop laughing at him because we were drunk and his face was swollen from having his wisdom teeth pulled earlier that day. Stanovich stumbled around the leaves and logs, still tweaked on painkillers and half a beer. He shouldn't have been out that night. It was hilarious, until we heard the cops sweep in from the back.

Goatboy stopped talking when we heard the dogs. Next, we saw Stanovich panic as he heard the barking behind a stand of birch. He thrashed his way out of his black CB parka with the fluorescent green stripe across the chest. It hung in the prickers as he crashed down the hill past us and out in the light above the cul-de-sac. Three cops stopped yelling at the muddy girls as one tall, thin cop took off after our friend— scratched, bleeding, coatless, in full sprint. Goatboy slurred, "Stanovich is fucked! That's that pig, what's his name? LaFerrier. He runs the Boston Marathon! Stanovich's done, kid, and I'm wasted. We hafta get to that yard fuckin' fast!" Sure enough, I saw LaFerrier closing on Stanovich near the Briley's basketball court as they flew into the darkness.

The dogs were getting near us up on the hill and then we saw the muddy girls flee the cops distracted by our doomed friend Stanovich. "Good for them," I thought, "looks like they were smart enough to wear good shoes for running tonight." And those girls motored down the sanded street. Their feet fell loud and fast! I couldn't see any cops chasing after us so I agreed with the Goat: "Fuck crawling, let's sprint for that yard." We thrashed and fell through about one-hundred feet of trees and bushes and made it to a back patio. I squeezed my ass under a gas grill, where the propane tank should've been. I was smaller back then. Pulling a blue tarp down, I saw Goatboy hide flat on his back at the base of a retaining wall. He slipped his white Adidas off and hid them beneath his jacket. "Shit, that mud is cold as hell!"

The house behind us was dark and quiet, so it seemed like we got lucky and picked a place where no one was home. But the police flashlights and barking dogs, clinking on their leashes, were only a few short yards in front of us We knew the path they were on led away from us, but it bent along the backyard we were in and then cut back to the school. I smelled grass stains and wet, cold earth, and licked at the blood from crisscrossed scratches on the backs of my hands, rubbed at the lash mark below my eye. I told Goatboy not to move, but he didn't seem to hear or didn't care to answer.

The next thing I know, I'm freaked out because I can just see a flashlight bouncing off the path toward us. There were a few raggedy holes in the tarp, so I can see a bit, but not everything. I'm about to panic and run for it, but then Stanovich comes hauling around the side of the house and into the back yard. He goes full speed past us to the next yard, but he trips over a garden gnome or some statue at the base of one of the mulched trees. Officer LaFerrier comes loping up slow behind him and the flashlight from the path is shining squarely on Stanovich's face, swollen and wincing. He's rolling on his back, holding his shin and the cops are laughing a little, prodding his ribs with their feet and flashlights. I can hear Stanovich swearing at them, but his mouth's too swollen and slow. He's just drooling and making strange shushing sounds—slurring and just getting more angry. It took all I had not to laugh out loud when LaFerrier said, "Who's the pig now, fatty? What the fuck is this kid's problem, eh?"

Later, when the cops cleared out, I crawled out from under the gas grill and poked Goatboy. No movement, so I hiss at him to put his sneakers on because we need to run. No movement again. I go over there and he's passed out cold, curled up a little bit against the retaining wall, all puffy in his black Triple F.A.T. Goose jacket with the hood up. Just passed out cold like a fat drunken goat, clueless about all the hilarious shit I just saw. I kicked him, he swore at me and then I gave him shit about how he could fall asleep with cops and dogs all around us—he didn't care. We started up Hovey to get to Lefty's on Rogers Street and I asked him, "Did you see Stanovich come flyin' around that corner and bash his shin on that garden gnome?"

"What!? Stanovich got bagged?"

"You idiot! He ran right past us, full speed, tripped on the gnome into the next back yard. LaFerrier caught him and cuffed him. The cops laughed at him for a while then dragged his sorry ass to the paddy wagon."

"You're just fuckin' with me. No way."

"I'm not, you retard. You're passed out ten feet from the cops, and Stanovich is hogtied all fat-faced and swearing at the cops right there like eighty feet away, right in front of us! I'll never forgive you for missing that. I'm serious."

"He was swearing at the cops?"

"He railed his shin off that statue and was tryin' to tell the cops to leave him alone, but he was only drooling and all mush-mouthed from the wisdom-teeth thing. Don't you remember anything? Are you fucking hammered off those two berry wine coolers you bummed off those Lowland girls? You moron! You have missed a moment in the life of Stanovich that will go down in history all because you can't hold your fucking drink. You lightweight son of a bitch..." I paused to see if Goatboy would let me keep piling on the insults.

All he slurred was, "Oh, man, you're right. I missed the whole goddamned fantastic spectacle." He sounded sad. Then he was back to his old angry, drunk self: "God fucking dammit! Nevermind you not forgivin' me, I'll never be able to live with myself for this shit! I'll give you fifty bucks if you let me tell people I saw it all go down! C'mon!"

"Okay, I can do that." And I took his money—totally knowing I'd just wait till next weekend to tell the whole school the truth. Goatboy had the cash from selling weed and mowing lawns. And as I took the bills he seemed to forget about Stanovich, and his loss. Then he said, "Let's go to Lefty's, get a basket of fries and find out who else got arrested."

When I finished this story in Ecuador, the bar was kind of quiet—even the loud kid from Arizona had trouble digesting the story. He was first to speak: "You mean, all y'all drank beer and ran from the cops all the time? Why?"

I ignored the kid. But everyone—the architect from Spain, the Ecuadorians, the guy from Belfast who were all used to the brutal force of their own police—looked to me for some kind of an answer. I just said, "Yeah, we had fun with it. But we didn't know any better. I would never mess with the cops like that in any other part of the world, to be honest. At this point," I said, "Stanovich himself is now a cop back in Seawell. So I can always go home and fuck with him!"

All the English speakers chimed in: "Nooooo! No way! Seriously, he is?"

The Spanish speakers looked a little freaked out by the English speakers' reactions and yelled for a translation: "¡Traduzce! ¿Qué dijo? Por favor, traduzce."

I translated for the rest: "Stanovich trabaja con la policia ahora." I was shocked by their disbelief that someone who enjoyed running from the cops so much, someone like my old friend Stanovich, could ever become a cop. The English speakers, the Spanish speakers, everyone was unhappy with the prospect of Stanovich working as a cop. To be honest, the whole crowd in the bar that night was fuckin' flabbergasted!

I was like, "Yeah, seriously, I'm not kidding. After that night he got caught he said getting bagged wasn't too bad, nor was being in a cell but he did say it sucked having to call his parents to get him out. And a few years after that night at the Briley, Stanovich had a string of terrible jobs at Nynex, and two banks and after taking one class at Seawell Junior College, he dropped out and joined the police academy. The fat bastard became a cop in our hometown."

There were still some odd gasps of disbelief. I chalk it up to some cultural difference that I still don't get. So I said, "If you guys don't believe me, you can ask him yourself. I'll go grab some post cards and you can write him."

That same night, and it was a little weird, we all wrote Stanovich post cards. I handed them out to a bunch of people that Stanovich would never meet. We all drank beers, sat around writing in this beachfront bar on the edge of the jungle in Ecuador and each person wrote notes like: "Stanovich, how could you? You are an enforcer of the State! Shame on you!" And "What about the night of the gnome? You should've listened to the gnome, man. Garden gnomes know their shit!" The best one was from that architect from Spain, she wrote, "¡I'm very disappointed in you, Stanley! I supported you when you ran from night school. You were bold. ¡You lost the race, but you had *duende*! Your old friend thinks highly of you, and I do two. Please re-dwell your choice of career. All my love, Chanchita." I don't know why she decided to sign it "Piglet," or how she thought Stanovich was named Stanley. It was probably my mistake that she thought we'd ditched night school classes because her English was pretty impressive beyond those minor mistakes.

Stanovich had worked as a cop for several years when I addressed and mailed about twenty post cards from the coast of South America. Oddly enough, he had just quit the force about two weeks before the cards arrived at his door. He said he got them over a two- or three-week span. When I finally ran into him, a year or so after he'd received them, he still hadn't figured out it was me who'd orchestrated the whole thing.

Stanovich re-told the story to a bunch of us one night while I was home visiting Seawell. "Yeah so there I am. I just quit the police force and the guys on the force are all pissed at me, claimin' they don't get it, 'How could you do it?' 'You're pissing away your pension' and all that shit. And then I start receivin' like a dozen post cards from Guatemala or Belize or somewheres. Every one of them's from strangers and in English, but a few were in Spanish, so I had an old Spanish teacher do some translating for me. I useta see Señor Donaghue in some of the Acre bars so's I would bring the cards with me, buy him a beer and he'd tell me they all said more or less the same thing: they all asked me how I could've become a cop and I'd joined the darkside an' shit like that.

"For like three weeks I'm readin' these things in my house, wonderin' how the fuck these people found me and how they knew about the garden gnome night and this shit I'd almost forgotten about. Now, I'd never left New England at that point and I hadn't talked to Sweeney in about a decade so I didn't figure it out for a couple months. I should've known right away. But no one ever said I was the sharpest tool in the shed, you know what I mean? But it didn't matter either way, because I was happier than a pig in shit—as they say in Pentucketville—to get those things. That's the best part about it. Every day I'd come home from the gym or the beach just hopin' there was another post card from a complete stranger on the floor of my front hall. It was a little weird because I wasn't even close to another job yet. I was just checking the papers like once a week. I spent more time beating myself up over my decision to quit the force. I was a drunken wreck, really, just shitfaced all the time and then there'd be these random notes telling me to basically do what I'd just done—quit bein' a cop. I didn't know why it was happenin', but the post cards made me feel like I'd done, for once, the right thing…just this one time, just once. After the fourteenth card I felt maybe I'd done okay.

"I took it as some sign from the heavens or whatever, you know what I'm sayin'? If there's people out there that I don't even know takin' the time to write to me and somehow tellin' me what I need to hear, somehow, like dispellin' my doubts—and that isn't even the part that freaked me out. What gets me is that all these cards arrived at the exact time I was ready to listen to what I already knew. You know what I'm sayin'? It's fucked—if you take some time to even think about it. And I took that time, my friends, fuckin' believe you me, I took that time.

"Back then, it made me realize the world isn't anything like we've been taught. At least, at that time, that's the kinda conclusion I came to—that some other shit's going on out there and I might get to check that shit out if I open my eyes. I mean, these people from all over the fuckin' place who I'd never known wrote me—understood me a little bit. And they're telling me, "Quit your job, come to...like, fuckin' Guyana or somewheres. They mailed me their fuckin' e-mail addresses! The whole time every one I know—my friends and even my family—were just bullshit at me for doing what I thought was right. It sorta screwed with my whole perception of things, you know?

"I even ended up buying a ticket out to Vancouver and going out to mountain bike in the rainforest across the sound. I figured I owed it to those strangers. I owed them something. Maybe I didn't need to pretend I should drink twelve beers in their honor in Vancouver each night, but I drank myself into a glorious stupor every night out there, and I loved it. I always wanted to do that—to go to Canada by myself.

"And you know what? Gah'head and laugh at me, but that's where I met my wife—in The Foggy Dew in Vancouver. So I'm not doubting the power of this whole thing that happened to me. I can't imagine my life without Ginny, so I'm not gonna forget this shit that happened to me.

"But it's hard. I seem to forget a lot—like when stupid pointless shit happens to me. Life's rough sometimes, and it's a lot more rough for other people—I'm kind of a lucky bastard—but I still get pissed and forget this crazy shit went on in my life. Like when I get road rage or when the weatherman repeats the word 'sleet' like ten fuckin' times in thirty-five seconds...you know, I just get crazy pissed-off for no good reason, just meaningless shit.

"I keep tryin' to think about those post cards, though. I tacked them up over the bar I built in the basement—and that's all I can do. I just take a deep breath, slip downstairs, crack a beer, drink and think about the fact that there's about fourteen or fifteen people out there who I will never meet who understand me a little bit. That calms me down most of the time when I'm all stressed out and want to kill some clown in a Camaro.

"When I do it right, I can almost see people chillin' in a bar in South America, like out in a jungle or on a beach somewheres—they're drinkin' beers for like twenty cents a bottle but somehow, some way they decide to write me a note way back when. Fuckin' God bless 'em. I mean it, God fuckin' bless life and how those cats live it.

"Without them I never e-mail the Dutch kid, or wherever he's from, and he never tells me to call the mountain bike guide in Vancouver and I never meet the guide's sister and I'm not married to Ginny right fuckin' now.

"Boys, you can call me a mystical new-age bastard if you want, I don't give a care. This is how it remains, and who am I to question any of it?"

04

THE REYMEN,

A.K.A. "The Tiny Cheiftains"

Reymen or Oakmen are associated with the Sweetrey Oaks of Seawell, the most abundant and long-living of the northern trees. Oaks are the only tree to bear acorns and this food was crucial as mast for pigs in rural Seawell as the canals were dug and the mills were built. Reymen feed on acorns, prying the caps off with grotesquely large forefingers and what looks like a horn growing from the first knuckle of that finger.

Generally, the Reymen hate all humans but poets of the Merrohawke River Valley. This hatred stems from the massive tree removal that occurred during the canal and mill construction throughout the region. Sweetrey Oaks and the Reymen represent fertility, creativity and are guardians of Celtic poetic mysteries. In some sections of the Acre, the oldest Sweetrey Oaks are called Ollave Oaks or Druid Oaks as a way to pay tribute to the regal and mystical nature of the ancient trees by invoking the names of the master poets and pagan priests of Celtic lore.

Reymen regularly glamour mushrooms and smaller cobblestones making the dangerous items appear as delicious foods in order to poison unsuspecting Acre residents (non-poets). Upon biting down the victim loses his or her front teeth instantly and lives as if in a haze for hours or sometimes days at a time. The human is unaware of the passage of time and, despite losing teeth, most survivors of the experience report a flowering of their imaginative existence, their creativity and spiritual faculties. Dozens of mill workers who spent time with the Reymen subsequently left their jobs, to the consternation of their families and friends, to become either poets, carpenters or shipbuilders. Reymen believe these livelihoods to be the most noble for a human to undertake. In fact, one

of the earliest documents from the knacker camps of mid–19th-century Seawell charts the nobility of livelihoods for all immigrants entering Acre City:

> *The traditions of Celtic Gypsies will be upheld in our new land.*
> *Poets, Storytellers and Arborists are held in highest regard in our*
> *camps and societies. Next are those descended from Kings and*
> *Chieftains of the old countries. Musicians, carpenters, shipbuilders*
> *are tertiary in their worthiness. Horses, cows, pigs and church*
> *dignitaries will also always be held in high regard in Acre City.*

There is a Sweetrey Oak on Clark Road in the Oakland neighborhood
of Seawell believed to be upwards of 350 years old. This tree was honored
by the Native Americans of the Merrohawke Valley, the Pentamucks, and
used as a meeting place during their time. At the start of the Revolutionary
War, Minutemen gathered here before marching off to Lexington to
fight the British. Millworkers and residents of the Oaklands annually pay
tribute to this tree with a children's parade and feast, echoing May Day
celebrations around the world.

It is believed that the Oakland neighborhood was founded by a band
of thirteen toothless men and women, enlightened devotees of the Reymen, who came to Seawell looking to create a life in the densest grove
of Sweetrey Oaks in all of New England. They found such an expanse
of Oaks off of what is now Wentworth Avenue. The grove skirted several
miles west and north to what is now Seawell State Forest. The Oak forest
encompassed much of central Seawell, south of the Merrohawke River
and was held sacred by the Pentamuck tribes of the region for generations.

To this day, an Oak wand hung above the front door of a Seawell home
honors druidic and poetic mysteries of Celtic origin, indicating that the
residents of the home celebrate and respect a rare connection to nature
that respects living and growing things through the turning of all seasons.

Thousands of New England poets have, over the years, made pilgrimage to Seawell and the Merrohawke River to ritualize their commitment
to a life devoted to poetry. Wading out to Thunder Islet, a sliver of

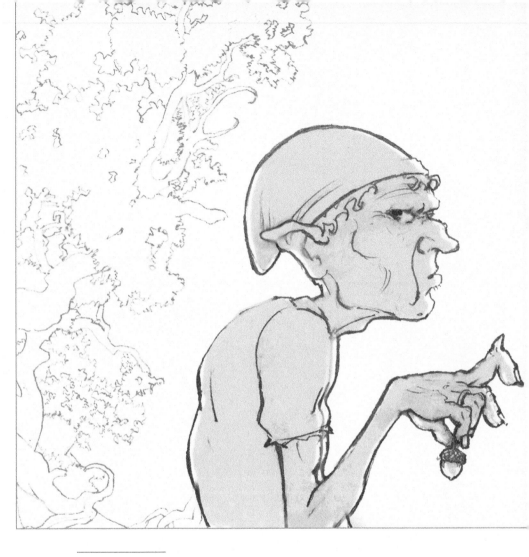

Erich Schumann was a gypsie from the Black Forest of Germany who was exiled to Boston, Mass., during scattered European efforts to destroy gypsie culture. After a few years in Boston, the renamed Eric Jones—due to his talent for languages, sketching, painting and storytelling—latched onto a group of Irish gypsies in East Boston and walked northeast for two days with them to Seawell. This group of mostly young men formed the kernel of the gypsie labor force that dug the city's miles of industrial canals. This drawing, entitled "Keeper of the Mast of the Muse, The Reyman" is the result of Jones' claim that he spent a week with the Reymen in the coastal oak forests of Southeastern Seawell (what is now the Oaklands Neighborhood). Jones produced this sketch in lieu of bail money for a somewhat sympathetic and romantic Chief Ferris Parker after the Seawell constabulary arrested Jones for "Vagrancy outside the bounds of the paddy camps." Back on the streets of the Acre, Jones recovered from his "ordeal" with the Reymen and his time in jail to make decent money selling his sketches of mill buildings and canals in Seawell and downtown Boston. Jones eventually opened a public house and inn called The Old Wardin House near city hall in downtown Seawell.

Image and history courtesy of the Ferris Parker Estate.

05

A CHRONOLOGICAL HISTORY
OF APOLOGIES

FROM THE MERROHAWKE RIVER VALLEY AND THE WIDER WORLD

1697: Just down the coast from what will eventually become Seawell, a judge and twelve jurors apologize for the Salem witch trials five years after the killings. The colony honored the victims with a day of fasting and prayer.

1711: Massachusetts offers restitution and compensation to the families of the victims of the Salem witch prosecutions and two families were rumored to have then moved to the Merrohawke River Valley. Those two families supposedly opened taverns with their money. The White Witch Tavern on Rock Street in the Acre *claims* to be the oldest drinking establishment in Seawell, built on the blood of the owner's wrongly executed siblings.

1770: Reverend Harvey Bain apologizes to the Pentamuck tribe of the Merrohawke Valley for refusing its gift of raw salmon eggs and sturgeon heads (normally reserved as a sacrifice for its gods). Reverend Bain makes due penance by wading out into the early summer waters of the Merrohawke River and bathing in the Pentucket Falls for one entire night. Reverend Bain nearly died from "[his] demons of repentance" or what is more commonly called "hypothermia."

1782: Seawell Mayor Maynard Felcher reportedly apologizes and offers to pay compensation to East Galloway for surreptitiously obtaining riverfront lands from destitute farmers and Native Americans during a particularly terrible drought. Felcher reputedly obtained the approximately 500,000 acres through a barter that involved barrels of ginger beer, four oxen and $78 worth of "knick-knacks," i.e. bolts of cheesecloth, eleven ball-peen hammers, twenty-five frayed quilts and "one country mile's worth of string." Officials in Seawell deny the report detailing the transaction and thus the veracity of the subsequent apology.

1858: The Seawell town council apologizes in *The Seawell Sun* for the death of surveyor Michael "Mick" O'Toole during a routine expedition to survey what is now Seawell State Forest. O'Toole was somehow tripped from behind by a town councilman, Whitford Ashley Bickford, and disappeared down a well. The body was never recovered, but O'Toole's prized mule, named "Salt Hill," reputedly refused to leave the scene for three days after his master's death.

1859: In the first public apology of a long list of public apologies for racially motivated statements or acts, Whitford Ashley Bickford admitted to purposely tripping Mick O'Toole, whom he unabashedly referred to as "that white nigger." Bickford famously said, "He's no better than that stupid mule and I aimed to put him in the mud, face first, where he belonged. I didn't know the well was there. Sorry for all the troubles I've caused, but then again there's plenty more bloody Irish knackers where he came from."

1868: Captain Louis Bagley apologizes for shooting rival fisherman and father of fourteen, Captain Louis MacDiarmid. Bagley commented, through tears, "I hated the man, but ought to've thought of his family." The shooting took place on the high seas so Bagley was never charged with a crime.

1871: Captain Bagley rescinds his promise to help feed Captain Mac-Diarmid's "half-orphaned" 14 children. Bagley sells his boat and moves inland to Andover gaining employment as a custodian at a private school.

1893: The U.S. government formally apologizes to the town of Seawell for not offering more federal reinforcements during the founders' original bloody battle with the Pentamuck tribe to wrest forest, riverfront and farming land from the natives. Thirty-seven men and two women died during the two-week skirmish. Thirty-two were Native American. The four Seawellians died in an unfortunate horse-drawn buggy accident involving an underground beehive and a birch tree that had fallen across the town's only passable exit road.

1894: The 28 Chinese immigrants running various laundry establishments in Seawell are forcibly encouraged to publicly apologize to the Acre neighborhood for lighting firecrackers during their traditional New Year's celebration and scaring the neighborhood children. The Irish residents of the Acre do not accept the apology and a mob promptly tramples two Chinese teenagers to death for their alleged role in the incident.

1894: Ashley Whitford Bickford, great grandson of the abovementioned Whitford Ashley Bickford, publicly apologizes for pushing a French Canadian mason from the three-quarters-completed smokestack of the Merrohawke Mills building. Peter Favreau, 27 years of age at the time, fell one-hundred feet to his death on a cobblestone sidewalk. No one of Favreau's family spoke enough English to comment publicly and they were encouraged not to press charges.

1895: Owners of the Loafe Cotton Mills apologize to the families of 70 millworkers shipped off to the Civil War in 1863 in exchange for federal tax breaks. The workers were told they would be given "temporary, higher-paying positions at a mill down South." All but one millworker was killed in action. The seventieth worker, Eoghan Murphy, was hanged by Union troops, in northern Georgia in 1864, after a failed attempt at desertion.

1888: Sheriff Buddy Whitley of Alabaster County, Arkansas, apologizes for physically intimidating (i.e. clubbing and whipping) four Loafe Mill overseers exploring the possibility of importing cheaper labor into their Seawell operation. The four overseers were found "in congregation" with 130 African Americans at a church picnic.

1896: A joint statement issued to mill workers (predominantly knacker children and teenaged girls from New England's farms) by the Loafe and Merrohawke mills' ownership teams:

> As we return to England to share Seawell's industrial advance-
> ments and progress with Europeans and the wider world, we
> deeply regret the consistent and numerous deaths and disfig-
> urements of our mill girls. We will recommend to all interested
> parties during our travels, as per your request, that the work
> week be shortened from six to five days and that the work days
> be shortened to twelve hours from fourteen. Your concern for the
> exhaustion of your fellow workers and the subsequent injuries
> and accidents is duly noted and upon our return in six months
> to a year we intend to investigate these potential solutions. For
> now, we thank you for your dedication and labor.

1900: Canada accepts a joint apology from the mayor of Seawell and governor of Massachusetts for organizing the movement of several thousand French Canadian farm laborers across the Maine border. Once across, they boarded a train to Seawell and accepted work in the mills, in violation of an agreement between the countries.

1902: Acre residents apologize for "unintentionally crossing" into the Rathmines neighborhood for waste disposal efforts during the previous twenty years.

1903: Sheriff Buddy Whitley Jr., of Alabaster County, Alabama, expresses regret for forcibly detaining and then shipping 400 African Americans to Seawell, Mass., to work in the Loafe and Merrohawke mills. He denies he received any compensation from mill overseers or owners.

1904: Loafe and Merrohawke Mill overseers apologize for privately compensating Alabaster County, Alabama, Sheriff Buddy Whitley Jr. for the delivery of "a cheaper, more illiterate labor force." Whitley refuses comment and is re-elected in a landslide victory later that year.

1907: Connecticut Valley farmer and father of eleven Stephen Rourke seeks an apology and reparations from the Loafe Mill owners for the death of five of his daughters while they were at work. His letter to *The Seawell Sun* newspaper receives no reply from mill ownership, editorial staff or readership. Rourke, a prosperous man, pays a special fee to run his daughters' five obituaries, with accompanying tintypes, in *The Seawell Sun* every day during Lent for seven consecutive years.

1910: At the ruins of the Merrohawke Mills, owner Robert F. Burkholder, drops to his hands and knees to express his remorse over the death of 342 mill girls (i.e., children and teenagers) during a fire in the company's largest mill. Later that year, upon investigation, it is discovered that mill overseers were apprised of the basement fire in the Merrohawke Mill but neglected to immediately inform the workers citing "production deadlines" while threatening physical violence to help quell employees' questions and concerns about the "smokey atmospheres" on the lower floors.

1911: The four Acre residents accused of arson during the investigation of the burning of Robert F. Burkholder's expansive home atop Grandfather Hovey (a large hill overlooking downtown Seawell) in the Oaklands neighborhood of Seawell refuse to confess. Each culprit uniformly admits witnessing "a strange, beautiful woman named Afterhours Jenny bragging of the deed in question outside the taverns on the edge of the Acre." The accused all claim: "We ain't sorry it happened and we hope he rots in the pit of Hell for what he's done."

1965: One thousand, nine hundred, sixty-five years after the death of Jesus Christ, the Second Vatican Council declares the Jews should not be labeled as the murderers of Jesus. They continue to hold fast to the idea that women may not become priests. The concept that their priests' vow of celibacy is busy creating rampant perversion resulting in the raping of tens of thousands of children by men deemed "closer to God than the layman" will not be discussed by the Council, the media, the government, the people, lawyers, judges and just about anyone who breathes (including the scarred victims).

1976: President Gerald Ford states that the imprisonment and/or "internment" of Japanese Americans during WWII was a hateful, racist thing and officially overturns the acts of former President Franklin D. Roosevelt.

1982: The Soviet ambassador to France conveys "unadulterated official regrets" to the French foreign ambassador in regards to a Soviet spy ship that ran aground during an October storm off the beach of Hossegor. French surfers, as well as visiting Australians and Americans, cannot hear the prattle above the roar of the perfect hollow waves spinning down a sandbank created by the hull of the Soviet ship run aground. Most ignore the fuel leakage and rainbow colors shining across the faces of the waves at this short-lived surf spot dubbed "Lenin's Lefts."

1982: France states that the Soviet apology regarding the stranded spy ship is insufficient, but the surviving crew is released and deported back to Mother Russia.

1983: Some kind of "International We're-Too-Late-But-We're-Trying Commission" demands that Congress works to create legislation offering a formal and official apology with compensation to formally imprisoned and/or "interned" Japanese Americans.

1984: After the Democratic National Convention, Rev. James Robinson apologizes to Jews for insensitive remarks made during his presidential campaign stop in Seawell.

1985: The United States officially apologizes to, well, just about anyone (with a conscience that still listens to their b.s.) for having assisted Nazi war criminal Franz Barbieski escape to Argentina to avoid prosecution after WWII. It is widely suspected that Barbieski, a.k.a. "The Fair Butcher," ordered the execution of more than 200,000 Jewish, Catholic and Gypsie men, women and children. The international press dubs the former Nazi "Mass-Murder Barbi."

1989: Brazil demands that the Soviet Union pay reparations for shooting down Brazilian Air flight 009 on September 9, killing all 212 passengers and 24 crew members. Brazilian foreign relations official Luis Teixiera states, "Brazil would not accept an apology even if the Soviet Union offered one. A bully is a bully. Brazil asks that the USSR simply give the families of the deceased some of the money it would normally use to buy the kind of artillery used to commit this senseless act fueled by fear and cowardice."

1989: During a speech to Seawell's WWI and WWII veterans, and specifically in reference to WWII, Seawell's City Councilwoman Reggie Rondeau inexplicably but intentionally echoes recent statements made by the Japanese Emperor Kamakura and states "it is unfortunate that there was a regrettable period in this century."

1989: The Merrohawke Region's United Indigenous Peoples Group formerly recognizes, but does not accept, the first apology from the United Church of Seawell for wrongs committed by the church during the past two centuries.

1990: The United Church of Seawell formerly offers its regrets, *again,* to the Merrohawke's indigenous people for wrongs committed by the church during the past two centuries, stating, "Regardless of the MRUIPG's non-acceptance we just want to say we're still sorry for all the Indians we killed, inflicted knowingly with small pox, robbed, tortured and marginalized as often as we could for so long."

1992: During his third re-election campaign, Nebraska Governor K. Weldon Beatrice offers an official apology for the 1969 Nebraska College shooting of six students protesting the Vietnam War (Beatrice was elected eleven years after the killings).

1992: Sweeney wants to apologize right now to his readers for quitting on this list. It's just too depressing to continue researching even though he's so close to digging into the pain and ignorance of our contemporary times.

I mean, seriously, I'm broken down by this whole thing even though some of it is almost somehow hilarious. I'm a confused, angry young man who is tired of being confused and angry. I'm exhausted, actually, and I type this through the kind of hangover that offers unparalleled clarity. For one, no more beer for me. I mean it this time. . .aww fuck, I suck for even typing that. But, what the fuck? I mean I haven't even tapped into the apologies and non-apologies and unaccepted apologies and 30-years-too-late statements that litter the '90s—South Africa, Cambodia, the Catholic Church and the slave trade, the IRA and RFU and so on. Nagasaki, Dresden, Hiroshima have been brushed under the rug. What about the Guatemalan massacres, El Salvador's civil war, Afghanistan, Che Guevara, the Congo, Bolivia, Cuba's a mess, Argentina and Chile's political massacres, Iraq, Sri Lanka, Zimbabwe, Malawi, etc., etc., etc.? What the Christ is a young man supposed to do? No one wants to even talk about this shit. And what would that do? Talking about shit doesn't make it anything other than talked-about shit, right?

I'll give you three more apologies that sum it all up on a person-to-person level because it's easy to get caught up in the international scale of suffering (see above). That's somewhat useless. Let's stay closer to home for the conclusion of this list of the finer points and niceties of humankind:

1978: A Vietnam war hero, and Seawellian by birth, Paul Anderson is arrested for his first of seven charges of operating while under the influence over the span of fourteen years. He is not charged for vehicular homicide.

1979: Anderson officially apologizes for killing a pregnant woman during the abovementioned accident resulting in his arrest. Melody Rivera, a 23-year-old, seven-month-pregnant resident of Seawell was instantly killed, along with her unborn child, in a crosswalk at 11 a.m. on a Tuesday on Jackson Street in downtown Seawell. Anderson ends his statement with, "I deeply regret this situation, and I'm sorry for the family, but I've done this before and I just don't know anything anymore. I don't know...."

1992: Today, the day I quit this list: Paul Anderson was arrested in downtown Seawell on Arcand Drive for his seventh and final operating while under the influence. He is drunk, as he has been every day since 1978, and witnesses saw him trying to ride a skateboard. He fell off a curb, cracked his head on the cement and slumped conscious but bleeding on the sidewalk until he was arrested. He was brought to the hospital and then released into the custody of Seawell police officers after being diagnosed with a minor concussion and the beginning of what *would have been* a long withdrawal from alcohol addiction.

Six hours after the arrest Paul is found dead in the drunk tank. Internal bleeding and head trauma are rumored to be the cause.

Paul lost his license to drive a decade previous. Not long after, a judge banned his use of bicycles after he was the cause of two traffic accidents in downtown Seawell while riding his Huffy drunk (the Huffy was actually stolen twice from the same nine-year-old, Little League-spectator named Billy "Tiny" Archembeault Jr.). Not long after the bike ban, Anderson was arrested downtown for operating an adult-sized tricycle while intoxicated during Seawell's Bluesfest.

1992: This very morning, the day I quit this list: His new stolen skateboard tucked under his arm as he left the bar, Paul said his last words: "If I get busted for riding a skateboard I can always get a pair of roller skates, right fellas?"

Paul Anderson has been busted in every way a human mind, body and life can be.

—Compiled by Sweeney O'Sweeney

06

THE LOOM BROOD

A.K.A. THE BAREFOOT IMMORTAL

One of the "orphan spirits" haunting Seawell; believed to be a maternal figure—though still a child herself when she was killed—for the spirits of mill girls killed when their hair or limbs were caught in looms or other such machinery. The Loom Brood is known as such a leader due to the fact that on the day of the harvest moon of A.D. 1894, this child of eight or nine years, the "slightest girlchild in the Loafe Mills" workforce, was called from her work to climb under a loom and reach up to extract a lodged bobbin from the workings. Once under the machinery, out of sight from the other mill girls and overseers, the system of looms sparked to life again catching The Loom Brood's hand. Her hand was drawn in, her arm followed and the mill overseers shut the mill down for a quarter-day in order to remove the mangled, blood-drained body of the girl. The girl's reported name was Brigid O'Malley. It is interesting to note that the actual name of this mill girl is unknown because most, if not all, knacker women and girls were unilaterally called "Brigid" by native Seawellians and regional Yankees.

The Loom Brood is usually found on the northern banks of canals, huddled by coldwater ivy hedges and blooming gorse thickets. Amanita Muskbush, when planted in Acre gardens, pay tribute to this spirit thus protecting the occupants of the household from premature death or maiming in the workplace. Wanton destruction of the canal banks, through human folly or accelerated erosion, often raises the ire of this spirit.

Within a quarter-mile radius, most mechanical vehicles will stall repeatedly until outside of the agitated Loom Brood's range. Signs that The Loom Brood lives nearby include block-wide pockets of static and electrical interference affecting primarily AM radio stations and analogue

Left: The Loom Brood's head and arms are mashed tangles of blood, bones, skin and hair. She often covers herself shyly when spotted, just before flying into a homicidal rage.

Seawell's most famous artist, Maddox "Maddie" Callahan, was hunting for shoe molds on the upper floors of the Loafe Mill ruins when she heard something outside the collapsing stairwell she descended. Always wielding a camera, she whirled and fired off the shot. Maddie froze, sensing what she might have caught on film. The artist says both she and the Loom Brood stood stock still listening and waiting for the other to move for more than an hour. Maddie still claims her victory in that game of "Headless Chicken."

Above:
"Headless Chicken"
Loafe Mill shoe molds, threaded rod and wooden pallet by Maddie Callahan

Image courtesy of 119 Gallery, Chelmsford St., Seawell, Mass.
From 119's two-person show entitled "The Last Frontier,"
featuring Seawell-based photographer/filmmaker Higgie Baby & Maddie Callahan

07

PEOPLE OF SEAWELL

SEAWELL'S SUMMER OF THE BELT, 1931

FOR SGT. DANIEL CRICK JR. (1920-1997)

The old man only knew how to be cruel. He was sure his kid told nothing but lies: "You were on that bridge, and you know the rules!" Blows rained each night no matter the kid's replies. Their tenement neighbors ignored the cries, above the sound of Mr. Crick's brown belt that flayed Dan's back to a palette of welts.

The bridge was an abandoned railroad trestle that spanned a canal off the Merrohawke. The kids jumped from the bridge, before it fell, and swam through dyes dumped beneath brick smokestacks. Dan never did. He saw his own scarred back in the blue, black and crimson water's blend—as his boyhood, that year, slumped to its end.

FAILED RITE OF PASSAGE AT SEA-LEVEL

BURNT DUNES CAMPGROUND, SEAWELL STATE FOREST

Acid Victim of the Appalachian Mountains you never told us your name. Baby-faced Navy-kid gone AWOL, where is your campsite? You chase visions of fragile minks through goldenrod fields at dawn.

Your tribal tattoos have not yet made you a man. You are narcoleptic beneath the Sweetrey Oak. You nod off, back to the rough bark; start awake, staring at wild mistletoe.

You have taken too many hits mixed with a touch of dust, and you mumble that your sister watches, that she is in the C.I.A. Red-headed stranger, you believe we are your friends, but this is campsite thirty-six.

Stop wandering the yellow meadows, take this cold can of ginger ale, come down from your lost altitudes.

It is high noon, let paisley and pied minks lie—the ground no longer seethes with quick rodents.

Acid Victim, the hunt's over. Unclench your jaw, sleep and dream. You have found your totem beast.

19-HOUR DAY

I once worked with a Cambodian that cut fish for a living in Seawell—cod and haddock, some salmon. Vann loved salmon. I saw him lick the length of his favorite knife while fill-iting★ forty or fifty pounds of salmon: he'd run the wide flat of his tongue right down the flat of the steel, looking at me and laughing loudly.

He was a good guy; we worked some fourteen-hour days, a few longer, together in that clamshack.

One time, he got pissed at our boss—Sean needled Vann pretty bad. He gave him shit about his accent, Asian women and how the hell he ever got the name "Vann." Sean would give him shit every time Vann came down to work with us. Sean liked Vann, and Vann liked to work for Sean. And when he got sick of Sean's shit, Vann'd say something about his weight to shut him up.

But that's just how it works in Seawell, you talk shit or most people'll walk all over you. Most kids learn to talk trash really quick around here.

So Vann was pissed at Sean's yappin' one long day near the end of June. I just kept quiet, and tried to skin and worm the fill-its of cod as fast as Vann was cuttin' 'em. I'm runnin' the fill-its through the skinnin' machine, then pickin' out the spiral worms with the tip of my knife.★★

★"Fillet" or "filleting" is usually pronounced "fill-it" or "fill-iting" by the fishermen and fishcutters in Seawell. The "T" is not silent.

★★I stood at a portable, electric light table—the type photographers use to study their negatives. With this weak light shining through the skinned fill-its of cod, small parasitic worms appeared light brown, like a ballpoint pen's ink tube curled into a spiral—like tiny shadows of knots in the bottom-feeding whitefish's flesh. My job was to run the fill-its through the skinning machine, dig all the worms out of the fill-it on the light table with my knife's tip, rinse the fill-it and pack it in a plastic container, weigh out each container-full and snap on a plastic lid. Later, I'd deliver the de-wormed cod to seafood restaurants all over eastern Mass. Overall, other than the people I worked with, the job was unpleasant at best.

Sean'd gone over to the packie and bought us some beers, 'cause we were in the twelfth hour of a nineteen-hour day. Vann was about six-beers deep and he was smokin' one-hitters all day as usual. He was a little stoned, hungry and tired when Sean, sober for seven years, started makin' fun of Asian drivers, his name—just the standard bullshit, no more hurtful than normal. But Vann was wasted and sick of cutting a freezer-full of fish. He snapped, just lost his shit. It was Sean, me and a livid Vann in a fly-infested, rundown clamshack out by Sun Valley.

I'll be honest, I was scared shitless! Vann weaved a bit, and waved his knife around, kinda at Sean, kinda at no one in particular.

He yells: "Go fuck you-self, Sean! I'm so sick of this shit, maaan. You never shut you mouth. Shut-the-fuck-up, maaan. I work all day for you...."

Sean put his own worn knife down, but he kept it within reach, I noticed. Sean worked with us sometimes on heavy days. He weighed over three bills. He was fat, strong and way quicker than you'd think—a big, tough bastard to be honest.

I was trapped in my corner, so I switched off the skinnin' machine, and hoisted the skinned cod fill-its in the plastic basket. I eyed my own knife in the scales and guts on the light table. Vann raved, and Sean stepped back then held his ground. He told Vann to, "Chill, buddy...."
Vann raved, "Sean, you fat fuck, I fuckin' stab you right here. I wi' gut you like this fish!"

He speared a cod's gills on the stainless steel counter.

Sean spoke, "Vann, take it easy, I..."

"Fuck you, you fat fuck! I wi' gut you, maaan. I fuckin' work hard, maaan. I drive down here and work and you never shut mouth all day!"

His English grew more slurred and choppy as he got more pissed. "I see my brother and two sisters killed. Bamboo spear! In my front yard when I was just small kid. A soldier...maaan..." He slowed a bit, so Sean shot me a look—I just lifted a finger to my lips, hoping that Sean would keep his loud mouth shut. Vann amped it up a little after he caught me making the gesture. He leveled the blade at Sean and sneered: "You don't know fuckin' shit, I see kids killed by soldier and I lose my family and I still work."Vann turned back to the heaped codfish, "I still work hard and you, fuckin'...."

All his rage, and the point of his knife shook at Sean; he left me alone. I was five-beers deep, twitching with exhaustion as Vann began to fade, "You Irish fuck, I see my family killed...my own eyes...I see blood, bamboo, fuck...shut you big, fat mouth..."

He lost his steam, hunching above the fish. Vann still held the knife point up, shaking at Sean. I wanted to grab another beer for him—a peace offering, but Sean beat me to it, which was good 'cause I don't think I could have moved if I tried.

"Vann, kid, I was just...fuck," Sean laughed, too loud, "You are scaring the shit outta Sweeney over there. Don't gut me, kid. I'll shut up. I'll go get more beers across the street."

Vann leaned on his yellow-gloved fists, and stared at the heaped cod, with his back to me as Sean cracked that last can of beer and slid it through a pool of cod innards and said, "If you relax, I'll..."

"Don't tell me to relax, you fat fuck. Just go buy. We need more beer."

"Okay, I'll shut my mouth. I will, don't worr-..."

"Yeah, fatty, you better buy us somethin' good—make it a twelver of Heineken this time!" I chimed in to try and make Vann laugh a little. He laughed weakly and we worked six more hours with cod and more beers and all kinds of exhaustion. I never knew what to say to the poor guy.

But, man, could he cut fish—the fastest knife to ever fill-it a cod, haddock or salmon that me or Sean had ever seen in Seawell.

ICE-PICK LOBOTOMY
For Sgt. Daniel Crick Jr. (1920-1997)

1941

The Depression raised him, had its effects, then he shipped out for the South Pacific. He saved his pay, but his father cashed the checks from his one kid—the Army mechanic.

1946

Shell-shocked, broke, Dan came home in a panic to an ignorant, remorseless father and a newfound medical procedure.

1986

In the condemned asylum, the blown leaves mix with onionskin and manila files. Four decades later, the homeless man grieves those years spent behind a pick-induced smile. He paws tools, restraints—rotting in a pile—as his stiff, chapped hands recount what he has lost: a life's summer, his snipped season of frost.

35-YEAR-OLD AT LEO'S PIZZA

"I told my friends not to butt–in so I'd just get beat up and then we'd leave. There was about fifty of them and three of us. 'Cuz there was no way I *wasn't* getting my ass kicked by this girl. I knew that.

"She just sat on top of me, pulled my hair and pounded on my face."

The story finished, she laughed, checked a calzone in the oven and carried on wiping the countertop.

THE VETERAN LOBSTERMAN

The sea smoke curls and unravels between the low hills of a four-foot groundswell, and he motors out to check his traps up north.

"I'll do the same down south tomorrow, then move some traps near Plum Island on Thursday—if the weather holds.

"These December mornings reveal the North Atlantic for what it is and what it might become."

The clear, sharp air freezes the hair in his nostrils before he inhales his morning menthol, the first of the day. "I try to wait for the sun to push its yellow face above the water before I light up."

A smooth winter sea rolls like cold venom that wrecks nerves, numbs warm bodies in about ten minutes flat. "It's bit men like me by the dozen each winter, men just like me and better men than me."

Sometimes he watches the sea smoke lift, as the backs of greenskinned waves grow and push shoreward. Liquid makes its way, and sheds the vapor, "...it makes its way no matter what—over, under, around or through."

"This life in my body won't last. The sea will warp and smother me soon."

He stares down the haze-tongued ocean as it waits for him to slip, and lures him nearer each morning. "I'm chained to it—when the winter sea smoke slips along the hull—my brother and crew tucked deep in the unmade bed of the North Atlantic."

But these are all just thoughts he thinks, "...things I tell myself on these coldest and shortest days—between the reefs, the banks...that perceptible turn of the tide."

—As told to Sweeney at the Madeira Social Club
    on Back Central Street by a soused Richie Gouveia★

★See note on Gouveia on page 343, Appendix A.

BEAUTIFUL NUISANCE

Margaret Tierney heaves the wide, green sash of a twelve-foot window in her condo that once was a textile mill—back when Seawell's workers were mostly mill girls or fishermen. Ms. Tierney dangles her feet down from her seat on the wide sill most warm summer evenings. Black canal waters divide the banks of mills for a mile and ripple with wavering red reflections of the ruined factory across the water. Ms Tierney's electric-yellow canary hops across forest-green paint, slick on the sill—chancing low, hovering leaps with tentative wings but singing with blear-eyed abandon, trembling with song. Ms. Tierney trills as well when happy: "I know I'm too old to hang my Irish-pale legs, these odd white sticks, out of my windows, but only the mill girls' ghosts in those old ruins can see me and my eccentricities."

Ms. Tierney taught elementary school, grade three, before moving to philosophy at the high school when she got the chance. She keeps canaries, but swears this "will be her last."

Her mother, Oona, bought a canary back on the day the mill closed its doors to begin its crumbling decline. Oona kept songbirds because she knew the mills had wrecked her lungs. She said they wrecked most mill girls' lungs and Oona watched four childhood friends die of asphyxiation—choking to death slowly on their own phlegm. She said, "Forced retirement is a well-lit mine-shaft, smelling of purgatory, filled with just enough oxygen to curse God and cough blood."

Oona's kids grew fond of chirps, serenades, excited pings from corner cages while the family's antique Victrola stood blue, mute, faded in the parlor. Dozens of birds outsang that heirloom through the years—birds named Aileen, Fergus and *Pogue Mahone*—but none could sing like her daughter's bird dancing in the light of its own calls, dancing with halting steps next to her on the same green sill.

Ms. Tierney tells, again, the story of going to dinner two years ago, how she rushed out the door, "And I'm not one to be late," she says, "Nor am I one to skip-out on a bill! It was my first 'chew-and-screw' my students tell me."

She'd recalled the windows were open, her last bird loose in the living room. Ms. Tierney rushed home to burst in with a frantic look around, and the bird perched on the sill among green beads of rain, its wings outstretched, the doorknob smashed the bricks and lightning struck at the instant she caught sight of her bird: outside, the corridor of water, the glassless arches of the ruined mill lit up, shock-white with a boom. The bird, about to leap, stunned, instead fell backward with a splash "no bigger than a sugarcube in a teacup," one wing stayed outstretched.

And Ms. Tierney believes this will be the last canary. She says, "I'm gettin' up there and (the renamed) 'Sugarcube,' God love him, is a beautiful nuisance for such a handful of feathers!" Some of this is true, some rehearsed and retold in a lilt remixed with mock-weariness. She's still spry enough to heave up the sash, cup Sugarcube from his perch and set him to dance on the green sill whenever she dangles her legs and looks for carp, bronze in the black canal. There aren't enough warm, quiet evenings for Sugarcube's songs and the lurch of his inch-high attempts at flight. Ms. Tierney barely laments the bird's gone blind from the strike. She's sure it's bettered his song.

The bird sings through late spring, summer, warm fall evenings, and often only cued by the breeze, only when cupped to the sill to preen and hop on Ms. Tierney's wide perch, beside her floral-patterned hip. "Come mid-winter," Ms. Tierney reports, "the little thing's so silent, so blind and alone, he'll test the air with a flash of song and it's as if someone's shone a harsh spotlight on my ears, if you follow me." During wet New England winters, Ms. Tierney watches iced canals catch sheets of snow. She isn't sure how she ended up across from the ruins of the place that fed her family and clotted her mother's voice with memories while spotting five-hundred handkerchiefs with blood. She keeps this blind canary to call down shafts of light, to dance in a cage, to hop beside her dangling white legs hung down evenings where nobody sees her. She devises lessons to teach the mill girls' grandkids that we're made of the stuff of long-dead stars—the stuff of blind, electric-yellow song.

ASPECTS OF CRICK, 1997

For Sgt. Daniel Crick Jr. (1920-1997)

Daniel Crick slept light, if he slept at all—park benches, ashen birds, his filthy clothes. He often dreamt of Houdini's escapes—the bronze coffin, the ghost house and milk can.

West Sixth drowsed through the dry height of summer the day Crick thought up a plain-faced sister: Ruth Ann loved him and worried herself sick over his shiftless habits and five-month binges. Passersby heard him tell her of the clipped peacocks who had the run of the estate. Passersby saw him churning flower beds. He trimmed shining, non-existent box-woods: "They let me work, and I get my work done, Ruth Ann!" he yelled at a backfiring car.

Ruth didn't approve. She frowned above him sprawled on cement, comatose near the curb.

Crick woke in the I.C.U. at Saint Anthony's, he was near the end of his intricate escape. And still he heard the soft, building drum roll of his sobered pulse in his head held in his hands. The nurses couldn't see through the white curtain as he slipped the tangled collar of life support.

Crick left, knowing he had no audience.

THY VS. TAYO, THE UNDERCARD
OR *"KIDS FROM THE FOURTH GRADE"*

Let's all sit here Indian-style; let's circle the flagons outside our old Oakland School. Inside this circle's where witnesses watched Thy fight Tayo. Sit, laugh, let's all drink until we piss and shit ourselves. Hold puke-soaked hands through buddy-system smiles. So neighborly. Let's playact drunken Marco Polo—blind heroes and loudmouth dodgers. Let's all wade through, tell tales, swill rum mixed with milk in half-pint cartons. Missing kids in black and white leer sideways, tilted as we drink liquid lunch, mixed-eighty-proof. Let's drink up, sing our long way back to nodding off at wheels and switches. Let's get drunk where once we circled, cheering Thy's first fight. It's sharing time: there's no "do-over-repeat" rules for saddest-day tales—sick nostalgia to take the stale cake and eat it too. Because we knew Tayo as a semi-pro, malnourished bully, brought up, up-and-coming, on a diet of rice and beans, stamp-bought milk, beating after beating at home.

Face it: Tayo wasn't fat, red-haired, bullying through his boredom. Spastic, tiny brown mirror of fists flashing, hashed with scars from when his mother's boyfriend burned him on the one orange coil still working on their stove. Face it, really, what made Tayo nearly flawless, marble-hard in his rage? Brothers, boyfriends, parents? Tayo never ate much, no one knew hungry, scared, sick and bullied like he knew those things. He was the Puerto Rican Prince of the Whipped.

The most-bullied bully back for ballast—thus Tayo the Prince stalked smart kids, white kids, girl kids, dumb kids, black kids, sisters, strangers, brothers, mutts, cats, frogs, ants, even Thy—the first Cambodian we ever saw at Oakland School.

Let's sit, drink in our cliques, kiddish and clueless. Even as it rains, sit, drink, sing:

Red Rover, Red Rover all our
fields have scabbed over! Red Rover,
Red Rover the paddies spill over!

Ignore "Fallout Shelter" signs with yellow-black triangles circled, stuck on brick school walls and doors to herd the free, the brave, the A-bombed deep to safety in numbness—those soft blue nap-time kindergarten visions, dreaming of first-world-wonder-full-regret. Who'll drink to saddest-day songs and these teacher-free histories treasured in our chests? Let's paste Thy's face here on asphalt—a newfound photo torn from Seawell's paper. Let's make rules! You hafta drink if Tayo's bullied someone close to you. You hafta drink when you say words that start with the letter "T." You hafta drink if "gook" or "chink" are words you've ever used as insults. Drink for "spic" or "*Mira, mira*" mimic-slurs. Don't wipe your mouth on sleeves of muscle.

Who is featured next to Thy on yesterday's front page? He frowns, his saddest-day-take-stale-cake life recalled for schoolkids penned in huge, hot auditoriums. Thy sits next to Seawellians, others who survived a genocide. "*Once upon a time,*" they whisper—even though this thing, genocide, is a constant—they bear witness.

Once upon a time there lives an eighty-something Polish woman who made it posing as an Aryan while her people died in gassed droves;

Once upon a time there lives a slim Rwandan man who watched boys dodge bullets then fall as prey for lions drunk on blood and flesh of lost boys—scared, running in the bush. He can't fathom how the grim man next to him can sleep while Turkish government officials claim the genocide in Armenia never happened. "This can't be," he says to strange kids. "I could not be sleeping, living, even breathing after someone would say genocide didn't happen in my country."

Red Rover, Red Rover all our
fields have scabbed over! Red Rover,
Red Rover sow crimson in clover!

Once upon a time, Seawell is nothing but a haven for all victims—twenty-eight flavors of violently dispossessed peoples. And Thy was one of the first victims—who we met as kids in *our* first world—fleeing genocide still raging through what he knew as *his* first world in humid, wet, green Cambodia.

This morning I spotted Thy's face—as the front-page story, reading, "Facing History and Facing Ourselves." I was slammed back to when Thy was thirty words into English—thirty years before this *Seawell Sun* story and photo where he's frowning next to other bullied ladies, gentlemen— these former tiny victims of brutality grown epic-and-forever. Thy's aunt, it reads, finally got him to Thailand, quickly bribing any body in the way, and then to Seawell and the growing refugee Cambodian population.

Red Rover, Red Rover all our
fields have scabbed-over! Red Rover
Red Rover the paddies spill over!

Three strange months later school threw Thy into Tayo's scar-hashed, brutal hands without a single friend or fellow Cambodian who could warn him, even just speak with him. "Chink" was not a word he knew as Tayo screamed it three-weeks straight at lunch, before school, after school and any moment teachers turned their backs. But something got through, in that third week. Catching the drift, Thy spoke finally in quiet tones: "I not from Chink. I'm other." Tayo laughed and mimicked.

Drink if any one here laughed that day, we were all there—so drink if you recall that pre-fight weigh-in when Tayo laughed hard enough to rile a former child soldier. From killing fields where automatic rifles helped him get enough food nightly for the sister still alive, to playing fields where he was picked last for all our games—kickball, TV tag, red rover, street hockey and baseball. Didn't we all grimace knowingly, seeing frowns descend then scurry over Thy's calm face? Remember Tayo pulling eyelids toward ears, dancing "chink-like," circling Thy's thin crossed-arm frame.

And I sometimes can't live with the rabid memory foaming in my mind.

Drink if bullies have snuck up and surrounded us adults. Drink to ditch the bullies wearing us down; drink if you think rock beats paper, paper smothers scissors, scissors just surrender, rise up, fall down, go fetal.

I wish Thy beat Tayo, but Thy and Tayo scrapped as boys do: fists flailed, missed their marks, eyes squinched shut, rolling headlocks, cheekbones scraped raw. Who won? No one? But now I know how it's possible neither kid looked scared, and why neither pissed down pantlegs.

Often, I drink till I trade my memories for other ones. Who'll drink with me till drunken recollection helps us face this history?

I want to cry with joy, remembering Thy scared as hell by Tayo's bully act—till they both square up, fists raised, circle some, then visibly pause, simultaneously piss their pants in fear—their first tastes of fear.

Red Rover, Red Rover send kid
soldiers right over! Red Rover,
Red Rover the bloodiest drover!

Instead, I'm sobered through knowing that these hungry, tortured and terrified babies had quelled fear by age nine, by the time fourth grade took aim to teach them what was next in this fuckstained world.

I recall Tayo's predictable spaz-rage but I'm haunted by Thy's demeanor—his refined, simple decision to fight the scarred child we all were afraid of. Thy was wearied by the scene. He felt driven to simply fight. No puffing his chest, or ripping his jacket off.

He quickly unzipped the one thin, beige jacket he owned, folded it and asked a girl to hold it without using words—peering up at her. She clenched it, unsure if it was okay to help this new stranger, then stood white-knuckled as the boys began their ugly mimicry—spattering knee socks and girls' saddle-shoed feet.

Red Rover, Red Rover send kid
soldiers right over! Red Rover
Red Rover sow crimson in clover!
Red Rover, Red Rover all our
fields have scabbed over! Red Rover,
Red Rover we're all in the clover.

08

THE LOAFE POOKA

Most sightings occur near winter and summer solstices, usually heard (though rarely seen) singing its mournful songs around the spring and autumn equinoxes. Since crumbling mortar and small chips from old bricks primarily make up the Loafe Pooka's diet, this species of Pooka usually inhabits old mill buildings and mill ruins. Many believe this creature is the patron faerie of the terminally ill. A grove of Coyote Elder or Cork Elder growing on the grounds of mill ruins is a sure sign that a Loafe Pooka lives nearby. This Pooka takes its wrath out on men and women who deliberately harm these trees without first asking permission with an offering or prayer.

This Pooka invariably haunts the dreams of any person unlucky enough to have chopped down a Coyote Elder. Once acknowledged in the nightmare, the faerie forces the victim to stare at his/her own suddenly manacled wrists until his/her future is foretold.

This story was told to Dr. Nicolas Panagiakis on June 13, 1983, by Jermaine LaForge himself. LaForge grew up near the intersection of Rock and Willie Streets in the Acre section of Seawell. The Knacker village there (one of the five main encampments in Seawell) was believed to be at least one hundred years old by that point. LaForge's encounter with a Loafe Pooka resulted after he destroyed a grove of Coyote Elder trees for extra parking near his home. The nightmares soon began for Mr. LaForge.

The Loafe Pooka usually appears with the head of a bull, possessing Ass ears in place of horns. It has a goat-like body. Its legs continually morph and transform depending on its temper, alternating between talons and cloven hooves.

Mr. LaForge says, "The first nightmare woke me in a cold sweat as the Loafe Pooka stood on a set of two blood-red, scaly eagles' legs with accompanying gray-barbed talons of exceeding strength and sharpness. The creature had a fearsome aspect. Its voice is deep, monotone and its face remains unequivocally placid. I was unnerved by its appearance and demeanor, to say the least, when I woke up. But I didn't think much of the dream.

"In the second nightmare my hands and wrists were forced through chainlink and I was trapped in a half-standing position unable to feel my numb fingers on the other side of the rusted fence. I somehow knew this was my duty, to simply wait—to bow my head and wait. The Pooka never mentioned why I was cursed, but I was shamed as if it was known by all that I had butchered a living, beautiful Coyote Elder. The Loafe Pooka told me my troubles would begin on December 22 and continue for a year and a day.

"This time I woke up afraid, unable to go back to sleep. I went out to the kitchen to fix myself some tea and whiskey and wait for my shift to begin three hours later at the mill. As I spooned two lumps into the black swirl of my cup, I noticed a chafed rawness on my wrists that persisted to different degrees until December 22, the beginning of my curse. That year, and you can ask anyone about this, was the worst of my life. I lost two dogs to traffic, one cat ran away and all of the plants surrounding my home either died or didn't flower.

"My neighbors and family tell me that I developed an 'unhealthy need' to follow the diagnoses, sicknesses, pain and slow deaths of a number of local children stricken with leukemia of one kind or another. I lived as 'in some kind of pall,' as my wife, Shannon, describes it."

When asked of her opinion of the Loafe Pooka and its habits, Shannon—along with every one of Mr. LaForge's closest friends—stated they'd learned a fair bit about the life and death of all natural things during that year and a day.

Shannon stated, "Since this experience, my husband has been a dutiful supporter of children's cancer charities and events. During the first year of his curse, he could only watch and mourn the slow, painful death of local children. Their deaths moved him deeply and he was nearly catatonic. He seemed frozen by a morbid fear of a kind he couldn't explain. Once his curse ended, he swore to never cut down or dig up another Coyote Elder, ash, apple or even a yew tree without asking permission from the Loafe Pooka. I don't know if I believe all this. But he's been a better man since this supposed hellish curse came to an end."

"The Loafe Pookah" by Jermaine LaForge
Welded found objects: tractor parts, mill machinery scrap. Hung on twenty-lb-test
fishing line on Wilder St. in the Rathmines neighborhood of Seawell.

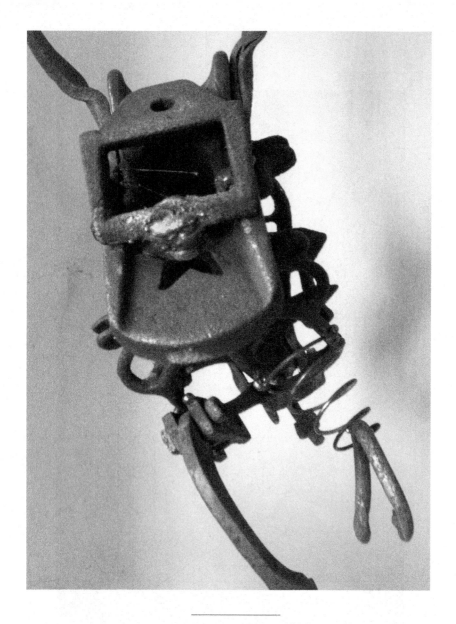

Jermaine LaForge made this piece five years before
he died of pneumonia. He walked up from his
nursing home, once a day during his last years, to his
family's old house. He let himself in the back door
and sat in his wife's favorite rocking chair to watch
his sculpture slowly turn in the weak light of the
stained glass window on the landing of the
front stairs.

Mr. LaForge kept his family's driveway, front walk and porch stairs shoveled clean and salted all winter, every winter despite the fact that his children and wife had all passed away and the house was no longer occupied. The Univeristy of Seawell purchased the house for offices and labs for the Psychology Dept. Mr. LaForge anonymously donated the money from the sale of his family home to various environmental charities. He died alone just weeks after the sale and donations were finalized. This sculpture was the only work of art he finished in his life.

09

PEOPLE OF SEAWELL'S SISTER CITY
The Seven Dreams of Pancho & Ramøn (Canoa, Ecuador)*

As told to Sweeney by Pancho Moneymaker

A hissing monsoon Saturday, gone dark under a cloud-heavy sky retching warm rain so hard the bus to San Vicente, stark beneath the streetlight, stops dead on the main street in my coastal town. Between two bars, Coco and Mambo, each thatched with palm on a frame of bamboo and jungle hardwood, all the cars, horses, bikes, donkeys and ATVs might need to be moored before this storm relents and heat jars me from bed tomorrow, hungover, unsure of the deeds I did or didn't do. I'm perched on a stool in the Mambo Bar, drunk on warm beer, dreaming up creeds that could prepare or protect me from the cruel cycles at work in this black sky on that wet street.

Ramón, the farmhand, can't see me through the schools of droplets swimming down in the dark, behind heat-fogged windows on his San Vicente bus. He spent his day, rawshouldered and replete with a poison-filled backpack, working to flush out and kill all the bugs feasting on another man's crop. When I spoke last year about the dangers, he'd cuss me and my "gringo professors" out, then prop himself on his burro's flank to better check off his more pressing needs: food, cash to lop off his growing debt, clothes for his kids, and to stick to his plan to open an electronics store in Caráquez. Eyes rheumy, and his voice flecked with phlegm, you'd think he'd listen a little more to an old friend, but when I went away to study I was dubbed a fraud by some in town. It's a chore to shoulder the insults. Somehow my schooling would muddy the clear waters of our old neighborhood bond. Even my friend Ramón, his face grown pocked and

---

*Pancho Moneymaker, I've figured out, is my twin—much like the original Sweeney's "Man of the Wood" was his fellow crazed hermit. Pancho is my Ecuadorian me.

ruddy from Caña Manabita, had abandoned our memories of jungle hikes back when we lived by Bella Vista. Now he's donned an expression of disdain—my oldest friend—when I say pesticides run invisibly slick on his skin, destroy cells to hasten his end before he's fifty. And though he can be a prick, Ramón and I have little cleaving us but this headlight-lit sheet of rain—flickering filmic and strobe-like. His face, or what remains of Ramón's formerly cherubic face is almost obscured by the fog and glut of water coursing down the idling, quaking hulk of the stopped bus. And I'm sure he can't see me, sitting, Pilsener in hand. This dark Mambo Bar only slightly drier with its slant of palm thatch keeping out most of the rain.

The life of Ramón grows like a rare, thorned plant, dreamlike in every direction—using pain to wound enemies and friends. He knows violent outbursts, drunken embroiled brawls and shame; shame brought to bear through evangelical cant imported originally by the gringos he hates. And Ramón's barbs back me from the slant of torrential rain between me in the throes of pre-*Carnaval* drink and him staring blankly from a rubbed-clear spot in the fogged window of his bus.

The thatch begins leaking above, like a tank of tepid water poured through a fist-sized hole. Five loud, pale gringas spill from the bar to flank the bus and dance drunk in the pelting godawful storm. One of the women wears a sleeveless shirt, now black and wet, her white arms writhe and pull at the sky. Roots reggae pulses while gringas flirt with natural disaster in craven light, beneath banks of rain. The lithe gringa's soaked skirt flings drops as she spins. Giving up her sober ghost, her limbs flow fast—a slim white body dancing for distance from her other plight: she laughs at all her former struggles, maybe a cubicled life or youthful divorce? Her dream fleshed out in flashing drops, in getting dizzy for dizziness alone. Shut-eyed in the gleam of dim headlights, she shook for the shaking—hiss of fat drops paying the monsoon season's *per diem* for this jungle town.

This *seems* like my life, unless as this unfolds tonight I learn I've begun to borrow bits of daydreams and nightmares others have orphaned in their unconscious run away from the jewels of their inner lifetimes.

Is that a smile or wince on the fogged and one-time angelic face of Ramón? Besides, is the lithe gringa, drenched, giving it up to the blackened sky...is she part of a moment in my existence, Ramón's nightmare or her own warm rain-sodden daydream? Did she dream this dance during cold, clear northern European nights? Is she emboldened by blaring rain and reggae or the beer in huge brown bottles, warm and cheap? The bus stands still—weak lights, drenched bodies, Burning Spear and the drops scintillating across the distance slowing this shared vision down like a film gone joyfully wrong.

Or at least, for my two cents, things grew and changed in those moments. Was time unwound for those of us staring out glass-less windows at the gringas? Yet that same moment looked hellish to Ramón, an impasse the bus driver would not attempt to leave behind. The driver stood near me taking nips at the bar, hooting at the gringas while in disbelief of the rain.

Ramón's nightmare, his Herculean chore, paused as he climbed down, slipped beneath dripping palm-eaves near me and asked for a pack of smokes. He swore at me first, "¡Verga!" then said he'd sprayed down fields all day. I was shocked he opened with the sore subject of pesticides, saying he "should shield his boys from the kind of life he has now—devoid of the things we'd dreamt as kids." It was hard to yield the floor to a man who'd been nothing but annoyed with me for years. But he didn't even wait for my ear. He spoke quietly through his destroyed throat, left no moment unfilled with words since debate was beyond him. He ordered a shot of sugar-cane booze and talked at length. Most of his hate seemed spent; but his garbled thoughts and speech didn't auger well for my understanding as to why he could suddenly stand the sight of local surfers grinding with gringas.

But he reached back, so I complied and recalled the days he described. Our shared memories rose through the ethers, elixirs and flies swimming around our heads. The rain spit and flared in the lights while Ramón leaned in the window to spin our former lives afloat again. He spared no detail since the bus driver drank with a thin fisherman named Yoél. The bus would leave when the driver was drunk.

So, two days became one in the hands of Ramón, as he would weave disparate experience like a unified, linear reality that couldn't be cleaved as our friendship had.

His dream began at mid-tide when we were nine and we waited for it to drain out, then fill back in for a high-tide, low-wind evening surf session. We were poor, didn't own surfboards, so we began the day-long search for a board to share later. We went to Juan Lee Hooker's* house and walked in. Juan's grandma perched on a stepstool by the stove in a kind of pose—like a statue with a spatula, in a lurch among coursing black smoke that reeked and rose from a pan of burning, black, overfried eggs. We pulled her back, her open eyes in repose, watering from the smoke. She shook on thin legs and told us about her condition: She had passed out one month before, one side of her face still sags to this day. Since then her ruptured brain has amassed still shots of her world. She'd seen two yolks, yellow and bulbous, and her vision held fast to that sight until we came in the door and ran to her rescue, lost in her head's climate of smoke.

Ramón collapsed these two days, rewrote the span of time between the old lady's standstill, spoke-like perception, her snapshot vision of the cooked eggs, and his own near-drowning. He had cloaked his questions, he said, all of these years—as he looked at the still-writhing gringas in the street, their inexorable dance—since questions worked against his belief in God. But he'd blocked out the bleat of his hungry kids for the last time, lying in bed, an unpaid workday stoking his sense of defeat.

He looked up, his faith gone, his eyes were dead: "Pancho, you learned something when you were gone. You know something like these girls. And I've never said how much I wish for our past. I feel like a pawn these days and I wouldn't wish my life on you, that careless girl stumbling like a silly fawn in the street or my worst enemy. But time flew until I'm left with only my bitter grudges. I want to bring back the old me, when I

---

*Juan Lee Hooker was the nickname of a boy Pancho grew up with who once wore the same John Lee Hooker concert T-shirt for three months. The shirt was his prized possession. He has been known in Ecuador as Juan Lee Hooker ever since. Juan Lee Hooker is a painter and a surfer and loved by all who know him.

knew why we loved the world—because of its broad smudges and in-consistencies. I want to walk, again, behind *Abuelita* as her brain fudges her world with freeze-framed moments, like a unique clock keeping time in her world.

"Remember how she said she could see our faces, hear us talk but our lips were still? She didn't know what 'now' meant anymore. We would walk behind her, stuck in static vision, but she could hear and allow her world to freeze, trusting we'd moved and not shucked our bodies to orbit her world from a place, a dimension parallel to hers. I felt unstuck and thrilled by this, as a kid, unable to trace any given explanations or answers back to their root of truth.

"We were young. Time and space grew limitless before us. But now a crack of thunder is just noise. The percussion of drops on the road just reminds me I've forgotten this black night will get back to blue. I've run dry mops through my mind and sopped up all remnants of wonder. I'm left with a gut-wrenching fear that gums-up my heart and reveals the bigoted blunder I've labeled 'my life.'

"Remember that surf session later that day—after we pulled her from under the egg smoke—back before all this aggression, when we were inseparable? Remember you saved me from those huge waves?"

I finished, stirred by Ramón's questions: "Nine green walls roared in like a train derailed and intent on drowning. No one tried, or could reach you, while the swells feathered in the broad riptide that dragged you south. But I paddled from the beach, cut-in on your dance with water—seven deep dives beneath those waves. I arrived tired, beyond speech, pushing you our borrowed board. The sea was alive with churned sea foam.

"A lull widened, between pulses of waves, but our lungs were burning like hives in our chests. We lurched sideways, an exhausted lean, across the green board. The quiet fizz of sea foam surrounded us as the reflective sheen of thousands of bubbles, mini sky-blue domes, frothed and popped. We had time enough to make out our mirrored heads in the bubbles as they roamed about in clusters, pushed by the board's small wake. No other sound encroached, our submerged feet flew like pitched hatchlings in wet wind. We thought to take our time as all around us our world was blue and repeating, fragile, clear, with our faces fired on liquid veneers—floating, reflective, see-through. Each convex reflection, a saltwater world, expired with a tiny sibilant breath—a fragile trance, churned moments. This reel of our youth was like inspired meditation: two blank slates afloat in their chance to mirror the rhythms and tacit hush of time. What pulled our eyes from this prophetic glance beyond the past or the future? What internal rhyme? Whose wisdom unfurled for us—these dimensions and worlds tangled in a cosmic heap—synchronous, sublime?"

10

THE CANAL HAG

A.K.A. "AFTER-HOURS JENNY" OR "THE LATE-NIGHT BITCH"

Associated with the Honeyash tree of Seawell which comes to leaf as late as the end of May and keeps a skirt of withered, yellow leaves through mild winters, the Canal Hag is a water faerie who displays many aspects of the White Goddess. She often appears to drunk men as a seductive woman with long blonde hair streaked with green, weed-like highlights. Her aliases, "After-Hours Jenny" or "The Late-Night Bitch," are evidence that she also takes on the appearance of a whore and/or she-wolf.

She lures lonely, unsuspecting drunks away from crowds filing out of the public houses and taverns in downtown Seawell and toward the cold, black canals laced through the city. She's rumored to nest on a bed of skulls and scalps deep in one of the hydropower tunnels under the Loafe Mills. The Canal Hag bludgeons her victim with a petrified Honeyash limb, then she quietly drags the unconscious man underwater. Once she drowns her victim, the Canal Hag's been heard to sing a dirge-like song while slowly waltzing with the lifeless body as it rises and spins to the surface of a canal. Brian MacCaulkin, a local reformed drunk has dubbed this dance "The Pressure-Drop Waltz," and he claims: "It's a terrifying thing to see and hear. The memory, it'll follow a person. It's the kind of sight and sound to keep any half-wit or better from frequenting the pubs past eleven p.m. for the rest of his life. 'Nothing good happens in Seawell after eleven,' as they say. I can vouch for that bit of wisdom."

After-Hours Jenny's violent outbursts often occur somewhere between mid-February and St. Patrick's Day. The rest of the year, her nature is described as more benign and she has been known to save small children from trolley tracks or out from under a car's bumper. Elderly Seawellians repeatedly describe a mysterious woman helping them cross busy cobblestone streets in the downtown area. Virtually identical descriptions have been recorded through the decades. Peggy Brigantia, former mill girl and resident of the Acre, described the Canal Hag in a *Seawell Sun* article in 1934, titled "The John-Street Jenny":

> She was rail-thin and kindly, the poor thing. Told me her name was "Jenny," and that she had "all day and all night to help me get across this terrible street." Told me she worked downtown and had moved there a long time ago. I assumed she meant the Acre, but she seemed too beautiful a thing to come out of that old shantytown. And I told her so—right to her face. She just smiled and wandered off toward the Merrohawke Mills.

The Canal Hag is honored when Seawell, Galloway and Lawrence compete annually in the American-Gaelic Games at rotating sites in Massachusetts. Irish, Scottish and Welsh Americans use hurleys made from Honeyash to compete in a hurling tournament before a crowd of tens of thousands. The hurleys, interestingly enough, are traditionally coated in butter and cured in a chimney for one year before being ready for use. In Seawell's recent past, British overseers at the mills were often enraged to find hundreds of their workers' future hurleys steeping on wire racks mounted secretly in their smokestacks. Most mill overseers would nonetheless leave the hurleys to steep, knowing the Honeyash wood to be sacred to After-Hours Jenny. Any brazen or greedy mill overseer who disturbed the hurleys would inevitably be found floating dead in a canal. Through the years Seawell's chief coroners recorded "heavy trauma to the head," "forcibly removed scalps" and "drowning" as the causes of multiple overseers' deaths. These causes of death, the calling cards of the Canal Hag, were rarely investigated in any depth by the local authorities.

Each New Year's Day, the locals of South Seawell ritually appease Seawell's Queen Fairie, the Canal Hag, by nailing a used hurley at the top of this ladder. In March, the same groups re-create the Canal Hag's ascent to the world of mankind. The youngster braving the dye-laden mud and carp-infested, freezing water in this photo is fourteen-year-old Maeve Cahill who was chosen to play the part of "After-Hours Jenny" for the 1978 St. Paddy's festival. Photogapher B. Froud says he remains perplexed by the unintended transparency of his main subject, Miss Cahill (his original negative shows no evidence of tampering). Miss Cahill's image survives here as fragile and illusory as her short life would prove to be. No further efforts to record this annual ritual on film have been made since 1978, as it is widely believed the Canal Hag was summarily offended by the taking of photos during the ceremony meant to honor her. Tragically, Miss Cahill was found dead (drowned and shorn of her long hair) three days after this photo was developed.

The Canal Hag sleeps away a spring snowstorm. This shot was one of only a few paperclipped to Dr. Nicholas Panagiakis' original onionskin manuscript, "Folklore of the Knackers of Acre City, Seawell, Mass." A photocopy of this image was clipped to each story that mentioned the Canal Hag, After-Hours Jenny, John Street Jenny or the Late-Night Bitch.

This photo is from the Seawell Historical Society's archives. The photographer is unknown, but on the back of the original there are faint pencil scratchings that read: "Jenny & the last Honeyash in the Acre."

11

PEOPLE OF SEAWELL'S SISTER CITY, PART II

PANCHO & RAMØN'S ENDLESS MEMORIES
OF THE HERE-AND-NOW (CANOA, ECUADOR)

AS TOLD TO SWEENEY BY PANCHO MONEYMAKER

Fat Tío made me promise I'd return the empties to his bar. So I swore I would as Ramón and I stepped into the thinning rain. The drunken gringas were still dancing, but paired off with local surfers and the scene grew calm—in concert with the weather as it relented.

A thick mist fell, but the storm had ripped brown palm fronds from their folds in the rooves. While water gushed and swelled over everything like a wordless psalm, I paused to eye Ramón as he removed his boots and surrendered his feet to the mud, barefoot like me, laughing a little, moving like a load had been lifted. I thought he might dance or skate across the wasted road down to the beach to drink our beer.

As we rinsed off our feet in the warm ocean, Ramón pulled out a roach as I pulled out a pinner. We laughed and he flicked his away. I lit mine and tried to reach for…to find a way to talk about my degree. When I look back, I'm stunned it was Ramón who'd drawn the truth from me, from behind the dimming cherry of that joint. I'd never breathed a word of the con I'd pulled, not even to my parents, who'd died without knowing. They were long since gone and I'd figured they were the ones I'd screwed over, so only they would care that I never finished school. But Ramón was a strange dude and he'd only grown stranger. I began to shiver a bit in my wet clothes as I started to mend and weave the truth.

First, I asked if he ever realized how much we'd learned from our old friend Roberto Sepulcros. The name alone took command and doused Ramón's face with softness. He seemed to bend his ear to my words. The task of the truth at hand became less of a burden in that split second. So I talked about the fact that Roberto's stand to save the dry tropical forest behind our home—our beloved squatter village, the slum called Bella Vista—was so crucial, so bound to my person. "He taught me where we are from and I learned all about our little dry ravine rising above El Río Chone's thrum and thrust through the Pacific's tides."

We'd seen a few gringo backpackers in Caráquez, but Roberto was different because he stayed in a lean-to right in Bella Vista. Our small rut of dust and shacks didn't have lights or running water but it sat surrounded by uncut and untouched square miles of the most rare and most stunning forest on the planet. Ramón and I were raised within this dormant miracle, a cloning of prehistoric nature, and we were unfazed until some sunburned, bugbitten Dutchman ignored the filth, the dust and spoke as if dazed by a beauty unseen by our town of fishermen.

He said, in laughable Spanish, "I want to lives here, on the edge of the woods. I want to crown a tree that touches the hill right here to gives entry to the jungle." And Ramón recalled the first words of Roberto Sepulcros because, all these years later, we loudly agreed, it was impossible to remove the sight and sound of him from our memory-drunk heads.

His first appearance…he was so tall and white, so patently harmless. The women and kids took to him like flies to fruit! We shoved, in spite of his protests, and crowded about him amid his hands and knees to blurt questions at him in such a flurry that he said we clearly outdid ourselves, and he blushed through his beet-red sunburn!

Ramón reminded me: "I want to lives here, on the edge of the woods. I want to crown a tree that touches the hill right here to gives entry to the jungle,"—how Roberto repeated the same absurd sentence! How that laughable phrase remains a running joke—though when it's meted out these days it draws laughs muted by memory.

But Roberto's knack for never feeling defeated by our tongue, the sun, the bugs or the poverty (i.e. both our sheer lack of money *and* learning) became his most endearing quality to everyone from Bella Vista's burning dirt streets. Ramón started to see my point of view as he recalled the days of hiking, the trips we took in the jungle, the sheer hours spent listening to him talk of the three rare types of jungle on our coast.

Although, I'd bent my ear to the jungle floor while Ramón's gripes with his vicious, drunken father simply dropped from my view. My turning away from Ramón's snipes these days reminded him, and now me, that I'd walked away with Roberto and left Ramón to fight his father alone.

Sitting on that beach, just soaked to the skin, drinking warm Pilsener all night I could see that I'd deserted my best friend for the forests. But the weed and beer combined just right in Ramón's heart to forgive me. In the end, maybe he recalled that my father would leave my mother, me and four sisters to fend for ourselves about two years after the cleaving of our friendship.

Maybe not. All we would care to recall that night, on that wet sleeve of sand below the forest's cuff of tree-lined darkness, was the Dutchman's way of jumping out of his skin whenever he'd see an undiscovered orchid. Or he'd ricochet from pawprint to pawprint while tracking the cat he believed had never been named.

Then he found one odd stray killed by a car, and it turned out to be that mystery cat—with a long, thin orange torso and a skull like a jaguar. We saw the furred mat of blood he held by the tail, how he was aglow with his find until the carcass disappeared before he could dissect it or snap a photo.

We never figured out if it was wild or if an ocelot had bred with a pet cat from the town. Roberto was visibly crushed—the only time we saw him down and out—for a month, until we found that lone toucan without a scientific name. His grant was renewed for ten years on that find alone, nevermind the near-discovery of the road-kill cat that became his Ecuadorian Yeti or *Chupa Cabra* of sorts.

He told us it must've been capuchin monkeys that stole the cat's carcass from his freezer. Who else would grab a decomposed mystery cat and stroll through town with the stench stuck to their clothes like glue?

Ramón and I laughed ourselves back from our old reality to the present—from the coups and quirks of Roberto's world—to our thirty-odd-ounce beers and another squall blotting out the blue water of the Pacific, at first light, dimmed and silvered by the clouds.

Ramón concurred, Roberto was the sole resource that we'd been lucky enough to tap as children inured, but not maimed, by poverty. The stunning view of the river and the sea had always stirred our pride as part of Bella Vista's crew of kids; we even had a special bird call we whistled low when we saw one or two locals we'd grown up with.

But after all, Roberto was the gringo who'd made it cool to learn the songs and sounds of animals to begin with.

Some dads knew the varied schools of fish, the currents and the waves but they had mostly forgotten the cyclical rule of the tropical trees and beasts. Even today, it's easier to feed and clothe kids and wives through fishing or shrimp farms. Most men thought it was ok to let the kids have the woods, content with their lives on the water watching for their lines gone taut.

The men of Bella Vista clean fish with knives worn down from years of cutting whatever they've caught in their nets and on gaffs made from a hubcap's hidden hook. They gut fish underneath palms we all were taught could provide decades of roofing for bamboo shacks. But corrugated tin and cinder blocks, some booze for most and prayer for a few, now brook against the fear of the jungles' myriad pox. And since we've driven the indigenous tribes to near extinction we sleep in our tin boxes having forgotten the things nature prescribes for all our needs and ailments.

But here Ramón stopped me and said only he and I ascribe to this; he wondered aloud if I had known this *before* I earned my degree. I said I had but I wanted to know if *he* had grown accustomed to this point of view as a kid with Roberto and if it was why he gave me hell for going away to school.

I talked and balked and told him I'd something I wanted to tell him since I'd returned to live and work on the coast. As I spoke, I felt like a snail smashed out of its shell—dropped by some bird—naked on a rock, exposed, the spiraling shards of my constructed, false life strewn here and there.

As kids we'd watched, engrossed, as hovering kites did this—since their curved, knife-like beaks weren't enough to pry some snails from their husks. My framework of lies split that morning—rife with beer breath and drymouth—the truth has a musk like a dying animal.

I slurred to my friend, "One year before I graduated the mask fell apart for me," I said, "so I put an end to my studies, left school quietly and used my father's monthly checks to wile and wend my way around South America.

"I'd excused my longtime lies by blaming my dad. But he'd come through on his promise to pay for school; confused by his absence in my life and his guilty need to make up for it with cash, I'd burned through his 'flight money,' as I called it, with a speed and precision that turned heads."

Ramón said, "Is this the first you've spoken…the first person you've told…."

The weight of my statement and the drugs were like cysts swelling his tongue to uselessness. "Get ahold of yourself, *caraverga*!" I teased. "It's true, I never got my Ph.D."

This bowled him over right there in the sand—though he knew enough to carefully set his beer upright before cracking up hysterically.

I laughed too, as wasted as I was, relieved that my secret just might be out—and I said in Spanish that "The frozen cat's out of the bag, eh?" And this phrase would delight Ramón for months since such an idiomatic expression is strange and senseless in Spanish, yet it fit so perfectly with our memories—our regression to our youth spent with "the gringo who never quit!"

Ramón spluttered, "The smell of your cat and its bag won't stick to me my friend. Because if I make it through this hangover I'll be sure to brag about your travels and lies and lack of degree to everyone on this coast. You don't mind if I drag you down, do you?"

Ramón was clearly giddy with the prospect of telling all the local guys I was a fraud. He loved my dishonesty and we recalled how we once adored good lies and practical jokes—when we used to take the world less seriously.

Ramón's eyes were lit with tears and laughter as he tried to make me tell him the hows and whys. He'd read my published articles in journals, but for the sake of his role as a hater he'd called it all rubbish through the years. He wanted to hear how I could write expertly of medicinal plants and shrubs if I hadn't earned my degree. I said it would have taken several years to finish up, but I was sick of living in the hood in Guayaquil, right near the school, at the top of a set of streets known as the "the den of thieves."

"The seventh mugging really was more of a swap for me—I gave thieves my money and received the shift in perspective needed to change my whole outlook and direction. I mean, no one grieves for lost cash if it's the seventh time you get rolled in front of your own flat! It's like kicking a door that's already open and leads out of town.

"There's no dole or welfare or effective system the poor can rely on for help here, so the desperation is unreal—as we learned in rural Ecuador. It's worse in the cities, I think, but my station as a grad. student let me forget about that until the muggings forced a reformation of my understanding.

"And it was time to scout a new route back to the forests of my home. The decisive moment arrived that night, and bore out while I was on mushrooms in my shabby room above the city: Around three a.m., a deranged storm rolled over Guayaquil. Maybe it was the 'shrooms that coupled with my revelation of change—stalking me like a chained dog at the end of its rope, circling until I fell in its range—I thought the clouds might devour the city, penned in by its own filth and violence. The distant buildings were dimmed and hidden by a distended tongue of a beast—the rain's pall pushing, insistent, scavenging the cement, nerve-lit bones on the far side of that collapsed, humongous slum.

"My resistance was gone that night, the weak call of a burgled car sounding in my ear, the storm would finish off the city—leaving a shiny, smeared trail scarred into the exhausted earth. Who'd know the trough was once Guayaquil? Would nature be sated with swallowing us whole?

"I almost scoffed at my notion, until I recalled the somewhat dated scientific discovery that certain kinds of snails, after eating other snails, are endowed (or fated to absorb) their victim's memory. The scale of this transference of shared memory hit my mind broadside and instantly derailed my thoughts of a Rainbeast eating the world in a fit of revenge; instead, I decided I didn't want my memories to transfer—the stabbings, and shit-stained accidents, addicts and scenes that would haunt most of my daydreams and nightmares. Us beasts gone upright, pacing the concrete cage, grown gaunt and obsessed with letting days slip away like greased piglets that grow into pig weeks and pig years. I behaved the same, grown flush with hypocrisies, and I knew the city would still be right here when the storm relented.

"But then the clouds had changed as bolts of lightning slashed like synaptic spears crawling from the folds and bulges across the range of my vision. Like gray matter, the clouds released their angry thoughts and blew out the senses—the strange neon eyes and ears of a skyscraper were snuffed in a curtain of black rain. I imagined we humans were no more than tiny pests who'd latched onto the skin and into the skull of a flea or some living breathing thing losing its mind and memory bit by bit, city by city. We'd be snuffed like parasites within the design of something beyond our meager senses and grasp.

"The lightning resembled synapses, the kind of electric thoughts that shed pure light and map brief insights, sightings of truth—the nature of things actually beyond truth.

"For me, a lapse of reason: It's not that I *believed* I was watching a storm devour mankind or that I was a part of the brain of some universal leeching beast; it was more a dousing of the buzz of logic—its hold on my mind's view of the world.

"Once I shushed my ego, as a Zen monk does, a kind of balanced nothingness unfurled around and through me. *Infinity* and *connectedness* were re-revealed as the only words to remind me that wisdom and things beyond truth lie etched on walls that can't be described with words.

"James Lovelock got close—like a kind of organic architect rebuilding the world of things until it shook and bled like any other animal— with his Gaia Principle.

"I knew this bluegreen rock was breathing and alive, but that night I recalled something I know by heart: The concept passed to me by Roberto and the indigenous people of Ecuador was the same as Lovelock's masterpiece of science!

"For age upon age, animals, people and plants have lived on this vast, round beast with an intuitive and sage-like knowledge of balance through connectedness. I swore that when I woke up in that same cage the next day, I'd quit studying science's efforts to prove what *La Pachamama*★ had already shown me.

"I knew I'd been blessed by the forests overhanging the tin-clad shacks of my town. I still feel like a blessed fool living in untouched wilderness. It's luck that I'd met a man that *lived* the Gaia Principle; a man who gave us his life without regret, who believed in the Buddhist's web of infinite jewels.

"He'd always said, 'In each jewel,' making a net with his hands, 'lies the reflection of all the other jewels. The nature of the universe is present in every cell, truth in all particles.' I'd leaned on that quote, quit school and left for my town and the jungle—I took the long way home—to dwell on its fringe and to maybe build that 'tree house crown' that Roberto never finished dreaming of."

In that instant, Ramón stood up and patted down his pockets for a light. The night had shoved off over the ocean and away from our squinting eyes. Time had lost itself above our lolling heads. Ramón said he felt "sour and exhausted."

He mentioned he might want to help build the tree house then he slurred, "I'm only nine hours late and today's my youngest's fourth... or...third birthday, I think. Why'd I do this to myself?" He closed one eye to look at me and then willed himself to stumble off—accusing himself of various stupidities.

Although, I heard laughter as he climbed from the beach to the shelf of shining mud, eroded ruts and plateaus of pebbles and rocks we called the beach road. Still, as he staggered east for the first bus along wet rows of shuttered bars and stores, I heard him. He whistled the call of *el gavilán.*

So before he could walk out of earshot, I widened my tongue to fill my mouth and whistle the call of the sparrowhawk*—that tiny but fierce hunting bird that gave us kids from Bella Vista our secret knock, a trilled watchword all our own.

One long look at the waves feathering in the breeze, and I knew a truce had been sounded out.

I needed to find a cave to descend into—cool darkness to induce the long sleep needed to soothe my pounding head. I was "*chuchaqui fatal*," ★★ and the hangover's noose would cinch mercilessly if I didn't get to bed.

I smiled and stumbled home toward my small farm, hitching a rough ride in a pickup with yuca bread and some water to help the effort. Jamming my forearm on the armrest I braced myself against the holes in the coast road's asphalt.

I felt naked, unarmed and elated as the truck sped north under knolls of sacred *Ceiba* trees.

I knew Ramón would soon visit. His ruined voice would extol, again, our *Ceibas*—Gaia's green, bejeweled bones jutting from the canopy's shifting flesh in this rarest forest. *El Gavílan* hadn't yet flown.

---

*The call of el gavílan, the sparrowhawk, is a shrill whistle: "kill-EEE, kill-EEE, kill-EEE."
★★"Chuchaqui fatal" (Chew-CHAH-kee fay-TAHL) is slang for the effects of a long night of boozing, in other words "a deadly hangover."

12

THE BOGBERRY TROLL, A.K.A. THE PIECE TROLL

This shy and swarthy creature plants Bogberry Vine at the base of the best of Seawell's graffiti murals to protect them—most often those including the letters M, U, I or N. Once in a great while, Bogberry will sprout at the base of a graffiti mural that lacks the abovementioned letters and this is considered the highest compliment that can be paid to an East Coast-based graffiti artist. Thus, Portland, Boston, Philly, NYC, DC, Charlotte, Atlanta and Miami graffiti artists make the once-in-a-lifetime pilgrimage to Seawell to test the sandy soil beneath its bridges, inside its trolley tunnels, along its alleys. The blessing of the Bogberry Troll is highly sought after and is known as the "Seawell Seal."

Seawell's most famous Piece Troll chiefly dwells in alleys, behind dumpsters or under railroad trestles. He, like most of his kind, is bearded and appears ungainly but can actually move swiftly and leap three-stories in a pinch. One of the most colorful denizens among Seawell's mythical creatures, this troll is never seen without a kelly-green cap, sky-blue vest and what look like odd-shaped scarlet stockings. On closer inspection, it's revealed that the creature's feet resemble those of a duck or goose. It is not believed that his webbed feet assist him in swimming since it is common knowledge that the Bogberry Troll abhors all forms of water. He is believed to be descended from the fairies that dwell in the mines of northern Wales and is most active, like his cousins, during the month of September.

The Bogberry Vine possesses stinging nettles proven to induce a painful, lasting, itchy wound to any who might wish to harm the murals of graffiti artists. Some of Seawell's Acre-dwelling storytellers insist that a deep enough Bogberry wound will rot flesh and sometimes require the amputation of fingers or toes. Graffiti removal companies in the region regularly report that their workers are often showered with sticks and stones while sandblasting murals, painting over them or cutting back Bogberry Vine.

The Bogberry Vine itself reveals the spiritual importance this creature holds among the knackers of Acre City. It is one of the only known trees in Seawell to flower and bear fruit at the same time. Similarly, visual artists (and all dedicated artists) represent one of the few versions of a modern human still actively engaged in achieving a balance (or simultaneous blooming) of their emotion (heart), intellect or logic (mind) and their capacity for imagination (soul/spirit). This is especially true for graffiti artists who face heavy fines and jail time for attempting to achieve balance in their lives through their underground art form.

A wreath of Bogberry passed over the crown and raised right thumb of a person will protect that individual from the corrosive power of evil runes and unreasonable laws or social responsibilities. The junction of the Correb and Merrohawke rivers was the site where Native Americans used the berry from this thorny vine to dye hides a rich, reddish purple—a color sacred to the regional tribes.

The Piece Troll dines on loaves of wet newspaper, flattened wax cups and he uses discarded straws to quench his slight thirst by drinking the drippings of wet spray paint from fresh graffiti murals. He only sleeps diagonally across defunct train or trolley tracks, his green-capped, bearded head touching one rail while his scarlet goose-feet touch the other parallel track. He guards these tracks with fervor during his vigil over the finest graffiti murals on the East Coast.

Bogberry nettles in the foreground, a stunning "AVES" piece in the background. This building, the Seawell Electric Co., was torn down one year after this photo was taken. No one's seen evidence of the Piece Troll in Seawell since the demolition.

Photo: Eddie "Tred" Eliot, 2006

13

CUFFED HAIKUS & CHAINED TANKAS

MOMENTS CAPTURED FROM MY ARRESTS AND THOSE OF
FRIENDS, ENEMIES & STRANGERS IN SEAWELL, MASS.

Her billyclub's butt end jabs
beneath a raised arm to chip
ribs, unfold fists and force prayer

Meditating, cheek
pressed to the cruiser's warm hood—
wind, sirens peel my reflection from windows

Should have sold it all
   or snorted it—all this time
for just mule-ing it from place to place

Dawn's ninth autumn in prison
      she still smells the Armor All'd
squad car, the stench of dried puke

—MCI Framingham
October 28, 1997 - October 28, 2006

Ray was enlightened—
   lifted from the pocked wet curb
  by a fist stuffed with his short black hair

Another bar brawl
  near full moon while the place blasts
"Tangled Up in Blue"
   I hope the blood hides my cheeks—
I blush as Officer Kim cuffs me

Old-timer goes: "Sis's Greek
  Easter dress tore, so I beat up one
Irish kid per week on principle that year"

"Malicious Damage
　　to a Motor Vehicle"
means I crow-barred every inch of his Monte Carlo

　　—*Leanne Alves, the Acre, Seawell, Mass.*

　　　　　　　Entry and exit plugged tight
　　　　　　　　in his thigh, he changed clothes, hid it
　　　　　　　then bled by design across the squad car's seat

It wasn't "Trunks" Indecent
    Exposure charge but the Jaywalking
ticket that got him worked up

We found more teens in the woods
    brought them in, damn kids cheered from their cells
like they were at some kinda parade

—*Smalltown police officer in rural New Hampshire referring to Seawell High students camping and drinking in his town*

Faded staggerings uptown
            to sleep on the couch, Sergeant Ruiz,
    old friend, woke him in a stranger's residence

"Trunks" is ah old-time boxah,
            still punch drunk, everyone's seen that clown
get pinched a buncha times fuh
            deckin' some random guy wearin' red
shawts in Kearney Sqweah—Trunks just sees that No-Name
    who knocked him out in sevinny-eight

—*Common answer for a typical question at McSwiggan's Pub*

Years later I'd forgotten
    the raid—under-aged, cuffed together,
paddy wagon brimmed—drunk friends laughed, cried

Right clog's heel thuds, echoes
    in the garage, Dawn's left hand holds it—
bludgeons Leanne's head blind and rhythmic

                         Electric skillet, spatula, stick-
                              on letters, lamination paper
                         Polaroid: sixty bucks, fake I.D.

Smitty was huge, cut,
　　　　ripped like a god when he got out—
　　but he froze slow, stabbed behind filthy snowbanks

In june-yuh high Vann got whaled
　　　　on three times a week by crackahs, niggahs and
　　spics beefoh he could speak a
　　　　wurdda English. He met some othah gooks that
　　jumped him in, and high school was diffrint.★

Cruisers flanked me, knees
　　　　on cobblestones—one fist cocked,
　　one around a throat, I froze　bathed in white light

★To get "jumped-in" is to be beaten severely as part of an initiation ritual into certain
Seawell gangs. If the boy survives the beating and takes it like a man, he becomes a
member.

Frank's mother would smack his head—
    so he stole tires from a Packard, made curfew,
fixed the flats, put 'em back the next day

                              Dawn dialed nine-one-one
                                    said "Eleven Elm," blacked-out—
                            he beat her bad while he had the time

University Ave. tenement
    kegger—from between two cops
  our host grins "Come back in ten, keg'll be here"

One man in one night
    beat and raped two teenaged girls,
  stabbed their mothers—no one called the cops

In her country, twelve-
        year-olds are often mothers—
here, her brother is a pedophile

Vann's thirty-six now
        no one's called him "gook" or "chink"
in twenty years—kept his mouth
        shut, did time and has a girl,
two kids—scared he won't survive getting jumped-out

His own brother called the cops—
    because he lost ten grand on Keno
one night tending their bar—the safe's dry

Cashier says "Suddenly we
see seven West Virginia I.D.s
this week? I'll keep it, kid—you can screw"

Shot in the neck Friday night—
hospital, gauze, pills—
back to school Monday morning

I broke that kid's face
with one left hook because he
bothered me with a small, damning voice

He'd never raised a finger
    but she was sick of the bickering—
he went out, she called in Domestic Abuse

They robbed those college kids blind—
    roulette table, blackjack and sports book—
these kids were thirteen, with moustaches

—*Cop overheard on Moody St., Seawell*

She's three and a half
        and only knows the police
take her uncle gangbanger away

I changed seats in the drunk tank
     when the wino's guts turned, boiled
before he leapt for the metal bowl

Every other year or so
        some couple decides to leave
their newborn in a dumpster

The Police Log says
  "Uttered a False Prescription"
—I just traded addicts pills for sex

It's a balancing
                    act as Fat Bookie Dan buys
        beers for Thin Cop Paul

        —*Witnessed by hundreds in The Temple Bar*

What about that kidnapping in Mexico?
        They propped the kid in the car, dead, stuffed her ribs
with drugs to cross the border—they're animals down there.

        —*Overheard outside Stan's Tavern,*
                Jackson Street, Seawell, 1991

14

SMOKESTACK BOGEY, A.K.A.
HEARTH FAERIE

Bogey's are originally associated with the letter B in the Celtic alphabet and connected to the tip of one's thumb in druidic lore. The Seawellian strain of this faerie is closely related to Rockwall Fays, ever-present in the rural country of New England and the outer Celtic isles. The Smoke-stack Bogey may appear in the sky like a horned bird and in the next instant it might resemble a harmless garter snake with large gray, mossy horns. It is believed to have hollow bones and soft gray ash, rather than blood, puffing through its veins and heart.

The average Smokestack Bogey is a very fragile, skittish creature—unless, it is trooping (moving about in a flock) with other faeries. If it finds itself in the company of dozens of other bogeys, it is a gregarious and mischievous thing performing acrobatic flight patterns. When in its snake-like form, it has been seen biting its own tail and rolling down hills at high speeds. Most Smokestack Bogeys survive on a diet of coal smoke or wood smoke and glowing Foxfire fungus (only found on birch stumps). This bogey drinks smoke much like a human enjoys a pint of stout—some Smokestack Bogeys even appear to sport "smoke bellies" from all the smoke that they consume. These bellies are a source of un-ending pride and the bigger the belly, the higher the social rank in their respective troop.

These creatures have such a sparse diet, however, that they are be-lieved to defecate only twice per year down the mouth of a carefully chosen smokestack—on the evening of December 24 (at the setting of the sun) and on the morning of January 20 (with the rise of the morning star). Due to the glowing nature of Foxfire, the staple of their diet, and since they troop together to shit, they leave an extensive, green, phosphorescent trail of excrement spiraling down the inside of their chosen smokestack. The specific smokestack varies from year to year, among the more than two dozen smokestacks towering above Seawell.

This green, glowing, spiral trail is rumored to be a map of the summertime stars in the northern sky. For Smokestack Bogeys are the physically larger cousins of Lithuanian and Celtic hearth faeries and it is common knowledge that all Hearth Faeries detest the cold and the winter months (which is why they simultaneously haunt and bless hearths, wood stoves, chimneys and smokestacks in and around deciduous forests the world over).

There are no known harmful effects or consequences from most interactions with this bogey, whether in its flying or slithering form. It is considered an exceedingly good omen if you come across one in a stand of birch trees. Sightings of thin exhalations of coal-black smoke and the sound of a slight but insistent wheezing indicate a Smokestack Bogey is nearby.

Cutting a switch from a Birch tree during the waning gibbous December moon and hanging the switch above the crib of a newborn reportedly brings good fortune and robust health for that child's first nine years of life. The Scottish and Spanish Gypsies of the Acre, and their scattered descendents, adhere to this practice without fail and Birch switches can be found in virtually all of their homes around Seawell. Some believers go as far as engraving Birch switches on their headstones to ensure a fortunate afterlife or rebirth.

A flock or "troop" of thousands of Smokestack Bogeys at sunset above
wintertime Seawell. Inset: The Smokestack Bogey, in its horned bird form,
prepares to contribute to a map of the stars.

Photo: Dottie Harrigan, 1978
Inset: Illustration by P. Kivlin, 1998

15

TRAVELS THROUGH THE DARK SEA

In Three Parts

PART I

Letter from a Ruined Desert

You're older now, and I write because it's the middle of another night—fitful, sleepless, lost-animal night. Owen, this Southern California beach town is crowded, and I'm shaken. I just woke to a straining, hoarse voice: "For the love of God, somebody please help me." It was a man's desperate whisper, and a phantasm of chills swept up my spine. My hackles were raised, I felt cagey, spooked. I heard Peter in the next room. He found his glasses, pushed them on his face and we went out the side door into the narrow space between the packed-tight homes. We shuffled with raspy feet, in our boxers, and wondered if we should call the police—squinted up and down the asphalt yard. We'd both woken up to pain that seeped from a shut-quick window or re-locked door, it dropped through the dark of our rooms. It shook us from deep sleep and we'd both heard it groan a second time: "For the love of God, somebody please help me."

So I write from San Clemente, where the waves shush the rocks. I can't sleep. Too many houses, too many strange people with basements and attics sealed against this ruined, seaside desert.

I've enclosed a never-sent postcard from Paris. I scrawled it during a night that woke and stretched back into its own pain—a long, lost-animal night. When the sun came up, I'd run out of wine and remembered you were too young to read. But who better to write than a child, when awakened from a drunken sleep by worldsong—life's spectral undertone of raw suffering? It was you or Christ, you or Muhammad you or Quetzalcoatl. At least I can find your address, and those aren't my gods, prophets or myths after all.

Paris, France, April, 1990:

"Dear Owen, I just woke up in my run-down hotel room to an animal wail. It's drawn-out, echoing through the wet, narrow streets. I drink wine from the bottle between the quarter-minute moans. I drank beer at Café Madrigal all evening, people-watched, then passed out alone in this sagged, musty bed…and there it is again! It's awful, wounded and half-human. This window sill's the cusp of the city's pent-up hurt. The panes hinge out over the street. Something wails at the restful through this mist. So few wake to pity, so few wake to fear. I'm awake. I'm terrified by this blind moan. I've begun to pity the mist. I can't speak French; I can't ask anyone. This night will never leave me alone."

—Sweeney

Transcribed by Dave Robinson from a letter mailed to Owen Kivlin.

PART II

THE LONG HAUL: *SEEN ON A RURAL ECUADORIAN HIGHWAY*

Here, the back pages of "*El Diario*" hold before-and-after shots from gangrene treatments. Electricity snuffs out daily with the rain. Yesterday I saw three fat men, a swaddled newborn and a young mother riding one four-wheeler on the coast road.

We bounce south, straddling backpacks in the eggshell-blue bed of a hired pickup—through a town grown kiln-hot as it can get.
A tick-hobbled quarter horse and oblivious burro rise above us, bending from their burdens of two thin men. Beneath five black vultures hunched in a fallen balsa, they stumble up a roadside ridge.

Our hundred-dollar fare split six ways, so we're hauled three-hours through one-speedbump towns, across exhausted bridges threaded by nameless rivers. Eight or nine bamboo shacks patched with bricks, tin and palm fronds huddle, strain against the ingrown flesh of the jungle. When the false wind dies during downshifts for speed-bumps, time feels maimed by a blight—by the gross weight of the sun.

The tick-hobbled quarter horse and oblivious burro weave above us, bending for their comatose-drunk cargo. They stumble up washed-out paths, rise beneath five black vultures hunched in a fallen balsa.

Drag your binge's dregs across the crumbling highway. Stagger rubberbooted, laughing, through your three-day bender's Sunday evening, tinted by our cough of suspended, blue exhaust.

Gear up beyond the pot holes across the girded bridge, by Spanish signs bragging of three waterfalls nearby.

Two-and four-legged stumbles, weaving stupefied in a saddle. Behind you, your sober friend? brother? uncle? has dismissed your drunken life with a wave. He's done this for us to see.

Leave this town, though I know you can't, please know blood will pool at the base of this sunbleached ridge. Feathered omens double in the sky, soar and double across your vision. Soon your thinned blood will mingle with the oblivious ribs, the burst cavity.

One of you will pull yourself through dirt and trash to beg for dimes, your stomach pressed to a filthy homemade four-wheeled cart. You'll wish for legs like those now tangled in your stirrups, any legs—dreaming of grotesque limbs from before-and-after photos you sleep underneath each sticky night.

PART III

The Diviners: *Seawell, Mass.*

Some of us've gone retro in our narcotic leanings: morphine lulls on toolshed rooftops, reddened sky marred by homemade fireworks over fall's fallen, unexotic gleanings. Some of us forgo forays into ourselves, but not on this night.

We hear warm rain drum out a foreign November across the public house's only window. Pints align, settle. Shrug-shouldered locals throw back stout to roll back pain:
His sister's gone haggard too young—a death crone cold on booze; my cousin's ex is back—his head's spun, he's broken kindling; a heroin-haunted uncle's made off with her three grand; an IRA gun-runner's buying beers, he's become bored with against-the-grain peace. And who'll diagnose this nagging anxiety digging a numb den in my thighs?

I play "Black Steel in the Hour of Chaos" to repair the barman's nerves, jangled by gun-toting visitors from Lynn. While I loudmouth up and down the pub, Al Green is declared *the* romantic of our time. She grooves, Indian-style, on a stool until we four cut out at last call for homesmoked weed and legal, bong-fueled visions from a bag of Salvia.

A final, small glass of Skye drops me off, sixth floor, in her green chair—neck stiff, mouth agape: I dream a sea-silhouetted jaguar stalking drowsy birds down the beach; But someone bleats, "A whisk of brown manes rearranged by whitecaps, and jade waves twist into taut harbor seals hauled out legless atop a rock collection scattered on your sill... dripping drapes...green sea foam."

Who'll walk south with me across

                          downtown—drunk, stoned, a pin-fixed
spraycan spitting white breadcrumbs

                     in our wake? Where hide the bald,
armed men from Lynn, Lynn, city

                of sin? Whose flinching hearts are
hooded against this sweet and

           heavy rain? How are we held,
swayed, staggered by a sliver

             of wild dog stilled by our footsteps?

Jetblack coyote stalking

            windless, inland paths near the
cemetery at dawn, you

         lope away from those of us
bound for bed till noon. Help us

           lure and sweet talk wild beasts back
into our dreams if only

       to better feel out our days.

16

THE JETTY FAY

This type of Fay dwells where land and sea meet—in manmade granite jetties, under docks and piers, near tide pools and rocky harbor mouths. Seawell knackers believe the connection between land and sea represents the conscious meeting the unconscious, respectively. It is where the solid, logical mind of our outer, social lives meets our shifting inner mind/soul. In Seawell, Seaside Blackthorns and Eastern White Poplars grow closest to the North Atlantic, thriving in mixed and sandy soil or rocky areas. Jetty Fays, known to be knowledgeable arborists, are often seen tending these trees. In fact, most Jetty Fays' coloration resembles the greens, grays and silvers of Blackthorn and Poplar leaves, as well as the shades of their granite-boulder homes or moss-covered pier-piling hiding spots.

During moments of trepidation or doubt within our passage between logic and awareness, similar to the jitters many experience before a long journey across an ocean, we should pray or make offerings to the Jetty Fay and wait for guidance. As children, humans are born in and closely connected to water but that connection may falter as we grow older and are burdened with more societal responsibilities.

Sailors, fishermen, lobstermen and their families often make offerings of fish scales and bones (or share a final meal of seafood together) at the base of White Poplars and Blackthorns the evening before family members leave on extended voyages. The Order of Reverent Lobstermen of North Seawell annually leave seven boiled, fully intact lobster claws arranged in a circle around a Seaside Blackthorn at the moment of full high tide or extreme low tide on the Autumnal Equinox (when light and dark, ocean and land are momentarily in perfect balance).

These rituals, among others differing slightly in the Oaklands neighborhood to the south, ensure that the Jetty Fay will watch over both the person gone to sea physically as well as those gone to sea mentally and emotionally. For the spouses or families left behind, the Jetty Fay helps to maintain a fully engaged social survival on land.

This tree is the northeastern-most Seaside Blackthorn in Seawell and has been a site of ritual for generations of fishing families. Many kids have cut their hands climbing into its canopy to see if their fathers' and uncles' and cousins' ships were returning after howling nor'easters.

Sweeney and his cousin Tommy Santos were once the focus of a highly public incident involving a half-constructed treehouse found one October morning in this Blackthorn's limbs. The nasty spikes on this tree's branches make it a terrible choice for the boys' dream treehouse.

Yet to this day Tommy Santos claims, "Sweeney had me buildin' the thing with him for the Jetty Fay, not for us. Our skin was laced bloody by that damn tree, and neither of us ever planned on spending a minute in whatever it was we were trying to build. We were nine, fahchrissakes, and we loved the Jetty Fay stories all the fishermen told. But it started rainin' so we went home to watch TV. We got community service for nailin' like five two-by-fours to that thing…and for skippin' school…and stealin' the lumber from some Lowland construction site. My dad wasn't too happy we left his tools out in the rain that time, either. Caught an extra beatin' for that stupidity, if I remember right. He might-even-ah whacked Sweeney once or twice for that one. My dad was a self-proclaimed 'generous disciplinarian.' Yeah, trust me, that guy really gave. He kinda never stopped givin', you know what I mean?"

Photo: Merrowhawke Seafaring Society—taken from the deck of the schooner Appledore.

17

THE DEAD-LETTER CROWN

Owen,

While living on the coast of Ecuador, I received in the mail the first eleven poems from a supposed heroic crown of sonnets. Last time I saw the poet Diana Marpessa, she'd told the bartender Oskar to keep feeding me thirty-two-oz. *Pilsners.* We'd been hanging out for a time at this bar called *Encuentro*, at about 10,000 feet above sea level in the capital city of Quito. She said she was going to the bathroom, handed Oskar 300,000 sucres (around $75) and walked out the back. That kept me and two friends drinking for a long time that night. The next night I couldn't find her in any of our high-altitude haunts. I knew she was gone, and I'd known she was leaving for a long time. The cocaine up there is too pure to be believed and it was easier to get than weed. I knew she wouldn't last at the opening pace she'd set.

The poems that follow were postmarked in Rochester, Minnesota, and arrived two years after Diana's exit from *Encuentro*. She'd cultivated habits, I'd cultivated habits; we lasted a couple years.

Last year, after reading her eleven poems approximately two hundred times, I decided to write the last four poems to simultaneously complete and corrupt her heroic crown of sonnets. I'm not a big love-poem poet, but sometimes, I mean, what can you do but write a few when you're in it? Once in a while you even have to look back, throw a crop of lines together and try to figure out what you once had.

Diana must've started writing this heroic crown while she was at the Mayo Clinic. She was a talented poet, published in respected journals by the age of seventeen. But she just about gave up on writing by the time she left me in Ecuador. She once told me she knew there was no money in poetry so she was going to become an absinthe sales rep in Egypt if she could ever stop drinking. She might be there now, I don't have any way of knowing. The fact that we both wrote poems probably kept us together much longer than we should've troubled.

The thing is, she was the only woman I ever really loved. And whether it was the infamous Ecuadorian mail system or her going back to drinking and drugs remains to be seen; I just know I never received the final poems that would've completed this heroic crown.

I wrote the fourteenth poem "One Evening Anchored in Baja" during a weekend when something was telling me that Diana would leave me no matter who I was or what I did. It's the only poem included that was written while I was with her. Somehow, this fourteenth poem ended up being about an evening that never happened in a place we never visited together.

Diana would've hated trying to complete the fifteenth poem of this heroic crown in a strict manner, by using the fourteen first lines of each poem exactly as they appear to make up the entire fifteenth sonnet. In turn, I tried to hate that symmetry too and simply took words and phrases from the fourteen poems to make fourteen lines, a fifteenth sonnet and a final stab at marking our time together. What happens on these final pages in these final poems of her heroic crown would probably satisfy her. But then again, what do I know?

After all this time, I'm still just some guy she left perched at a bar at 10,000 feet beneath the flank of an active, green volcano.

—Sweeney

FIRST LOVE OF MY LIFE

I've never been the sort of woman to ask questions of myself. I lack the capacity for wonder. I've got reflexes: my palm moving toward my mouth like chapped gravity cupping a solar system of pills. Mars-red orbs, moon-gray ovals adopt diminished orbits through my cavities. I'm after burned-out, staring down a false frontier.

At thirteen years old, how could I know these pills would cross-pollinate my head and heart with lead? What if I'd known my liver would bloom with off-white, gentled poisons? Each dry heave kinks my spine, plucks up my anthem: "I love me, I love me not. I love me. I love me not."

—Diana Marpessa

SECOND LOVE OF MY LIFE

Self-loathing is a Christian anthem best sung while sober. My penance was steady, maintained benders for two and a half decades. I'd elected drink my salve, used it for years while kids around me grew up, grew angry and wilted early: practiced trophy wives, plastic gossip hounds, workaholic husbands, cradle-robbing sleazebags. Sobered for spells, I heard the weak concern of friends. All my years of guzzled reason, and they whined:

"You were always a little crazy, always went too far." "We were worried, but we didn't know what to say." "You were always so pretty, why'd you need to drink?" Drunk, just like me, they used to spit up their desires and regrets. But I'm done listening. And they're done wearing their hearts like ruined garnishes stuck on their sleeves.

—D.M.

DETOX

Up the ruined sleeves of a dying Oak, the heatbug's drone makes me hear dry husks and feel cracked shells. If I catch its reverb in my bones, I feel a hammer crack an anvil—the earache's ode.

If I bit the heatbug's song, it'd snap and spill embers and acid rain like entrails. This gray braid of night and Kool smoke outside my window can't beat back the dogstar heat, these dried green leaves.

This thing, with its drumhead and cynical skin, calls to break my coiled thirst. Dirt-hatched chakra, root-fed monk, audible black hole—are you the last living *castrato* hidden in the twigs? Why cry like a claw clawing at my hide? Hush your anonymous dirge, this sky-cured concrete tide.

—D.M.

THREE PAYPHONES IN WINTER HILL
2002

I can't hush this anonymous dirge—the dial tone ebbs through the wires like a hollow tide. Yellowed fingertips can't navigate these numbers, won't punch the touchtone phone so we can talk. I can't.

You're nearby for once, back in Mass.—your letter shakes out the details in my nettled fist. The paper unfurls with my DTs like weak signals for failure in a lost language of flags.

Each time the drone dies and the line goes dead I hang up to the slack sounds of summer traffic. The black handset's held to my muddled head as warm rain taps at leaves like AM static. Unnerved, I head into the nearest bar—to self-division—scared stiff by who, in me, made this split decision.

—D.M.

LOST FACES
MINNEAPOLIS, MINN., 1994

We didn't decide to split up and run right then. We kept it together, star-crossed as hell, when we were mugged the night we met. Hits of E and beer after beer 'til we were broke then cups of water 'til the club closed. We walked the ten or twelve blocks back up to Central, to where the city stays awake. But we never made it: glinting mica sidewalks and warm fog slowed us till they yelled, ran up on us, pressed the gun near club-numbed ears. "Any temple in a storm, huh, guys?" you said, quietly to yourself, patting your pockets down in the dark. No laughter. Nothing. The four of us were without faces—less like crossed stars, more like frail black spaces.

—D.M.

LOST FACES

SEAWELL, MASS., 2002

I crossed up my steps, frail stumbles through blackened snowbanks under some streetlights and dim winter stars. KJ, the bartender, said—once he knew we met out West—"Any friend of Sweeney's a friend of mine."

We drank most of the night—after-hours lockdown in The Skeff—me haunting the ghost of you because I can't shake it all off. I can't face my shitty, haggard reflection between the shelves and bottles, so I leave.

Under a green star on Dutton Street, two kids run up and hedge me in—more nervous kids acting tough, with rags of breath rising from the pits of their hoods. Caught on the edge of the Acre, wishing I was in Winter Hill, as another gun flags my eyes down toward my temple. I hand it all over, run-through by the thought that I'd never been any kind of friend to you.

—D.M.

LOST FACES, POLICE LINE-UP*

MINNEAPOLIS, MINN., 1994

I remember thinking: "None of these faces are friendly, and none of them look familiar." The detectives dragged me out of work. They'd caught the kids with my AmEx card sleeping late in the Hilton's suite. "I never saw their faces," I said, "Too dark. Too drunk." "Just take a stab," the cop urged. "At who?" I thought, clinging to my blindness like that was some kind of high road. They called you in next. Later, over beers, you told me you ID'd them.

My heart turned like it was sick; I heard a murmuring begin. It blended with my belief that you'd pointed at any black face you could find. I hated you for doing it during the first months as we fell in love. I hated myself more because that's what I know best.

—D.M.

---

*This poem is evidence of either the early irreparable rift between us or severe memory loss caused by alcohol, because Diana knew I had better than twenty-twenty vision. To think she thought of me as a racist is too much for me to take. I studied every inch of those two black teenagers' faces out there, sobered, in the dark.

COMPLETE DARKNESS
IN THE NORTH COUNTRY, 1994

My whole childhood I hated my life, my town, but I loved knowing the black paths strung through the Northwoods' needled beds. Moon-faced, weasel-eyed, I was a bitch of a teen humming along with the mosquitoes past midnight.

I remember the weeks I watched as an East Coast city boy learned to get lost in my woods. But you stayed, that winter, to help me chop and sell nine cords of wood. I told you I had no parents, that I was woven grass, a few flowers, some salt water.

It was all drunken ragtime we talked and slurred. From our couch, the old Mercury's backseat, I could keep chanting how high just to see if you'd leap. One month you were my halfman–halfbird, the next I played the hag in our weird courtship until I lead you astray on our South American trip.

—D.M.

COMPLETE DARKNESS
ON A SPRING AFTERNOON

It didn't matter where we strayed on whatever trip, you leapt into my insane itineraries as if they were *your* flight of fancy too: Bundoran for winter surf and the Olde Bridge Bar, Vancouver Island bud-harvest work. We must've lost track of time when we got to the Andes? I don't know. You just leapt when I leapt, but then led when you felt I would follow. When I caught myself, I left. But that bar in Quito wasn't the first time, just the last. I want to describe the first for you because I can't leap any longer:

Back in the Northwoods, as you slept off a late-spring bender, I'd skulked away down an overgrown trail. I was getting out. Three miles deep, I slipped off a huge fallen Oak face-first onto the furred back of a black bear gorging on berries. We tumbled to all fours, snout-to-nose—two petrified animals weighing some new thoughts: It seemed I'd mugged myself as the bear shuffled off tilting shamed looks over its shoulder.

—D.M.

COMPLETE DARKNESS

ON THE NORTH COAST, 2003

But when I look back now, it's clear that *I'm* some kind of gutless, blind hunter-gatherer who's finished with your heart. I'd finally bled us dry, without ceremony, in that Quito bar, *Encuentro*. And I flew out of Ecuador wishing my plane would get smashed to bits on the side of a mountain, obsessing on our final night on the beach in Canoa. We'd split up to gather driftwood, then back at the fire, I never spoke because I couldn't find the words for the silhouette of the cat running across the low-tide sand—a jaguar down from the jungle hunting sleeping sea birds. Its power and speed turned the wide beach into a no-man's land: I knew it could kill us no matter what we did. Instead, I saw it bolt south with an onslaught of speed and a small feathered heart in its mouth.

—D.M.

TWO UNSENT LETTERS
2002

Dear S O'S, I took the express up to Seawell during an onslaught of regret—I knew you weren't there. I got drunk and some bartender you know gave me your p.o. box, but said you never check it. I already wrote about this—getting mugged when I left The Skeff—and it makes no sense for me to write you now since my last letter was returned anyway. I'll toss this thing with my unfinished poems and start wondering where you are: King's Island? Canoa? Hokkaido? Thurso? I wonder why I care.

Hey S O'S, it's been six weeks since my last returned letter. Since then, I realized my life's a dead letter any way you read it. So I'll finish this one and mail the eleven sonnets written here in "Rochestah," as you'd say. They've put me in the Mayo Clinic—I'm manic and puking a bit of bile each day, but "any temple in a storm" right? I'm almost dried out but swollen—a husky paper tiger milling around a shabby diorama.

Love, D. Marpessa

P.M. SONNET, BEFORE THE WINTER SOLSTICE
CORREB RIVER, SEAWELL, MASS.

The snowflecked river swells by the husk of a mill that stands condemned. Buoyed by the blue weight of dusk, an owl's wide eyes peer from a sill of granite. Snowflakes swarm around the defunct mouths of smokestacks. Behind her swiveled glare she hesitates, searches the naked web of limbs for the perch that will support her stare. The light obstructs her hunt, but the sky's gray ebb tugs her from this roost toward bare trees spliced with cold. Her talons rain, like a clutch of blades, on this longest night woven from absence; the night that's crossed with a woof of shortest days, tread by hushed wingspread. Nightly, she descends wind-rungs and raids the frailest trails strung like lace through filigrees of frost.

—Sweeney O'Sweeney
2003

A.M. SONNET, AFTER THE WINTER SOLSTICE
Downtown Seawell, Mass.

Crows drift and thread wind-cuffed trails through the sky; they call above a falcon as it roosts. Spooked by the bird, the crows plummet through rye-colored light draining dark from the icicles hemming slate eaves. The fire station's bell tower sits damped beneath the bird, who scours but stalls while the warp of night abates. Ads for "Tooth Powder" and "Phoenix Beverage" lie painted on walls built of red brick—unveiled, archaic spiels lit by the rising sun and bleaching toward gray absence. Later, near the cold day's blunt peak on a field of paint that flakes and peels, midday drafts heft the shadow of the bird—his instincts kindle, flare, as he rises to hunt.

—Sweeney O'Sweeney
2003

ONE EVENING ANCHORED IN BAJA

The ruby planet's face will rise and flare above the fingering, stubbled headland that gestures to the south—a reddened hand reaching for, holding the Pacific's darkened stare.

Afloat, we'll gawk at the spilled luminaries of the bright Milky Way that spin and pull away—despite our stares—like the red jewel of Mars, trawling its luster on the seas.

For now, lie back in the yaw of this rose evening, lean with the boat's sway; lie down with closed eyes as the tide climbs to the moon's fluent clock. I'll slowly lick salt from your tanned chest, leaning close to the rush of your heightened, sharp sighs commingled with waves mouthing reef and rock.

—Sweeney O'Sweeney
1999

ME AND MY OFF-WHITE WITCH

She was my kinked anthem. Diana walked like gentled poison—drunk, pretty and wilting under the spell of ruined hearts on her sleeve. I'd seen her cry once, beaten by a braid of radio static and the tropical heat's drone, stuck in traffic, late for our train. And now this one letter she's sent shakes out her life:

As if speaking quietly to herself, she pats down eleven pockets to find the burden. I drank, snorted and popped just like her; she forgets we prayed in haunted temples together—slept days, fled bar tabs and hotel bills, high on our murmuring blindness. But I was happy to go astray as the halfman-halfbird in her leaping-hag refrain.

Then she slipped away, knowingly mugged herself again in the Andes. I'd wished her plane crashed in that leap, that she was smashed gutless by her mute regrets. But there's no sense in breeding paper tigers from bile. I'd already faked I was manic, flew to a roost to watch her weave a life from absence spliced with the colder solstice. Drifting, I stalled so her darker instincts might drain. She was my poet of ashen thoughts, my luminary leaning on our luster but pulling away beneath the moon's fluent clock.

—Sweeney O'Sweeney
2003

18

MIDDLEAGED MALE PLAYING KENO AT THE BAR

A.K.A. PHILOSOPHER–COKEHEAD

"I got a system" he says to whoever
sits next to him. "I figured this out
and I got this system but it ain't
workin' 'cause it feels like there's static
running through my legs—my bare
toes are twitching in my socks,
like there's snow from the TV
filling my feet, filling my two direct
connections to the Earth.
I bet-ya the best,
like those guys Hank Aaron and Orr,
felt all five toes on each
foot like they were individual
prongs plugged into the unknown moves
of the universe. I bet-ya
the best know the way
through the dark.
Ya know what I'm sayin'?"
Clearly, no one knows
what he's saying. But
whenever he's not in the bathroom,
whenever someone sits next
to him he says,
"I got this system because

I figure the bookmakers are busy
runnin' numbers through everythin'.
And what is this thing
here at the bar between
you me and all these beers?
It's just a complicated, invisible pile of
smells, thoughts, everyday tragedies
and the wagers we think
might give us another handful
of minutes in the rain
on the sidewalk just outside
the bookmakers' open door.
Ya know, when I was over ta' England
in '87 it always looked like a New
Year's party just went by outside
the bookies' place with castoff tickets
like tickertape
dandruff left to blow away.
That's the largest organ in our system ya know.
They tell me the skin's the largest organ
in my can't-take-it-with-you
parade-float of a body.
S'cuse me I gotta piss
like a racehorse."

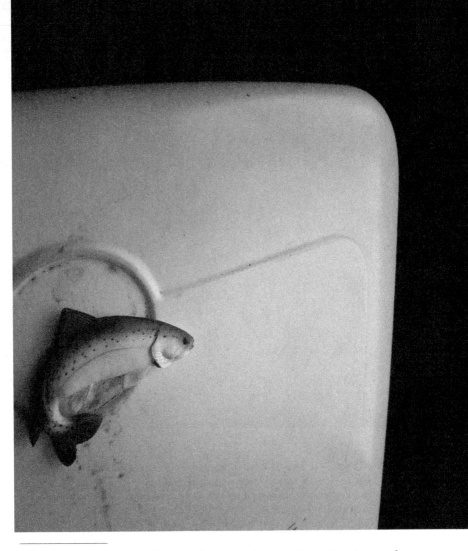

Sweeney befriended many of the high school kids who regularly drank in the out-of-bounds area of Farannan Golf Course (since Sweeney and friends once did most of their underage drinking in that same forest). One of the newer generation of young drinkers was taking a photo class at Seawell High and asked if he could take some photos of Sweeney's drydocked boat, the Kemp Aaberg. The above photo captures the antique contraption known as "The Icebox," which was actually a busted '50s refrigerator that Sweeney kept padlocked on the uppermost, tiny, observation deck of his boat. Most of the year, New England was cold enough to keep the contents inside fresh (mainly cheap cans of Mexican beer and pony kegs of Canadian lager). During the summer months, Sweeney and his friends stocked The Icebox with block ice to keep provisions at proper temps. Most guests were required to bring either beer or block ice to be allowed to come aboard the Aaberg. All guests universally and loudly complained of having to haul their gifts across the golf course, into the woods and up three ladders to the uppermost deck.

This photo is the only interior detail of the Aaberg that exists. Sweeney and Mickey "Goatboy" Obregon pulled the engine from the trawler before moving it to the out-of-bounds forest at Farannan, and once the boat settled beneath the trees they soon installed this Fisher woodstove above the gutted engine hold. As the story goes, Sweeney accepted the stove as payment from two middleaged French Canadian junkyard owners in the Pentucketville neighborhood. After a few hundred hands of 45s (Seawell's official card game) Mr. Gagne and Mr. Archembeault, of Guy & Tiny's Pentucketville Salvage Emporium, badgered Sweeney into calling it even if they delivered the Fisher stove to the hole-six tee box at Farannan. With a simple design— long and narrow, with a convenient cooking feature that involved a stepped top panel—the Fisher warmed several Aaberg winters while helping to produce some quality stews and supposed hangover cures during the years Sweeney lived in his boat on stilts in those woods.

Photos: Anthony Ferreira, from "In Maple Tree Sugar, Details from Life Near the Northern Kingdom"

19

AUTODIDACTS IN ADIRONDACKS

"It was one of those years when the ravens flew down from the Northern Kingdom's frozen pine forests. I always believed that DDT's destruction of hawk and eagle eggs gave those black geniuses their widest range through Seawell. It's ravens and northern fur seals that claimed Seawell and the Merrohawke's mouth as the southern limit of their winter migrations. They never seem to visit us during the cold months anymore."

Michael O'Dowd says this, or some version of this, to me every time I bump into him. He says it after his famous, friendly greeting "Hey, Sweeney, how you been? You stayin' outta trouble?" I say hello, of course, but I would never speak of trouble and whether I'm in it or not. I know he doesn't give-a-care because so many winters ago Mike gave me the keys to his, to Seawell's, Kingdom of Seals and Ravens (so to speak). He talks of symbols and northern forests to goad me into telling him of waves I've found. He also hopes to remind me of the day he helped me become my own man in the frozen wake of my parent's migration. If there was one old-school surfer—one of the original Seawell locals—I revered as wise, it was Mike O'Dowd. He surfed because the need to surf bored through him so strong you could see it in his movements through his moments on land. But especially in the ocean that chews apart the beaches and rock reefs of New England, you could sense O'Dowd felt at home.

Deep winter surf sessions result in a kind of suspended span of time; and you can forget Seawell and the seasons because they've spun and tilted away once a wall of half-frozen water's about to flood your hooded wetsuit, boots and gloves with hellishly cold liquid.

And the day O'Dowd speaks of when we meet…the sea smoke appeared at six a.m. My wetsuit was frozen stiff, and slicked with paper-thin ice on the clothes' line—shaped like a shining black bird folding a wing above a carcass. I recall working some lines from one of my poems over in my mouth. I shivered in my heavy coat: "The dead thing's summer or the sun and all things green and blooming." I'd been stuck on the poem for weeks and I was betting on a surf in the cold ocean to help me move through my stumbles and wasted efforts—some days I just need to get wet. Yet it's impossible to know the full effect of the North Atlantic on the Seawell portions of my life—I mean fully, with my head and heart—it's impossible to fathom the depth of the shaping that that half-frozen wilderness has had on me. But Mike helped me to learn we're honed by tides, wind, waves, sandbars and rips.

It's been said that we modern kids never know the moment we become women and men. Well, maybe girls feel the tides of their hormones pushing them to womanhood, but most boys drift between boyhood and the rank of man-child, never drawing up to adulthood. The prison they'd put me in had space for the sphere-less, for the kids without province, and so many of my friends. They're tucked away at a young age—blacks, hispanics, Southeast Asians and some white man-kids—in out-of-sight holding-pens. Stuck in their violent, hopeless dual existences—physically developed but absent of any of the emotional, spiritual or intellectual maturity that flowers in kids made aware of their spheres as adults. But my North Atlantic pulled me into the next phase of my life while it moved in its own fields under the moons, low pressure, storm fronts and its steady calling to me through all seasons. And O'Dowd ritualized it for me, in a way, on that day in the '80s, before I went to prison, still mired behind the passage of my parents.

If you think back to the story Brian Mello tells in the prologue—the one about the night he found me alone in my empty house, asleep on the only ratty couch the movers left me—well, what I describe *here* happened a few months later in February after a high school basketball tournament. It was the same sort of night of drinking and screwing around that Mello details, but Seawell was banked deep and soft, snowed-in to the gills. The difference, for me, was I thought that the waves would be epic the next day. None of my friends from school surfed in the winter.

They were all summertime surfers and only a few could surf at all. I'd given up trying to get them to buy wetsuits when I was younger. That winter I had just moved to the Kemp Aaberg—the dry-docked boat I bought from Gerry the Russian. I sometimes still slept at my old house on that ratty couch because it was still for sale and the realtor was a distant cousin who didn't care if I slept there now and again. I hadn't told a lot of my friends about my boat in the trees. I was just a kid stuck in some shifts and changes; and that night of drinking sticks in my memory because it was one of the first times I revealed that I lived in a boat alone out in the woods on the golf course.

Back then, we'd sometimes scrounge beer and play wiffle ball, "Winter Rules"—that's what we called it because we'd wait for the windiest nights, throw four or six black strips of electrical tape around a wiffle ball and try to play some innings on Farannan's third fairway (not too far from my old and new houses, or boat or whatever). Pitching a wiffle ball during a nor'easter is just stupid, if not impossible. So trying to hit a ball in howling winter wind and snow is even more ridiculous. But we had beer, and running around like a pack of idiots in a foot of wet snow was the real goal. Winter Rules wiffle ball's more like cricket, I guess, since we'd surround the batter and pitcher and play that any contact would count—foul tips were singles, solid foul balls in any direction were doubles while line drives and fly balls that weren't caught in the air were triples and anything over the fielders' heads was a homerun. Each batter gets three pitches and everyone takes a pull on their beer for each new batter, each hit and each swing-and-miss. Only the worst trash-talking about mothers and ex-girlfriends is allowed, but no one can hear shit anyway because we played in the middle of high winds and snowstorms. The final rule we made to keep the game moving and to keep all the drunken fielders involved is if two different fielders catch two pitches in a row, pitches that sailed wildly away from the batter in the gale, then the batter is out and the person who catches the second wild pitch bats next. It's a ridiculous game, as I said; and most likely, drunk teens from Seawell are the sole animals capable of playing it (habitually...

to the point of starting leagues). In the summer, Seawell hosts the City Golf Tourney; in the winter, Seawell teens get drunk and compete in the Winter Rules Tournament, open to the public (i.e., all under-aged drinkers). Lowland, Sun Valley and Pentucketville kids would all field co-ed teams versed in the sport and its odd winter mutations. Games were played on all three courses any weekend night with winds over twenty knots or a snowstorm that's predicted to drop eight inches or more on the Seawell region. I recall this night of Winter Rules because it was the first time we used an orange wiffle ball (with strips of electrical tape) as the game ball and it made a huge difference in the quality of drunken play. Seriously, it did. We could track a pitched-ball or hit-ball so much better. Oh, and it was the first time I played Winter Rules sober since that nor'easter was pushing in some decent swell for the next day. I had a couple beers, but I didn't drink much so I could be up at six a.m. to catch Seawell's sandbars at the right tide with some good wind (hopefully) and no other surfers in sight.

The next day I woke at five to handcrank my old weather radio for the buoy readings (this was years before the internet reports and cams we have now). The buoys off Portland, Maine, and Boston told me it was big—a couple feet overhead and the wind was northwest, which is pretty ideal for Seawell Beach. Low tide was at nine-oh-nine. All looked good, except that it was mid-winter and the air was eighteen with the water temp. hovering around thirty-six—menacing, to say the least.

"The dead things these cold days are summer, sun and all things green and blooming" chimed in my head as I found my stiff wetsuit on the rope I'd strung between two pines above the bow of my boat in the woods. I cursed myself for not bringing my suit in by the woodstove the night before, but it was going to be six-to-eight foot with no one out, so I shook the suit briskly and it made sounds like heavy wet wings as the ice cracked, flew on the wood stove, hissed, evaporated fast. My mind began to race with liquid visions of barrels and floaters across the tops of waves bending down a sandbar I'd surfed by myself all autumn and winter.

My suit wasn't warming up much, but I threw it on and pulled my boots and gloves on as fast as I could. It was later, around seven-thirty, just past first light at that time of year. Minus tides, spring tides as they're called, help groom Seawell's groundswells over five feet so I just felt if the wind would hold and stay out of the northwest I was going to be a contented kid in a candy store, without a doubt.

All suited up, I jumped off the Kemp Aaberg's stern. Three feet of new snowdrift swallowed me up to my waist. I lifted my six-foot-three Bonzer, that Mike O'Dowd shaped for me that fall, tucked it under my black wetsuited arm and ran through the Rey Oaks onto the rough of the sixth hole of the course. I traced the edge of the woods laced, every branching inch, with powdery snow. I had a path I liked to thread— along the back corner of the course and the out-of-bounds stakes—it was a tendency I'd developed from watching too many documentaries about foxes, lynxes and other predators of the northern woods. I picked up my pace to warm up my legs, and I rose over and through a thicket of dune rose, then dipped quickly into a brown and yellow copse of Poplar and Blackthorn saplings with their dead leaves scratching and rattling as my surfboard's fins, tail and leash brushed against tips of sheltered twigs. I eyed the open ground of the snowed-in course under weak morning light. Little glints flashed from the snow-warped lips of the sand-traps and the northwest wind began playing at the top of the canopy. The false storm fell, padded down, fleecing the fiercely blue sky with drifts and clouds of shining snowdust. As I crossed the seventh green, stopping at its high point to get my first peek at the waves, wind and progress of the ebb tide, I could see two others checking the same sandbar I planned on surfing. If I hadn't recognized the van, I would've melted back into the trees, until they decided to surf somewhere else. Back then, the few surfers that knew enough to check Seawell Beach didn't know the tides that well—how they worked across its changing sandbars—I always tried to paddle out while no one was checking my spots, hoping I'd get to surf all alone. Beachbreak, cold-water winter surf is not inviting to the masses because you punch through walls of freezing water, eight-feet high, thick, roiling and ceaseless to even make it out to the peak—before you even catch a wave. Most guys—during fall, winter and spring—would go out up at the points to the north where you can paddle around the incoming sets and trains of white-water. Though, back then, there weren't nearly as many surfers in New England so guys would look for friends and other surfers to paddle out with—me, I always want to surf alone the way Edward Abbey preferred to walk in the woods. I'll still take a flushing of wintertime Atlantic down my wetsuit and the white noise of huge surf over small talk and idle gossip. I'll surf alone through all the seasons, but winter's best. It's getting cleaned-up, rolled, humbled by sets of indifferent waves pushing me around like a speck of numb dust.

On this morning, though, Mike O'Dowd and Ray Johnson must've seen me on the crest of the green before I slipped back in the trees toward the dunes to jog the quarter mile down the beach to my sandbar. The two of them had hidden behind a dune, backed the van out of sight and popped up when I got closer. They both waved me up the beach to them, now waiting by O'Dowd's van. They were laughing at me a bit. I'd known these guys a while. I mean, O'Dowd had shaped the board I had under my arm. And they knew Seawell's waves better than anyone. And they knew my habits: "Hey Sweeney," Mike grinned, "you stayin' outta trouble?"

Again he flashed his tooth-deficient hockey grin. He'd lost a few teeth playing for a junior team in Quebec. "Tryin'," I answered, "But you guys know me; It won't be long now."

I pulled on my hood to let them know I wanted to get in the water right then. Ray, instead, gave me a decent shot to the gut and laughed. So I dropped my board in the snow and dunegrass tufts, tried to take a breath and dropped him with a hard tackle at the knees. We'd just started to wrestle when Mike boxed us, in turn, right on the ears.

Stung, we paused, looked up at him: "C'mon, you fuckin' goons. Knock that bullshit off and let's smoke that joint. This sandbar ain't gonna start workin' for forty-five minutes. We got some time." O'Dowd was still quick and strong as an ox from his hockey days, roofing and surfing. He was always exhausting himself with work, it seemed, saying, "If you know how to work hard, you're a good man—that's all I know." Then he'd laugh his sarcastic laugh, and I'd always grown up believing that old-school Seawellian notion. Until this day I'm describing, anyway. It's the old New England Yankee-Puritan dourness surviving to this day; and it's all most people care to know in Seawell. These Puritan guys were the same prudes that almost killed surfing when they sailed to Hawaii to convert the locals and deem their culture "savage and sinful." Thank Allah they failed and people like Jack London and Duke Kahanamoku saved, spread and revived surfing and the waterman culture.

These concepts and histories were the first items we discussed while passing around the joint of Puerto Rican kine bud they had smuggled back from their trip to surf Rincon and Gas Chambers the previous week. Both Ray and Mike always took winter trips to Costa Rica, Puerto Rico and Mexico: "Gotta surf in just trunks at least once each winter," Ray chirped about every time I'd bump into him at the bars or at a football game. I used to meet these guys after each trip to check out their photos and hear their stories. When I first started surfing, Pat Kivlin introduced me to them. They're hardcore East Coast surfers and I owe much of my knowledge of surfing to Pat, Ray and especially O'Dowd.

"Mike O'Dowd, the Toothless Tom Curren! Hey, Mike, did all your style disappear with your teeth?" I'd yell at him after he'd get a really solid wave. O'Dowd knew I could fight, so he let me get away with giving him some carefully timed shit—when I knew he was mellowed out or just about to go to the islands or something. But when I say he "knew I could fight," I don't mean there was a chance in hell I could take him. O'Dowd was Seawell's most vicious and feared brawler. He got more fuckin' dangerous the more pain he was in. Quebec Juniors had beat the fear of pain clear out of his head. He was, in a word, *deranged*—when he decided it was time to fight. Back then, as it's been written, I brawled. Back then, O'Dowd...he was in his own class and he was forty-five years old. No one anywhere remotely near Seawell that liked to scrap would even look his way. You bought O'Dowd a beer and steered clear of his mile-wide mean streak. But after coming out of a tube, when I'd see him grinning to himself, I'd yell my timed "Toothless Tom Curren" crack and he'd just reply with a raised middle finger.

And now inside this madman's powder-coat black van was a mini surf shop with bits of sandpaper and ragged corners of fiberglass cloth strewn on the floor, his custom-built shelves, seats and dash. The back had a space heater for which he'd hijack juice through three or four extension cords (on the shelves) connected and strung through bushes and trees along the side of some stranger's yard and into their outlet on the side of their home. O'Dowd had a house in the Lowlands but he rarely slept in his bed if there were waves. He'd drive to the Outer Banks for a hurricane swell, surf all day, nap away rush hour and drive north through the night to, say, New Jersey to surf the same hurricane swell the next day. And he'd done this so many times, it was laughable—all the way up through our breaks, New Hampshire, Maine to Nova Scotia (where he'd stay with his relatives for a month or more). O'Dowd was a legendary bruiser, shaper and junior hockey player from the Seawell bars down to Hatteras and back to Cow Bay. You can tell I revere the guy. And as we sat in the Adirondack chairs in the back of his van it occurred to me that he wasn't even that good of a surfer! I mean, he pulled the odd dry barrel and roundhouse cutback but, really, here was a guy who slept in his van two-hundred nights a year, roofed for his travel money, shaped his own boards (and he was a much better board-maker than surfer) and got wet all winter long in the North Atlantic, Caribbean and Pacific. He was and still is as committed a surfer as any pro or warm-water-raised surfer. In all my travels, no one's come close to his unadulterated love for the ocean, waves and the act of riding them on his feet, stomach, while injured, ill, in any weather with or without friends and with or without a board of any kind.

Now, I was stoned to the bejeezus as this all occurred to me. So I pulled out of my daze and knew not to reveal my revelation—that being the best at something doesn't mean shit if you don't care about what you're doing, right? And this was half of my rite of passage that snowy spring-tide day. O'Dowd told me to get in his van *because* he'd never asked me to before. But he'd known I'd get what he was telling me without saying a word.

O'Dowd, and Ray for that matter, smoked me up then sent me out alone to surf my sandbar. They laughed, "Ga'head, Sweeney, it's all yours since you were trying to hide in the trees to get it to yourself anyways. We'll burn this twin joint of kine and watch. This is your one free pass." As I said, I was baked. I was power-baked and reeling from my recent epiphany in the fold-out Adirondack, but the fact that these original locals were just gonna let me surf eight-foot, offshore, low-tide perfection by myself was mind-blowing! I was tongue-tied as I climbed out the back of the van. I snapped out of it, brought to my senses by the frigid air.

I threw my leash on my ankle, looked for a rip to help pull me out the back when the next lull between sets arrived. In the two or three minutes I stood in the snow on the frozen sand, before running across the low-tide flats to paddle out, I accused those guys of many crimes and misdemeanors. *Had they seen a shark?* No way...too cold for sharks. *Did they know a better spot and would take off only to give me shit next time we saw each other?* Probably. *Was the wind supposed to switch and blow apart these perfect waves?* I didn't think so, but there was no way to be sure. *Maybe they had fucked with my leash, wetsuit or board while I was flipped out on that kine bud?* Wait, that must be it! *They laced the weed...but they'd puffed the same as me, I think. That must be it, I'm so fucked...but I can hold my weed...*though that was the end of my brief, violent bout of paranoia because I saw the lull I'd been waiting for. I ran down the beach and punched under the third wave of a four-wave set, did one more duckdive, was blitzed by the fucking frozen water and made it out with the rip to the peak I'd been watching.

Then, it began. I knew the drill, instantly, because I was sucked by a horrendous current pulling me from north to south at an impossible clip! A horn honked over and over, carried on the offshore breeze like cold, bloodless laughter. I laughed hard myself, because it was going to take all my prowess and strength as a young, stoned-about-the-gills surfer to even stay in position long enough to catch the meager quota of waves necessary to justify paddling out on that winter morning. But Mike and Ray, I have to give them credit, stayed around to see if I'd get up-current again. They wanted blood, maybe, but I was determined to catch at least one decent wave—a barrel, huge floater or turn that would tide me over till the next surf session.

Those bastards sat there and honked at every set that rolled in and right by my windmilling, exhausted, frozen self. Although, around ninety-or-so minutes into the test, after three or four over-the-falls and suit-flushing, bone chilling wipeouts (more honks endured) I managed my only real ride of the ritualized and watched session. I lobster-clawed and scratched into position to backdoor the last wave of a seven-wave set. As I caught and popped to my feet I set my inside rail at takeoff. Halfway down my eight-foot wall of green, groomed water I heard nothing, no honks. I gave a half-pump of the rail to gain a bit more speed because ahead of me the wave already heaved and warped as it hit our sandbar with a gorgeous silent harmonic pitch. It hollowed and walled for at least twenty yards. In an instant I was encased in a rolling barrel of liquid, my head was emptied of thought and I only saw sunlight down the line as the water spun around me, gurgled under and behind me. Briefly, I felt my self rising with the wave's face, rising against gravity with no drop of water out of place around me. My empty body felt in tune with something. But five or six seconds in that tube were warped, stretched thin and then bloomed in my mind, in concert with all my meager senses until I was slung at the light as if pitched on wet wind that lifted, pushed and then dropped me back into wintertime. Out of the shade, back to weak sun, I turned off the shoulder of my one real wave. I remained standing on my board until it came to a sluggish stop, sinking beneath my tangible joy. No honks, silence, just nothing—as I submerged to waist-deep...chest-deep in the icy North Atlantic. I reached for the rails of my board and let it rise to meet me as I lay back down to float, turn and be swallowed by the next shove of white-water. I hurtled toward the beach, and bellied to shin-deep, walked up to the van. O'Dowd rolled down his window. Ray just shook his head at me as O'Dowd barked, "Finally someone who knows how to fuckin' operate the boards I make. Your balls have dropped, kid. Nice wave. Now stay outta trouble; because before enlightenment there's roofing houses and paying your damn taxes, after enlightenment...there's roofing and taxes."

The two of them took off—no doubt to surf some secret spot that turns on when the tide is on the rise. I walked back to the Kemp Aaberg not knowing where I was, but smiling the smile of the green monk in fresh, frozen robes.

THE END.

APPENDIX A

Owen,

As I mail you this manuscript, my response to your book *Sweeney on-the-Fringe*, I'm imagining that most readers, especially those in Seawell who knew me, might've said something like the following if they ran into you in McSwiggan's or The Skeff:

> *Hey, Owen, good to see you! I read your book. Congratulations! No, seriously, good for you. There's some good stories in there. I really like the stories. You got Sweeney down just right, seriously. I loved it. I mean, I don't read much poetry so that was, you know, kinda not my speed. But the whole thing was great, man. You writin' another? What's your next book about?*

So, this thing I'm mailing you from my South American outpost is basically a book of poems I've disguised as paragraphs and prose. This way, you see, I get to do what I love and also mess with all the people I grew up with who made fun of me for reading and writing so much poetry. It was all in good fun, I know. They were just teasing, but it always made me feel a bit insane to love something that so many people, even artists, claimed was dead.

Please, if you get a chance, publish this disguised version of my poems—the prose version of *Sweeney At-Sea*.

Thanks, my friend,
Yardbird

SWEENEY'S NOTES
ON THE FORMS OF HIS POEMS
COMPILED BY DAVE ROBINSON FROM SWEENEY & OWEN KIVLIN'S LETTERS

"PAGAN'SONG" is unrhymed iambic tetrameter.

"RUNNING FROM COPS" is blank verse.

"PEOPLE OF SEAWELL" is a mixed bag. Within that grouping of poems I used a few forms:

> "SEAWELL'S SUMMER OF THE BELT, 1931" and "ICE-PICK LOBOTOMY" are Rhyme Royal poems loosely based on my paternal grandfather's life.
>
> "ASPECTS OF CRICK, 1997" is also about my paternal grandfather's final few days, but it's blank verse couplets.
>
> "FAILED RITE OF PASSAGE AT SEA-LEVEL" is free verse.
>
> "19-HR. DAY" is blank verse.
>
> "35-YEAR-OLD WORKING AT LEO'S PIZZA" is free verse.
>
> "THE VETERAN LOBSTERMAN" is blank verse. Richie Gouveia used to get smashed with me and we'd try to tell stories and jokes in unrhymed, iambic pentameter. Sauced Frost vs. Soaked Shakespeare, but only in the Madeira Social Club on Back Central Street where no one would bug us. He was pretty good at it, actually. Better than me, no doubt, but never wrote any of it down I don't think.

"BEAUTIFUL NUISANCE" is blank verse because that's
how old Irish ladies sometimes sound in Seawell when
they're not yelling at you for everything under the sun.

"THY VS. TAYO, THE UNDER CARD," like ninety percent
of it is in trochaic tetrameter—until a section near the
end, where I flip it to blank verse.

"PEOPLE OF SEAWELL'S SISTER CITY, THE SEVEN DREAMS OF PANCHO &
RAMÓN" is *terza rima*.

"PEOPLE OF SEAWELL'S SISTER CITY, PART II, PANCHO & RAMÓN'S
ENDLESS MEMORIES OF THE HERE-AND-NOW" is also *terza rima*.

"CUFFED HAIKUS & CHAINED TANKAS" are as advertised, except different. I
mean, they're written to be the opposite of normal haikus and tankas in
that they present moments that are void of traditional, pastoral, Buddhist
epiphanies of emptiness or true nature. They're more like nontraditional,
urban, western litanies of the everyday ego. They're stretched out a bit
more than Japanese haikus and tankas, too. Distantly related, really, in their
opposition. "Same difference," as Seawellians are apt to say. Or maybe
they're not alike enough to be opposites or something like that. Same
difference, yeah, whatever. Nevermind.

"TRAVELS THROUGH THE DARK, IN THREE PARTS" is another mixed bag
of poems:

> "PART I: LETTER FROM A RUINED DESERT": is in syllabics
> for the California narrative and the Paris letter is syllabics,
> too (nine & seven syllables per line, respectively).

> "PART II: THE LONG HAUL": Don't have it in front of me,
> but I think that one was pretty much syllabics.

"PART III: THE DIVINERS": starts out in syllabics for a couple lines, mixes in some longer accentual lines and goes back and forth between the two until the last section of stepped lines. In the final section, I mix and link the lines with accentual and syllabic features.

"THE DEAD-LETTER CROWN": Mostly Italian sonnets, some holding tighter and truer to the form than others. There might be a couple English sonnets in there. I forget. I don't think I can fuckin' read those things again, to be honest. I know they all have a "turn"—one of the main things that make sonnets endlessly interesting. Diana and I differed in our preferences for rhyme, meter and formal or informal poetry but we drunkenly and repeatedly agreed on that point. We both loved to set up conflicts and problems and try to work the words through the turn toward some kind of new direction or resolution. We were pretty good at it on paper, just not so good at it in our relationship.

"MIDDLEAGED MALE PLAYING KENO AT THE BAR, A.K.A PHILOSOPHER COKEHEAD" is free verse with a touch of syllabics to keep it honest.

"AUTODIDACTS IN ADIRONDACKS": And in the final race, it'll be blank verse to win, place and show. Put the rent money on that trifecta.

CARDINAL'S OFFICE
66 BANKS DRIVE
BOSTON, MASSACHUSETTS

MR. SWEENEY O'SWEENEY
C/O MR. PATRICK KIVLIN
415 MORNINGSIDE DRIVE
SEAWELL, MASS.

Dear Mr. Sweeney,

On behalf of the Cardinal's Office here in Boston, I am responding to your correspondence sent two months ago, within which you request excommunication and express that you have decided to forsake your faith in Catholicism in favor of a naturalist spirituality. Although we are saddened to learn that you find the Catholic faith to be so unaccommodating and lamentable, we will certainly respect your decision.

It may be comforting to know that your baptism, first eucharist and confirmation are irrevocable as they are sacraments that impart a permanent grace and spiritual character. If you wish, you may ask the parish or church where the sacraments were dispensed, and thus memorialized, to annotate the records in regards to your abandoning of the Catholic faith.

We hope that this letter will be of help to you, and will pray for you as a fellow member of the human family.

Sincerely yours in Christ,

Reverend Victor J. Langher
Secretary to the Cardinal

Detail from "View of Seawell" by Eric Jones, 1850
(See page 221 for more on Jones' work & biography.)

This is a corner-section detail of an expansive drawing by Eric Jones, formerly Erich Schumann of the Black Forest Travelers of Germany. Jones almost always depicted artists in the act of creation within his works. He believed a day would come when "Seawell shall be colonized and dominated by poets, painters, musicians and sculptors. It shall be an age of enlightened politicks [sic] and cultural extravagance to make New York High-Society Circles covetous of our Northern Kingdom by the Sea."

Detail courtesy of the Ferris Parker Estate

BOOK III

SWEENEY AT-SEA

A FAILED SCREENPLAY

WRITTEN BY DAVE ROBINSON &
OWEN KIVLIN

EDITOR'S NOTE

What follows is a working draft of a screenplay based on the first two books about Sweeney O'Sweeney. Ellen McCann & Dana Shirley were the two chief creative forces behind the project, serving as director and executive producer respectively. The following screenplay is NOT the final edited version they were using to film. That version is nowhere to be found. Dana Shirley insists Sweeney himself stole the hard drive that contained the final draft during his final day on set as a Creative Consultant. It's also possible Ms. McCann destroyed the only copies of the final screenplay. No one knows for sure, but Sweeney was rumored to say the inconsistencies and inaccuracies of this script were getting to be too much for him to stomach.

In any case, the project ultimately failed. A couple of the surfing scenes were filmed during the first week of production. Bootleg footage of the pro-surfer stunt doubles appears and disappears every few years.

As the reader will see, at various intervals this script is interrupted by the story of Director Ellen McCann's battle with mental illness. Even if Ms. McCann had won her battle there were rumors the film was doomed from the start.

ACT I

INT. - LOWER HOLD OF WARSHIP - THE EVE OF D-DAY, 1945

PETTY OFFICER HARRIS "HARRY" O'SWEENEY a black-
Irish,ruggedly handsome 24-year-old paws at a large
maroon hardcover - the ONLY book in PETTY OFFICER DANNY
WILLIAMS' kit.

P.O. WILLIAMS is a rail-thin, bookish, nervous kid. He
looks no older than 16.

> P.O. O'SWEENEY
> Willayyy! You can bring one book onto
> this deathtrap of a boat and you
> take this giant "Collected Works of
> Bakunin"? What's wrong with you, kid?
> Nothin'?

> P.O. WILLIAMS
> What's wrong…nothing, yes, well, it's
> part of a series of 24, a subscription.
> I own about fourteen books like that
> and ten more are to be sent to my
> house, already paid for.

> P.O. O'SWEENEY
> Hmm, you're a strange bird, Willy.
> Just like I thought.

> P.O. WILLIAMS
> Just like you thought…?

Interrupting. Handing back the book with care.

> P.O. O'SWEENEY
> "Williams," what is that name, Welsh?

> P.O. WILLIAMS
> (meekly)
> Umm, it's actually Engl...

> P.O. O'SWEENEY
> (not listening)
> The Welsh, I got some Celtic Welsh in
> me. My mother's father's side. Lookit,
> I know for a fact that the Welsh play
> cards. The Welsh are good for the
> cards, Willy. You wanta play some
> poker? The guys are gettin' a big game
> goin' in like ten minutes. You must be
> dyin' to play some 5-Card-Stud.

> P.O. WILLIAMS
> Umm, I don't have much money…

> P.O. O'SWEENEY
> …Oh boy, here we go with the routine.
> Reelin' me right in. You don't mess
> around, do you? Lookit, Willy, I'm not
> a 5-Card-Stud kind of guy. 45s is my
> game, so save the routine for someone
> who has a chance, huh? C'mon, if you're
> unlucky and you get up against it Ican
> back you. You can write me an I.O.U.,
> pay me later. Let's go.

SMASH CUT TO:

INT.-LOWER HOLD OF WARSHIP-CARD TABLE-SAME

P.O. O'SWEENEY looks calmly across a HUGE PILE of
toothpicks at the only man still sitting at the table.

P.O. WILLIAMS SWEATS visibly.

P.O. Williams pushes the rest of his toothpicks into the
pot.

> P.O. WILLIAMS
> (quietly)
>
> Call.

The surrounding soldiers catcall and laugh, some wince
and shake their heads.

P.O. O'Sweeney raises his eyes from his cards and
SHEEPISHLY shows his hand: Queens over sevens, a FULL
HOUSE.

There follows incredulous laughter and happy curses from
these BABYFACED boys.

Sweeney STEALS a PAINED look at so many young faces
staring out of the smoky darkness.

P.O. Williams seems oddly RELIEVED.

He shows his 3 KINGS.

> P.O. WILLIAMS (CONT'D)
>
> I can't pay. Wait, did I beat you? No,
> that's a full house. You win but, like
> I said, I can't pay.

No one listens but Sweeney, the men laugh and swear at
the outcome.

> P.O. O'SWEENEY
>
> I know.

> P.O. WILLIAMS
>
> I want to. I just don't have it.

P.O. O'Sweeney calmly nods, stands and slips effortlessly
through the crowd into the darkness.

INT. LOWER HOLD-P.O. O'SWEENEY'S BUNK-SAME

There are empty canvas hammocks, swinging
hypnotically,everywhere.

O'Sweeney glides in stride onto his back in his hammock.

P.O. Williams STUMBLES after him, trailed by a group of men.

P.O. O'Sweeney has a satisfied, almost paternal air about
him as he lights a cigarette.

> P.O. O'SWEENEY
> Willy, you look like death warmed over.
> We'll talk, kid. Don't worry yourself
> sick over it.

P.O. Williams is visibly GRATEFUL.

> P.O. O'SWEENEY (CONT'D)
> We get one more hand dealt to us in the
> morning, huh? It all hinges on that.
> Let's try to get some rest.

P.O. Williams' head is on a swivel between the crowd and
O'Sweeney. A flicker of FEAR spasms across his face.

> SMASH CUT TO:

EXT. D.DAY-NORMANDY-AMPHIBIOUS LANDING CRAFT-Day

Massive theater of war ERUPTS — explosions, machine gun
fire, terrified screaming, etc.

P.O. Williams shoves his way back to the stern through a
crowd of SCARED soldiers PACKED TIGHT in a flat-bottomed,
rectangular amphibious landing craft.

The boat is still tied to the port side of the huge troop
transport ship.

P.O. Williams reaches the pilot, P.O. O'Sweeney.

O'Sweeney is a statuesque vision of stubbled, chain-smoking CALM amid BLOODY CHAOS.

> ### P.O. WILLIAMS
> (screaming)
> O'Sweeney, this is your second run,
> correct? What's it like? Some of the
> men are saying it's fucking hell in
> there. Excuse my French…

O'Sweeney takes a cherry-red drag off a Lucky.

> ### P.O. O'SWEENEY
> (shouts)
> WILLLLLLLLAAAAAAAYYYYY! Man, I
> thought you had me last night! You're
> the current big loser on this boat,
> too! What in-the-hell were you doing
> that deep into the pot with three
> kings? Seriously, do you know what
> your backers would do to you if you
> tried that shit where I'm from, back
> in Seawell? Nah, I'm just teasing you!
> I was your only backer! HAHAHAH! What
> the hell you gonna do with a fist nearly
> full of kings? Fold? Not in a million
> years. The best part is you played
> it all out without a dime to your
> name, huh? That's my favorite part,
> my favorite moment on this fantastic
> cruise (sobering a bit).

Williams relaxes a little, accepts an offered cigarette
from the pair O'Sweeney lights off the cherry of his last.

> ### P.O. O'SWEENEY (CONT'D)
> Willy, I rolled one hundred and one
> cigarettes for today. Giving them all
> away until I have only my own last pack
> of Lucky's left. If we make it through,

I mean WHEN WE make it through today,
we're gonna quit smokin', right? Filthy
practice, this tobacco, huh?

Waving at all the carnage around him, O'Sweeney SHOUTS
maniacally.

                    P.O. O'SWEENEY (CONT'D)
                  (shouting)
          FILTHY, FILTHY PRACTICE, THIS SMOKING!
          "GOR-RAM FILTHY PRACTICE!" THAT'S WHAT
          MY MOTHER ALWAYS SAID! HAHAHA! SHE
          NEVER SAID "GODDAMN," BUT SHE MIGHT IF
          SHE SAW THIS PLACE, HUH? BUT WHAT A
          GOR-RAM FILTHY PRACTICE, THESE LUCKY'S,
          HUH?!

                                        CUT TO:

EXT. - D.DAY - TROOP TRANSPORT SHIP - SAME

O'Sweeney throttles and steers away from the main troop
transport toward the beach.

PULL BACK TO REVEAL O'Sweeney's boat is one among
HUNDREDS.

The SCALE of the theater of violence staggers the mind.

                                        CUT TO:

EXT. - D.DAY - SAME

O'Sweeney pilots with P.O. Williams at his elbow.

                    P.O. O'SWEENEY
                  (lying through his teeth,)
          Willy, I didn't see too much up there
          but I figured out how you can pay me
          back.

Before a sound comes out of Williams' confused mouth,
O'Sweeney holds his hand up to shut him up.

Williams leans in to listen, then JERKS his head around as a babyfaced man nearby SCREAMS, crumples, helmet clattering.

Another soldier grabs the fallen man's collar, pulls him up, PUNCHES him in the back of the head.

Someone else SLAPS the boy twice across the face.

Williams is JARRED by the headpunch and the slaps.

O'Sweeney grabs him by the collar.

> P.O. O'SWEENEY (CONT'D)
> Lookit, you gotta give me your books
> for payment. We don't have a lot of
> time so you gotta give me your books
> and we're even. Fuckin' even-Steven.

> P.O. WILLIAMS
> What books? What the hell?

> P.O. O'SWEENEY
> You know that stupid, thick maroon
> Bakunin's Collected Works you got?
> Here's the deal, and you aren't in any
> kinda position to say "no" so just nod
> your head so I know you're gettin' it.
> After we both survive this day down the
> beach…

> P.O. WILLIAMS
> "Down the beach," what the fuck are
> you talking about?

> P.O. O'SWEENEY
> Shut the hell up, Willaaay! "We're
> goin' down the beach!" Thick
> Massachusetts Irish Catholics! Even
> when we're drivin' northeast to the
> coast for the day, the dense fucks
> say the same damn thing: "We're goin'

down the beach!" Heads like rocks, and
that's what you and me need today—heads
and hearts dense as rocks. Willy, you
hear me? You and me are goin' down the
beach right now. Gimme a nod…good. And
when we get back to the States you're
givin' me all those books you got back
home. Agreed? AGREED!?

                P.O. WILLIAMS
           (sputtering, confused)
What's wrong with you? We're both
gonna die, it's bedlam out there! But
yeah, yeah, you can have the books. Ok?

                P.O. O'SWEENEY
Good. I'm about to hit my assigned
sandbar here! Tell me who you got. Tell
me who I got waiting for me back home!

                P.O. WILLIAMS
You want me to tell you the authors'
names?

Williams points at the approaching beach above and beyond
the huddled, helmeted heads of his fellow infantrymen.

                P.O. O'SWEENEY
Christ, Willy! We don't have time. Tell
me who I got waiting for me! Do it!

                                CUT TO:

EXT.-D.DAY-SAME

P.O. O'Sweeney grounds the transport, throws a lever to
drop the entire bow of the rectangular landing craft.

The bow wall starts to fall and machine gun fire
RICOCHETS off the outside of it.

Men wince and whimper, a few steel themselves until…

The bow wall drops down toward the beach, allowing gunfire to invade the boat.

Soldiers SCREAM, drop and about half rush forward into the waist-deep water carbine rifles held above their helmets.

P.O. O'Sweeney pulls Williams up by the collar, two-handed.

> P.O. O'SWEENEY
> Willaaay! No ducking your debt now, kid! Fifteen seconds and you gotta follow these kids down the beach! The water is NOT fine. Spit it out, you fuckin' three-king loser!

> P.O. WILLIAMS
> (voice rising to a scream)
> Arthur Conan Doyle, Voltaire, Chekov, Henry James, Balzac, Bakunin, umm, goddammit…

> P.O. O'SWEENEY
> …Oh fuckin swill! Willaaayy, you don't have any poetry? I don't need fiction or facts. Gimme the poets, kid!

> P.O. WILLIAMS
> (laughing despite himself)
> Shit! You're a lunatic. Keats and Hopkins and Byron and Whitman and Blake and, ahh, fuck this!

SMASH CUT TO:

Williams SCREECHES like a rabid animal.

He turns & SPRINTS into the water.

We see him make it to the sand, then make it to some meager cover.

O'Sweeney turns starboard, VOMITS all over the steel wall.

DISSOLVE TO:

EXT. - D.DAY - SAME

A SERIES OF IMAGES:

O'Sweeney picks up boatload after boatload of YOUNG soldiers.

Drops them off into near guaranteed slaughter in the shallows.

Whenever the boat is emptied, O'Sweeney vomits.

The boat's full, then empty, but for the blood and guts.

O'Sweeney DRY-HEAVES. BILE streams from his bent-over form.

Finally, O'Sweeney grimly scuffs at and toes some intestines off the bow and into the water.

CUT TO:

INT. LOWER HOLD, MAIN TRANSPORT SHIP-P.O. O'SWEENEY'S BUNK-NIGHT

O'Sweeney SWAYS in his hammock with a grimy, tear-streaked face.

He's WIDE AWAKE.

TREMBLING fingers shake out, FUMBLE his last Lucky onto his chest.

The swaying of O'Sweeney's hammock and MOSTLY EMPTY hammocks around him becomes hypnotic.

Sweeney weakly gropes for his dropped Lucky.
BANGING, CLATTERING emanate from deep inside the ship.

FADE IN:

INT.-GROUNDSKEEPER'S TOOL SHED, GOLF COURSE—OUT OF BOUNDS
AREA-SEAWELL, MASSACHUSETTS-EARLY '90S-EARLY MORNING

BANGING, CLATTERING emanate from OUTSIDE the shed.

SWEENEY O'SWEENEY (the grandson of P.O. O'Sweeney) has
long dark brown hair, stubble. He has just DREAMT his
grandfather's D-Day experience.

Sweeney groggily responds to BANGING, CLATTERING.

He lies tangled and NAKED under a colorful MEXICAN
BLANKET,SWAYING IN A HAMMOCK.

> SWEENEY
> (to himself)
> Jesus. Again with that fuckin' dream? I
> was never even there and Grampa's been
> dead for years.

Sweeney stands, wraps the blanket around his waist.

He's in PERFECT surfing shape: lithe, muscular, tan.

BANGING, CLATTERING continues.

> SWEENEY (CONT'D)
> Who the hell is that? No one knows I'm
> out here…

One end of the HAMMOCK is tied to a spike driven into the
top of massive wooden shelving attached to an old oak
workbench.

On the workbench lie Sweeney's GRANDFATHER'S MAROON
BOOKS: "The Collected Works of Bakunin," "Blake,"
"Whitman," etc.

Dozens of empty beer cans, half-smoked joints, wrenches,
hammers, mowers blades, weed whackers, bongs, etc.,
compete for space around the books.

CUT TO:

EXT. - SWEENEY'S LANDSCAPING SHED - SAME

Two Mormon teenaged missionaries BANG on the GARAGE DOOR
of the shed.

They're wearing the standard uniform, they hold Bibles.

ELDER SMITH, 18, Blond, portly, sweating more with each
knock. He's clearly in charge.

ELDER JOHNSON, 18, blond, thin, tall and nervous.

> ELDER SMITH
> (hissing)
> They said he'd be in here. Knock again,
> brother.

> ELDER JOHNSON
> (spitting back)
> Let's just go! This is a crazy person,
> here. You know what they all say about
> his drunkenness and fighting. Let's go
> back to the projects in the Acre and
> talk to some Southeast Asian gangsters.
> At least we know they'll just ignore
> us, maybe laugh in our faces. We don't
> know what this Sweeney O'Sweeney will
> do. They say he gets drunk and sleeps
> in the trees!

Both boys look up at the trees fearfully.

CUT TO:

INT. - SWEENEY'S LANDSCAPING SHED - SAME

Sweeney presses an ear to the garage door.

He stealthily peeks through a grimy window, gives an
approving frown, scratches at his stubble and CRAZY
BEDHEAD.

He looks up thoughtfully at a dozen SURFBOARDS in the rafters.

>   SWEENEY
>   (to himself)
>   OK, boys, the tide's almost out. I
>   gotta get down the beach. Let's give
>   you what you evangelical, delusional
>   fucks deserve.

Sweeney dons a shit-eating grin, readjusts the MEXICAN

BLANKET over one shoulder, toga-style.

>   **CUT TO:**

EXT. - SWEENEY'S LANDSCAPING SHED - SAME

ELDER JOHNSON BANGS on the garage door one last time.

>   **CUT TO:**

INT. - SWEENEY'S LANDSCAPING SHED - SAME

Sweeney squats, grabs the garage door handle by the ground.

A NAIL JUTS out next to the handle Sweeney holds.

Sweeney thrusts upward with all his strength, THROWING the door above his head.

>   SWEENEY
>   (shouting over a simultaneous ripping,
>   tearing sound)
>   GOOD DAY lovechildren of Joseph the
>   Fraud Smith…

>   **CUT TO:**

EXT. - SWEENEY'S LANDSCAPING SHED - SAME

POV of the two Mormons - staring at a BUCK NAKED Sweeney.

The teens gasp, then hold their breath.

CUT TO:

POV from behind Sweeney. Beyond his BARE-ASS the Mormons stand, frozen, jaws on the ground.

A large piece of Mexican blanket FALLS from the nail that tore it from Sweeney's body.

Sweeney stands stock still for a beat.

His arms are raised above his head, the blanket covers ONLY HIS HEAD.

Sweeney slowly begins the CHICKEN DANCE.

He belts out the CHICKEN DANCE SONG, flapping his elbows,bending his knees up and down, turning round and round.

> SWEENEY (CONT'D)
> DAH NAH NAH NAH NAH NAH NAH, Welcome
> to what has become, DAH NAH NAH NAH
> NAH NAH NAH, unfortunately for you two
> kids, DAH NAH NAH NAH NAH NAH NAH, an
> R-rated Polish wedding reception! DAH
> NAH NAH NAH NAH NAH NAH...NAH, NAH,
> NAH, NAH!

Sweeney continues the dance and the song.
He follows the horrified kids as they begin to stumble away.

CUT TO:

EXT. DAY - CANOA, ECUADOR, OUTDOOR BAR ON THE BEACH

Sweeney sways in a HAMMOCK, beneath palms, raises a 32 oz. brown bottle of beer to his mouth.

We can read the label: "Pilsener, El Cerveza de ECUADOR."
He tells the story to a crowd of locals and travelers.

                    SWEENEY
                (laughing a bit)
        And I have too much of a hangover to
        deal with these kids. Elder so and so
        was right. And the stupid Chicken Dance
        was the only thing I could think of
        doing once that damn nail ripped my
        blanket off.

                                        CUT TO:

EXT. - SWEENEY'S LANDSCAPING SHED - SAME SERIES OF IMAGES
_____

Sweeney's really getting into the chicken dance.
The Mormons snap out of their shocked state.

They WINCE as Sweeney squats to do the dance properly.

Covering their eyes with their forearms.

Stumbling away as Sweeney flaps his elbows.

Sweeney's still belting out the melody.

He shouts it after them as they run away.

                                        CUT TO:

EXT. FARANNAN GOLF COURSE - RAISED GOLF TEE - DAY
_____

Sweeney's "Chicken Dance" song echoes over the course.

GOLFER #1 downswings and violently hooks his tee shot
into the woods.

The other golfers on the tee LAUGH hysterically.

                                        CUT TO:

EXT. - CANOA, ECUADOR - SAME SERIES OF IMAGES
_____

Everyone LAUGHS harder as Sweeney translates to Spanish
for the locals.

Outside the fence of the outdoor bar two DIFFERENT Mormon teenaged missionaries walk by.

They look in on the laughter as if they KNOW they are being laughed at somehow.

Sweeney waves magnanimously.

The laughter reaches its zenith as everyone in the bar seeS the Mormons.
The boys hurry away with ties a-flapping, sweat-stained, slightly worried and disgusted at the same time.

                                        CUT TO:

EXT. - FARANNAN GOLF COURSE - SAME

Sweeney chases Mormons across a fairway, ties a-flapping,sweat-stained, slightly worried and disgusted at the same time.

Golfers on the tee above yell at them.

The Mormons stumble and slip in mud.

Sweeney see this, slows down.

He turns and does a little jig for the angry golfers on the tee, giving them the finger.

Elder Johnson DROPS his Bible as the Mormons help each other out of the mud and keep running.

Sweeney picks up and THROWS THE BIBLE into a pond.

BOTH Mormon boys witness the throw, wide-eyed, HORRIFIED.

                                        CUT TO:

EXT. - RAISED GOLF TEE - SAME

ALL THE GOLFERS witness the throw, wide-eyed, IMPRESSED.

                    GOLFER #1
          Christ! You see that throw? He's still
          got the best arm north of Boston.

Golfer 1 shakes his head in disbelief.

                    GOLFER #1
               (suddenly angry, but still
               in awe of the throw)
          He shoulda nevah quit baseball to begin
          with. He no-hit us twice his senior
          year. And we all knew he was high as a
          kite on the mound the second time. What
          the fuck is wrong with that guy?

All golfers nod and murmur agreement.

                    GOLFER #1 (CONT'D)
          I'm hittin' another. That first one
          doesn't count. That was a duckhook
          caused by a certifiable loon. So fuck
          all of you, I don't care.

More laughter and begrudging agreement from other
golfers.

                    GOLFER #2
          You know, whenever Sweeney takes off to
          surf or whatever-the-fuck he does with
          his time, he sends back poems to my
          wife's cousin's kid? He's fucked in the
          head. Completely wacked.

                    GOLFER #1
          What are you talking about?

Setting up another ball on a tee.

                    GOLFER #2
          Yeah, I read 'em. Poetry's not really my
          thing, but some of 'em are pretty good.
          All about the jungle and some broad he
          met who drinks even more than him.

Golfer #1 gets visibly angry, again, as he does a
practice swing.

> GOLFER #1
> Ok, shut the fuck up Emily Dickinson.
> I'm about to crush this thing down the
> middle.

Golfer #1 begins backswing.

> GOLFER #2
> (to the others, quietly)
> Emily's Dickin...who?

Laughter erupts again as Golfer #1 hooks another off a
pine tree right back to the front of the tee, ten feet
from their 4 pairs of IDENTICAL saddle-shoe golf spikes.

> **CUT TO:**

EXT. - FARANNAN GOLF COURSE - SAME

The two Mormons turn in the distance, realize they've
lost a Bible.

Sweeney's still lazily pursuing them. Dancing a bit,
waving to other golfers, shaking his junk, playing the
fool.

Elder Smith's anger reaches an apex.

> ELDER SMITH
> Sweeney, you lunatic! You are
> cursed for this! You are surely
> going to hell and will never be saved.
> No matter what you do, you are a cursed
> man!

> **CUT TO:**

EXT. - CANOA, ECUADOR - SAME

Sweeney and PANCHO MONEYMAKER exit the outdoor bar
together.

PANCHO MONEYMAKER is Sweeney's South American twin. Tall, shoulder-length brown hair, in perfect surfing shape. He speaks fluent English, albeit with an accent.

They walk down onto the beach to check the waves for an evening surf session.

> PANCHO MONEYMAKER
> So what do you think? Did you get cursed by those kids? Didn't you go to prison around that time?

> SWEENEY
> Ahh, I don't know. I leave that part out when I tell it now. Kind of a buzz kill at the bar, ya know? Curses and shit, I don't know. It's hard to say. I know that very day they cursed me, I went surfing and got my first shot in a surf magazine.

> PANCHO MONEYMAKER
> Really? That shot in "Surfer Magazine"?

> SWEENEY
> (regretting mentioning it)
> Umm…I don't know, I think…

> PANCHO MONEYMAKER
> The bottom turn on that overhead wave from Hurricane Brandon?

> SWEENEY
> No. Nevermind. I mean, I didn't think much about those Mormon kids till a couple months later. There was a lot of surf that late summer and fall and I was drinking a ton…and fighting a ton… but that photographer was up from the Outer Banks filming some East Coast pros on Seawell Beach.

INT. - SWEENEY'S LANDSCAPING SHED - SAME SERIES OF IMAGES

Sweeney has his wetsuit half-on as he pulls down tatters of his Mexican blanket from the garage door.

He grabs a surfboard with a Bonzer fin set-up and runs outside.

He runs barefoot, fast, down a path in the out-of-bounds woods parallel to a fairway.

He gets to the rocks behind the 7th green, scampers nimbly down onto the sand.

Looks up to see photographer RICKY ELIOT setting up his tripod and super-long lens up high by the dunes.

RICKY ELIOT is a stocky man in his mid-30s, wearing surf trunks, a longsleeve T-shirt and a brown canvas sun hat. He's capable, practical.

> SWEENEY
> (angry)
> Hey, what the fuck are you doing here?
> Get that fuckin' camera outta here!

> RICKY ELIOT
> (shouts right back)
> You must be Sweeney. I heard about you
> from Mike O'Dowd.

Sweeney makes his way up the soft sand to Ricky, STICKERLESS SURFBOARD under his arm.

> SWEENEY
> (softening a bit)
> Oh yeah? What'd that toothless prick
> have to say?

> RICKY ELIOT
> He said to, umm, I don't know quite how
> to put this. He said to tell you, and I

quote, "Shut the fuck up, Sweeney. Just
go surf and let this guy do his job. He
won't name your spot in the magazine."

Sweeney is surprised by this, but his anger subsides.

> SWEENEY
> Oh, I, ahh, well, O'Dowd makes the
> calls around here so I guess you got
> the green light.

> RICKY ELIOT
> Oh, cool. Thanks. I appreciate it. And
> we definitely won't name this spot. Has
> anyone ever shot for the magazines here?

> SWEENEY
> Nah, no one ever follows hurricane
> swells up past Jersey or Montauk. Fine
> by me. You guys can stay down south.
> We get waves, but it's colder up here.
> I think some guy from "Surfed Out"
> magazine was here in the '80s, but he
> got skunked.

> RICKY ELIOT
> Well, we didn't get skunked today, did
> we?

> SWEENEY
> Definitely not. That's solid six- to
> eight-foot groundswell and northwest
> winds on just the right tide.
> (Fired-up) Look at that set! It's going
> off right now!

> CUT TO:

EXT. SEAWELL BEACH - DUNES - SAME

PRO SURFERS 1, 2 AND SETH COLLINS slowly walk through the
dunes, STICKER-COVERED thrusters under their arms.

They look even more hungover than Sweeney.

SETH COLLINS, the best of the three pros, has a black eye.

>   SWEENEY
>   Oh, shit. I remember that guy. Did
>   I do that?

>   RICKY ELIOT
>   (laughing loudly)
>   Don't worry, Sweeney. You slapped
>   Collins around, but he gave himself
>   that black eye. Actually passed out
>   onto his own kneecap sitting in the
>   front seat of my car. I've never seen
>   anything like it.

>   SWEENEY
>   Hmm, why'd I slap him around? I forget.
>   I had a couple shots of the Doctah
>   early last night. It's all a little
>   foggy.

>   RICKY ELIOT
>   Collins is a good guy, but he can't
>   hold his liquor and he gets arrogant.
>   You went easy on him, but I didn't
>   realize until this morning that it
>   was you, that you were Sweeney. This
>   morning, some of the locals told me
>   they were surprised you didn't ruin his
>   night right off the bat.

>   SWEENEY
>   Yeah, Seawell's a city but a small town
>   all at once, ya know? I usually only
>   try to fight guys who like to brawl or
>   guys who deserve a beating. Collins
>   isn't a fighter, just a loudmouth. I
>   grabbed him before someone else did, ya
>   know?

                    RICKY ELIOT
                  (laughing)
          You literally just pinned him like
          you were his big brother. You gave
          him eight or ten slaps to the face.
          You were talking to someone over
          your shoulder about your bookie the
          whole time you had him pinned. I doubt
          Collins even remembers.

                    SWEENEY
              (tunes out, whispering to himself)
          Oh shit, that's right! I owe Rousseau
          500 bucks. Damn.

                    RICKY ELIOT
                  (raising an eybrow)
          Just go surfing. I'll handle Collins.
          Forget about him. He probably won't
          even paddle out. I did a trip to
          Mundaka with him last year. This is
          nothing new.

                    SWEENEY
          Ok, then. Cool. See you later. I'll get
          you a pint down at McSwiggan's later if
          you guys stick around tonight. Him too,
          I guess.
              (nodding at a queasy Collins)
          No hard feelings.

                    RICKY ELIOT
          See you at the pub, man—as soon as I
          run outta light. Have fun. Get some
          barrels for me.

Sweeney turns and SPRINTS over the lowtide flats.

                                        CUT TO:

EXT. - CANOA, ECUADOR - HIGH TIDE LINE - DAY

                    PANCHO MONEYMAKER
          So, it was that day! The whole story
          in the magazine was about this
          "unidentified" surfer north of Boston
          who out-drank and ripped harder than
          all those pro surfers.

                    SWEENEY
          Yeah, but that article, the editors
          took some shit out on Collins, I think.
          He wasn't a bad guy…

Pancho starts figuring it all out while he talks

                    PANCHO MONEYMAKER
          Man, that was my favorite article I've
          ever found in a surf magazine. It's the
          only article based on an "unidentified
          surfer." The whole thing revolves
          around a nobody, a nothing…

As he reminisces, we…

                                        FLASH CUT TO:

INT. PANCHO'S BEDROOM - DAY - YEARS EARLIER
_____

A teenaged Pancho lies on the ground, fully engrossed in
the SURFER MAGAZINE in front of him

                    PANCHO (Voice Over)
          I learned English so I could read
          that whole article. I'm not kidding.
          And that was you! *Cara de verga*!
          (Subtitle flashes: "Cockface!") I
          should've known.

TIGHT ON PHOTO of Sweeney in magazine.

                                        CUT TO:
_____

BACK AND FORTH FROM SWEENEY TALKING AND THE YOUNGER
PANCHO POURING THROUGH THE MAGAZINE, THE PHOTOS OF A

BEAUTIFUL GREEN HURRICANE SWELL LEAPING OFF THE PAGES,
PANCHO'S STUBBY FINGERS FOLLOWING EACH LINE OF TEXT AS HE
STRUGGLES WITH THE ENGLISH WORDS, ETC.

> SWEENEY
> Wait, like I was sayin', Collins actually
> rallied and surfed great that day and…

> PANCHO (V.O.)
> Fuck you, Sweeney! You bastard. That
> story is fuckin' legendary. Even down
> here in the jungle! You son of a…did
> you go back and drink with those guys
> that night?

> SWEENEY
> Yeah, I met up with them. I won a grand
> on the Pats to lose by 17 in the 4
> o'clock game that very Sunday. So I
> took them out and showed them the real
> Seawell dive bars.

> PANCHO (V.O.)
> The photos from that story…in those
> shitty bars…those awesome waves…the
> story…but your face isn't in any of
> the photos.

> SWEENEY
> Yeah, I made a deal with Ricky
> Eliot that he could run only two or
> three photos of me surfing and that I
> couldn't be identified at all. So he
> kept his word and ran three shots of
> me. No portraits, nothin' with my face
> in it.

> PANCHO (V.O.)
> There's only TWO shots of you in that
> article, *verga*. (Subtitle flashes:
> "Cock.") I know it. I have it at my
> house, still. It's three photos of

Collins, two of the other guys, two of
you and that opening spread of that 10-
foot, empty, perfect, green wave just
barreling.

CUT TO:

EXT. - CANOA, ECUADOR - HIGH TIDE LINE

SWEENEY
What the fuck, Pancho? You're a surf
geek, huh?

PANCHO
Yeah, I am. Just like you, so shut
up. You just hide it better. Let's go
get our boards back at the bar. It's
getting good out there.

Sweeney looks out at the waves, then back to Pancho.

SWEENEY
(quietly, but smirking)
Pancho, you know that empty, hollow
wave in the opening spread?

PANCHO MONEYMAKER
Yeah.

SWEENEY
I came out of that one.
PANCHO MONEYMAKER
No. NO! (rapidfire) Oh no, no, no, no,
no, no, no, no. (begging, looking up to
the skies) *No, por favor, no!*

As they approach the bar's gate above the beach, Pancho
inexplicably takes off RUNNING through the tables, around
and then behind the bar. He disappears, digging through a
shelf.

SWEENEY
What are you doing? I'm not drinkin'
until after we surf.

Sweeney grabs his board from the outdoor rack by the bar. Pancho returns with a ragged surf magazine, pointing at a page, calling over other local surfers as he stumbles, stunned toward Sweeney now waxing his board.

> PANCHO MONEYMAKER
> You…*hijo de puta*…Son of a…

Sweeney tucks his board under his arm, leans over Pancho and points at the photo he's showing everyone around him.

> SWEENEY
> Yeah, whaddaya mean? I thought you were
> a surf geek, amigo? Don't you see me
> behind the curtain, there? I'm deep.

The crowd of local surfers all know the article, it's infamous. They SUDDENLY BREAK UP INTO JOYOUS LAUGHTER AND CURSING. Not a single person ever saw that Sweeney was in the barrel in the article's CAPTIONLESS opening spread photo.

Local surfer kids are staring up at Sweeney, mouths agape.

> PANCHO MONEYMAKER
> You, you shoulda gone pro. Why wouldn't
> you do such a thing if you could? You
> were good enough to go pro.

> SWEENEY
> C'mon, man. Let's just go surf. I
> don't know. Put that stupid magazine
> away. I got beers to get to when the
> sun goes down.

CUT TO:

EXT. - CANOA, ECUADOR - HIGH TIDE - LINEUP - SUNSET

Sweeney and Pancho sit astride their surfboards.

Both men laugh and talk, completely at ease as large waves pass under them and detonate on the inside sandbar.

                    PANCHO MONEYMAKER
                 (speaking to another local)
         *Si, si! Sweeney estaba en el tubo en
         esa photo!*

SUBTITLE: *"Yeah, Sweeney was IN THE TUBE in that photo!"*

Pancho turns to Sweeney as Sweeney paddles for a wave.

                    PANCHO MONEYMAKER(CONT'D)
              You bastard! That's a deep, deep tube!

Sweeney sits up, lets the wave go to a little kid. He's
more at ease, even smiling, now that he's in the water.

                         SWEENEY
              Yeah. Ricky Eliot thought I'd like that
              he ran that photo as an empty wave
              with no caption. You can just make out
              my silhouette in that thing if you
              look wicked close. But I came out of
              it, *verga de mono*. (Subtitle flashes:
              Monkeydick) Believe me. Second best
              barrel I've ever had at my home break.

Sweeney strokes effortlessly into the next wave.

ALL the surfers SWIVEL to watch him going down the line.

He RIPS the wave apart, perfect combination of power and
fluidity.At the same time, the wave behind it DETONATES
and completely destroys a local surfer sitting on his
board who was too busy watching Sweeney surf.

He surfaces, looks around, no one saw it. He gives a
laugh of relief.

All is quiet at sunset except for the sound of the waves.

                                        CUT TO:

EXT.-AERIAL SHOT OF CANOA, THE BEACH, THE TOWN THE
SURROUNDING JUNGLE-SUNSET

_____

EXT. BEACH - CONTINUOUS

A girl, FLOWPI LUQUE, and two boys, local kids, hoot on
shore as Sweeney gets a tube.

He exits the barrel.

Kicks out of the wave near shore.

Steps off into shallow water.

The two boys run to him for high-fives.

Sweeney's laughing and very surprised when FLOWPI RUNS
AND TACKLES HIM from the side at the knees.

She's smiling and wants five from Sweeney too as they
both splutter and splash in the shallows.

The boys laugh and pigpile on Sweeney and Flowpi. Small
walls of whitewater roll them all around.

Flowpi SPEAKS DIRECTLY, QUIETLY to Sweeney. We can't
hear.

Sweeney is STUNNED as one of the boys pulls Flowpi out of
the pigpile.

Sweeney waves at the boys to take his surfboard out for a
few waves.

SWEENEY
(distracted)
Cuidado, niños, cuidado con la tabla.
(Subtitle: "Careful, kids, careful with the
board.")

Sweeney walks up toward the bar, stopping now and again
to look back at Flowpi playing in the shallows.

CUT TO:

EXT. - CANOA, ECUADOR - HIGH TIDE - LINEUP- SAME

Pancho watches Sweeney walking up the beach. He turns
back to some locals bobbing, astride their surfboards.

                    PANCHO MONEYMAKER
            Quizás él está hechizado, pero
            claramente el está conectado al mar.

SUBTITLE: "Well, he may be cursed, but he's clearly
connected."

                                            CUT TO:

EXT. - CANOA, ECUADOR - SUN-BAKED, DIRT ROAD IN TOWN -
EVENING

Sweeney and Pancho walk together, surfboards under arms.

A HUMONGOUS PIG runs in front of them and up the muddy
road.
                    SWEENEY
            Hey, what's going on with that girl
            tackling me?

                    PANCHO MONEYMAKER
            Who? Flowpi?

                    SWEENEY
            Yeah, are those her brothers? How old
            is she?
                    PANCHO MONEYMAKER
            Cousins. They look after her, sort of.
            They're just kids so they're not very
            good at it. She's like 9 years old.

                    SWEENEY
            What's going on with her?

                    PANCHO MONEYMAKER
            She's got some mental problems, I hear.
            But there aren't any good doctors
            around here. Down in Guayaquil, maybe.

But her father took off and her mother
works six or seven days a week. Her
mother tells everyone the behaviors are
going to go away. I talked to her about
Flowpi. I keep an eye on her and her
cousins.

                    SWEENEY
Does she surf? She was freaking out
over that last wave I caught.

                    PANCHO MONEYMAKER
Yeah, she surfs. She's really good.
Better than her two cousins. And
they know it. Those two little
shits try to keep her out of the
water as much as possible. I heard
a British surfer describe her
surfing perfectly. He said, "The
ocean suits her."

                    SWEENEY
You know what she said to me?

                    PANCHO MONEYMAKER
She talked to you? That's cool. She
doesn't talk to many people. She
babbles to some imaginary friends or
something. What'd she say?

                    SWEENEY
I heard it, loud and clear, she said,
"I know how alphabets are born." What
the hell does that mean?

                    PANCHO MONEYMAKER
You might be able to surf, man, but
your Spanish sucks. She didn't even
talk to you, did she? Are you fuckin'
with me?

> SWEENEY
> I wish I was. What does it mean? How
> are alphabets born? It's like a Zen
> poem. Has Flowpi been to Kyoto? Are
> there Zen priests around…Nevermind,
> there aren't even paved roads, how
> could she spout Zen koans at me?

> PANCHO MONEYMAKER
> (distracted)
> Zen what? Fuck you, she didn't even
> talk to you. You didn't even tell me
> you were in that barrel in the mag
> until I forced you. *Es un chiste,*
> *vergacorta?* (Subtitle: "Are you joking,
> littledick.")

> SWEENEY
> I think I wish she didn't talk to me,
> man. I'm not kiddin'. "I know how
> alphabets are born"? What the...?

CUT TO:

EXT. - BAHIA DE CARáQUEZ, ECUADOR - BUS STATION - DAY

Sweeney lifts his huge backpack from a tricycle taxi.

He pays and tips very well as Pancho pulls up in his own
tricycle taxi.

Sweeney pays Pancho's driver.

> SWEENEY
> Pancho, this guy's going to wait for
> you so you can get back to the ferry.
> It's too damn hot to walk.

> PANCHO MONEYMAKER
> Thanks, hombre. My liver's glad to see
> you finally go, but my tired feet are
> going to miss your free spending ways.

                    SWEENEY
          I'll miss this place. Gotta get back
          and do some tree work this spring and
          summer. I'll be back next winter or the
          one after that.

                PANCHO MONEYMAKER
          Ok. Don't forget us…hey, where are your
          boards?

                    SWEENEY
          Oh, yeah, I wanted to ask you to look
          after them. Flowpi has the bonzer. Make
          sure her cousins don't take it from
          her, ok? She's an amazing little kid,
          especially in the water. She needs a
          board. I'll make enough money up in the
          trees in two days' time to buy another.

Sweeney starts toward his bus as his backpack is THROWN
under the bus with the other luggage.

                PANCHO MONEYMAKER
          Yeah, okay. Cool. So you're climbing
          trees again when you get to Seawell?
          Good. But where's that other board you
          let me ride?

Sweeney steps on the bus, starts up the steps, looks back
out at Pancho, SMILING.

                    SWEENEY
          No sé, fuckface. No sé.

SUBTITLE: I don't know, fuckface. I don't know.

                                      JUMP CUT TO:

EXT. - BELLA VISTA - PANCHO'S TREEHOUSE-DAY

Pancho runs into his wall-less living room.

Flowpi lies in a hammock. She pretends not to hear

Pancho, she stares at the STUNNING view of Bella Vista, Bahia, the rivermouth beyond and the coast up to Canoa.

Sweeney's TWIN-FIN lies on the floor next to her.

Flowpi laughs, jumps out of the hammock and TACKLES Pancho at the knees.

> PANCHO MONEYMAKER
> (laughing)
> Vamos a surfear, Flowpi! Vamos a Canoa!
> Hay olas grandes! Por qué no? Poco a
> poco, Flowpi, poco a poco!

SUBTITLE: "Let's go surfing, Flowpi! Let's go to Canoa! The waves are huge! Why not? Little by little, Flowpi, bit by bit!

> FLOWPI
> (laughing)
> Si, si, si, Pancho! Sweeney dijo que yo
> soy como tu nueva sombra en la tierra,
> en los bosques y en el mar! Y él me dió
> su tabla de surf que tiene mi pintura
> del gavilán!

SUBTITLE: "Yeah, Pancho! Sweeney told me I'm like your new shadow on land, in the forests and in the ocean. And he gave me his surfboard, the one with my painting of the sparrow hawk on it!

Pancho, shakes his head and gives Flowpi a big hug.

He picks up the board, lovingly. They both look at Flowpi's EXQUISITE painting of a SPARROW HAWK.

> PANCHO MONEYMAKER
> Oh, niña, estás hablando más y más, no?
> Qué chévere, mi sombrita! Y tú puedes
> pintar como una maestra! Qué hermoso!

SUBTITLE: "Oh, kid, you are talking more and more, no? That's so cool, my little shadow! And you paint like a master. It's so beautiful."

Suddenly, from the other side of the treehouse, we hear the call of the sparrow hawk (kill-eee, kill-eee).

Pancho and Flowpi whistle the call in simultaneous response.

Pancho belts out a rough version of the Chicken Dance as he and Flowpi begin an approximation of the dance in celebration.

Flowpi's two cousins SPRINT in RIGHT PAST THEM to the surfboard on the floor and begin babbling excitedly about it.

The two boys join the singing and dancing above Bahia & the emerald, forested coastline.

                                          CUT TO:

EXT. - SEAWELL, MASS. - BUDDING CANOPY OF AN ANCIENT OAK TREE - DAY

A SERIES OF IMAGES:

It's windy and Sweeney is NOT harnessed to the tree he has climbed. Smoking chainsaw in one hand, ancient yellow-tinted Smith ski goggles on, no hardhat, no work gloves.

We FOLLOW a giant limb he cuts as it FALLS to the ground where MICKEY "GOATBOY" OBREGON looks on.

MICKY is a small but wiry, work-hardened 20-something. Sweeney's oldest friend. He constantly paws at a small goatlike beard on his chin.

Sweeney cuts another branch with DEFT chainsaw work.

As the limb CRASHES to the street we...

                                       JUMP CUT TO:

EXT. - SEAWELL, MASS. - NIGHT

Tight on a townie's bleeding face as it CRASHES to the

street.

Sweeney leans over him, BARELY BOTHERED.

> SWEENEY
> Hey, fuckhead! Don't get up. Crawl to
> your retard-friend's car and go back to
> Galloway.

Sweeney goes to check on Micky lying on the sidewalk in front of "The Skeff," a Seawell bar. He helps him up.

> SWEENEY (CONT'D)
> How the fuck's that eye of yours,
> Goatboy? (not waiting for an answer) What
> the fuck did you say to that clown
> anyways? He wanted to rip that goat-
> head you got right off your tiny body!

> MICKY
> Fuck you, Sweeney, but thanks for
> grabbin' that guy. It wasn't even him!
> His buddy, that little weasel eyed
> fuck, grabbed Spiro's sister's left
> tit. I punched him in the temple.
> SWEENEY
> Shit! All this for Voula's famous tits
> that nobody's ever seen? I didn't even
> see the punch. He was out cold. Wish
> I'd seen you do that, dammit.

> MICKY
> Yeah, I never got someone with one
> shot. But, Jesus Fucking Christ! His
> buddy, that big fuck you tore up, he
> fuckin' nailed me before I knew what
> was up.

Sweeney and Micky laugh hilariously and walk into the bar.

The locals inside ROAR and LAUGH as they enter.

The door slams and we…

CUT TO:

A SERIES OF IMAGES:

Goatboy playes Tower of Power's "Back on the Streets" on a dive bar's juke box as all the boys toast Sweeney...

Sweeney takes a shot of Jameson.

Sweeney defends smaller guys getting picked on.

Sweeney checks the waves at dawn. It's flat.

Sweeney downs beers at night.

Sweeney gets arrested, cuffed, thrown in a cruiser.

Sweeney defends a young woman getting harassed.

Sweeney buys a few rounds.

Sweeney jokes with the cops. Gets arrested again.

Sweeney fights and drinks some more.

We see him surfing tiny waves on a classic longboard.

He surfs with perfect style through gray weather and bad conditions.

His face looks ragged, a little restless.

CUT TO:

INT. - HARBORSIDE BAR - DUSK

Sweeney and Micky sit at the bar looking out the bay window at Seawell Harbor.

                    MICKY
          It's been flat as hell this summer, huh?
          No surf whatsoever.

                    SWEENEY
        Tell me about it, kid. It's killing
        me. I just want some head-high waves
        and it's been like six weeks of Lake
        Atlantic around here.

Micky checks his watch, cranes his neck to look out the
window.
                    MICKY
        This shouldn't take too long.

                    SWEENEY
        What's the deal with this guy?

                    MICKY
        I don't know. He's Barry. He's
        a fisherman. We were callin' him
        Barishnikov, but now he's just Barry
        the Russian. I forget his real name.
        Doesn't matter.

BARRY THE RUSSIAN enters, crosses toward their table.
He's a short, WIDE man with ice-blue eyes, brown chopped-
short hair, woolen sweater, fishgut-stained jeans.

                    SWEENEY
              (under his breath)
        Barry the Russian, unreal. It's
        seriously a laugh-a-minute with you,
        Goatboy.
                    MICKY
              (getting angry)
        Oh yeah, Sweeney, well you can go
        fu…

Barry the Russian arrives at the table.

                    MICKY (CONT'D)
              (changing his tone)
        Barry! How the hell are ya? This is
        Sweeney, the guy I told you about.

All stand and shake hands, mumble hellos.

                    SWEENEY
          You want a beer, Barry?

                    BARRY
              (thick Russian accent)
          Tequila Sunrise, please, thank you.

                    SWEENEY
          Ok, sounds good. You like Kurt Russell
          or Sly Stallone better?

                    BARRY
          Eh? Who is this Russell?

Paul, the Bartender, passes near the table with ice in
two 5-gallon buckets. The establishment is otherwise
empty.
                    SWEENEY
          Huh? Oh nevermind. Paul! Good timing,
          man. More beers for me and Goatboy
          here, and a Tequila Sunrise, if you
          would be so kind.

                    BARRY
          Thank you. So I have boat here and
          these Fish & Game men are, um
              (searching for the right phrase),
          breaking my balls. Do you want a boat,
          Micky? Or should I call you Goatman?

Sweeney coughs a laugh, just stops himself from spitting
out his beer.

                    MICKY
          Oh that's great. Just great. Fuck you,
          Sweeney. Barry, call me Micky. And, no,
          I don't want a boat.

Pointing at Sweeney like he's disgusted with him.

                    MICKY (CONT'D)
This loony prick does. He wants your
boat. He wants to live in it out in the
woods. He's a nutbag, but he might be
just the nutbag you're lookin' for.

The bartender throws the drinks down.

                    BARRY
Sweeney, you would like the boat?

                    SWEENEY
Yep.

                    BARRY
Would you like to see it first or has
Goatman shown you?

                    MICKY
I already showed him the damn thing,
Barry.

                    BARRY
Well, it's *your* new "damn thing" if you
can get it out of harbor by Wednesday.
It's Sunday. Can you do that?
                    MICKY
I have a feelin' WE are gonna give it a
shot, Barry.

                    SWEENEY
Yeah, you're damn straight you'll be
helping me, "Goatman."

Looking back at Barry.

                    SWEENEY (CONT'D)
You want any cash for this vessel,
Barry? 'Cause I don't have much, to be
honest.

                    BARRY
          No. No. Just take it away and you can
          have it. Someone stole engine parts and
          it leaks oil now. These Fish & Game
          ballbreakers. I, ahh, just take it.
          Drain oil. It is yours. But do not ever
          put it in water. It is no longer worthy
          of the sea, as you say here.

                    SWEENEY
          Neither am I, man. Who is? Shall we
          let the Doctah witness the handshake
          that seals the deal, then?

Sweeney rises, signals for Micky and Barry to stay
seated.

Walks to the bar.

                    SWEENEY (CONT'D)
                 (shouting)
          Three shots of the Doctah, barman! I am
          the proud owner of a new boat! I have
          my sea legs, I have a Goatman! My sea
          legs are stretching and strengthening
          before you as we speak!

Micky shakes his head, paws at his chin-beard.

Barry, finally lightens up and even looks bemused.

Sweeney plants the shots of the Doctah in the middle of
the table.

Barry and Sweeney shake hands…WORK-BEATEN hands.

All three down their shots.

                    BARRY
          It is schnapps, yes? Peppermint?

Micky's realizing what he's gotten himself into.

Micky shakes his head, wincing.

                    MICKY
          It's a long fuckin' Sunday night and a
          longer Monday morning is what it is,
          Barry. Fuck schnapps sideways.

                    BARRY
          How do you fuck schnapps, what is it,
          sideways?

                    MICKY
          Neverfuckingmind that, Barry. We call
          it "the Doctah" around here.

Sweeney hold his glass high, empties the last drop of
Doctah onto his tongue. He BEAMS at both men at the
table.
                                        CUT TO:

EXT. – FARANNAN GOLF COURSE – NIGHT
_____

Sweeney, still beaming, is mud covered and laying down
sheets of rotted, splintering plywood under the wheels of
one side of a too-small boat trailer.

Micky shakes his head at him from the other side of the
undersized, bowing trailer.

                    MICKY
          We ain't gonna make it to the out of-
          bounds on hole 6, man. I'm tellin' ya
          right now.

                    SWEENEY
          Kid, we're almost there. Let's just do
          this. We just gotta get those sheets
          of plywood from Spiro. It's fifty yards
          more. We got an eternity, all the time
          we need, to go like 100 yards. We're
          golden, kid.

                    MICKY
               (disgusted, mocking)
          "We're golden, kid, we got an eternity,
          kid." I'll give ya a fuckin' golden
          eternity, Kerouac. Look at this mess!

PULL BACK TO REVEAL 200 yards of fairway and the rough is
GOUGED deep with tire tracks from the truck and trailer.

A full moon's lighting the course up like noontime.

                    SWEENEY
          I didn't know you read Kerouac's
          Buddhist texts, Roshi Goatboy. Wow.
          Anyways, I told you I'll fill in all
          those tire tracks, seed them, whatever.
          It'll be fuckin' no problem whatsoever,
          kid. You know better than I do grass
          grows back fast. Some chickenshit
          fertilizer, c'mon. Now gimme that plank
          you're holdin' for this stuck wheel,
          man.

Micky's irate, pointing with four fingers at the
destruction.
                    MICKY
          Don't patronize me with that "you know
          better" shit. And YOU'LL fill and seed.
          It'll take YOU till Noon tomorrah to do
          that BY YOURSELF and Mr. McGuirk, Dr.
          Leahey, Judge Quinn and Alderman Dowd
          have their regular Monday tee time at
          seven sharp, you fucktard. Every one of
          them in that foursome hates you. They
          want you banned from Farannan. They've
          each asked me to fire you like ten-times
          over.

Micky picks up the requested PLANK, pretends to brain
Sweeney with it.

Sweeney flinches slightly.

                    SWEENEY
          Yeah, but…

                    MICKY
          Shut up or I'll give you a golden plank
          right across the back of your eternally
          thick Irish head! Me, you and Spiro are
          gonna be here till the sun comes up
          hiding this boat and throwing band-aids
          all over this disaster. Did you even
          tell Spiro what's goin' on?

Sweeney reaches across the trailer hitch for the plank.
Micky INTENTIONALLY keeps it out of reach.

                    SWEENEY
          No way, man. He'd be miles from here
          by now if he knew there was work to
          do. And stop worrying about those
          clowns at 7 a.m., kid. You're the head
          groundskeeper's son and everyone knows
          you do all the work around here. If you
          say it was joyriding kids in a Chevy
          Celebrity blasting KRS-ONE that tore
          this place up, they'll listen. Tell 'em
          you been workin' all night to fix
          it. They'll lap up that "hardnosed
          bluecollar kid" bullshit, like dogs,
          kid. Like dogs.

                    MICKY
          Jesus, Mary and Josephine, how the fuck
          did you talk me into this?

                    SWEENEY
          'Cause they won't let us play 45s
          in your groundskeepin' shed anymore and
          I need a place to stay since my parents
          took off.

                    MICKY
          Yeah, it's called an apartment.
          Normal people live in APARTMENTS! And
          everything you own is outta the shed
          tonight. TONIGHT.

                    SWEENEY
          We must resume our winning ways out
          here. Give me that plank and no more
          bitching. Gimme the plank, man.

Micky keeps the plank well out of Sweeney's reach.

                    MICKY
          If you even test me on this then it's
          gasoline, a match and a big pile of
          your stuff, kid. Wetsuits, books,
          your stupid 3-speed bike, that ratty
          hammock, mexican blankets, booze, your
          bong. I will torch the shit out of it
          all.

                    SWEENEY
          Ok, man, of course. Relax. Tonight.
          Stuff's out tonight. No problem.
          (Reaching out) The plank?

Micky starts to hand over the plank. Thinks better of it.

                    MICKY
          Asshole. I'm gonna hafta walk those
          members, especially Dr. Leahey, INTO my
          shed so they can see that all your shit
          is gone. Don't you get it? Half these
          golfers want to lynch you, half love
          you. I'm on the fuckin' fence at this
          point, myself, you dickhead. (Subtitle
          flashes: "Cabeza de verga")

                    SWEENEY
               (quietly testing Micky)
          'Cept for my surfboards, kid. Those

things can stay in the rafters, right?
That was the deal. I won't have room on
the S.S. Kemp Aaberg. You hafta tell
Leahey you started surfin', that the
boards are yours, and they gotta stay.

> MICKY
> (voice rising)
> HOLY MOTHAH OF GOD, I'VE NEVER
> FUCKIN'LIKED YOU. WHAT THE FUCK? GO
> FUCKIN' FUCKYASELF!

Micky WHIPS the PLANK at Sweeney's midsection.

Sweeney gamely dances back. Wood clanks off his shins. He
goes down, laughing and cursing.

> SWEENEY
> (grunting with pain)
> Man, we'll be drinkin beers and playing
> 45s in a couple hours in the galley of
> the Aaberg. You're MY partner, kid—I
> call it. Fuckin' take it easy. This'll
> all be behind us if you stop beatin'
> the shit outta me and let me work.

Micky leaps over the trailer hitch.

Sweeney's on his back, fingers interlaced over his shin.

Micky grabs him by the shirtfront with one hand, bouncing
him off the ground.

Still pointing four fingers back at the damaged course.

Sweeney laughs harder.

> MICKY
> BEHIND US? BEHIND US LOOKS LIKE A PACK
> OF WILD BOARS ON A COKE BINGE CAME
> THROUGH BEHIND US! FUCKING THICK IRISH
> FUCK!

Sweeney's laughing really hard now, unfazed.

                    SWEENEY
                (between laughs)
            Coke-binging boars! Yeeeeaaaaaahhhh
            boyeeeee!

As Micky falls to the ground with one last slap to
Sweeney's head, Spiro beeps and bellows from the road.

                    SPIRO
                (shouting)
            Are you guys already wasted or what?
            I didn't steal this plywood for my
            health! Hurry the fuck up, everyone's
            already at the bar!

Micky, lying in the grass next to Sweeney, smiles
knowingly.

                                        CUT TO:

EXT. - FARANNAN GOLF COURSE - OUT-OF-BOUNDS WOODS NEXT TO
HOLE NUMBER 6 - EVENING
_____

Sounds of laughter and clinking bottles emanate from the
boat.

"The Kemp Aaberg" is painted on the back of the boat.

                                        CUT TO:

INT. - THE KEMP AABERG GALLEY - SAME
_____

Sweeney, Micky, Spiro and Tommy Santos play 45s by a
hurricane lamp's yellow light.

TOMMY SANTOS is Sweeney's first cousin—a 280-pound
bruiser wearing a too-tight "Seawell Beach '89" T-shirt.
He's bald, heavily 5-o'clock-shadowed at all times. A
dangerous townie.

Tommy points at Sweeney and Micky methodically, again and
again, while talking.

                    TOMMY SANTOS
We're playin' Cutthroat after this
game. No more partners. You and Sweeney
fuckin' cheat so bad at partners it
makes me naw-shus.

                    MICKY
                (unfazed, impatient)
Oh, shut the fuck up Santos, you fat
fuck. Me and Sweeney been 45s partners
for so long we don't even need to
cheat. You just suck at cards. Go back
to the Lowlands with that inferiority-
complex shit.

Tommy GLARES at Micky, and opens his big maw to respond.

                    SWEENEY
                (not looking up)
Play fucking cards, Tommy, and don't
even say it. You got all the focus of
a drunken housefly and you've had like,
what, three beers? That's why you
fuckin' lose all the time. You don't
even remember what cards your partner,
the Greek Easter-bunny over here,
played.

                    TOMMY SANTOS
Hey, easy, of course I remem...

                    SPIRO
                (snapping out of a daze)
What? Is it Greek Easter already?
Fuckin' first thing tomorrow I gotta get
a card for my Yia-Yia!

Sprio grabs a pen and scrawls "Greek Easter" on the back
of his hand.

                    SPIRO (CONT'D)
                (voice cracking with worry)
        My Yia-Yia will kill me if I forget.

Micky and Sweeney break up laughing.

Tommy shakes his head at his loopy partner, shoots
Sweeney a lightning quick middle finger.

                    SPIRO (CONT'D)
                  (catching on)
        Hey, bein' Greek's better than bein' a
        Portuguese refugee or an Irish potato-
        eatin' fuckin'…

Spiro ducks an empty can flung at his head, calmly
deflects another in front of his face with the edge of
his hand.

Spiro utters ninja-esque noises, wipes beer from his
face, smiling.

                    SPIRO (CONT'D)
        Shit. That woulda left a mark! How the
        fuck am I s'posed to talk to girls at
        the bar with a welt on my face? Whoever
        threw that is lucky I'm a brownbelt and
        I've studied the art of restraint.

                    SANTOS
                  (incredulously)
        What's wrong with you? You're
        certifiable. For one, I never see you
        talk to girls at the bar. You fuck
        goats. You been givin' Goatboy the eye
        all night. You're a goatfucker, through
        and through. And, two, stop with that
        "brownbelt" shit. You quit afterschool-
        karate like ten years ago.

                    SPIRO
        Hey, easy. It was five years ago. And

that dojo was corrupt, I told you that.
And, by the way, you're talkin' like
I'm the Bill Clinton of goatfuckers.
No cigars from me, Goatboy. Sorry to
disappoint you. Not tonight, not ever.

Laughter all around.

Spiro starts to throw a card down, stops…

                    SPIRO (CONT'D)
          Wait, whose turn is it to throw?

Santos looks up at Spiro, winces, throws a 4 of spades.

                    SPIRO (CONT'D)
          After all this bullshit waiting and
          griping, that's the card my fuckin'
          partner throws. How the…

                    MICKY
                (interrupting)
          SHUT UP, Spiro! You guys can't fuckin'
          TALK about the cards played. You know
          that shit.

Sweeney throws the ACE OF HEARTS.

Spiro drops his forehead to the galley table,
despondently.

Santos has to laugh. He throws his cards down.

                    SANTOS
          Let's just get that woodstove in here
          now. I gotta go out to the cooler to
          get a beer anyways. Fuck this game. I
          wanta get down to McSwiggan's soon.

                    SWEENEY
          Yeah, me too. Those Galloway fucks have
          been out and about. I want to fuck up

one of those goons—the guy with the
cauliflower ear.

Santos SNEAKS a sideways look at Sweeney sensing
something's wrong. He stands, they all go onto the aft
deck of the boat.

CUT TO:

EXT. - FARANNAN GOLF COURSE - FAIRWAY - NIGHT - SAME

The four men walk away in the distance.

> SANTOS (Voice Over)
> Man, that fuckin' woodstove weighed
> a ton. It'll be good when it's cold,
> though. You really gonna stay in that
> boat this winter?

> SWEENEY (V.O.)
> Yep. The last of my family are gone for
> good; I'm on my own. I don't pay much
> for rent to Goatboy back here. It's a
> good spot for me.

> SANTOS (V.O.)
> Yeah, you're a loon. You'll fit in fine
> out here. Although, speakin' of that,
> what's with you drinkin' and startin'
> fights left an' right lately? You're
> actually gonna pick a fight with a guy
> with cauliflower ear? What's wrong with
> you, nothin'?

> SWEENEY (V.O.)
> I don't know, man. There haven't been
> any waves all summer. I'm antsy. I
> actually want to get outta Seawell for
> the winter but I lost that bet I made
> against Boston College. I'm kinda goin'
> feral.

CUT TO:

EXT. FARANNAN GOLF COURSE - SAME

Sweeney and Santos walk together, a little ahead of
Goatboy and Spiro. All are horsing around: stepping on
the heels of each others' shoes, tripping each other,
throwing empties, etc.

                    SANTOS
          Feral, huh? Well knock it fuckin' off.
          I'll loan you five hundred bucks. Take
          a week and go down to, where is it,
          Hatteras or somewhere and get some
          waves. You're buggin' me lately.

Santos pushes Sweeney, who stumbles to the side laughing.

                    SANTOS (CONT'D)
          I'm sick of bailin' you out in all
          these brawls. And would you stop with
          the stupid bets against B.C. football
          just because it's a Catholic school?
          That's fuckin' stupid.

                    SWEENEY
          Yeah, I know, right? They do suck,
          though. By the way, you seem to
          forget that I saved you last week
          when that kid split your lip.

Sweeney deftly drops back a step and kicks Santos's back
foot sideways so it catches on the back of his other leg.

Santos nearly falls to the ground, grunting with the
effort.
                    SANTOS
                 (sheepishly)
          That kid was quick, man. You know I'm
          about as fast as a brick shithouse
          comin' apart in the wind.

Santos throws a no-look, straight right out at Sweeney's

head. Sweeney ducks in-stride and keeps talking like the punch never happened.

Sweeney dances around the walking Santos, throwing a blur of combination punches. Santos tries to remain oblivious to this STUNNING display of left hooks, jabs, right hooks and short uppercuts that LIGHTLY pepper his ribs, chest and arms.

> SWEENEY
> I was savin' that kid from YOU, to be honest. You woulda crushed that skinny prick once you got your mitts on him. But I'm there for you, no matter who it is. You know that.

> SANTOS
> Same to you, you loony bastard. Same to you. Let's go get hammered.

> **SMASH CUT TO:**

INT. - DIVE BAR- SEAWELL - NIGHT

TIGHT ON THE FACE OF A HUGE TOWNIE known as "The Monstah" as he gets shoved violently forward, smashing his mouth on the back of someone's head in front of him at the crowded bar.

He bleeds from his lip, grows impatient, continues to try and order his drink in a civil manner.

The Monstah tries to ignore the fray behind him.

He's talking to the tops of his buddies' heads around him.

> THE MONSTAH
> Hmmm, that must be Sweeney, huh? I outweigh the guy by eighty pounds, what the fuck is he thinkin'?

WE FOLLOW Tommy Santos as he comes pushing his way around the rectangular bar to subdue a visibly drunk Sweeney.

Santos gets Sweeney to other side of the bar, pushes him toward a pool table.

Santos waves away a shot of whiskey offered to him.

> TOMMY SANTOS
> Nah, looks like I'm done drinkin'.
> I gotta babysit now. Just give me a
> Miller Lite.

CUT TO:

INT.-DIVE BAR-SAME

GALLOWAY TOWNIE #1 leans in to hiss a warning at the Monstah.

> GALLOWAY TOWNIE #1
> Should we just get outta here?

> THE MONSTAH
> Yeah, bro, I'm not up to it tonight
> either. I still got a fucked up hand
> from last week. One more for the road
> and we'll get the fuck…

The Monstah's interrupted by a red Solo cup BOUNCING off the side of his head.

He turns around to find Sweeney, who has eluded his friends, shoving him hard back hard against the bar.

Galloway Townie #1 takes a swing at Sweeney who turns his chin just out of range and immediately throws an elbow in high and tight to send Galloway Townie #1 to the floor in a heap.

> THE MONSTAH (CONT'D)
> (resigned)
> Here we go.

HISPANIC BOUNCER herds Sweeney, Santos, Spiro and Micky out to the street through the FRONT DOOR.

                    HISPANIC BOUNCER
          Sweeney, this is like the fourth fight
          for you in a month. If the cops come
          you're definitely getting pinched, you
          stupid fuck.

                       SWEENEY
          Shut up, Rousseau, or I'm coming back
          for your sorry ass when I finish these
          assholes off.

                    HISPANIC BOUNCER
          Rousseau? Do I look French Canadian? If
          you come back tonight I'll cave your
          thick Irish head in with the Yaz bat
          over the bar.

Hispanic Bouncer SLAMS the door and LOCKS it from the
inside.
                                              CUT TO:

EXT. - PATIO, DIVE BAR - NIGHT
_____

Other bouncers herd The Monstah and his friends out to
the SIDE PATIO through another door. They clatter into
plastic tables, chairs, snapping umbrellas.

                      IRISH BOUNCER
                  (thick Irish brogue)
          Somehow you geniuses picked the only
          guys in the bar that DON'T carry guns.
          Now FUCK OFF back to Galloway before I
          call the cops.

Irish Bouncer SLAMS the door, LOCKS it from the inside.

                                              CUT TO:

EXT. - SEAWELL, MASS. - STREET AND SMALL PARKING LOT NEXT
TO DIVE BAR - NIGHT
_____

Sweeney, Spiro, Santos and Micky scramble over one
another to get around the corner to fight the Galloway
crew.

They stop in their tracks at the sight of the group.

They're outnumbered by three or four Galloway guys.

> MICKY
> God fucking dammit, Sweeney. Again! You
> fuck me over like clockwork. You're the
> fuckin' Rolex of the fuckin'-people-
> over world I apparently live in.

Sweeney doesn't appear to be listening. He's focused,
quiet.

> MICKY (CONT'D)
> Sweeney! I'm talkin' to...ah, fuck
> you. (to himself) Let's just get
> this over with.

                                          CUT TO:

A SERIES OF IMAGES:

Micky & Spiro pair off with one or two guys each.

Santos goes straight for The Monstah.

Townie #2 & TOWNIE #3 are about Sweeney's size, they head
straight for him.

Sweeney fakes a right cross at Townie #2 and sweeps the
ground for an ankle pick on the guy on the right, Townie
3.

Townie #3 goes down on his back before he knows it and
Sweeney is on him with a jab that SPREADS his nose across
his face.

Townie #2 pales, but goes for Sweeney anyway.

Sweeney's up & dodging until he can circle a bit and grab

Townie #2's shirt, hockey-style. He pulls him into a
stiff uppercut on the point of his chin.
Townie #2 is done and Sweeney lets him down EASY by the
shirt.

Micky is rolling around on the cement with a Townie. It
looks pretty even.

Spiro's stuck in a headlock by Townie #4. He's catching
sloppy punches to the top of his head. He's punching his
adversary ineffectively in the ass-cheek over and over.

Sweeney's moving smoothly through the fray until a random
spectator holds him back from getting involved in the
Santos vs. Monstah fight.

Sweeney grabs the guy's wrist, twists it behind his back
and shoves him into the crowd. EVERYONE BACKS OFF.

Tommy's doing so-so against the Monstah but as he goes to
throw a punch he SLIPS in a puddle and does a half-split.

The crowd GROANS, laughs.

Tommy falls to his back, breathing hard, holding his
groin.

Sweeney steps in.

                    SWEENEY
              (half-sober, serious)
          Why don't you go the fuck back to
          Galloway before you get hurt, man?

                  THE MONSTAH
          Sweeney, you're a joke. If I leave
          I'll send back my little sister. She's
          uglier and almost as tough me. She'll
          fuckin' ruin your pretty face for free.

Sweeney looks down at a Solo cup between his feet.

The Monstah looks down too, and DOUBLETAKES at Sweeney's
feet. He's wearing Rainbow brand sandals, flip-flops.

In one impossibly smooth motion, Sweeney crouches, flicks the cup at The Monstah then leaps from his crouch behind the cup.

As the cup hits The Monstah lightly in the face, AGAIN, Sweeney connects with a straight kick to The Monstah's solar plexus.

The Monstah crumples to one knee, the wind KNOCKED from his body.

He's on one knee, trying to keep his eye on a pacing Sweeney who seems to have gone FERAL.

> SWEENEY
> (taunting)
> If you're feelin' froggy...then leap, suckah.

The Monstah gamely staggers upright, though he still can't breathe. He is finally ANGRY.

Sweeney ducks away from the Monstah's haymakers and scrabbling attempts to grab him.

Sweeney connects with one or two punches, even tries a bodyshot.

The Monstah's regaining his wind and is surprisingly light on his feet, absorbing punches, waiting.

SMASH CUT TO:

TIGHT ON The Monstah's right incisor coming clean through his upper lip as Sweeney connects flush with a left hook.

Blood SPATTERS on rows of spectators.

CUT TO:

EXT. - ONE BLOCK FROM THE BAR - APARTMENT WINDOW ABOVE A BURNT-OUT CAR - SAME

Elder Jones and Elder Smith lean out of a tenement

window, looking for the commotion.

There are a few Southeast Asian gangsters smoking and drinking on the stoop.

                                             CUT TO:
EXT.-PARKING LOT, STREET - DIVE BAR - SAME

                    BIG-HAIRED GIRL
                  (screeching)
          Shit! Is it in my hair? Open your eyes,
          you bitch! Look! I fuckin' just got
          this perm like five hours ago and now
          there's blood in it!

The crowd JEERS as she STALKS off toward the two Mormons leaning out their window in the distance.

Big-Haired Girl gives the crowd the finger back over her shoulder.

                    BIG-HAIRED GIRL (CONT'D)
                  (shouting)
          That's fuckin' it! I'm movin' in with
          my cousin Tricia in Southie. Fuck
          Seawell, and fuck you, Sweeney!

                                             CUT TO:

EXT.-ONE BLOCK FROM THE BAR, APARTMENT WINDOW ABOVE A
BURNT OUT CAR - SAME

Elder Jones tenses instantly as he hears Sweeney's name.

                    ELDER SMITH
          C'mon, let's go. Sweeney's at it again.

                    ELDER JOHNSON
                  (mocking)
          "Sweeney's at it again?" What? You
          think you're in the Justice League or
          something? I haven't gone outside after
          dark more than twice in two years in
          this awful dying city. Why would I go

out there now? A rerun of "Perfect
Strangers" is starting in a minute. I'm
not going anywhere.

>   ELDER SMITH
>   (not listening)
> C'mon, brother, follow me. And that
> TV show is sinful. You know I don't
> approve.

ELDER JOHNSON hangs out the window for a beat, looks down
at a couple of Asian gangsters smoking a blunt on their
stoop.

>   ELDER JOHNSON
> Yeah, well I don't approve of getting
> killed by drunk madmen. (to the
> gangsters) I'm never rooming with this
> guy again.

The gangsters laugh, oblivious to the commotion at the
bar.

>   **CUT TO:**

EXT. - PARKING LOT, STREET - DIVE BAR - SAME
_____

(SERIES OF IMAGES Continues)
The Monstah appears hurt. He's bent over, taking shots.

Sweeney is lightning quick. No signs of fatigue.

He moves in and out of range, between parking blocks, on
and off the curb.

He's effortlessly luring The Monstah through these
stumbling blocks, waiting for a misstep and a window to
strike.

Sweeney misses a chance, but The Monstah pretends to
stumble again and bends forward at the waist toward
Sweeney.

Sweeney tries to finish him with a swing at his temple.

He MISSES BIG and follows through too far.
The Monstah grabs the back of Sweeney's sweatshirt.

It looks bad, for an instant, but Sweeney slithers out of
his sweatshirt, arms above his head.

The Monstah loses his balance, the sweatshirt in his
fists.

Sweeney stands shirtless, bloodied, all muscle, lean,
sweating, gleaming. He looks possessed.

Sweeney dodges a punch, steps quickly to the right, a
half step, and gets an angle for a fully extended right
hook that lands flush on the jaw of The Monstah.

The crowd quiets, in shock.

The Galloway townies are stunned, mouths agape, they
pause from wiping blood off their hands on their shirt-
fronts.

Tommy (still holding his groin on the ground), Micky and

Spiro's expressions all swing from worry to PRIDE.

The Monstah's foot slips off the curb and his forehead
grazes the cinderblock wall of the bar as he goes down in
a heap.

The Monstah's beyond dazed, but his eyes are open, he
scrabbles to one foot, falls.

It's over and the crowd starts shuffling away to cars and
back in the bar.

CUT TO:

EXT. - DIVE BAR - SAME

                         SWEENEY
                      (screaming)
               Get up you fat fuck! This isn't
               Galloway, you lightweight.

Santos sees Sweeney's beyond keyed-up. He limps over to
sweep him up in a bear hug, subdues him.

>   TOMMY SANTOS
>   (loudly, growing softer)
>   IT'S OVER, it's over, it's over. The
>   cops'll be here. Come back in the bar.
>   It's over, it's over. Come back inside.
>   Beers inside, man. It's over. Beers on
>   me, inside. Inside, man. Let's go.

Sweeney FAKES that he's going in the bar, struggles out
of Santo's arms, LEAPS toward the seated Monstah.

Micky and Spiro step in front, but they clearly don't
want to touch Sweeney.

He's CRAZED.

>   **CUT TO:**

EXT. - DIVE BAR - SAME

A SERIES OF IMAGES:

Elder Smith is running, breathing hard.

He comes up behind Sweeney.

Tight on Tommy Santos' SHOCKED face as he sees the
Mormon.

>   TOMMY SANTOS
>   (erupting)
>   OH SHIT! DON'T GRAB…

Elder Smith GRABS Sweeney's left arm from behind, up by
his shoulder.

>   ELDER SMITH
>   Sweeney O'Sweeney, You owe me a Bible…

Sweeney wheels, throwing a nearly blind yet perfectly
placed right hook that Elder Johnson accidentally leans

into with his mouth WIDE OPEN.

Elder Smith DROPS, jaw shattered. He's a lifeless heap
even BEFORE CRACKING his head on a parking block.

Spiro, Micky and Tommy are instantly on Sweeney, pinning
him down.

They appear SICKENED by what they've just seen.

JUMP CUT TO:

EXT. - PARKING LOT, STREET - A VOLKSWAGON JETTA - SAME
The Monstah is being stuffed in the back of the Jetta.

It peels out with the doors banging shut on the fly.

CUT TO:

EXT. - PARKING LOT, STREET - SAME

Two cop cars, lights flaring, sirens cut off, screech to
a stop.

Elder Johnson is pacing between his unconscious fellow
Mormon and the pile of men holding Sweeney down.

He bends to look at his roommate's smashed face.

He walks back to the pile of bodies on top of Sweeney.

He bends to SCREECH in Sweeney's face pinned on the
cement.

> ELDER JOHNSON
> (hysterical)
> SWEENEY YOU ARE CURSED! I CAN'T, I
> CAN'T…

Four cops jump out, push aside Elder Johnson.

The cops peel Spiro, Micky and Tommy off Sweeney.
They pepper-spray Sweeney and cuff him.

Sweeney struggles in a FRENZY, like an animal.

COP #1 points at Elder Smith, unconscious and bleeding profusely into an oily puddle.

>   COP #1
>   Call an ambulance, that kid's fucked.
>   And somebody grab that other religious
>   freak so we can get a statement. Calm
>   him the fuck down! Are these fuckin'
>   Mormons or something? Jesus, don't they
>   know not to send these virgin fucks to
>   this part of Seawell? Get him in the
>   bar and kick everyone else out. KICK
>   EVERY FUCKIN' CLOWN OUT!

COP #2 yells for the dwindled crowd in the street to disperse as COPS #3 & #4 enter the bar screaming at everyone to leave.

>   COP #2
>   Alright, everyone fuck off! I don't
>   care what the rest of you have to say
>   about this circus. Get in your fuckin'
>   cars. DON'T GO BACK IN THAT BAR! DO
>   NOT! You! Hey, fuckin' idiots. DO NOT
>   go in there, I said. Sweeney's fucked.
>   He's goin' to jail, you wanna go with
>   him?

                                        DISSOLVE TO:

INT.-MERRIT HOUSE OF CORRECTIONS-SWEENEY'S CELL

We see a series of images beginning with Sweeney doing pushups, RAPIDFIRE, on his KNUCKLES on the floor of his cell.

His head is SHAVED, but he's starting to grow a BEARD. We see one bunk stacked solid with BOOKS: Weldon Kees, Rimbaud, Basho, Joseph Campbell, "The Tibetan Book of the Dead," Robert Frost, Issa, Elizabeth Bishop, Denise Levertov, Brendan Behan's "At Swim-Two-Birds."

The camera lingers on two books: both bent, dogeared, both facedown and spread open: "THE POEMS OF SWEENEY PEREGRINE," BY TREVOR JOYCE & "SWEENEY ASTRAY" BY SEAMUS HEANEY.

We hear Sweeney count off 199, 200 pushups. He pops to his feet with catlike reflexes, slips into the desk's chair and slides the "DSM IV" out and begins studying "Schizoaffective Disorder, Bipolar Type."

                                                    CUT TO:

INT. MERRIT HOUSE OF CORRECTIONS, PHONE ROOM - DAY

                         SWEENEY
               Yeah, I found the diagnosis I'm going
               for. Don't you fuckin' mention this to
               anyone either, assface, ok?

Micky sits on the other side of the glass, listening intently. He looks shaken.

                         MICKY
               Of course I won't fuckin' say anything.
               But you better be sure you want to…

                         SWEENEY
               Kid, I've missed too much time outta
               the water and wasted too many years
               of my youth, you know what I mean? I
               haven't done anything. I haven't been
               anywhere. I'm fuckin gettin outta
               Seawell winters once and for all.

                         MICKY
               Man, you traveled more than anyone
               I know. You'll be out in a while,
               travelling. You know you can always
               work for me. We make bank when you work
               for me. That government money might not
               be enough to travel on anyways, right?

SWEENEY

Well, it'll be close. It's like 650
bucks a month or so and I'll just do
tree work under the table for you
during the summer and fall.

MICKY

Under the table? I don't know, man, you
sure? Just stay on the books and we'll
split the business up 50/50. I got
plenty of work for us.

SWEENEY

I know what I'm doin'. Don't tell
anyone and don't even bring it up with
me anymore. Seriously. I gotta sell
this whole process starting today.
Today's the six-month anniversary of
that beatdown I gave that Mormon. This
is the first step. TODAY.

MICKY
(nervously)

Did you, I mean, some of the guys think
you meant to…. Man, you wrecked that
kid's face so bad, I mean…I never seen
you do somethin' like that before but
you were so fuckin' angry. I seen you
angry before, but not that fuckin'
angry. Your own cousin, man…Tommy won't
even talk to me about you. He almost
killed me last month when I brought
that night up. You were just wasted,
right? You didn't mean it, right? We're
like family. You can tell me, man.
Please tell me.

Sweeney places the phone down on the desk, drops his head
into his hands.

Micky is perplexed, hurt, phone glued to his ear.

Sweeney looks at Micky as we hear the Pogues "And the Band Played 'Waltzing Matilda'" quietly begin.

Sweeney picks up the phone, holds it at arms length.

He's singing the lyrics, swaying.

> MICKY (CONT'D)
> What? I can't hear you? What the fuck are you doing?

> SWEENEY
> (loudly into phone, in
> unison with song)
> "And the band played 'Waltzing Matilda'
> as we sailed away from the quay. And
> amidst all the cheers the shouts and
> the jeers we sailed off for Galipoli…"

Sweeney slams the phone down. Flails wildly as guards rush to grab him.

Though it's all an act, he throws a convincingly horrifying fit as he screams the same phrase over and over.

> SWEENEY (CONT'D)
> BUT I DON'T BELIEVE IN ANY OF THEM!

The guards manage to drag the screaming, twitching Sweeney from the room.

Micky looks unsure of what he's just seen and heard from his old friend.

He stares at the forgotten phone in his hand.

> End of Act I

THE STORY OF THE FAILURE OF THIS SCRIPT IN HOLLYWOOD & BEYOND

PART I

"Who was this man you slept with, anyway?' Dana asked her wife on the drive home from the fertility clinic.

"What? Who? What are you talking about?" Ellen laughed, "The imaginary man, you mean?"

"Yes, of course. You've always insisted you've never been with a man. 'All women, all the time, on my TV.' That was your signature line in college. It always made me laugh to hear a lesbian use a David Lee Roth line from the 'California Girls' video. It's still funny to me, Ellen, yet now after all these years of laughter I find out you've been sleeping with an imaginary man?"

Ellen appeared unruffled as she engaged in this banter with her wife: "Well, yes, I mean according to Dr. Thorpe, the new deviously liberal doctor you found for us, I have been befouled by the member of a man."

"Dr. Thorpe has written here that you and this man 'tried multiple times' to have a baby. 'Tried multiple times' in layman's terms indicates a lot of hetero fornication that I frankly don't approve of, my dear. And finally, after all that effort, you were deemed infertile. Is that how it went? Is that why we are now eligible for our insurance to cover the costs of this second effort at artificial insemination? Damn right-wing fundamentalists to the hell of their own making if you want, but when you are done with that effort at damnation, I still want to know who this imaginary man was."

"Dana, before we go any further, I want to assure you that I've considered that the phantasmal phallus of said man was at fault so many years ago—that it was not I who was infertile. What I've found however, after much soul searching, is that both scenarios are true: I am infertile and yet a dick that never existed cannot do the job for which dicks were created. Better that should've gone without saying, possibly."

Ellen flashed an impish grin at Dana after quickly checking the rearview mirror for a view of their sleeping toddler, Nora.

Dana, thrilled at this grin as a sign of a welcome return to their stress-free, pre-pregnancy past, continued, "Regardless, Ellen, I want you to know I find myself inexplicably and imaginarily jealous of this hallucinatory dong from your past."

"Allow me to fan the flames, then, Dana. This lone stranger from my past was an amalgamation of men, specifically the visages of a young Ernest Hemingway and Rock Hudson."

Dana snorted a laugh, stifled it and stole a glance over her shoulder at Nora in her car seat. Still asleep. "Interesting combination. One of the chosen went crazy and killed himself and the other spent his public life in the closet until he very publicly was forced out of the closet by contracting and then dying of AIDS."

"Well, you asked. I have dubbed my imaginary friend 'Sir Ernest Rock, and you'll have to admit, your lesbian proclivities aside, that the chosen combination makes for one very attractive nonexistent individual."

"Yes, Hudson Hemingway would be too waspy of a name. Good work staying in touch with your Catholic, blue-collar heritage. But I notice you've knighted this hybrid man?"

Ellen paused for effect, "As you know firsthand, any man who would put his dick, imaginary or not, in me would need bravery and boldness equivalent to that of the entire Round Table, no?"

"In a world filled with uncertainties and illusions of all flavors, Ellen, I believe what you've just said to be a given—yet another truth that ought go without saying."

Ellen and Dana's conversation about imaginary lovers concluded as they left downtown Chicago for the farmland south of the city. Nora, dreaming of hailstorms and lightning underneath the aural gauze of her mothers' laughter, woke crying at the first clap of dreamt thunder.

Nora's cries heightened to hysteria within a half mile. Ellen pulled to the breakdown lane, white-knuckling the wheel, wincing at the din. Dana climbed in back laughing to herself, soothing Nora with hugs and cooing.

It was a memorable car ride for Dana in particular, because it was not only the first time she learned the name of her future adversary but also the last time she witnessed her wife at ease in their shared roles as mothers, wives & professionals. They were mid-stream in the development of their feature film based on the books Sweeney on-the-Fringe and Sweeney at-Sea by Dave Robinson & Owen Kivlin.

Nora soothed, and now babbling like a brook, Dana noticed the white knuckles and offered to drive. Ellen slumped to sleep in the passenger seat within a half mile, only stirring to retract drool with a shushing slurp as they turned toward their refurbished farmhouse in rural Carbondale.

All sentient, inanimate and imaginary things began their daily assault on Ellen's mental and emotional state after that car ride. The responsibilities of directing a feature film of Sweeney's life were a particular bane to her.

This was a revelation to Dana, as Ellen had never appeared ruffled by any aspect of their professional lives. She had formerly been the picture of ease and expert composure. In some Hollywood circles, she was known as "The Natural."

Rumor has it Redford himself gave his blessing for the use of the nickname after co-producing a documentary with her about snake-oil salesmen in rural 19th Century America.

Ellen's otherworldly talent and résumé of films and projects, despite the early end to her career, will stand the test of time.

Dana, a wonderful producer and director herself, chose to be in Ellen's professional shadow. After mental illness scratched away the final crumbs of mortar holding their careers and personal lives together, Dana would reconstruct a distinguished career in Hollywood in spite of being a working single mother of three.

It wasn't long after the abovementioned car ride that Ellen began riding the "Sir Ernest Rock joke" like a rusted three speed bicycle she found in the trash heap at the back of her mind. Sir Ernest Rock became, in name only, a part of Ellen and Dana's daily lives during Ellen's pregnancy with the twins.

During the second trimester, as morning sickness faded behind a haze of lethargy and crazed appetite, even little Nora began to spook Ellen. Nerves, long since frayed, warped into an attitude of disgust toward their waddling child. It weighed on Ellen that two of her self-described "lowgrade eggs" (originally harvested for her first pregnancy with Nora) were now planted and growing in her womb. Nora, in other words, was the first of triplets—all redheaded and pale as the moon. Aileen and Gerty, Nora's sisters, arrived seven minutes apart a full three years after Nora was born.

Dana, who deemed them the "Gap Triplets," which became the diminutive "Gaplets," was overjoyed by the science fiction-as-modern-medical-fact aspect of her childrens' birth stories. These were special, interesting details that she would contemplate to help buoy her spirits during the most difficult times of raising three children under four years old (to say nothing of the increasing burden of Ellen's descent into insanity).

Ellen's mental health seemed assailed by the existence of her three red-headed children. All three possessed unique personalities, none of which pleased Ellen. She was soon revolted by their mere presence. Two six-month-olds and a three-and-a-half-year-old inexplicably plagued her ability to get through a day. Ellen was no longer herself.

Dana's and Ellen's final conversation about the Gaplets consisted of a failed effort by Dana to repurpose the seemingly remnant-Catholic parochialism of Ellen's experience of the twins into something more positive.

Dana pleaded, "Ell, you remember how difficult it was to get you pregnant again? We had to stack the house with the eggs we had left. It was the only choice they gave us back then. Aileen and Gerty were harvested as eggs in Boston and planted in your womb in Chicago. It's like we all made the same road trip out here to our new life together, but at different times."

Ellen did not respond. Ellen remained glazed over—silenced by her paranoia and her unharnessed detachment.

"C'mon, Ell, I'm just kidding. I'm just trying to get you to see how lucky we are with these three little rubies. It's not too strange that they ended up being the Gaplets, is it?

Let's just get through this Sweeney film and then we could do a documentary on the kids and the politics and medical wonders of artificial insemination. It's time we did another documentary anyway. It'll be a cinch."

As a reluctant finale to her rhetorical effort, Dana climbed on Ellen's old bicycle in an effort to obtain some semblance of a reaction from her wife: "I guess only Sir Ernest Rock missed out on that family road trip, huh?" Ellen still glazed, whispered, "I should've adopted with Ernie years ago when I had the chance. I wish I'd never let

him go. I miss him."

Dana hasn't much time to mourn the loss of her former wife to insanity. She has even less time to visit her at the home nowadays. Ellen lives in a large, borderline luxurious, out of-the-way facility for the mentally ill in the small town of Breeze, Illinois. She is heavily sedated and on constant suicide watch. She is close enough for regular visits, though those are suspended by doctor's orders until further notice.

Any and all visitors inadvertently jab at and inflame Ellen's paranoia, even through the cloud of chemicals designed to quell and calm.

ACT II

CUT TO:

INT-MERRIT HOUSE OF CORRECTIONS-CAFETERIA-MORNING

TITLE FLASHES: EXACTLY ONE YEAR LATER

As "And the Band Played Waltzing Matilda" continues we see Sweeney's mental state reflected in his physical appearance:

His HAIR HAS GROWN SHOULDER-LENGTH AND MATTED, along with a now mammoth, unkempt beard.

Sweeney sits at a metal table, at ease, eating GRAY OATMEAL.

Other prisoners just behind Sweeney's bent form watch him and laugh a bit nervously, rolling their eyes at him.

In tight on Sweeney as he tenses up as if someone speaks to him from his immediate left.

He looks left.

> SWEENEY
> (muttering, gravel-voiced)
> Something broke inside you, kid, didn't
> it?

Turning his gaze straight ahead. His eyes blaze with an odd look.

                    SWEENEY (CONT'D)
                 (loudly, clearly)
        Yep. Something's broken.

PULL BACK to reveal NO ONE sitting in chairs on either
side of him.

Sweeney turns his head to the right.

                    SWEENEY (CONT'D)
                 (muttering, gravel-voiced)
        You fucked that kid's jaw up; Put him
        in a coma. Nearly killed him, didn't
        you?

Gazing straight-on again, Sweeney's hands have gone limp,
the knuckles around his spoon drag through his bowl of
oatmeal.
                    SWEENEY (CONT'D)
                 (loudly, clearly)
        Yep.

Suddenly looking up above the table with a violent
jerking of his head.

                    SWEENEY (CONT'D)
                 (loudly, clearly)
        What? What? Don't talk to me from
        up there, you fuckin' asshole. At
        least have the decency to come down
        to my level. (Voice rising an octave in
        disbelief) You fuckin' floating heads
        got a great sense of humor. Always
        sneering, muttering.

Snapping his head down and to his left.

                    SWEENEY (CONT'D)
                 (muttering, gravel-voiced)
        You really got your oats, now, eh?
        You're eatin' your oats, now, huh kid?

Looks straight ahead.

> SWEENEY (CONT'D)
> (begging)
> Oh leave me the fuck alone, you guys,
> huh? Please. Just let me have a
> breakfast to myself for once.

Looking right and then straight up again.

> SWEENEY (CONT'D)
> (muttering, gravel-voiced)
> Oh, you'll eat your oats now. Eat 'em
> up. You're gettin 'em now, huh kid?

> CUT TO:

INT. MERRIT HOUSE OF CORRECTIONS, PRISON PSYCHIATRIST'S
OFFICE

DR. DUFFY is a slim, bespectacled brunette in her mid-
30s. She has an INTENSE but ATTENTIVE aura as she studies
Sweeney. She takes no notes, though she has pen and pad
in hand.

> SWEENEY
> Yeah, the medicine helps cut down on
> the sightings. No doubt about it.
> Medicine and exercise.

Sweeney bends in his seat, rolls one pantleg halfway up
his calf.

> SWEENEY (CONT'D)
> But I'm in a bit deep, kid, a bit deep.

> CUT TO:

INT.-MERRIT HOUSE OF CORRECTIONS-SWEENEY'S CELL

Sweeney is escorted into his cell, sits on the bunk.
He sits perfectly still, his HAIR AND BEARD ARE LONGER,
CRAZIER, FILTHIER.

He spits out a pill and hands it between the bars to a

hand from neighboring cell.

He drops to his back on the floor for RAPIDFIRE crunches.

A knowing smile lights up his face.

                                        CUT TO:

INT. - MERRIT HOUSE OF CORRECTIONS, PRISON PSYCHIATRIST'S
OFFICE - SAME

                    DR. DUFFY
                (interest piqued)
        YES, I did happen to grow up in
        Seawell. I live in Boston now. However,
        I wonder why you ask so many people you
        meet where they are from?

                    SWEENEY
        I don't.

Sweeney bends in his seat again to roll up the other cuff
of his uniform. He FUSSES to match the length of both
cuffs.
                    SWEENEY (CONT'D)
                (laughing)
        Cuffs, Cuffy. Dr. Cuffy, I'm in deep,
        huh?

                    DR. DUFFY
        Maybe. But could you elaborate for me?
        I've heard you ask everybody where
        they're from?

                    SWEENEY
        No. I ask everybody what part of
        SEAWELL they're from. I don't give a
        shit where they're really from.

                    DR. DUFFY
        Really? Why Seawell?

Sweeney bends, quickly rolls both cuffs up to his knees.

                    SWEENEY
            (absorbed with his cuffs)
Oh, everyone's from some part of
Seawell--some of 'em just don't know
it. (raising his voice) MAN! I AM IN DEEP
HERE. I'm gonna need a shovel, maybe a
mop.

                    DR. DUFFY
            (checking an annoyed tone)
In deep what, Sweeney, what?

                    SWEENEY
Oats, oatmeal. Goddamn oatmeal's about
shin-deep in here. (Snapping out of it
for a second) The kid on the Farina box
is from Seawell. You ever heard that? I
did. I met him once at a frat party at
Seawell State.

                    DR. DUFFY
            (genuinely interested)
Really? I never knew that.

Rolling down his cuffs to half-calf length again.

                    SWEENEY
They should give us all capri pants
in this place, for Christ's sake!
At the very least high-waters should be
standard issue. Yeah, the
Farina kid. Yeah, he was alright, I
guess. He was from the Rathmines
neighborhood, his parents farmed
him out as a baby-model. He was like
five years older than me when I met him.
I fuckin' knocked him out, though, for
not givin' me a keg cup one night.

                    DR. DUFFY
            (checking her shock)

Oh, and why would you…

                    SWEENEY
          Nah, I'm just kiddin'. I almost
          drilled him, but I was just in high
          school back then. I decided not to
          punch him. I just invited him over
          to the groundskeeping shed to play
          cards.

                    DR. DUFFY
          Oh, you became friends? That's nice.

Sweeney rolls his cuffs partially down--left then right.

A BEAT. He rolls them right back up--right then left.

                    SWEENEY
          Yeah he was in a frat so me and my
          friends had this hidden roulette
          table and I told him about it once
          he had a coupla beers and we let
          him take a bunch of money at cards.

Sweeney stands, then sits. Looking at his cuffs the whole
time.
                    DR. DUFFY
          You were in high school and you had
          an apartment or, er, a shed, with a
          roulette table? Wait, you let him
          win money off of you?

                    SWEENEY
          Well, it was the groundskeeping
          shed on the course and then I put
          an old boat on beam ends behind it
          to live in. I've never lived in an
          apartment. The Farina Kid, that's
          what we called him, he came over to
          the shed. Anyways, we took all of
          The Farina Kid's money that night.
          Him and all his Seawell State

fratboy friends lost their shirts.
The roulette table, cards, bit of
dice. We got 'em drunk, took their
moneyand dropped them off on the other
side of the river where they
belonged.

Sweeney rolls the cuffs all the way back down. Seems
satisfied.

                    DR. DUFFY
          Is the oatmeal gone?

                    SWEENEY
          I wish. It's low tide. Believe me,
          high tide oatmeal-style ain't gonna
          be pretty.

                    DR. DUFFY
          What's Seawell like these days? I
          don't get back to visit very often.

                    SWEENEY
                (turning on the charm)
          It's the same as it's always been,
          trust me. Everyone makes fun of
          anyone from a different neighborhood.
          We brawl, we drink,
          we are proud of our city.

                    DR. DUFFY
          And the Heads are which
          neighborhood, did you say? The
          Lowlands? Is this because you've
          fought with so many men from that
          neighborhood?

                    SWEENEY
          Yep. Definitely some kind of
          payback because I always brawled
          with Lowlands kids. They were the
          only ones stupid enough to keep
          agitatin' me. Well, them and

Galloway kids. I fuckin' hate
Galloway guys.

                DR. DUFFY
Just out of curiosity, Sweeney,
what neighborhood am I from in
Seawell?

                SWEENEY
        (laughing)
Lady, if you don't know by now...
(Changing to mock seriousness) Nah,
I'm just foolin'. You probably grew up
in the Oaklands like me, didn't you?

                DR. DUFFY
        (failing to check a smile)
Yes, how...did someone tell you...

                SWEENEY
Yeah, you probably grew up off of
Grandfather Hovey.

                DR. DUFFY
        (distracted by a memory)
I forgot about that name for that
hill.

                SWEENEY
Oh yeah, that's what everyone calls
the huge hill up near my house.
It's where some of the, um, more
well-to-do families live.

                DR. DUFFY
        (nostalgic)
I forgot. I haven't thought of
that hill since I went sledding
there as a child. Did you grow up
on Grandfather Hovey, Sweeney?

                    SWEENEY
        No, I grew up next to Mr.
        Blackstock's Garage, the car repair
        place, near Lefty's bar. Then we
        moved near the marshy side of the
        golf course. But I always walked up
        to Grandfather Hovey to sled and do
        the can trick to cars and stupid
        shit like that. Oh, excuse me.
        Language. Sorry.

Sweeney stands abruptly, nervously.

                    DR. DUFFY
        That's alright. Um, are we done for
        the day? I'd like to talk more
        about the Heads, if we could. Next
        Wednesday is the anniversary of
        your arrest for the fight, so…

                    SWEENEY
              (suddenly uncomfortable)
        Yeah, uh, no. We're done.
        Next Wednesday is *theeeeee* Big
        Wednesday. Six months left after that.
        The Heads, my buddies, will be back on
        Wednesday. All three in full-force. And
        I'm s'posetah see you that day too, so
        I hafta get back to my cell and read
        and get ready and stuff. I have to get
        through that new Zen book I got.

As Sweeney is already moving past her and out of the
office.
                    DR. DUFFY
              (flustered)
        Ok, then. Yes. Get ready then. Go
        and meditate. Keep that practice
        going. Read up on Zen, if you can.
        I'll see you in a week, on Big
        Wednesday. (exasperated) I mean,
        I'll see you next Wednesday, then.

CUT TO:

INT - SAME

In tight on Sweeney as another knowing smile creeps across his bearded face.

                    SWEENEY
          Yep, you'll see me then...unless I
          see you first around the neighborhood,
          Duffy.

In close on Dr. Duffy surprised, but welcoming of the familiarity.

CUT TO:

INT. - MERRIT HOUSE OF CORRECTIONS - COUNTER WINDOW - DAY

Sweeney receives his clothing and Rainbow sandals back from a guard. His hair is long, thick, unkempt and he has a MASSIVE BEARD.

Dr. Duffy stands nearby watching Sweeney's every move.

                    DR. DUFFY
          Sweeney, remember, I would have
          already diagnosed you with
          Schizoaffective Disorder, Bipolar
          Type but the State requires another
          opinion. This could be a tricky time
          for you. Try to avoid stressful
          situations, even if it means only
          working part time. Surf as much as
          you can, since that's something that
          grounds you in nature. Do the things
          that ground you.

                    SWEENEY
          Don't worry, Duffy. The waves are
          massive right now and I gotta get it
          at low tide. So thanks for everything,
          really. I hope I never see you again!

                    DR. DUFFY
                  (laughing)
          Sweeney, I don't really want to see
          you around here either. Go get in
          the water and please don't stray
          from your meditation practice.
          Meditating every day will keep you
          balanced out there as it did in
          here. Refrain from the beers for a
          while, huh? (Beat) That'd be good.

                    SWEENEY
                  (simultaneously)
          That'd be good.

They both laugh. There's a hint of tenderness between
them. Dr. Duffy's still worried about Sweeney as he is
released.

                                              CUT TO:

EXT. - TWO LANE COUNTRY ROAD - FALL - DAY
_____

Sweeney walks quickly along the shoulder of the road, his
back to the oncoming traffic. He holds his thumb out,
occasionally breaking into a trot, spinning, looking for
oncoming cars. The leaves are ABLAZE with fall colors.
Sweeney's hustling to get to the beach to surf.

                                              CUT TO:
EXT. - SAME
_____

A RUST-POCKED blue 1980 Jeep Cherokee pulls over.

MINNESOTA PLATES on the back as Sweeney climbs in the
cab.
                                              CUT TO:

INT. - CHEROKEE'S CAB - DAY
_____

DIANA MARPESSA is a beautiful woman in her mid-20s, with
thick blond hair and a face that needs no makeup. Her
INTENSE eyes fix on Sweeney.

                    DIANA
          Where to, stranger?

                   SWEENEY
              (frozen by her beauty)
          Uh, East. East toward Seawell
          Beach. You can just drop me near
          Farannan Golf Course. I gotta get
          in the water.

                    DIANA
          East it is. It's freezing though,
          the water, this time of year, isn't
          it? Why would you go swimming?

                   SWEENEY
          I'm not swimming. I'm gonna surf,
          when the wind switches. It's been
          too long, I need to surf in the
          worst way.

                    DIANA
          People surf around here?

                   SWEENEY
          Yeah, everyone says that. If you
          have a good wetsuit the surf is
          great in the fall. And it's gonna
          be epic today. The best is you can
          always surf alone in Seawell.

                    DIANA
          Alone, huh? That'd be nice. I like
          walking around in the woods alone
          at night. It's kind of similar.
          Bears, sharks, hypothermia, very
          little control--not much to do but
          float through it. I can handle the
          bears and the woods, but I can't
          deal with cold water. How big are
          the waves today?

Sweeney takes a good, long look at Diana. He's impressed.

                    SWEENEY
          Um, there should be some 15-foot
          faces on the sets. And you get used to
          the cold water. Where are you from,
          anyways? Didn't I see Minnesota plates
          on this old thing?

                    DIANA
               (bristling)
          This "old thing" is "Large Marge
          the Blue Barge." She and I have
          circumnavigated North America twice
          without a single breakdown beyond
          what I can fix with my own hands.
          Show some respect, nameless hitchhiker.

                    SWEENEY
               (wincing)
          Hey, I apologize. You're right, Marge
          did deign to pick up my sorry ass. I'm
          Sweeney, by the way. What part of Minny
          are Marge and Diana from anyways?

                    DIANA
               (feigning anger)
          Don't call it "Minny." I live in a
          little cleared-out splotch in the
          Northwoods called Longville,
          Minnesota. There's about 600 of us
          in town. We're outnumbered by bears
          and mosquitos. And how'd you know
          my name, by the way?

                    SWEENEY
          I heard "the Minnesota girl" was
          around again this year. You and I
          did some shots last year during the
          City Golf Tournament. You don't recall?

                    DIANA
That was you? I remember someone
NEARLY outdrinking me. I heard you
fell down some stairs near the loo?

                    SWEENEY
                 (proudly)
I JUMPED down those stairs, I'll
have you know. Cleared eleven
stairs and one passed-out friend at
the bottom. I won some money with
that leap. I woulda bought you some
more Doctah with my 23-buck's worth
of winnings but…

                    DIANA
Yeah, that shit's the worst
schnapps I've ever had. You won't
catch me drinking that again.

Sweeney gestures at the backseat piled high with clothing
and camping gear.

                    SWEENEY
Don't denigrate the good Doctah,
you might change my opinion of your
obviously classic good taste. Is
that a stuffed possum or a fur coat
under there?

                    DIANA
                 (sarcastic)
Classic good taste, that's
hilarious. And that's a coywolf.
He's sleeps under my stuff.

                    SWEENEY
Coywolf? Nice. You know, I just did
a stint away from surfing for a
while so I gotta get in the ocean
as much as possible to heal up a bit.
But after that, maybe--you can

drop me off up here by the fence,
thanks. But after that--my mental
and spiritual convalescence--maybe I'll
come out to look for work
around Longville. I like bears and
trees. You know of any jobs out
there?

> DIANA

Yeah, c'mon out. You can chop some
wood for my family or something.
I'm starting back home later
tonight. Me, my wolf and Large
Marge the Blue Barge, that is.

> SWEENEY

There's a chance I'll head to South
America for the winter, so maybe
it'll be next summer when I get out
there. Will you be in Longville
then, when the surf's flat around
here?

> DIANA

Yeah, I'll be there then. I'm not
comin' back to Seawell if I can help
it, that's for sure. And we got better
schnapps than the Doctah, city boy.

> SWEENEY

Talk to you later, then. Too bad
you and Marge are leaving tonight.
There's a welcome-home party for me
at McSwiggan's. It'd be nice to
have a few drinks with you.

> DIANA
> (rolling her eyes)

It'll take a more than a few beers
for your charm to work on me, man.
I've heard about your exploits
around Seawell. This isn't my kind
of town.

                    SWEENEY
          Hmm, busted. Then, um, you ever
          been to Ecuador? Come on down to
          visit me once I get there in
          January. Surf lessons, maybe?

                    DIANA
               (flashing a stunning smile)
          Probably not. First come visit the
          Northwoods up in "Minny," as you
          call it, and I'll help you find
          work. I got a little money saved,
          maybe we might travel well
          together. Who knows? What's this
          welcome-home party bullshit about
          anyways?

Sweeney climbs out of the car, leans on the open window
to continue flirting.

                    SWEENEY
          Oh, I don't know. Just some friends
          from the neighborhood. At this
          point, I have no godforsaken idea
          where I'm coming from and after
          running into you I'm not too sure
          what's next. But, um, maybe I'll
          come find you when the snow melts.
          And stop calling it "Minny." A
          local told me that was stupid.
               (Locking the door, patting the
               roof, walking away, calling back)
          See you at McSwiggan's later!

Sweeney effortlessly hops a six-foot chain-link fence and
down onto Farannan Golf Course. He slips OFF his flip-
flops and begins SPRINTING across the fairways. Diana
watches for a LONG TIME.

                    DIANA
          Yeah, right. Nice ass, though.

INT. - SWEENEY'S LANDSCAPING SHED - FARANNAN G.C. - DAY

It's cloudy and a flurry of snow falls as Sweeney enters
to find Micky on the floor, sharpening the blades on a
36-inch lawnmower.

> MICKY
> (overtly casual)
> Oh, hey Sweeney. How's things?
> Still rainin' out there?

> SWEENEY
> You mean snowing. Yeah, it's still
> snowing and you owe me 35 bucks for
> the fuckin' cab ride, asshole.

> MICKY
> I was s'posetah pick you up from
> jail at Noon. It's 7-fuckin' a.m.
> I'm not payin' shit.

> SWEENEY
> Yeah, well, I got out a bit early.
> Leo Luque let me go so I wouldn't
> miss the incoming tide.

> MICKY
> (incredulous)
> You got a prison guard to let you
> out early, 'cause you didn't want
> to miss the tide? How the fuck…
> (beat) Forget it, I don't wanna
> know.
> SWEENEY
> Leo's from the Oaklands neighborhood
> and he owed me one. I neglected to
> mention to him that I wanted out early
> because the waves were good.

                    MICKY
Oh, they're good. They're huge!
Wind's not s'posetah swing west
until later this morning, though.
The beachbreaks are too big, man.
Let me drive you up north to the
pointbreaks. Give those noodle-arms
of yours a chance to flail you into
a wave or two before they fall off,
fuckin' jailbird.

                    SWEENEY
              (happily surprised)
Sounds like you been surfin' a bit,
Micky. Learnin' the lay of the non-
land, eh?

Micky wipes his wrench clean and points it at the
rafters.

                    MICKY
Someone had to use all your boards
while you were gone. Didn't want
them to go to pasture just yet, yah
know?

There are vintage singlefin longboards, thrusters,
Bonzers, twinfins and one yellow singlefin '70s
shortboard off to the side by itself. It nearly GLOWS.

                    SWEENEY
Wow. I'm impressed, but you didn't…

                    MICKY
              (exasperated)
Oh, fuckin' relax. I didn't touch
your magic board. The Hot Buttered
has remained un-fuckin'-sullied. I
did get wasted once and sing it
some Midnight Oil lullabies. I was
shellacked that night, though!

Sweeney's listening, but already ascending a wooden

ladder to grab the yellow Hot Buttered surfboard.

> SWEENEY
> I've been waiting to get back on
> this board for like two years now.

> MICKY
> Yeah, no shit. Wax it up. Your
> wetsuit's in that locker. Suit up
> and let me drive you up to Fox Head
> or Wagon Train's…with this tide.

> SWEENEY
> I'm surfing here, man. Fuck the
> points, the clowns and the crowds.

CUT TO:

EXT. LANDSCAPING SHED, FARANNAN GOLF COURSE - MORNING

Sweeney stands outside in FLURRIES of snow barechested,
wetsuit folded down over his legs. He pulls it up from
his waist and forces his arms into the sleeves one at a
time. The attached hood goes over his head, he zips up
the back of the suit, pulls the hood OFF, takes the Hot
Buttered with BARE hands, crouches, lays the board across
his knees and waxes it from tail to nose. He then pulls
on his gloves, looks at his boots in the snow and KICKS
them aside.

Micky throws open the garage door of the shed. The riding
mower he was working on ROARS to life.

> MICKY
> (yelling over the mower)
> You gotta wear the boots, man. The
> waters' like 45 degrees or so. It's
> cold as hell out there.

Sweeney ignores Micky, but scowls a bit. He stands
and lovingly inspects the rails, tail and GLASSED-ON
singlefin. He STARES DOWN Micky, slips the board under
his arm.

                    MICKY (CONT'D)
          Okay, okay, don't fuckin' bite my
          head off with that look. Jesus,
          just don't expect me to swim and
          save your crazy ass. Take this
          leash, at least.

                    SWEENEY
          No leash plug, kid. Never had one,
          never will.

                    MICKY
          You gotta swim in 15-foot closeouts
          and borderline arctic water temps,
          (voice rising) you fuckin'
          melodramatic moron. This ain't the
          tropics.

Sweeney's jogged off, leaving dark green footprints in
the SNOWDUSTED grass.

Micky RUNS to a wall-mounted ROTARY PHONE by his
workbench. Dials.

                    MICKY (CONT'D)
               (yelling)
          Yeah, Little Rocks. What? (beat)
          Right fuckin' now, man. Just got
          outta the pen and he's running down
          the beach as we speak. (beat)Lissen,
          O'Dowd, you just get here with Ray
          Johnson or without him. I don't care.
          I can't fuckin' help the guy if he
          loses his board, it's too big for me.
          You can grab him.(beat) (quietly) Yeah,
          I KNOW he doesn't need our help but you
          wanna see what he does with his first
          wave just like me. I know that much,
          fuckhead.

Micky SLAMS the phone down, darts around in a frenzy.

                    MICKY (CONT'D)
                  (to himself, loudly)
        Can I catch him? Fuck it, I'll take
        the mower. It's a piece of shit anyways.

Micky grabs the wetsuit BOOTS, throws the mower in gear
and CHIRPS the tires as he heads out into the LARGE
flakes of snow now falling THICKLY like a curtain across
the open garage door.

                                              CUT TO:

EXT. SEVENTH FAIRWAY-FARANAN GOLF COURSE-DAY
_____

PULLED-BACK PANORAMIC THROUGH THE SNOWFALL, MICKY'S ON
THE MOWER ON THE FAR RIGHT EDGE OF THE SHOT. HE IS SLOWLY
CATCHING UP TO SWEENEY AHEAD OF HIM NEAR THE FAR LEFT OF
THE SHOT. STARK IN HIS BLACK WETSUIT, YELLOW BOARD UNDER
HIS ARM, HE MOVES WITH STEADY GRACE. THE FOREST BACKDROP
BEHIND THEM STILL SHOWS ORANGE, REDS AND GOLDS OF AUTUMN.
WE LISTEN IN ON THEIR CONVERSATION BEFORE SWEENEY CLIMBS
DOWN THE ROCKS AND ONTO THE SAND TO PADDLE OUT INTO THE
UNADULTERATED, HALF FROZEN FURY OF THE NORTH ATLANTIC.

                    MICKY (Voice Over)
        Jesus, man, how're those feet?
        Don't punch me in the throat or
        anything, but I brought those boots
        if you've changed your mind.

                    SWEENEY (V.O.)
        Can't do it, man. I kinda miss my
        board when I wear boots. I haven't
        surfed in so goddamned long. I miss
        the feel of the wax on the deck.
        Can't do it.

                    MICKY (V.O.)
        Alright, you got those crazy eyes
        right now. I know what that means.
        I actually chased you down to give
        you the last buoy report I heard on

the weather radio this morning. So
humor me for a minute, if you will?

FADE IN:

EXT. - TOP OF THE GRANITE-BOULDER SEA WALL BEHIND SEVENTH
GREEN - FARANNAN GOLF COURSE/SEAWELL BEACH - MORNING

Sweeney gives Micky a low, sideways five before hopping
nimbly down the boulders. The snowfall has diminished. As
his feet hit the sand Sweeney's grows calm, CONTENTED.

CUT TO:

SWEENEY'S P.O.V.

Sweeney splashes ocean water on his face and jumps on
his board. He paddles out through many, many nasty walls
of churning whitewater. He steadily, slowly, expertly
paddles through the pounding, freezing surf as we hear
Micky detailing the particulars of the SWELL OF THE
DECADE in Seawell, Mass.

> MICKY (Voice Over)
> Seriously, humor me for a sec. The
> water's about 45, I'd say. It was
> choppy this morning, but this snow
> squall's probably changed the wind.
> Knowing you, you lucky fuck, it
> will go west like right now.

> SWEENEY (V.O.)
> Lucky? This lucky fuck just did two
> years in prison...

> MICKY (V.O.)
> You know what I mean. Anyways, the
> tide's pushing over the mid-tide
> sandbars with the storm surge. It's
> probably a 12- to 14-second period
> swell and the outside sets will be
> feathering way out there. If that wind
> actually goes west, it'll clean-up. But

it's gonna be too big to surf at this
spot, man. You know it, I know it, and
about three other people in New England
know it. None of us want any part of
it. Why do you?

Sweeney is now duckdiving under huge green walls of
water, detonating a few feet from his face. Over and
over...

> SWEENEY (V.O.)
> (Sarcastically)
> Hmm, I wonder why? Did I not just
> mention that whole prison thing?

> MICKY (V.O.)
> (unruffled)
> Whatever. The pulses are pretty
> close together, like five minutes
> between them. This is from three,
> not one, but THREE huge low
> pressure systems combined over the
> North Atlantic. It's 15-foot and
> bigger on the sets.

We see Sweeney finally make his way to the outside,
sitting astride his board.

The WAITING GAME for just the right wave begins.

> SWEENEY (V.O.)
> Goatboy, Jesus, I didn't know you
> REALLY started surfing. You got it
> down, huh?

> MICKY (V.O.)
> I been keepin' an eye on it for you
> while you were gone. A seal couldn't
> beach its fat ass around
> here without me seein' it.

CUT TO:

EXT. - LINEUP-LITTLE ROCKS-SEAWELL BEACH - DAY

Sweeney sees a set coming in. Several large waves pass
under him. He turns for the final wave of the set.
Paddles a bit, changes his mind. Sits up on his board.

                                        CUT TO:

EXT. - ON THE TOP OF THE GRANITE-BOULDER SEAWALL BEHIND
SEVENTH GREEN-FARANNAN GOLF COURSE/SEAWELL BEACH - DAY

Micky is sitting on the mower. He sees Sweeney start to
paddle, he starts to stand on the seat, craning his neck,
biting his fingernails.

                                        CUT TO:

EXT. - LINEUP - SAME

Sweeney fights against the current to stay in position.
Paddles, sits up, has to lie down and paddle more.
Paddles, sits up, etc.

                                        CUT TO:

EXT. - ON THE TOP OF THE GRANITE-BOULDER SEA WALL - SAME

There's no snow, dimmed sunshine leaks through the clouds
over the ocean now. The waves and water have silvered in
the light. Micky's still sitting, somewhat bored, on the
mower. He squints, leans forward to look south way down
the beach at a FLAG above the dunes.

                        MICKY
                    (to himself)
              No shit. Un-fucking-believable.
              Look at that flag. This guy has
              some fuckin' connection to the
              ocean I don't even understand.
              Unreal.

                                        CUT TO:

EXT. - LINEUP - SAME

Sweeney looks at the same FLAG now blowing OUT TO SEA.

He grins. He turns to await the next pulse of waves.

                                              CUT TO:

A SERIES OF IMAGES:

Sweeney paddles furiously for the HORIZON. He digs UP
the face of the first wave of the set. It's 12-foot,
feathering in the now-stiff west wind. A BEAST of a wave.

He barely makes it over the vertical lip of the wave.

The next five or six waves come through, getting BIGGER
and BEASTLIER.

Sweeney's getting STRONGER as he paddles.

Sweeney punches under and through the throwing, thick lip
of the penultimate wave of the set.

Micky is jumping and waving both arms over his head,
whistling like a madman.

Sweeney's not getting the signal.

Micky's gesticulations grow WILD.

Sweeney has STOPPED. He is the picture of STILLNESS IN A
MAELSTROM sitting astride his yellow board.

Micky's LOST IT like a toddler tantrum--fists clenched at
his side, jumping, screaming, slipping, ALMOST falling.

He regains his composure for a second, locates Sweeney in
the lineup.

Immediately jumps with both booted feet to TRY to break
the springs on the seat.

He continues screaming at Sweeney to paddle.

Sweeney remains still, facing down the green and silvered
wintry monster bearing down on him.

Sweeney's green, intense eyes are taking it all in.

He remains CONTENT as he is SUCKED UP the face of the
BIGGEST wave of the day.

The lip feathers in the stiff west wind.

It's about to break on his head.

In one FLUID motion he turns, puts one black-gloved hand
up near the nose and PULLS the board under him just as
he's lying down.

He's using the buoyancy of the board to PROPEL him into
the wave without a single paddle. NOT ONE STROKE.

Micky SEES what is happening--that Sweeney is TAKING the
wave without paddling.

His LIPS PART, he's mesmerized.

Sweeney rises to his feet, effortlessly late-drops into
the trough of the pitching wave.

He bottom-turns up to mid-face on the wave and his BARE
FEET KICKSTALL the singlefin.

Sweeney sets the inside rail and STANDS TALL in a huge,
churning barrel.

He slips forward a bit on the board, a picture of
composure and style in the teeth of the barrel.

Micky is now perfectly STILL, up on the seat of the
mower, FIXATED on what he is witnessing.

                                              CUT TO:

EXT.-SEAWELL BEACH-DAY

We see a pulled-back shot of the length and majesty of
the wave as it wraps around Sweeney and walls up for
thirty yards in front of him. Sweeney is in the tube
for around ten seconds--an INCREDIBLE tube. He flies
out and carves on the shoulder back toward the chruning
whitewater. He looks left and right and LIES DOWN on his

belly on the board in the wall of whitewater. He coasts a
bit, angles left while the wave is REFORMING into a ten-
foot, sandy inside bone-crusher. It's a nastier, thicker
second section. He paddles two or three times and slips
to his feet again, drops back into the right hander as it
hits a shallow sandbar. Sweeney roller-coasters across
the steepening wave, he manages an off-the-lip that
perfectly sets him up for a second tube. He throws an
understated soul-arch bottom-turn and sneaks under the
frothing lip of the thick, mean wave. Sweeney is engulfed
again. He disappears from sight.

SMASH CUT TO:

EXT.-ON THE TOP OF THE GRANITE-BOULDER SEAWALL BEHIND
SEVENTH GREEN-SAME

Micky REMAINS perfectly still, standing on the seat of
the mower. FIXATED.

SMASH CUT TO:

EXT.-SEAWELL BEACH-DAY

WATER SHOT OF SWEENEY IN THE SANDY, FOAMY, GRINDING TUBE.

Sweeney is crouched, his leading arm extended but
relaxed, his trailing arm bent and caressing the face of
the wave bending tightly around him. He is SLACK-JAW-
RELAXED.

He weaves masterfully to SQUEAK out of the barrel just
under the crashing lip as the wave closes out in a few
feet of water. Sweeney gets clipped in the head, but
stays on his feet, arms draped loosely at his sides. He
is the MATADOR allowing a final, close pass of the bull.
For a moment, he stands tall and then LIES back down
and bellies the board into ANKLE-DEEP water in front of
Micky.

CUT TO:

EXT.-ON TOP OF THE GRANITE-BOULDER SEAWALL BEHIND SEVENTH
GREEN-SAME

Micky is wide-eyed. He involuntarily raises his arms over

his head, but SLIPS and FALLS off the mower.

                                              CUT TO:

EXT.-SEAWELL BEACH-DAY
_____

Sweeney, at the edge of an angry ocean, puts his board
under his arm. Shakes his head at Micky's antics.

He starts walking away, stops, looks back out to the
waves.

He cups some ocean water from the shallows, rubs it
roughly on his face.

Sweeney stares back at Micky, then turns, JOGS slowly
down the beach AWAY from his friend.

                                              CUT TO:

EXT.-SEAWELL BEACH-DAY
_____

In the distance, Sweeney disappears into the dunes.

                                              CUT TO:

EXT. - MCSWIGGAN'S DOOR - NIGHT
_____

Diana sheepishly hands a bouncer her I.D. She looks
AMAZING.
                        MCSWIGGAN'S BOUNCER
                  Oh, so you're the Minnesota girl.
                  Wow. Go right in. Sweeney was
                  right. Jesus Christ.

Diana's embarrassed but pleased. Pauses to reinstate her
cool demeanor, enters the bar and spots Sweeney in the
far corner.

Diana smiles just as…

Sweeney's face breaks into a grin.

                                              CUT TO:

EXT. - MCSWIGGAN'S DOOR - CLOSING TIME

The bouncer who spoke with Diana is now yelling at everyone in front of the bar to go home.

Behind him Sweeney and Diana slip out of the door, arm in arm, STUMBLING, beers in hand.

                                              CUT TO:

EXT.-SEAWELL-RESIDENTIAL STREET-DAY

Sweeney's up a tree, working for Micky who is at the base of the tree dodging branches as they fall.

>   SWEENEY
>   (yelling)
>   Here comes that damn ice cream
>   truck again. The floating heads
>   demand a Sno Cone, Micky.

>   MICKY
>   (rolling his eyes)
>   Oh, wouldja stop it with that fuckin'
>   invisible-heads shit you been pullin'
>   on me? Just take a 5-minute breather
>   if you need it, asshole. And since
>   when did you start likin' Sno Cones,
>   you always got Screwballs from the ice
>   cream truck since we were kids…I never
>   seen you get anything but Screwballs…

Sweeney scrabbles down the tree, drops to the ground, catlike, and interrupts Micky.

>   SWEENEY
>   The heads aren't invisible. I see
>   'em clear as day, buddy. And I hear
>   they want a goddamned Sno Cone and
>   an orange Fanta. Me, I'd take the
>   Screwball eight days a week but you
>   know these heads get mean if I don't
>   listen.

                    MICKY
            (hesitant, mildly shaken)
        Just shut the fuck up and get your
        ice cream and get back up that tree
        and finish!

                                    CUT TO:

EXT.-SEAWELL-RESIDENTIAL STREET-DAY
_____

Four little kids, 9-years-old or so, the CAPANETTI AND
SWENSON BROTHERS, hide in the bushes in the yard Sweeney
walks through to wave down the truck.

Sweeney ambles over to Micky's dump truck and grabs a
fistful of change from the dash.

                    SWEENEY
                (yelling)
        Micky! I took $2.73 in change. I
        owe you.
                                    CUT TO:
_____

                TIMMY CAPANETTI
                (whispering)
        Shut the hell up, you guys! The truck's
        comin'! And don't move. The other three
        boys ignore Timmy. All in various
        stages of sunburned muddiness, they are
        too busy laughing and punching each
        other in the arms and legs.

                                    CUT TO:

INT.-ICE CREAM TRUCK-DAY
_____

JAY SCANLANN, a curly haired, late-teen, whistles along
with "The Sting" as it plays over the loudspeaker on the
truck he's driving. He is content.

                    JAY SCANLANN
        Ahh, the landscaper discount for this

guy. Sweeney's a nut, but he's a good
customer. Fuck his boss, though.
Micky's an angry prick…

We hear BANGING AND CLATTERING as something gets tangled
in the wheels and axle of the truck. Scanlann slams on
the brakes, throws it in park, and jumps out of the truck
right in front of Sweeney. He leaves the door OPEN.

He and Sweeney look at the tangled fishing line and soda
cans in the front axle of his truck.

> JAY SCANLANN (CONT'D)
> (quietly, intensely)
> Can Trick, again. Dammit. Sweeney, take
> whatever you want. Leave the money on
> the dash. This summer-long battle ends
> here and now. Here and fuckin' now.

Scanlann leans back in the truck for a Super Soaker
squirt gun--a water cannon, really. He SPRINTS around
the front of the truck and STALKS down the other side,
looking around the tail-end of the idling truck. He's in
full-on assault mode.

> JAY SCANLANN (CONT'D)
> (shouting)
> Get ready you little shits! This
> attack's fueled by piss 'n' vinegar.
> It runs in my family! You're mine!
> YOU ARE DEAD! I made enough money
> this summer already. I can chase you
> little bastards until school is back in
> session! No more can tricks
> for you guys!

Sweeney hears all of this, pretends not to be listening.

CUT TO:

EXT.-SEAWELL-RESIDENTIAL STREET-DAY

In the shade of the bushes, the laughing stops. The boys

fearfully peer down at Scanlann.

                    TIMMY CAPANETTI
          Did he say he had his family's piss is
          in that squirt gun?

                    CHRIS SWENSON
                      (worriedly)
          No, I think it means he's wicked mad at
          us. I hope, but I'm not sure. Vinegar
          smells terrible, too.

                    TODD CAPANETTI
          What? Shut up, you guys! I don't give a
          shit! He ain't gettin' me.

                    BERT SWENSON
          Yeah, he's downhill from us. We can
          nail him!

All the boys GRAB from a pile of water balloons in the
mulch, BURST from the bushes in front of the house above
the ice cream truck. As they throw and hit Scanlann
several times, he slips in the grass, stands, gets closer
to them. He's getting within range and fires. The boys
scatter, squealing, swearing at him. They retreat uphill,
away from the street. Scanlann pursues, laughing and
angry at the same time as we…

                                        CUT TO:

EXT.-SEAWELL-RESIDENTIAL STREET-DAY

Sweeney watches Scanlann chase the boys around the back
of the house. He looks up at Micky, high up in a tree.
Sweeney calmly climbs up the steps of the truck, SHUTS
the door. He PLACES the $2.73 in a cup on the dashboard,
grabs a SCREWBALL from the freezer, sits in the driver's
seat, turns "The Sting" up as loud as it will go. He
CHIRPS the tires on the truck as he takes off without a
word to Micky, watching from up in the tree, mouth again
agape.

A bug flies into Micky's mouth.

                    MICKY
              (coughing, sputtering)
         Fuck, argh! My craziest and oldest
         friend is turning me into a fuckin'
         (cough) frog. Where the fuck does
         he think he's going in that thing?
         Probably a beer run. (coughs) I
         hate that fucker. Was that a horse
         fly? Fuck.

                                              CUT TO:

EXT.-VARIOUS ROADS, HIGHWAYS, BYWAYS ALL HEADING WEST-DAY

WE SEE A SERIES OF IMAGES AS SWEENEY DRIVES WEST TO HIS
UNKNOWN DESTINATION. HE DRIVES DAY AND NIGHT.

                                              CUT TO:

EXT.-HIGHWAY-DAY

The ice cream truck passes a huge sign on the highway
that reads: "Welcome to Minnesota".

                                              CUT TO:

EXT.-COUNTRY ROAD-DAY

Vibrant WILDFLOWERS crowd both sides of the country road
below a sign: "Welcome to Longville, MN, Pop. 645".

                                              CUT TO:

EXT.-FRONT YARD OF A LOG CABIN-DAY

We see DIANA MARPESSA come out of the cabin as Sweeney
pulls the truck up to the house. She's blonde, tan,
ethereal, almost WITCHY in her beauty.

Sweeney doesn't move from the driver's seat.

He's entranced; his eyes follow Diana's every step as she
approaches the truck.

She slinks up to the wide window of the ice cream truck.

Just as she's about to mock-order an ice cream, Sweeney flips on the "The Sting" and she bursts into laughter, shaking her head at the crazy man who just drove up.

Sweeney gives her a "come-hither" look as he stands and moves toward the freezer. A PROFUSION OF WILDFLOWERS fills the 3 open freezer doors. The back of the interior of the truck is bursting with wildflowers.

Diana is in awe, moved. She opens the door to the truck and steps in as Sweeney removes the three huge bouquets from the freezer doors, closes the doors, scatters a thick bed of flowers over the top of the freezer.

Diana kisses Sweeney hard on the mouth.

Moments later, lingering through the end of that first kiss,Sweeney lifts Diana onto the corner of the freezer. She reaches out with one long, tan LEG and hooks it around him.

She pulls him in and wraps her other leg around him.

                                              FADE TO:

INT.-MCSWIGGAN'S PUB-SEAWELL, MASS.-DAY

A Seawell Townie has a fistful of Jay Scanlann's shirt, finger in his face, BUMPING him against a wall. Next to them, out the window, it is SNOWING.

                    JAY SCANLANN
                  (defiant)
            Fuck off! He did steal my fuckin'
            ice cream truck at the end of the
            summer. I know the guy better than
            you, you fuckin' ape. AND I saw him
            pull away in the truck, so calm the
            fuck down.

The Seawell Townie's enraged and rears back with a cocked fist.

The fist BEGINS flying forward SMACKS Scanlann at the
same time the Seawell Townie TAKES a punch to the TEMPLE
and drops like a sack of bricks.

CUT TO:

INT.-MCSWIGGAN'S-SAME
_____

Tommy Santos stands above the Townie, shakes out his
massive paw of a fist, picks up Jay Scanlann off the
floor. He dusts him off a bit, sits him up on a tall
ROTATING CHAIR, his BACK to the bar. Scanlann shakes
out the cobwebs and puts two fingers up, signaling to a
framed photo of TERRY O'REILLY for THREE beers.

> TOMMY SANTOS
> (laughing)
> I was gonna say, "Did he getcha, kid?"
> But I think it's clear he caught you
> with one.

Santos PHYSICALLY TURNS Scanlann on his stool to FACE the
bar. Scanlann smiles a bit, hand still in the air.

> TOMMY SANTOS (CONT'D)
> (wincing)
> Yeah, O'Reilly's not here, man. The
> bar's over this way. I left my
> stethoscope in the truck, but I

> TOMMY SANTOS (CONT'D)
> think you'll survive. Might have a
> shiner, might not. Skull a beer,
> that always helps me. Sorry I
> couldn't get to that goon quicker
> than I did. I been turnin' a deaf
> ear to all the Sweeney talk in the
> bars this winter, mostly. They talk
> about that guy more now than when
> the fuckin' loon was hangin' around.

Jay Scanlann gets his THREE cans of Narragansett tall

boys, opens one with his left hand, hands Tommy the
second and sets the third cold can on his RAPIDLY
SWELLING eye.

                    JAY SCANLANN
          Yeah, I try not to talk too much about
          the whole ice-cream-truck thing but
          this fuckin' sack of shit wouldn't go
          away. Thanks, by the way.

                    TOMMY SANTOS
                 (distracted)
          Huh, for what?

Jay points at the out-cold Seawell Townie in a heap on
the floor.
                    TOMMY SANTOS (CONT'D)
          Oh, for that useless pile? Yeah, no
          problem. Like I said, I woulda gotten
          him sooner but I don't know you. I
          heard you say it was YOUR ice cream
          truck so my ears pricked up. Do you
          know your alleged assailant?

                    JAY SCANLANN
          No, I don't know him. Does every
          goon, no offense, in Seawell think
          Sweeney's the man or something.

                    TOMMY SANTOS
          Ha ha, very funny. This goon right
          here, I'm Sweeney's first cousin.

                    JAY SCANLANN
          Sorry, sorry, I couldn't resist.
          You're a big fucker. And what with
          your premature baldness, stubble
          and lack of a discernible neck, you
          know, I just assumed you two goons
          were acquainted.

> TOMMY SANTOS

Premature baldness? That's a nice
way to put it. Spring chicken on
the inside, I'll tell ya that much.
Seriously, though, a lot of idiots
around here do hold Sweeney's
fighting and drinking skills in
somewhat high regard. Personally, I
don't give a shit about that stuff
anymore.

Jay stifles a laugh, snorts a bit of 'Gansett out his
nose.

> JAY SCANLANN
> (scoffing)

You laid that 250-pound fucker out
like it was your job!

> TOMMY SANTOS

Shut up, you know what I mean.

> JAY SCANLANN
> (coughing)

Actually, not yet I don't.

> TOMMY SANTOS

Well, I'm gettin' to it. I just
want to hear what happened to my
cousin Sweeney the day you lost
your truck.

> JAY SCANLANN

What happened? I didn't lose it.
That bastard stole it. I know where
it is. It's with him, wherever that
is. And what happened is he climbed out
of his tree, got inside my truck and
drove off. Micky, you must know Micky?
Yeah, he says he probably drove to
California or somewhere to surf.

                    TOMMY SANTOS
        Well, I'm gonna set you up with a
        shot of the Doctah to set that
        rattled brain of yours straight and
        you're gonna tell me the whole
        story start-to-finish.

The nameless guy on the floor stirs a bit & Tommy signals
to the bartender. The bartender comes around the bar,
pulls him to his unsteady feet and guides him, gently, to
the door and a waiting taxi outside.

                TOMMY SANTOS (CONT'D)
        They don't need bouncers around here,
        with a guy like Chicky behind the bar.
        Fuckin' masterful. Anyways, what was
        I sayin'? Oh yeah, Micky's a good guy
        and we still hang out here and there,
        but he's so pissed at Sweeney for
        taking off that he can barely talk
        about the guy without flying into a
        rage. I need to hear if my cousin has
        finally lost it and whether I need to
        go find him or not. Bring him back to
        reality with a couple of slaps about
        the head and shoulders, you know what I
        mean?

                    JAY SCANLANN
        I think I know exactly what you
        mean. I was gonna go home, but I
        got time. What do you want to know?

                    TOMMY SANTOS
                (softening, concerned)
        Well, you know how Sweeney is. Um…

Tommy cracks his knuckles on both fists, loudly,
methodically. He doesn't want to know the truth about
Sweeney's mental status.

                    TOMMY SANTOS (CONT'D)
               Ah, um, what was he actin' like
               that day? Has he fuckin' lost it?
                                        CUT TO:

INT.-LOG CABIN-LONGVILLE, MN - NIGHT
_____

Sweeney and Diana sit by a CRACKLING woodstove.

                    SWEENEY
               So what do you do all winter in
               this place? You been living here
               for how many winters in a row?

                    DIANA
               I've been here the last three winters.
               I sit around, drink coffee, write a
               lot of shitty short stories and I chop
               wood. I chop endless amounts of wood. I
               hunt little for food, mostly deer.

                    SWEENEY
               Hmm, I write a lot of shitty formal
               poetry in my boat back in Seawell.
               Not much hunting, not big on
               hunting. And walking around with a
               gun in Seawell is just asking for
               it. But I chop wood all winter, too,
               actually. Gotta feed the stove.

                    DIANA
               I'll tell you what. This winter, you're
               definitely chopping wood and from what
               I've read of your work, you'll be doing
               some shitty writing, too.

Sweeney plays it off like he's unhurt. Diana might be the
only person who cuts him.

                                        CUT TO:

EXT. FRONT MEADOW OF LOG CABIN-LONGVILLE, MN

Sweeney and Diana chop wood, most of the trees are bare,
snow flurries fall. Diana runs the log-splitter, Sweeney
swings an axe in front of cords of CHOPPED wood as
well as a MASSIVE pile of logs waiting to be split and
chopped.

>   DIANA
>   See what I mean? We're gonna chop
>   wood like 25 days of each month,
>   eight hours a day. You really going
>   to stick this out with me for the
>   winter?

>   SWEENEY
>   Yep. Cord after cord. We should make
>   a bunch of money and head to South
>   America for a month or so in March.
>   There's good waves, weather and wind in
>   northern Ecuador in March.

>   DIANA
>   Maybe, but we'll see. If we get
>   hammered by storms we might not
>   make enough cash. I have money
>   anyways, my father's loaded. If it
>   gets too bad, we can just take off.

Looking askance, this is the first he's heard of this.

>   SWEENEY
>   Well, if you're loaded and I've got
>   a little saved up right now, tell
>   me again why we're chopping wood
>   for the next three months?

>   DIANA
>   (suddenly angry)
>   Because it'll keep us out of

trouble for the winter, that's why!

                    SWEENEY
               (teasing)
     But I like trouble, you knew that when
     I told you I was coming out here, huh?
     I'm not much of a fighter these days,
     but I still have ten thousand beers to
     drink in a thousand places. Can't waste
     my youth now can I? That would be a
     shame, a damn shame, huh?

                    DIANA
               (still angry)
     Well then fuckin' take off, eh? You
     don't have to stay if you don't want to
     be here.

Sweeney drops his axe, throws his hands up in submission.

                    SWEENEY
     Wait a sec, take it easy. I'm just
     teasing, just trying to figure out what
     we might get up to together in the near
     future.

He goes over and takes her in his arms. She's
halfheartedly hugging back. Her hands are COVERED in
GREASE from the log splitter.

                    DIANA
     Ok, ok. I'm sorry. I've just been
     doing this for a few winters by myself.
     It helps me empty out my head and stay
     out of the bars down south. I do have
     money to do whatever I want, whatever
     WE want, but that's the problem with
     me.

                    SWEENEY
     What is? Money doesn't seem like
     much of a problem to me.

                    DIANA
                  (quietly)
        Most of the time, I can't stop
        doing whatever I want.

Sweeney takes a firmer hold of Diana to talk her down;
she's shaking and he's not sure why. He begins swaying
ever so slightly with her in his arms, his chin on top of
her head. The only sound other than his voice are several
woodpeckers at work on a dead tree by the cabin. He sways
more and more as Diana relaxes.

                    SWEENEY
                  (soothingly)
        Me, too. Me, too. I'm the same way,
        Dee. Don't worry about it. We'll
        just stay here then. Don't worry so
        much about it. I'm sorry I brought
        it up. We'll just finish out the
        winter here and think about going
        somewhere in the spring. I only
        have to get the ice cream truck
        back to Seawell, get arrested for
        it and start that final stage of
        diagnosis. Won't take that long.

Diana tenses a bit at this subject. Sweeney, still
swaying, changes course a bit.

                    SWEENEY (CONT'D)
        Forget about that, forget I even
        said it. We can go wherever we want
        this spring. My insanity thing will
        take care of itself. You said
        something about Tofino up by
        Vancouver. There's waves and weed
        there, I like that idea. Let's forget
        all of it and just have a good night
        here in the woods. It's getting dark.
        We got a lot done today. Let's call it
        a day, go inside, split that case of

Leinenkugel's Red you bought us.
We'll have sloppy sex later and
pass out. This is our immediate
goal, Diana. We must have goals.
The sex'll be so good we won't even
remember it.

Sweeney gives a little thrust of his pelvis at each
turn of the waltz. Diana is laughing a little, relaxing
back into their isolation together. The only sounds
are Sweeney's soothing voice in the wind and the over-
achieving woodpecker's relentless knocking.

> SWEENEY (CONT'D)
> When the woodstove goes out and we
> wake up frozen and swearing like
> landlocked sailors, we'll be forced
> to stoke the fire and jump each others'
> bones once again to stimulate mutual
> warmth. Hangover sex is only slightly
> worse, though more therapeutic, than
> sloppy sex. We must survive this winter
> together, Diana. Together. We do this
> all the time, huh? Like every single
> night. Why not tonight? Isn't this what
> Northwoods Winter Romance is all about?
> You've taught me well. You're like the
> Obi Wan Kenobi of log cabin romance.
> I am but pliable clay in your capable
> hands. I'll have sex wearing a blacked-
> out flight helmet if you tell me to.
> Remember that time I kissed your chest
> and you gave a wave of your hand and
> whispered, "These are not the breasts
> you're looking for," and then I went
> down on you for like two hours? You've
> got me in your sex-jedi grasp. Do we
> have any weed left? We can get high
> and play some 45s. You like Crazy 8s,
> actually. Crazy 8s shall be commenced
> whence our highness is achieved. Two

crazy high useless poets playing Crazy
8s to stave off the darkness. We're
good at this shit. You know this. We're
the Sloppy-Sex Allstars. Look at us
now: We're already doing the Waltz of
the Woodpecker. (Suddenly shouting at the
woodpecker on the side of the cabin) Fuck
you, redheaded stepchild of the Great
Northwoods. I despise you and your
kind!

Sweeney throws a piece of wood from the WAIST-HIGH
woodpile at the bird, startling it.

Diana is now taking Sweeney's bullshit in stride,
laughing. She runs inside, returns with two opened
bottles of beer.

                                          CUT TO:

EXT.-MAMBO BAR ON THE BEACH-DAY

An EXHAUSTED Sweeney carries two bottles of beer over to
the hammocks where Pancho is waiting.

                    PANCHO MONEYMAKER
          I think we'll be able to go for a
          surf later. Maybe we should go easy
          on the beers and see what the waves
          look like at high tide.

                    SWEENEY
               (raggedly, dismissively)
          Fuck that. I'm not surfing later,
          I'm getting hammered all weekend.
          Starting now.

                    PANCHO MONEYMAKER
               (worried)
          Yeah, you can have mine. I want to
          surf later. Flowpi and her cousins
          are coming up from Bahia to surf. I
          told you. Remember? Flowpi's been
          bad lately. She's talking to her

imaginary friends all the time and
forgets her board when she comes
down to the beach to surf. I'm worried
about her. I'm doing that mural with
her. She loves to paint and draw so I
want to keep her busy in one place. You
want to help us?

                SWEENEY
Yeah, yeah, I said I would, but not
this weekend. I brought that new
board for Flowpi. We'll keep it here
in case she forgets hers. I'll do that
mural in a couple weeks or something.
It's too hot. I gotta get my head
together anyways.

            PANCHO MONEYMAKER
So you want to tell me what happened in
Minnesota?

                SWEENEY
Fuck Minnesota! I don't want to
talk about Diana. I got outta there
early for a reason.

            PANCHO MONEYMAKER
Alright, whatever. What about
returning the ice cream truck? Did
it all work out? Are you getting a
monthly check from your government
now?

                SWEENEY
            (brightening)
Yep. It went down just like I
needed it to. I brought that truck
back to the very yard I took it
from, up on Parkview Ave. I went up
to the old lady's house, the
Garrets', because I knew she'd
be home. She's a shut-in, but

she remembered me and handed her
cordless phone out to me. I called
Goatboy and told him I had Jay
Scanlann's money for the Sno Cone.
Micky called Scanlann and they came
by and saw me and they were all
bummed out that Scanlann had to
call the cops and say I'd returned
the truck. But then, even better, a
cop drove by as we were talking on
the street. The cop knew Scanlann
and the story of the truck and just
cuffed me right there. It was
perfect. It saved poor Scanlann
from having to call them on me.
got all his insurance money sorted out
and I got what I really wanted.

                PANCHO MONEYMAKER
Did you see Dr. again? How's
she doing? Is she still looking good?
Did you tell her I want to meet her?

                SWEENEY
            (laughing)
No, you fuckin' perv. You've never
even seen a picture of the woman...

                PANCHO MONEYMAKER
Yes, but you are a poet. You once
drunkenly recited an ode to her
beauty...

                SWEENEY
I what? I did? Well, she's hot but
I don't remember doing that. In any
case, it doesn't matter. She doesn't
know you exist and, more importantly,
she got me my monthly SSI checks. I
made sure all my symptoms were still

accurate and on display and I got that
final arrest on the anniversary of
punching that Mormon kid in the head.
She ate it up and got me my checks. I
had to spend a few nights in lockup and
then a few weeks at Darville Hospital
but it was fine. I stayed off the meds
and just focused on the goal.

                PANCHO MONEYMAKER
So you were in an insane asylum, sober,
after you and Diana had, umm...

                    SWEENEY
                (angry, quiet)
Yeah, I left her. I had to do the
whole thing on the anniversary like
I said and I was gonna wait till the
spring, like 6 months later, but some
shit happened in the late fall. It was
a very sober, lonesome couple months
in Darville. I almost started taking
the meds they gave me each day but I
stuck it out. I just let myself get
fuckin' angry at Diana and I let it
simmer in me. I read a ton of books.
I went back to the Brontë sisters
and some Virginia Woolf. I just read
their books and got pissed at all the
stiff, humorless characters in their
stories. I just went numb without the
drugs and no booze at all. I dried
the fuck out, is what I did. I was
like a stalk of some kind of halfdead
weed fallen over in the corner of the
ward. No one paid any attention to
me except for a guy in a faded red
Irving Fryar Patriots shirt. He kept
telling me, every fuckin' day, "Take

the over on the Dolphins at Buffalo,
they can handle the weather this year.
Forget the weather. Take the over.
Forget the weather." I almost called
a bookie just to make any bet I could
after three weeks of the guy saying
that shit.

                    PANCHO MONEYMAKER
          So it worked, but was it worth…

Before Pancho finishes, in SPRINTS Flowpi and her two
cousins. She is ecstatic to see Sweeney and gives him a
big hug while babbling a million questions in Spanish at
him and at Pancho. Her cousins follow, jumping around
Pancho and Sweeney with questions and laughter and happy
commotion.
                                        SMASH CUT TO:

EXT. – LINEUP, CANOA, ECUADOR – DAY
_____

Flowpi is up and riding on what appears to be a BRAND
NEW BOARD. Pancho and Sweeney stand in ankle-deep water
watching, smiling. Pancho has his board under his arm,
Sweeney holds a 36 oz. bottle of Pilsener beer.

                    PANCHO MONEYMAKER
          Have you even ridden that board,
          Sweeney?

                    SWEENEY
          No. That's ok. Although, Flowpi
          only put a smidgen of wax on the
          thing. I have no idea how the hell
          she's not slipping right off it.

                    PANCHO MONEYMAKER
          I know. She gets her feet right on
          the two tiny spots she waxed. It's
          unbelievable. Why don't you pound that
          beer and try the new board?

                    SWEENEY
          Nah, not today. I gotta get drunk,
          gotta make up for lost time in the
          asylum, huh? Do me a favor, tell
          Flowpi to come in so I can wax that
          board right for her.

                    PANCHO MONEYMAKER
          She won't listen. She can't get out
          of the water until she's exhausted.
          She's the same as you. Look at that
          roundhouse!

Flowpi reels off a smooth backside roundhouse with a
rebound off the foam.
                    SWEENEY
          She's so little! I wish I surfed
          like that at her age! You know
          what's worse? Ahh fuck it, just go
          surf Pancho. Forget it. Go get some
          waves.

                    PANCHO MONEYMAKER
                 (hesitant)
          Ok. I'll get a couple waves with
          these kids and meet you in the bar
          later. Watch Flowpi, though. Keep
          an eye on her with me, ok?

                    SWEENEY
          Yeah, of course. I'm gonna sit
          right up there in the sand.

Pancho jumps on his board and paddles out as the sun sets
beyond him. Sweeney turns and PLODS up onto the sandy
hill at the high tide mark. He's close enough to watch
and hear Flowpi having the time of her life on his new
board.

                    SWEENEY (CONT'D)
                 (to himself)
          She surfs like me AND has real

imaginary friends that won't leave
her alone. Fuckin' just like my
faked imaginary friends in the pen.
What the hell is this little kid
all about?

Flowpi kicks out of a wave and looks to the beach to see
if Sweeney is watching.

Sweeney starts to raise his bottle in tribute, stops. He
waves and throws a hang-loose sign to her instead. She
turns to paddle out for more. Sweeney downs the last of
his bottle as Leo Gordo arrives with a new 36-ouncer.

> LEO GORDO
> Hola, Sweeney. Flowpi es increíble,
> no? Qué bien que surfea, parece que
> vuela! Exactamente como tú, amigo. No?

Subtitle: Hey, Sweeney, Flowpi is incredible, no?
She's so smooth, she looks like she is flying. Just like
you, huh?

> SWEENEY
> (dropping head in hands)
> Claro, claro. Y más de lo que tú sabes,
> Leo.

Subtitle: Clearly, clearly. And more than you know, Leo.

> **CUT TO:**

EXT.-MAMBO BAR ON THE BEACH-NIGHT

A drunken Sweeney has his arm around a drunken Pancho.
They sway on their barstools. Leo Gordo is behind the
bar, polishing glasses, drinking with them but not nearly
as hammered. It's a good vibe with lots of backpackers
and locals drinking beer, mojitos, cuba libres,
caparinhas as roots reggae pulses.
> PANCHO MONEYMAKER
> So you left Diana in the cabin? Did
> you chop all that wood?

SWEENEY

What wood? Fuck the wood. Fuck her.
I drove all the way out there in
that ice cream truck--you ever
drive a shitty old ice cream truck
on the highway? It sucks. Actually
it's about the same as most trucks
down here. You fucks have it worse,
way worse! You might as well all be
driving ice cream trucks down here
all day long! Be safer than the
four-wheelers and shitbox trucks
you have!

Pancho and Sweeney crack up laughing at this. Leo Gordo
looks confused.

PANCHO MONEYMAKER
(pleading)
Why'd you leave her, Sweeney? I HAVE
seen a photo of Diana. There's no way
I'd leave that beautiful woman alone in
a cold cabin.

SWEENEY
(resigned, slurring)
She left me, man. She left me and
then wouldn't admit it. No note,
nuthin'. You really want to know? I
guess you might as well know.

FADE TO:

EXT. - FRONT YARD OF LOG CABIN IN THE DEEP NORTHWOODS,
OUTSIDE LONGVILLE, MN - DAWN

Late fall, it's WINDY, dark, and sunrise lights ragged
storm clouds dragging across the eastern sky. The UNCUT
woodpile is gigantic. It's nearly as big as the cabin

that Diana slinks out of. She shuts the door slowly and
silently, adjusts her backpack, then moves lightning
quick off the porch, across the clearing, into the woods.
She NEVER LOOKS BACK.

                                            CUT TO:

INT. - LOG CABIN - HALF HOUR LATER - SAME
_____

Snow flurries swirl and the violent wind rattles the
small window. Sweeney wakes with a start. Diana is NOT
next to him in bed. He quickly tends the woodstove,
shoving some kindling and a log inside. The WIND crashes
at the windows. The kitchen table is clear, the mantel is
orderly. There is NO NOTE anywhere in the small cabin.
As Sweeney reaches for the handle of the front door, he
hears Diana SCREECH in the distance.
Sweeney drops the blanket draped around him. He runs out
into the front clearing in his boxers and unlaced boots.
Diana is SPRINTING out of the woods--TERRIFIED, silent.

                        SWEENEY
                What's going on? Diana? Where were
                you?

Just as Diana CRASHES into Sweeney's arms we…

                                        SMASH CUT TO:

EXT. - TRAIL IN THE FOREST - DAWN
_____

Trees CRACK, creak and sway in the battering wind.
Flurries begin to fall, swirl amidst the blowing leaves.
Just as Diana climbs nimbly over a HUGE fallen tree
across the trail, she pauses to look up at a CRACKING
LIMB falling from a tree.

                        DIANA
                    (muttering to herself)
                Fuck. Just what I need. Goddamned…

She SLIPS off the top of the fallen log and down the
other side.

She lands on the BACK of a BLACK BEAR foraging for roots, its head buried under huge mushrooms growing off the side of the fallen tree.

Both roll away from one another onto ALL FOURS. Diana's eyes slowly leave the ground to peer through long tangled locks.

Her face is frozen behind the thin curtain of hair.

The bear is stock still, only sniffing hesitantly. Both are frozen by the shock of the contact.

Their noses are only a FOOT away from one another. The wind howls, the flurries swirl between them.

The bear begins backing away, unsure of what is before him.

Diana moves a hand to push the hair from her face.

The bear freezes, GROWLS.

Diana goes CATATONIC.

The bear begins backing up again.

We hear the eerie kids' voices singing the beginning of Smog's song "Hit the Ground Runnin'."

Once the bear is ten feet away, it turns slowly and walks tentatively, pauses, then scampers away. The bear keeps throwing ASHAMED looks over its shoulder back at Diana.

Diana WAITS until the sound of the scuffling bear fades. She stands, her body shakes involuntarily--like a beast waking up.

She steps on the half-eaten fungus on the tree and VAULTS back over onto the trail back to the cabin.

Her feet, in unison with the chorus, "hit the ground RUNNING.

                                                    CUT TO:

INT.-LOG CABIN-LONGVILLE, MN-NIGHT

A fire roars. Empty Leinenkugel bottles are scattered everywhere. Sweeney is sober-drunk. Diana is wasted and weeping openly. Sweeney hides that he's despondent. But he knows it, he feels it--Diana LEFT him.

> SWEENEY
> (consoling)
> Well, it's been three days now. You can't keep up the pace with the beers, really. What else is eating at you?

> DIANA
> (instantly furious)
> Fuck you! A 300-pound fucking black bear contemplated eating me! If it happened to you, I'd be wiping your ass for you till next week!

> SWEENEY
> (getting testy)
> Ok, ok, I already told you something like this DID happen to me in Ecuador with the jaguar on the beach. I didn't land on the thing's back, but it did freeze me in my tracks when I saw the fuckin' thing. I know a little…

> DIANA
> You don't know a fucking thing. I'm done. I'm going to sleep. You sleep on the floor. Don't even come near this bed. I'm done.

> SWEENEY
> (quietly)
> You were done three days ago. You were done before that bear ever had the misfortune of meeting you face to face. (beat) Fuck this.

Diana crawls into bed clumsily holding two full beers, a lit cigarette between her teeth.

> DIANA
> (slurring, resigned)
> I heard that. Bring me that pipe
> before you go to bed, then fuck
> off. I'm staying up tonight.

Sweeney turns, faces the woodstove, warms his hands, polishes off half a beer. He looks at the clock--3:33 a.m. He turns up the stereo and Smog's "Hit the Ground Running" comes back on.

Sweeney grabs a beer, opens it, goes over to the bed and delicately removes the lit cigarette from Diana's mouth. She's passed out. He takes the two beers out of her clenched hands, throws a quilt over her. He steps outside with three beers, takes a drag on the cigarette.

                                          CUT TO:

EXT.-MAMBO BAR ON THE BEACH-NIGHT

Sweeney wipes some tears from his drunken face with the backs of both hands, orders a round for all the locals at the bar.

> SWEENEY
> Leo Gordo, my friend, sprinkle the
> infield!

> PANCHO MONEYMAKER
> Leo, I'll get this round and then
> that should do it. Don't let this
> drunk bastard buy all these people
> more drinks. He needs his money.

Pancho grabs his and Sweeney's Pilseners first, ushers Sweeney to the hammocks in a quiet part of bar's yard.

> PANCHO MONEYMAKER (CONT'D)
> So how long was it until you left her?

                    SWEENEY
Who? Oh, yeah. I was gone about a
day later because the anniversary of
decking the Mormon kid was coming up
and I had to get back to Seawell and
be arrested on that exact day with the
truck full of rotten ice cream and
shit.

                PANCHO MONEYMAKER
This is the last question I'll ask
on this matter, amigo. Have you
talked to her since?

                    SWEENEY
Well, I left a note on the mantel while
she was passed out.It pretty much said
I would be down here in Canoa by now
and that she owed me like two grand for
the wood I chopped. I figure she might
track me down at some point to pay me
back and torture me some more. You
know she has the time and the travel-
chops to actually show up here. I kinda
hope I never see her for the rest of
my life. Then again, whenever the bar
phone rings I catch myself looking
up to see if Leo's gonna pass me the
phone. I'm a fuckin' godawful mess.

                PANCHO MONEYMAKER
You'll be OK, I think. I don't blame
you for being a mess. No one would. You
need to get back in the water, though.
I'm sure of that. Swell on the way, the
locals are saying.

                                    CUT TO:

A SERIES OF IMAGES (WITH VOICE OVER):

Sweeney surfs HUNGOVER at dawn by himself and then shakes
off the rust with pancho during an evening session. He
surfs a little better, each dawn and dusk. He's painting
a mural with the kids, then surfing brilliantly. He
paints another larger mural and surfs some more (finally
surfing, laughing with the kids).

> SWEENEY (V.O.)
> Yeah, I'll paddle out soon enough.
> When those waves get here in a couple
> of days I should be on it. I almost
> surfed the little high tide chest-high
> waves I saw today. But then I just
> drank a beer for breakfast. I'll sober
> up soon when the waves arrive. We can
> surf in the morning when the wind's
> good. We'll paint a mural with Flowpi
> and her cousins if the wind goes
> northwest. I'll sweat all the beer
> out in the fuckin' scorching streets of
> Bahia. I'll be surfed out, sweaty and
> good as new. Soon as I can, I'll forget
> all about my white witch. Soon as I
> can, I'll forget her.

End of Act II

THE STORY OF THE FAILURE OF THIS SCRIPT IN HOLLYWOOD & BEYOND

PART II

Dana believes that when Nora, Aileen and Gerty turn seven and five respectively they will be old enough to accept the lie that Ellen is dead. For now, they know that "Mom is ill and needs to rest."

Dana plans on orchestrating a funeral for the benefit of the girls. It will be good for them to meet all of the friends and family who never had a chance to say goodbye to the version of Ellen that is long gone.

Ellen knows she is medicated, she feels struck-down, an inert shell whose inner workings have been gutted via the spectral machinations of a natural world she no longer comprehends. In fact, Ellen believes she is actually stuck in the basement of a wrecked house—held captive by her spooky, cloned children.

Six months after Dana was forced to institutionalize Ellen, she sold their Back Bay condo in Boston. The Gaplets had never known the condo as much more than an office and playspace during brief trips back to Massachusetts, but it was the original property their mothers purchased just before getting married. Dana and Ellen, however, had begun their life together in the Back Bay—they had been exceedingly happy for many years in that space.

In order to clean out the property, Dana hired movers and rented a storage unit. The movers were to take everything out but the contents of two rooms that served as offices on the third floor. All but Dana's and Ellen's work-related materials would be boxed and put into storage. Dana's office was the first on the right upstairs, followed by a left-handed bend in a long hallway that ended with three small steps up to a landing in front of a hexagonal room at the very back of the condo. Five of the six walls in Ellen's library boasted chest high bookshelves with a small window above. The entrance was centered in the sixth wall.

When the movers called to say they had finished, Dana booked a flight out of Chicago and packed up the Gaplets. After a fussy, overheated flight to Martha's Vineyard they visited with family for a few days, then Dana jumped on the ferry to Boston.

She began sifting through their vast collection of things accumulated and now virtually abandoned in the Back Bay. It was the first time she had been alone for a weekend, without the kids, in two years. The silence descended on her after she finished the several-hour task of sorting through, organizing and clearing out her old desk.

Glass of cloudy tap water in her left hand, Dana stopped in the upstairs hallway to better attune ears to the utter lack of cacophony. She reasoned it wasn't wholly unpleasant, though a little foreign—like the time she put her running shoes on the wrong feet, tied double-knots and stepped into the late-night empty dormitory hallway at UCLA. It had taken her a few moments then to seek out the true source of her discomfort.

In the bored-out hallway connecting her office with Ellen's, Dana paused to look down at her feet once again. She smiled softly at their bareness, their rightness, then decided to tackle the bedlam in the room Ellen had always called her "library." She had planned to save it for Sunday afternoon or evening, possibly after a night of steeling herself to the task with cheap beer at The Delux. Yet something called to her in that quiet moment, in that bent and emptied passageway. Dana turned and returned to the stereo in her own office. She cued up and cranked the Cure's "Disintegration" on cassette and entered Ellen's abandoned sanctuary. Stepping into the darkened room, eyes adjusting, she caught sight of a tall, rail-thin, twisted figure leaning over the desk. Dana jumped back, slapping hard at the wall for the circular dimmer switch. With the other hand, she reached for the vase on the tiny table outside the door. She couldn't get ahold of it. She stuck her head into the hallway to find it. The movers had packed it.

From the threshold, she stole a look back into the now well lighted room and she eased off her fight-or-flight reaction..

Again, Dana smiled at her own oddness.

A massive stack of books grew from the hardwood floor up the left side of the desk, climbed above it, then twisted and teetered over Ellen's Blueberry

Apple monitor.

Green shades drawn, blinds closed, as they had been for years, Dana suddenly found she stood in a symmetrical pocket of brightness. It was like standing within the luminous idea of her wife as her former, functioning, sane self. Dana understood all at once how deeply she connected this library and Ellen's work with the sane version of Ellen.

Dana felt as if she'd been up all night and now her eyes demanded to quit the artificial light. She just needed to lie down. She hadn't napped in years. But since there were no Gaplets capering about, she contemplated a siesta while staring down the stack of books. But there were no beds or couches left in the condo to aid her effort to rest.

With a sigh, she instead picked her way amongst the clutter on the floor, narrowly missing a red pushpin with her smallest toe. Dana crouched and began counting the books from the bottom of the towering stack and as she slowly stood she swung her head around the back of the column, leaning into a posture that mimicked the twisting stack. She read the bindings as she went, all of them. There were thirty-seven, first-edition, hardcover copies of John Gardner's collection of short stories, "The King's Indian."

"Thirty-seven? Ellen has thirty-seven first cousins," Dana said aloud, cutting through the pulsing tang of guitar and wailing voice of Robert Smith: "Remembering you standing quiet in the rain / As I ran to your heart to be near / Andwe kissed as the sky fell in, holding you close / How I always held close in your fear."

Each and every copy was bookmarked with a length of simple black ribbon. The marked story was titled: "The Ravages of Spring."

Dana sat at her wife's desk and began to read, sure she was unfamiliar with the story.

Slack-jawed at the finish of the tale, Dana closed her eyes and let her head sink onto the surface of her insane wife's desk. She slept for a spell.

When she woke she didn't immediately stir. First she came to the realization that she was not only familiar with the story she had just read, she had lived it.

Dana forced herself to pick up her head and look around to get her bearings.

She half-expected to find a mad scientist and his youthful, redheaded clones surrounding her.

No.

Next, she thought of the whereabouts of her children.

No, not here either.

Finally, she looked in the nearest mirror. She nearly pressed her face to the mirror's surface. Dana held her breath.

Breathing out, Dana recognized the glint of knowledge in her reflected eyes as they fogged-over for a moment. She finally knew where her wife had gone.

For years, Dana had the passing thought (hope, even) that the insane Ellen believed herself run away with Sir Ernest Rock living a new life devoid of children and her wife.

But now Dana knew the truth: Ellen believed she was trapped in a basement with unnatural strangers (her redheaded Gaplets) and a mad scientist (Dana herself, her doctor?). Their previous lives together--as snake-oil--filmmakers, mothers, partners—had been blown to ragged bits and down upon her hunkered head. Ellen's mental illness had been some kind of natural-world phenomenon, frighteningly thorough and expert in its talent for destruction. The illness was masterful in its carving of a distinct path of burned-out chaos within and without Ellen's head. Anyone who loved her risked destruction as well. To have known both versions of Ellen was to understand the callous, animal indifference of the observable universe.

Dana realized this story, her life with her wife and the Gaplets' mother, was simply finished. The End.

There was no climbing out of that basement for Ellen. There would be no licking of wounds, extending of hands down to the Gaplets to help them up and out. Whether Ellen lived long or died in a week was irrelevant. In either scenario Dana knew she and the Gaplets were all, at least partially, trapped in Ellen's delusional basement with her for the duration of each of their individual, mortal lives.

With the Back Bay condo gutted of things and memories, Dana mailed thirty-four black-ribboned copies of Gardner's short story collection to Ellen's remaining first cousins. She kept three books for the Gaplets. She didn't want a copy for herself.

Someone would read this story aloud at Ellen's upcoming fake funeral. Everyone could follow along. There was a slim chance the story could be a map for others, showing them the basement into which Ellen fell.

Later in life, Dana hoped this same strange piece of art-as map could somehow guide her girls up and out of that same hole their mother Ellen could not escape. After all, Dana had learned, you can never be sure which way art will take you when it takes hold.

ACT III

CUT TO:

EXT. – EDGE OF BAHIA DE CARáQUEZ, ECUADOR – SUNSET

At the end of the cement road, just before the dirt road
up to Bella Vista and Pancho's treehouse, we see Flowpi
being teased by her two cousins and a few neighborhood
boys. The teasing soon turns to bullying.

> FLOWPI
> (furiously)
> Dame mi tabla! Sweeney me dió esta
> tabla!

SUBTITLE: Give me my board back! Sweeney gave me that
board!

> COUSIN#1
> (laughing)
> Cállate, loca! Me voy a Canoa con
> mi hermano, no contigo!

SUBTITLE: Shut up, crazy girl! I'm going to Canoa with my
brother. You can't come.

CUT TO:

A SERIES OF IMAGES:

Sweeney comes to the top of a stairway up above and
behind the kids as they start pushing her around and

throwing rocks at her to make her run away.

Sweeney RUNS down the stairs.

Just as a good-sized rock is about to hit a crying, hysterical Flowpi, Sweeney CATCHES it and FAKES a return throw.

Most of the kids scatter. Flowpi's cousins are FROZEN by the sight of Sweeney.

Sweeney SILENTLY points at them, directs them to sit on the curb by the sea wall.

One cousin comes over with the board under his arm and gently puts it down next to Flowpi.

Flowpi SCREECHES incoherently, spitting in his direction.

Sweeney catches her gently, TRIES to calm her. She shakes with rage, talking a blue streak, unable to look at anyone.

It's as if she doesn't know he's there. She sits in the sunbleached dirt, where the cement ends, tears streaking her face, talking, shaking, talking to no one in particular. Sweeney just sits with her.

The last sliver of sun drops below the sea's horizon.

        Flowpi's pulling, stretching Sweeney's shirt over her bent knees in front of her as she sits next to him. Her brown face is streaked with tear-tracks, smudged with sunbleached white dirt from wiping her face over and over—a near indigenous embodiment of Sweeney's faked insanity.

Sweeney sits stock-still, letting Flowpi get it all out.

The streetlights above buzz and flicker to life, they are yellow-orange in the blue twilight.

The cousins try to shuffle off. Sweeney just shoots them both a look. The cousins sit, dejected. They shiver a bit in the suddenly cool, nighttime air.

The tiny waves on the other side of the seawall shush and crash, shush and crash.

Sweeney has his arm around Flowpi now. She has quieted. Her head drops onto his shoulder. It's nighttime, THOUSANDS of bugs and moths are SWARMING around the one streetlight above like it's the last light on the planet.

Sweeney scoops Flowpi up. As he stands, he nods at her two cousins and then the surfboard. Cousin #2 picks up the board. They follow Sweeney as he starts up the dirt road that winds through the hillside and the shanty town of Bella Vista.

There are no more streetlights. The tropical forest hanging over the shantytown is alive with bird, animal and bug noise. As the four make their way by faded shacks and fences, a 200 pound PIG runs across the road. Electric light leaks out of shacks on stilts with only split-bamboo trelliswork for walls.

A woman in a cinderblock shack next to a cement soccer field peers down from clinking glasses, a kitchen card game in progress. She throws down her cards and runs a drink of water down to Flowpi, still half-asleep in Sweeney's arms.

NIEVE is a twenty-something, raven-haired Ecuadorian. She has Mayan blood, dark skin, almost-black eyes, high cheekbones and an oval face centered by a brilliant smile. She appears familiar with Sweeney right away. She wears simple, faded jeans and a white sleeveless shirt. Her natural radiance is chased from her face by her instant concern for Flowpi.

> NIEVE
> Agua, mija, agua. Cuidado, poco a
> poco, no? (looking at Sweeney with
> a quick smile) Es un proceso, no?

SUBTITLE: Water, my little one, water. Be careful, little by little, no? It's a process, no?

Flowpi, after stirring just enough to drink, rests again in Sweeney's cradled arms.

Sweeney begins crying, unable to wipe the tears from his face for fear of jostling the girl.

Nieve looks inquiringly at the two silent cousins then back at Sweeney, offering water.

> SWEENEY
> (grimly)
> No, gracias, Nieve. Los niños no
> tienen sed en este momento. Gracias,
> mil gracias. Y más tarde,
> si tienes un poquito de sopa, puedes
> traerla para Flowpi? Nos vamos a la
> casa de Pancho por la noche.

SUBTITLE: No, thank you, Nieve. The boys aren't thirsty right now. Thank you, a thousand thank yous. And later if you have a little soup for Flowpi? We'll be staying at Pancho's house tonight.

> NIEVE
> Claro, claro. Voy a visitarlos
> en una hora, mas o menos y llevo la
> sopa. Que pasó?

SUBTITLE: Of course, of course. I'll visit with soup in an hour or so. What happened?

Sweeney swings his crying face back and forth between the ashamed, barefoot, ragged boys and Nieve.

Just before he speaks he pauses to read the faded, flaked lettering on a rickety wooden fence behind the cousins: "*Paz, Amor, y Vida.*" Subtitle: "Peace, love and life."

Sweeney points a hand, from under Flowpi's knees, at the fence as he begins talking to Nieve.

> SWEENEY
> (pointing)
> Yo tuve un plan para pintar mañana con
> Flowpi un mural con un mensaje como

ese. Pero Bella Vista está llena de
sufrimiento como el resto del mundo, y
los niños...el mundo ESTÁ sufriendo pero
estos niños no entienden. Yo tengo el
mismo sueño de sufrimiento, un sueño
sobre la realidad de mi abuelo, pero
cuando me despierto hay más sufrimiento
de otro tipo, pero es el mismo. Tú
entiendes, Nieve? No? Si, claro, tú
eres de Bella Vista. Tu entiendes.
Que linda y simpática! Qué
simpática! Pero los primos son
cabezas duras. Tienen las cabezas
llena de tierra. Flowpi está en el
centro del sufrimiento, no? Si,
si. Flowpi está sufriendo cada día
como una poeta, no? Sin defensas,
como una poeta que no podría pagar
por las zapatillas. Y ahorita ella
necesita ir a dormir. Discúlpeme,
señora, no puedo explicarme. Gracias,
Nieve. Hasta pronto, no?

SUBTITLE: (Sweeney pointing at sign) I had a plan to
paint a mural with a message like that one tomorrow with
Flowpi. But Bella Vista is full of suffering like the
rest of the world, and the kids...the world IS suffering
but these kids don't understand. I have the same dream
about suffering, about the life of my grandfather, but
when I wake up it's more suffering of a different kind,
yet the same. You understand, Nieve, don't you? Of course
you do, you grew up in Bella Vista. You understand.
Look at you, look at how beautiful and kind you are. So
compassionate. But these kids have heads like rocks.
They have heads full of Earth. Flowpi is the center of
suffering, isn't she? Yes, Flowpi is suffering these days
like a poet. Defenseless like a poet that can't afford
sandals. And now she needs to go to bed. Excuse me, miss,
I can't explain myself. Thank you, Nieve. See you soon,
right?

EXT.-THE STEPS BEHIND PANCHO'S TREEHOUSE ABOVE BELLA
VISTA NIGHT

Sweeney whistles the call of the sparrowhawk, "kill-eee,
kill eee," the Bella Vista neighborhood's signal. Inside,
someone responds. Pancho quickly appears at the top of
the steps.

> PANCHO MONEYMAKER
> Hola, what's…oh, mierda! Que paso?

SUBTITLE: Hello, what's…oh, shit! What happened?

> SWEENEY
> I'll tell you later. Flowpi just
> needs to rest for the night here.
> Her idiot cousins will clean one of
> the rooms out for her and then they'll
> clean the rest of the house. I haven't
> said much to them, but they're feeling
> sufficiently terrible for doing this to
> Flowpi. I think they should work off
> the shame a bit before they go home. I
> need a fucking drink. You got anything?

Pancho carefully takes Flowpi from Sweeney's arms,
turns and goes up into the treehouse. Sweeney follows,
plodding. He signals for the boys to go in before him.

> PANCHO MONEYMAKER
> (quietly over his shoulder)
> Yeah, I got a bunch of beer in the
> fridge. I'll join you. I'll get her
> settled in a hammock while the boys
> clean. (gently whispering) Oigan, primos,
> limpien el cuarto en frente de la casa.
> Apúrense! Los llevo a su casa despues
> de que ésta casa esté limpia.

SUBTITLE: Hey, you two, clean the room at the front of
the house. Hurry up! I'll walk you two home after this

whole house is clean.

Sweeney settles into a hammock with a perspiring 36-oz. bottle of Pilsener. He sways on the edge of the wrap-around porch overlooking the shantytown and nighttime skyline farther off before the rivermouth and the dark mass of northern jungle beyond. Buildings, cars and boats sparkle. Flecks of light in the distance. A cool breeze shifts through the canopies of nearby trees.

Pancho sits in an old kitchen chair, facing Sweeney and the view beyond him. He cracks his beer.

SWEENEY
(sighing, eyes closed)
Right now I can hide out in this
breeze, but tomorrow, and the day
after that the sun will be back to
burn us down to nubs of meanness…

Cousin #1 tries to slip by silently on the porch. He eyes the hammock warily, broom in hand. Sweeney's tired eyes snap open, the boy yelps like a wounded dog and stops in his tracks.

SWEENEY (CONT'D)
(saddened, closing his eyes again)
Los dias de violencia han terminado,
amigo, para mi, para ti y para Flowpi.
Entiendes? Nadie va a sufrir con mis
manos. Limpia la casa, anda a tu casa y
mañana vamos a hablar sobre tu prima.

SUBTITLE: The days of violence are done, my friend--
for me, for you and for Flowpi. Get it? No one's going
to suffer by my hand. Now clean the house, go home and
tomorrow we'll talk about your cousin.

Sweeney gently rests his hand on the boy by the hammock.

SWEENEY (CONT'D)
Paz, amor y vida, hombre, no? Y
mañana tu, tu hermano y yo vamos a

pintar ese mensaje en una pared gigante
en la ciudad para Flowpi. Vamos a
trabajar como burros todo al dia.

SUBTITLE: "Peace, love and life," man, right? And
tomorrow you, your brother and I are going to paint that
message on a gigantic wall in the city for Flowpi. We are
going to work like donkeys all day tomorrow.

                                        CUT TO:

Pancho's face looks worried as Cousin #1 shuffles by. The
view soothes him a bit and he drinks with Sweeney as they
look out at the night falling on the coast.

                                        CUT TO:

Pancho stands, takes Sweeney's empty bottle in hand with
his empty bottle. He opens a fresh one, hands it to
Sweeney, gives his hammock a little shove with his knee.
Sweeney opens his eyes, swaying, more relaxed, watches
Flowpi's two cousins slip in behind Pancho who is still
looking down at him in the hammock.

                    PANCHO MONEYMAKER
            Sweeney, my old friend, I'm sorry
            to say this but Leo Gordo at the
            Bambu Bar in Canoa left a message
            at my mother's house for you. He
            said Diana called from Quito early
            this morning. You never went back
            to Canoa today, right?

                    SWEENEY
                (eyes closed, pained)
            I didn't make it back like I
            planned and I'm not going back
            tonight. I know that much.

                    PANCHO MONEYMAKER
            Well, for now, I'll walk these two
            home and tell their parents we need
            them tomorrow…early. Will that work?

                    SWEENEY
          Yep. For now, that'll work.

                PANCHO MONEYMAKER
          Can you get Flowpi into the front
          room on the bottom bunk in a few
          minutes? She hates the top bunk.

                    SWEENEY
                 (exhausted now)
          I can do that.

Sweeney covers his eyes, squeezes his temples with one
hand.
                PANCHO MONEYMAKER
          But don't forget the mosquito
          netting on the bed for Flowpi,
          okay? When the breeze dies it will
          be bad here with the moscos. And
          Sweeney, I'm sorry to have to
          tell you about Diana. I think you
          were okay without her, but what do
          I know? I'm sorry.

Sweeney takes a deep breath. Looks out at the glittering
city and coastline. Points.

                    SWEENEY
          Not your fault, man. Pancho, you
          remember that first time you showed
          me Bahia? You showed me that giant
          Galapagós Tortoise living in the
          schoolyard, the markets, the different
          neighborhoods, the beaches, the harbor,
          you remember? I never told you but all
          that stuff was great, but for me I
          couldn't stop looking at all the hotel
          highrises and condo buildings that
          are just sitting there empty because
          of that earthquake a few years ago.
          Remember me staring and staring at

them? You were giving me shit about
looking at them so much. I never told
you how they remind me of all the old
mill buildings in Seawell. I grew up
around massive boarded-up brick mills
in Seawell. Remember that first day in
Bahia? You taught me all the bird calls
you use with the kids from different
neighborhoods? Remember my first day
on the coast down here? Ahh fuck it,
whatever, you have to get those two
idiot cousins of Flowpi's home. Get
going, I'll talk to you when you get
back and I won't forget the mosquito
netting on the bed. But, hey, come back
soon okay? Don't leave me up here
to drink alone for too long.

            PANCHO MONEYMAKER
    Ok, be back soon. I'll get some
    more beer, too.

Sweeney swings his legs out onto the floor, slips his
flipflops on and looks up at the two cousins. They are
still and silent. They know something else is wrong,
but don't understand English. They look at each other,
concerned for Sweeney.

Sweeney sticks one open hand out and smiles a genuine
smile at them. They run over and each give him five.

As Pancho and the boys turn and leave, they walk around
the house and down the hill in front. Sweeney whistles
the call of the Sparrowhawk, all three answer in unison—
"kill-eee, kill-eee!"

Sweeney is tense, but he has to smile at this. He stands
and goes down the porch to the hammock holding Flowpi,
still dwarfed by his surf T-shirt, still dusty and
sleeping.

He picks her up and gives her a kiss on the forehead as
he starts whispering to her. We can't hear what he says

as he continues to whisper and tucks her into the lower
bunk in a small comfortable, dimly lit room with two
bunkbeds and netting hanging from the ceiling above each
bunk.

Sweeney shuts off the light, takes a step back toward
his beer. Pauses, turns the light back on and unties the
mosquito netting around the bottom bunk, he lets it drop
to the floor. He crouches to check the bottom of the
netting to make sure it's sealing off the bed. He runs a
hand over the netting, looking for holes.

Flowpi wakes up for a moment, looks out at him crouched,
checking the netting with such care. Sweeney doesn't see
she's awake for a moment.

He sees her awake. She flashes him a smile and a weak
hang loose sign.

Sweeney stands, reaches up to the cord hanging from the
bulb, pauses, flashes a smile and a hang loose sign back.

> SWEENEY
> (whispering)
> Dulces sueños, Flowpi. Tengo que ir
> a Quito mañana. No vamos a pintar
> el mural hasta la próxima semana.
> Hasta pronto, en una semana más o
> menos. Okay?

SUBTITLE: Sweet dreams, Flowpi. I have to go to Quito
tomorrow. We're not going to paint the mural until next
week. See you soon, in like a week or so. Okay?

Flowpi is already asleep again. She didn't hear a thing
Sweeney said.

Sweeney pulls the cord, the light goes out, the noises
of the jungle take over. The view is still OVERPOWERING.
Sweeney makes his way back toward his hammock and beer.

> SWEENEY (CONT'D)
> (to himself)
> Doesn't matter. Pancho will fill

you in. Just rest up. I'll be back
in a while with a steady flow of
money for you and your family. I'm
almost as tired as you are, kid. I
can't carry it anymore. You can use
the money more than me anyways.
(exasperated) Goddammit, I'm
SO...FUCKIN'...WORN...THE...FUCK...OUT.

Sweeney slips back into his hammock on the porch, sways,
takes a long swig, takes in the view. He PICKS AT the
Pilsener label a little. He's mumbling, almost asleep.

                SWEENEY (CONT'D)
             (to himself)
Somehow, some fuckin' way, my head
makes every dream a nightmare. I
swear to god, if I don't figure some
shit out, this fuckin' dream isn't
gonna leave me alone.

Sweeney sleeps.

                             CUT TO:

INT.-PANCHO'S TREEHOUSE-SAME

A short time later, Sweeney is sitting up in the hammock,
tense, feet on the floor. There's quiet chatter from
Flowpi's room. Something has changed drastically. He
stands, goes to smooth down his shirt...he's shirtless.

                SWEENEY
      (nervously hissing to himself)
Mierda! I mean, shit! The kid still
has my shirt on. It's like I'm some
kinda gringo-weirdo sitting up here
by myself drinking beer shirtless!
Dammit! How could I forget she was
coming up here? I'm a fuckin' moron.

There is quiet chatter and laughter, female voices, in
the now lit-up bedroom.

Sweeney is tip-toeing on the wraparound porch, trying to decide what to do. He can't find lights in the rooms he enters, he can't find a stitch of clothing to wear. He goes to take a pull of his almost empty beer, catches himself, runs to the kitchen table, puts the bottle down like it's on fire…but quietly. He paces, sticks his head in and out of the same rooms.

> SWEENEY (CONT'D)
> (whispering to himself, frantic)
> Where the hell does Pancho keep his shirts? He only has like five! Do tree houses have closets? Sweaty bastard ruins shirts in like a week. What am I gonna do?

The light goes off, Nieve steps out onto the porch, holding a towel and bowl of water. She looks back in, gently chides Flowpi about going back to sleep. Her whispered Spanish has a lilt to it.
Sweeney comes around the corner, stops in his tracks, staring at her wide-eyed, much like Flowpi's cousin froze under his gaze only an hour before in the same exact spot on the porch.

> NIEVE
> Estas bien?

SUBTITLE: You okay?

Nieve slips close to him, past him and into the kitchen. She puts the bowl into the sink. She walks to the fridge. Sweeney looks at his hands, he doesn't know what to do with them. Nieve looks in the fridge. Sweeney quickly crosses his arms, frowns, puts them in pockets that don't exist in his surf trunks. Nieve looks up. Sweeney throws them behind his back quickly, awkwardly.

> NIEVE (CONT'D)
> Hay más cerveza. Quieres más?

SUBTITLE: There's more beer. Do you want another?

                        SWEENEY
                    (trying too hard)
            Claaaaaahhhhroooo.

Nieve laughs, and flashes an awkward hang-loose sign as
she speaks.

                        NIEVE
                (laughing at Sweeney, gently)
            Tú hablas como una surfista desde Canoa.
            Pero tú eres Sweeney, no? Los surfistas
            desde Bahia hablan de ti. De dónde
            eres? Argentina, si? No es seguro,
            pero tú eres otro amigo de Pancho y
            la Pachamama. Las dos fuma marihuana
            en los bosques, son compadres con los
            monos, y también con las mujeres de
            Europa que visitan Canoa. Es verdad?
            Si? Ahorita estas muy tímido, pero tu
            eres un buen tipo. Te conozco.

SUBTITLE: You talk like a surfer from Canoa. But you're
Sweeney, right? Where are you from? Argentina? (mocking)
I'm not sure, but you are another friend of Pancho's y
Mother Earth. (laughing) The two of you smoke weed in the
woods, you are friends with the monkeys as well as the
European female backpackers that visit Canoa. True? Yes?
Right now you are shy, but you're a good guy. I know you.

                        SWEENEY
                    (embarassed)
            Umm, hmm, well, no, soy de los Estados
            Unidos…y, um, discúlpeme pero le di mi
            camiseta a Flowpi y estaba pensando
            sobre…compadres de los monos? Quién
            dijo que nosotros…

SUBTITLE: Umm, no, I'm from the States and, um, pardon me
but I gave my T-shirt to Flowpi and I was thinking about…
companions of the monkeys? Who said that we…?

Mercifully, there's a sudden Sparrowhawk whistle from the
back steps, "kill-eee, kill-eee".

Nieve, enjoying herself thoroughly, returns the call with
perfect pitch.

                    SWEENEY (CONT'D)
            Pues, ELLA es de Bella Vista. Yo no
            mucho más.

SUBTITLE: Well, SHE is from Bella Vista. I know that
much.

Pancho saunters into the room, arms filled with bottles
of beer. He stops cold, a knowing smile darts across his
face, then he sashays over to the fridge looking the two
of them up and down.

Impossibly, Sweeney is even more embarrassed. He and
Nieve simultaneously blurt out greetings at Pancho, in
Spanish and English respectively.

                    NIEVE
            Pancho! Que pasa? Todo bien? Tu
            amigo estaba hablando sobre los
            monos…

SUBTITLE: Pancho! What's up? Everything good? Your friend
was talking about the monkeys…

                    SWEENEY
            Pancho! Where the hell you been?
            This woman is roasting me like…

Everyone breaks into laughter and Pancho, looking
confused, slowly puts down the beer and holds up
Sweeney's T-shirt that Nieve had stashed in the fridge.

                PANCHO MONEYMAKER
                (confused but suspicious)
            Qué pasó?

Nieve flashes a mischivieous smile.

                         NIEVE
                (embarrassed, feigning innocence)
          Qué? Qué? Pero Sweeney se apareció
          muy…muy, umm…cómodo.

SUBTITLE: What? What? But Sweeney just looked so…so,
um…comfortable.

                                            CUT TO:

INT.-PANCHO'S TREEHOUSE-A BEDROOM WITH EMPTY BUNKS-NEAR
DAWN

Pancho is trying to keep Sweeney behind some mosquito
netting. Sweeney thrashes a bit between trying to
drunkenly explain all that is going through his head and
all that happened since sunset.

                        SWEENEY
                       (slurring)
               But she's so little, man. I'm not
               even sure kids can be or have
               Schizoaffective Disorder, like I
               have. I mean "fake-have." You know
               what I'm sayin'?

                    PANCHO MONEYMAKER
                  (less drunk, soothing)
               Si, si. Go to sleep, man. Whisper.
               Go to sleep. It's almost the sun
               coming up now. Flowpi is asleep, still.
               Even the birds and bugs are. Listen…

Sweeney cocks his head as if to listen, but immediately
carries on, jabbing at the net with his finger at the
netting to make his points.

                        SWEENEY
               C'mon, fuck the bugs and the bees,
               man. I'm talkin' about how those
               tall empty hotels and condos of
               Bahia down there are like the
               vertical axis, man. They are the

vertical axis to the long horizontal
condemned redbrick mills of Seawell,
man. It's like I'm on some kind of
graph of my past and future and I suck
at math. How did I get on this axis
tonight, you know what I'm sayin'? I'm
at like zero with Diana coming to find
me in Ecuador…ECUADOR!

        PANCHO MONEYMAKER
          (hissing)
Cara de verga! Shhhhh! Cayate gringo!

SUBTITLE: Cockface! Shhhhh! Shut up, gringo!

          SWEENEY
          (laughing)
I'm in Ecuador and she comes and
finds me on the night I see Flowpi
go down. Like, I can't go back to
Diana and railing lines of coke in
some club in Quito and blowing
through our money and then going
back to Seawell to get more. You
know? Did I tell you they almost
caved Flowpi's fuckin' head in with
the rock, Pancho. Did I tell you
that? I caught that rock and I think it
woulda killed the girl. She was already
knocked down in the dust, right down
there by those empty, tall buildings.
Right at the start of the dirt road,
where the cement ends like my past
life and my…what the fuck am I talking
about? Fuck, man, what am I gonna
do about Diana. Fuck her! What am I
gonna do?

        PANCHO MONEYMAKER
I don't know, but you need to go…I
need to…

                    SWEENEY
                (conspiratorially)
          Did you see Nieve tonight, amigo?
          Wow. Where does she live? I mean, I
          know she grew up here but I haven't
          seen her…Jesus, Jesus Christ was
          she hot as hell or what?

Pancho gives up the fight at the turn in conversation
toward Nieve. He's smiling but exhausted.

                PANCHO MONEYMAKER
          Oh man, here we go. Go to sleep,
          man. Remember, she thinks we're
          companions of the monkeys. And
          besides, you got a long road to
          Quito tomorrow. I give up.

                    SWEENEY
                (settling down)
          Nieve? Why did she put my shirt
          with the beer? Wait, why am I goin'
          to Quito tomorrow? Today? I don't
          wanna go. Fuckin' Quito, maaaan. I
          already said that, though. Wait!
          Who thinks I'm from Argentina, by
          the way? I should go there if
          people who look like me people that
          place. Jorge Luis Borges is the
          man. Ireneo Funes, man. That's the
          fuckin' legend right there. Buenos
          Aires it is, then. Fuck Quito and
          Diana. Is it light out? I'm so tired.
          Pancho you need some sleep, man.

Pancho is long gone.

                SWEENEY (CONT'D)
                (whispering, almost asleep)
          Where are all the bugs and the
          bees? (in a sing-song voice) I
          don't hear you.

EXT.-AIRPORT TAXI STAND-QUITO, ECUADOR-DAY

Sweeney looks at a clock outside the airport that reads
3pm. He waits for Diana. She is a no-show.

Clock shows 4pm, Sweeney throws his small backpack in the
backseat of a taxi, climbs in after it with a knowing,
dejected look on his face.

> SWEENEY
> Buen día. Por favor, hay un bar en
> la calle Juan León Mera se
> llama "Encuentro." Gracias.

SUBTITLE: Hi, Please, there's a bar on Juan Leon Mera St.
called "Encuentro." Thank you.

As the driver pulls away into the Quito traffic, beneath
the emerald green flank of the Pichincha volcano, Sweeney
hardly looks out the window at all.

Beaten before he has begun.

> SWEENEY (CONT'D)
> (exhausted)
> I don't know if I can make these
> leaps with her for much longer.

CUT TO:

INT.-ENCUENTRO BAR-EVENING

There are a few Ecuadorians and a couple of European
backpackers sitting at the small bar above a tiny dance
floor and DJ booth. Roots reggae plays loudly.

Diana sits with her back to the door, she is drunk and
has two cans of Henieken in front of her, a few more
empties beside those.

Sweeney takes a step into the bar, PAUSES just over the
threshold. He sees Diana. She hasn't seen him. He ever so
slightly begins to start an ABOUT-FACE, but hesitates.

                    DIANA
          Oh shit! What time...*Qué hora es*?!
          Mierda! I have to get to the airport!
          Oh this could be bad, really bad...so
          bad. Dammit! This could be so bad.

Sweeney is moved as he witnesses Diana panic about
forgetting to pick him up. Diana jumps up, WOBBLES, and
before she can decide to not go at all Sweeney speaks up.

                    SWEENEY
          It could be, but it isn't. Not unless
          you don't have my money for cutting
          all that wood. Actually it'd be worse
          if I find out I've missed happy hour.
          Bartender! Line 'em up and let's drink
          'em up so we can catch up. Por favor,
          cuatro Heniekens!

Diana relaxes, finding her balance against the bar. She
bursts into a stunning smile then RUNS and JUMPS into
Sweeney's waiting arms. She buries her head in Sweeney's
neck, kisses his face all over.

                    DIANA
                 (muffled)
          I'm sorry, so sorry. I'm so sorry, I'm
          sorry. I had one goddamned thing to
          do today and I screwed it up. I'm so
          sorry, Sweeney.

                    SWEENEY
          Ahh, don't worry about it. I knew where
          to find you, didn't I?

                    DIANA
                 (slight slur)
          I'm so glad you flew up here, I'm
          so glad to see you. I never should've
          tried to leave you in the woods like
          that. Things have changed, you'll see.
          I have all my money now, and we can do

whatever we want like we talked about.

Sweeney's face changes when he hears the news that Diana has cashed in her trust fund. He's not entirely comforted by the news.

> SWEENEY
>
> We don't have to talk about money. We have some time now to figure things out. I want to take you down to the coast to meet Pancho and this little girl I met, Flowpi.

Diana pulls away. She looks at him accusingly for a moment, turns and heads back to her barstool.

> DIANA
> (cooled)
>
> Who? I don't want to meet some little spic hussy you're giving surf lessons to.

> SWEENEY
> (exasperated)
>
> Oh, wow. What was that, like 45 seconds of 'nice to see you'? Relax, I'm talking about a 9-year old girl that has all the real mental issues I've been faking for the last few years. And what's with the racist shit? How long have you...

> DIANA
> (interrupting)
>
> Wait, hold on, sorry. What the hell is wrong with me? Hold on, let's start this over for the second time tonight. Give me a minute. I'm going to use the bathroom and I'll be back in five. Forget about what I just said. Just forget that, it's a bad inside joke between me and

the bartender, Oskar. (yelling)
Oskar! Dos cervezas por favor.

Oskar approaches, opens the beers. Reaches out a hand to
shake Sweeney's.

                    DIANA (CONT'D)
          Oskar, Sweeney. Sweeney, Oskar.
          un momentito, hombres.

Diana heads back to the bathroom. Sweeney watches her go
for a moment longer than normal. He swings his head back
to Oskar, takes a long pull of a beer.

                    SWEENEY
          Me gustaría pagar la cuenta de mi
          novia, por favor, Oskar. Cuánto cuesta?

SUBTITLE: I'd like to pay the bill for my girlfriend,
please, Oskar. How much do I owe you?

                    OSKAR
          Oh, no es necesario, Sweeney. Ella
          no paga nada aqui. Y tú tampoco.
          Las cervezas no cuestan nada aquí
          para ti.

SUBTITLE: Oh that's not necessary, Sweeney. She doesn't
pay anything here. And you, too. Beer doesn't cost a
thing here for you.

Sweeney looks puzzled, for a moment grateful, but then
suspicious.

Diana exits the bathroom wiping stray grains of COKE from
her nose.
                    SWEENEY
          Si? Gracias pero por qué es la
          cerveza...

                    DIANA
                (quickly, dismissively)
          Oh don't worry about it, Sweeney.

As they say in the Northwoods,
"when you find the gift horse drink
with it, nevermind looking in its
mouth" or whatever it is.

Diana plants a kiss on Sweeney's mouth.

Oskar moves off.

Peter Tosh's "You Can't Blame the Youth" BLARES.

Sweeney shrugs it off reluctantly, finishes off his first
can. He and Diana begin to patch things up over their
beers.

                                              CUT TO:

INT.-ENCUENTRO BAR-SAME

TITLE: FOUR HOURS LATER

The entire bar crowd greets a 20-something coke dealer,
ANGEL, like an old friend who's been gone for months.

The first few chords of The Shod's "Fuckin' Around" come
on the sound system as if it's Angel's entrance music.

He's handing out business cards, greeting strangers and
friends warmly. He has long hair--a friendly, baby-faced
local no different than the other locals.

                         CROWD
                   (shouting in unison)
                  Angel! Angel! Angel!

The scraggly, pale Canadian DJ is looking over records
and virtually head-banging as the first CHORUS of the
song HITS THE BAR.

Sweeney grabs his two beers from the bar as Diana jumps
back in HIS arms, then PULLS him to the dance floor.

The rest of the crowd, all double-fisted with cans of
beer, packs the tiny dance floor with Sweeney, Diana and
Angel at the center, BOUNCING.

The bar has ROARED to life and it's completely
infectious.

Sweeney and Diana have reconnected, they are leading the
bar in song.

With each chorus, all the Ecuadorians try to sing along
in broken English with Diana and Sweeney.

                    SWEENEY & DIANA
                 (shouting)
        "I wanna have some fun...

                    CROWD
                 (shouting)
        BUT I JUST KEEP FUCKIN' AROUND!

                    SWEENEY & DIANA
                 (shouting)
        I'm tryin' to get shit done...

                    CROWD
                 (shouting)
        BUT I JUST KEEP FUCKIN' AROUND!

                    SWEENEY & DIANA
                 (shouting)
        Don't wanna be a bum...

                    CROWD
                 (shouting)
        BUT I JUST KEEP FUCKIN' AROUND!

As the final chorus ends, Diana takes a quick look around
and then leads Sweeney into the women's room to do some
lines. With Sweeney's first real snort we...

                                        CUT TO:

INT.-FIVE-STAR HOTEL BEDROOM-NIGHT
_____

Sweeney snorts a line off Diana's stomach, up toward her
breasts, he finishes with a lick along her neck, kissing

her jaw and then Diana attacks him with her own long kiss, tonguing him into submission below her.

We pull back as Sweeney speaks to reveal a beautiful room littered with bottles, beers and coke. Beyond is a stunning nighttime view of QUITO.

> SWEENEY
> (fiercely, quietly)
> We're back at it, aren't we? Back at it in…where are we? Ahh, fuck it. This is still Quito, right?

CUT TO:

INT.-FIVE-STAR HOTEL BEDROOM-NIGHT

The room is nearly identical to the Quito room. Sweeney and Diana roll around in bed once again.

> SWEENEY
> (laughing, quietly)
> Ahh, fuck it. This is still Quito, right?

> DIANA
> (laughing)
> Buenos Aires, mi amor, Buenos Aires and we leave in two days for Santiago, Chile. Get your head on straight.

> SWEENEY
> Why? Why the hell would I ever want to do that?

CUT TO:

INT.-ANOTHER BAR-BUENOS AIRES-THE NEXT AFTERNOON

> SWEENEY
> I think I might go over to the Borges Center after these beers. Do you want to go?

                    DIANA
               (ignoring Sweeney)
          Señor, aguardiente por favor!

                    SWEENEY
               (resigned)
          Alright, I'll see you later then.
          Be back in a couple hours. Can I
          have some cash? I don't get my SSI
          check for another few days.

Diana impatiently shoves Sweeeney A LOT of money and
throws him a quick kiss on the cheek. She downs her shot
of aguardiente and leans into the first of the two beers
with a little too much strain on her TIRED face.

And her attention is instantly elsewhere.

Sweeney pauses, shakes his head at this hint of her
desperation. He turns toward the door and shrugs it off.

He steps into the sunshine, looks around the beautiful
buzzing streets of Buenos Aires. A bit of relief chases
the worry from his eyes.

He takes a long pull from a beer.

A balding, bespectacled businessman walks by, looks up at
Sweeney drinking his beer. Their eyes meet.

Sweeney instantly hands him his unopened beer. They CLINK
cans.

Over Sweeney's shoulder, through the door, Diana turns in
time to see Sweeney sharing his beers in the sunshine on
the sidewalk outside the darkened bar.

                    SWEENEY (CONT'D)
          Salud, amigo!

                    BUSINESSMAN
          Gracias, hombre, y salud!

The businessman takes a drink with Sweeney and then walks
on his way with the beer and a friendly look back over
his shoulder, raising his beer in salute to Sweeney.

> SWEENEY
> (radiantly happy, to himself)
> You gotta love Thursday afternoons
> in South American cities. Taxi!

Climbing in the back of a cab.

> SWEENEY (CONT'D)
> Paz, amor y vida, no? Por qué no?
> Es un proceso. Poco a poco, verdad

SUBTITLE: Peace, love and life, no? Why
not? It's a process. Little by little,
right?

> TAXI DRIVER
> (perplexed)
> Qué? No entiendes, señor. Qué?

SUBTITLE: What? I don't understand, sir. What?

> SWEENEY
> (laughing)
> Paz, amor y vida, señor, en cada
> momento de nuestras vidas, no? Al
> Museo de Borges, por favor, señor.

SUBTITLE: Peace, love and life, sir, in each moment of
our lives, right? To the Museum of Jorge Luis Borges,
please, sir.

CUT TO:

INT.-FIVE-STAR HOTEL BEDROOM-NIGHT
The room is again littered with cans, half-smoked joints,
etc. Sweeeney and Diana are back at it.

                    SWEENEY
Ahh, fuck it. This is still Quito,
right?

                    DIANA
Rio, mi amor. We were in La Paz and
now Rio. We take the leap in two
days for that stupid waterfall in
Guyana that you are dying to see.
Then we hop back to Quito in the
clouds. Get your head on straight.

                                    CUT TO:

INT.-FIVE-STAR HOTEL BEDROOM-NIGHT

Sweeney and Diana are NOT back at it, but climbing
wearily into bed. Diana's turns her back on Sweeney who
is lying on his side.

                    SWEENEY
        (an exhausted attempt at levity)
Ahh, fuck it. This is definitely NOT
Quito. You have around 300 mosquito
bites on your arms and the back of your
legs.

                    DIANA
        (simmering with anger)
No shit, Sweeney. I didn't come
down to South America to go check
out some shitty waterfall in the
jungle. I could've stayed in the
Northwoods with those mosquitos.
They're worse up there and you
would've come to me when you ran
out of money. I'm so tired, I don't
even want to talk to you.

                    SWEENEY
        (resigned)
Run out of money? Are YOU the crazy

person in this equation? I thought
I was the one getting monthly SSI
from the government? And for the
record, one more time, I've never
NEEDED a cent from you. Happy to
help you snort and drink up your
trust fund, but let's not pretend…

Diana LEAPS out of bed. Sweeney instantly regrets opening
his mouth and begins gathering a blanket, knowing the
impending outcome. Diana picks up and SMASHES a half full
bottle of aguardiente off the wall. She goes silent.
She is rageful, teetering on the edge. Sweeney is CALM,
RESIGNED.

                    DIANA
              (matter-of-factly)
          Get out.

                    SWEENEY
              (impatient & sarcastic)
          Yeah, yeah. No shit. You kick me
          outta bed every other night now. I
          have to learn to shut my mouth if I
          want to get laid, or even get a
          pillow for that matter.

Diana slams the bedroom door. She weeps loudly.

Sweeney stands, blanket in hand, staring at the door.

                    SWEENEY (CONT'D)
          When am I gonna learn? That was a
          lovely evening of exhaust and filth and
          crying babies on the bus. If we stayed
          in the jungle like I wanted, we'd have
          fallen asleep to the sound of howler
          monkeys roaring in the valley. Instead…

Another SMASH AND CRASH from the bedroom. Sweeney begins
setting up the couch for himself. Diana is still wailing
and crying.

                    SWEENEY (CONT'D)
                (wincing)
        Actually, by now I'd probably be
        kicked out of our little lean-to
        and halfway up a tree with a jaguar
        snacking on my thighbone.

We hear one more LESSER SMASH from the bedroom. Then
quiet.
                    SWEENEY (CONT'D)
        Oops, I think she's out. (in a weak
        imitation of Howard Cosell) "Frazier goes
        down!" I'll just get up in a few hours,
        clean the place, replace the liquor.
        She won't even remember this. (laughing)
        It'll be a long two-hour flight to Quito
        if she does. Ahh, happy hour in Quito
        once again.

Sweeney rolls over to sleep. It is quiet. The sun rises
outside the window perched high above Rio's coastal city
scape.

                    SWEENEY (CONT'D)
                (whispering)
        Yep, happy hour cures all ills in
        this house of insanities. Real and
        imagined.

                                        CUT TO:

INT.-ENCUENTRO BAR-QUITO-EVENING
_____

It is happy hour. Everyone swarms around Diana and
Sweeney, welcoming them back to Ecuador. They are
peppered with questions about where they've been, what
they did, drugs, clubs, bars etc.

Per usual, Diana orders two shots of Caña Manabita and
four beers. She looks rundown. Her hands SHAKE. Her voice
QUAVERS. She feigns smiles and laughs. She's not all
there.

Sweeney is carrying on with his old Quito friends, but he eyes Diana WARILY.

                    DIANA
              (saccharine sweet)
          Sweeney, babe, I forgot. You
          probably don't want your Caña shot
          just yet do you. You like to have
          one at sunset, don't you?

                    SWEENEY
          Yeah, I'll have one with you now
          since we're back…

                    DIANA
              (pretending deafness, still pours it
              on thick)
          I'll just have that one for you
          then, my dear. There we go, now.
          Here are your cans of Heineken.
          Welcome back to Quito, darling.

                    SWEENEY
              (exasperated)
          Oh, Jesus, can we just have a good
          night back here with everybody? I
          told you I was sorry for the "crazy"
          comment. It's been a rough
          circuit for both of us lately. Can
          we just…

Diana fires back the second shot, pushes her two beers to Sweeney. Waves at Angel, the coke dealer, hops off her stool and gives him a big hug and kiss.

Sweeney gives Angel a genuine half-hug and handshake. He bears no ill-will for anyone involved with Diana's proclivity for constant stimulation.

Angel and Diana head off toward the women's room to do some lines. Sweeney turns back to the bar and begins to corral his FOUR BEERS.

Sweeney leans into the first of four. Two long swigs and it is gone.

He looks at Oskar with a wry grin on his face.

> SWEENEY (CONT'D)
> Un sueño o un desastre, hombre? Yo
> no sé.

SUBTITLE: A dream or a disaster, man? I don't know.

> OSKAR
> Es un proceso, si? Poco a poco,
> amigo. Como se dice en la costa,
> no?

SUBTITLE: It's a process, right? Bit by bit, my friend.
As they say on the coast, no?

Sweeney gives Oskar a suspicious glance, then flashes a broad smile as...

> **CUT TO:**

EXT.-QUITO-PHONE BOOTH-LATE AFTERNOON

> SWEENEY
> Yah, Pancho! Amigo, dos semanas...no
> más. Si, yo tengo un cheque en el
> banco y habrá otro en dos
> semanas. Diana y yo vamos a Canoa
> en dos semanas!

SUBTITLE: Yah, Pancho! Man, two weeks, no more than that.
I have a check in the bank and there's another check in
two weeks. Diana and I are going to Canoa in two weeks!

Sweeney is clearly ecstatic to talk to Pancho again. He
hangs up the phone and rushes back toward Encuentro.
He looks back at the sun setting over Quito and the
Pinchincha volcano.

He ALMOST bumps into an indigenous family--father,
mother, and small girl around nine or ten years old. They
are all wearing traditional felt hats and the father is
carrying a huge bundle of purple TIMOTHY FLOWERS.

                    SWEENEY (CONT'D)
             Oh, perdoneme, perdon. Disculpame!
             Soy un gringo, un mono loco!
             Perdón!

SUBTITLE: Oh, pardon me. Pardon. Excuse me! I am a
gringo, a crazy monkey! Pardon.

The little indigenous girl BURSTS into laughter sounding
out like a BLAST OF SONG above the city's coughing
noises.

Everyone is STUNNED at the sound.

Everyone smiles down at her.

Sweeney and the girl's parents begin laughing more and
more as Sweeney does a little Chicken Dance mixed with a
monkey dance mixed with a dance of joy.

As the laughing subsides, Sweeney is about to rush off
but he remembers something and begins patting down his
pockets. He takes something small out of his pocket and
hands it down to the girl.

                    SWEENEY (CONT'D)
             Oh, si, para ti. Una tablita de
             surf. Es balsa. Para tu llaves, pero
             en forma de una tabla de surf…

Subtitle: Oh yeah, this is for you. It's a little
surfboard. It's balsa wood. For your keys but like a real
surfboard…

Confused looks all around.

                    INDIGENOUS GIRL
             LLaves? Oh, pero no usamos llaves.

SUBTITLE: Keys? Oh, but we don't own any keys.

She, sadly, tries to hand the keychain surfboard back to
Sweeney. She is unfailingly polite with the strange, tall
gringo in front of her and her family.

                        SWEENEY
            No, por favor, es para ti. Por
            favor, si no tienes llaves…es
            una cosa, como un juguete, para ti.

SUBTITLE: No, please, it's for you. Please, if you don't
have keys…it's a thing, like a toy, for you.

Nervous laughter.
                    INDIGENOUS GIRL
            Oh, gracias. Un juguete? Pero, qué
            es esto? Cuál es la funcion?

SUBTITLE: Oh, thank you. A toy, but, what is this? How
does it work?

Sweeney pauses at the question. He's rocked by the
question really. He looks slowly from face to face to
face of the family.

                        SWEENEY
            Es difícil que explicar, es un
            símbolo de una tabla mas larga,
            um, pero…no se.

SUBTITLE: It's difficult to explain, it's a symbol for a
larger surfboard um, but…I don't know.

They all laugh at Sweeney a little, though respectfully.
The girl's father PUTS DOWN the HUGE bundle of timothy
flowers he carries on his back. He takes off his felt
hat, wipes the sweat from his brow on his sleeve.

                   SWEENEY (CONT'D)
                    (awkwardly)
            Sabes, las olas en el mar, pues…

SUBTITLE: You know the waves in the ocean, well…

                    INDIGENOUS GIRL
                      (sweetly)
              Si, si? He visto una foto.

SUBTITLE: Yes, yes? I've seen a photograph.

                        SWEENEY
              Pues, cuando un hombre…o una niña
              como tú…quieran subirse

SUBTITLE: Well, when a man…or a little girl like you…
wants to ride…

                    INDIGENOUS GIRL
                    (understanding)
              Oh! Es una silla! Una silla para,
              (still confused) para…o dijo "una
              tablita" para…las olas? Pero…no
              entiendo? Papá, entiendes?

SUBTITLE: Oh! It's a saddle, for…or you said "it's a
little table" for…the waves? But I don't understand?
Papa, do you understand?

The little girl stares up at her father for some kind of
explanation. Her father SHRUGS. He begins to pick up the
waist-high bundle of flowers off the sidewalk.

                        SWEENEY
              No, un momentito! Por favor, no es
              importante. Yo hice esto con
              mis manos…

SUBTITLE: No, wait! Please, it's not important. I made
this thing with my hands…

INSTANTLY, the family members understand. They look at
one another knowingly. The little indigenous girl is
beaming, now, she is a bit shy beneath her gratitude for
the small gift.

                    INDIGENOUS FATHER
                  (somewhat brusquely)
         Gracias, señor. Tú eres muy amable.
         Gracias.

SUBTITLE: Thank you, sir. You're very kind. Thank you.

                       SWEENEY
         De nada. Es una…cosa para su niña.
         De nada. Pero, señor, las flores
         cuanto cuestan?

SUBTITLE: You're welcome, it's a…thing for your daughter.
You're welcome. But, sir, how much for the flowers?

                                          CUT TO:

INT.-FIVE-STAR HOTEL BEDROOM-QUITO-NIGHT
_____

The bed BURIED UNDER TIMOTHY FLOWERS.

Two PLANE TICKETS are BALANCED on the crest of the
mountain of flowers atop the bed.

Sweeney stands in the door, he smiles, goes back and
PROPS UP the surprise for Diana, the flowers and the
tickets.
                       SWEENEY
                    (to himself)
         Vamos a Canoa! Vamos a surfear.

SUBTITLE: We're going to Canoa! We're going surfing.

                                       JUMP CUT TO:

INT.-ENCUENTRO BAR-LATE NIGHT
_____

Sweeney sits ALONE at the bar. EMPTIES FILL the space
around him on the bar.
He is despondent.

Oskar wipes clean the far corner of the bar, stealing
empathetic looks at Sweeney.

Sweeney raises a finger in Oskar's direction.

As Oskar brings over a 32 oz. bottle of Pilsener.

> SWEENEY
> Ella esta volando a America. Yo sé.
> No entiendes, pero yo lo sé.

SUBTITLE: She's flying to America. I know. I don't understand, but I know it.

> OSKAR
> (sheepishly)
> Lo siento, Sweeney. Pero, pues, no
> sé. Las mujeres. La vida. No sé.
> Pero es un proceso. Ella te dió mucho
> dinero, cerca de mil dólares. No está
> todo mal.

SUBTITLE: I'm sorry, Sweeney. But, well, I don't know. Women. Life. I don't know. But it's a process. She left you a lot of money, over a thousand dollars. It's not all bad.

Sweeney's drunk. He stands, takes out the wad of bills and gives Oskar a HUNDRED DOLLAR BILL. He holds the wad up, points at it, points at the back door. He does this again and again, drunkenly.

> SWEENEY
> (incredulous and in English)
> She just left this and walked out
> the back? She just left this and
> walked out the back?

Oskar tries to hand the money back to Sweeney.

Sweeney gives him a disapproving look and slides it back across the bar to Oskar.

> SWEENEY (CONT'D)
> Estaba comprándole flores y los
> boletos para Canoa. (in English)

And, and, just getting my head on
straight like she useta tell me to
do.

SUBTITLE: I was just buying her flowers and our plane
tickets to Canoa.

Sweeney repeats this to himself, mumbling, drunkenly
as he wanders out the front door with one last wave to
Oskar.

                    SWEENEY (CONT'D)
                (shouting)
        Visítame en Canoa, hombre. Tú
        puedes a surfear mientras yo bebo
        en la playa! Adiós!

SUBTITLE: Visit me in Canoa, man. You can surf while I
drink on the beach! Adios!

                                        CUT TO:

EXT.-TRICICULO-STREETS OF BAHIA DE CARÁQUEZ-EVENING

Pancho and Sweeney sit side by side as they are pedaled
down toward the river, past all the apartments, bars,
stores and hostels of Bahia. It looks like the streets of
Havana, Cuba. Every now and then, someone whistles a bird
call at Pancho, he answers the varying calls precisely.

                    SWEENEY
                (asks, but his heart's not in it)
        What bird was that?

                    PANCHO MONEYMAKER
        You know that was the *hornerito*.

                    SWEENEY
        Like an oven bird? Which neighborhood
        whistles that one? Nevermind. Frost
        has a poem about the ovenbird in
        New England. They whistle "teacher,
        teacher" up there. A mid-woods bird.
        Whatever. We gonna make it to

the water taxis before they shut it
down for the night?

>   PANCHO MONEYMAKER
>   (saddened)
>   We should. I don't have cash for a
>   taxi up the road though. We'll hitch.

>   SWEENEY
>   Nope. I got cash. We'll get a taxi.
>   For some sick reason, I wanna make
>   happy hour at the Mambo Bar.

                                        CUT TO:

EXT.-MAMBO BAR ON THE BEACH-NIGHT
___

Sweeney is morose at best. He cheers somewhat as the
beers go down. And the beers go down fast and furious.

                                        CUT TO:

EXT.-THE BEACH-CANOA-DAWN
___

Pancho drops a pile of driftwood next to a face-down,
shirtless, passed-out Sweeney. He stokes the fire, shakes
his head at the sight of his friend.

>   PANCHO MONEYMAKER
>   (sighing)
>   I gotta go to bed, man. I stopped
>   drinking like seven hours ago.
>   Haven't slept on the beach in a
>   long time. We're lucky a jaguar
>   didn't get us down here. I'm glad
>   you talked me into having a huge
>   fire. You were wasted, but that was
>   a good idea.

Sweeney grunts an assent. Pushes himself up to his knees.

His eyes are shut. His face is ENTIRELY PASTED WITH SAND.

He reaches up and clears the sand from his eyelids.

His eyes flicker open. He leans over, dry heaves.
Pancho stands a bottle of water and a small bottle of
aguardientes in the sand.

> PANCHO MONEYMAKER (CONT'D)
> Get some rest, man. Sleep it off.
> There's waves coming in a few days
> and Flowpi will want to see you as
> soon as she hears you're back. I
> know you don't want to hear this
> right now, but my advice is to NOT
> let Nieve find you until you dry
> the fuck out.

> SWEENEY
> Oh, man, I don't even want to think…

> PANCHO MONEYMAKER
> I know, I know. I'm just giving you
> some sage advice. I know the women
> around here and you will never know
> any more of them if you don't dry the
> fuck out. Get back in the water, figure
> out what you want to do around here
> with me. What projects you want to get
> involved with? Murals, jungle tours,
> surf lessons, whatever. I'll be back in
> a couple days when there's waves. Come
> by the treehouse in Bella Vista if you
> can sneak by Nieve's parents' house
> without them catching sight of you.
> Good luck. Seriously.

Pancho gets up and takes off back toward town. Sweeney
rises. Walks into knee-deep ocean water, falls, tries
weakly to rinse away the night, the past week, the past
six months. The past.

                                        CUT TO:

EXT.-BAHIA DE CARÁQUEZ BANK-DAY

Sweeney walks out of the bank, wobbling a bit. He takes a
pull from a fifth of Caña Manabita. He walks across the
street toward the river. Flowpi sits in the shade at a
seafood stand.

Sweeney buys her some ceviché. He gets himself a small
bottle of beer.

The sounds of cars, buses, tricycle taxis, the water
taxis behind them on the river drown out Flowpi and
Sweeney's conversation.

Sweeney sloppily hands Flowpi HUNDREDS of dollars.

Flowpi takes it, but looks around nervously to see if
anyone is watching them exchange money.

She gets up, Sweeney hails a tricycle taxi for her and
she gets in and heads off.

Sweeney gets up and walks down the pier toward the long,
narrow water taxis. He heads across the river, back
toward Canoa.

                                                    CUT TO:

EXT.-CANOA, MAMBO BAR ON THE BEACH-DAY

Nieve storms down the dirt street by the bar, she goes
past the fence, onto the beach and stops at the bar's
beach gate. She peers into the sparse crowd. She is
intensely searching.

Sweeney is SLUMPED on a barstool, back to Nieve and the
beach.

As Nieve KICKS OPEN the gate TW Walsh's "Young Rebels"
KICKS IN on the bar's soundsystem. Nieve gets everyone's
INSTANT ATTENTION—except Sweeney.

Pancho strolls in behind her and he is holding Flowpi's
hand.

Flowpi looks SHAKEN and ASHAMED, as if the spectacle
might be her fault.

Sweeney is too inebriated to care about the noise behind
him.

Everyone SNATCHES their drinks and DANCES for shelter as
a RAGEFUL Nieve approaches.

Sweeney is PUZZLED to see Leo Gordo ducking into the
kitchen with a hiss of warning for him.

As Nieve SHOVES Sweeney off his stool onto one knee…
we pull back to reveal perfect 6-foot waves breaking in
front of the bar along the rivermouth sandbars as…

Nieve chews Sweeney out in front of everyone, pointing at
him, pointing at the waves, back at him, at the surfboard
rack, at the waves and then repeatedly at Flowpi and
Sweeney. Back and forth at Flowpi and Sweeney.

She is LIVID. We cannot hear her. Finally, she takes
Sweeney's bottle of beer and dumps it all over him.

Sweeney hasn't moved from his spot on one knee in the
sand at the base of the bar stools.

                                          CUT TO:

INT.-PAÍS LIBRE HOTEL POOL-MORNING
_____

Sweeney is out cold in a chaise lounge.
We hear the gate creak open.

Sweeney doesn't move.

In walk Pancho AND Flowpi's two older cousins who stand
meekly behind him with a large BUCKET.

The two boys both strain to lift it above Sweeney.

We've yet to hear these two boys speak other than in
excited jibberish and babbling at Flowpi.

Pancho prods Sweeney with his foot.

Nothing. No movement.

                    PANCHO MONEYMAKER
          Ok, niños, háganlo.

SUBTITLE: Ok, boys, do it.

The boys both hoist a five-gallon bucket of clear liquid
and DOUSE Sweeney with it.

Sweeney LEAPS AND SPINS with his old agility and a speed
that startles the boys and even backs Pancho up a bit.

                    SWEENEY
                 (sputtering)
          What the…it's burning my eyes! What
          did you…for the fuckin' love of god!

The two boys run out of the room, just starting to crack
smiles. Pancho remains, crosses his arms in an attempt to
steel himself to the task at hand.

Sweeney is dripping and livid.

                    PANCHO MONEYMAKER
          It's sugarcane booze. My uncle made it.
          He makes the best in Manabí.

                    SWEENEY
          Why the hell would you…oh, ok, I
          get it. I've been drowning my
          sorrows anyways, right? Fuck you,
          Pancho, now I'm a walking fire
          hazard and you wasted all that
          moonshine…

                    PANCHO MONEYMAKER
                 (angry)
          A waste! A WASTE! Go rinse off in
          the shower and then look in the
          fuckin' mirror. You're lucky I
          didn't let Nieve in here. She'd

kick you in your useless balls, you
drunk fuck. I don't know what to
hope for you anymore. Mierda!
Cara de verga, borracho! TAKE A SHOWER
RIGHT NOW!

SUBTITLE: Shit! Cockfaced drunk!

Pancho is pacing angrily, not even looking at a subdued
Sweeney.

Sweeney looks the part of the worn-thin alcoholic.

Sweeney steps into the tiny bathroom's miniscule shower
stall. He seems to know what's coming and is ready to
take it, albeit under the cover of the drizzling water.

Pancho steps in the bathroom, he's SEETHING.

Sweeney reaches up to adjust the ELECTRIC WATER HEATER
above the nozzle! He gets SHOCKED!

>   SWEENEY
>   Ahh! For fuck's sake!

>   PANCHO MONEYMAKER
>   Serves you right, dickhead! What
>   the hell were you thinking giving
>   Flowpi five hundred dollars in broad
>   daylight in Bahía the other day? She
>   could've been killed and thrown in
>   the river by any one of the desperate
>   fuckers living over there! If anyone
>   had seen you do that…cops, soldiers,
>   bums, thieves, anyone would've robbed
>   that defenseless child!

Sweeney steps out of shower, dripping, towel around his
waist and out into the room.

>   SWEENEY
>   (sobered)
>   I don't really remember…

                    PANCHO MONEYMAKER
          Yah, I know you don't. Do you even
          remember Nieve knocking you off
          your barstool yesterday afternoon?

Sweeney looks wistful for a moment, then gives a weak
shake of his head. He doesn't recall.

                    PANCHO MONEYMAKER (CONT'D)
          Yah, I know you don't. Everyone
          here used to think you were the
          man. Now Flowpi's mother told me
          she can't spend any more time WITH
          ME! WITH ME! You've nearly ruined
          like three lives with one, extended
          bout of feeling sorry for yourself.

Sweeney pulls some surf trunks on under his towel.

                    SWEENEY
               (sheepishly)
          She can't hang out with you? Why
          the…
                    PANCHO MONEYMAKER
               (fuming mad)
          No talking, dickface! Fuck. You
          would think you're Latin or something
          with the way you carry on
          about this addict girlfriend of
          yours. This Diana isn't even your
          girlfriend any more, you're just a
          self-pitying Irish moron. (beat)
          But we'll fix that.

                    SWEENEY
          Where are we go…

Pancho GLARES at Sweeney.

                    SWEENEY (CONT'D)
          Right. I'll shut up.

Pancho grabs a gallon jug of water from Sweeney's shelf and a towel from the railing outside the room. He stomps off.

Sweeney steps into the BRUTAL sunlight.

                                              CUT TO:

EXT.-DIRT STREET IN CANOA-DAY
───

Sweeney follows behind a marching Pancho. They arrive outside a cinderblock shack with a patched tin roof and flaking paint job.

Nieve steps out of the house and stares down Sweeney.

It doesn't take much.

Sweeney is sweating out booze, shirtless in the harsh light. The sun is beating him to a pulp. His hands tremble.

Pancho speaks harshly while pouring half of the water all over Sweeney's head and shoulders. He throws a T-shirt into Sweeney's face.

                    PANCHO MONEYMAKER
               Go in and apologize to Flowpi's
               mother for putting the only child
               she has, actually the only person
               left in her entire family, in
               danger by trying to be a rich,
               drunk gringo fuck. (beat) Don't use
               that language. Figure it out.

                         SWEENEY
               What? I'm not going…

                          NIEVE
                       (to Pancho)
               Vas a recordar esto?

SUBTITLE: Is he going to remember this?

PANCHO MONEYMAKER
Si, si. Hoy es el día

SUBTITLE: Yes, yes. Today is the day.

Nieve turns with a catlike swiftness and SLAPS the
defiance from Sweeney's face.

He holds his face, now turned directly at the dark open
doorway.

There is SILENCE.

A DONKEY clops down the street and past the three frozen
individuals.

SWEENEY
Ok, ok. Ya me voy. Basta ya. Basta
ya.

SUBTITLE: Ok, ok. I'm going already. Enough. Enough.

Without looking back at his two infuriated friends,
Sweeney towels off quickly, pulls a shirt on, tucks his
long hair back behind his ears and enters the shack.

FLOWPI'S MOTHER sits still at a small kitchen table.
There are buckets, tupperware and cups EVERYWHERE for
catching water during rainstorms.

Sweeney approaches slowly, taking a quick glance up at
the HOLES in the tin roof, at the buckets and cups all
over the floors and tables.

There is a small TV, a 30-yr.-old refrigerator, a tiny
sink, some magazines, a ratty couch, a few framed and
cracked photos of Flowpi with her father.

The level of poverty is staggering. But the clear
effort to make a home out of nothing is simultaneously
heartwarming.

Flowpi's Mother is a solid woman, dressed in her kitchen

uniform. She has a hairnet on, she is less than pleased
with the man in her home.

> SWEENEY (CONT'D)
> Señora, discúlpeme. Lo siento. Por
> favor, mi amigo Pancho es un maestro
> único para su niña. Y Flowpi debería
> aprender de él. Y...yo...yo no tengo las
> palabras para explicar mi culpa. Por
> favor, con su permiso, me gustaría
> trabajar aqui en su casa mientras Uds.
> están trabajando en la cocina. En un
> mes, más or menos, podria reparar el
> techo, las paredes y otras cosas. Con
> su permiso.

SUBTITLE: Ma'am, excuse me. I'm sorry. Please, my friend
Pancho is an unparalleled teacher for your daughter. And
Flowpi should learn from him. And...I...I don't have the
words to explain my guilt. Please, with your permission,
I would like to work here at your house while you are
working at the kitchen. In a month, give or take, I could
repair the ceiling, the walls, other things. With your
permission.

Flowpi's Mother says nothing. She SIGHS, stands and
leaves the house to go to work down the road in the
kitchen of the Bambuu Bar.

Sweeney is at a loss. He stands for a moment in the empty
shack. He takes one last look around at the desperate
conditions.

He walks toward the bright doorway.

                                              CUT TO:

EXT.-DIRT STREET IN FRONT OF FLOWPI'S HOME-DAY
_____

Sweeney steps into the light, blinded. He is wilting.

There is no sign of Pancho or Nieve.

Sweeney shuffles and slumps down the dirt road past a
TINY PIGLET chained to a stake in the ground, surrounded
by trash and rancid food scraps.

                                              CUT TO:

EXT.-CANOA TOWN HALL-EARLY MORNING

Sweeney stands with a 10-ft. ladder on his shoulder.
Another man, in a work uniform, stands next to Sweeney.

                    SWEENEY
          No, no, señor no voy a pintar un
          mural con los niños. No hoy.
          Necesito la escalera que reparar mi
          vida. Poco a poco. Hoy yo comenzo.

SUBTITLE: No, no, sir I'm not painting a mural with the
local kids. Not today. I need the ladder to repair my
life. Bit by bit. Today I begin.

The man looks confused but laughs it off.

                    SWEENEY (CONT'D)
          Ya vuelvo a las cinco con la escalera.
          Y las misma manana, si es
          posible.

SUBTITLE: I'll be back with the ladder at 5. And the same
tomorrow, if that's possible.

The man nods, frowns and shrugs Sweeney on his way.

                    SWEENEY (CONT'D)
                 (yelling back over his shoulder)
          Mil gracias, señor! Mil gracias.
          Hasta pronto!

SUBTITLE: A thousand thanks, sir! See you soon!

                                              CUT TO:

A SERIES OF IMAGES:

Sweeney sweating out the brutal, tropical heat on the
rusted tin roof. He is replacing the tin.
Days go by, Sweeney works early in the mornings and
through the evenings and late into the nights.

Whenever Flowpi's Mother approaches…Sweeney takes off as
fast as he can.

Flowpi is nowhere to be seen.

The PIGLET chained to the stake is getting BIGGER.

                                              CUT TO:

INT.-PANCHO'S TREEHOUSE-NEAR DAWN
_____

Sweeney sneaks up on a sleeping Pancho inside a mosquito
net.

Pancho opens his eyes and ROLLS OVER. He's turned his
back to a crouched Sweeney whispering through the
mosquito net.
                         SWEENEY
                      (whispering)
              Pancho, Pancho! I know you can hear
              me. (beat) Anyway, I need you to
              ask Flowpi's Mother if I can work on
              the walls and flooring? You have to ask
              her. I'm afraid I'll go in some morning
              and it'll be her day off and she'll
              scream and I'll jump and she'll
              strangle me.

Nothing. Silence.

                      SWEENEY (CONT'D)
                       (begging)
              C'mon, man. I got a whole new roof
              on her place. She must be warming
              up to the idea of this by now.

                    PANCHO MONEYMAKER
          Flowpi's Mother doesn't take days
          off. She can't afford to. Two shifts
          a day, six days a week. Church and an
          evening shift every Sunday. She makes
          around two thousand dollars per year.

                        SWEENEY
          Per year?

Pancho speaks to the wall. He won't move or look at
Sweeney.

                    PANCHO MONEYMAKER
          Yes, fuckface. That's why giving
          her daughter a quarter of a year's
          pay on a busy street in a sketchy
          city is such a bad idea. Yes, fuckface.
          Her only daughter could've been killed
          and robbed for 500 bucks. It's hard
          to blame the guys around here robbing
          tourists. Thieves have kids, too.
          People are DYING of malaria around
          here. Malaria and starvation are both
          very treatable where you're from.
          Around here, 500 bucks might be the
          medicine that saves some desperate
          father's only son. And in Bella
          Vista, my neighborhood, where I
          live right now, 500 American
          dollars is more like half a year's
          pay. Around here, you are still a
          fuckface and you have a long way to
          go. I can't help you with Flowpi's
          mother. She is just starting to
          allow Flowpi to come visit me again
          and I don't want to mess that up.
          Get outta here, for Flowpi's sake. What
          is it you gringos say? "Fuckin' screw."

Sweeney rises slowly. He's hardly listening as he leaves.
The reality of life in coastal Ecuador has hit him hard.

He leaves Pancho's room.

                    PANCHO MONEYMAKER(CONT'D)
                 (to himself)
            Why is that moron whispering anyway? I
            live alone in a treehouse on a hill on
            the edge of a jungle. Fucking cabron!

                                          CUT TO:

A SERIES OF IMAGES:

Sweeney passes the GROWING PIGLET with ladders, hammers,
bamboo flooring, etc. He stops every time and pours water
or throws food scraps in the piglet's direction.

Sweeney alternately patches walls, replaces the tiny
windows in the shack, installs the bamboo floor…

…and RUNS from the approach of Flowpi's Mother each and
every time.

The neighbors smile, despite themselves, as they watch
Sweeney scamper away every day.

Flowpi's Mother TRUDGES to and from work twice a day
through muddy streets, downpours and the searing heat of
the tropics. Every day.

Sweeney only appears when she has walked a block away.
A few neighborhood kids begin waving to Sweeney each day
as he passes the MUCH LARGER PIGLET chained to the stake
across from Flowpi's house.

The PIGLET FINALLY allows Sweeney to approach it.

He gives it a scratch it between the ears.

                    SWEENEY
                 (quietly)
            Oye, puerco, estas contento con la
            basura debajo del sol, durante la

lluvia? Cada mañana y noche, estás
contento? (beat) Si, si, si, puerquito.
Yo? Yo no estoy contento. Pero estoy
trabajando y es un proceso, verdad?
La satisfacción es un proceso. Hablas
inglés, puerquito? Language is a
process. Nuestra vida juntos en esta
calle de fango…Nuestro vida es una
calle de fango. La calle de fango.
Calle de mud. The long and winding
mud, my friend. The long and winding
suffering of the mud of every moment of
my life.

SUBTITLE: Hey, pig, are you content with this trash
beneath the sun, during the rainstorm? Each morning and
night, are you content? Yes, yes, piglet. Me? I'm not
content. But I'm working and it's a process, right?
Contentedness is a process. You speak English, piglet?
Language is a process. Our life together on this street
of mud…Our life IS a street of mud. Mud Street.

SWEENEY (CONT'D)

NUESTRO vida, puercito, nuestro
vida.

SUBTITLE: OUR life, piglet, our life.

CUT TO:

INT.-FLOWPI'S FAMILY ROOM-EVENING

Sweeney is touching up the bamboo flooring in the corner.
He is on his hands and knees, head jammed into the
corner, back to the front door. He grunts with the effort
of placing the final piece of flooring flush with the
wall.

Flowpi's Mother steps in the house.

Sweeney is startled.

They both take a quick look around the place as Sweeney
stands and gathers his tools quickly, clumsily.

                    SWEENEY
          Ya me voy! Ya me voy. Perdóneme, lo
          siento. Ya me voy. Necesito una hora
          más manana y yo terminaré.
          Pero ya me voy, lo siento.

SUBTITLE: I'm going! I'm already gone. Pardon me, I'm
sorry. I'm already gone. I need one more hour tomorrow
and I'll be finished. But I'm already gone, I'm sorry.

                  FLOWPI'S MOTHER
          Esperate, espera un momentito,
          Sweeney. Siéntate. Siéntate, por
          favor. Un momentito, por favor.

SUBTITLE: Wait, wait a tiny moment, Sweeney. Sit. Sit,
please. One tiny moment, please.

Sweeeny sits, instantly if not awkwardly, at the
kitchen's miniscule table.

Flowpi's Mother steps to the refrigerator. She takes out
a large bottle of Pilsener beer and brings over two SMALL
glasses.
                    SWEENEY
          No, no cerveza por mi, Gracias,
          pero no. Tiene te?

SUBTITLE: No, no beer for me, thank you, but no. Do you
have tea?

Flowpi's Mother pours the beer into the tiny glasses
anyway, ignoring Sweeney's protests.

                  FLOWPI'S MOTHER
          Si, si, si, por qué no? Por qué no?
          Mi casa está linda y SECA!
          (laughter) Seca es mejor que linda pero
          linda está bien también. Vamos
          a beber cerveza juntos porque mi
          casa, las casa de Flowpi es una
          casa en realidad ahora. Antes de tu

y su trabajo nosotros vivíamos en
una choza. Y mañana no vas a trabajar
aqui. Tu vas a pintar un mural con
Pancho y Flowpi en Bella Vista. (in
broken English) Pancho y Bella Vista
needs you. Y my…como se dice?…my
daughter needs you. Manana, manana.
Entoces, salud! Paz, amor y vida,
verdad? Paz, amor y vida are a process.
Poco a poco, como Pancho le gusta
a decir.

SUBTITLE: Yes, yes, yes, why not? Why not? My house
is beautiful and DRY! Dry is better than beautiful,
but beautiful is good too. We are going to drink beer
together because my house, Flowpi's house is a real house
now. Before you and your work we lived in a shack. And
tomorrow you aren't going to work here. You are painting
a mural with Pancho and Flowpi in Bella Vista. Pancho
and Bella Vista need you. And my…how do you say it?…my
daughter needs you. Tomorrow, tomorrow. So, cheers! Peace
love and life, right? Peace, love and life are a process.
Little by little, as Pancho likes to say.

Sweeney is humbled. He takes the small glass of beer and
CLINKS glasses with Flowpi's Mother. He is redeemed and
a huge smile spreads across his face as the VERY LARGE
MUDDY PIG comes trotting into the shack, its broken CHAIN
dragging behind it.

Both Sweeney and Flowpi's Mother are startled.

The pig looks them both over, turns and departs--its feet
clicking across the brand new bamboo floor.

Both Sweeney and Flowpi's Mother begin laughing
hysterically.

                                              CUT TO:

EXT.-A FENCE IN BELLA VISTA-EARLY MORNING.

Sweeney, Pancho and Flowpi are a bit sleepy. They yawn,

stretch, look down on the rivermouth at the small waves
coming in at the southern beach. At their feet are piles
of paintbrushes and cans of paint of all colors.

Bahia de Caraquéz twinkles in the early morning light.

> PANCHO MONEYMAKER
> La pared está allá, al fin de la
> calle. (pointing down the hill at
> the edge of Bahia) Y hay otras
> personas que vas a pintar con
> nosotros.

SUBTITLE: The wall is there, at the end of the street.
And there are some other people who will paint with us.

> SWEENEY
> (excited to get started)
> Ok, vamos! Tenemos mucho trabajo
> hoy, no? Quién va a pintar con
> nosotros, Pancho?

SUBTITLE: Ok, let's go! We have a lot of work today, no?
Who is going to paint with us, Pancho?

Sweeney and Pancho pick up the cans of paint. Flowpi puts
a HUGE bundle of brushes on her back, they are bristling
in every direction out of a makeshift backpack like a
bushel of Timothy flowers.

> PANCHO MONEYMAKER
> Well, at around nine one of the
> classes from the closest school is
> coming out. That's like thirty kids
> and two teachers. Leo Gordo is
> supposed to come down from Canoa.
> He's from Bella Vista originally,
> umm...are you even listening?

Pancho whistles the call of the sparrowhawk (kil-eee,
kil-eee) and starts to follow Sweeney down the dusty
road.

Flowpi hangs back for a beat, then she answers the call with her own whistle.

Sweeney and Pancho STOP and turn back to look at her. She is radiant through her shyness, grinning from ear to ear.

                                              CUT TO:

EXT.-MURAL WALL, OCEANSIDE STREET-BAHIA DE CARáQUEZ-MORNING

Tower of Power's "Back on the Streets" accompanies a series of images:

Sweeney and Pancho and Flowpi all slap whitewash on an eight foot-high retaining wall across the street from the ocean, just south of the mouth of the Rio Chone.

They rest in the shade of the wall. It is completely whitewashed, a blank canvas.

Pancho looks at his watch, it reads: 9:15.

He looks up to see a flood of children rush down the stairs at the start of the wall. They scream and laugh and grab at all the brushes.

Flowpi appears to be overwhelmed…until Sweeney reassures her, gives her a hug.

Sweeney then dives into the mass of kids and gets them all painting a carpet of leaves along the bottom of the wall.

They slap reds, greens, yellows into all the bold black lines Sweeney, Pancho and Flowpi have readied for them. It's paint by number.

There are the black outlines of four Ceiba tree trunks separating the wall into THREE white sections above the carpet of leaves.

Leo Gordo appears, we see him add in the green leafy canopies of each Ceiba tree.

He lifts Flowpi up to get the higher spots filled with green.

Sweeney and Pancho are filling in the trunks of the Ceibas with their distinct shifting grey-green hue.

Pancho squints up at the sun, almost at its midday zenith.

Leo Gordo heads off up the road toward work, laughing about the amount of green paint covering his jeans. His white shirt is SPOTLESS.

Flowpi RUNS up and SLAPS HIS BELLY, leaving two perfect, green HANDPRINTS on his imposing midsection.

Sweeney and Pancho exchange a look, smiling at Flowpi's interaction with Leo Gordo.

                                              CUT TO:

INT.-PANCHO'S TREEHOUSE KITCHEN/DINING ROOM-NOON
_____

Sweeney and Pancho sit at the table, dripping with sweat. They drink water as Flowpi slips off her chair and goes to the railing of the house overlooking Bella Vista.

She gives the call of the sparrow hawk, looks back at Sweeney and smiles mischievously.
Sweeney is curious, but silent.

Pancho rises from his chair.

                    PANCHO MONEYMAKER
              Hace calor, amigo, no? Y es la hora
              de la siesta. No más trabajo hasta
              dos o dos y media más o menos. Flowpi,
              estas cansado?

SUBTITLE: It's hot, man, huh? And it's time for a siesta. Let's take a break for two, two and a half hours or so. Flowpi, are you tired?

                          FLOWPI
                   (giggling uncontrollably)
          Claaaaaaahhhhroooooo, Pancho. Si, si,
          si. Me voy a la casita.

SUBTITLE: Clearly, Pancho. Yes, yes, yes. I'm going to
the little house to sleep.

                          SWEENEY
                        (hesitantly)
          Ok, then, I guess I'll take that
          hammock over there where there's a
          breeze. It's so damn hot I don't…
          The two ignore him, knowingly smiling
          at each other as they disappear around
          the corner.

The wooden steps beneath their descent CREAK LOUDLY.

For a beat, we hear the sounds of the nearby jungle—a few
birds, some capuchin monkeys, then a DONKEY BRAYS.

Silence.

The steps CREAK AGAIN.

Sweeney is curious, but too exhausted to move.

Nieve walks around the corner.

Sweeney is stunned.

She gives Sweeney a come-hither nod. She wants him to
follow her.

Sweeney JUMPS from his chair.

                      SWEENEY (CONT'D)
                  (whispering to himself)
          I never liked naps anyway.

                                             CUT TO:

EXT.-PANCHO'S TREEHOUSE-THE PATHWAY DOWN THE HILL-SAME

Sweeney walks down the creaking steps. He looks for
Nieve.

She slips behind the massive, smooth trunk of a Ceiba
Tree.

Sweeney catches a glimpse of her before she disappears.

He walks down the path, around the trunk.

Nieve holds a BUCKET OF ICE WATER.

Sweeney stops puts his hands up in a gesture of
submission.

                    NIEVE
          No tenemos nieve aqui en Ecuador,
          pero tenemos hielo. Mucho hielo.

SUBTITLE: We don't have snow here in Ecuador, but we have
ice. A lot of ice.

Nieve DRENCHES Sweeney with the bucket of ice water.

Sweeney screams like a child. He is shocked and dripping
wet.

There are hundreds of ice cubes surrounding him on the
ground.
                    SWEENEY
                  (muttering)
          Woo, that is fucking freezing.
          Wicked...fucking...cold.

                    NIEVE
          Tsk, tsk, tsk, Sweeney. Such dirty
          language. You shouldn't speak like
          this in front of a woman.

                    SWEENEY
          When did you learn English? Nice
          work. You know, I never thought I would

need a wetsuit on the equator. It's
like duck-diving a wave in January up
in Seawell. Jesus Christ that's cold!

LIGHTNING QUICK, Sweeney snatches several ice cubes off
the grass and LEAPS at Nieve.

He manages to get one or two cubes down Nieve's shirt.

She laughs and screeches delicately at the touch of
the cubes, and with surprise at the sudden nearness of
Sweeney.

Nieve gives him a quick, inviting kiss on the lips.

> NIEVE
> (suddenly whispering)
> Besito? Por qué no? Es un proceso,
> no?

SUBTITLE: A little kiss? Why not? It's a process, no?

Sweeney is immobilized for a moment, listening to her
sultry whisper.

Leaning in for kiss, Nieve SHOVES ICE DOWN HIS SHIRT.

They tumble and laugh a bit more, ending with the long
kiss BOTH have been waiting for.

CUT TO:

EXT.-THE MURAL WALL-AFTERNOON

Sweeney and Nieve stand together staring at the
unfinished mural.

> SWEENEY
> What do you think? Tomorrow we're
> going to paint two or three animals
> from the jungle between the trees.
> Maybe some monkeys, a jaguar, some
> bats, maybe toucans or harpie eagles or
> something?

Pancho and Flowpi approach, kicking up dust on the road
out of Bella Vista.

                    NIEVE
          Well, I like that idea. It's simple
          and beautiful, but don't forget
          about the protest tomorrow.

                    SWEENEY
          That's tomorrow? I thought it was
          next week.

                    NIEVE
          Tomorrow. Tomorrow we are protesting
          for trash collection
          trucks to come out every week from
          Bahia. This way we can clean up
          Bella Vista and stop burning trash
          in the ditch. And then next week we
          are going to protest for electricity
          and street lights.
          There are a series of protests
          planned. Didn't Pancho tell you?

                    SWEENEY
          Yeah, but I've been kinda, um, busy
          so I sort of forgot what was going
          on down here. Did the American couple
          that owns the land out here
          agree to sign it over to Bella
          Vista yet?

Pancho and Flowpi arrive.

                    PANCHO MONEYMAKER
          No, not yet. But they will, I
          think. They have hired some of the
          police to "watch over" the protests.
          I heard this today from the mayor of
          Bella Vista. But we have to start

somewhere. Tell me, Sweeney, what do
you think of Nieve's English? Not bad,
huh?

Sweeney looks at Nieve with unadulterated admiration.
He tears his eyes away from her for a moment to answer
Pancho.

                    SWEENEY
          Claaaaaaahhhhhroooo, Pancho. Claro
          que si.

SUBTITLE: Clearly, Pancho. Of course.

They all laugh a little as Flowpi starts shoving brushes
into their hands, impatiently. For a kid, she's about as
all business as you can be.

                    FLOWPI
          La pared, el mural, por favor.
          Blah, blah, blah, Uds. estan peor
          de mis (making quotes in the air)
          amigos imaginarios.

SUBTITLE: The wall, the mural, please. Blah, blah, blah,
you guys are worse than my "imaginary friends."

For a moment, the self-deprecating humor takes the adults
by surprise but then they all crack up laughing.

Flowpi breaks into a huge smile as Nieve leans down to
give her a huge hug.

As they begin painting, Sweeney lets Pancho in on his
strategy.

                    SWEENEY
          I was thinking, Pancho. The hired
          police only have this one way into
          Bella Vista so why don't we paint
          a message that'll stick in their heads.
          Let's add some lettering here, let's
          send a message.

CUT TO:

EXT.-THE MURAL WALL-THE NEXT MORNING

Some PHOTOGRAPHERS from "El Diario" take photo after
photo of the wall. We can't quite see what the finished
image is yet. But there are heart-stoppingly beautiful,
detailed paintings of JUNGLE ANIMALS in some sort of
intricate pattern between the painted tree trunks, above
the schoolchildren's carpet of leaves and below Leo
Gordo's green canopies.

CUT TO:

EXT.-THE MURAL WALL-LATER THAT MORNING

Three truckloads of SOLDIERS in full riot gear drive past
the MURAL. The trucks all have to SLOW DOWN as the cement
ends. The trucks bump and roll onto the washboard dirt
road up to Bella Vista.

The soldiers mutter to each other. Many are clearly
IMPRESSED.

Dozens point, staring at the MASSIVE, GORGEOUS MULTI-
COLORED MURAL.

The dust behind their trucks begins to settle and THROUGH
IT we see the 100-YARD-LONG, EIGHT-FOOT-HIGH MURAL.

The largest most elaborate block letters read:
     "PAZ AMOR Y VIDA!"

Subtitle: "Peace, Love and Life!"

The next largest, less elaborate cursive letters read:
     "Bienvenido a Bella Vista!"

Subtitle: "Welcome to Bella Vista!"

And the smallest cursive letters read: "Tenemos nada,
pero nuestro nada es su nada tambien."

Subtitle: "We have nothing but our nothing is your
nothing too."

The HUGE block letters forming "Paz" "Amor" and "Vida" are filled and overflowing with a litter of JUNGLE ANIMALS in intricate patters and colors.

The animals' faces are serene, sublime.

It is instantly evident the work has been completed by an artistic GENIUS.

                                                    CUT TO:

EXT.-THE MURAL WALL-SAME

As the last motes of sun-bitten dust float down we FOLLOW THEM to the bottom right of the mural where, in small cursive letters it reads:
        "Las Letras y Animales por Flowpi, edad: 9, desde Bella Vista"

Subtitle: Letters and Animals by Flowpi, age 9, from Bella Vista

The scope and achievement of the mural is MIND-BOGGLING and OTHERWORLDLY in its beauty.

                                                    CUT TO:

EXT.-BASKETBALL COURT-CENTER OF BELLA VISTA-DAY

There is a small podium and microphone. The reporters are gathered nearby as all the WOMEN of Bella Vista make up the crowd of protesters.

The basketball court doubles as a soccer field. It is OVERFLOWING WITH WOMEN and their CHILDREN. The soccer goals on each end underneath the warped hoops are full as well.

Pancho stands, in a suit, with the Mayor of Bahía de Caraquéz behind the podium.

Sweeney and Nieve and Flowpi observe from the side of the crowd of local women. They occupy the shade of a scraggly tree.

Flowpi looks NERVOUS.

A few women question Nieve. They don't believe Flowpi
actually painted the mural. They speak AS IF FLOWPI ISN'T
THERE OR CAN'T UNDERSTAND.

                    NIEVE
               (annoyed, clipped tone)
          Si. Si. Una otra vez. Flowpi
          pintó las letras y las animales. Es
          su mensaje, es su mural. Nosotros
          solamente ayudamos.

SUBTITLE: Yes, yes. One more time: Flowpi painted the
letters and the animals. It's her message. It's her
mural. We only helped.

Flowpi is ignoring the attention, both good and bad.

Her eyes move to Pancho and the Mayor.

THEIR EYES follow the SOLDIERS as they climb down from
their trucks behind the crowd on the road.

The soldiers look around nervously at ONLY WOMEN AND
CHILDREN ON THE SOCCER COURT.

                                        CUT TO:

EXT.-BELLA VISTA-SAME
_____

A quick series of shots show that there are little
gatherings of the men of Bella Vista but they are trying
to keep away from the protest.

They peek out from houses and down from porches.

They play cards, drink sugarcane booze.

A few work on a run-down pickup truck.

Several ROLL THEIR EYES at the women, a couple give
dismissive waves.

It is clear that the protest and the effort to take back

the hills of Bella Vista from the American landowners
will be up to the WOMEN of Bella Vista.

CUT TO:

EXT.-BASKETBALL COURT-CENTER OF BELLA VISTA-SAME

Pancho steps to the microphone. He is NERVOUS.

He looks over at Sweeney and Flowpi.

Flowpi is beginning to behave ERRATICALLY. She starts
talking loudly with no one in particular.

Sweeney is eyeing the soldiers who, for their part, look
uninterested in the proceedings.

Except for one ANGRY SOLDIER who is gripping his PISTOL
in his holster tightly.

The veins on his forearms are straining with the grip.
His neck muscles are bulging as he works his jaw.

There is some inexplicable hatred behind his GLARING at
an oblivious Pancho.

Sweeney is far from oblivious, studying, memorizing the
soldier's boyish, angry face.

CUT TO:

EXT.-BASKETBALL COURT-CENTER OF BELLA VISTA-SAME

Pancho signals to Nieve and she LEAVES Flowpi's side and
begins handing out ice cold Coca-Colas from a cooler.

The soldiers are generally happy with the gesture.

The one ANGRY SOLDIER declines a Coke from Nieve.

He doesn't take his eyes from Pancho, who begins
speaking.

CUT TO:

EXT.-BASKETBALL COURT-CENTER OF BELLA VISTA-SAME

We hear Pancho's soothing, positive voice. As he starts
his speech, we see a series of images.

> PANCHO MONEYMAKER (V.O.)
> Bienvenido el Alcalde de Bahía de
> Caráquez. Bienvenido a su pueblo en
> el bosque, en la frontera de su
> ciudad, bienvenido a Bella Vista. Y
> la policia del estado, bienvenido a
> su pueblo. Vamos a tener siete eventos
> de protesta en el próximo mes y medio.
> Uds. van a vistarnos cada fin de
> semana. Somos pescadores, artistas,
> granjeros en las granjas locales, y
> como Uds. Somos padres y madres con
> niños como sus niños. Somos pobres,
> estamos cansados y queremos, como Uds.,
> electricidad, agua limpia, calles sin
> basura. Pero no tenemos pistolas o
> dinero para los politicos—perdóneme,
> Alcalde—pero queremos ser felices,
> como Uds. Entonces, bienvenido a Bella
> Vista, durante nuestros eventos de
> protesta donde nosotros vamos a obtener
> nuestros derechos sin violencia, sin
> pistolas, pero con la fuerza de nuestro
> amor por esta vida y nuestra casa aquí
> en Ecuador. Este es un evento de paz y
> amor, un evento de protesta por gente
> pobre pero fuerte.

SUBTITLE: Welcome, Mayor. Welcome to our town in the
jungle, on the border of your city, welcome to Bella
Vista. And to the state's police, welcome to our town.
We are going to have seven protests in the next month
and a half. We are fishermen, artists, cowboys who work
the local cattle farms, and like you we are fathers and
mothers with children like your children. We are poor,
we are tired and we want, like you, electricity, clean
water and streets free of trash. But we don't have guns

or money for the politicians—no offense, Mayor—but we
want to be happy, like all of you. So, welcome to Bella
Vista, during our protests when we will obtain our rights
without violence, without guns, but with the strength of
our love for this life and our home here in Ecuador. This
is an event of peace and love, an event of protest by
poor but strong people.

Flowpi is now GESTURING wildly and beginning to YELL at
her imaginary friends.

A couple of local WOMEN glance her way, but go back to
chattering nervously and quietly with the soldiers.

Both the women and the soldiers are listening to Pancho.

Sweeney is neither listening to Pancho nor noticing that
Flowpi is in the early throes of a Schizo-affective
episode. Still, he watches the one ANGRY SOLDIER.

Nieve is too busy handing out Cokes and easing the
remaining tension amidst the crowd of sweating soldiers.

                                              CUT TO:

EXT.-BASKETBALL COURT-CENTER OF BELLA VISTA-SAME

Sweeney finally takes his eyes off the one ANGRY SOLDIER
as Flowpi's voice rises to a screech and she begins to
TEAR at her own hair.

Sweeney DROPS to a crouch next to Flowpi to whisper to
her calmly just as Nieve arrives to SWEEP Flowpi up into
her arms.

Sweeney GRABS a Coke from the hand of a THIRSTY SOLDIER
who has just opened it and is about to take a sip.

                      SWEENEY
                (pointing up at Flowpi)
            Sorry, uh, Perdoneme, amigo. La niña
            esta enferma. Un momentito, hombre.

SUBTITLE: Sorry, uh, excuse me, friend. The child is sick. One moment, man.

The THIRSTY SOLDIER is stunned, for a moment he seems to understand, but then looks around at his fellow soldiers starting to smile and laugh at him.

Sweeney hands the Coke to Nieve, who heads off toward the rickety steps of a shanty where an older woman is waving.

Sweeney turns back to the smaller THIRSTY SOLDIER who is growing angry in his slight embarrassment.

                    SWEENEY (CONT'D)
                    (apologetically)
            Lo siento, amigo. Un momentito. Ya
            vuelvo, ya vuelvo.

SUBTITLE: I'm sorry, friend. One moment. I'll be right back, right back.

Sweeney moves quickly, smoothly, between the soldiers toward Nieve's abandoned cooler. He looks over his shoulder as…

The two women take Flowpi into the cool interior shade of the nearby bamboo shanty on stilts, trying to soothe her.

Sweeney grabs THREE COKES out of the ice.

He slips back through the crowd of fatigued soldiers and back to the THIRSTY SOLDIER.

The ANGRY SOLDIER has now joined the THIRSTY SOLDIER, they whisper conspiratorially.

                    SWEENEY (CONT'D)
            Ok, lo siento amigo. Aqui, dos para
            ti, uno para mi.

SUBTITLE: Ok, I'm sorry friend. Here, two for you, one for me.

The THIRSTY SOLDIER is instantly appeased.

                    THIRSTY SOLDIER
            Gracias, ok. Gracias, hombre. No
            hay problema.

SUBTITLE: Thank you, ok. Thanks, man. No problem.

Sweeney's gaze now shifts to the ANGRY SOLDIER still
flexing his jaw and SEETHING with a barely subdued rage.

He is trying to stare Sweeney down.

Sweeney has seen this all before. He remains unfazed.
Sweeney looks back at the THIRSTY SOLDIER.

                    SWEENEY
                (smiling, rapidfire)
            Hombre, tenemos sed, verdad? Pero
            solamente uno o dos estamos
            enojado, si? Hace calor? Como en
            un horno. No puedo estar enojado
            debajo del sol. Quién esta mas anojado?
            Su amigo aqui o este sol increíble?
            Es como un instrumento de tortura.
            Soy un gringo blanco, un honky. Sabes
            esta palabra "honky"? Si? Ok, entoces
            yo odio este sol mas de un soldado de
            estado. Paz, amor, y vida como decian
            aqui en Bella Vista donde no hay
            dinero. Pero en America, donde tenemos
            dinero, estamos como monos con dinero
            que sale de cada agujero, decimos "paz,
            amor, Coca-Cola y mas amor por favor."
            Cuanto cuesta por el amor, mas amor,
            verdad?

SUBTITLE: Man, we're all thirsty, right? But only one
of us is angry, yes? It's hot. Like an oven. I can't be
angry beneath this sun. Who is more angry? Your friend
here or this incredible sun? It's like an instrument
of torture. I'm a white gringo, a honky. You know this
word, "honky"? Yes? Ok, so I hate this sun more than

any soldier of the state. Peace, love and life as they say here in Bella Vista where there's no money. But in America, where we have money—we're like monkeys with money sticking out of every hole—we say "peace, love, Coca-Cola and more love, please." How much does it cost for love, more love, right?

The THIRSTY SOLDIER laughs hard at the crazy gringo. He shakes his head and looks over at the ANGRY SOLDIER who still seethes.

It's as if he hasn't heard a word of Sweeney's attempt to relieve the tension via bullshit.

Sweeney and the THIRSTY SOLDIER exchange a knowing look. They both raise their eyebrows, shrug a little bit.

> SWEENEY (CONT'D)
> (changing the subject)
> Oooohkaaaay, entonces, es un proceso.

Sweeney offers the ANGRY SOLDIER his unopened Coke. Sweeney, of course, is silently rebuffed and gives it up.

He turns, pats the THIRSTY SOLDIER on the shoulder, and walks toward the shanty.

In that moment, Nieve steps into the door frame, she waves frantically in Sweeney's direction and then in Pancho's.

They both RUN over.

> CUT TO:

INT.-BAMBOO SHANTY-SAME

Sweeney, Pancho and Nieve sit around the bed in which Flowpi is now peacefully resting.

> NIEVE
> She was having a conversation with
> her imaginary friends. She kept
> yelling at them. Something like, "I

know that soldier is mad, but I'm
too little to help. I know he's
mad."

                    PANCHO MONEYMAKER
Well, she seems fine now. We should
keep her away from the protests
from now on, I think. Who was she
even talking about.

                    SWEENEY
          (shaken)
I know who she was talking about. I
have no idea how she zeroed in on
this one guy, but he is an angry
bastard. It was like 'roid rage
with this one soldier. He wanted to
kill someone. I had my eyes on him the
whole time. What, were there
like 75 soldiers there or something?

                    NIEVE
I gave out around fifty cokes.

                    SWEENEY
Maybe she picked up on me staring
at the guy. Out of sixty or so
soldiers, I guess she could've
picked him out. But I never saw her
staring at him or even looking his
way.

                    PANCHO MONEYMAKER
Well, like I said, at least she's
ok now.

                    SWEENEY
          (sadly)
She might've picked up on how angry
I am. I wanted to break the guy's

jaw for being so angry.

                    NIEVE
              (soothingly)
     You should just try to forget it,
     Sweeney. Don't be so angry either.
     That soldier is just doing his job.

                    SWEENEY
     Yeah, but he's itching to use that
     gun.

                    PANCHO MONEYMAKER
     Sweeney, that soldier is just a
     young, poor kid from some town near
     here just like Bella Vista. You
     have to forget about him and just
     help us keep these protests peaceful.
     It's the most important
     thing for Bella Vista, for Flowpi,
     since this is her neighborhood.
     Comprendes, amigo?

                    SWEENEY
              (smiling, relieved)
     Ok, I got it. What'll we do with
     Flowpi next weekend, though. She
     spends every day with us.

                    NIEVE
     I'll just take her up to Canoa and
     we'll go surfing or I'll get her
     some lunch and ice cream and get
     her mind off things down here. Her
     mother will be glad for that.

                                   CUT TO:

EXT.-BASKETBALL COURT-CENTER OF BELLA VISTA-DAY

_A SERIES OF IMAGES: contrasting the protest with the
laidback surf vibe of Canoa just up the road:_

Nieve and Flowpi on the beach in Canoa.

Pancho leading all the WOMEN of Bella Vista in an orderly protest march around Bella Vista.

The ANGRY SOLDIER remains vigilant and menacing amongst an otherwise uninterested group of soldiers.

Nieve and Flowpi eating ice cream and talking and laughing in the hammocks of the Mambo Bar in Canoa. The WOMEN of Bella Vista hold up homemade SIGNS in Spanish protesting the lack of clean water. They sing and demand their rights, the rights their children deserve.

There is a scuffle between a few baby-faced soldiers and some of the WOMEN of Bella Vista which PANCHO and SWEENEY squash peacefully.

                                    CUT TO:

EXT.-BASKETBALL COURT-CENTER OF BELLA VISTA-EVENING

Sweeney and Pancho jump out of a taxi and stop the departing trucks, filled with sweating, tired soldiers.

                    PANCHO MONEYMAKER
          Amigos, momentito, momentito, por
          favor.

                    TRUCK DRIVER
                  (furious)
          Muévete, ahhh! Muévete! Tenemos que
          ir. Tú y su mujeres con sus derechos
          y mierda. Estamos cansados. Mueve al
          taxi, ahorita!

SUBTITLE: Move it! Ahh! Move! We have to go. You and your women with your "rights" and shit. We're tired. Move the taxi, right now!

Pancho and Sweeney open the taxi trunk and take out several CASES OF PILSENER BOTTLES.

> TRUCK DRIVER (CONT'D)
> Ok, posiblemente podemos esperar un
> momentito.

SUBTITLE: Ok, we can wait a moment, possibly.

Every single soldier is smiling as they accept the 32 oz.
bottles of beer from Pancho and Sweeney.

All but ONE. The ANGRY SOLDIER refuses, scowling.

> CUT TO:

A SERIES OF CONTRASTING IMAGES CONTINUES:

Flowpi surfs a four-foot wave flawlessly on Sweeney's
fish with the sparrow hawk painting.

Nieve watches, wading in the shallows. She praises
Flowpi's ride with the shrill call of the sparrow hawk,
"Kill-eee, Kill-ee!"

The WOMEN OF Bella Vista hold signs, march in solidarity.

They call and respond with various demands about their
fundamental right to electricity like the neighboring
city of Bahia.

They, too, end the protest songs and shouts about their
equal rights to trash collection with the shrill call of
the Bella Vista's sparrow hawk, "Kill-eee, Kill-eee!"

> CUT TO:

EXT.-BASKETBALL COURT-CENTER OF BELLA VISTA-MID-MORNING

Title: The Seventh & Final Protest

We see dozens of protest signs standing up against a
courtside bamboo shack.

They read: "Give Us Our land", "American Landlords Not
Welcome," "We Were Here First," etc.

The WOMEN of Bella Vista are looking out of doors and windows. Only A FEW are on the court, by the podium, waiting to start.

The MEN of Bella Vista are staying out of sight, some drinking Caña Manabita and Pilsener beers despite the early hour.

CUT TO:

EXT.-THE PATH DOWN FROM PANCHO'S TREEHOUSE-SAME

Pancho, Sweeney and Nieve walk down from the treehouse, kicking up the white dust behind them.

Pancho carries more signs. Sweeney has paint cans and brushes in his arms.

> NIEVE
> (worriedly)
> Flowpi wasn't at her house this
> morning. Last night she told me she
> would be ready at seven to go for a
> surf with me. It's strange. Her
> mother was already at work so I
> couldn't talk to her.

> PANCHO MONEYMAKER
> (distracted)
> I don't know. She probably…I don't
> know. But we have to at least get
> this protest started in a half
> hour. Then we can go look for her.

Sweeney is silent, worried.

CUT TO:

EXT.-BASKETBALL COURT-CENTER OF BELLA VISTA-TEN MINUTES LATER

Pancho, Sweeney and Nieve walk onto the court. They drop their signs and supplies. They turn to say hello to the few WOMEN on the court.

Pancho is ebullient and charming, at the same time encouraging and determined to help these women see their protest through to save and improve their neighborhood shantytown.

> PANCHO MONEYMAKER
> (loudly)
> Poco a poco, no? Hoy es importante
> para el futuro de Bella Vista. Gracias
> por su apoyo y determinación,
> mujeres. Gracias. Los niños de
> Bella Vista van a…

SUBTITLE: Bit by bit, no? Today is important for the future of Bella Vista. Thank you for your support and determination, ladies. Thank you. The children of Bella Vista are going to…

                                              SMASH CUT TO:

EXT.-DIRT STREET BELOW THE COURT-SAME

Two MEN, both stumbling drunk, roll out of a shack. They are wrestling and trying to punch each other. Neither is very capable of landing a punch, neither has the upper hand.

Pancho SPRINTS to break up the fight.

Sweeney STAYS PUT on the edge of the court above the drunken scene.

He looks in the distance, down the road, where the 3 trucks full of SOLDIERS bumps off the pavement and onto the approach into Bella Vista.

> SWEENEY
> (whistling)
> Kill-eeee! Kill-eeee!

Pancho has just been bowled over into the dust by the two drunk men. He looks up at Sweeney, spitting dust.

SWEENEY (CONT'D)
(shouting)
Los soldados están aquí! Necesitas
de mi ayuda?

SUBTITLE: The soldiers are here! Do you need my help?

Pancho signals for Sweeney to come down.

Sweeney SPRINTS and immediately TAKES OUT both men with
some polished wrestling moves. He DOES NOT HURT them.

The men hardly know what's going on before Sweeney stuffs
one in a shack on one side of the road. He shuts the
door.

He GRABS the other drunk and CARRIES him into a shack
across the street. He shuts that door.

Pancho is talking to two different men, dusting himself
off.

He is repeatedly pointing at the two shacks across from
one another.

PANCHO MONEYMAKER
Por favor, necesitamos un día sin
pelear! Yo sé que los dos hombres
tienen un problema con la esposa
de un tercer hombre pero no hoy.
Por favor, no hoy. Pueden mirar
las puertas de las casas por una
hora? Voy a volver con comida y
cerveza para los dos en una hora mas
o menos, ok? Y cerveza para todos Uds.,
ok? Gracias, mil gracias.

SUBTITLE: Please, we need a day without fighting! I know
that those two men have a problem with the wife of a
third man but not today. Please, not today. Can you two
watch the doors of these houses for an hour? I'll be back
with some food and beer for these two men in an hour
or so, ok? And beer for all of you, ok? Thank you, a

thousand thank-yous.

As Pancho finishes talking the two men into guarding the
doors, the police trucks pull up and STOP.

Pancho turns and returns to his charming, ebullient self,
brushing the dust and dirt off his clothes.

> PANCHO MONEYMAKER(CONT'D)
> Hola! Bienvenido a Bella Vista y al
> día final de nuestros eventos de
> protesta! Hoy las mujeres van a
> cantar y gritar sobre sus jefes,
> los Americanos que compraron muchos
> hectáreas de este bosque y la costa.
> Y nosotros entendemos que han
> pagado por su presencia aqui hoy.
> No tenemos dinero, pero hemos
> preparado una comida grande con mucha
> cerveza y vino para todos de
> los soldados. Las mujeres están
> cocinando para nosotros ahora en
> sus casas. Entonces, bienvenido al
> evento de protesta. Disfruten las
> canciones de protesta y después
> vamos a comer y beber por el futuro…

SUBTITLE: Hello! Welcome to Bella Vista and the final day
of protests! Today the women are going to sing and shout
about your bosses, the American landlords that bought all
these hectares of jungle and coastline. And we understand
that they have paid for your presence here today. We
don't have any money, but we are able to give you a huge
meal with lots of beer and wine for all of the soldiers.
The women are cooking for us now in their houses. So,
welcome to the protest. Enjoy the songs of protest and
afterwards we are going to eat and drink to the future…

SMASH CUT TO:

EXT.-SHACK ON ONE SIDE OF THE SOLDIERS-SAME

The door of the shack OPENS WITH A SLAM and out stumbles one of the drunk men from before.

He is oblivious to the presence of the soldiers.

He is armed with a RUSTY MACHETE.

He stumbles out into the blinding sunlight, right into the fender of the first truck full of soldiers.

Everyone laughs. Everyone but Pancho and Sweeney.

They exchange worried looks.

The TRUCK DRIVER throws his idling truck in reverse and moves it out of the way of the drunk man.

The drunk man stumbles, impossibly, to the front door of the shack across the road wherein lies the other drunk, his mortal enemy.

He begins weakly HACKING at the wooden door on the shack.

He slurs curses and challenges, all incoherent to the amused soldiers.

As Pancho walks over toward the man to subdue him, the ANGRY SOLDIER jumps down from behind the truck and STOPS Pancho from intervening with an open hand on Pancho's chest.

Sweeney begins to move toward him.

The ANGRY SOLDIER takes out his pistol and WEAKLY waves it in Sweeney's direction.

Sweeney stops in his tracks, throws his hands up as...

                                        SMASH CUT TO:

EXT.-SHACK ON THE OTHER SIDE OF THE ROAD-SAME

The MACHETE DRUNK leans back for a two-handed chop.

Instead, the door of the shack BURSTS open and knocks him

onto his back in the dust.

The other drunken man staggers into the light.

He is holding a RUSTY OLD REVOLVER.

Groans of surprise and more laughter rise from the ranks
of the soldiers. Most still peer from the back of the 3
trucks down at the drunken, embroiled nonsense unfolding
before them.

> PANCHO MONEYMAKER
> Sweeney! There aren't any guns for
> miles around here. These fucking
> idiot soldiers have all the guns.
> How did you manage to shove this
> drunk bastard into the only shack
> with a gun? How did he find it? He
> can hardly walk!

Sweeney shrugs sheepishly, backs off a few steps.

Only the ANGRY SOLDIER seems completely content to let
the drunken gentlemen fight.

He gives Pancho a SHOVE back toward Sweeney and turns his
attention toward the two drunks, now squaring off and
stumbling AWAY up the road.

                                              CUT TO:

EXT.-BASKETBALL COURT-CENTER OF BELLA VISTA-SAME

A few more WOMEN have gathered on the court. They number
around a dozen or so and they are all worried that
this violence will disturb their effort to protest the
treatment of their people and their neighborhood.

A couple of kids on the court STOP kicking around a
soccer ball. They all pause to look at the soldiers, the
fight, the machete, the gun.

They've seen it before. The kid with the ball DROPKICKS

it into the net. They go back to kicking the soccer ball around.

Nieve watches the kids, she moves to shoo them away to safety until SOMETHING flitting across an open window in the shack near the court catches her eye.

Nieve RUNS to the window and leans inside to look around.

Flowpi SNEAKS out the door of the shack when Nieve LEANS IN the window. She hides behind a tree.

Nieve returns to the court, extra wary.

Behind her on the hillside, we see Flowpi sneaking, from house to house, tree to tree in an arc that would bring her to the hill just above the altercation in the dust.

CUT TO:

EXT.-ROAD BELOW THE BASKETBALL COURT-SAME

MACHETE DRUNKARD and REVOLVER DRUNKARD are circling one another erratically.

Pancho is following them with the intent of breaking up the fight.
He motions to Sweeney, starting to move, to stay still.

Sweeney listens and freezes as ANGRY SOLDIER with his gun STILL DRAWN passes close by.

He takes a moment to sneer in Sweeney's direction though he is smart enough to stay out of his reach.

The drunk combatants' orbits are off-kilter, to say the least, and together they wobble off the road into a muddy ditch.

Now, just below the verge along the basketball/soccer court, they both seemed overmatched by the mud

Both look down at their shoes stuck in the deep mud.

PANCHO MAKES HIS MOVE to disarm the man with the revolver

at the same moment MACHETE DRUNK swings down at REVOLVER
DRUNK.

MACHETE DRUNKARD just MISSES HIS MARK and thwacks the mud
at Pancho's feet.

Pancho quickly WRENCHES the revolver from REVOLVER
DRUNKARD.

> PANCHO MONEYMAKER
> (enraged)
> OYE! CABRON! Cuidado!

SUBTITLE: Hey! Bastard! Careful!
Pancho raises the revolver to shoot one round in the air
to get BOTH drunkards' attentions.

A SHOT rings out.

But PANCHO CRUMBLES into the mud, screaming.

> **SMASH CUT TO:**

EXT.-ROAD BELOW THE BASKETBALL COURT-SAME

A SERIES OF IMAGES:

ANGRY SOLDIER's revolver drops to his side. It's SMOKING.

He tries to holster it CLUMSILY.

For the first time we see ANGRY SOLDIER isn't much more
than a FRIGHTENED BOY in soldier's clothing.

And the rest of the soldiers are SHOUTING, LEAPING from
the trucks.

Meanwhile, the WOMEN of Bella Vista are YELLING,
SCREECHING, BURSTING out of doors, CLIMBING OUT of
windows to get to the scene.

They SWARM from all directions, converging on the dirt
road.

The soldiers see this and A FEW pause again; they look to
each other for leadership rather than rushing to their

comrade's side.

The anger has disappeared from ANGRY SOLDIER'S face.

He instantly realizes he's crossed a line.

For a beat, it is possible no one has his back.

Sweeney snaps out of his FROZEN state.

He FOCUSES his intense gaze on ANGRY SOLDIER as dozens
and dozens of women begin streaming past him.

Sweeney starts fording the RIVER OF WOMEN between him and
ANGRY SOLDIER who is now FROZEN.

We hear the GROANS of Pancho as the first WOMEN surround
him and lean over him, jostling, crowding.

A dozen or so SOLDIERS begin moving toward ANGRY SOLDIER.

Their HEARTS are not in the effort to part the RIVER OF
WOMEN filling the road.

SWEENEY is solely INTENT on getting to ANGRY SOLDIER.

He wants blood.

Pancho SCREECHES in pain.

Sweeney is closing in from behind on ANGRY SOLDIER whose
SHAKING hand rests on his NOW-HOLSTERED GUN.

The TRUCK DRIVER closest to the action has his forehead
on the steering wheel. He is praying, hands clasped
together in front of the steering wheel and his crop of
black hair.

Sweeney reaches out over a WOMAN passing by, he is ABOUT
TO GRAB ANGRY SOLDIER.

HE IS INCHES FROM TEARING HIM APART.

Suddenly a flash of COLOR BEHIND SWEENEY sweeps beneath
his outstretched arm.

Sweeney takes a LOUD SLAP to the ribs from below.

He looks down to KILL whomever it is.

IT IS FLOWPI. SHE IS ON EDGE.

She GRABS HIS HAND.

Sweeney pauses.

> FLOWPI
> (wagging a finger)
> No más.

A SERIES OF IMAGES:

At that moment, ANGRY SOLDIER spins to see Sweeney, WHO IS LOOKING DOWN, STUNNED THAT FLOWPI IS THERE.

The angry soldier grips his GUN TIGHTLY.

His hand SHAKES VIOLENTLY NOW.

Sweeney is looking at Flowpi, then up at the soldier. He seems trapped, unable to act.

The ANGRY SOLDIER is still SHAKING, GRIPPING HIS GUN.

Just BEFORE he can pull the gun or decide to back off…

TWO SOLDIERS GRAB HIM BY HIS HAIR AND ARMS. They YANK him away toward a truck, THROW him in the CAB with the PRAYING TRUCK DRIVER.

Flowpi PULLS Sweeney away from the TWO SOLDIERS dragging their quarry away toward the trucks.

The PRAYING TRUCK DRIVER looks up, surprised.

He GROANS, as his situation has gotten worse.

Pancho GROANS.

A dozen soldiers half-heartedly approach the WOMEN with

their ARMS LINKED surrounding Pancho in the mud.

The WOMEN all TURN THEIR BACKS on the soldiers, some of
them no more than boys.

> SOLDIER
> (weakly to the women)
> Es un proceso, lo siento pero
> tenemos que interrogar a Pancho.

SUBTITLE: It's a process, I'm sorry but we have to
question Pancho.

The jostling and crowding WOMEN, the ENTIRE GROUP, FALL
and PILE onto Pancho writhing in the MUD.

> WOMEN OF BELLA VISTA
> (shouting in unison)
> NO! NO! NO!…

The soldiers are FLABBERGASTED.

Pancho, now at the bottom of the monkey pile, winces but
he manages a smile.

Flowpi leads Sweeney up onto the verge above the pile of
WOMEN.
All the MEN of Bella Vista linger LAMELY in doorways and
windows.

NONE approach the scene.

The soldiers mill and wander on the outskirts of the PILE
of PROTECTIVE WOMEN.
Occasionally, a soldier halfheartedly tries to pull a
WOMAN from the PILE.

The effort is met WITH THE INTERLOCKING OF ARMS AND LEGS
AND SHOUTING.

Flowpi slips a foot in front of a SHOCKED Sweeney's legs
and pushes from behind.

SWEENEY TRIPS into the short side of the PILE OF WOMEN at

the bottom of the verge.
Flowpi LEAPS IN THE AIR to land on Sweeney, who is on top
of SEVERAL WOMEN.

They are not far from Pancho, but several more women pile
on.

Sweeney tries SHOUTING FOR PANCHO IN SPANISH.

It is a cacophony of Spanish and a confused chanted
chorus of "no's".

Sweeney embraces Flowpi protectively, smiling for a
moment.
                    FLOWPI
          Inglés. Usa Inglés, Mono lento!
SUBTITLE: English. Use English, you stupid monkey!

                    SWEENEY
              (sheepishly)
          Yeah, right. Good idea. Pancho! I
          have Flowpi here! Tell us you are
          ok!

Sweeney digs into the pile, wiggling his way down through
arms, legs, buttocks, breasts, faces, hair.

                 SWEENEY (CONT'D)
              (shouting)
          Pancho, are you ok!? It's Sweeney.

Nothing.

Several soldiers give up on the edges of the pile.

They return to their trucks, exasperated.

The pile is MASSIVE, MUDSOAKED and CHURNING.

Children have appeared and are running to jump in.

At the sight of the children, MOST soldiers give up.
Throw up their hands sheepishly.

Sweeney and Flowpi are still struggling along the mud and
shit and filth of the ditch.

Sweeney is getting upset, he starts to exert his
strength.

Flowpi calms him with a giggle and a pinch to the arm.

She is POINTING.

Sweeney rolls over and is FACE-TO-FACE with PANCHO.

Pancho smiles through a mask of slathered mud.

> PANCHO MONEYMAKER
> (matter of factly)
> I'm fine. I'm fine. Hola Flowpi.
> Comó estás?

Flowpi BURSTS into laughter, as do a few women nearby.

Sweeney is bewildered for a moment.

> PANCHO MONEYMAKER(CONT'D)
> He shot me in the leg, my calf.
> It's not bad. It hurts like hell,
> but I'm very sure the bullet just
> grazed me.

CUT TO:

EXT.-DITCH BELOW THE BASKETBALL COURT-SAME

A tropical sunshower BURSTS from the clouds overhead just
as the soldiers' trucks cough to life.
The WOMEN and CHILDREN all CHEER.

Someone begins chanting: "Paz, Amor y Vida, Paz, Amor y
Vida!"

Subtitle: Peace, Love and Life, Peace, Love and Life!

The WHOLE pile joins the chant.

The chant ECHOES down the hill, CHASING the soldiers out
of town.

The TRUCK DRIVER reaches over and SLAPS ANGRY SOLDIER in
the back of the head like the shamed BOY he is.

                                                  CUT TO:

EXT.-THE PILE-SAME

Flowpi grabs Sweeney's hand, she grabs Pancho's hand.

Both men are laughing and CRYING.

The three wiggle and roll and squirm to the edge of the
pile, they help each other out of the mud.

They drop, exhausted onto the grassy verge of the court,
letting the sunshower drench them.

They are CRUSTED with mud, nearly indistinguishable from
the rest of the WOMEN AND CHILDREN PLAYING in the mud.

They laugh and sing, throw mud at one another.

They KNOW Pancho is ok.
Above the pile, above the RETREATING trucks filled with
soldiers, we see IMMENSE flocks of PELICANS flying north.

HUNDREDS UPON HUNDREDS of graceful birds bank on the
wind, shift and rejoin in symmetrical patterns strung out
across the sky above the rivermouth, the northern coast
and endless jungle.

FLOWPI chirps to Pancho and Sweeney, pointing:

                         FLOWPI
                    (excitedly, ecstatic)
                 Aqui, mira! Ahora Uds. Saben donde
                 nacen las letras!

SUBTITLE: Here, look! Now you know where alphabets are
born!

Sweeney is RELIEVED, something RELEASES in him. He is
JOYFUL, wiping the mud from his grinning face.

                    PANCHO MONEYMAKER
                       (contentedly)
              Aquí--en este momento, mis amigos--este
              es el poema de nuestras vidas.

SUBTITLE: Here--in this moment, my friends--is the poem
of our lives.

                    THE END.

CREDITS ROLL

As the credits begin,

A SERIES OF IMAGES:

Sweeney, Flowpi and Nieve walk down the dirt road toward
the rolling waves at the mouth of the Río Chone.

They are caked in mud. Laughing, stolling, kicking up
dust in the sunset's light.

They reach the beach at the bottom of the shanty town.

Melvern Taylor's "Working Stiff" accompanies the three
friends splashing and washing the dried mud away.

Flowpi and Nieve catch a few waves on longboards. The
Pacific Ocean at sunset suits them just fine.

As Melvern Taylor's song ends, Money Mark's "Tomorrow
Will Be Like Today" takes us through to the credits' end…
as Sweeney, Flopi and Nieve gliding across the faces of a
tiny, perfect waves.

THE ORIGIN OF THE FABLED SURF FOOTAGE
FROM WESTERN IRELAND

Casting went with a relatively unknown stage actor from Wales named Dylan Mirthing for the role of Sweeney O'Sweeney in the film. Mirthing was a young, handsome, talented actor on the cusp of fame. He had recently been fired from a Welsh National Theatre production of "The Ice Man Cometh" for drinking too much cider. Well, reports have it that it was cider for breakfast, porter for lunch and (if he made it that far into the day) bourbon for dinner. Mirthing was 23 years old when he was let go from the National Theatre.

He was from a family of some renown in Wales. His mother was Cornish and a famous comedic television actress in Great Britain before she died young. Mirthing's father was of royal descent in Wales and had been bitterly and famously dubbed the "Earl of Absenteeism" by his son.

Mirthing summered in Cornwall with his mother's people in his youth. He had a darker look than most Welshman, which is what caught the casting agency's eye initially. He tanned very nicely, which helped with the surfer-look and even Sweeney's Black Irish origins. Most importantly, Mirthing grew up surfing in the cold Cornish waters.

In films that involve surfing, it is crucial to get the smaller details depicted properly and the crew believed they would be able to feature Mirthing's surfer physique in shots as well as film him carrying a board, waxing a board and so forth. Mirthing was familiar enough with these things to carry them off without much strain.

The surf-action-shot consultants planned on filming pulled back and/or water-level action shots of Mirthing, as Sweeney, paddling for waves, catching waves and even beginning to pop to his feet. At this point in the action sequences they planned to cut to shots of Dave Rastovich and/or Joel Tudor, the pro surfer stunt doubles, who would do the actual surfing on the face of the waves.

Mirthing as a somewhat experienced surfer was a bonus for the project, and he didn't mind the colder air and water temperatures in Western Ireland since he was used to Cornwall's similar conditions.

However, getting wind of the full extent of Mirthing's limitations as a surfer was a stunning setback for the production crew, and possibly the death knell of the film. When an actor is cast chiefly because of his experience as a half-decent surfer, the idea that he can't swim never crosses anyone's mind. Everyone assumes surfers are good swimmers.

Mirthing passively dropped a crucial hint to the crew the evening before the first surf-scene shoot. He mentioned he had grown up wearing a leash and a wetsuit while surfing. He never went in the water without those two tools. Wetsuits are apparently quite buoyant and helped to float Mirthing through his early years in the water. The star also said he'd never experienced a broken leash in waves of any size in Cornwall.

This was one of the last things Mirthing said to the crew the night before the failed shoot and his subsequent firing.

The morning in question involved filming a longboarding scene in some three-foot surf. The wind, tide and waves were all aligning for a chance to capture some quality footage. The crew was operating on flawed intelligence that placed Mirthing in bed by 1 a.m. the night before the shoot. It was said he was only "reasonably inebriated." The crew had witnessed him rise-and-shine out from under far more alcohol and far less sleep in the previous two weeks. No one was worried.

Yet at 7 a.m. as the high tide filled in on the reef, and the winds remained perfect, all waited on the cliffs above the surf spot and Mirthing remained absent.

The surf was at least twice as big as it had been forecast, so a shortboarding session was added to the scheduled longboarding shoot to round out the collection of action footage. Dave Rastovich and Joel Tudor surfed at first light (the crew couldn't keep them out of the water for long whenever the waves were good). Mirthing, on the other hand, was nowhere to be found.

Two hours later—after the ideal tide, wind and swell window for the shoot had closed—the lead actor was located blacked out on the floor of the make-up trailer. He and two attractive Irish make-up artists were found nude, limbs entangled, sleeping soundly.

They had been at it all night and found themselves predictably, self-admittedly "not at the top of their games." Empty bottles of Powers whiskey and tall cans of Tenants lager littered the trailer.

To sum up, it was an unoriginal drunken imbroglio involving a leading man, female make-up artists, booze, Cheez-Whiz, a half-dozen cigarettes laced with hashish and a DVD of the Australian soap opera "Home and Away" running on a loop on a portable television.

As Mirthing was dragged out of the trailer—with what is best described as an amateur make-up job all over his lips, jaw and neck—he confessed he'd known the waves would be bigger that day. Then he screamed to no one in particular, "I can't bloody swim!" Some believed it was meant as a scathing and brilliant impersonation of his father's manner and expression.

Mirthing stumbled off the set for good in the middle of a garbled soliloquy about the values of a good surf leash. All of this strange biography was confirmed by the Earl of Absenteeism, who visited the set later that week in a failed bid to save his son's job.

The tone deaf Earl stated matter-of-factly, "I can't recall Dylan ever surfing without a leash," he went on, "nor do I believe he can swim very well at all. If you would only shoot these scenes in an ocean of lager, all would be well. I can assure you of that."

In fact, after Mirthing was fired, it was revealed he was specifically unnerved by the scheduled scene that involved longboarding without a leash (as Sweeney never longboarded with a leash and was an accomplished open-ocean swimmer).

This lack of a leash was an authentic detail that couldn't be altered, per Sweeney's production-note request. Fearing the loss of his board in the larger surf the next morning, Mirthing dragged the McChicks (as he'd dubbed the pair of Irish make-up artists) to the beach at 3 a.m. to check the waves and smoke hash. Mirthing told the McChicks that the swell was much, much bigger than forecast. The McChicks noted Mirthing's drinking became frenzied between 4 and 6 a.m.

The entire production crew begrudgingly gave Mirthing high marks for effort—though watching "Home and Away" episodes and repeatedly having sex with both women did little to calm the film star's nerves and he essentially passed out by first light. Conversely, stunt doubles Rastovich and Tudor surfed enough to produce ample stock footage and made the improvised shoot a success. Each part of the process of catching a wave was caught on film from multiple angles because the two surfers refused to get out of the water until dark.

The swell kept building enough to work through all tides so Rastovich lit a huge bonfire on the beach, surfed for hours, got out and warmed up by the flames, ate, rehydrated and surfed for hours and then repeated the process one more time in the late afternoon. Tudor was of like mind. They grew enamored with that little-known, remote reef beneath the cliffs of Western Ireland.

Later in the week—footage checked and rechecked—production decided to recast the part of Sweeney O'Sweeney.

The Earl of Absenteeism was told to inform his son, reportedly drying out near Tintagel in Cornwall.

Despite losing their leading actor, most of the crew went out drinking in Bundoran at The Olde Bridge Bar to celebrate the events of that week of work. Rastovich and Tudor flew to France to surf a new swell soon after that. The Irish make-up artists, the McChicks, were given a second chance.

The women proved to be great company and incomparable members of the production team once the spell of Mirthing wore off everyone involved.

Plaza Monumental
TIJUANA
"A la orilla del mar"

Feria Tijuana 2000

Domingo — 4:30 p.m.

27 AGOSTO DE 2000

Surfing 5.00 Dlls. WELCOME TO

RANCHO SALSIPUEDES

OCEAN FRONT

CAMPING
SURFING
HORSE BACK RIDING
CABING FOR RENT

FIRE WOOD
TRAILERS SITES
SPECIAL EVENTS
PARTYS

ENJOY YOUR STAY

THANK YOU

N° 814

Camping 6.00 Dlls.   Mon. Tue. Wed. Thur. Fri. Sat. Sun.

...INCOMPARABLE!

ENRIQUE **GARZA**

El tigre de Cadereyta

GUILLERMO GONZALEZ **CHILOLO**

El líder absoluto del escalafón taurino Mexicano
por primera vez en Tijuana

y

CESAR **CASTAÑEDA**

El Tijuanense ídolo de ambas Californias

Lidiando arrogantes toros de

6 ARROYO HONDO 6

PROPIEDAD: JOSE MIGUEL LLAGUNO GURZA
DIVISA: VERDE, ROSA Y NEGRO

Book IV

SWEENEY
SOUNDING
AWARENESS

From the Travel Journals of
Sweeney O' Sweeney

Transcribed by
Dave Robinson

01
MOUNTAINS

It's impossible to be ready for the sweetness of strangers—from eleven-teen-year-old boys who can't tether their smiles, to rough-cut young men wearing their dreams on their sleeves.

When Mario found out I surfed, he told me he wants to leave these Guatemalan mountains for good. He wants to learn to surf with his uncle who lives on the coast in Nicaragua. Mario works in his family's market, which transforms into an impromptu bar at seven each evening. The farmers' sons, the twenty-somethings, drink Gallo beer and wait for illustrated e-mails from Nicaraguan beaches. It's evidence of the strange power of surfing—to find people who love it as much as I do, though none of them have even seen the ocean in person.

These lifelong and landlocked friends play *fútbol* in the street, school-yards and tiny pitches on the sides of the peaks. These young men drive like suicidal maniacs all over the mountains, across rivers, through the jungles. Some even get paid to drive rebuilt American school buses hand-painted in elaborate patterns and colors. It's like Ken Kesey's Further Bus went south and multiplied, taking on a familiar expat edginess.

The buses are recycled from the U.S., but the drivers are local Gua-temalans, boys barely men, whose sweetness and earnest natures are as disarming as their driving.

Mario made the trade, *un cambio*, with me in half a heartbeat.

> Trading surf wax for
> A town soccer jersey—market
> Cashier goes shirtless.

I've always hoped he and his old friends got their chance to go to Nicaragua to use that wax.

In the mountainside town square, I stumbled across an oddity—a taut volleyball net with chalked lines marking the court. When I asked Mario who used it, he told me to come and play later in the evening. Everyone under sixty seemed to love playing. It was a strange thing to see way up in the nowhere mists hiding that town. The young men took over from the kids and the elderly around eight, under the orange glare of sodium lights encased in shifting clouds of jungle bugs.

I was lucky enough to visit between religious festivals during a quiet time of the year. A French-Canadian couple was in town as well. Only us three gringos to sit back and observe life in that part of the world.

I recalled seeing the couple at Tikal amongst the ruined temples and sun-scorched courtyards. They were nice enough. We shared a few dinners, a bus ride and some travel stories. The husband, Dale, was a hockey fan like any Quebecois would be. We talked about the finer points of pond hockey in northeastern North America. He told me he surfed in Nova Scotia and central Maine while back home. They were headed to Peru to surf later in the their six-month trip.

Dale seemed like a good guy until I watched him play volleyball in the tranquil plaza. I was reminded of the utter lack of sweetness in adults hailing from our part of the world:

> A six-three gringo
> Spikes like it's his job!—no locals
> Over five-eight for miles.

The drivers of Guatemala's buses are one thing; the fare collectors are another breed of pragmatic daredevil entirely. Bolted all over the roof, sides and fenders of the transformed school buses are sturdy handles. This doesn't make any sense until you ride in an overcrowded bus hauling down a jungled mountainside. There are Mayans every couple of miles who get on, the bus is near capacity from the start. But the driver jams anyone and everyone on board, large bags are given to the fare collectors to stash on the roof. No money changes hands immediately. People board through the front door until the front and middle are loaded down. Passengers are helped up and down, in and out through the back emergency exit of the school bus until it's stuffed.

The worn forest-green leather seats built to hold two American children now host three adult Guatemalans on each side of the aisle. The two halves of the adults that can't fit on the seats hang out into the aisle.

> Our row's seventh is wedged
> On knees in the aisle, wall-to-wall
> In the speeding schoolbus.

The aisle, the sole feature of the bus meant for passage, is made impassable via passengers—a river of limbs, laps and bouncing humans.

Kids and grandmothers fill the stairwell up front, block the back exit. It feels like mayhem exemplified until you look out the window you're pressed against and see it is a one-thousand-foot drop off the edge of the crumbling road to a trickle of glinting river in a jungle valley. It's then you understand that you've never known what true mayhem is. And finally the young apprentice to the driver punches in to earn his wage. He is rail-thin, long-armed and knows he is immortal that day on that wet mountainside. The description sounds melodramatic, but if you saw it in person you'd allow for it:

> Fare collectors climb out
> Doors and windows—spidering
> Rain-slick yellow hull!

At last this, you think, is true mayhem in its highest form. Even I, a gringo who'd been raised to believe he'd live forever, had to stop watching this morbid show the first time I saw it.

This everyday existence no one around me wasted an ounce of wonderment on.

Her black-eyed mother wore a hand-made Tyrolean hat that reminded me of the guy on the Peroni beer label. She was cool toward me, but obliged because it was a long bus ride that afternoon.

> Sharing one headphone with
> A Mayan child as wide open
> As her mother's shut tight.

The Beastie Boys and then Getz & Gilberto triggered smiles on the girl's face that distracted me from our imminent gory death at the bottom of a ravine.

No words passed between us. She spoke little Spanish or English. I didn't and still don't know a single word of her indigenous language. But we parted as friends when we reached their stop. The girl's mother even smiled a little in thanks as I waved goodbye.

Maybe it's similar to what Frost said about a poem versus confusion, and music is a momentary stay against ordinary mayhem?

Earlier in that trip, in another country with a range of larger mountains and volcanos, I crossed into the Southern Hemisphere for the third time in my life. The forests seemed thinner in that part of Ecuador than they had been in Guatemala, but the indigenous people wore similar alpine hats and scrapped at making a living any way they could.

Crossing the Equator—
From the rim I see a whole town
On the crater's green floor?

When I found out the volcano I was standing on was active, I waved to the bus driver to leave without me. I picked my way down the crater wall to find a bed. I couldn't move on without spending a night in the mouth of a volcano. There were planted fields, fallow fields, horses, cows, pigs, donkeys and roads laced all over that most temporary of dance floors. The townspeople told me I was good luck, because the evening cleared of mist and clouds. There were no hotels or hostels in that crater, but I found a family with a spare bed. After settling my gear, my host family and I lit a small fire out in a field to stave off the chill while watching the night sky put on a show above the rim. We burned old fence posts, since there were so few trees growing in the crater town. I talked about Seawell and surfing, they described life on volcanic soil. We ate grilled guinea pig off skewers, a local delicacy. I saw one other glinting fire far across that spread of thin crust on a rare and exceptionally clear night along the equator.

Out come the stars—
Slow-churning sparks or reflections
Of this warm cup's fires?

Back up north in Guatemala, I spent a few months with an indigenous family near San Andrés Semetabaj. Grandmother, grandfather, daughters, sons-in-law, grandkids all in one three-room abode with slapdash additions and winding hallways.

Many Guatemalans who are old enough to remember the '80s don't want to talk to an American about their country's government-sanctioned slaughter of the Mayan people. But they all have stories. I spent a lot of time busing, hitching and walking through the high places—just listening. Most of the farms I visited welcomed me openly. The children were jumping with excitement at the sight of a gringo. Some understandably reticent adults usually warmed up and told me about their crops, kids and grandkids. A few eventually went further to describe what the government did to their families so recently.

> Hitching through mountain
> Farms: corn, beans, snowpeas and
> Unmarked mass graves.

Since my trip to Guatemala was unplanned, I hadn't read up on the history and culture. I was going off memory. That's part of the reason I toured the jungles and mountains—to learn about the place I'd dropped myself into. I didn't have the heart to tell any of the locals I didn't know much about their struggles—that I was just a kid in 1982 when it all happened so far from Seawell, Mass.

Instead, I kept my ears and eyes open trying not to offend anyone through my ignorance.

I carried extra cigarettes and candy everywhere I went as icebreakers. I'm apolitical by nature, and inclined to root for the underdog in any fight. Often people in that realm sensed this, I think. Also, like many people born and raised outside the U.S., most Guatemalans softened visibly when they learned I was a poet. There's a deeper and basic reverence for writers and artists in countries beyond North America.

These Mayan peasant farmers would smoke with me, sit in the sun, smile while I taught their kids to play baseball. I never minded whether they shared their stories of genocide with me or not. I was just glad to spend time and talk. I wasn't on any kind of fact-finding mission, no journalist's instinct.

I needed many years of reflection upon that walk through Guatemala before I could begin writing this travelogue.

One evening, I was making my way back down to my host family's house in San Andrés Semetabaj. I hitched whenever possible, walking for miles across forested and farmed valleys in between rides. A mini-pickup appeared behind me. When it pulled over, I counted sixteen indigenous passengers in the bed, holding on to the head-high rack and piled upon one another. I climbed on, gratefully. The wind wouldn't allow for much conversation so I studied sunworn, grinning faces, homburg hats, fedoras, scarves, shawls, a vintage Run DMC windbreaker and pairs of eyes squinting against the wind's watering. We took on even more locals, the truck bowed with the weight.

At my stop, mostly everyone got out. I helped a wrinkled elderly woman down:

> Teachers taught us Mayans
> Vanished—but this toughened peasant
> Makes twenty in this truck's bed?

She trundled off with a pack of cigarettes I offered, smiling toothlessly. She might've been ninety years old. I have no way of knowing, we'd only exchanged a thank-you and you're-welcome. My host and guide, Florencia, saw me give away the pack. She said she knew the woman. Her name was Ximena, everyone knew Ximena. She used to be tall and beautiful, she used to be married and live on one of the biggest farms around. Everyone knew her because Ximena's:

> Six kids rode an army
> Chopper to the sea—dropped from
> A height to smash them all.

I was told this was what the government soldiers did so they weren't bored by the repetition of killing their indigenous countrymen and women. I was told that Ximena's story was well known in Guatemala. How could they forget? By slaughtering Ximena's kids, the U.S.-backed Guatemalan government claimed to be fighting guerilla warfare and the indigenous support system for that warfare.

I tried to sleep that night, failed, got up to drink beer and listen to whatever nighttime noises I could find. Just a few odd birds singing "poo-tee-weet" repetitively for hours. It could've been a recording of birds on a loop. It was too dark to find the source. How could I know for sure?

Eventually, I went back to bed and pulled the mosquito net into place. There must've been a small hole somewhere in the netting. I must've been feeling a little deadened, a little knocked-loose:

> Haven't fought a fly or
> Hurt a man for years—I kill two
> Mosquitos inside my net.

I took a moment to reckon with my foolishness then got back up to drink at a small table in my room until sunrise. I passed out as the room brightened.

I never said a word about any of it to anyone in Florencia's home, out on the farms or in town. How could I? There is nothing sensible for anyone to say, least of all an American in Guatemala.

Florencia's grandkids knew something was wrong, I'm not sure how. I woke sweating out Gallo beer at Noon to a donkey braying along with Pink Floyd's "We Don't Need No Education" blaring at an ungodly volume from across the street.

There were old political-campaign T-shirts from the town piled with some flowers and candy outside my door—left there by Florencia's grandkids and their neighborhood friends. The kids must've seen the T-shirts I'd traded for in Ecuador and realized they had some similar shirts saved somewhere.

I stood staring down in the bright sun—at the flowers.

They left me goddamned flowers because they sensed something was wrong. There was a shakily written note asking me to feel better, asking me to wait around for the kids until they got home from school so I could watch over them swimming in Lake Atitlán. They had been dying to show me how well they could swim since I'd arrived.

Three green volcanos cup
The blue polluted lake—shining wet
Kids yell for me to dive!

These children of the needlessly damned. It's impossible to be ready for the sweetness of strangers.

02
FORESTS

When I was a kid in Seawell, Mass., we didn't have any wilderness near enough (other than the North Atlantic). A lot of the kids I grew up with read comics to escape the urban nastiness—the bullies, the older drunk siblings and uncles, the stolen bikes, the fights or abuse from parents. I read some comics, too. I liked the X-Men, but I was never a fiend for comics like the other kids on Hazel Street near my house. For me, Farannan Golf Course was the next best thing to real wilderness and escape.

One year I cultivated weed up on Vancouver Island with a Japanese surfer I met in Ecuador. People in British Columbia told me they grew up reading comics—but they read them to *escape* the unending wilderness surrounding their worlds.

After my Japanese friend and I made some money off a crop of White Widow, I took a boat trip down to the San Juan Islands in the Straight of Juan de Fuca at the northern end of Puget Sound. It was wilderness all around—orcas hunting salmon schools as big as football fields, minke whales diving under our bow, bald eagles everywhere, sea lions, seals and one of the San Juans was peppered with white tailed deer. I camped on a forested island for a week or so and had a run-in with a deer that reminded me of my favorite comic book story—a passing detail, really, but one I've never forgotten. I haven't read the comic it appeared in, but one stifling summer day as a kid skateboarding around Seawell, Mass., I overheard Marc Mueller telling Nicky the Hack about it.

Here's how I remember it: Wolverine—a potentially vicious individual, though a good guy at heart, and one of the core X-Men—used to hone his skills by stalking deer deep into the wilderness. He would track a doe or buck for miles without being noticed by the animal. Slowly, painstakingly, silently he'd creep up on the foraging, docile creature only to startle it with a pat of his hand. He never harmed the deer, only practiced his own stealth and patience by approaching one to touch it.

That little overheard detail of a much larger story stayed with me into adulthood. Then on the San Juan Islands, I spotted a tiny deer on a hillside above the trail I was hiking. During that week, I'd noticed deer keeping a wary distance but rarely bounding off at the sight of humans. I decided I'd try to stalk that deer on the hillside, just like Wolverine.

It took hours, but I moved slower than I ever have while concentrating on my breathing. Steadily, I approached. As I got within thirty yards, I paused each time the deer paused in its foraging. The tiny thing seemed to know I was there since there wasn't a lot of cover on offer above that trail.

It moved deeper into the woods, farther up the hillside, but didn't appear frightened. I inched along in my slow pursuit over the thick, dry carpet of oak leaves. The deer stuck its head into a bush to get at some greener leaves. I stepped around the trunk of a huge tree and I suddenly heard the sound of a deep buzzing.

Bees!

I crashed downhill, getting my feet off the underground hive as fast as I could. I'd taken one sting to the side of my neck. I cursed under my breath at the sharp pain.

Once I'd removed the stinger, I looked back up the hill to see how close I'd come in my failed effort. My disappointment faded as I saw the deer still feeding higher up the hillside. I began a new approach, giving the underground hive a wide berth.

On the way up, I recalled my old landscaping boss laughing at me for getting stung two weeks in a row mowing the same lawn on Luce Street in Seawell. Once we found it, Goatboy burned the yellow-jacket nest with some gas and a single match. The elderly homeowner's eyes waxed like full moons behind his screen door at the sight of a six-foot flame snaking upward from a hole in his green-carpet lawn.

I remembered Goatboy's surprised mutterings, as the flame leapt:

"Jesus, I hope there's no gas line down there. Let's get outta here before this guy says anything. Anyways, we got lawns to mow."

Almost laughing out loud at the memory, I found myself back within twenty yards of this deer on an island in the Puget Sound. The little thing again sensed I was there: twenty feet, fifteen, ten—I went stock-still each time the deer raised its head from the brush to chew. When the deer jammed its whole head into a tangle of brush one last time, I noticed we were surrounded by thorns as big as my thumb. But this felt like my twice-in-a-lifetime chance.

I crept within an arm's length. Stopped.

I looked to see if there were any hikers below, witnesses to what was really happening. Anyone? Anything? Nothing?

> The ragged fawn, orphaned
> Maybe, strips the brambles of leaves—
> Ignores my quick touch!

That night I drank some Rainier cans by a campfire. I'd found a little clearing on a peninsula jutting out into a lake near the center of the island. I could wake up in the morning, have a cold swim and then build a small cooking fire to dry off by. I had a few too many beers, staring at orange flames, occasionally wandering away to study cricket-shattered silence from atop a huge downed pine jutting out into the water.

> Above a moonlit lake
> Two owls talk from black treetops—
> Miles apart.

Back at camp, the owls quieted by the weight of what to say next, I stoked the coals before chucking a log of oak on to brighten the underside of the swaying pine boughs above me.

Flames spark upward
To red eyes spiraling down! —
Treed raccoons descend.

A mother raccoon and three little masked cubs scratched down thin trunks and dropped into my flickering ring of firelight. They paused on the pine needles, dipping heads, sniffing at me and the warmth of the fire. The family moved on into their realm of nighttime forest.

I once met a woman who loved to wander in the northern woods of Minnesota, up by the Boundary Waters. Lila didn't own a flashlight but knew all of the paths, the rocks, the roots. Even with my good eyes I sometimes had to feel my way around that place in the pitch black—arms outstretched, warding off temporarily invisible tree trunks.

The summer I met her I'd seen black bears and coyotes up close in the meadows, on the trails. I was told to watch for bobcats and just to the north wolves were said to have returned. The long calls of the loons out on Little Boy Lake sounded almost spectral to my ears.

I wouldn't say I was attracted to Lila. Nothing ever happened between us. I was more in awe of her, enraptured while witnessing her deep connection to such a wild place.

I shared a tent with her and a wilderness guide named Rowland. Lila and Rowland grew up a few hours south and had moved up there by the time we met. They were old friends and they watched over me a little bit, I admit. It was early in my days as a city kid gone feral. I still drank a lot of beer and got lost in the trees now and again.

We'd all ended up living in the woods in the same tent for around two months on the outskirts of Longville. My girlfriend, Diana, had made it clear I was no longer welcome in our cabin a few miles away. The weather was still reasonable.

I met Rowland in a bar in Winona. I stuck out, he said. He could see I didn't know where I was going that night. I met up with him the next day and we fished a little. He introduced me to Lila and she said I could stay with them.

I don't know what Lila and Rowland's excuses were for being way out there. Why ask? It was a comfortable exile for the three of us for a time. We had a reliable tent and a backseat from an old Mercury Cougar propped up in the needles in front of our sleeping quarters. We'd sit around a small fire or citronella candle and talk, smoke weed, maybe we had some beers now and again. Every so often, one or two of their friends would hike through a small meadow into our pinewoods to find our tent and hang around for a couple of hours. None of us had much money, as I recall. We couldn't buy beers whenever we wanted. Sometimes we couldn't find a ride to the liquor store in Longville. We were content.

Lila showed us paths through the dark and we stealthily borrowed a canoe from the nearby kids' camp.

Wide awake on my
Back in the bottom of the boat—
Welcoming vertigo.

We portaged to hidden lakes below bats flying erratic paths while feasting on infinite swarms of mosquitos.

Canoe ripples warp
Reflections of bats unblending
Between streams of stars.

Back in Seawell, Mass., we say the rain's "coming down sideways" when it's especially bad out over the North Atlantic. At the altitude I found myself outside Mindo, Ecuador, everything was drenched by mist. The giant centipedes in the cloud forest shone black and wet. Humidity sapped through all layers of waterproof clothing. Shoes were pointless and sometimes lost to the mud. The endless green leaves dripped while the gaps in the canopy looked stuffed with rags of fog.

I had a mission, though, and a guide who'd abandoned his sandals to the mud near the top of the trail. He and I laughed that we'd even found the river:

> Forget the trees—
> Up here you can't see the forest
> For the clouds!

Two ascending hikers gave us some odd looks as we lugged our strange gear to the valley floor. My guide assured me we'd be fine, that he'd consulted all of the maps and had hiked miles downriver along the very bank we stood on. There was nothing but jungle and one cable-car crossing (for cattle or humans). I trusted him and agreed to run the rapids. I hoped we didn't discover a waterfall he'd missed in his previous forays downriver. After all, he rolled and smoked his own joints like a two-pack-a-day man smokes Luckies. Maybe I'd made a mistake? I got on the river anyway and my doubt vanished.

> Green kingfisher on a
> Wire stares down—why run rapids
> On old inner tubes?

Shaking from the cold and laughing at the end of our two-hour run, I only freaked out *after* crossing a huge valley in a different, high-altitude cable car. I'm not sure I would've ridden above that expanse of forest, through the undersides of the clouds, if I had known what powered the contraption on the other side.

We paid our toll to the owner of the cable car ferry, seated in an old Chevrolet's front seat propped up on the floor of a three-walled shack. He ran the whole system off an old truck engine mounted under a flimsy tin roof on the east side of the valley. There was a gearshift, even a muffler extending out and around one wall of the shack to keep the exhaust away.

Terrifyingly functional.

In Guatemala I shared a ride in a van with a woman I'd met in the small city of Antigua. We were both going to Tikal and Semuc Champey, so we traveled together. Her name was Kat and she was from Tasmania, raised on a sheep ranch—about as far away from Seawell as one can get on the planet.

The driver of the van sensed the kind of instant connection Kat and I had made, somehow, as we all sat shoulder to shoulder in the front seat. He said to her, assuming we were already a couple, "I can see in your eyes how much you love this man."

Kat and I were embarrassed by his insightful overestimation. I was in my early thirties at the time, and I sat there like a mute child. Kat was suddenly bashful as well.

We rode through the jungle for hours to get to Tikal. The driver's candor was typical in a place where the people had every right to treat outsiders with suspicion as a rule.

As we found Tikal's main courtyard, a large outlandish animal ran by us on all fours looking for scraps in the grass. It wasn't tame, definitely as wild as the unending landscape of trees around us, but inured to travelers.

It was so alien to us we weren't sure if it was a kind of canine, feline or giant rodent. The sight of this thing rendered two adults inarticulate in two languages. We weren't sure how to formulate a question about the creature.

Kat gave it a try anyway, asking a Guatemalan couple lying on a blanket in the shade:

> Qué es eso?' 'Es un
> Bizoté.' 'Si, pero, comó un perro o un gato?' —
> 'No sé, como un Bizoté.'

"What's that beast?" "A *Bizoté*."
"Yes, but canine or feline?" "I don't know—
like a *Bizoté*."

I've felt the same way about a few things in my life. Some days things seem wholly independent of each other—and I can go on pretending I am just myself the way I see myself. But when confronted with something like a *Bizoté* (so entirely foreign to my version of my universe), it is sudden insight that *everything* is beyond my meager understanding.

Everything is connected. *Everything* is one thing—and it's laughable that we humans don't know what this "one thing" is or why it exists at all.

During our ride to Semuc Champey the next day, the same driver asked us to guess how old he was. His grin was as impish as a grin can get. We'd just picked up two more backpackers to fill up the van.

The driver's assistant answered for us, "You're older than the temples at Tikal!" He cackled at the driver, before climbing out the window to tie down two more packs, "You're older than my *abuelita* and she shits dust!"

The driver went straight-faced for a moment, paused for effect, then calmly pulled a lever on the steering column—soaking the baggage handler in a mix of windshield wiper fluid and water. His friend screeched curses above us on the roof as we approached forty-five mph on the narrow mountain road. No one in the van besides Kat and I noticed this hilarious skirmish.

Impish grin restored, the driver repeated, "How old am I?"

Flustered by the potential of seeming rude, Kat was unable to answer. I'll be honest, I thought he was forty or forty-five at most. So I guessed thirty-five to be polite. But I told Kat later I wouldn't have been surprised if he'd told us he was even a bit younger. Kat asked him if it might be his birthday, and a significant enough one for him to ask us such a question.

We were both wrong. He said, and I'll never forget the moment or the man, "I'm seventy-five." We were incredulous. But Pedro, the now-drenched baggage handler climbing back in the window as we approached a mountain tunnel, insisted it was true: "*Es verdad, El Viejo sin Edad tiene setenta y cinco años.*"

Kat and I took one long look at each other before the van flew into the mountain's unfinished, unlit tunnel.

> After-images
> Of her large blue eyes drift across
> Sudden darkness.

A minute later, deep into the tunnel, our dim headlights lit up a support column in the *middle* of the road. There was no other traffic and it was suddenly a strange, otherworldly place underneath that mountain.

As we got closer we heard a roaring sound and the post began writhing! The driver slowed to swerve around it:

> From the jagged rock
> Ceiling, thick as a trash can—
> A column of water!

Another half-mile out of the tunnel and another hour on mountain roads, finally we swam at Semuc Champey. The stepped pools of blue water were warm and clear as water can be above bone-white sand. Yellow fish schooled in the shady corners.

> Small fish hover
> Below rock overhangs—drifting
> Birch leaves in blue skies.

I've never spoken to Kat again, not since we parted in Guatemala. The last thing we shared at the very end of our two weeks together, was the sight of a Guatemalan family climbing the moss-slick steps of the tallest ancient temple in South America.

We'd gone back to Tikal for another look. Hundreds of dangerous steps, no bannisters, ropes or safety measures of any kind. Climb at will. We were shocked to see a grandmother, sweating in the tropical heat, make it to the top:

> Wearing her Sunday best
> *Abuelita* summits, descends—
> In two-inch heels!

There was a 300-degree view of nothing but jungle canopy out to the horizon—no sign of humankind beneath a billion leaves. Only a few other temples jutted from the blanket of green below our vantage point.

> Jungle's grown up once
> Again, submerging Tikal—endless
> Seascape of treetops.

George Lucas shot footage of this same view in the '70s to use as the setting of the rebel base on the planet Yavin 4 in "Star Wars"—another perfectly familiar yet alien part of the Earth.

We both knew the next day Kat was off to Guatemala City to start back toward Tasmania. I would bus north from Guatemala along the Mexican coastline, alone with my board bag again—Puerto Escondido, some secret spots near Huátulco, La Ticla and on to Baja on an overnight ferry across the Sea of Cortez.

The last things Kat and I said to each other weren't very memorable, though we were not eager to part.

I know neither of us has forgotten the approach of those distant thunderstorms above the swelling trees. Tikal's ancient city and temples had been covered in mud and vines for centuries and then excavated by scientists and looters.

Mayan poets and priests recorded histories and conquests of other cities by building Tikal's massive temples in tribute to their leaders. They filled fig-bark books with hieroglyphics that tell stories of the stars in time, wars and kings, heroes and sacrifices.

Kat and I felt all of this and sat in awe for a time, rooted to the top of a pile of rocks:

Howler monkeys roar,
Thunderheads crash, drag curtains of rain—
Temple Four's stones tremble.

03
VILLAGES

At night, the hotels and hostels of South America lock their doors. I often drink beer wherever they'll serve me as late as they'll allow. I play some pool if I find a table, or talk to whatever travelers end up in the same remote outpost. I usually seek out surf spots less revered than others. I like less of a crowd and more of a local feel to the sessions.

Canoa, Ecuador, has a slight Western Caribbean reggae vibe in the water and beachside bars. Mild strains of marijuana, laid-back local surfers, warm water and waves every day—I couldn't care less if other international surfers write off this beachbreak or not. I love that surf town almost as much as Seawell. There's no denying it. But don't press me to talk about the boat-access reefs north of there because I won't. I told the locals I'd keep their secrets.

There's a family-owned and -operated hotel in Canoa called Hotel País Libre. It's four stories of palm-fronds and jungle hardwood over-looking the rivermouth and cliffs at the north end of the beach. I've spent many months there at $10 a night in a corner room with a view of the pool.

The nighttime security guard lets me in around eleven, locks up be-hind me. Victor has a bad limp. I see him in Bahia de Caráquez sometimes, which is where he's from—as well as where the thieves that try to rob the hotel come from. His leg hardly bends inside his semi-military jumpsuit. Victor's a nice guy—a bit older than your average Ecuadorian hotel security guard. Eventually he chose to tell me what happened to his leg.

I wasn't ready for the story.

Victor said he was riding on a motorcycle with his young wife fifteen years before. They were in Bahia de Caráquez, a place that reminds me of

Havana, Cuba—the faded pastel buildings, crumbling roads and old cars.

A taxi pulled out from a parking spot for a U-turn, Victor told me that quiet night. I'd brought a 32 oz. Pilsener beer back from the bar on the beach for us to share. I doled it out in two small sweating glasses. I slumped back in a wicker chair, Victor sat back into another across from the reception desk, his sawed-off shotgun across his lap.

Before reaching the crux of his story, Victor paused and reminded me to return the empty beer bottle to Leo Gordo at the bar so he could get the deposit back. I promised I would.

Victor went on to tell me how he and his wife were catapulted off their motorbike the day the taxi cut them off. His femur snapped across the yellow bumper. His wife flew over his head, over the hood of the car and into the gutter. Her head struck the curbstone and she died instantly.

I sat there stunned, sobered, no longer slumped in my chair. Victor said, "It was lucky she died because she wouldn't have been able to handle that our baby girl died that day."

Witnesses later told Victor his wife somehow never let go of their child as she was flung to the street. They had to pry her arms from the infant's body.

I was quiet. After several minutes, I waved a moth from in front of my face and said I was sorry. I filled his glass, sipped at mine, filled his again and again. I wished I had more to give, but I didn't. No one does when a thing like that is spoken.

Victor finished by adjusting his stiff leg with a grimace, saying, "Later that day, the day I woke up, the day I learned they had both died, I had to call my cousin in Spain and borrow money for the surgery. They were going to cut my leg off if it wasn't for my cousin in Spain. I was able to pay him back a few years later."

Later that week, a thief from the city climbed into the hotel's yard. Victor heard his feet hit the flagstones by the outside showers, so he limped hurriedly through the hotel's dark, empty restaurant to the sliding glass doors in back. He saw the teenager climbing to the second floor's balcony railing. My room was on that floor at that time. I was the only person staying in the hotel.

Ten thousand frogs, birds, bugs
Shriek awake this world for good—
Four a.m. shotgun blast!

Victor was let go from his security job a few weeks later. The owner,
Andrés, explained to me reluctantly that Victor was a little too old, a little
too reliant on warning-shot gunblasts in the middle of the night. Andrés
was a kindhearted man, his regret at the decision he'd had to make about
Victor played across his face.

No one in Canoa felt good about him losing his job. But Victor truly couldn't move very well, he was in pain most of the time and even
though he rarely showed it, he also lugged around more sorrow than I
could each day.

Once, he solved a problem in the hotel's stairwell for me using only
a flathead shovel. I hadn't known what to do when I'd found the largest
spider I'd ever seen perched shoulder-high on a stairwell wall. It was almost as big as a dinner plate and far hairier. I was afraid the woman I was
with would see the thing and want to leave town.

Hotel País Libre's decks, hallways and stairs are open—designed to
let the wind blow through. No one can afford to screen windows or get
every doorjamb flush with the floor. Reptiles, insects and birds are permanent guests—it's part of life on the edge of the jungle by the beach.

I couldn't kill the spider myself as a Buddhist. So I told Victor. I didn't
really ask him to do anything, but the hairy thing weirded me out, and I
thought I should tell someone it was there on the wall.

The day before, I'd caught a matchbox-sized beetle crawling in our
room with a paper cup and the palm of my hand. When I released it on
the deck, it unfolded wings I didn't know it had and fluttered past my
face revealing a stinger the length of a needle on its rump. The bugs were
getting to me that month.

Moments after I told him about the spider, Victor went up the stairs
with a shovel. I winced as the flat of it smacked against the wall. That
terrifying thing was venomous *and* sentient. It wasn't hurting anyone.

A tarantula as
Big as my face stills itself—
Fuses my bones with fear.

As a younger man, people in Seawell thought I was pretty fearless for fighting goons and surfing in the middle of winter. I guess I keep it together through some fearful moments, at others I'm a timid animal like anyone else.

I have no idea why Victor got up each morning. I wouldn't know how to ask him that. Nor could I ask how a person watches his wife and infant daughter die in a pointless accident and limp on to kill venomous spiders and fire warning shots above thieves' heads without complaint? All to keep drunken gringos safe?

When I think of Victor's daily experience, everything seems as senseless as it can get.

Writing this all down right now, remembering it vividly, I feel vaguely insane. Where the hell is Victor now, ten years since?

And people wonder why drink is one balm of choice for me? When you're the kind of person who sees clearly that questions beget nothing but more questions, soon questions beget booze.

During a different trip to Canoa, I met two non-surfing brothers who'd just reunited for the first time in six months or so. Dana came north to Ecuador via the jungles of Peru where he'd volunteered to study and protect endangered spectacled bears. Tim came south from Arizona just to travel and connect with his little brother. We talked of where they were from, how they grew up and we all ended up hanging out for a few weeks. It eventually came to light that Dana, as a baby, drank milk all day every day for years on end. He waddled around with a bottle in his mouth all his waking hours. Wouldn't sleep without one in his arms. The whole family called him "Milkmonster Dana." I loved it.

He was around six-foot-four and rail thin. The tops of his feet were all torn up and infected from the rubber boots he wore while lugging tranquilized bears up and down muddy trails in the Peruvian jungle. Milkmonster now limped down the muddy streets of Canoa each morning and evening to soak his bare feet in the Pacific to try to heal the cuts. He couldn't put on shoes for the pain and he stubbornly refused medicine.

It was borderline gory.

His older brother said not to worry about him, Milkmonster Dana did as he pleased—as a rule. It wasn't really my place to say much anyway. But the tropics are not kind to open wounds; you might go to sleep one night on the mend and wake up the next bright morning with a cache of insect eggs tucked into your feet.

Evenings, whenever I saw him in town, I exaggerated my Boston accent to distract him from his limping: "Milkmonstah Danah! Let's get a beeeah and poh-ah some rum on those feet! It's on me, Doctah Sweeney!" He would laugh and then find his brother Tim and we'd get some beer and sit on the beach.

One cloudy afternoon, after we'd finished a hike in the virgin rainforest north of town, we all went to the beachfront bar next to the rivermouth. We were exhausted from the heat, mud and hills we'd climbed on our hike. We'd picked some limes along the way and were trying to recruit attractive female New Zealanders to our cause of mojitos & caparinhas on the beach later that night. All except Dana. He was quiet, per usual.

We told the Kiwis that we'd seen a harpie eagle, one lone venado (a tiny deer endemic to those forests) and a troop of black howler monkeys. They seemed eager to take the hike with us again later that week. Dana had gone for beers at that point. The rest of us claimed low-slung hammocks with a view of the surf and debated a swim out front. Upon handing out our beers, Dana mentioned quietly that we should follow him:

Milkmonster swears a
Baby black howler is hiding
In the bar's rafters.

We were reluctant to get up from our hammocks, thinking he might be trying to steal the best spot. Curiosity prevailed so we followed him over the soft sand toward the sounds of the women in the kitchen preparing for the dinner rush.

> Ten-thousandth time I lean
> On a bar, things change—an orphaned
> Monkey climbs my arm.

I cradled the trembling creature in my sweatshirt. He was only the length of a hardcover book with two long arms, legs, perfect little feet and fists. I caught a glimpse of his needle teeth after he calmed down and yawned. At that age, around four or five weeks old, a baby howler monkey looks exactly like a miniature mountain gorilla rather than a howler. It was a beautiful and eerie experience.

> Pitch black eyes
> Swaddled in my cradled hands—
> The near-human stare.

I held that terrified monkey for four quick hours, its leathery hands gripping the tips of each of my thumbs, until the owner showed up and took him back to his cage.

Tim left for the U.S. a week later but Milkmonster Dana stayed on in Canoa, changing his plane ticket once his feet healed. He decided to learn to surf. He was quick on the uptake and could catch waves and get up on a shortboard in a few days. Impressive ability and effort, really.

Until the waves got bigger, that is. A couple of weeks into his apprenticeship in the Pacific, we woke to eight to ten-foot surf with offshore winds. Canoa is a high-quality beachbreak that can handle bigger days with less current than New England beaches. It's unique because there really are no riptides. I've never seen a single one in all the years I've visited. The local kids swim in the shorebreak and never get pulled out—north and south by the currents, yes, but never out to sea.

Still, paddling and positioning become more challenging whenever the waves get bigger. There's a lot more water moving around while you punch under a dozen walls of whitewater once you step off dry sand. It can be draining for the uninitiated.

I saw Milkmonster as we both paddled out under a last roiling wave to get outside. We sat up on our boards. I was happy to see he made it all the way out to wait for the next set. He was such a mellow character and he loved the ocean and surfing more and more each day. He admitted to me he was worn out by all the paddling, but he took the ocean's beatings with good-natured shrugging and sheepish grins.

I don't care how good a person gets at surfing, Milkmonster had already absorbed the lesson of humility that the Pacific offered. Rare is the surfer who rips *and* shrugs off the inevitable humiliation that comes with time spent in the ocean. Given my choice, I'd rather surf with a beginner awake to humility than just about anyone else.

Milkmonster, it turned out, was having trouble sitting on the beach while the waves were so good—while watching so many good rides by the locals. He was hooked. It was too late for him already! Something in his newfound understanding of the contentment possible in the act of surfing conjured up mischief in me—it all happened fast as I started to warn him of an approaching set of waves. The first was huge, crumbling and crashing halfway down its face about twenty yards beyond us. I told Milkmonster to go for it, to paddle as hard as he could. For an instant as I yelled to him, I thought the wave would reform as it reached us—maybe allowing him to glide into an easy take-off. In the next instant I saw it was not going to be easy, the wave was clearly about to steamroll his flailing form.

My last thought: "Milkmonster's pretty athletic, he's a good swimmer. He can handle…" Then the wave doubled up and absolutely crushed him. He disappeared under the whitewater and his board shot to the sky.

I paddled deeper to line up the next wave—laughing, smiling, maybe groaning a little.

I figured I'd see him on the inside after my wave. I didn't end up finding him for two hours, but Milkmonster filled me in on the beating over some cold beers (sheepishly put on my tab) at sunset:

"It swallowed me, bounced
Me off the sand then ragdolled me—
Nothing to be done."

He was worn out when the wave let him surface in waist-deep water around one-hundred yards from where it hit him. The current whisked him a mile down the beach when he tried to paddle back out. He couldn't get back outside past the whitewater so he just kept going south.

I still laugh at the mock anger of Milkmonster Dana that evening. The Kiwi girls ate up the story, some of them having taken similar thrashings in the surf that day.

Everyone detailed their exercises in humility and encouragement doled out in unequal doses by the Pacific. Dana and I told them once the swell died we'd find our local guide and take them on a jungle hike to find some howler monkeys and eagles.

We had a couple more beers and went to bed early, agreeing to do it all over again the next day.

The next morning was Milkmonster's twenty-third birthday. I was around ten years older than him. He'd told me at that time he wanted to be a writer. Apparently he'd found the copy of Owen Kivlin's *Sweeney on-the-Fringe* I'd left with Leo Gordo for the bar and hostel's library. I'd brought a copy to Canoa because some of the locals are mentioned in it.

I was a little embarrassed by Milkmonster finding the book, and took it from him. Instead I asked him to read the manuscript I was working on during that trip to Canoa. I told him I'd rather have him read my writing than stories about me told and written by my friends. I felt weird about it, I explained. I'm not sure if he understood.

In any case, Milkmonster had been raised as a Christian Scientist and his father had just died a year ago right around his son's twenty-second birthday. After six months of walking around in a grief-stricken haze, Dana dropped out of college and volunteered to save spectacled bears.

His roots in Christian Science might've explained his reluctance to get medical attention for his feet—as the founder Mary Baker Eddy taught illness was an illusion that could be healed through prayer. But ultimately Milkmonster rejected the religion his parents had chosen for him. In my estimation, this conglomeration of surprise grief and the bizarre strictures of Christian Science had produced an interesting young writer.

Dana and I spent a couple of months critiquing each other's writing projects. We surfed almost every day because there are waves down there every single day, you just have to hope for the wind to work. We also volunteered a lot of time with Pancho, who had taken a liking to Milkmonster.

Pancho and I, in fact, put together a great little party for his birthday. We invited a few of the local surfers who had met Milkmonster, some cute Dutch backpackers, the Kiwi women, one lone German architect from Munich and a Japanese guy who lived in Canada and grew weed for a living. Most of Pancho's farming cronies showed up and we had a memorable gathering in Hotel País Libre's back yard.

It was impromptu and last-minute because most of us surfed until around three, when the northwest wind came up and blew out the surf. The swell looked to be fading.

At dusk, the local Ecuadorian musicians arrived. They consisted of a seventy-year-old singer-guitar player and another younger local who also played guitar. They couldn't find the third member of their group, he was suspected of being on a bender in Manta an hour to the south.

We all cracked open our Pilseners and sat at some tables on the grass next to the pool. It's a quiet, fenced-in yard next to the river and we were content to hear some local music.

Pancho laughed out loud, when I realized I'd forgotten half of the payment for the musicians. As the singer took my forty dollars, he patiently informed me that he was physically unable to sing until he had a bottle of local sugarcane moonshine to warm up his vocal chords. He pointed at his throat and shook his head sadly. Clearly he was parched.

Milkmonster, the birthday boy no less, leapt up to run for liquor. It took five minutes for him to return breathless, barefoot, with the bottle.

In the meantime, those of us from all corners of the Earth sat and listened to the night sounds rise and mix with darkness descending over the town and coast:

> Old man purses his mouth
> Until *Aguardiente* arrives—
> Pretends to tune strings.

> "*Guantanamera*"
> Tree frogs, birds and bugs sing—
> Guitar strings at dusk.

Later, after the men finished their songs, we would stroll down the street to the bar on the beach. But during the performance, I looked around at the smiling, swaying strangers around that yard:

> Consecrating all our
> Births with beers and songs—wistful, yet,
> At the sunset's wink.

This calm and connected period in my life—sleep, eat, surf, write, read, hike, drink, laugh, sleep, repeat—is difficult to re-create with disparate people in any foreign place. You need to stumble on a group of individuals busied with idleness and appreciation of the life surrounding them. These calm and connected days are all I crave as I grow older.

04
COASTS

> Each dawn I wade, swim
> Or paddle across the muddy
> Rivermouth—eyes wide.

I'd found a remote surfspot in Mexico. I kept forgetting to ask a local if there were alligators or caymans or crocodiles in that part of the country. For the life of me, I couldn't be sure. I spent a lot of time thinking about it. I had to cross the river to get to the surf spot each morning, and each morning I realized I'd forgotten to ask what lurked. There weren't any bridges or boats. The river was narrow but, depending on the rain in the mountains above the town, it could swell to triple its size overnight. There were usually birds wading and fishing where the freshwater hit the ocean. In that part of the country the tidal change was never big enough to separate the rivermouth from its running into the shallows of the sea.

One morning I waded through knee-deep water, unable to see my feet, near thousands of shore birds hunting minnows and shellfish. The next morning:

> Nine vultures stamp flower
> Patterns in mud, plucking the soft
> Gut of a sea turtle.

I never saw an alligator. Though I hung out with a couple of the surfers from that part of the world for a few months, I never remembered to ask. I've since checked maps and habitat range, but I still can't be sure. Maybe there were sharks I should've been more worried about? Probably.

There were plenty of light green iguanas in the brush at the edge of the driftwood-strewn beaches. I'd walk up the coast to swim by myself and lie in the shade of a cliff with a hole in it that housed some bats sleeping not too far from the high tide line. After sunset I would walk along a hillside above a grove of tall swaying palms by the riverbank's flats.

> Fat fireflies like green sparks
> Weaving through the slender black trunks
> Of coconut trees.

Three weeks into my stay, as I made my way back across the river after surfing the long, left-handed, cobblestone pointbreak, a local kid started yelling at me. A group of huts and lean-tos stood on the sand next to the river. These often were washed away by the river or the ocean, so they remained simple structures of bamboo and palm fronds with a narrow dirt road cuting through them and ending at the river.

I don't remember the kid's name, but he was a little punk. I remember liking his attitude and fearlessness. He surfed whenever he could borrow a board. But he seemed to spend more time mocking the gringos and backpackers who trickled through town on their way north and south to more well-known mainland Mexico destinations.

The day he yelled at me, I stopped and squinted into the dark shade of a hut tucked back behind some empty hammocks. It was still early in the morning, cool and quiet but for his screaming. All I heard was "Sweee-NEEE! Sweee-NEEE! Qué eees meening-fah-KING?" I didn't know who it was at first, and I couldn't tell if the person was using Spanish or English to accost me.

Squinting harder into the shade, I saw that it was my friend, the punk kid. So I guessed it was probably broken English. He'd been asking me questions about English words for weeks: "wax," "buds," "swim fins," "rum (not 'ron')" and "campfire" versus "bonfire." The kid helped me with Spanish words, too. I couldn't recall the word for "bat" the day I found that high-tide cavemouth up the coast. He told me, condescendingly of course, it was "murciélago"—to this day, one of my favorite words in any language: The hint of the word "murky," as bats are, at the start of the word; the ascent on the accented third syllable, the lone "e"; and the way the word finishes with an open vowel sound reminding me of the inherent open-endedness of flight.

In any case, after about fifteen seconds of this kid repeating his question—screaming it at me, reclined in his hammock (always the cool kid)—a few adults nearby caught his meaning before I could and they started laughing uncomfortably. I tried to gauge what was going on with them while trying to decipher what was being shouted at me.

I was still dripping wet from paddling across the rainswollen rivermouth on the lookout for toothy, floating driftwood so I had to check my head. It took an extra second or two to shift to this test in translation. I finally figured out my shrill nine-year-old friend was asking me to explain what "fucking" was.

I shook my head at the kid, refusing the requested explanation. I took a moment to shrug in the general direction of the adults (who shrugged back as if to say, "True, no one knows what to do with this kid.") Shuffling along the sunbleached dust to my own hammock, I couldn't help but laugh at the audacity—that a nine-year-old had managed to bewilder me with so little effort.

I paid the equivalent of four dollars a day for a wall-less shanty right on the soft sand of the beach. I guess the name for it is a "*palapa* hut"—four posts beneath a roof framed with tree limbs. I usually pack a hammock and two lengths of rope when I travel in the tropics. It's extra weight, but I sleep in it for weeks or months if I find a consistent, remote surf spot.

This hidden coastal town claimed to be mosquito-free as a way to draw travellers and stray surfers off the highway. It was a stunning beach that featured two surf spots—one decent beachbreak for west and northwest swells and a world class left that appeared during summer south swells. I paid my taxi driver to take me all the way to the sand from the highway (when we found the right turnoff). On the bumping muddy track west I asked him just how and why there were no mosquitos. We had just passed a fading hand-painted mural of a giant mosquito in a red circle with a slash through it. He just shrugged and said he didn't know why, something to do with the river he thought. I smiled. It was getting late, I was staying the night no matter his answer.

As the sun set, I locked my backpack and surfbag to a post in my palapa and ran across the sand to the beachbreak. Twenty minutes and three decent waves later, I had washed off the grime of buses, stations and city streets. I rinsed off in a little bath house on the sand. A half dozen pale geckos crawled up the walls of the shower stalls, stalking the bugs orbiting the light bulbs.

A fresh south swell was supposed to arrive the next day. If I was lucky I would get a chance to surf the lefthander just out of sight across the rivermouth.

It was already dark when I strung up my hammock and sat at the little plastic table beneath my *palapa*. There were two plastic chairs rounding out my collection of furniture. I didn't expect any company. No games of 45s on this night. Instead I read some Thich Nat Hahn, the only book in English I could find down there. Then I played solitaire without cheating and waited for the onslaught of mosquitos.

I put my cards away and suited up for the first, experimental sleep in the open air on the beach—long pants (as they're called in Seawell), my one pair of socks, a long-sleeve T-shirt that read "The Windy Hills" and a baseball hat to pull over my face. The hammock swayed, the nearby waves lulled me toward sleep.

No bugs yet?

Massive sand crabs threatening me from below? Check.

A sleeping stray that looked a lot like the Muppet dog from "Fraggle Rock" curled up in the sand beneath me? Check.

Mosquitoes?

Wake in my hammock on
The beach under a palm-frond roof—
Roll over, check the surf?

The waves looked fun from my hammock. And then I remembered the bugs! I quickly ran my hands over my face, neck and under my shirt to find the expected topography of bites.

No bugbites at dawn!
So I surf each south swell, then sleep—
As one night becomes months.

I regret not bringing Muppet the Dog back to the U.S. when I finally left that quiet part of Mexico. I miss him. He was the cutest and gentlest dog I ever found in Central and South America. The beach life suited him and he seemed healthy, happy—unlike most strays.

I once believed surfing made me different than non-surfers (and, further, that growing up as a cold-water surfer made me different than warm-water surfers). The wild and wooly ocean beat those delusions out of me over time. I assumed others were learning to let things and their egos go through the humility the ocean forces on every surfer.

But I've been dropped-in on and hassled to no end in the decades I've surfed around the world. Too many hassles to believe there's wisdom of any quality arising from the undisciplined, repetitive pursuit of a quantity of perfect waves.

One of the many reasons I decided to quit surfing involved a Venezuelan twenty-something sharing an isolated, beautiful lineup with me. We couldn't see a city, town or house for miles and miles in any direction. It was a perfect tropical morning with very small, very average waves. Most surfers would sleep in on a morning like that, wait for the next swell to arrive. Rest.

I just wanted to get wet, stretch out the paddling muscles a bit. To this day, I don't truly understand why this other surfer was in the ocean that morning. It wasn't for the waves (they sucked), it wasn't for the expansive views (barely noticed over a perma-scowl). I'd only hung out with this surfer once or twice in a group with some Chilean and Argentineans I'd met—old friends traveling together during a break from university studies.

In the water that day, I realized I was meeting the Venezuelan version of Dale, the six-foot-three French Canadian volleyball hero mentioned at the beginning of this book.

Except this Venezuelan woman was a good surfer, as good as me— maybe better. I'd seen her ripping up a shallow reef break a week earlier. She was fearless and talented. These could be the reasons she wanted to assert her dominance without any provocation from me. Who knows? I certainly don't paddle around and rank surfers according to skill while sharing a tropical lineup with them.

I do my best not to drop in on anyone and steal their wave. If it happens, I apologize and give that surfer one or two waves as reparation. Any other kind of cutthroat behavior is better suited for a football field or boardroom.

Surfing represents the antithesis of competitiveness for me. It's not even a sport in my experience. It's usually not an art form, either. But it approaches art at its best and it most certainly can be transformed (with meditation and single-minded focus) into a Zen practice—just as "temple archery" has been in Japan.

I suppose, for many, surfing is a simple and endlessly creative interaction with nature. And that's more than enough. In fact, that's the essence of its allure and magic. It was never more or less than that for me. "The Innermost Limits of Pure Fun," as the genius filmmaker George Greenough showed us.

Ever since I was a little kid in the cold waters of Seawell, Mass., surfing was an immersion in nature, an escape from stringent society into an intentional act of creativity.

But I don't surf anymore. Not since that Venezuelan woman gave me her worst. My Zen practice asked me to let go of surfing, so I have. As a younger man I often gave people like that Venezuelan the satisfaction they searched for via confrontation.

Seawell was nasty, like any East Coast blue-collar city, and I couldn't afford to lose too many fights. I learned how to take people out—big guys, little quick guys, cement-headed guys, wrestlers, boxers, idiots with weapons. Truthfully, I'm not proud of much from that time in my life. But those things are long gone and I wouldn't be writing any of this if I hadn't experienced them.

Here and there I defended some people and helped a few innocents by beating the shit out of their tormentors, but mostly I fought for thrills and as an ill-conceived form of therapy.

Regardless of intent, I mainly caused a lot of suffering.

But this day in Mexico was too beautiful for me to be distracted by suffering. I simply imagined this Venezuelan woman was ignorant of common courtesy.

I wouldn't rise to the bait. I paddled a little up the beach. Ten minutes later, she seemed to end up near me again in our vast field of ocean. Soon after, she hassled me out of another tiny wave. Maybe I stared at her as she kicked out of that wave. I don't think I cared enough to? But maybe she caught a quick stare of disbelief and took it as a challenge? Who knows?

I didn't wait around. I caught a little right and rode it down the beach to wash her out of my mind. I kicked out, then paddled even farther away. I wasn't rattled yet. I waited for more waves by myself, watching some little kids splashing around the beach with a soccer ball.

I noticed the Venezuelan had gotten out of the water and walked my way. I caught a wave. As I paddled back out, I saw she was wading back in to paddle out toward me. She made no eye contact, spoke no words. I knew what was happening.

I just paddled for the very next wave to get it over with.

It was barely a thigh-high ripple of a wave. The Venezuelan went for it and cut me off. I think I laughed out loud. I can't be sure.

Either way, I caught and rode the next wave to the beach on my belly. I didn't even stand up on my final wave as a member of the "surfing tribe," as they say.

The tribe, I'd learned, is a sad joke.

I walked back to town, gave my board to an eleven-year-old named Jonathan. He had been borrowing my boards every day for months. He was ecstatic. I told him he could keep the board and then asked where his cousin Tania's house was. He told me and paddled out to catch a few waves before his school day began.

I grabbed my favorite board, my Bonzer, and walked to Tania's house. I asked her mother to give it to her daughter who'd already gone to school. Once I explained that Jonathan had my other board and I was leaving that day for America, she was happy that her kid would be able to spend every day in the ocean with her cousin.

She said she could get her to do her schoolwork now, ask her to get straight A's in order to be able to use the surfboard. That seemed fair to me. School's mostly drudgery, so kids need to be bribed sometimes.

I mentioned that I hoped Tania and Jonathan never dropped-in on anyone, ever. I'm not sure she understood, but no matter.

On the way back to my *palapa* hut, a local surfer I'd met caught up to me and said he'd seen what happened in the water. He said a few of the locals were going to have a talk with the Venezuelan woman. I wasn't moved to join the fray.

The whole thing felt like it was happening to someone else, that I was just witnessing it and failing to stay clear. I mean, it never matters who you think you are. Any person at any moment imagines you the way he wants to and reacts how he chooses. I felt like I'd just come to recognize a new way in which I *didn't* exist—there were, in those days, many examples of my insubstantialness piling up around me.

Surfing was as fruitless to me as my ego on that day. Even if I'd screamed at that woman and cut her off on every wave she went for during the next week (and none of the locals would've faulted me), I still would've felt a little bit erased.

But it's all felt different since that day, because I'm no longer afraid of the feeling of erasure.

I simply packed up my gear, gave my board bag to a friend to sell or trade. I gave all my wax to another local who always asked for a little from me out in the lineup. It's hard to find surfwax in the jungle.

I caught a ride out of that Mexican town and bused up the Pacific coastline. I had to wait a day or two for the next bus north, so I went scuba diving outside of Sly Stallone's Acapulco vacation home, replete with helicopter pad. I had a wonky BC vest that wouldn't inflate and deflate reliably. I sank and rose unsteadily during the whole dive, at one stage almost impaling myself on a bed of sea urchins. I held myself afloat horizontally with one hand, my other busied with the button to inflate the vest.

> One finger on the reef
> In a garden of purple spines—
> Echo of my breath.

The vest tightened slowly, slightly—lifting me away.

Later, I drank some beers here and there in the city—wandered around looking for interesting bars, clubs, parks or galleries. I found Acapulco's once-famous cliff diving show. I'd originally seen footage of it as a kid on "ABC's Wide World of Sports," but I caught the nighttime version involving torches and a huge crowd of tourists on the cliffs.

It remains a death-defying spectacle. I enjoyed it, but still felt a little detached somehow.

On the way out of that neighborhood, I found a shop owner who claimed he was a retired cliff diver. He was a nice, drunk guy with a beer belly that made it look like he was hiding a motorcycle helmet under his rhinestone cowboy shirt. We talked for an hour or so.

> The old cliff diver
> Breathes heavy—underneath bloodshot
> Eyes and memories.

I haven't ridden a surfboard since those days in Mexico.

Maybe I resented that Venezuelan woman for a couple of months after the incident and my decision to let surfing go, but I got over that with some thought and effort. She wasn't to blame. After all, she wasn't unique.

I realized at the time I had little control over my perceptions of self. I meditated on this new kind of nothingness every day for months after that Mexico trip.

I bused up the coast some more. Spent a couple days in the frenzy of Mazatlán. I snorkeled with a boatload of tourists by the Isla de Venados off the coast of the city. I swam toward the tip of the island by myself till the current grew too stiff. When I turned around to swim back:

> Current sails purplish
> Jellyfish at my bare chest—blurting
> Curses up my snorkel!

That evening—nursing some ugly, burning welts—I boarded an overnight ferry out of Mazatlán across the Sea of Cortez. I had booked a flight out of Baja back to Seattle. The ship was crowded with Mexican families familiar with the trip across that narrow bit of ocean. I found my third-class seat up on the third deck in a huge room with hundreds of red, reclining seats. I put my book and a small empty backpack on my seat to save it. I tried to beat the crowd to whatever food they sold on the ship. No more than ten minutes later, I came back and a severe-looking Mexican woman had moved my book and bag to the floor, claiming the whole row for her family. This bothered me more than the misguided Venezuelan.

I took her stuff off my seat as she stared me down, murderously. I'm not exaggerating for effect, either. This lady was no joke.

I showed her my ticket, pointed and said in polite fluent Spanish that this was my seat and I would be back soon. She was surprised by my Spanish, maybe softened a bit by it. I was too tired to care.

I left to watch the sunset from an out of the way vantage point on a steel bench on the top deck, starboard side. I noticed some birds following our giant ship as it pulled out of the harbor. The sunset was long, drawn-out and added some nice brushwork to the spectacle of a flock of gannets hunting a school of fish off the front of the ship.

> Seabirds ascend on
> The prow's breeze, glide and divebomb blind
> Fish riding bow waves.

I never went back inside the ship. Never went back to my seat to claim it. I slept on the narrow steel bench on the fourth deck, outdoors all the way across the Sea of Cortez. Didn't even need a blanket, it was perfect out there. I kept thinking of John Steinbeck, that I would have to read that book he wrote about that body of water. I still haven't, but I will.

I woke with a red sunrise over Baja, a little stiff from my night on the steel bench. The wind was slight and quiet.

On land, feeling stripped-down and light on my feet, I decided to cancel my flight and hitchhike or bus my way up the Baja peninsula back to the Boat Ranch, south of Ensenada on the Pacific coast. I didn't know when or how I would get up to Seattle after that, but I'd figure it out. If I could reach the Boat Ranch, I was betting I'd run into a few of the guys who surf the south swells at Cuatro Casas and Shipwrecks each summer.

I got a long ride outside of San Juan from a tiny Australian surfer named Rory who'd saved for a year to fly to L.A., buy a Volkswagen van and surf Baja by himself. He wore a yellow Gath helmet when he surfed on the one board he'd brought, a nine-foot-six longboard. He told me he hated the helmet but, since he surfed completely alone most of the time, he was afraid he'd get knocked out by his board or hit a rock and drown in the middle of nowhere.

Rory and I had a great time during the week and a half we traveled together. I didn't tell him I knew how to surf, or that I'd quit recently. A few days into the trip, we found a pair of swim fins for sale on the side of the highway on a fold-out table covered in pots and pans, spatulas and giant dented spoons. I bought the fins because Rory insisted he'd teach me to bodysurf. He'd seen I was a good swimmer, told me it'd be fun for me to try. I was exhausted that day, I grabbed the things so we could get back in the van and I could get some sleep.

I pulled the fins on a couple days later and swam out to Rory at a left-hander he had to himself one evening. Three or four seals were swimming around him, unhappy with his invasion of their kelp beds. I snuck up on the Aussie and barked at him. He jumped, almost fell off his board and cursed me effusively.

I asked him to tell me what he knew about bodysurfing (as if I'd never tried before). It was just a lark for me as he gave me a basic lesson about keeping my head up, kicking like mad, angling at takeoff, planing on my inside hand, rolling to use the side of my body to stay higher on the steepening face of a wave. He pointed out some rocks and shallow spots on the reef to watch out for as the tide dropped. He gave a pretty good breakdown of the basics, actually.

I pretended to miss a few waves. He remained encouraging. I let him catch his own set wave and when he was on the inside I caught a medium-sized one with perfect shape and angled at take off, planed on my left palm and rolled on my side to speed down the line up high on the wave's face. I stalled on my belly in the pocket of a bowling hollow section, slipping out of the barrel onto the face again. I kept going until I passed him standing on the rocks in thigh-deep water. I wanted to catch the look on his face.

He was justifiably stunned and started hooting at me like a crazy person! I opened my mouth to tell him I'd pranked him, but then just let it go because I was so surprised at how ecstatic he was for me right then.

It was a selfless species of joy.

During the drive north, Rory told me he thought he'd witnessed something rare in the surfing world—a natural dropping into the fold, later in life. According to him, I'd found my previously-unknown-yet-already-mastered art form.

He was a naïve guy in some ways, incredibly experienced and capable in so many other ways. There wasn't a cynical bone in Rory's yellow-helmeted body.

A day or two later, the van broke down and we sat on the side of a dirt road miles from the coast and even further from the highway. We sat in the summertime desert's heat for a day and a half waiting for someone to drive by. No one came.

We ran low on water so we were forced to walk inland that evening as it cooled down. We walked all night, slept in the shade of some rocks the next day and hiked half of the next night.

At the end of our hike on the second night, I kicked at a plant out of frustration and exhaustion:

> Yucca spine pierces
> My second toe's cuticle—
> Fierce pain burns my foot!

I had to sit on the sandy ground, remove my boot and pull out the needle with some tweezers from our tiny first-aid kit. It was a bloody disaster by the light of a headlamp, but we kept on. The sun would be up and scorching soon.

Climbing and descending gave me some trouble, the flat ground wasn't too bad. I grew dog tired and my limping was getting more pronounced. Neither of us spoke about infection.

I think Rory and I both realized we'd best find some help soon. We had another twenty-four or thirty-six hours left in us at best. Coming down a small hill spiked with dead yucca, I spooked an animal out of hiding:

> Black-Tailed Jack Rabbit
> Bolts five-feet high—lands twenty
> Feet from my boot tops!

Rory thought my frightened face was pretty funny. When he caught his breath after laughing himself hoarse, he reminded me that Baja was far less harsh than the outback of Australia. I didn't know either way, so I didn't say much about it.

At the same moment the rabbit leapt, Rory had also spotted lights from a cattle ranch in the distance that I hadn't yet seen. So he was laughing a little in relief as well.

We slept in a rocky ditch—a scar from a flash flood during the spring—until the ranch showed signs of stirring to life. We didn't want to frighten or upset anyone in the early morning darkness.

It was a terribly thirsty and long walk in the dark, but maybe not the worst thing I've ever gone through. I was only in pain for the last few miles.

After feeding us and letting us shower and rest, two ranchers drove us back to the Australian's van (an eight-hour drive) and fixed our flat and our engine. They spent around nine hours working on the engine and one blown tire for us. We paid them with what we had—sunglasses, surf clothes and Eighty-eight dollars' worth of Mexican currency between us.

Have you ever seen a wiry, seventy-three-year-old man wrench a flat off its rim with a crowbar and sledgehammer? Chupo found the puncture using water poured along the tire's surface out of an old beer bottle. He patched the hole from the inside with rubber cement, wedged the tire back onto the rim, inflated it and made sure the bead was perfect.

It was mind-blowing and ordinary as the day is long all at once.

I reached the Boat Ranch near the town of Jaramillo on a Saturday morning. The gate was chained and padlocked and the waves were small but looking to get better on a dropping tide. I picked my way down the eroding cliffs to get in the water and glide across a few small ones.

I had the place to myself.

Rory and I had parted at the edge of the highway when we found the dirt road I was searching for. He was going farther north to a couple spots he heard about near Santo Tomás.

Floating in the lineup that day at Cuatro Casas, I wondered if Shipwrecks to the south was picking up more swell. No way for me to check, too far to walk by myself. I was done with walking in the desert anyway.

I caught a few fun waves, dodging kelp as I slid along the lumpy rights. After three or four rides I felt rejuvenated. I resigned myself to staying the night back in Jaramillo at an old friend's place (if he still lived there). Martín was once the King of Thieves in Jaramillo, also known as the Town of Thieves. He'd let me stay the night if he wasn't yet drunk when I found him. If he was really drunk he wouldn't recognize me, wouldn't be able to distinguish me from the voices he heard while hammered. Martín scared a lot of people with his drunk and unstable antics. As I remembered all of this, I caught one last wave down the line.

Clambering onto shore, I could see some dust kicking up north of the point. Someone was driving by Cuatro Casas. If there was a south swell arriving soon, surfers would be pulling in to camp on the cliffs for the night. If I was lucky, it would be someone with a key to the Boat Ranch and I would get to sleep in an old trawler's teak-wood cabin like I often did as a younger man.

Turned out the approaching truck was driven by a guy who started the Boat Ranch, John Staley. He was one of the originals. He'd towed several of the old boats down to that spot and propped them up on barrels and beam ends. He drove to Mexico from San Clemente almost every south swell from April to October. He knew Martín in town, Martín's wife, Lety, and a lot of the other locals on that coast. The few fishermen living on the cliffs always looked forward to seeing John because he bought lobsters whenever they beached their dories nearby. He always had extra Tecate and Pacífico for his friends as well.

John was excited once he recognized me. His Spanish wasn't that good so he needed my help. Something was urgent. He handed me a cold Pacifico Ballena and yes-yes'd me about a ride up to the States, but assured me there was swell on the way so we'd go on Monday or Tuesday after the waves died down. I was fine with that. I was pretty excited to have connected with someone from the Boat Ranch I knew.

But John and I didn't talk much, he just pushed and pulled me over to a fisherman's shack out on the cliffs at the tail-end of the Cuatro Casas lineup. There used to be a big arch of sandstone that stuck out into the water right near the shack—a high-tide spot called Arches that only broke on big south swells. The arch had fallen into the sea, but I'd seen a photo of it once in a surf magazine from the '60s. The wave still appeared for a couple of hours a few times each summer.

A fisherman named Lipo (Lee-poh) and his wife lived there—they were older and their kids had long since moved to Ensenada, three hours or so to the north. Cobbled together from cinderblocks, tin, aluminum siding, cloudy glass and bricks, their home stood about fifteen or twenty feet from the ever-eroding edge of the desert cliffs above the high-tide line. They lived as close as you can get to the Pacific without toppling in.

John insisted he needed me to translate for him and Lipo about his sick wife's medicine. Emperatriz, or "Empe" as he called her, was ill with some kind of serious stomach issue. I never really figured out if it was a flu bug or related to her diet, maybe dehydration or just old age and the harsh setting taking their toll.

There's no hospital, medicine, food or water for miles and miles in that part of the desert. Lipo ran his gas-powered generator for a few hours each night so he and Empe could watch some television or read the paper. But Empe, Lipo said, hadn't been able to do anything for days.

They'd made a run to a drugstore up the highway three days before and the washboard dirt roads had wrung out almost all of her remaining energy. They didn't find any drugs that worked for Empe and she hadn't left the car since that day.

Empe wouldn't allow Lipo to carry her the last few feet into their home. Instead, he managed to pull the car around the shack, along the cliffs (a big risk), then he backed it up to the seaside wall of their home.

During Empe's final few days, he swung the two giant doors of the Caprice open to catch a crossbreeze for her. At night, he piled blankets on her in the back seat and crawled in to comfort her. She barely slept, he said. But when she did he tried to drink tequila quickly so he could get some sleep as well. Lipo looked like this was riding him hard.

When I looked inside the rusted Caprice Classic, Empe sat with her hands folded in her lap in a blue rectangle of shade. I spoke briefly with her, she rasped something about "*una via...*" I couldn't catch all of it over the rising northwest wind and John and Lipo's stunted efforts at conversation. Empe was gray, fading—skin like tissue paper.

> Her pain stitches
> A pall of dust and shade across
> Her backseat deathbed.

I could see the worry creasing Lipo's wind-burned face. He was telling me quietly to tell John that he couldn't leave his wife, couldn't go out to sea for fish, couldn't go in to town with or without her. He described her howl on the washboard roads, how he couldn't do that to her again, how he'd never forget that sound.

They were going to run out of staples in a few days. John told Lipo we'd make a food, water and gas run for him the next day if they were okay for the night. I caught a little relief flitting across Lipo's eyes.

This made me take a clear-eyed, long look around at the empty kiln of a landscape surrounding their home. The "four houses" of the surf spot's name had dwindled to three over the decades. There were some seasonal surf camps here and there. No question, it was a harsh place to live year round. I'd only managed six consecutive months myself all those years earlier at the Boat Ranch when I first left Seawell.

I slipped into the front seat of the Caprice and tried to talk with Empe one last time. I tried to gauge her pain. It was impossible, as she barely looked at me. Flies crawled across the scarf she wore on her head.

I decided it would be best to tell Lipo which medicines to give and when.

Out in the merciless sun, John reached into his brown bag, pulling out three jars of pills, pointing at his own gut and chest and head. John looked in at me, asking me to tell Lipo: "If you can get her stomach settled and she ate a few good meals with lots of water she might be okay."

I started to climb out so I could translate when Empe spoke out the far door of the car to no one in particular. Her voice strained with needling pain: "*La via de elegancia, la via de elegancia.*"

She sounded like a dried branch of cholla cactus when a low stiff wind catches in its mesh of cracks and holes.

> I explain the drugs
> That might help—but he knows morphine
> Is all she might need.

She'd lost interest in eating, water and medication. No one needed me to translate our mutual understanding of this plainest of unspoken facts.

Empe died the next evening, just after the sun went down when the air started to cool—several hours after the south swell arrived on the reef below the cliff.

Only John and I had been in the water the day Empe died. No other surfers showed up that weekend for the swell—odd for that time of year in Northern Baja.

We didn't feel like going in the water while Empe was so close to dying right there on the cliff above where each ride ended in deeper water. But Lipo asked us to. He said Empe had always liked watching the surfers, so why not that day?

"*¿Por qúe no? ¿Es un proceso, no?*" I caught myself thinking for a moment.

Late in the morning on the day Empe died, John paddled slowly next to me as I kicked with my swimfins up and over the shoulders of eight-foot swells in the deeper water in front of the Caprice Classic where Empe still sat.

Our hair was still dry in patches as we reached the take-off spot for Cuatro Casas. The Caprice was pointed right at John and I as we took off and shared perfect waves for a couple of hours.

We are silent in
The surf—we wonder if Empe
Sees us glide and splash.

When we got out of the water and walked up the incline, past Lipo's rundown boat with its mismatched oars and leaky outboard, we saw him lurch into Empe's car. Barefoot, we ran up to his shack.

I took John's board and hung back. He knew Lipo better than I did, and I didn't want to intrude.

I walked back to the Boat Ranch to rinse off with rainwater collected and piped to a showerhead. The water was warmed from the morning sun shining on the storage barrel.

John walked back to me, his wetsuit now peeled to his waist, with a confused look on his dripping-wet face.

"Is she ok?" I asked.

"About the same, I think."

"What happened? Why did Lipo jump into the Caprice?"

"He said he heard her whispering something and thought she was finally dying. She hadn't said anything to him since howling on those washboard roads. He figured that was it—that she was dying. He's pretty shaken."

"Jesus. That's rough. I didn't want to say anything yesterday. What's it, like five hours to a decent hospital? She doesn't look like she's going to make it much longer. She didn't even bother to tell me how much pain she was in yesterday afternoon. I couldn't get her to talk. What did she say to Lipo?"

"He said she pointed out at the ocean and said, '*La Via de Elegancia*.'"

"Huh. That's what she said yesterday. Not to me, really. She whispered it out the door of the car just before I helped you explain those medications to Lipo. '*The Path of Elegance*, maybe? '*The Way of Elegance*' is a better way to say it, I think."

"What does that mean? Anyways, Lipo told me he has no idea what she's talking about. Maybe a street she remembers from Ensenada as a kid? Maybe from San Miguel de Allende? They traveled there one time when they were younger. I guess Empe's aunt was a famous painter or something. Lipo's not sure what Empe's saying, but he seems to think she's not going to make it through the night."

"I don't know," I said. "I feel like I've heard that phrase, 'La Via de Elegancia.' What's the name of that street in Ensenada lined with all the brothels and bars?"

"What?"

"Nothing…nothing."

THE END.

The View like the sky, leave it as it is.
The Meditation like a mountain, leave it as it is.
The Action like the ocean's waves, leave it as it is.
The ocean can be busy or still, but it never leaves its bed.

—Supreme Resting
Lama Surya Das quoting
"The Light of Wisdom, Volume 1"
Commentary by Jamgön Kongtrül,
Root Text by Padmasambhava

BOOK V

SWEENEY
IN-CLEAR-LIGHT

FROM THE TRAVEL JOURNALS OF
SWEENEY O' SWEENEY

TRANSCRIBED BY
DAVE ROBINSON

chapter 01

I chop wood most days, split kindling with my hatchet. The wood stove my cousin and I installed in my dry-docked trawler in the forest does yeoman's work to fight back the cold. Seawell, Mass., can get frigid for months. The other day, some of the water I hauled across the golf course and through the woods froze in my arms before I reached my boat.

It's quietest out here once the birds have gone on their various migrations. When I see a straggler lingering in the trees, I listen. Their songs remind me of friends who rarely visit now.

Felipe, my redheaded friend from the Oaklands neighborhood, used to come out each week to play 45s and drink bottles of beer. He's raising a family now. He digs for old records and listens at home with what little spare time he finds:

> Late winter evening,
> The cardinal tilts its head
> To the wind's music.

Cooped up for too long, my discipline lags. I walk into downtown Seawell to place bets or go drinking. Soon I remember why I remain hidden in my boat, the Kemp Aaberg, for long stretches of time.

Living in the out-of-bounds woods on a golf course—meditating, bodysurfing Seawell beach a bit, writing some poems—has changed me in so many ways. Downtown Seawell, with its myriad sadnesses, sent me looking for shelter regularly as a younger man. After recovering, each time, I unwittingly dove headfirst back into the ongoing current of suffering. These days I float more than struggle, but this change is the fruit of determined practice.

Still, I do get lonesome out here now and again. Downtown Seawell quickly reminds me of everyone's lonesomeness.

Hand pressing the side
Of her head, sitting in a snowdrift—
The ambulance arrives.

They say the seed of our death is the only thing granted to us at the moment of our birth—suffering is the reliable transport between the start and finish of a lifetime. Feels right to me. Seawell, its people and this dust mote of a planet, remain essentially the same while our chosen illusions are in a state of constant flux. Though I'm learning it's more that Seawell, people and the world are changing incessantly. Nothing but change and change is nothing but suffering in a universe that's everything and empty all at once, right? That's physics and Buddhism for ya! But I don't really know anything, to tell you the truth.

Canine icicles guard
Snowbanks in the alley behind
My bookie's barbershop.

ᗣ ŏ ᴜ ᠁

But there is a way out of suffering; that's the second thing I learned when I looked into Buddhism. I try to find ways out each day, different methods for all the different moments.

Years ago, some construction project gone awry, a company dumped hundreds of granite columns and rough tablets in a swamp in East Seawell. I often visited the place to climb and sit atop the quarried bits of stone by some overgrown railroad tracks. Jutting, immovable and sinking sculptures everywhere you looked—like jumbled thrones for a lost king and his certifiable advisers.

I explored that place for many years, but I was only able to write one or two satisfactory haikus about my visits. Both happened during a windless flurry of snow, the swamp not yet fully frozen for the season. I wrote them almost without thinking in threadbare sheets of snow on two granite slabs:

> Dusk on the solstice—
> Idle chickadees scold
> The hungry woodpecker.

Of the Western poets, I always thought John Keats captured best the fleeting nature of human life. Carved in a tombstone that does not feature his name, his epitaph reads: "Here lies One Whose Name Was Writ in Water."

Leaving that swamp, I knew the wind would blow, more snow might fall or with a few minutes of sunlight, my words would fade from the face of that abandoned granite.

> Here walks one
> Whose name is writ in
> A dusting of snow.

chapter 02

If it is a bad winter for surf and the weather is as raw as usual, I'm usually stir-crazy by early spring. Even now, I drink too much beer. Back in the day, I liked to drink beer *and* fight in the bars, pubs, taverns and dives. Anywhere, really. Those days are gone. Not much bothers me enough to make me angry anymore.

Yet I can't shake the hold the ocean has on me: I'm forever bothered by the day-in, day-out sight of a flat cold North Atlantic.

Most animals I see at this time of year seem impatient with the sour weather as well. A few birds return as the snow melts and mud season sets in around my boat in the trees.

> Sparrows hop through
> Budding thickets into weak sun—
> Three flinch at my glance.

Ͳ ୪ ℧ ♏

I set a small, flat rock beneath an old oak in the garden cemetery on the edge of South Seawell. I sit on it, back against the rough trunk, to read or meditate in the sun. Each year I'm more grateful for the season's turning. Once, a favorite animal of mine nearly ran headlong into my seated form on the rock. She was eight feet away by the time she caught sight of me at the base of that huge oak. We shared, for an instant, the distraction brought on by that mild day:

> Red fox slips between
> Gravestones and daffodils—veers
> Downhill from my stare.

ᛏ ᚤ ᚢ ᛘ

Leaving Seawell on foot or hitching rides brings me through farms and fields in the surrounding towns. I take extra apples in my pack, twist them in half with my hands to feed to any horses I find.

> April hailstorm sails
> Across fenced-in meadows—spooked
> Mares gather and bolt!

Spring in Massachusetts is harsh for travel, more so if you are unable to leave where you live.

> Long tails and manes flying,
> Corralled horses can only run
> In circles for their fear.

chapter 03

Fresh out of apples, far from home and lost in the sameness of factory-farm cornfields, I met an elderly farmer. He'd always lived in that corner of southern Illinois with his wife in an old white farmhouse surrounded on three sides by a forest. I found the place lush in mid-summer, the weather unseasonably cool and dry all the days of my visit. The sun and shade in his yard allowed for perfecting summer laziness and easy contemplation.

I lifted the two-year-old daughter of a friend from the grass. Leaving the adults with their gentle gossip and banter, I chased songbirds along the edge of the trees to make the child laugh.

Sam, the white-haired rangy farmer, couldn't pick the Dalai Lama out of a police line-up, yet he was clearly a Zen adept. He radiated calmness, resided in an abiding nature.

As a younger man, Sam converted his basement into a barroom and later into a casual gallery cluttered with hundreds of his oil paintings. He gently mocked himself, showing us the landscapes—the harvest of his late-onset hobby.

Sam had fallen in with flashes of beauty—as if aware they were of questionable company—surrounding him in that part of the world. He laughed at and forgave himself in the same breath all afternoon:

The old farmer tells us:
"Whatever, I love it, Whatever…"—
Adopting greatgrandkid's slang.

chapter 04

The poet Weldon Kees disappeared or killed himself near the height of his creative powers. He's always been one of my favorite artists—a painter, jazz musician and poet with a clearly autumnal interior existence. He was a dark realist working out his mortality on the page, piano and canvas. I always felt he'd discovered how to be lost and found all at once—he felt such despair for the human condition, but he took care to express the qualities of that condition as a kind of flaring energy in his poems. Such a razor-thin line between the suffering and enlightenment each moment of the day offers us.

> *A good night for the fireplace to be*
> *crackling with flames—or so he figured,*
> *crumpling the papers he could only see*
> *as testimonials to long plateaus of emptiness*

> —from "The Heat in the Room"
> by Weldon Kees

An old friend of mine, Marc Mueller, a talented poet and lifelong surfer from Seawell (there are few of us caught dabbling in both), came to visit when I lived out west. We surfed Cuatro Casas and Shipwrecks in Baja, and San Onofre, Trails or Sunset Cliffs while north of the border. When the Pacific went flat, we drove east for an hour up to seven thousand feet and into the old mining town of Julian, California. The town sits in an alpine forest that even gets a bit of snow in winter—all this so close to the coastal desert, beaches and sunshine of San Diego.

We ate apple pie, ice cream and drank beer before visiting an old bookstore. I bought a National Geographic *Guide to North American Birds*, gently used. I think Marc bought some of Edward Abbey's essays. As we walked back through town in perfect crisp fall weather, we saw some locals dressed as cowboys and whores re-enacting a famous shootout from Julian's past.

We drove out of town, farther east, and down the mountainside dropping us into high-altitude desert near the Blair Valley's dry lakebed. That part of the Anza Borrego desert cools down enough in the fall to allow for camping.

We ate some mushrooms and set up camp at the base of a five-hundred-foot pile of sun-bleached boulders and cacti. As the mushrooms took hold, we climbed to the top, keeping our eyes peeled for rattlesnakes and scorpions. The green, twisting ocotillo stretched ten or fifteen feet into the air and resembled seaweed in a slack current. The sunset empurpled everything below on the alkali lakebed. We could look into Mexico to the south.

It was a great thing, to be high with one of my oldest friends during that still evening. As we picked our way down through prickly pear and cholla back to cold beers at our camp, I told Marc about the time I found an old fire pit nearby. It was tucked behind a boulder half the size of a boxcar, beneath another ridge of boulders. It was a secret campsite for those slipping north over the border.

I saw a group of immigrants nearby once, they call them "illegals" these days, resting out on the dry lakebed at sunup. I felt silly for backcountry camping alone and getting drunk under the same stars lighting their hidden route north.

Fleeing suffering their
Ten thousand fires painted this rock—
Old matchbooks, empty fifths.

ᛏ ᛟ ᚢ ᛘ

The night Marc and I camped, we drank beers and built our fire in a small steel tub propped at an angle on stones to keep stray sparks and embers in check. It gets cold up there once the sun goes down.

We snapped off white creosote twigs from the branches around us, lit them in our fire and studied their burning. They seemed to writhe in pain as the flames climbed and consumed them, creeping toward our fingertips.

Late that night in our tents we both heard some kind of large creature come into our camp, panting and circling us as we tried to sleep. Neither of us said anything about the animal as we broke down camp in the early, hot sun.

The creature showed itself as we rolled up our sleeping bags and we both laughed:

High desert autumn—
Raven wingbeats sound like wolfbreath
Outside my tent near dawn.

ᛏ ᛟ ᚢ ᛘ

Later that fall, drunk and alone in that same valley, I was shocked by the midnight appearance of kangaroo rats hopping throughout my camp. Their burrows riddle the sand around the creosote shrubs, but I'd never seen any other sign of a single rodent before that night. Suddenly, hundreds surrounded me by the fire. I double-checked that all my gear was zipped up tight and then enjoyed the spectacle.

Packing up my truck at dawn, I had another visitor who must've assumed I was a giant rodent for the taking:

> The desert kit fox
> Ignores offered water—devours
> A rolling apple whole!

Marc Mueller wrote a long poem about our hike to the Kumeyaay people's ancient mortero sites, agave roasting pits and pictographs on massive boulders nearby. But the two verses I like best focus on a chimney crack between two rock faces topped by the nest of a great horned owl. After listening to the birdcall most of the night, we decided we had to find its nest. We wouldn't have known it was there but for the piles of regurgitated remains.

> Desert dusk, a scrim
> of rock; sun mushrooms and bruises
> the bleached eyrie.

> Last night's owl questioned
> The whole valley, but said nothing
> Of its litter of bones.

> —from "Desert Disrepair, A Poem for Edward Abbey"
> by Marc Mueller

When I returned east later that season, I made money raking leaves in North Seawell. All day out in the cold wind and weakening sunshine—not a bad way to make more money to travel.

Great flocks of geese and ducks pull each other across the sky heading

south over the Atlantic as they do every year. Vultures, hawks and falcons
soar and slowly spiral south above meadows and marshes. But the crows
aren't going anywhere, they'll stick out the rough weather. Crows are
intelligent but are at their best when they let their form in flight be as
slapdash as the wind wishes:

> Fall winds on the headland—
> A blue-bird day for crows laughing at
> All these dogs on their chains.

♈ ♉ ♋ ♌

I visit an old Coldwater Oak tree south of Seawell each autumn I'm
home, usually after the leaves are down. It's several hundred years old,
with a massive and ancient elegance. The trunk's circumference is nearly
fifty feet and its canopy must hang one hundred feet above the ground.
There are very few Coldwater Oaks left in New England, as this lone
mature tree survived the blight from late in the 19th century. I've never
seen another of any real size.

One evening in late October, I found it brimming with starlings.
There must've been one thousand birds in the bare branches, and the
racket they made drowned out all other noise in that forest. I sat to listen,
to drown out the clashing thoughts in my own mind that day.

Ten minutes later, with the birds still at their voluble best and my
mind settled somewhat, a lone crow landed on an upper branch to make
its feelings known:

> Deafening chatter
> Stops dead at one crow's raw command—
> October light on starlings!

chapter 05

As a kid in Seawell, I did a lot of things besides surfing during the colder months. Wetsuits were bad back then and I just enjoyed doing anything remotely fun with whoever else was interesting. My friend Nicholas Leblanc and I played pond hockey whenever possible. Nicky was French Canadian, so he had an innate love for all things hockey. But he's gone now; he died from cystic fibrosis in his mid-thirties. It was hard to watch him go, even though he'd suffered enough, even though all of us old Seawell friends knew he was going to die young if no cure was found. We were told this in junior high. We were told, by a teacher who had lost his own child, that Nicky had no more than five years—according to the doctors in Boston. Nicky beat out those kinds of predictions for a couple of decades running.

I have great memories of riding around Seawell and the Merrohawke Valley looking for "good ice" to play some shinny with him. We called him "Nicky the Hack" or "the Hack" or just "Hack"—partly due to his chopping and slashing on the ice, partly due to his omnipresent cough. It was a sort of rough offering of compassion from his oldest friends. Nicky didn't mind the name, he told me that much. He knew we loved him, kindnesses be damned (as they oftentimes are in Seawell among those who've known each other for too long).

The Hack didn't surf, but these searches for good ice with him always felt similar to looking for a surf spot to me—this checking of ponds and lakes and swamps around Seawell. You need the right tide, wind, swell size, period, swell direction and current for a winter surf session to come together around here. The Hack and I sought out ponds in or out of the wind, in or out of the sun, maybe one with a stone retaining wall on one edge to shoot the puck off. We eyed our thermometers with suspicion morning, Noon and night. We hoped to find one with the snow already whisked away by the wind. When we finally chose a pond, we shoveled and swept snow, hoping to uncover perfect ice underneath.

These days I often seek out good ice by myself. I miss all of my friends who've died young: Nicholas, Vann, Steve, Cam, Ted and Eileen. Drugs, drinking, car accidents, genetic disease, heart attacks—I keep skating, bodysurfing, writing, traveling and meditating partly because the repeated loss of friends—of these kids—has given me insight. I'm at least grateful to be more aware of the things that matter.

And skating with a stick and puck slapping at a huge sheet of good ice, whether night or day, is the closest I've come to meditation in action (other than surfing). You move, you glide through space without thought and little effort. It seems unnatural to think of anything more than what is going on right in that very moment:

> Skateblades cut shining
> Nighttime ice—heartbeats splinter
> With each groan from my weight.

Everything slips away the moment there's an attempt at grasping anyway.

> Moonless night, blackness beneath
> Frozen pond—the two-faced mirror
> Catches emptiness twice.

ᛏ ŏ ᚢ ᛘ

I met the poet David Budbill a couple of times. He sometimes travels south to visit and read at a college about an hour outside of Seawell, up in the woods. Budbill knows the look of a long winter in New England. There's a cosmic futility that forces itself out into the open during the cold and dark stretches:

> I can't say the sun is going down.
> We haven't seen the sun for two months.
> Who cares?
> —*from the poem "The Sixth of January"*
> *by David Budbill*

And Budbill's friend and fellow poet of the North, Hayden Carruth, tried to help us all through:

IT'S TRUE

> The night left flowers
> of snow in my plum tree. Now
> the wind is rising.
> —*from Hayden Carruth's book "Doctor Jazz"*

chapter 06

I met a Japanese backpacker in Canoa, Ecuador, during my second visit there many years ago. Like me, he preferred traveling alone, surfing alone and sitting around in the evenings drinking Pilsener, the local beer.

We took a memorable trip up to Mompiche and caught six- to eight-foot left-handers that lined up in perfect symmetry for three days. We'd catch the wave at its peak just beyond exposed volcanic rock, drop in and bottom turn into the tree-sheltered hook of a small bay. The point hosted a tall, vine-draped jungle that blocked the prevailing northwest winds.

The wave, wind, reef, sand and trees came together to produce a little isolated magic for us up by the border of Colombia. Out past the tip of the point, we had to contend with wind-chatter on the face of the wave. Our first bottom turns cut through the chop in the trough as the wave broke above our head and walled up in front of us for the length of a few football fields. After the wave swung in under the shelter of the jungled point, there wasn't a breath of wind and the water went smooth. It was like surfing across the lens of a 400-yard-wide magnifying glass focused on a perfectly shaped sand bank.

While we visited, most of the locals were surfing in a national contest in Montanita many miles to the south. We rented the last cabin on stilts right at the base of the point—so close to the ocean that the whitewater washed under, six feet below us, as we slept.

Two weeks later, back in Canoa, as another huge swell arrived we were told, that very cabin had washed away into the Pacific.

Some years after that trip, I traveled to Tofino in Western Canada to find my Japanese friend. Matsuo Kobayashi was not easy to find, since he made his living developing rare and powerful strains of marijuana in the forests of Vancouver Island. He'd actually dropped out of university in Kyoto at the age of nineteen and migrated to Canada with his family's reluctant blessing. Matsuo made himself into a talented, self-taught botanist. His buds were highly sought-after each summer and he lived a humble, cash-only existence with his surplus funds buried in the dirt of his massive backyard. "I cannot open a bank account. Legally, I can only send so much money home to my family. I don't know what else to do with all of it," he once told me.

Matsuo hired me for a spring and a summer that year and we took almost daily hikes into the wilderness to plant seeds and tend to his plants with Roshi, his silver Labrador retriever. Roshi weighed about seventy-five pounds and had been trained by Matsuo to do two things: sniff out our trail back to the truck once we'd planted our seeds and frighten off curious black bears during our hikes in and out of the bush.

Usually the bears we saw were already running away from us and our snarling dog. Twice, I dropped the fifty-pound bag of soil I carried on my shoulders because I thought I was about to be mauled. Matsuo Kobayashi never dropped his soil or tools.
He hardly slowed his pace through the forest whenever Roshi flushed something out of the deep woods with sudden ferocity.

I felt I aged five years during these few brief instances of involuntary terror. My Japanese guide was more stoic. During the first encounter I will relate here, Matsuo was singing a Tom Waits song quietly to himself and I don't believe he missed a beat when the abrupt crashing began in the brush.

I recovered my frayed wits as Matsuo plodded past me up the narrow trail, crooning: "You...can never hold...back spring," he whistled the clarinet's notes, "you can be sure I will never stop believing...the blushing rose that will climb, spring ahead or fall behind, winter dreams the same dream every time. Baby you...can never hold back spring."

> Wake of trembling
> Needles—scared fawn doubles back,
> Melts into the pines.

Weeks later, as I walked ahead of Matsuo trying to keep pace with his dog:

> Roshi's growl and sudden
> Thrashing drops my heart in the dirt—
> A small buck skips away.

Roshi trotted out of a thicket with her wagging tail slapping branches and trunks—proud as punch. Her "master" hiked by my frozen form, tossed his dog a treat for doing her job while telling me, "Well, I don't get too upset in the bush these days. Not like you, anyway.

> "But don't worry, my friend,
> I feel my death will show the same
> Results as yours."

chapter 07

The first days of summer in Seawell are long affairs of light. I like to get up in the cool darkness, around four-thirty in the morning, if there are waves:

> Shelf of watery clouds
> Reflects June's faint sunrise beyond
> Green waves soaked through with light.

After a couple of hours of bodysurfing, I'll eat some eggs and cheese on toast, drink black tea and drive two or three hours inland. It's quietest during a weekday before the schools release the kids for summer. I find and climb a tiny mountain, sure to be one of the oldest on Earth.

On the bald summit I eat lunch, meditate a little and try to absorb the sight of the northern forest folding along ridges and mountainsides.

> Longest-day sunshower,
> The low valley quilted green—
> Rain beads on birch leaves.

I descend and drive back to the coast to bodysurf past sunset and on into the tranquil darkness, looking for an early moonrise. The ocean is often still cold at this time of year, the west wind slackens at dusk if I'm lucky. This leaves the North Atlantic smooth as stained glass, silvering and tinted orange under the last light from beyond the Avalon Marshes:

Lull between waves—summer
Raindrops splash to blend concentric
Moments with orange light.

chapter 08

I've spent a lot of time in the coastal desert of Baja when the Pacific is flat. It's nearly as beautiful. But when the waves arrive from the southern hemisphere in late summer and early autumn, combing the rock reefs and lonesome points, that desolate part of the world casts its spell.

South swell hits Baja
Yucca signposts pull me offroad—
Fires, cold beers, the smashed coast.

I surf past moonrise, a white trembling path on the sea. Racing along walls of water at high tide, other travelers light fires above the shoreline tumbling with smooth round stones. Strangers sit on the edge of the sandstone cliffs, drink beers, whistle and hoot at every turn I make on my inside run—the waveface warbling with backwash off the gray cobble.

One more wave—always, *always* one more wave. After paddling out under the risen full moon, sitting up on my board, I realize I'm no longer alone in the water:

Fall migrant's apple-
Sized eyeball peeks at me—where's
The calf's gray mother!?

ᛏ ᛜ ᛋ ᛗ

I love the city of my birth, but it is an unquestionably edgy place. I've always felt the need to be on guard against thieves, addicts and enemies while at home. These are some of Seawell's living scars and I accept them, but all this wears on my tolerance.

Yet I know a woman so effortlessly compassionate she remains calm and selfless within the steady, diverse donnybrook known as Seawell, Mass.

She remains young, beautiful and unassuming in my mind's eye—floating through, while fully engaged in the fray. She always told me she wasn't perfect:

> November winds
> Rustle the ash-blonde city willow
> Singing for empty swingsets.

Even so, I wish I were more like her. I try, most days. As they say in Ecuador: "*Es un proceso.*" What else can you do, really, if you already recognize the folly of the ego? Long ago, as a child, I lost interest in leading an unexamined life.

Most days I try to cultivate enough humor and stillness to watch everything and everyone I know (including myself) disappear through death. I achieve moments of insight and calm. I laugh at myself a few times each day:

> Rake golden piles
> Then sit still—birch leaves scatter
> Across squares of lawn.

I'm working to dispel that supposedly inevitable pang of terror—to be better prepared and accepting of my death. It isn't easy:

The rake combs at weeds,
Scrapes stones—a jangle of tines
Carries on a cold breeze.

chapter 09

Downtown Seawell is buried—muffled by falling, deepening snow. It gets dark around four beneath these last clouds dragging behind a nor'easter. Ten thousand streetlights and windowpanes cast weak collective light that reflects off the blanket of snow, then back down off the ceiling of low clouds. It's my favorite time to walk the streets in heavy boots, coat, gloves, hat and a hood. After a few hours outside, it becomes impossible to resist a couple of beers in a warm, deserted public house when you look in and see an empty seat by a roaring fire. I wrote this poem while drinking a pint of the black stuff in the "snug" of The Skeff Bar in the Acre neighborhood:

> Snow-clotted skies glow
> Above a rough geometry—
> The snowbanked city.

Eventually wind, false thaws and city workers get rid of the bulk of the snow. Freckled with bits of trash, the brown matted grass appears again. Who knows for how long? The brick eaves of the mill buildings remain edged with ice and warped snow. Things look pretty dingy, though the weather can always turn for the worse:

False squalls at the bus
Stop—New Year's Eve winds rip snow
Sideways from mill ruins!

I have to bodysurf, play pond hockey or flee to the tropics each year to get through the winter. Practicing meditation every day works best to keep me from getting bogged down. But I'm an undisciplined animal—a great ape, really. I distract myself with voracious reading and writing, or beer and weed or meeting friends at the pub.

Walking home one frigid evening after bumping into some guys from the old Oaklands neighborhood, I found myself tapped into beautiful, cold, dead Seawell:

Sewer caps crusted with rock-
Salt, cracks echo down frozen canals—
Dry wintertime darkness.

It's an especially long walk back to my boat in the forest when it is below zero by the North Atlantic. But the wood stove my friends and I installed (where the Kemp Aaberg's engine used to sit in the cabin) has yet to fail me.

I sleep the sleep of the dead after beers, weed, Irish storytelling sessions, a frozen walk home and some woodstove-warmed food.

Cast-iron skillet
Fries russets on my blazing stove—
Winter's late-night supper.

chapter 10

After a "wicked bad winter," as we say, spring sometimes doesn't know what it's doing. Really none of us do.

On the flat, raw days when I can't bodysurf, think, meditate or write, I reread "For Once, Then, Something"—Frost's response to the critics who wrote of his supposed limitations as a poet-thinker. It is funny and sad that an artist of his caliber could spend a lifetime looking deeply into things to create works of art only to be told by strangers that his way of looking was all wrong.

In the end, criticism is just one flawed diamond trembling in an infinite web of connected jewels (to use the Buddhist metaphor). You can't get trapped staring at one shiny facet for too long when the flawed *and* flawless are all the same pulsing thing. Frost knew that. After all, "For Once, Then, Something" is about wondering at the well's mouth *while* hauling the water (probably just before wondering *while* chopping some wood). The practical Buddhist point of view helps connect with the practical Frost.

When I read the poem, I'm reminded that I've spent too much of my life afraid that my blindness and ignorance would be revealed to everyone at some time. If, I feared, it hadn't shown itself plainly already. Doubts are ordinary and expected, but I suppose I had phases when I let them trouble me too much.

One of my favorite living poets taps into the futility of fearing our own blindness. As Basho and Walt Whitman wrote of fields and graves and grass, so does Denis Johnson:

...the grass becoming green

does not remember the last year,
or the year before, or the centuries
that kept passing over.
          —*from the poem "Spring"*
          by Denis Johnson

𝕋 𝕠 𝕦 𝕞

The grip of winter weakens along the North Atlantic as spring slips
north along the coast. Dozens of condemned mills in Seawell remain
gutted, miles of mills, but the bars and restaurants brim with formerly
cooped-up locals.

The first mild days of May and early June wrench open ten thousand
stuck windows. Cherry blossoms, bluff willows and crocuses have opened
their soft doors.

June leafshadow freckles
Yellow smokestacks—laughs spill from bars
Across wet cobblestones.

I used to crave the return of calmer weather, but I know now it means
long spells of flatness. And I want to bodysurf when it is warm out, not
stare at Lake Atlantic. I wait until after the summer solstice to fly to South
or Central America for the Pacific's southern hemisphere swells.

In the northeast, spring dusks lean into long twilit evenings while
the cold water repels the fair-weather surfers for a few more weeks. The
bulk of cottages and beachfront homes remain vacant till school's out.
There are moments of balance and solitude to be found at this time of
year—when the sun slides far enough north to set behind the Sun Valley
neighborhood:

Lone surfer waits to watch
May's sunlight igniting distant
Insides of empty homes.

And once these quiet beaches brim with sunburned families—everyone trying to get outside all day, to unwind, to forget about work for a week or two, then I look for a few other signs that I should go. My favorite is catching sight of my namesake bird on the hunt again down from the Arctic. The Irish poet Trevor Joyce translated the story I modeled my life after in his 1975 book, *The Poems of Sweeney Peregrine*. And I'm fortunate enough to see migrating peregrines perched on the tallest smokestacks or stooping in the skies above Seawell's downtown streets and canals:

Springtime's great wanderer
Wears a bluegray cloak and dark hood—
Peregrine shits then flies.

chapter 11

I always heard stories of my older cousins and my mother waiting all winter during the '50s and '60s for their two weeks down the beach at my Grampa Sweeney's house. The rest of the year an assortment of tenants filled the place.

Eventually the house sold to someone outside the family, then my parents owned it briefly. I even lived there by myself for a short time as a teenager. And my oldest friend Paddy Kivlin bought 415 Morningside years after college loans released him back into the world.

We went to McSwiggan's Pub to celebrate the purchase. For me, it was like having the house back in the family. I loved and hated the place.

I loved that my mother, each summer, couldn't help telling me again about that house overflowing with cousins, aunts and uncles—tramping to the beach every day, swimming for hours, hunting for crabs at the rocks, getting chafed by the sand, washing it all off with outside showers in the backyard. The adults would grill burgers for dinner or buy fried haddock down the street, maybe lobsters when they had the money. It was time to drink cans of Narragansett lager and play poker or 45s late into the night. The kids ran around till they dropped on a couch or carpet, three or four to a sandy bed. The youngest cousin slept in the bottom drawer of a dresser, padded thick with beach towels, for the first three summers of her life.

And when Paddy Kivlin told me he bought the place, I also remembered I hated it as the locus of my immediate family's disintegration. But

I let that feeling pass the moment we raised our glasses to toast: "To 415 Morningside. It's back in the family, the only…" We might've said more but a local at the bar heard my toast and blurted, "415 Morningside? That's old Harry Sweeney's place. I used to live there. He rented it to me for a song. You bought it, huh? Good for you! Let me get you kids a pint of plain on me."

He was an old, old regular at McSwiggan's. He bought us two pints of stout and stood to leave. As he went he almost said it to himself, "Poor guy, Harry. Nicest guy you'd ever meet. Wouldn't hurt a fly. Told me he'd rent it to me for a song. And he did. He did. Poor guy never could stand the sound of the waves. I thought of buying that place for myself a few years ago. I passed. I don't know why people don't hold onto it; I should've bought it myself."

The old man pulled on his windbreaker and said, "Poor Harry couldn't even look at a beach after what he went through at Normandy. I miss him. You kids take care of that old house. It's a gem. Nice talkin' to ya, and remember what Harry always said to me: 'A pint of plain is your only man.'" He shuffled off through a suddenly stilled night.

Paddy and I hadn't said a word. We were dumbfounded. Not only had this stranger known my Grampa, he'd quoted him with a line by the Irish writer Flann O'Brien. O'Brien was one of the first to use the Sweeney myth in his novel *At Swim-Two-Birds*. The book prominently features an insane Sweeney character and the line "A pint of plain is your only man" in a poem repeated throughout the book. Paddy and I had each read his book back in the days when I was orchestrating my insanity diagnosis in prison.

There was suddenly more depth to this full-circle cycle Paddy had started by purchasing the cottage at 415 Morningside. Things were falling into place beyond our control, beyond logic.

I told Paddy Kivlin, right there in the bar, that I'd never heard my grandfather use that quote, but he was a well-read man. Did it mean he knew the legacy of the Sweeney name? He was already gone when I'd chosen to use the story of King Sweeney as my myth to live by. But did my

Grampa know it would become the fabric for my spiritual evolution—that these books Owen Kivlin and I had written would be written? Impossible, right?

My head was spinning, Paddy looked no more stable than I. We ordered another "pint of plain," to settle our minds.

I began telling Paddy that I'd never equated my Grampa with the kind of deep, daily suffering this stranger had just framed for us. I'd known that Grampa got his dose of cold reality, maybe more than anyone deserves, during D-Day. And it's true that Grampa lived through decades of summers in Seawell and never went down the beach. Not once.

We sat at the bar for a long time that night. We let the breadth of it settle and sink in: Grampa had rarely spoken of the day he had watched so many good men, kids really, suffer and die right in front of his eyes as he dropped them into the fight at Normandy. He told my mother about it—more like confessed it to her—three weeks before he died from emphysema and a third stroke. He'd drowned in his own phlegm. Everyone thought it was a horrible way to die; we were stunned by the extended pain he went through. The indignity.

When he passed, my mother cryptically told the family that Grampa saw this kind of death coming his way, that he told her he'd "earned it." She said no more. In the depths of our grief, we were remiss in not asking why he felt this way. He'd also smoked Luckies until he was seventy-five. Maybe we pinned it all on that habit? I'm not sure.

But it became clear to me that night at the bar that Harris Sweeney had lived as a pitiable man who refused all pity.

And "pitiable" is not a word I've ever considered in describing my grandfather to anyone.

Days later, after our pints of plain, I found myself reading to excess, thinking, sitting around trying to digest this new facet of a person I thought I knew so well. I came across a character in a Richard Brautigan poem:

Widow's Lament

It's not quite cold enough
to go borrow some firewood
from the neighbors

—*from Richard Brautigan's book*
The Pill Versus the Springhill Mine Disaster

These days, I wonder if it was ever "cold enough" for my grandfather. If and when it got too cold who did he turn to? These thoughts won't leave me alone.

Oddly, like most humans, I need to relearn the things I've been taught. Again and again, it seems. I'm a bit thick, but that's okay. Yet everything you know and love (or even despise) can change forever between just a pair of shallow breaths. Bit of a paradox, this life.

Years later—after the McSwiggan's local bought us a pint and gave me insight into a person I thought I knew so well—I had a similar experience out behind Grampa's cottage.

I woke before dawn on the summer solstice, an unseasonably hot and humid day to come. But there were waves, a fresh mid-range ground-swell. Paddy Kivlin had long since sold 415 Morningside. It was out of the family for good. I guess I forgot that fact on this morning, since the waves were supposed to be so good.

Since it was years before I finally quit using surfboards, that morning I climbed off the Kemp Aaberg and grabbed a 6'3" Bonzer from my pile of boards in the weeds. I walked through the woods and down the beach for a sunrise surf session by myself, stopped when I heard a musical thread of song slip through the inland trees. I shook out the last cobwebs of sleep and listened again.

There it was—some kind of distant falsetto of a rhyming song peppered with laughter or was it crying? A slight wind stirred the dewy saplings at my knees, blotting out the threnody for a moment. Then it trickled back through the ensuing stillness. I moved toward the hidden source.

I know I've read and written too much of the fairie denizens of Seawell's urban, coastal and forested realms. I was obsessed with books on the subject as a younger man, yet here I was being lured away from the surf by this ethereal song.

I was run through by what I saw beyond the tree trunks and brush in the backyard of my Grampa's old cottage, my family's old summer stomping grounds, Paddy's and his son Owen's old house. It didn't make sense at 5:45 in the morning, but there it was:

> Strange children captain
> The gray boulder I first sailed
> Through Grampa's old yard.

The kids, a boy of around six years old and his little sister of around four, had rigged a wooden plank off the old stove-sized boulder near the stonewall marking the tree line. They were at a game of pirates, while their father slept on a chaise lounge on the screen porch behind them. He dozed in his boxers and a threadbare T-shirt. His two children already wore their bathing suits, shirtless in the dim light. The prospect of going down the beach had them up before the sun. I could relate, standing in the trees with my surfboard under my arm, my wetsuit peeled to my waist. I let the few mosquitos have their fill for fear of disturbing the scene before my eyes. I waited to hear, knowing full well, yet waiting—unable to go down the beach until I learned that they were the source of the otherworldly song I'd caught through the oaks.

The older brother made his way out onto the plank slowly; it creaked and bent as he hung his ten toes over the edge. His back was to me. His younger sister somehow looked so much like Owen Kivlin at that age! It was as if Paddy's son Owen, my surrogate nephew, was singing again in front of me like he used to in that very yard, on that same boulder, so many years ago.

The girl's voice bubbled over with giggling and a freshness as it echoed off the back of the old house and poured through the summer canopy and pre-dawn gloaming. At the very moment she sang the final word of the old rhyme, her brother jumped off the wooden plank and down into the mossy sea of the backyard:

"Ride away to Seawell,
Ride away to Lynn, careful when you
Get there you don't fall *IN*!"

I remained for a minute, until their duet of laughter subsided and they switched roles—the convicted and already drowned rose from the moss to become the executioner-poet.

Shaken, I turned to go for a surf.

T̄T Ŏ ∪ ♏

I caught several good, hollow, back-lit waves that morning. Came out of each and every barrel I attempted, a rare thing. Yet I wasn't all there. Each wave offered more than the instantaneous bliss of getting barreled. Each tube seemed to be unwinding everything inside me I'd known before. Droplets of water beading on the deck of the board winked in the sun then washed away in a moment; spray off the lips of the waves more like thin manes on white horses surging toward the beach; the ultra-clarity of the ocean water all the way down to the sand bar.

Not a soul appeared on the beach for miles and miles during the entire experience.

After so many great waves by myself, feeling transported, I strolled back to my boat in the woods. I took an outside shower, changed, then drove three hours to a tiny inland mountain per my solstice ritual. At the top I drank a can of beer, rested, woke from strange dreams I couldn't recall.

I had some black iced tea from my sweating thermos and tried to meditate. My mind wavered, so I laughed it off and gave over to the lone memory cycling through my soothed but restive head. It was a childhood scene that played out each time I asked my Grampa to please go down the beach with me, "just this one time." He was gentle, suffering my childlike persistence without ever revealing his own daily struggles and pain: "Nah, not today. Not for me, pal. Not for me, pal-oh-mee-noh. But you should go. Go down the beach every chance you get. Have fun. The weather around here never stays the same for long. Go down the beach while you can."

I descended my tiny mountain in northwestern Mass., hearing his wheezy voice in my head as clearly as my own breathing. I drove east to Seawell for a dusk surf session to finish off that strange day. And it happened that very night. I was jarred back to reality—life's no more than a brief bout of suffering—while riding the evening's diminished surf on my longboard.

The first heat wave of summer broke then. I'd seen signs of thunderstorms from the mountaintop and then watched them roll in fast over the water. Fat, black clouds gathered above the crowded, summertime spots.

The heat failed, thunder rose and rumbled just a few miles north of my sandbar. A white bolt of lightning slashed down and struck the sea.

I called it a night—actually, a long weird day came to a close right at that moment. The downpour washed the salt from me as I walked back to my boat tucked in the darkened and flash-lit woods.

I thought again of Grampa just before sleeping. Soon after I woke the next day, the waves already gone, I learned some more about that storm from the previous evening.

Lightning touches down,
June's heatwave breaks—the struck girl drowns
still leashed to her surfboard.

The girl was only fourteen years old. She was named Ollave. Everyone in Seawell that surfed knew Ollie. And she was the only "Ollave" I've ever known. She was a quiet kid with thick brown hair, ocean-combed, who fixed surfboard dings and worked the register at a North Seawell shop—the local shop rat. Surfing and the North Atlantic both expanded and marked the boundaries of her world (as they did for me at that age).

There were no surfers close enough to Ollie to notice she was blasted off her board and into the water. There were no surfers for miles. The lifeguards had gone home at four.

Ollie's parents never had to worry or wonder of their child's suffering. She died quickly, while unconscious, stunned lifeless as her lungs filled with water.

My friend Ticky, Ollie's uncle, went back to the beach to look for his niece's flip-flops and towel. He found them perched on a smooth, round boulder. Wrapped inside the rain-soaked bundle were tiny bone-white shells Ollie collected for her youngest brother every time she went surfing.

Even the most stoic local filing through O'Farrell's Funeral Home to pay their respects wept when they saw those sea shells around Ollie's brother's frail neck.

chapter 12

I've been a ragged traveler for a long time: the coasts of North, Central and South America, Ireland, Spain, France, southern England; the forests and deserts of the world; the cities of Madrid, London, Paris, Quito, La Paz, Vancouver, San Francisco, San Diego; Baja's point breaks and shipwrecks, Puerto Escondido's sand bars, Puerto Rico's urchin-infested reefs.

I decided to slow down and go inward with Emerson, Frost, Bishop, Levertov, Dogen, Basho, Issa and Hakuin. Whether or not I'd ever left Seawell, this traveling inward has mattered most. I wish I'd done it sooner. Oh well, "whatever."

I've stocked up on winter wetsuits. I fixed up the old boat in the forest where I live quietly and simply. It's come in waves, my awareness and my practice of leading (and then letting go of) an examined life.

A long time ago, I heard the poet Li Young Li say that meditation as we think of it—sitting, breathing, becoming aware—is for amateurs. I had some beers with him at a college just north of Seawell once. He was right in that I'd have to start there, of course. But when he told me I must meditate while changing a shitty diaper, or after witnessing an accident in the street, to make meditation work—well, through my practice I've found that's not a specific enough description of what can happen if you do meditate each day.

The thing that makes meditation useful to me is it helps me recognize when I'm fully aware during the good moments and the bad (before I slip back into my everyday sleepwalking mode, tugged this way and that way by thoughts and emotions). Once meditation helped me recognize my awakenings, I stopped fighting so much and consented to these kinds of moments.

The Zen master Albert Low calls this "surfacing" and says, "If, instead of resisting, we remain quiet and still, while alert, we will find that there will be moments of surfacing even in the darkest experiences."

The trick is, I can't observe my surfacings and then hold on to that observation. Actively seeking to gain insight is a trap I repeatedly set for myself. Instead, I welcome the surfacing, no seeking—I simply agree to these moments of awareness. This is how Zen masters begin to usher in their enlightenment, their awareness of ultimate reality through all moments.

> Beyond old graveyard walls
> Grass and leaves hide forgotten stones—
> Neglected granite teeth.

We can choose to surface because, whether infants or corpses, we already float.

> Flock of plovers
> Skims waves, banks on October wind—
> Feathered flake of ash.

♈ ♉ ♌ ♏

Not too long ago, I made my way back east. I hitched the final 300 miles to the edge of the coastal city of my birth. No one knew I was coming. I crossed above the Merrohawke River on foot around three in the morning. It was a warm, late October night. Not a single car passed me on the bridge far above the clinking lines of the sailboats moored in Seawell Harbor.

The bay is golden
Under bridge lights, yet fall's full
White moon still slithers.

I could see a luminous fogbank offshore. I watched it approach and swallow the mouth of the harbor. I waited, noticing it was cold enough to watch my breath—tracking small puffs forming and dissipating each time I exhaled:

No wind on the bridge
But masthead lights sway below like
Candles on caked fog.

Three-quarters of the way across, I saw some kind of large animal leap onto the road and then off into the brush of a boatyard. I followed. The fog thickened and mists gathered in the low places of the Avalon marsh. The flashing speed of the animal on the road surprised me—I thought it might be an Irish wolfhound or a coywolf. Through the bushes, marsh and trees along the river, I caught glimpses. I kept seeing bits of a white flank. My backpack no longer felt heavy as I trailed the animal through vacant lots, down a few alleys. Slipping around ruined smokestacks through hip-high weeds I tracked the unhurried creature through the condemned industrial wilderness, the miles of twisting and boarded-up mills that frame the center of Seawell between the merging Correb and Merrohawke rivers.

I'd found my way home, but it wasn't along any path I recognized. The animal looked to be mostly white. It had grown more cautious in its movements but seemed to have a specific destination in mind. It followed invisible and familiar paths. Every so often, it passed through a cone of light thrown through the fog by the lamp posts. Finally, it picked its way behind some low brick walls and then into one of four crumbling Loafe Mill buildings on the banks of the Merrohawke. I picked up my pace once it was all the way inside the wrecked building.

When I stepped into the ruins, it took some time for my eyes to adjust to the inky blackness. I had been maybe fifty yards behind the animal and now I could find no sign of it in that massive, dripping expanse. I stood perfectly still for long minutes. Then I heard a crunch of glass a few hundred yards away at the far end of the ground floor.

I walked deeper into the labyrinthine mills, realizing I'd yet to see another human once I'd crossed the bridge over the harbor. No homeless sang drunk by the river, no revelers stumbled out of after-hours bars—it was a strange and quiet Seawell. Following the sound across the mill through the mouth of a gaping hole in the bricks of the back wall, I stepped into a gigantic overgrown courtyard. I'd never seen this walled-off parcel of Seawell so close to the rivers and downtown. It was silent. No city or harbor or river sounds penetrated the place.

A few dozen trees, an isolated forest of forty- or fifty-year-old ditch apple, rey oak and fragile birches had grown up there undisturbed, their trunks sheathed in mist. Autumn had turned all the leaves varying shades of yellow and they began ticking lightly under a small breeze. Broken windows and seven-story walls loomed over the preserved wasteland, boxing out everything I thought I knew as home.

But there was no animal in sight. Possibly the thing crouched in the yellowed, tall grass. Maybe it had re-entered a different cavernous segment of the mills. I slipped off my pack, sat on it, leaned back against a smokestack then lit a small fire from old wooden crates, sticks and bits of cardboard I scrounged up. I was sure I'd lost the animal.

Time passed, I suppose I let myself drift on old memories while staring up at that rectangle of dim stars. To be honest, I wasn't sure how to get out of there safely. I hadn't thought about it on the way in, trailing that beast. Now I thought it better to wait for first light before picking my way through the pitch-black mills with their wonky, half-collapsed floors and rotten wooden stairwells. I must've slept. I'm not sure, but some sound stirred me and I saw my little fire had guttered out, smoldering by my feet. Someone or something moved in that vast, withered yard. I kept still, scanned with my eyes and saw that the rectangle of sky had brightened above me. To my left, something moved. Slowly I turned my head, following the curve of bricks I leaned against at the base of the smokestack. Nothing. No one was there, but I froze as I inhaled a strong, familiar scent:

Sudden stench of skunk
By the red smokestack! Yet the flash is
Just an albino buck?

It had leapt over the low sill of a giant, smashed window and stood next to me in the grass. I cannot explain why the buck looked past me, almost over my shoulder, at my smoking pile of ashes then shifted its cloudy eyes to my face and *didn't* run.

There was no fear, no movement for a long moment. My breath caught, I was snared in my frenzied senses. My nose told me to flee from an angry skunk. My eyes, at the same instant, locked sidelong on the bulk and heft above me—poised effortlessly beneath a stunning twelve-point rack.

Eggshell sky behind pink
Eyes—a flickering daystar
Tangled in antlers!

I let out a plume of breath and the white stag snorted a larger cloud. As it faded, the animal turned and walked diagonally across the yard, stopping, craning its neck up, lifting forelegs out of the grass to pluck a ditch-apple off a branch with its mouth. The tree shook back and shed a curtain of hundreds of small, flickering leaves. The buck slipped through trunks of the forest and back into the mill through the hole in the redbrick wall.

I put my fingertips down into the dirt to stand and follow the deer back through the ruins, vacant lots, boatyards, and upriver across the bridge—out of Seawell forever. But I couldn't get up beyond my knees. I wasn't sure where the stag would walk and something alchemical in that first light had ignited each stalk of yellowed grass and every flickering leaf. It all grew golden, luminous as a fine mist began falling.

As I crouched, thinking about how far that buck had traveled for a few ditch apples, I was struck by the memory that a person could be sentenced to death for chopping down an apple tree in ancient Ireland. Had I read that somewhere?

Somewhere laughter echoed back from brick walls as I realized I couldn't even remember what was in my bag; so I looked up to the let the mist dapple my face.

I didn't know how long my eyes were shut, or if they had been at all. I opened them wide to a now-cloudy rectangle of spitting sky. I slumped back against the bricks, looked down at my tattered backpack—my current throne in the dust.

Things around me were tinged with light.

I felt elated, almost unhinged with happiness.

Had I been hiding in this canopy—my attachment to the illusion of me-ness—for forty-five years? Was I just descending now to hack down this fruitless tree?

It felt like free-fall in a vast space without walls, beyond time. More maniacal laughter echoed through the fall-gilded yard. I wouldn't have known I was laughing if not for that echo.

I felt all of my limbs and trunk thump to the earth in the span of a heartbeat.

I'd gotten the death penalty I'd always wanted.

Taking my hatchet and water bottle from my pack, leaving the rest behind, I said aloud to nobody:

> I just found
> A bed for this blanket
> Of Autumn rain.